"One thing I like about Jane Lindskold's books is that she plays fair with her readers. It doesn't matter that she's writing a series; each book will still stand on its own and be a satisfying read, for all that it adds depth and texture to what went before."

—Charles de Lint

"Blind Seer's wisdom is Firekeeper's center of gravity in the machinations of court life, while his huge size and blue eyes are a constant source of distress to the "civilized" circles they attend. Wolf and young woman converse effortlessly, offering a running commentary on the idiosyncrasies of human behavior, which, unfortunately, rarely attain the ethical imperatives of a well-led wolf pack. Exploring the wrenching adjustment required of a feral child in the first novel, Lindskold looks at another aspect of the so-called feral dilemma in *Wolf's Head, Wolf's Heart*— the relationship of a human with a non-human intelligence—an exploration of the question that John Lilly posed in the '60s about the urgency for learning to communicate with dolphins because, 'If we cannot communicate with non-human intelligence on earth, how can we expect to communicate with non-human intelligence from another world?' . . . Once again, Lindskold has written a book to take in slowly, to savor—a good, long read."

—Barbara Riley, *Santa Fe New Mexican*

"Without question, the best I've seen from this author."

—*SF Chronicle*

D1459836

TOR BOOKS BY JANE LINDSKOLD

Through Wolf's Eyes
Wolf's Head, Wolf's Heart
The Dragon of Despair

WOLF'S HEAD, WOLF'S HEART

WOLF'S HEAD, WOLF'S HEART

JANE LINDSKOLD

A TOM DOHERTY ASSOCIATES BOOK
NEW YORK

This is a work of fiction. All the characters and events portrayed in this book are either products of the author's imagination or are used fictitiously.

WOLF'S HEAD, WOLF'S HEART

Copyright © 2002 by Jane Lindskold

Edited by Teresa Nielsen Hayden

Map by Mark Stein based on an original drawing by James Moore.
Family tree art by Tim Hall

A Tor Book
Published by Tom Doherty Associates, LLC
175 Fifth Avenue
New York, NY 10010

www.tor.com

Tor® is a registered trademark of Tom Doherty Associates, LLC.

ISBN: 0-812-57549-0
Library of Congress Catalog Card Number: 2002067247

First edition: August 2002
First mass market edition: August 2003

Printed in the United States of America

0 9 8 7 6 5 4 3 2 1

For Jim, my angel on Earth
and
For Dad, Gwydion, and Haley,
three of Heaven's newest angels

ACKNOWLEDGMENTS

As always, there are more people to thank than I can easily remember. My husband, Jim, must be thanked first for providing his increasingly sophisticated critical and editorial assistance—and his unflagging patience and love.

Phyllis White of Flying Coyote Books is owed thanks both for help finding good sources on wolves and for the Tower at Worldcon 2000. Geoff from Fish and Wildlife in New Mexico made it possible for me to participate in a wolf capture. Tom McCarrol and Pati Nagel insisted I needed a Web site and helped me get it up and running. (Check it out at www.janelindskold.com)

On the publishing front, Kay McCauley offered good counsel when I needed it. Fred Herman earned my undying gratitude by answering the phone. Teresa Nielsen Hayden taught me new things about the inside of the editorial mind.

To all those friends who offered support during this difficult past year and gave me the strength to keep writing—Yvonne, Sally, Weber, Sharon, Jan, and Steve among them—I offer my thanks and my hopes that you enjoy the story.

And, finally, I want to thank the Los Alamos Five and all the other readers who wrote me this year for reminding me why I like writing books.

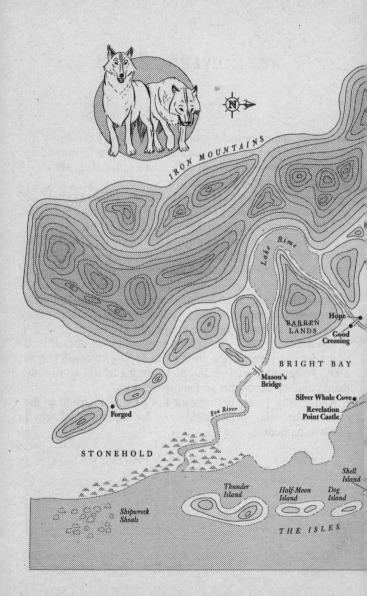

IRON MOUNTAINS

N

Lake Rime

Hope

BARREN LANDS

Good Crossing

BRIGHT BAY

Mason's Bridge

Silver Whale Cove

Fox River

Forged

Revelation Point Castle

STONEHOLD

Thunder Island

Half-Moon Island

Dog Island

Shell Island

Shipwreck Shoals

THE ISLES

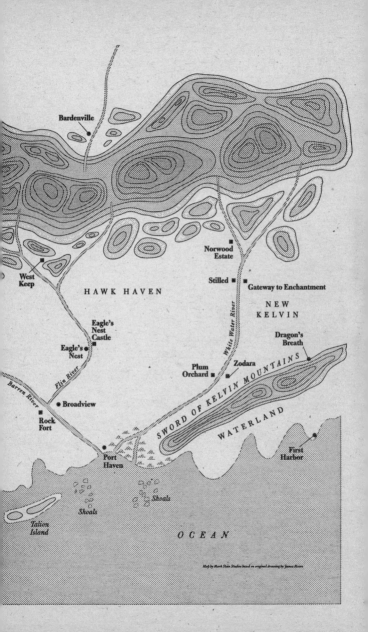

Bardenville

Norwood
Estate

West
Keep

HAWK HAVEN

Stilled

Gateway to Enchantment

NEW
KELVIN

Eagle's
Nest
Castle

Eagle's
Nest

Dragon's
Breath

Plum
Orchard

Zodara

SWORD OF KELVIN MOUNTAINS

Flin River

White Water River

Barren River

Broadview

WATERLAND

Rock
Fort

First
Harbor

Port
Haven

Shoals

Shoals

*Talion
Island*

OCEAN

Map by Mark Stein Studios based on original drawing by James Moore

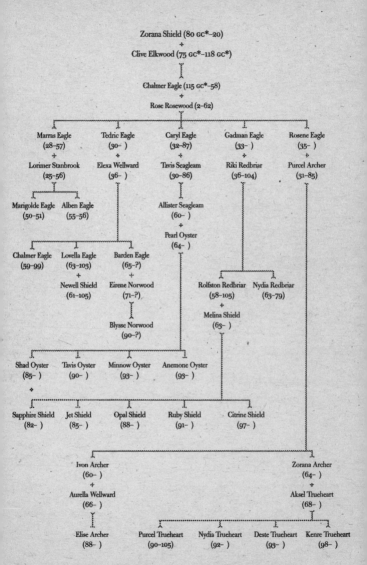

Zorana Shield (80 GC*–20)
+
Clive Elkwood (75 GC*–118 GC*)

Chalmer Eagle (115 GC*–58)
+
Rose Rosewood (2–62)

Marras Eagle (28–57)
+
Lorimer Stanbrook (25–56)

Tedric Eagle (30–)
+
Elexa Wellward (36–)

Caryl Eagle (32–87)
+
Tavis Seagleam (30–86)

Gadman Eagle (33–)
+
Riki Redbriar (36–104)

Rosene Eagle (35–)
+
Purcel Archer (31–85)

Marigolde Eagle (50–51)   Alben Eagle (55–56)

Allister Seagleam (60–)

Pearl Oyster (64–)

Chalmer Eagle (59–99)   Lovella Eagle (63–103)   Barden Eagle (65–?)
                        +   +
                        Newell Shield (61–105)   Eirene Norwood (71–?)

Rolfston Redbriar (58–105)   Nydia Redbriar (63–79)
+
Melina Shield (63–)

Blysse Norwood (90–?)

Shad Oyster (85–)   Tavis Oyster (90–)   Minnow Oyster (93–)   Anemone Oyster (93–)
+

Sapphire Shield (82–)   Jet Shield (85–)   Opal Shield (88–)   Ruby Shield (91–)   Citrine Shield (97–)

Ivon Archer (60–)
+
Aurella Wellward (66–)

Zorana Archer (64–)
+
Aksel Trueheart (68–)

Elise Archer (88–)   Purcel Trueheart (90–105)   Nydia Trueheart (92–)   Deste Trueheart (93–)   Kenre Trueheart (98–)

* GILDCREST COLONIAL CALENDAR (ALL OTHER DATES HAWK HAVEN CALENDAR)

BOOK
ONE

I

LYING ON HIS BACK in the darkness of his bedchamber, King Allister of the Pledge listened to his wife's soft breathing.

Pearl was pretending to be asleep, even as he was. Twenty-two years of marriage made fairly certain that neither was fooled. Those same twenty-two years made certain that each would maintain the farce.

He wondered if the same things kept her awake. There had been so much. The war—King Allister's War, they were calling it now, as if he had started it. And maybe he had. He had certainly done his part to end it.

The coronation earlier that day—all those people kneeling before him, swearing oaths. Some had been truly happy, he thought, but others . . . He thought he'd seen all the faces that men turn on each other, but he had seen a new one now . . . the eyes had been flat, holding no expression at all, while lips smiled or frowned; you could almost taste the calculation going on behind them. He'd never had power before, so he'd never seen this bland face that ambitious men turn to power.

But why should he fool himself? Ignoring the true reason for his sleeplessness was as ridiculous as this game of pretending to Pearl that he was asleep. At least that game served some purpose; at least each could believe the other might be resting.

Valora's letter. Whether his eyes were opened or closed Allister could summon the text of it before him, seeing it as glowing silver words against velvet black, though the real letter had been neatly written in prosaic black ink upon fine vellum. He'd first discovered the letter—and the queen's treachery—soon after their arrival.

Allister Seagleam, king in all but crown, had arrived with his family and retainers at Silver Whale Cove mid-afternoon the previous day. The castle itself—a massive stone structure along whose walls both rounded and square-built towers alternated—had been built close to the water, on a high point jutting into the cove. Named Revelation Point Castle for some event in Bright Bay's colonial past, it was the traditional seat for rulers of the area.

They were hardly through the arched stone gateway before they learned that Queen Valora, the former Queen Gustin IV, had departed on schedule as promised, taking with her rather more of the castle staff than was polite, and leaving those who remained in an uproar as they prepared for the formal coronation that was to be held the next afternoon.

The Keeper of the Keys, an elderly Pelican whose family had held the post since the days of Gustin I, had been the first to hint that all might not be right. He'd knelt in front of Allister, offering his homage as was his due and duty.

"I'm Ivory Pelican, Your Majesty," he'd said, extending in front of him a square, flat cushion of dark purple New Kelvinese silk upon which rested a highly polished bunch of keys. "My title is the Keeper of the Keys."

"I recognize you," Allister had said, "and confirm you in that title and its tasks and honors, unless you have reason to wish to be relieved of them."

He'd recited that formula many times in just the few hours since his arrival at the castle. The entire thing would need to be redone subsequent to the formal coronation, but these interim oaths were necessary, confirming that he wasn't out to strip everyone of their rank and privilege just because he'd managed to strip the queen of her throne.

All the other times the person so reassured had made some small speech of thanks and had then hurried off to do whatever needed to be done—maybe pausing along the way to reassure kith and kin that their particular royal stipend wasn't about to be stopped.

This time, though, Lord Ivory had rocked back on his heels and given his king—for although not yet formally crowned,

Allister Seagleam effectively had been king for these twenty-odd days—a look that might have been sly, but that just might have been a bit sad.

"Well, Your Majesty," Lord Ivory had said, keeping his voice low, "if you can spare an old man a few minutes, I believe there is something you should see."

Allister had found those minutes. Accompanied by Shad, his eldest son and heir, and a brace of trusted guards, he had followed where the old Pelican led.

Any onlooker would have immediately seen the likeness between father and son. Shad was as fair of skin and hair as his father, but where Allister was lean and with a vaguely scholarly untidiness to his bearing, Shad had inherited House Oyster's rounded lines from his mother. When he'd been a boy, the uninformed had often mistaken this apparent plumpness for softness, but now that several years at sea had put muscle on him, Shad showed promise of a whale-like solidity that did not preclude grace.

But where they were most alike was in a frank curiosity regarding the world around them, a curiosity that Shad did not bother to conceal as Lord Ivory Pelican led them into reaches of the castle that before this day had been the private quarters of the now-deposed Queen Gustin IV.

Allister was less a stranger to the castle. His father had been Prince Tavis, brother to Gustin III, third in line to the throne after his elder sister, Princess Seastar—that is before Gustin III had finally fathered his little Valora, a child born fairly late in his life, after others had become ambitious for the throne.

Prince Tavis had never held much hope that he or his son would be king. Indeed his own mother, Queen Gustin II, had entered into a pact with King Chalmer of Hawk Haven to wed Tavis to Chalmer's daughter Caryl in a pledge for peace between the kingdoms. The pact did not include the power to enforce those ideals. Perhaps that was why it had failed.

But Tavis's son by that marriage had frequented the royal castle as a child, escorted by his father, who—much though he resented being a playing piece in kingdom politics—would not let his son be dismissed as an inconvenient nonentity.

Prince Tavis had made certain that his son would bear a title—that of duke—and hold lands he could pass on to his own children. More than that, he could not do; and when he died at sea, a comparatively young man of fifty-six, it was whispered that he had welcomed death.

By then, however, Allister had made peace with his odd place outside of the usual order. His was no Great House, yet he was first cousin to the queen. He attended sessions of court, held office, sailed for a term in the navy. Each of these roles gave him access to different parts of the labyrinthine castle, yet he could swear that he had never before even seen the door to which Lord Ivory led him that day.

"This, Your Majesty," said the Keeper of the Keys, "is the door to the Royal Treasury."

Allister frowned. He knew perfectly well where the treasury was. He'd been in and out of it many times in his early twenties, when he did a stint as an auditor. Lord Ivory saw the frown, and thinned his lips over old teeth in what a shark might call a smile.

"The *Royal* Treasury, Your Majesty," he repeated. "The one that only the monarch goes into. The crown jewels are kept there . . . and other things. She who is now Queen Valora made a visit here before she left. She said she had to leave the crown for you."

"And you keep the keys for this treasury?" Allister asked.

"I do." Lord Ivory shook out a fat silver key from the bunch on his ring. "Shall I open the door for you?"

Allister knew Ivory Pelican was toying with him and disliked the game, but he couldn't see any reason not to play along. The crown that had fit Valora's dainty head would look ridiculous on him, but two of the former Gustins had been male, and one of their crowns should do. He had no wish to add having a new crown crafted to the reasons for delaying his coronation.

Besides, there were things other than crowns among the crown jewels of Bright Bay, and Allister felt ice in his gut at the thought of finally seeing them.

"Open the door," he said, hiding his sudden fear with brusqueness.

"One moment, Your Majesty." Lord Ivory selected a smaller, rather utilitarian key from his bunch and used it to open a wooden cabinet tucked in an alcove along the hallway. "You will need light."

He drew out several triple-wicked candles set ready in a silver-gilt candelabrum. Lighting them from one of the wall sconces, he extended the candelabrum to the king.

"Give it to Shad," Allister said. "I'd like him to come with me."

"Only the monarch goes into the treasury." Lord Ivory protested.

"Someday Shad will be king," Allister said firmly. "I think I'll start a new tradition."

He glanced at the guards, longtime retainers from his own estate. As of yet, he didn't know who he could or could not trust from the castle guard. He didn't quite trust Valora not to leave behind some faithful retainer with orders to slip a knife between his ribs.

The captain of the guard, Whyte Steel gave Allister an almost imperceptible nod. He, too, was seeing assassins in every shadow.

Muttering protests, Lord Ivory unlocked the door. Thanking him, Allister stepped over the threshold. He could hear Shad behind him. The young man's breathing came quick and excited, but to any less proximate to him than his father, Shad probably seemed quite calm.

Lord Ivory shut the door behind them, but Allister was certain that with Whyte Steel on the other side it would open again. Then he turned his attention to the chamber.

It wasn't large, maybe five feet to a side, but there were six sides, each of equal length. As if to make up for its comparative smallness, the room was very high. The windows at the top of each wall were narrow slits. Set halfway up each wall was a pale block of stone carved with intricate patterns.

Allister had seen their like before, elsewhere in the castle. They were remnants of Old Country magic, enchantments that—if tales more than a hundred years old were to be believed—had once shed a soft, clean light all through the building. It was said that such routine magics had continued to function for years after the Plague, but had gradually failed because no one remained who knew how to renew their power.

Ever quiescent, the carved blocks inspired awe, but they could not hold Allister's attention long, not with the huge treasure cabinet that was built into half the room demanding his attention.

The cabinet was crafted from polished maple the reddish-gold of honey, and fit neatly into three angles of wall. Its doors were closed, but a silk ribbon braided in the sea green and gold of the royal house hung from the faceted crystal door pulls. Two keys depended from the ribbon: a silver one, twin to that which Lord Ivory had used to open the door to the treasure room, and a smaller, golden one set with emeralds.

"Well, I see that the king need not always bring the Keeper of the Keys whenever he wishes to change his hat," Allister said, trying to lighten his own mood. "How kind of Valora to leave these behind. Shall we see what is in the cabinet?"

Shad nodded.

As expected, the golden key opened the cabinet, revealing that the doors had been cleverly hinged so that they folded back into a neat packet that did not impede access to the interior, even in this small space. Good workmanship, perhaps from the days when the Old Country still ruled, but nothing that a competent carpenter could not do today.

Within, three sets of shelves were revealed. To the left, on the highest shelves, were the crowns worn by the previous Gustins. Allister recognized several as those worn by Valora's father. He guessed that the other set of masculine-styled crowns had belonged to Gustin I, also called Gustin Sailor. There were many of these, as if Gustin Sailor had enjoyed showing off his newly won privilege. That fit what Allister had heard of the man—his own great-grandfather.

Below the crowns there were a few scepters, but these had never been much used in Bright Bay. Allister recalled Prince Tavis saying that his own mother had said they were damned heavy to hold for long periods of time. She had preferred a gavel of solid oak with which to hammer for silence. The lower shelves on this side were empty, waiting for future monarchs to fill them. Allister felt a momentary surge of awe when he realized that he and Shad would be among those to hold that honor.

The right-side set of shelves held much more prosaic treasures: ornate boxes containing rings and bracelets, jeweled weapons, pendants, and other such pretties. These were personal property of the kings and queens of Bright Bay. Seeing slight scuffing on one empty section of shelf, Allister guessed that Valora had taken away her own boxes. He wondered if she had made free with anything belonging to, say, her father or grandmother.

Allister barely glanced at the jewelry, his attention claimed by a set of closed doors in the center of the central unit of shelves. Here again a key waited for him on a braided ribbon. It was also gold, its ring shaped like the fat body of a whale, the teeth worked cleverly into the whale's spout.

Allister doubted that a twin of *this* key rested on Lord Ivory's ring. Indeed, he had seen it before, dangling on a chain worn at the throat of his grandmother, Queen Gustin. She had never been without it.

Twisting the key in the lock, Allister opened the cabinet. Beside him, Shad turned from peeking into the various jeweled boxes, waiting to see what must be kept trebly locked away. Both of them suspected they already knew.

The center door creaked slightly when Allister opened it. Inside there was nothing but a roll of pale vellum tied with a bright blue ribbon. Impressions in the plush velvet showed that once there had been something else kept here, something that had left an indelible mark on the fabric.

Even before he unrolled the scroll, Allister knew that he had been betrayed. All that waited was to learn how severely.

"My Royal Cousin," began the missive in what he recognized as Valora's own hand. It continued:

> *Yes. This is where they were kept.*
> *I wonder—how long after your arrival did you wait to seek*

*the Royal Treasures? Did you run immediately to gloat over
what you had won? Somehow, knowing you, even in my
darkest moments I cannot believe that this was the case. Even
if the treasures were on your mind, you would be too
courteous, too polite to the claims of those who had awaited
your arrival to simply order them away.*

*Knowing you, I suspect that you had to be reminded that
there were treasures for you to claim. Did Pearl say that she
needed a crown for her pretty head? Did some flunky hint
gently that you were overlooking something important? Or did
it take the Keeper of the Keys offering his fealty to suggest
that you seek out this room?*

*I told old Ivory to remind you, you know. That much I've
done for you. Actually, I've done a great deal more. My last
gift to the people I was born to rule is taking from them the
shadow of Old Country magic. Those three trinkets have been
the excuse for war, not just recently, but from the days of our
great-grandfather Gustin Sailor.*

*So I've taken them with me. Now, no one will have reason
to fear Bright Bay. If they choose to fear me, isolated on my
Isles, well, the ocean is my moat.*

*How will anyone know what I have done? I shall tell them.
On the day of your coronation, letters will be delivered by
hand to the rulers of Stonehold, Waterland, New Kelvin, and
Hawk Haven.*

Enjoy your reign, Cousin, long as it may last.

The letter was signed, "Valora, Queen of the Isles."

Allister had made no effort to hide the scroll and so Shad
finished reading moments after he did.

"She's angry, isn't she, Father?" The young man tried to
smile, but the expression failed to reach his eyes.

"She is," Allister agreed. He let the scroll roll shut. "Fortunately, for us, enough of the nobles of Bright Bay have remained loyal that she is unlikely to try to retake her throne by
force. Even if she makes an alliance . . ."

He rubbed his free hand over his eyes, feeling a headache
coming on. There were so many possibilities. Valora could

ally herself with one of Bright Bay's rivals—Waterland came immediately to mind. Of course, she put herself at risk, then, unless she could keep them from taking over in the guise of giving aid. The threat of Old Country magic might be enough. Then again . . .

Once more Allister rubbed his eyes.

"Bring the candles closer, Shad. I want to see if we can guess what was here."

Shad obeyed and the warm yellow glow illuminated three distinct depressions in the velvet. The first was roughly rectangular, about as long as Allister's hand from the heel of his palm to his longest fingertip, but only as wide as three fingers. The second depression was the largest: a face-sized oval set upon a long handle. The third was quite small: a perfect circle blurred at one edge, as if whatever had been there was irregular in shape.

Father and son studied these ghost images for a long moment; then Shad ventured:

"I'd say the smallest impression is of a ring. I've seen the like in Mother's jewel box."

"A ring," Allister agreed, "with some sort of setting. Yes, that seems likely. What do you think of the other two?"

Shad shook his head. "I'm less certain, but the large one could be several things: a fixed fan, a hand mirror, even a mask on a stick."

"Good guesses," Allister said. "You have a sharp eye. The last one could be too many things—even a small box holding something else entirely. We must ask, especially among the older courtiers, and see if anyone has ever seen these treasures. Unhappily, Gustin Sailor kept them a secret, so it is possible that no one currently alive but Valora herself may have seen them."

"That seems likely," Shad agreed with a sudden grin. "You saw the expression of horror on Lord Ivory's face when you said you were bringing me in here with you. Clearly, you violated some antique precedent."

Allister stared at the rows of crowns, giving in for a moment to the very human impulse not to think about something too horrible to contemplate. Then he turned to his son.

"Let us continue violating precedent, then." He handed Shad the key to the Royal Treasury door. "Bring your mother here when she has time and ask her to select crowns for both of us. She has a good eye. Tell her to feel free to choose jewels to wear as well, but to remember that we do not wish to appear like gaudy conquerors, only to express proper respect for the dignity of the occasion."

Shad nodded. "I can do that." He paused, toying with the key. "But, Father, what are we going to do about *that*?"

A toss of his head indicated the empty cabinet where three ensorcelled items should have rested.

Allister took the whale key and relocked the cabinet.

"We certainly cannot send a fleet to chase Valora down and reclaim them. We don't even know for certain what we seek, and she is right: The ocean is now her moat."

The king considered further as he helped his son shut and relock the polished maple doors, then handed him the gold and emerald key.

"I will write King Tedric of Hawk Haven. As he is our ally, he deserves to know of this development from us, even if our letter cannot reach him before Valora's does. Doubtless hers is already in Eagle's Nest, awaiting the appropriate date for delivery. Then, we shall go ahead with the coronation and then begin plans for your wedding to Crown Princess Sapphire."

"Shall I tell her," Shad asked hesitantly, "what has happened?"

"Do," Allister replied decisively. "Sapphire is present as her kingdom's representative to our coronation. Make certain that she knows that you are informing her officially, at my request. Sapphire is a proud girl, quick to feel a slight."

"Proud, yes, but brave, too," Shad said, "to come here in advance of her people with just a small honor guard."

"I'm glad you appreciate her courage," Allister said, "since you will marry her before the moon turns full again."

Shad nodded. "I do. I only wish things were simpler."

King Allister squeezed his son's shoulder. "We've accepted—some would say usurped—a throne and a kingdom. Nothing will ever be simple for us again."

IN THE DARKNESS OF HIS BEDCHAMBER, King Allister tossed, unable to keep up the pretense of sleep any longer. Beside him, Pearl sighed and moved close to him.

"It will be all right, Allister," she said, with the same soft certainty that she had once used to banish their children's night fears.

"Will it?" he asked, and was surprised by the harshness in his own voice.

"It must be," she said. "We must make it so, whatever it takes."

"I feel a fool, trusting Valora." It wasn't the first time he'd said this, not even to her.

"We had no choice," Pearl said, accepting some of the guilt as her own, "as we saw it then. Maybe even Valora herself didn't know what she intended to do. Maybe the impulse to claim the treasures came to her only when the time came to relinquish her kingdom and her power."

But King Allister of the Pledge, remembering the angry fire in Valora's ocean-blue eyes when she finally agreed to surrender Bright Bay's throne and accept a lesser kingdom in its place, thought that Valora had known even then what she would do, and cursed himself once more for not anticipating her treachery.

II

 DESPITE THE STRONG, CHILL WIND blowing in from the bay, the young woman remained perched upon the castle parapet, her dark brown eyes gazing out over the waters of Silver Whale Cove. Perhaps for warmth, perhaps for companionship, her right arm was flung around the neck of the enormous grey wolf seated beside her, his elegant head higher than her own.

"So much water," she said at last. "Derian told me it would be like this, and that the ocean beyond this bay makes the bay itself seem a cattle pond by comparison."

"And Queen Valora is fled over that ocean," the wolf added, "taking with her these magical treasures we have heard so much about."

He laughed, a dry sound that to most human ears would have sounded like nothing more than a faint snort. His blue eyes danced with amusement as he continued:

"And so this Valora steals a victory at a time when all expected her to flee tail-tucked, like a yearling too full of springtime strength who has been pounded by the One Male."

"I wish, Blind Seer," the young woman said a trace re-proachfully, "that I was as certain that what Queen Valora has done is amusing. Both King Tedric and King Allister are very stern these days. Crown Princess Sapphire hides her rage but thinly. I have heard that the seamstresses who are fitting her for her wedding gown tremble when they must approach her."

"True, sweet Firekeeper," the wolf agreed. "Our friends are worried, but then there is nothing more humiliating than being bitten on the nose by prey you had thought dead. The kings are old Ones who think about the consequences, but Sapphire only feels the shame."

Firekeeper shared Blind Seer's laughter this time before re-turning her attention to the bay.

"There will be no running after Queen Valora to bring the treasures back. I understand that now. I had not thought there was a river so wide that it could not be forded or swum, a pond so broad that one could not run around its edges to the other side."

A raised voice from inside the castle interrupted their dis-cussion.

"Lady Blysse! Lady Blysse!"

Firekeeper, who had accepted Blysse Norwood as a name to which she would answer, groaned.

Blind Seer commented slyly, "Crown Princess Sapphire is not the only one who snaps at the seamstresses, eh, Firekeeper?"

In reply, the young woman punched the wolf in the shoulder. Swinging her long legs down from the stone wall, Firekeeper called to the woman inside:

"I am here. Wait and I will come in to you."

A kerchief-covered head popped out one of the narrow windows in the castle's stone wall. The woman's face beneath the covering was shriveled with age and lined from sour temper.

"Lady Blysse!" she shrieked. "What are you doing out there?"

Firekeeper answered, just a slight note of exasperation in her voice, "Looking at the water."

"Be careful! You'll fall!"

Deeming this last not worthy of reply, Firekeeper paused in her descent only long enough to make certain that Blind Seer had leapt safely down from their shared perch. The wolf, however, experienced no more difficulty with the descent than she had, despite the fact that he was easily the size of a small pony. Nature had blessed him with dexterity, flexibility, and a singular lack of imagination regarding risk—traits Firekeeper shared.

Thus, when Firekeeper and Blind Seer slipped through the window into their room, it was the waiting tirewoman who was pale and shaking.

"I really must protest!" she began, her voice shrill.

"I wouldn't, Goody Sewer," came a male voice from the doorway. "She doesn't understand."

Firekeeper, who indeed had been growing frustrated, brightened at the familiar voice.

"Derian!" she cried in relief. "The meeting then is over?"

Without standing on ceremony—a trait Goody Sewer clearly disliked—Derian Carter strolled into Lady Blysse's room. He was a tall youth, possessed of dark red hair tied back by a black ribbon into a fashionable queue, and fair skin dusted with freckles. Hazel-green eyes that could be as changeable as the sea twinkled now with laughter.

"We are in recess," he replied. "When did you arrive?"

"Early this morning," Firekeeper said, "in a wagon with Doc. Blind Seer permitted himself to be covered with blankets, but still the horses shied when they caught his scent. I had to snarl at them most fiercely."

Derian Carter, more inclined than most to take Firekeeper literally, grinned.

"We asked for you," Firekeeper continued "but we were told you were in a meeting. A note was left for Doc and he told us what it said."

"The meeting was King Tedric's business," Derian said in a tone of voice that warned her not to pursue the matter further. Then he turned his attention to the tirewoman, who had been listening, curiosity warring with impatience.

"I beg you, Goody," Derian said, "to refrain from scolding Lady Blysse even when she acts in what must seem to you a foolish manner."

"But if she falls!" the woman began.

"No one will blame you," Derian soothed. "I assure you. No one who knows her well maintains for long the illusion that anyone but Lady Blysse is responsible for her actions."

Goody Sewer frowned, her critical gaze fixed on the young woman with clear dissatisfaction.

Lady Blysse Norwood did not fit the usual image of a young noblewoman. Lean and slim, almost to boyishness, Blysse wore scuffed brown leather pants cut below the knee and a matching leather vest. Her bare feet were dirty and callused. Her only adornment—if such a practical item could be classified thus—was a sheathed hunting knife in whose pommel gleamed a large, deep red, cabochon cut garnet.

"I came here," the tirewoman explained, "to fit the young lady for her gowns and found her perched out on the parapet!"

"Did she come inside when you called?" Derian asked.

"Yes," the woman admitted grudgingly.

"Then all is well," Derian concluded. "Please, go ahead with your fitting. I won't get in the way. I have a few minutes before I need to return to my meeting."

Firekeeper hid a grin, but Blind Seer, cheerfully aware that no one but Firekeeper would understand what he said, commented,

"Fox Hair is determined to pull the woman's tail. What has she done to him?"

"If," Firekeeper replied in the same language, *"she has been acting toward him as this castle's staff did to Doc when we arrived, she has been treating him as if he is as untrained and untried as I was when first I came forth from the forests."*

"Well," Blind Seer said philosophically, *"when the moon was last full this seamstress served another mistress, and her pack and Derian's were vowed enemies. Not everyone has taken well to the changes."*

Firekeeper nodded and, to the evident shock of Goody Sewer, began undoing the carved toggles that held her vest closed over her small but definite breasts.

"Lady Blysse!" the woman shrilled.

"Derian has seen me without clothes before," Firekeeper said with a patience she didn't feel and continued to undress.

Derian, however, perhaps feeling he had teased the woman enough, politely turned his back.

"I have been Lady Blysse's personal attendant these last six or so moonspans," he explained, "but my starveling waif has become a young lady. I shall remember her modesty even though she does not."

The tirewoman, who—no matter what she pretended— could not have failed to hear the stories of how Lady Blysse had been discovered in the wilds west of the Iron Mountains early the past spring, sniffed but did not pursue the subject. Indeed, Goody Sewer's easy acceptance of Blind Seer—as terrifyingly huge a wolf as any storyteller could dream—gave lie to her pretended ignorance and haughty indignation. That she trusted Blind Seer not to make dinner of her meant she had heard something of Lady Blysse's peculiar history.

"Try this gown on first" was all the tirewoman said. She held up a long-sleeved gown in dark blue fabric, banded at wrist and throat by ribbons in the Kestrel sky-blue and scarlet.

"I had the pattern cut along the measurements the post-rider brought, but there will certainly need to be alterations."

Firekeeper, now naked except for her underclothing, stepped into the gown and let the woman fasten it. As she stood, trembling slightly at the proximity of a near stranger, she asked Derian: ·

"How is Elation? We have not seen her since we arrived."

Derian's tone grew worried as he replied, "She was with me until shortly before I arrived at the city," he said. "Then she took off. Last I saw her, she was flying west."

Firekeeper was also concerned. The peregrine falcon had taken quite a liking to Derian and wouldn't have left him without good reason. Still, she decided there was no need to worry the young man further.

"The hunting birds," she offered, "migrate like most other wingéd folk. It could be that her blood called her."

She grinned suddenly, remembering how once Derian had not believed her when she said she could understand what animals said to her.

"It's not as if Elation could tell *you* where she was going," she added.

Derian chuckled. "That's true. How are you feeling these days? You look well."

"Doc says that my wounds are healed," Firekeeper replied, "though I will have some new scars."

A sniff from the tirewoman indicated that she had noticed the liberal patterning of scars across Firekeeper's skin. Not a one of the young woman's limbs was free from the silver and white lines: some mere gossamer tracery, a few heavily seamed with scar tissue. Two comparatively fresh scars—one on Firekeeper's back, the other along her thigh—remained livid red, fading along the edges into dull pink.

With his back turned, Derian's expression couldn't be seen, but his voice expressed his satisfaction at the news.

"Well, you can't expect to get away without any marks. You were nearly dead from your injuries and even Doc's healing talent can't free you from all the consequences of your impulsiveness."

Firekeeper recognized the teasing note in Derian's voice and let the apparent insult stand, though, coming from another, the accusation that she had acted without thought would have been a fighting matter.

At a prod from the tirewoman, Firekeeper raised her right arm so that Goody Sewer could adjust the pins in that sleeve.

"Doc has gone to learn what is expected of him for the wedding," Firekeeper said to distract herself. *And to see if he can "accidentally" meet with a certain young lady*, she thought, but she said nothing, respecting Sir Jared Surcliffe's dignity.

"Doubtless," Derian said, "he will take the time to familiarize himself with the public areas of this fine castle."

Again, something in Derian's tone—this time a warm undercurrent of laughter—made Firekeeper suspect that he had understood her unspoken thoughts as well as what she said aloud.

"I hear that we were among the last of the Hawk Haven wedding guests to arrive," Firekeeper continued, realizing to her astonishment that she was making conversation—a concept she would not have understood five moonspans before.

"Only the mother of the bride," Derian said, a note of tension entering his voice, "has failed to arrive. Some say that she will not attend, recently widowed as she is."

"Furious at her daughter," Blind Seer commented, *"if the truth would be known."*

Derian, of course, didn't hear the wolf's comment, and went on:

"Lord Rolfston's death is less than two moonspans past," he said, "but still many consider Lady Melina's absence a bad omen for the marriage."

Goody Sewer spoke around the pins held in her pursed lips. "How can it be a good omen if the mother of the bride—the proximate ancestress—refuses to attend? I say that Duke . . . King Allister should postpone the wedding until appropriate mourning for the bride's father is ended and her mother is willing to attend."

"You aren't the only one who thinks that," Derian said easily, "but King Allister is of another mind—as is his son. If Shad is willing to risk bad omens on his wedding day, I say we should support him. It's important to seal the truce between Bright Bay and Hawk Haven."

Goody Sewer could hardly disagree without seeming openly disloyal to her new monarch and his heir apparent, but her silence was eloquent. The chime of distant bells made any reply unnecessary.

"Time for me to return to the meeting," Derian said. "See you later, Firekeeper."

"I hope so," Firekeeper replied.

Firekeeper smiled after the retreating figure. It was good to be back with her first human friend. In the wash of pleasure she barely heard the tirewoman's question.

"Excuse me," she said politely. "I wasn't listening."

"I could tell that!" the older woman griped. "I said you can take off that gown and try on the next one."

Firekeeper cooperated, being careful not to damage the fabric or snag the ribbons. The next gown Goody Sewer handed her was the silvery grey of a wood dove's plumage, and deliciously soft. It reminded Firekeeper of the first fabric she'd ever touched—a lamb's-wool shirt Derian had given her.

"Who was that arrogant redhead?" the tirewoman asked, twitching straight the gown's long skirt, then lowering herself on creaking knees to pin the hem. "I've seen him about these past several days, ever since the contingent from Eagle's Nest arrived, but never to speak to. He gives himself airs."

Firekeeper thought that a less true thing had never been said about her friend and she carefully framed her reply.

"He's Derian," she said, smoothing the sleeve of the gown against her arm, "Derian Carter. Some are calling him Derian Counselor since the war."

She bared her teeth in a gleeful grin that was not completely kind.

"He's one of Earl Kestrel's retainers and youngest counselor to King Tedric of Hawk Haven," she continued, taking wolf-like pride in the strength of her pack. "A very important person."

The astonishment and consternation on the tirewoman's face when the old woman looked up from her pinning was precisely the reward for which Firekeeper had hoped.

LADY ELISE, HEIR APPARENT TO THE ARCHER BARony, thought she would break something if she stayed in the same room with her temperamental second cousin one moment longer. Quickly, on the excuse of fetching something from her own rooms, she stepped out into the hallway and pulled the heavy oak door firmly closed.

It wasn't that Elise didn't feel a certain degree of sympathy for Sapphire, the young lady admitted to herself as she hurried along the polished flagstones of the corridor. The strain on Sapphire had been unrelenting for several moonspans, ever since the competition for who would be named King Tedric's heir apparent had been brought to a head when Earl Kestrel had brought out from the western wilds a young woman he claimed was the sole survivor of Prince Barden's ill-fated colony.

True, Elise herself had been under some of the same strain as Sapphire, but in the end she had been able to return to her familiar, comfortable responsibilities. It was Sapphire who now found herself heir apparent to the thrones of not one but two kingdoms, who in a few days was to marry a man she hadn't even met until two moonspans before. It was Sapphire who was learning that the prize was not nearly as sweet as it had seemed when it hung out of reach.

Reaching the suite she shared with her parents, Elise quickly slipped inside. Her father, she knew, was attending the council called by King Tedric—part of Sapphire's bad temper was that wedding preparations had made it impossible for her to attend the entire meeting. Elise hoped her mother would be with Queen Elexa, whose frail health had suffered during the journey from Eagle's Nest.

The central parlor was empty when Elise entered, but the door to her own room opened almost immediately and a slender woman in her mid-twenties stepped out and curtsied.

"Good afternoon, my lady."

Elise smiled tiredly. "Good afternoon, Ninette. Are my parents about?"

"No, Lady Elise. Your father is still in council. Your mother left word to say she will remain with Queen Elexa until shortly before the banquet this evening."

Elise smiled, feeling a little guilty at her sense of relief. It wasn't as if her parents were responsible for Sapphire's mood.

"I can only stay for a moment, Ninette," Elise confided. "I'm fleeing my cousin and made the excuse I needed to fetch my embroidery."

Ninette, who had known Crown Princess Sapphire for long enough not to be completely in awe of her new title, grinned wickedly.

"I do have something that might distract you, Elise," Ninette said, dropping her formal manner as she often did—with Elise's heartfelt approval—when they were alone. "You had a visitor while you were away. Sir Jared Surcliffe came to call. When he found you weren't in he left a note."

Elise felt herself flush and covered whatever excitement she might have shown by speaking, perhaps, she feared, too quickly.

"So Sir Jared and Firekeeper have arrived from Hope," she said. "That's wonderful! Did they have a safe journey?"

Ninette was too aware of her poor relative's debt to Baron Archer's family to blatantly tease Elise, but her pale brown eyes shone with mischief as she made her apparently routine report.

"Sir Jared said that they had some difficulties with Blind Seer in the more populated areas, so they avoided all the settlements along the post-road and camped instead. He—Sir Jared, I mean, not the wolf—looked brown and healthy."

"Didn't Sir Jared and Firekeeper," Elise asked, more as a prompt than because she really needed to know, "take lodgings with Hazel Healer in Hope?"

"That's right," Ninette agreed, "and Sir Jared says that Hazel sends her greetings to both you and the crown princess."

"And Firekeeper's wounds?"

"Are healing nicely," Ninette said, "and she hopes you'll come and see her. She didn't want to come by herself because your parents might not like Blind Seer in their quarters."

Elise nodded, wishing Ninette would stop prattling and give her Sir Jared's note. "That was considerate of Firekeeper." Then, "You said Sir Jared left a note?"

Ninette relented and pulled a folded and sealed missive from her apron pocket.

"Here it is. He wrote it here when he found you weren't in, saying he didn't care to disturb Princess Sapphire."

Elise grinned, wondering if Jared had learned of Sapphire's fit of temper when King Tedric dismissed her from the meeting to have her wedding gown fit and to rehearse the responses for the ceremony. That Prince Shad had been similarly dismissed had not sweetened Sapphire's mood a whit, though it showed that he was being given no special privileges.

Elise took the note, noticing that the wax was impressed with Sir Jared's arms: a hand outstretched with the palm impaled by arrows. Deciding that she would not care to be questioned if either of her parents returned unexpectedly, she drifted into her bedchamber.

"Ninette, see if you can find my embroidery. Then there's no reason for you to miss the fun, so bring your own kit and come along to Sapphire's sitting room. Perhaps having a larger audience will remind her of her dignity and force her to behave."

As Ninette bustled about finding the requested items and putting her apron aside, Elise finally broke the wax seal.

"Lady Archer," the missive began with rather foreboding formality; then the hurried scrawl relaxed into a more conversational tone.

"I hope this finds you well. Firekeeper and I arrived early this morning, along with Blind Seer. Fortunately, cousin Norvin had done as promised and we found the guards prepared not only to accept my rather ragamuffin charge as Lady Blysse Norwood but also to admit a giant timber wolf into the castle walls. There are times that having Norvin Norwood, the Earl Kestrel, throwing his weight around makes life a lot easier.

Race Forester had come down from Hope a few days earlier, and he and Ox met us in the stables and took over the horses and luggage. Apparently, the combined pressure of the wedding guests and the fact that Queen Valora took about half the castle staff with her has put quite a strain on hospitality. They told us that Derian and the earl were in some high-level meeting, but that we might find you free.

While staying with Hazel Healer, I availed myself of her extensive library and her even more extensive knowledge of herbs and simples. I wish I'd known half of what I do now before King Allister's War began. There'd be a few more soldiers recovered from the aftereffects of their wounds. Ah, well, next war.

Here, Jared seemed to think he might have been too flippant, for there was a blot where he had let the quill rest and his tone when he resumed was much more formal.

Knowing your ladyship's sincere interest in the healing arts— as evinced by your labors in the infirmary following the battles—I would be happy to share with you some of the knowledge I have acquired. I am currently quartered with Earl Kestrel's party. Perhaps out of concern over Blind Seer we have been given an entire tower in the northeastern portion of the castle. A message sent there would find me and I would be honored to call upon you at your leisure.

I remain your servant . . .

The letter was signed simply "Jared Surcliffe," but he had added his title—Knight of the Order of the White Eagle—as an afterthought.

Elise sighed. She hadn't quite figured out if Sir Jared—
"Doc" to his friends, and she had thought herself one of those
friends—was interested in courting her or not. After her experience with Jet, part of her had no interest in romantic entanglements, but she did like Doc and didn't wish to
discourage him if he was interested in her.

Elise started to reread Sir Jared's letter, then realized that
both Ninette and the crown princess were waiting for her. She
scribbled a quick reply inviting Sir Jared to call on her at his
convenience. As she sealed it with the House Archer crest, she
worried that she had been too formal, but decided that it was
better than being too familiar.

"Ninette," she said, handing the letter to her maid, "find
someone who can deliver this to Sir Jared's quarters. He's
staying with Earl Kestrel's party in some northeast tower."

"I know where that is," Ninette answered promptly. "One
of Earle Peregrine's servants was complaining that Kestrel had
been given an entire tower when they had to make do with a
couple of suites. I explained about Blind Seer, but I don't think
they were mollified."

Elise shook her head. Up to this point, most of Hawk Haven's Great Houses had chosen not to interact too closely with
Earl Kestrel's peculiar ward, not wishing to grant her more
legitimacy than was her due. House Peregrine, Elise's
mother's birth house, had been more friendly than most, so
this new stuffiness didn't bode well. Firekeeper, although she
had not been chosen the king's heir, remained one of Tedric's
favorites, and had been chosen by Sapphire as a wedding attendant over more highly ranked ladies. Apparently, this irked
at least some of the representatives of King Tedric's Great
Houses.

However, all Elise said to Ninette was "Meet me in Crown
Princess Sapphire's suite as soon as possible. Don't stop to
gossip overlong with Valet."

"Yes, my lady," Ninette said, a trace offended.

Elise put a hand on her shoulder. "Thank you, Ninette. I'll
need all the support I can get."

Mollified, Ninette bustled off. Elise took up the bag con-

taining her embroidery, squared her shoulders, and went off
to rejoin her cousin.

FIREKEEPER STILL COULD NOT UNDERSTAND the hu-
man penchant for eating in company. Even less so, she could
not understand the human desire to combine business and
meals.

True, a wolf pack shared a kill, but not from any great desire
to do so—rather because any who departed the scene would
be unlikely to get a share. The Ones ate first and if, as was
often the case with smaller prey like a deer, the Ones devoured
most of the meat, the rest of the pack was left with the hide
and bones—and sometimes not even that.

Any wolf who made a solitary kill was not required to share
with the rest. Indeed, the pack would have thought such generosity unnatural. Only puppies were given greater consideration, as Firekeeper—ever a pup in the ranking of her pack—
knew well. She would have starved if the others had not
brought her a portion from kills made too far away for her to
join the pack. Even so, she did not repay this indulgence by
sharing the products of her own efforts at fishing or hunting.
That was neither required nor expected.

Since she had come to live with humans, Firekeeper had
learned that they did not exist on the same feast-or-famine
regime. Indeed, many moons had turned their faces since she
had felt the gnawing depths of true hunger. However, this had
not changed her basic nature. She struggled—mostly to please
Derian—not to bolt her food and almost always remembered
that growling when a person spoke to you was not a proper
response.

Today, at the banquet where King Allister was hosting the
many nobles gathered in anticipation of the marriage of his
son and the crown princess of Hawk Haven, Firekeeper was
having trouble remembering her manners.

Wisely, Derian had made certain that Firekeeper had something substantial to eat before getting dressed for the banquet. Therefore, Firekeeper was not precisely hungry. However, the sight of the fat roast pigs carried to each table made her almost pant with eagerness. The juicy roasts were surrounded by heaps of carrots and potatoes. Deep pottery bowls of apple sauce were set at each end of the table, along with trays of sliced bread and butter.

Firekeeper's early dinner had consisted of several bowls of thick seafood chowder and a hunk of fresh bread. That repast was forgotten now that quantities of juicy flesh were near. It was probably lucky for decorum that Blind Seer had been convinced to stay behind in Firekeeper's rooms, for the wolf would most certainly have overcome his shyness at the presence of so many strangers before the lure of so much food.

Firekeeper growled softly in her throat as Earl Kestrel, the host for this table, paused to make some quip to the woman on his right before beginning to carve. Derian, elevated from the servants' halls to a place at his master's table by his favor in King Tedric's eyes, nudged her.

"You can't possibly be hungry," he said, pitching his words for her ears alone. "Not after what you've already had to eat."

"He's so slow!" Firekeeper protested.

"And you and I will be among the last served," Derian reminded her, "as our relatively low rank requires. Cultivate patience."

"I could *eat* Patience," Firekeeper grumbled, referring to the grey gelding that was the only horse indifferent enough to its own fate to willingly carry her.

"Pretend," Derian suggested, "that Earl Kestrel is the head of your wolf pack and that if you leap on that pig before he's ready to let you he'll beat you bloody."

Firekeeper tried, but it was difficult. Small, hawk-nosed Norvin Norwood, dressed neatly in breeches and waistcoat of sky-blue brocade over shirt and hose in scarlet, looked anything but threatening. His silvering black hair and neat beard were freshly trimmed. His pale grey eyes twinkled at the jests of the woman beside him, yet there was an intensity about him, a feeling of a strung bow, that reminded Firekeeper that this little man had charged into battle against men twice his size and that they—not he—had fallen.

Such rememberings kept her under control until a dish with thick slices of pork and heaps of vegetables was set before her. Firekeeper even managed to eat with what she thought was dainty control, wiping her fingers on a chunk of bread and cutting potatoes into quarters before raising them to her mouth.

Except for Derian kicking her periodically when he thought she was getting too enthusiastic, Firekeeper was content until a light, fluting voice said:

"Goodness, Earl Kestrel, do you starve your poor ward?"

The speaker was a woman past her first youth seated about halfway down the table. She was wearing a bright yellow gown laced with pale green ribbons. Ropes of smoothly polished amber beads were looped around her rather long neck and two large amber nuggets depended from her earlobes. Hair a slightly darker shade of honey-gold than the gems had been twisted into a towering coiffure threaded through with a few more amber beads.

Firekeeper had been introduced to her when the guests came to table and now struggled for the woman's name. After a moment, it came to her: Lady Ceece Dolphin, a noblewoman of Bright Bay, scion of one of their Great Houses. She was sister to a duke, Firekeeper recalled. No one of any real importance, as the wolf-woman saw things, for neither Lady Ceece nor her children would come into the family's title. Indeed, Firekeeper thought title alone hardly any reason to grant someone respect. Humans, she had learned, thought otherwise.

Earl Kestrel answered Lady Ceece, his tone free of rancor.

"We don't starve her," he said, "but the poor child was near starvation's edge when I found her in the wilds this past Horse Moon. She has yet to overcome her enthusiasm for a well-filled plate."

Lady Ceece replied somewhat grudgingly, hearing her own

rudeness in the earl's courtesy, "Well, she certainly doesn't look overfed."

Sir Jared Surcliffe, Earl Kestrel's cousin, commented, "We only arrived today after several days' hard travel from Hope. I'm famished and the food is excellent. Cousin, would you cut me another slice from that roast?"

Even as the wolf-woman admired how the two men had clipped the barbs from Lady Ceece's words, Firekeeper considered the tensions evident in the large banquet hall. She was no stranger to social tension, having been brought into Hawk Haven as Earl Kestrel's piece in a play for the throne of that kingdom. The tension she sensed here was different. She slowed her attack on her plate of pork as she tried to sort out the reason for that difference.

Certainly, the strife over the throne of Hawk Haven had been bitter enough. There had been tears and screaming, bartering of lives for some imagined advantage, even hints that murder could be done if the prize was certain enough. Yet beneath it all there had been a sense that those who fought were all bound by a common interest.

It had been, Firekeeper thought, excited by the comparison, like wolves fighting over a kill. There had been no question who owned the kill. It belonged to the pack—or in this case, the kingdom. The question was who would get the best portions.

When the struggle had been resolved, almost everyone had settled back into their old patterns. A few bore wounds—Elise's disillusionment over Jet Shield was one such—but they were as no more than the routine slashes and cuts one wolf might give another. If trouble arose, the pack would rejoin, rivalry forgotten until the new crisis was past.

Here, though, the gathered nobility of Bright Bay and Hawk Haven were not yet a pack except by the commands of their kings. True, the nobles of Bright Bay had sworn oaths to uphold the new-made king, Allister of the Pledge, and his son and heir apparent, Shad Oyster. Part of that swearing was the understanding that Shad would someday reign not only in

Bright Bay but in Hawk Haven side by side with his betrothed, Crown Princess Sapphire.

In Hawk Haven the change had been less apparent. King Tedric still ruled, though his white hair and wrinkled features made clear that he could not last many years longer. His heir apparent had been drawn from approved ranks and those who had been passed by in her choosing—most notably Elise and Firekeeper herself—were pleased with the selection.

However, though Hawk Haven's nobility had been willing to accept King Tedric's selection of his heir, many had been less than pleased at the truce he had made with his nephew Allister. Until just that past summer Bright Bay and Hawk Haven had been sworn enemies. Now they were allies, their union into one nation reigned over by Sapphire and Shad a thing many of those gathered there could anticipate living to see.

And not all of them, Firekeeper thought, *are pleased at the thought of that seeing. Truly, this is not a pack gathered here to share a kill. It is a grouping of many packs, chancing on the same good hunting grounds and trying to decide whether or not to share the herds.*

The realization did nothing to quiet Firekeeper's soul, and she wondered whether Earl Kestrel was very brave, or only very foolish, to sit there and laugh.

III

THE WEDDING WAS A GRAND AFFAIR. As it was also in some sense the wedding of their two kingdoms—though that part of the marriage would not be consummated until both King Tedric and King Allister were become ancestors—made it an even more important event. For any of the heads of Bright Bay's five Great Houses to refuse to attend would be tantamount to declaring that the oaths they had sworn to King Allister were so much air.

None made that choice, though House Lobster had a new head—Duchess Faelene, the younger sister of the previous duke, Marek.

Old Marek Lobster had chosen to ally himself with Queen Valora. Indeed, he hardly had a choice, since his son, Harwill, was married to the queen and had taken the new title of King of the Isles. The uproar in House Lobster had been quite fierce, a source of gossip in both court and streets, but it had been simply a more public version of the choices being made in each of the noble families.

Yet old Duke Lobster was present after a fashion. Newly retitled Marek, Duke of Half-Moon Island, he had come as the Isles' representative to the wedding. To refuse him would have been to threaten the tense neutrality between the two realms. Duke Half-Moon's retinue was small, almost humble. He had brought no guards, no more servants than were perfectly proper for himself alone. As he was a widower, he did not even have a wife accompanying him.

In addition to his sister, several formidable women of Duke Half-Moon's generation were present. Foremost among these was Grand Duchess Seastar Seagleam, the late Gustin III's sister, and King Allister's aunt. Lesser in rank but perhaps more interesting to the gossips was Lady Brina Dolphin. Smiling with gracious vindictiveness, Lady Brina made herself highly visible at every gathering.

Gustin III had divorced her in order to marry Lady Viona Seal, who would bear him Valora. Valora's defeat was seen by many—including those of the Seals who had allied themselves with the Isles—as House Dolphin's vindication.

Although Shad and Sapphire would celebrate their marriage a second time before the nobles of Hawk Haven, several of Hawk Haven's noble houses had chosen to send representatives to this wedding as well. The Great Houses of Goshawk and Gyrfalcon were each represented by their Heads. Such would be expected of Goshawk and Gyrfalcon, for Sapphire was a granddaughter of those houses. Duke Peregrine, Queen

Elexa's brother, had planned to attend, but illness—really nothing more than advanced age—had forced him to send his heir. Wellward's example, however, shamed the remaining houses into sending at least a token representative.

Earl Kestrel was present for his house, but also at the express invitation of Princess Sapphire, who had desired that Lady Blysse serve as a wedding attendant. The Barony of Archer was represented by the entire family, again because Princess Sapphire had wished Lady Archer to be a member of her wedding party.

Still, no one really expected any of Hawk Haven's Great Houses to challenge King Tedric's choice of heir. Their protest would be against the public promise that someday the two kingdoms, rivals these hundred years and more, would be united.

"And so," said Firekeeper to Blind Seer as she mused over these complexities while bathing the morning of the wedding, "they sniff each other's backsides, trying to decide whether they are to be friends."

"And Lady Melina's absence and that of her children," the wolf replied, "becomes the raw wound in this great love-fest—a wound with dirt in it, for Duke Gyrfalcon, her own elder brother, is here."

"Here and howling to the moon about his sorrow that his younger brother Newell turned traitor," Firekeeper agreed.

"A loud howl does not mean a true hunter," Blind Seer said pedantically, "only an open mouth."

Firekeeper's brow furrowed. She, too, had trouble trusting the head of a family that had whelped both Newell and Melina Shield.

"Elise says that after the wedding, everything will be all right."

"Which wedding?" the wolf asked.

"I don't know."

The gown Firekeeper was to wear as a wedding attendant featured two parts: an underdress with a gently scooped neckline and long full sleeves, covered by a floor-length surcoat. The ensemble's essential simplicity—necessitated by the short length of time which the hastily recruited corp of seamstresses had been given to do their work—was disguised by the richness of the New Kelvinese silk from which it was made. The underdress was snowy white shot with silver, while the surcoat was an elaborately patterned crimson brocade.

The wolf-woman struggled into the underdress without much difficulty, but was glad when Derian knocked at her door as she was trying to reach the lacings at the back.

"May I?" he asked, running the cords expertly to and fro.

"If you don't," Firekeeper said practically, "I don't know who will."

"You're welcome, too," Derian said, thumping her gently on top of the head with his knuckles. "Today of all days, mind your manners."

Firekeeper sighed. "Must I wear these?"

She held up two dainty slippers, sewn from the finest dyed leather and decorated with scarlet tassels.

"You must," Derian replied without hesitation.

"And the hat?" Firekeeper said hopelessly, pulling on over her tousled hair a sweet little conical headdress bordered with a modest padded circlet.

Derian looked up from tying a bow at the top of her lacing and laughed heartily.

"Yes," he said when he had his breath, "you must wear the hat, but not like that. You look ridiculous."

"I feel," Firekeeper retorted, a trace sulkily, "ridiculous."

"Here," Derian said. "I'll show you how to do it right. Thank the Horse that I have a sister!"

He plucked off the offending headgear and took a brush to Firekeeper's hair. The thick, brown mass had grown a great deal since the early spring when she had stopped chopping it short with a hunting knife, long enough to be pulled back into a short queue—if she pinned back the stray ends that tended to tumble into her face.

"Today," Derian said, "a queue won't do. Not only is that a man's style, but you can't have a little bush sticking out from under the hat. We'll fan your curls out so . . ." He arranged her hair to his satisfaction, "then put the hat on, tilted slightly to the back so the circlet frames your face and the cap covers the dome of your head. There! Now that's pretty."

He showed Firekeeper her reflection in the mirror. She studied herself for a moment, then nodded reluctantly.

"That *does* look better," she admitted. "But why wear a hat? We'll be inside the castle. It won't rain."

"Because," Derian said cheerfully, "the crown princess wants you to wear it, the earl wants you to wear it, and you don't want to cause trouble over such a little thing—not since you agreed to be an attendant."

"I didn't know I'd need to wear a hat and *shoes*." The latter were a particular sore point and she glowered at the inoffensive slippers.

"You'll be happy enough for boots when winter comes," Derian predicted. "Consider this a rehearsal."

"Never needed boots before," the wolf-woman growled.

"Correction," Derian said. "You never had them. I assure you, you'll find them a great improvement over wrapping rabbit skins around your feet."

From where he had been dozing in the sunlight, Blind Seer yawned and chuckled.

"Derian is right," he said. *"You'll take boots when winter comes. Consider this dressing fancy protection against a different kind of cold."*

"Now look at yourself," Derian said, turning her before a full-length panel of polished silver, "and tell me you don't look quite the lovely lady."

Firekeeper again studied her image in the mirror. She still had difficulty with the idea that reflected images bore any relation to reality. Still, she had to admit that the person in the mirror looked rather like the other ladies she had seen bustling about the castle. She nodded grudging acceptance and let Derian fasten a pearl and ruby choker about her throat.

"Thank you," she said.

"And now for the crowning glory," Derian said with a chuckle. He extended her Fang, the hunting knife that had once belonged to Prince Barden. "I'm told you have permission to wear this strapped around your waist beneath the sur-coat."

"That's right," Firekeeper replied smugly. "My Fang does not leave me. Princess Sapphire agreed and even had a new belt made for it."

"Wise," Derian said, casting a critical glance at the weather-stained leather of Firekeeper's more usual gear. "Really we're going to have to teach you how to maintain leather."

Once the new belt was strapped loosely about Firekeeper's hips, the knife was not very visible. The part that was most so—the hilt with a large cabochon-cut garnet in the pommel—might be mistaken for a peculiar piece of jewelry.

Now that her own costume was complete, Firekeeper examined her friend's attire. Derian was dressed in knee breeches, waistcoat, and frock coat, all of a deep forest green. The color set off his red hair nicely. His stockings and shirt were off-white, and the silver buckles on his brown shoes shone with polish.

"You look a gentleman," she said approvingly.

"My mother helped me select this outfit along with several others when I went home after the war," Derian said. "She has a good eye for expensive clothing."

"And ambitions for her pup," Blind Seer added. The wolf was in a rather sour mood because, despite Firekeeper's repeated requests and Princess Sapphire's approval, he had been barred from the wedding.

Firekeeper knelt next to him and rubbed his head, ignoring the coating of fine silvery-grey hairs this left on the red brocade of her surcoat.

Derian forbore from commenting on this sartorial offense, only sighed.

A rap at the door summoned them. Elise, attended by Ninette, waited in the corridor. She was dressed identically to Firekeeper. The combination of strong red and silvery white went well with her fair complexion and made her golden hair seem to glow. Ninette was clad in a neat gown of salmon pink. Ironically, it was more elaborately embroidered than the one worn by her mistress, since it had come from her existing wardrobe, rather than having been hastily pieced together for the occasion.

Firekeeper gave Blind Seer a parting hug and hurried to join Elise.

"You look lovely," Elise said, reaching out to brush the worst of the wolf hair from Firekeeper's surcoat. "Now, remember, take small steps."

Firekeeper sighed, recalling lessons in deportment.

"Have a good time, sweet Firekeeper," Blind Seer called after her.

To all the listeners but one, his words came as a low, mournful howl.

IN THE INTERESTS OF POLITICAL HARMONY—and because all had assumed that it would be augmented by her mother and three sisters—the bride's party was very small. It consisted of Elise, Firekeeper, and the groom's young twin sisters, Minnow and Anemone.

These last were perfectly identical, still slight and slim, with straight silvery-blonde hair and eyes of a translucent green. Whether or not they would be beauties was still open to question, but there was no doubt they would be striking.

The little girls had celebrated their twelfth birthday four days before and were still trying to live up to the solemnity of their great age. Most of the time they managed, but every so often they would burst into pealing giggles. They were giggling when Firekeeper, Elise, and Ninette entered the room where all the bridal attendants were to wait before processing into the Sphere Chamber for the wedding.

Dressed in gowns of identical style to those worn by Firekeeper and Elise—though their underdress was gold-hued silk and their surcoat a sea-green brocade with a watery texture to the fabric—the twins had crowded up to a door and were peeking through a crack, giggling at what they saw.

Curiosity overcame Elise's first impulse, which was to drag the little girls back and remind them of the solemnity of the occasion. She noticed an older woman seated in a corner keeping a careful eye on them and decided that they must not be quite out of line. The woman had "old nurse" written in every line of her pleasant face and would not have brooked disorderly behavior.

"What are you looking at?" Elise asked, gliding toward the twins. The new slippers that had been supplied with the gown were superbly crafted. She made a mental note to learn the cobbler's name before she went back to Eagle's Nest.

Minnow—or was it Anemone?—started back guiltily, but both twins' gazes were bright with excitement.

"We were looking at the people coming into the hall," Minnow said. "It's so funny watching them."

"They bow to each other," Anemone added, "and say nice things but when they think no one can see them, the *looks* on their faces!"

"Certainly you've seen the like before," Elise said. "You've grown up in this court."

"Not really," Anemone said with charming honesty. "Father's title was duke before he became king, but it was just a courtesy. Everyone knew that we—his children, I mean—weren't going to be anything, so we didn't get invited to these big events."

"Father was," Minnow clarified, "and Mother, but not us. Anyhow, we were too young even if anyone had wanted to invite us. The ball on Bridgeton was the first time either of us went to a formal event."

And, thought Elise a trace bitterly, *because everyone thought your father might become king—though then they thought he was destined for Hawk Haven's throne, not Bright Bay's—then everyone wanted to treat you like ladies.*

She pushed the memory from her, knowing that her bitterness came from the memory of Jet Shield—then her betrothed husband—dancing attendance on the two little girls.

"Then was the coronation your first court event?" Elise asked.

"Pretty much," Anemone said, "and then we were sitting in front with Father and Mother and didn't get a chance to watch the guests."

Firekeeper had been standing back diffidently listening to the conversation. There was something guarded about her posture, a tension that reminded Elise that the wolf-woman was even less familiar with such events than the twins. *They* at least had been raised on the fringes of such things. Firekeeper had lived at Hawk Haven's court, but had always been a stranger there.

"Does everyone remember," Elise asked brightly, "what we practiced at rehearsal? Shall we run through our parts one more time while we wait? Ninette, you stand in for the crown princess."

Ninette did so, blushing slightly. Elise suspected that internally her maid was counting down the moments to when she could be excused to join the other favored servants on the back tiers of the balcony reserved for them.

They had just finished going through their parts and Ninette was straightening Firekeeper's cap, which had come askew again, when a herald in green and gold strode into the room. The nurse paused in the middle of inspecting the twins to make a deep curtsy.

"The Crown Princess Sapphire," announced the herald rather unnecessarily, for the lady in question was immediately behind him.

If the attendants' gowns had been chosen for simplicity, that must have been to free more seamstresses to work on the bride's gown. Although not so ornate as to be at odds with those worn by her attendants, Sapphire's gown was an elegant tribute to the dressmaker's art.

Her undergown was close-fitting scarlet silk, cut square across the shoulders, but fairly high to the throat—modest yet revealing. The shimmering white surcoat was quite elaborate, possessed of hanging sleeves that trailed to the floor, a sweeping length to the back that recalled a cloak, and elegant fur trim that began at the square neckline, then decreased slightly down the front to create a dainty breastplate before splitting into two sweeping rows that accented the wearer's hips.

Crown Princess Sapphire was no mere slip of a girl. Wielding a sword and handling a warhorse had made her broad in the shoulders, muscular in the arms. The clinging silk of the gown hinted at the strength of her long legs.

Like her attendants, Sapphire wore a headpiece, but whereas theirs were maidenly caps, equally suitable for either the little girls or the two slightly older women, Sapphire's shouted her importance—a jeweled crown laid over a veil that framed her forehead and spilled down her back almost to her elbows. Sapphire's blue-black hair was even longer, falling past her hips, a vibrant contrast to the surcoat's silver-white.

She looks wonderful, Elise thought, *and yet somehow odd. I suppose it's because I never thought to see her wed wearing any color but blue.*

Indeed, there was nothing blue in the bride's ensemble unless her own brilliant eyes could be counted. She spun before her attendants and the gown flowed with the motion. The gemstones in her crown glimmered in the light from the high windows.

"It is," Crown Princess Sapphire said smiling, "the most beautiful dress I have ever worn, and well worth all the fuss."

Elise grinned. "I hope you make certain the seamstresses hear your praise."

"I have," Sapphire assured her. "I'm even wondering if there is some award we can give them. Bright Bay has awards for everything, it seems. I've nearly gone mad memorizing all the subsidiary titles and honors."

Only the rapidity of Sapphire's chatter showed the nervousness she was feeling. At this small betrayal of vulnerability, Elise liked her a great deal. She liked her even better when the crown princess put out her hands to the other three.

"Minnow, Anemone, Firekeeper. Ladies, you all look wonderful and do great honor to your families."

Minnow said, "Lady Archer has had us practice our parts and we did perfectly."

"You have the gifts?" Sapphire asked.

The others nodded.

"Well, they shouldn't keep us waiting much longer."

Sapphire looked as if she wanted to go peek out the door, but restrained herself with an obvious effort at self-control. Ninette took pity on her and slipped out the back, coming in to report a few moments later.

"The kings and queens have just entered the hall and taken their places. The musicians are beginning the groom's processional."

"Then," Sapphire said, battlefield-efficient, "we should take our own places."

Crossing to stand before the doorway into the hall, Minnow and Anemone stood side by side, hands folded around small but intricately carved boxes. Elise and Firekeeper stepped a few paces behind them, accepting from Ninette two boxes of their own. Sapphire took her place behind them.

The crown princess did not carry a box, but instead held a small basket containing several small items, all swathed beneath a puffy fabric tissue.

And in some form or another, Elise thought, *every bride carries those same trinkets in her wedding. There is a leveling to it—a reminder that princess or milkmaid, we are all simply women.*

She heard a few nervous giggles from the twins. Beside her, Firekeeper's breath came fast and shallow.

"Don't be afraid," Elise reassured the wolf-woman, keeping her voice soft.

"I try," Firekeeper said, her tones gruff, "but I can't help it. I *am* afraid and more afraid because I don't know why I am afraid."

Elise gave her a quick hug. "It's natural. Relax into it and remember, we're just decorations. Everyone will be watching Sapphire and Shad."

"Thanks, cousin," said the crown princess dryly, but whatever else she might have said was interrupted by the double doors opening and the swelling of the music into the bride's processional.

Minnow and Anemone stepped forward, perfectly in step, perfectly in cadence. They moved out through the doors.

There may be some advantage to being twins, Elise thought, *when it comes to coordination.*

Then it was her turn. She walked slowly through the doorway, keeping her gait even and easy. To her relief Firekeeper matched her movements. The wolf-woman had a natural grace that compensated for her fear.

They passed through the double doors and into the Sphere Chamber. The room gave the illusion of being perfectly round though, of course, the floor was flat. The white marble walls curved upward, interrupted on two levels by half-round openings that led into viewing galleries. At the back of one of these, Elise knew, Ninette would be hurrying to her reserved place.

Long, narrow windows pierced the rounded walls at several levels. Today they had been left open to relieve the stuffiness of so many people in an enclosed space.

Peeking up at the galleries through her lashes, Elise thought she glimpsed Derian Carter's red head at the front of one of the first-tier balconies. Was that Sir Jared next to him? It was quite likely. Though neither possessed the rank to be seated lower down, both had won the favor of the bride and groom, as well as that of their auspicious parents. With this came invitations to the ceremony.

The more important wedding guests were seated at floor level in a great circle, their seats placed on shallow risers surrounding the low, raised dais at the center of the room. When the Sphere Chamber was being employed as a throne room, only half of its space was used. Sections of the seating area facing this theoretical "front" had been reserved since the time of King Gustin I for each of the Great Houses. Lesser personages were seated at the back and edges.

Today, since the entire room needed to be used, the carved wooden screen that backed the royal dais had been removed, permitting those seated behind a clear view—although more often then not they would be looking at the backs of the participants. Here were seated the foreign diplomats, the members of the monied—if not titled—houses, and anyone else who could not be refused an invitation to the ceremony without fear of giving offense.

King Allister needed to be even more careful than would be usual for such an event, since he had yet to ascertain who were his staunch allies and who gave support but grudgingly.

The royal dais was plushly carpeted in an ivory white only slightly darker than the marble walls. An honor guard jointly captained by Sir Dirkin Eastbranch of Hawk Haven and Sir Whyte Steel of Bright Bay surrounded the dais.

The armed and armored soldiers faced the assembly. They alternated guard to guard, one in the silver and scarlet of Hawk Haven, the next in the gold and green of Bright Bay. Ironically, though they stood the closest to the participants, they alone would see nothing of the ceremony, for their gazes would remain fixed outward.

Firekeeper beside her, Elise paced down the aisle. Aware—despite her assurance to Firekeeper—that all eyes were upon them, Elise glanced neither right nor left, but kept her gaze level and centered on her destination.

The royal dais was well worth looking at. At the center of the circle the two kings stood shoulder to shoulder, old Tedric at the left, leaning a bit on an ornate staff, Allister standing straight and looking more like a worried father than a king. Their queens stood beside them, Elexa frail but lovely in an ethereal, cobwebby manner, Pearl round and rosy, her head held high to balance the unaccustomed burden of a crown, her eyes bright with what might have been tears.

At Pearl's shoulder stood her son Tavis. The youth seemed to have grown taller and thinner in the few moonspans since Elise had seen him last—but then boys sprouted like that at fifteen. With his shock of dark golden hair, skinny torso, and slightly stooped posture, Tavis rather recalled a spring dandelion. Elise suspected that when the prince grew more comfortable with his new height and learned to stand straight, he would instead bring to mind a young puma. Certainly those stormy blue eyes seemed destined to haunt girls' dreams.

A few steps in front of Elise, the twins reached the dais,

curtsied to the monarchs, and then turned aside to stand alongside their brother.

Sadly, no children remained to stand at Queen Elexa's side, though she had borne two sons and a daughter and lost her health in doing so. However, when Elise and Firekeeper rose from paying their respects they took their places beside the queen.

Knowing that all eyes were turned to Sapphire, now halfway down the aisle, Elise sneaked out a hand and squeezed the queen's fingers—Elexa was her great-aunt and had always been kind to her. The queen gave Elise's hand a quick, birdlike squeeze in return.

At the center of the arc made by the two families, Crown Prince Shad waited for his bride. At twenty, he was three years younger than Sapphire. A fair-haired, serious young man, he had been a commissioned officer in Bright Bay's navy before his father won the throne. Although Shad was now crown prince, he had chosen to be wed in an elaborate dress version of his naval uniform—declaring himself for what he had won by his own merits rather than for the high position he would inherit.

The knee-breeches, waistcoat, and frock coat in dark green were not too different from what Shad would have worn in any case, but the shirt and hose were fine natural linen rather than the shimmering golden silk he would have worn as heir apparent to the throne.

The one alteration to Shad's uniform was in his headgear. Instead of the tricorn worn by lesser officers, Crown Prince Shad wore a crown upon his fair head. It was less elaborate than the Hawk Haven heirloom worn by Sapphire, but no less a declaration of his royalty.

When Sapphire reached the royal dais, Shad took her left hand and together they made homage to the monarchs. Then, gracefully trading clasped hands, they presented themselves to the assembled nobles, progressing round the circle so that they would be visible to all.

The applause that greeted this gesture was loudest, Elise thought, from the theoretical rear where the foreign diplomats and their parties were seated. It would have been unthinkable to move the rulers of Bright Bay's Great Houses from their traditional places at the front, no matter how important foreign alliances would be to the new king.

Now, in a move choreographed to present less back to the assembly, the two families broke their arc. The bride's party moved to the left of the dais and faced inward, while the groom's party moved to the right and did the same. The maneuver went well, and as the lowest ranked of the "floor" guests had been seated at this point, they would not be likely to complain about backs turned to them. It was enough honor that they were on the ground level at all.

Bride and groom remained at the center, facing each other.

It's going well, Elise thought as King Allister of the Pledge stepped forward to join the bride and groom.

"It is my great honor and privilege as both head of my house and head of my family to officiate at this wedding," he announced. His voice carried easily through the now-hushed room, so well that the heralds posted at the back to repeat what was said held their silence.

"We are here," King Allister continued, "to begin a new family, a family of two that will, with blessing and fortune, someday be a much larger family."

The traditional words took on a new meaning in the context of this particular wedding.

True enough, Elise thought, *for if King Allister's wish comes true, Sapphire and Shad will be heads of a very large family indeed—that of the new kingdom of Bright Haven.*

Looking out over the crowded room, she could tell that she was not the only one to have this thought, nor was every thinker pleased by the revelation.

"From the time of those ancestors who are but names in our personal litanies," King Allister went on, "we have celebrated the union of two individuals into one family by the filling of a pouch with small items symbolizing our hopes and dreams for the newly married couple. This pouch is then the first thing placed in their family shrine. Someday, when they, too, join the march of ancestors, their pouch will be moved into their heir's family shrine, thus granting continuity."

As King Allister finished speaking, Prince Shad cleared his throat. Like his father, he spoke loudly and clearly, his words heard throughout the hall.

"My dear Sapphire," Shad said, "I ask you to accept the pouch I have had prepared for this day."

He presented to her a small bag about the size of the palm of his broad hand, holding it high so that all of the assembly could at least glimpse it.

The wedding pouch was woven of gold thread, fringed with long strands of tiny, faceted emerald and ruby beads. Silver was never used in the making of these pouches, because of its tendency to tarnish; if family heraldry necessitated it, something white took its place. For this pouch the silver of Hawk Haven's coat of arms was represented in the strand of priceless matched pearls from which the pouch depended.

There were gasps of astonishment and awe as Shad held up the costly thing. Most wedding pouches were made of glove-soft leather and embroidered with costly treasures. This pouch was a treasure in itself.

Sapphire glowed with delight as she extended her hand as ritual demanded to join Shad's on the strap.

"I accept your gift," she said, her tones ringing and clear. Then in a softer voice she said, "Shad, it's just lovely."

Murmurs of delighted approval eddied through the Sphere Chamber as those in front repeated Sapphire's words to their neighbors.

This part of the ritual completed, Elise felt her heart beating faster. As the senior attendant, she would be one of the first to offer her gift. The parents, however, came first.

"My son and daughter," King Allister said, with those words accepting Sapphire into his family, "Queen Pearl and I offer you the hope of children, even as we have been blessed with children of our own."

Queen Pearl stepped forward when her husband spoke and dropped a small ivory carving of an infant into the open pouch.

She quickly kissed both her son and his new wife before stepping back to her place.

King Tedric spoke next and despite his best efforts, his words did need to be repeated by the heralds. King Tedric was clearly accustomed to this and paused between each phrase so that the heralds' voices seemed a natural echo.

"Daughter and son," he said, "you are entering into a great adventure. Elexa and I knew each other hardly at all when we were married. Over time, we have come to understand each other and to know that the greatest strength a marriage can have is the power to listen—not merely with the ears but with the heart as well. Learn to put yourself where the other stands, to not think of your own reply and advantage, but of what the other one is saying. Listening with ear and heart will bear you through all trials, through all manner of sorrows, and enhance all of your joys."

He concluded his speech by helping Queen Elexa walk forward, he leaning on his staff, she leaning on his arm.

Elexa placed in the pouch a tiny carved image of an ear and a heart bound together by a slim cord of twisted silk threads. Again the bride and groom accepted the parental kiss—though in this case the age difference made it seem grandparental.

My turn, Elise thought, and stepped lightly forward.

"Cousins," she said, "my gift is the wish for health for both of you and for all of your offspring."

Elise wanted to say more, but her mouth was drying with the sudden awareness of all those gazes—not all of them friendly—centered upon her. Panic made her heartbeat rush in her ears and she thought she heard a distant howling. Then she recaptured her confidence.

"Although you will have many treasures," she continued, realizing that the pause had been long only for herself, "health is the greatest of them. Without health, the shine of gold dims, the sparkle of gems turns dull. With health, every sunrise, every fresh breeze, every glow of firelight becomes a treasure beyond counting."

She stopped then, having done her best to paraphrase similar speeches she had heard given. From the little wooden box she had carried up the aisle she removed a piece of amethyst carved in the likeness of an androgynous figure breathing in deeply—the traditional image of health.

After bestowing the ritual kiss, Elise stepped back into her place. She discovered that she was biting the inside of her lip, for now the time had come for Firekeeper to do her part.

The wolf-woman hesitated for the barest moment. Then she stepped forward, her head held high. Watching Firekeeper move, Elise thought she seemed haughty; then she realized that what she had taken for arrogance was a listening alertness. Firekeeper was following the routine as rehearsed, but clearly her whole mind was not on the task at hand.

Firekeeper halted in front of the bride and groom. Her voice when she spoke was loud enough to carry, but strangely rusty-sounding. Elise realized that she had rarely—if ever—heard Firekeeper raise her voice, unless she was calling to Blind Seer—and then she was more likely to howl.

"Sapphire and Shad," Firekeeper said, omitting titles but speaking with an affectionate warmth that removed any trace of disrespect from the address, "I am to offer you the wish for wealth and I do that because I am supposed to, not because I think you will need it."

There was a soft chuckle at this, doubtless because of the abundance of gems and precious metals in evidence among the royal party.

Oh, soft-pawed Lynx, Elise thought in despair, *she's forgotten her part.*

"I offer you," Firekeeper continued seriously, "another wealth—one you have shown already, so I don't give it to you, I wish you to keep it. This wealth is the wealth of courage. Be strong and brave and faithful as you were in war, even now when there is peace. That is what I wish for you."

She placed a shining gold coin in the bag—the traditional fallback money with which every family gifted the newlyweds. After this she added something that only the bride and groom saw.

The wolf-woman smiled and solemnly kissed the astonished twosome, then padded back to her place. Through all of this, even her carefully worded speech, she never lost that bow-strung alertness.

Elise wondered if anyone else recognized Firekeeper's attitude for what it was. Glancing about, she saw Sir Dirkin Eastbranch looking from side to side, frowning.

After this, the ceremony proceeded without any interruptions to the ritual course. Prince Tavis stepped forward next and offered the couple the gift of wisdom. Giggles vanished into wide-eyed solemnity, the twins offered their eldest brother and his new wife the gift of happiness. Then it was time for the bride and groom to offer each other their secret wishes—each for the other.

Sapphire began, her strong fingers curled around the token in her hand so that none might glimpse it and so denature the power of the wish.

"Shad, I offer you my secret wish for our union." Sapphire's words were ritual, but the ringing note in her voice made them unique to this marriage. "I give it to you because from this day forth whatever I do, I do as part of something new—a new creation called 'us.'"

She slipped her trinket into the bag. Clearing his throat, Shad spoke in turn. Although the words were the same and his delivery less polished, he too spoke with sincerity.

Stealing a glance about the hall as Shad slipped his secret into the marriage pouch, Elise noted that many of the watchers were wiping away tears. The hostile looks had softened, too, blunted perhaps by the intensity of the two young people in front of them.

Incongruously, Elise thought she heard a distant, mournful wolf's howl. Again, she was in a position to note the expressions on other faces and realized that the sound wasn't merely her imagination. Surprise, annoyance, curiosity danced across face after face. The one face Elise couldn't see was Firekeeper's, for the wolf-woman still stood at her shoulder but through that slight contact she felt the other tense.

The ceremony was moving into its final phase and no one was about to interrupt it to deal with a disconsolate wolf. Indeed, many of the guests probably thought the cry was that of some hunting dog out in one of the courtyards and had already dismissed the noise as a minor annoyance.

Sapphire certainly recognized that lupine voice, but she did not permit anything to distract her from this important moment. As Shad had produced the pouch at the beginning of the ceremony, she drew something from her little basket.

"Now," she said, the single word a triumphant clarion, "dear Shad, we have received the good wishes of family and friends. With this needle and thread let me close the pouch so that these good wishes may sustain us through a long and fruitful marriage."

Shad drew the two edges close together, holding them for Sapphire's ease. As he did so he recited,

"What we here have drawn together let no person, no force, no cause in all the world pull apart. Together we are sewn. Together we shall remain."

On the final words, Sapphire ended her stitching and tied off the thread. As it snapped, the assembled guests broke their long silence by chanting as with one voice slightly furred about the edges:

"As these two so wish it, let it be so."

Bride and groom embraced and Elise felt tears blur her eyes.

Caught in the joyful moment, she thought the shouting that filled the hall was that of spontaneous applause. Only when she heard someone scream, heard the crash of metal upon wood, and saw Firekeeper leaping toward the bride and groom did she realize that something had gone terribly wrong.

IV

 FROM HIS SEAT IN THE FRONT ROW of a first-tier balcony, Derian Carter saw the assassins attack. Unfortunately, he was unable to do anything to prevent them. All he could do was lean forward and add his voice to the hundreds raised in spontaneous cries of warning.

"Look out!" he heard himself yell, and even as the words were ripping their way from his throat he thought how foolish they were.

Jared Surcliffe was on his feet trying to leave the balcony, his efforts slowed by those guests who were crowding forward for a better view.

"Let me through!" he commanded, pushing his way through. "I'm a doctor."

Such was Sir Jared's authority that the panicked mob did part—at least sufficiently to let him squeeze by.

Derian kept to his seat, knowing that by the time he reached the floor whatever was transpiring would be over. Instead, he set himself to witness every motion, for perhaps that testimony would prove of some later use.

Even as Sapphire had broken the thread with which she had stitched closed the wedding pouch and the assembled guests had spoken their joint blessing, four pairs of men had suddenly risen from their places among the rows of foreign guests.

No one commented or made move to stop them as they crossed the few steps that took them to the front. They were foreigners and couldn't be expected to know the details of the ritual. Indeed, the fact that they were garbed and equipped in a similar fashion suggested that they were special attendants, moving to escort their honored masters to congratulate the bride and groom.

One man in each pair bore a stout, heavily ornamented walking stick. Upon reaching the front row, he swung this at the guard closest to him, a fast, hard, practiced move that was hardly signaled by his body language until the action was already under way.

Although not expecting any such attack—indeed, distracted by the need to pronounce the ritual blessing—each guard automatically moved to block the walking stick with the elegantly beribboned spear he held in one hand. As the guard did so, the true nature of this seemingly insane attack came clear, when the second man of each pair dove for the space now opened in the ring of guards.

Sir Dirkin and Sir Whyte had positioned the guards so that each had the space of a broad-shouldered man between him and the next. This was partially so that the guards would not block the view of those very important guests seated in the lowest, closest bank of seats, partially so if action was called for they would have room to move. Shoulder-to-shoulder looked very impressive on parade, but it made bringing sword or spear into play rather difficult.

Three of the assassins who moved for the openings their partners had created leapt onto the dais with ease. The fourth was tripped by the butt end of the spear held by the guard at the other end of the gap, a quick-moving fellow whose reward was a knife thrown to bury itself to the hilt in his throat, fountaining blood over his white scarf.

The guards wore breastplates painted with their personal arms over dress uniforms that included highly polished helms, but no one had thought full armor—including highly uncomfortable neck protection—necessary, since the guards' role was to be ceremonial and preventative, not combative.

Having lost one knife, the assassin rolled clear of the spear point another guard thrust at him. Derian saw a look of studied panic on the assassin's face and realized that the man knew he was doomed, that his only wish was to cause sufficient distraction that those who had broken onto the royal dais would have time to perform their task.

Fascinating as that struggle was, Derian's gaze was drawn irresistibly to where the assassins raced toward the bride and groom. Long knives shone bare-bladed in the torchlight. Shad had grasped Sapphire and thrust her behind him—a gallant impulse but one doomed to failure, for the warrior princess was determined to remain at her new husband's side.

Bride and groom had taken their stations for the ceremony near the center of the dais, away from the encircling ring of guards, but the rest of the royal party stood near the edge. With remarkable clarity of purpose, the guards nearest to the monarchs bounded onto the dais, putting themselves between danger and their rulers. Other guards helped the threatened wedding celebrants down from the dais—all the celebrants, that is, but one.

At the first crash of spear and staff, Firekeeper—who Derian had noted seemed edgier than even her nervousness at taking part in the ceremony could account for—had leapt from her place next to Elise, racing to intercept the assassins. Her Fang was in her hand and a furious howl tore from her lips. All illusion that Firekeeper was a gentlewoman vanished with that cry. She was animal fury entrapped by a long gown.

The distant howl that answered hers did nothing to sustain the gentlewomanly illusion.

Firekeeper stumbled slightly against the swathing fabric of her skirt, but she didn't pause to tear the gown short. Instead, with another howl, she flung herself onto the closest of the three assassins. The man was slimly built and the impact staggered him, but he retained his balance. Flailing he steadied himself, simultaneously bringing into play a slightly curved knife with a curious, dull sheen to the blade.

Derian heard the words that ripped out of his own throat as distantly as if they'd been uttered by another person.

"Firekeeper! Poison!"

Whether or not she heard him, the wolf-woman twisted away from the knife blade's first thrust. Unworried about the niceties of civilized combat, she then bit the assassin solidly on the throat. Blunt human teeth might not do the damage of a wolf's fangs, but buried in unprotected flesh they did cause pain.

The assassin yelled. Against the general uproar that now filled the Sphere Chamber, Derian could not differentiate that single voice, but he saw the man's mouth open, revealing stained and broken teeth. The knife in his hand came down, snagging in the swathing scarlet fabric of Firekeeper's surcoat.

Firekeeper had wrapped one arm about her victim's shoulders, forcing him to bear her weight. Her teeth still worrying his throat, she brought her Fang up and into his side. It skidded against some hidden armor, sliding up uncontrolled for a moment before she readjusted.

Releasing the man's throat, Firekeeper spoke to the assassin. Again, Derian had no idea what she said, but he was struck by the curious calmness on her face. Elsewhere on the dais, fear, anger, and horror were evident, even on the faces of the professional soldiers. Firekeeper alone fought as if she were hunting—purpose dominating her actions.

Whatever she said to the assassin cowed him. The knife slipped from fingers suddenly nerveless. He slumped. Firekeeper snarled at him and he dropped to the carpeted floor, arms and legs spread wide.

Without another glance at her victim, Firekeeper turned to defend the prince and princess, but that battle was over.

Sapphire leaned against Shad, the silver white of her surcoat dyed scarlet, the scarlet soaked with blood. The high heirloom crown had fallen to the floor and her hair spilled in a dark curtain that hid the nature of her injuries from immediate inspection.

Shad held his newly wed wife close, his face pale with shock. Still, his control was that of a battlefield commander. He saw that some of the guards who were trying to enforce order on the panicked mob of what had been wedding guests were pushing back a single man determined to get forward. In a bellow trained to carry over storms at sea, Shad shouted:

"Let the man through! That's Sir Jared of Hawk Haven. He's a doctor!"

The guards, who must have been hearing something similar from Doc's own lips, let Sir Jared through immediately. The mob quieted as one at the sound of the crown prince's voice, their panicked shouts fading to a dull murmur so that for the first time Derian could sort individual voices from the general noise.

As Sir Jared half-ran through the parting crowd he nearly slammed into the one figure who moved to intercept him.

"Elise!" he said in surprise.

"I'm here to help," the young woman said stubbornly.

"Good," Doc answered without pause. "Get someone to fetch my kit or any med kit. Mine's in my room."

Sir Jared hadn't stopped moving even as he spoke. Elise

turned to obey his orders and found an inconspicuous brown-haired man coming toward her, the requested kit in his hand.

Derian had no idea how Valet, Earl Kestrel's personal attendant, had gotten past the guards, but Valet had the gift of always seeming to be in the right place at the right time. Doubtless the guards had responded to his purposefulness as something welcome in the madhouse around them.

"Valet!" Elise exclaimed in relief.

"Sir Jared's medical bag, my lady," Valet said, handing it to her with a short bow.

Elise spared no time in thanks, but hurried to where Shad had lowered Sapphire to the carpeted dais. Valet crossed to Firekeeper's side.

The wolf-woman stood with her foot solidly planted in the small of her captive's back, clearly waiting lest she be needed. However, the other assassins had been well and wholly dealt with.

Faced with the potential murder of Shad and Sapphire as penalty for anything less than thoroughness, the guards had not attempted to take prisoners. The two other assassins who had reached the dais were dead, their blood spreading to stain the snowy carpet crimson. The one who had failed to cross onto the dais was also dead, bludgeoned by several guards impatient to revenge their fellow's death.

The four club wielders had fared only somewhat better. Two had been knocked out almost immediately. A third had apparently experienced a surge of initiative and had moved toward King Allister. The king's guards had made short work of him.

The fourth club wielder had fled into the crowd, but had made the mistake of choosing the section of seats occupied by the denizens of Bright Bay's minor but extremely warlike Shark Barony. Required by law to always bear arms, the Sharks proved that their elaborately bejeweled belt knives were more than decoration.

In fact, Derian thought, the speed with which the assassins had been dispatched spoke poorly for the entire plan. What a waste of eight lives—for the three assassins who had survived would doubtless be executed. What purpose had the attack served?

True, Sapphire was wounded—perhaps badly—but there was ample medical assistance near. True, there would be those who would speak long and loudly about the ill omens of this wedding. Still, that alone didn't seem enough to merit such an act—not when the same eight assassins could have done their work elsewhere and with greater hope of success.

Frowning thoughtfully, Derian turned and joined those few remaining wedding guests who were now filing from the balcony.

What purpose *had* the attack served?

ELISE TOOK THE MEDICAL BAG from Valet and, snagging her skirts in one hand, raced up those same steps that, what seemed like a hundred years ago, she had mounted with all due decorum, worried only about the many eyes watching her every move.

A small group was clustered around the crown prince and princess, but Elise shouldered her way through without ceremony.

She extended the bag to Sir Jared. He glanced up, the worried frown on his face making his Kestrel family nose look even more beaky than usual.

"Hand me several small separators, would you? Then get out the blue bottle labeled sterilizing wash—the blue one, mind."

Elise did as ordered, finding the requested items easily. Sir Jared had given her some emergency medical training when the recently ended war was in the offing and she'd become familiar then with his personal organizational system.

She became rather worried when he requested the blue bottle of sterilizing wash. From past experience she knew that this was the concentrate he kept and usually diluted before use. Indeed, a glance showed her that there was a pale green bottle containing the dilute solution ready in the bag.

Sir Jared used the separators to hold open the edges of a long nasty slash that began low on Sapphire's right rib cage and extended below her right breast, rising into her left breast and stopping just below the aureole of her left nipple.

"Princess," he said to his patient, "this is going to burn worse than salt and vinegar. I suggest you scream."

Crown Princess Sapphire was, despite the amount of blood she had lost, quite evidently conscious. However, she was so pale that the white oval on her forehead had vanished into the general hue of the surrounding skin. Her reply was prefaced by a small, defiant smile:

"I'll take your suggestion, Doc."

The fingers of one of Sapphire's hands were wrapped around Shad's. He squeezed them gently.

"Ready?" the young groom asked his bride softly.

Doc, however, knew better than to give warning. With a nod of thanks to Elise, he took the blue bottle and splashed the undiluted solution into the open wound. It coursed down from the peak of Sapphire's breast, flowing through the wide slash and across her side.

Sapphire screamed, a shrill, raw sound, and promptly passed out.

"Well, that's for the good," Doc muttered. "Lady Elise, let's remove the fibers from the cut while she's out, and then close. Someone get us some better light."

Elise didn't know who obeyed the knight's command, but the area over them brightened almost immediately. Working quickly lest Sapphire reawaken, they used tweezers to remove the worst of the intrusive material lest it foster scarring and infection.

"Let's close now," Doc said.

Elise nodded and turned to remove clean needle and heavy thread from the kit bag. In the near distance, she could hear a self-assured voice insisting:

"But I am Lord Rory Seal, the Royal Physician, the medical attendant to the royal family. I insist on being let through to the crown princess! I would have been here sooner, but I was seated—quite improperly—toward the back and couldn't get here."

Firekeeper's husky voice answered him.

"Doc is with them. Others are hurt. Go there."

Lord Rory was clearly indignant. "I tell you. I am the physician to the royal family! The title has been in my family for seventy-five years!"

"Go."

Firekeeper must have made some threatening move, for when next heard, Lord Rory's voice was slightly more distant, but complaining still:

"Treating guards and vassals is beneath me! I am physician to the royal family!"

Elise sighed. Firekeeper possessed a fine sense of hierarchy but no patience at all with those who had not proven themselves to her personal satisfaction.

Holding the edges even, Elise held Sapphire's wound closed while Doc stitched through the pale flesh. A certain tension in the muscles under Elise's fingers told her when the crown princess returned to consciousness, but since Sapphire chose to play possum, Elise respected her wishes.

"Unhappily, there still may be a scar unless we are very lucky," Doc said, placing his hands over the wound. The vague look of intense concentration that indicated he was using his healing talent came over his face. "But the breast was not cut deeply and should still function, and the poison on the blade should have been washed out of the flesh. We are fortunate that her wound bled so freely and the knife didn't tag an organ or the circulatory system."

Shad looked relieved. "Thanks, Doc."

He bent to kiss Sapphire's face.

Sir Jared started to smile, aware of the honor inherent in the prince's informality; then he stared at a small ripped patch on the young man's left shoulder.

"Why didn't you tell me you'd been hit?" he snapped, holding the young man in place and taking a closer look at the nearly bloodless puncture wound.

"It was only a small cut," the prince protested. "She . . ."

Without pausing for words, Sir Jared grabbed for a knife to clear away the torn remnants of the prince's waistcoat and shirt. When this action was completed, he bent Shad forward with one hand and held him in place.

"Blue bottle," he barked at Elise. Then to the prince, "Where poison may be concerned, there is no such thing as a small wound."

"Yes, sir," Shad said. What Elise could see of his face suddenly looked young and scared. "Sapphire was so covered with blood and my wound didn't hurt very much . . ."

Shad's apology ended in an abrupt shout of pain. Sir Jared had splashed the remainder of the undiluted sterilization wash into the puncture wound.

"I apologize, Prince Shad," Jared said, letting his patient sit upright again. "But I didn't care to delay longer."

He sopped a bit of cloth in the solution running down Shad's back and pressed it over the wound.

"We'll need," he said, "to keep this rag right here until I can get more solution. Lady Elise, if you would hand me some of the long bandaging strips?"

Elise did so. As she finished helping Sir Jared tie the bandages snugly in place, she became aware that the small crowd gathered around them—which before had mostly consisted of guards—had been augmented. The queens Pearl and Elexa were now present along with a man with silvering hair who must be Lord Rory.

"*I* wouldn't have overlooked the crown prince's injury," he was saying to Queen Pearl. "I know my duty to the throne of Bright Bay. Ever since my grandsire's day when our family was first honored with this position, we have taken the health and well-being of the royal family most seriously . . ."

Queen Pearl nodded absently, almost, but not quite, ignoring Lord Rory entirely. Without regard for her gown, she knelt on the blood and medication soaked carpeting next to Sapphire and Shad.

"I'm sorry I couldn't come earlier. We had to do something about the panic and," she glanced up at Lord Rory who was now expostulating to a blank-featured guard, "we knew you were in good hands."

Sapphire, no longer feigning unconsciousness, lifted a hand and took Pearl's.

"Thank you, Mother," she said simply. "We never doubted your concern."

Shad, still holding Sapphire's head on his lap, nodded agreement.

"And," quavered Queen Elexa, her anxiety apparent despite her best efforts to remain calm, "what is your assessment, Sir Jared?"

The doctor rose respectfully to his feet and bowed, even while making his answer.

"I am hopeful," he said, "that both will recover. Princess Sapphire has lost a great deal of blood and should be given liquids—especially beef broth and teas containing strengthening herbs that I will supply—and restricted to bed. Prince Shad . . ."

Sir Jared looked grave. "Prince Shad may have taken some poison into his system. I recommend that he be kept quiet for at least a full day. Exertion would speed any poison through his system. With Your Majesties' permission, I would like to inspect his wound again as soon as he is settled in bed."

Elise had spent enough time with Queen Elexa to realize that the sudden tranquility that descended over her features was more indicative of concern than any hysteria would be.

"I see," Elexa replied very softly. "Pearl, what do you suggest?"

"The young people's suite," Bright Bay's queen replied, "has been prepared for them. However, it is hardly furnished as an infirmary."

Elise saw both Shad and Sapphire look vaguely embarrassed and realized that this should have been their wedding night, the consummation of their union. Doubtless, Jared's concern about exertion spreading poison—not to mention the raw nature of Sapphire's wounds—would make that final ritual impossible.

Queen Pearl continued, "There is a room here on the ground

floor that could be refurnished as an infirmary. Then they would not need to be carried as far."

"Is it," Queen Elexa asked, "secure?"

"We will make it so," Pearl said firmly.

Peripherally, Elise noted that stretchers were being brought into the Sphere Chamber. Doubtless some servant as efficient as Earl Kestrel's Valet had anticipated the need.

After kissing her son and his bride, Queen Pearl rose to give orders. Shad looked about somewhat anxiously.

"My father," he said, his voice making the words a question, "and the others. Tell me, who else was injured?"

Firekeeper, who had been standing a few paces away in watchful silence, took it upon herself to answer.

"Two guards were killed," she said, "and three others wounded enough for a doctor's care. The kings were not hurt—the guards made sure of that."

Her expression was grave. Looking up at her report, Shad and Sapphire saw the ruin of Firekeeper's gown and generally disheveled appearance for the first time.

"They attacked you?" Sapphire asked, a slight note of incredulity evident despite the weakness of her voice. Elise thought she might have even been jealous.

Firekeeper, however, replied with a short, barking laugh.

"Oh, no. They no attack me. I attack them."

"Lady Blyssé," Queen Elexa said with a fond smile for the wolf-woman, "captured one of the assassins. Even now, he has been taken for questioning."

The ice that entered the queen's smile promised nothing good for the man.

The arrival of a servant with the news that the infirmary would be prepared by the time the crown prince and crown princess could be carried to it ended the conversation. Sir Jared departed with the stretchers, speaking politely to the still vociferating Lord Rory.

Elise remained behind, unwilling to get in the way. She stood a long moment staring down at the red stains splattered over the once snowy carpet. Firekeeper came to stand beside her.

"Why?" she asked, her query as simple as a child's. "Why?"
Elise met the confusion in the dark brown eyes squarely.

"I don't know," she replied, "but I have all sorts of terrible suspicions. Come with me. We'll get you cleaned up and change into simpler clothing."

"No dancing tonight?" Firekeeper asked a trace sadly. The wolf-woman loved dancing and music above all other human arts.

"No dancing," Elise said. "Not of the sort you mean, but I dare say we'll have much fancy word dancing before this is concluded."

Firekeeper sighed. "Such is so much easier with wolves."

The distant echoing howl of Blind Seer, still trapped in the tower above, gave lie to her words.

"WE HAVE SOME INFORMATION," King Allister said to the nobles and counselors crowded into a meeting room rather too small for a gathering of this sort. Usually, the Sphere Chamber would have been used, but it was still being scrubbed clean after the events earlier in the day. "I have called you all here to me in order that rumor be squelched as rapidly as possible."

The king of Bright Bay swallowed a sigh and an impulse to rub the back of his hand across his eyes. Even such a small display of the grief and exhaustion he felt could be misinterpreted. Instead, he sipped from the goblet of watered wine on the table before him and surveyed the gathering.

Most of those here before him were members of his own kingdom, representatives of the houses and families who had been invited to the royal wedding. There were also, however, members of the Hawk Haven contingent. He recognized Baron Archer and his daughter, Elise, Earle Peregrine, and Earl Kestrel. Derian Carter was also present, as was his right as king's counselor. So, rather surprisingly, was Lady Blysse, her great grey wolf leaning against her leg and crowding the aisle.

These King Allister was comfortable with. He was less happy, given what had been discovered about the assassins, to have the diplomatic representatives present, but they were—not only the dignitaries from New Kelvin, Waterland, and Stonehold, as must be expected, but also from the Isles. To oppose a representative from the Isles attending the meeting would have been too close to an accusation—an accusation for which, as of yet, there was no proof. So fronted by friends, probable enemies, and those whose motives were as yet unclear, King Allister must give his report.

At least he felt certain of King Tedric, who sat to his right, his expression weary, bland, and vaguely concerned. Between them they had decided that King Tedric would keep silent, act the role of the shock-broken dodderer, and see what he could learn from the expressions of those gathered before them.

Putting down his goblet, King Allister continued:

"Doubtless rumors are growing with each breath that passes. I charge you to join me in ending them."

Duke Oyster, the king's father-in-law, indicated that he wished to be recognized. Allister did so, knowing that Reed Oyster was flaunting his own new importance by demonstrating to his fellow heads of house that he could interrupt the king.

"Your Majesty," Reed said, the tones of a practiced orator rolling out despite the muffling effect of the crowded chamber, "one of the most damaging rumors is that your royal self and the crown prince were both slain or mortally wounded. Do you intend to address this?"

Allister replied, "I myself will appear later today to address the populace. My captain of the guard, Whyte Steel, is making security arrangements. Crown Prince Shad is keeping to his bed for the time, under the advice of his medical attendants."

There was a flurry of motion as others signed for recognition. This time the king chose not to acknowledge them. He had done his part for Pearl's father and further cemented the support of that important ally. However, even for political reasons he was not about to turn this audience into an interview. Too much could get out of hand.

"Pray wait," he said firmly, "and listen to what I have to say. You may find your questions answered. In any case, this room is close and overfull. Despite the coolness of the autumn, we certainly do not wish to remain contained at tight quarters any longer than necessary."

A ripple of laughter acknowledged the wisdom of this last statement. When the gathering had stilled, King Allister went on, this time staying to the items on his prepared statement.

"First of all, I am pleased to report that both my son and his bride are recovering from the injuries sustained in the attack."

He went on to itemize the injuries in some detail, having decided that enough people would have seen the blood that pretending at less gravity would only incite the rumors he was trying to quell.

"Poison," he added, "was used. However, owing to quick action on the part of the attendant physicians, we may hope that its effects have been neutralized."

Ancestors, he thought, *grant that this prayer is granted!*

King Allister knew from consulting with Sir Jared Surcliffe that both victims were still in danger. Indeed, although the knight's healing talent could speed the mending of flesh and bone, it could not neutralize poison. There was some thought that it could even hasten the poison's effect by making healthy the flesh that would carry it. Still, Princess Sapphire's color was returning nicely, and Shad, scared by the risk he had inadvertently taken, was remaining dutifully in bed, his younger brother Tavis doing duty as both trusted attendant and watchdog lest the crown prince forget himself.

"Although both Prince Shad and Princess Sapphire are expected to recover," the king continued, "we did not escape without losses. Several of our guards, both those of Bright Bay and those of Hawk Haven, were injured. Two men were killed."

The king eulogized those who had died in the course of protecting him and his family. As the words flowed easily from his lips, he found himself wondering which of the studious and sorrowful faces before him was nothing more than a mask. Certainly someone here knew the truth behind the attack.

"Lastly," Allister said, "we have determined some facts about the assassins. Thanks to the quick actions of several of the guards and of Lady Blysse Kestrel, who took it upon herself to go to the bridal couple's defense . . ."

He paused while those present craned around to stare at Firekeeper. Stories of her fighting skill, greatly exaggerated, were some of the favorite about the castle and town. These the king felt no desire to quell, for he hoped they would protect her. For the same reason, he had agreed to let Blind Seer, the wolf, have fairly free run of the castle and grounds—as long as he remained with his mistress.

Firekeeper claimed, though Allister kept his private doubts, that it had been the wolf's howl that had first alerted her to the possibility that evil was afoot.

"We have captured alive three of the assassins. Under careful questioning, they have admitted their identities and nationalities."

He allowed himself to enjoy the drama of the moment. Not a word of this had gotten out, he was certain. Beside him, King Tedric appeared to be drifting to sleep, his wig slipping slightly over his forehead. Allister wasn't fooled, but he hoped that others were.

"The assassins were Waterland residents. They belonged . . ."

King Allister was forced to bang the base of his scepter on the table to restore silence, so great was the outcry at this announcement. Cries of "Treachery!" filled the room, countered by fervent denials from the members of Waterland's diplomatic contingent.

Anticipating some such reaction, King Allister had alerted the guards closest to the Waterland contingent's seats to be ready to defend them. The guards did their part valiantly, though their stiff, wooden expressions showed how they felt about putting themselves between those who might have arranged for the deaths of their fellows and just retribution.

Order restored, King Allister scowled at his audience. Peripherally, he was aware of King Tedric blinking and straightening his wig as if the commotion had awakened him from a doze.

"If," Allister said icily, "I had proof that the distinguished representatives from Waterland were aware of the assassins presence among their servants, I assure you that they would not be sitting so comfortably in this hall.

"The assassins belonged," Allister said, picking up where he had left off when interrupted, "to a subclass within Waterland unfamiliar to those of us who reside in Hawk Haven and Bright Bay. As you are all aware, Waterland advocates the practice of slavery."

There was a low growl at this, but no one spoke aloud, not wishing to attract the monarch's wrath. Still, the residents of both Hawk Haven and Bright Bay had ample reason to be aware that Waterland practiced slavery. Prisoners from naval engagements, if not ransomed, were routinely sold at the general market. Many were never heard from again.

The breadth of the White Water River where it separated Waterland and Hawk Haven made slave raids difficult if not impossible, but all along the kingdom's northern border parents frightened disobedient children with tales of slave raiders who swooped down and took those who didn't know their place. There might have been some truth to those tales, but King Tedric had not been able to say for certain.

"There are two classes of slave," Allister went on pedantically, "the born slave and the 'found.' Sometimes, as it has been explained to me, if a born slave shows particular talent for physical arts—strength or grace or courage—that slave is offered the chance to train as an assassin. If the assassin slave then performs a 'job' successfully, he or she is given his or her freedom.

"I will not pretend to understand the finer points of this peculiar and, to me, distasteful system. It has been explained to me that such assassins are commonly employed in Waterland to decide matters we would assign to legal courts and local custom."

The Waterland ambassadorial party looked rather angry at this, but King Allister continued blandly on:

"The assassins who attacked my son and his wife were these assassin slaves. As of yet, we have not determined their owners. When we do so, perhaps we will learn more."

"Surely," exclaimed Duke Oyster in exasperation, "the members of the distinguished contingent from Waterland *must* know who owns their own attendants!"

The senior Waterland ambassador was a corpulent man who looked as if he had never missed a meal, but had taken care to eat plenty in anticipation of the possibility. Since Allister had confirmed that the assassins were from Waterland, he had been steadily—almost frantically—signaling to be recognized.

Given that the assassins had worn Waterland colors, he had probably already found himself on the receiving end of a good deal of angry questioning. Before this, he could save himself by replying—in all honesty—that the kings had requested he hold his silence until the meeting. Now he must justify himself or face the consequences.

"Your Majesty," he said, nearly groveling once Allister had acknowledged him, "I beg your leave to explain some essential details regarding this matter."

"Speak on," Allister replied cordially.

"First of all," the diplomat, one Opulence Alt Rosen, said, "you should know that I had no part in choosing my entourage."

There were mutters of disbelief, but Opulence Rosen forged on, huffing a bit as if he were running uphill.

"I was already in this part of the world, serving as an observer for my government during the recent military events. When the joyous union of the two heirs was announced, I, of course, included the news in my report home. In interests of saving costs, I was told to remain and represent Waterland at both weddings. However, several members of my entourage were to rotate home in order to report more fully. A new support staff was sent out so that I would not be unduly inconvenienced."

Earl Kestrel made a slight scoffing sound that could easily have been ignored, but Opulence Rosen chose to respond as if questioned.

"I assure you, sir, that I had nothing to do in the choice of my new staff. I was somewhat surprised by its size, but decided that this must indicate the honor in which my government held the weddings."

"Staff, you say," Duke Oyster said, ignoring protocol once more. "Does that mean these killers had other skills?"

Opulence Rosen smiled weakly. "They did, but to be honest, their primary role was as honor guards. As such, they were an extension of my formal costuming, as it were."

"If His Majesty will permit," the Waterland diplomat continued, "I discerned some disapproval when the question of slavery was raised. I would beg your leave to explain further how the custom of the assassin slave arose. I would not wish your people to think we of Waterland value human life lightly."

King Allister nodded. He'd heard this explanation already and knew that Opulence Rosen would do himself no favors by giving it, but he had no desire to appear to be censoring any information related to the assassination attempt.

"Speak," the king replied, "but remember that this is not a lecture hall and keep to the point."

"Thank you, gracious Majesty," Opulence Rosen replied, bowing deeply before continuing to the assembled group, "As many of you already know, Waterland has no hereditary nobility. All that a father can pass to his son or a mother to her daughter is the wealth—whether in property, goods, or coin— that the family has accumulated. Our rulers are made up from a consortium of the most wealthy adults in the land.

"I shall spare you the details," Opulence Rosen added hurriedly, sensing the less than patient mood among his listeners. "What is essential for you to know in order to understand the place of the assassin slave in our society is that we place so great a value on human life that each person is accorded a monetary worth. Slaves who wish to acquire their freedom may purchase it or earn it. In this way, the estate is not diminished in value.

"However, not all slaves have the means to earn their worth in coin. Our wise founders felt there should be other means for them to earn their worth. Taking a risk of one kind or another can provide one of these means."

"Such as killing someone," interrupted Baron Shark.

The diplomat smiled in a thin facsimile of geniality.

"Yes, that's right, or building dams, or any number of other dangerous jobs that—since they create the risk that the owner might lose his or her entire investment—need to be compensated for in coin."

"And your point," King Allister prompted dryly, "is?"

Opulence Rosen flushed, though whether in anger or embarrassment was difficult to say.

"What I wish your people to realize, Your Majesty, is that the owner of an assassin slave may choose not to use that slave for his or her own needs. However, in all fairness to the slave, we believe that the slave should be permitted to employ its complex and exhaustive training before it becomes useless through age or injury. Thus, the assassin slave's services are often hired out to another contractor.

"I mention this most particularly because I wish you to understand that discovering the owners of these slaves who acted here during the wedding may not lead you to whoever set them on the good prince and his bride. They may have been contracted out to another party and the original owner may be innocent of any complicity."

Duke Oyster snapped out, "Tell me, Your Opulence, do you hire these assassins to foreign contractors?"

"I," Alt Rosen answered carefully, "do not currently own any assassin slaves, nor, given my earnings as a foreign representative for my nation, would I think it wise to hire them abroad. However, there are in Waterland who do so, who even *prefer* to do so since such contracts have fewer domestic ramifications."

Red-faced with fury, Duke Oyster surely would have said

more, but King Allister hammered once again for silence.

"Thank you, Opulence Rosen, for clarifying the place of the assassin slave within your society. Let me further inform those gathered here—since Your Opulence has already assured me upon this point—that you and your associates will be assisting us in every way possible as we work to track down the original owners of these slaves. Indeed . . ."

The king permitted himself a humorless smile. "Indeed, Opulence Rosen will be remaining with us in Bright Bay indefinitely while other members of his party return to Waterland to undertake the necessary research. Since we are greatly concerned for Your Opulence's safety in these troubled times, we will be assigning guards to follow you wherever you go and to remain close to you at all times. In this way, your safety will be assured."

King Allister stopped, sipped his watered wine. He didn't need to actually say the word "hostage" to make his intent clear to everyone present. To the man's credit, Alt Rosen concealed his dismay quite well.

"I thank Your Majesty for your concern for my person," he said.

Bowing stiffly, he resumed his seat.

King Allister nodded graciously, then resumed addressing the general assembly.

"That concludes my remarks regarding the current tragic happenings. If there is some rumor I have failed to address, I have some few moments remaining before my next appointment during which I may attempt to answer your questions."

Taking this opportunity, Duchess Pelican asked about the possibility that the canceled festivities—a ball and several banquets—would be rescheduled. The king regretfully announced that the events would not be rescheduled out of respect for those who had died in defense of their monarchs.

This decision was well received. The next question was less easily dealt with—all the more so because it was raised by young Derian Carter, who was apparently unaware that he was treading on sensitive ground.

"Your Majesty," the red-haired youth said seriously, "what

puzzles me is why the assassins chose to strike during the wedding. Surely there would have been better times and places. Did your interrogation reveal anything that might help this make sense?"

Had King Allister believed the young man was playing at politics he would have given some bland answer, but that wouldn't do in the face of Derian's evident sincerity. Brushing him off would raise more questions than the young man's query had brought out into the open.

"A bit, Counselor Derian," the king replied. "The ceremony enabled them to get near to all of their targets at one time. Even at a banquet or ball, the parties in question would have been more spread out.

"The targets," Allister went on, anticipating the question, "were first of all the bride and groom—preferably as one. Then myself and/or King Tedric, followed by my younger son Tavis, my daughters, and, if the assassins' luck extended so far, any ranking nobles within reach. Since the queens are not in line to either throne, they were relatively safe. Since successful assassination would have thrown one or both of our allied nations into chaos, it is impossible to deduce from those orders who the contractor for the assassinations might have been."

A sort of guilty thrill went through the audience as all the members realized that they had been in at least some danger. Earle Peregrine of Hawk Haven, representing her quite elderly father, asked:

"And have measures been taken to protect the targets?"

"Considerable measures," King Allister assured her, "including plans for the dispersal of this noble company so that we will not remain so vulnerable."

That provided an ideal note upon which to end the meeting. Suddenly, everyone was eager to get out of the crowded room. As they left, Allister overheard anxious discussions beginning as to how soon it would be polite to take leave of both castle and city.

Allister retired alongside King Tedric. Once they were vanished into a more private area, the old monarch looked at his nephew and smiled sardonically.

"You put the wind up them nicely, Allister. You have the makings of a fine king."

"I put the wind up, all right," Allister agreed, "but I must wonder how that wind will fill their sails and to what harbors it will drive them."

V

ONCE AGAIN, FIREKEEPER and Blind Seer sat upon the parapet, but this time instead of facing the bay they faced inland. This time, instead of watching the roar and crash of the seemingly endless waters, they watched a receding stream of humanity as most of the wedding guests departed the castle at Silver Whale Cove.

As before, the young woman sat with her arm flung around the neck of the great grey wolf, and those who looked back upon the castle and chance glimpsed the sight shivered in themselves, remembering her bloodied hands and gown, and the rumors that she had attacked an assassin with her *teeth*. The fact that these rumors were true did nothing to stop them from being enhanced.

Despite the numerous persons who had witnessed the attack, more than one forwent the evidence of his or her own eyes in favor of the lurid tales that told how the wolf-woman had ripped out the assassin's throat with fangs suddenly as sharp as a wolf's own. Never mind that the man had been taken from the Sphere Chamber alive and walking—albeit somewhat stiffly—under his own power. Enough dead men had been carried away to "prove" the tales.

Firekeeper knew something of what was being said and, far from being troubled by it, was amused. Had the tales been told about Blind Seer she would have been infuriated and worried, for the wolf could not speak to defend himself. She, however, could do so and would do so, confident in not only the protection of two kings and their heirs apparent but in her own strength.

Firekeeper, still in her teens and already the slayer of several powerful men, remained rather innocent. She did not realize how little the strength of a single person mattered against the tides of politics or how little the protection of kings and their heirs might count when fear came alive.

But this afternoon two days after the wedding of Crown Princess Sapphire and Crown Prince Shad, Firekeeper wasn't thinking about fear and its consequences; she was more concerned about the immediate question of who had tried to kill two people she rather liked. She had not had time to meditate on the question in privacy, though she had listened to several heated discussions of the matter. Now, taking advantage of the fact that no one needed her to sit with an invalid or threaten a prisoner or any other of the many tasks that had enlivened these past few days, she took the time to think about what she had learned.

Wolves regularly attacked their rivals in power, so the idea of killing to gain position was neither alien nor repulsive to her. The use of assassins she had filed as yet another of the curious tools—like swords and bows—that humans created to make up for their lack of personal armament. What she still had to puzzle through was the subtle strategies involved in killing those who were expected to *inherit* power rather than those who held the power itself.

It had been explained to her by Derian and Elise that Shad and Sapphire were not only people themselves but emblems of the truce between their nations, that killing them might devastate that truce, that at the very least the confusion and backbiting that had reigned in Hawk Haven in the months before King Tedric had chosen Sapphire as his heir could be expected to begin again, that . . .

It had all been explained and when explained made sense, but to Firekeeper's way of thinking, which was still rather direct and inclined toward personal violence when frustrated, the sense was in violation of everything she wanted to believe about how things should be run. The human way of doing things seemed far too complicated and had a tendency to end in foul actions like wars.

"Of course," she said to Blind Seer when her thoughts had led her this far, "in the wolf way a wise old One like King Tedric would fall prey to the first young pup with spring-hot blood. That would be a pity."

"True," the wolf replied, "for as I see it where wolves need strength and hunt-wisdom in their Ones, humans need something else, a type of wisdom that touches on things other than whether the prey can be safely taken."

Firekeeper mulled over this for a time. "You're right, but humans wouldn't need that different wisdom if they weren't always biting at each other. Once wolves decide who are the Ones and where each is placed within the pack, then they are wolves together. Humans don't seem to understand that they are a people."

"I think," Blind Seer replied, narrowing his blue eyes against a sudden gust of wind, "that is because they are not. Even wolves challenge each other when one pack crosses the territory of another."

Firekeeper sighed and said in the tone of one making an admission much against her will, "You are refusing to let me make simple and comfortable generalizations, dear heart. As much as it tastes of gall in my mouth, I must admit you are right."

The wolf huffed out his flanks in a deep laugh, which the woman shared, but, even as she shared Blind Seer's laughter, Firekeeper wondered if he could understand how much her desire to see the wolf way as a better way than that followed by the humans came from her deep desire to continue believing as she had until that previous spring—that she *was* a wolf.

To believe otherwise was unsettling; more than unsettling, it left her uneasy, prey to nightmares in which fires and almost-forgotten faces played too great a role. Only when she calmed herself with the repeated refrain that no matter her shape and what others might call her she—Firekeeper—was a wolf did those uncomfortable memories (for when she was asleep she knew them to be memories) leave her alone.

Moreover, and this was something that Firekeeper had hardly admitted even to herself, as she watched her friends and acquaintances dance their courtship dances she wondered at how indifferent she was to human ideas of beauty and suitability. It never occurred to her that she was young to have such feelings, since by wolf years—even those longer years lived by the Royal Wolves of which Blind Seer was one—she was quite mature.

Firekeeper had always seen herself as a pup to the wolves of greater strength, stealth, and speed, but now among humans she could judge herself—never seeing the incongruity of using those same qualities as her basis for judgment—as a great wise One. Even a man in armor and bearing a sword might fall before her—as she had proven when she had battled Prince Newell, the traitor of Hawk Haven. Conveniently, she chose to overlook how severely wounded she had been in that battle and how had it been a battle fought wolf to wolf some third challenger would have finished her before she might howl her victory before the pack.

Saying nothing of this confusion of thoughts, many hardly shaped into words, Firekeeper merely hugged Blind Seer harder and said as she had so often said before:

"I will never understand humans."

Blind Seer, though not quite four years old, was already wise enough to know that nothing he could say would be a suitable reply to that statement. He thought, however, that as long as Firekeeper continued to think thusly, she would indeed never understand humans.

"Why," Firekeeper said, raising a question she had meant to ask for some time but had continually put off in the chaos of the preceding two days, "did you howl me warning during the wedding?"

"I caught a scent upon the wind," the wolf replied directly, "a scent of one who might have borne you or the others ill-will."

He did stop speaking then, dangling the information just out of her reach as he might have a bone. Wolves, like humans, were fond of teasing.

"Who?" asked Firekeeper, tugging the short fur behind one of his ears in mock threat.

Had they been somewhere less precarious than on the edge of a castle parapet, doubtless the wolf would have pounced her and they would have wrestled for a while until one or the other won temporary dominance. Blind Seer, however, was not one to risk himself or his beloved packmate for a game. He surrendered graciously, folding down his ears to protect them from further pinching.

"It was the scent of the woman they now call Queen Valora," Blind Seer replied, "she whom they called Gustin IV when we first met her. The scent came to me over the waters as I sat out on the parapet over the bay where we had sat that first day."

Firekeeper sat up so suddenly that her balance might have been threatened if it had not been schooled by sleeping in the treetops on many a lazy afternoon.

"Valora! Was she in the castle?"

"I don't think so," the wolf said, "for her scent was faint and mixed with the salt scent of the waters. When I looked out, I saw many ships. I think she was there on one of them, out on the waters, waiting to see if the killers did their work."

"But you never scented her inside the castle?"

"No fresh scent," the wolf assented, "and I have checked as we have gone hither and yon these past days. Her scent lingers in a few accustomed places, but it is all old and dead."

Firekeeper's first impulse had been to leap down from the parapet and head inside to seek out someone—perhaps King Tedric—and tell him what she had learned. However, between the motion and the thought she paused.

Derian now believed that Firekeeper could understand what Blind Seer said to her, but he had long experience of her company. Also, though he might not realize it, there were times that he himself came close to having ears to hear such speech. His hearing was best with horses and their ilk, but even that came closer to an uncanny understanding of their needs and motives rather than spoken words.

Derian's special perceptiveness, however, was more a handicap than an advantage in Firekeeper's current dilemma. He alone seemed to realize how clearly she understood Blind Seer. Elise seemed willing to grant the wolf greater than usual intelligence and perceptivity. Most of the rest of Firekeeper's human circle simply took comfort in their belief that the feral woman had greater than usual control over her unusual pet.

"Someone," Firekeeper said, pausing with one leg on either side of the parapet on which she had been sitting, "should be told what you scented, but who would believe us?"

"Derian," the wolf replied, some of her own doubt in the cant of his ears, "might believe us, but could he get anyone else to believe?"

"And what good would that belief do us?" Firekeeper added. "You yourself say that Queen Valora didn't come into the castle. Perhaps she merely wished to observe the festivities from a distance. Humans often like to look upon what gives them pain—consider Doc's mooning over Elise."

Blind Seer sighed agreement. In this, at least, he was willing to assent that humans were incomprehensible, even by one who wished to comprehend them.

"Still," Firekeeper said reluctantly after a further pause, "I should at least tell Derian. It is possible that Queen Valora knew of the assassins—perhaps they were even her tools—and hoped to come into the castle when the killing was done."

Without further discussion, they left their vantage point. Some of the departing guests, looking upward and seeing the vanishing blur of grey fur and brown leather, hastened their paces without conscious volition, glad to be leaving a place where wolves and wild women walked unchecked and unchallenged.

❀

DERIAN CARTER SET DOWN THE QUILL with which he was writing a letter to his parents when Firekeeper and Blind Seer walked into his room unannounced. The young woman's expression was lit from within with a strange intensity, an intensity he fancied he saw mirrored in the gaze of the blue-eyed wolf.

"You alone, Fox Hair?" Firekeeper asked.

The query was no mere politeness, Derian realized. Blind Seer was sniffing as if to catch any intruder's scent, and Fire-keeper moved to check behind the window hangings.

"I am," Derian assured her, "though I might not have been. You really should learn to knock. I could have been enter-taining."

Firekeeper wrinkled her brow for a moment. "Oh, you mean you could be with someone I shouldn't see you with like the kitchen maid at West Keep, right?"

She grinned wickedly and Derian was reminded of his younger sister, Damita. He glared at Firekeeper as he might have at Dami under similar circumstances. He hadn't been aware that his charge, then barely capable of speaking simple phrases and seemingly caught up in a flood of new experi-ences, had been aware of *that* harmless flirtation.

Firekeeper's expression became suddenly grave.

"You *are* alone, Derian. I . . . we . . . have something very serious to talk to you."

"Tell," he corrected mechanically. "Yes, I'm alone and if you shut the door securely no one should be able to overhear us."

Firekeeper took him at his word, checking the door and even sliding the bolt shut so that no one else would walk in unannounced.

Frankly curious now, Derian waited while she settled herself on the carpet before the fire and rested her arm on Blind Seer's back.

"You remember," Firekeeper began, "how on the morning of the wedding, during the wedding, Blind Seer howled."

"Certainly," Derian replied. "I thought he was sulking be-cause he hadn't been invited."

Firekeeper shook her head, her solemnity unbroken though usually she would have returned some teasingly defensive remark.

"No, he no sulk. He trying to tell me something, to warn me to be careful, that he smelled something he didn't like."

"Go on," Derian prompted when she paused.

"What he smelled was . . ."

Again Firekeeper paused.

"Go on."

"He smelled Queen Valora."

Though the words were out, Firekeeper did not relax. Indeed, she stiffened further as if expecting her account to be challenged. Given that she was saying she was reporting for a *wolf*, Derian could understand her defensiveness. Still, he'd seen too much of the sympathy—of the apparent communication between the two—to automatically dismiss what she said as fancy.

"Where did he smell Queen Valora?" Derian asked, deciding that this was the safest question.

"Out on the water, out on the bay," Firekeeper said. "The wind was coming from that direction," she added as if this was crowning proof.

Derian felt himself starting to frown and struggled to keep his expression neutral.

"As I recall," he said, thinking aloud, "there were a good number of boats out there."

"Many," agreed Firekeeper, who still had trouble with numbers higher than ten. "I see them while I get dressed. Elise say later than many want to come to wedding but cannot and so go to water to watch building as if watching building was watching wedding."

She looked as if she found this idea rather incredible, but was willing to countenance that Elise understood humans better than she did.

"I remember something similar," Derian agreed, "and you are saying that Blind Seer caught and recognized one scent among so many at such a distance?"

Firekeeper nodded stubbornly.

"He say so. He could do so."

"But he caught no other scent?"

The wolf huffed out through his nose—a rather disdainful snort. Firekeeper replied (fleetingly Derian wondered if "translated" might not be a better term),

"He say he smell many other scents but no other one that is so very important not to say maybe dangerous. He cry warning to me so that I be on guard."

"Why would he think that Queen Valora would bear you any grudge?"

Firekeeper looked impatient for the first time. "Not me, Fox Hair, no, but she bear this grudge—a fat, heavy one, I think—for King Allister and King Tedric and many others. If it is going to rain, more than one gets wet."

"I see," Derian answered rather lamely.

He was trying to decide what to do with this peculiar information. Could he expect anyone to believe that a wolf—no matter how impressively large—could have isolated one scent from so many and at such a distance?

He realized with a start that he hadn't even considered that most would doubt that Firekeeper could understand Blind Seer's report or that the wolf had the intelligence to positively identify the scent of a woman he had only seen at a distance. At least he assumed that Blind Seer had never been close to Queen Valora. Who knew where he and Firekeeper had been during their nighttime rambles?

One thing at a time.

"Firekeeper," he said, "what do you want me to do with this information?"

"I think," she said uncertainly, "that someone should know, especially since the killer slaves come to the wedding."

Derian nodded. "Did you have anyone in mind?"

Firekeeper grinned triumphantly. "I tell you!"

Unable to help himself, Derian laughed. "You minx! Now it's my problem! Is that what you're saying?"

Firekeeper sobered. "I wish I feel it that simple. Maybe it nothing. Maybe Blind Seer smell wrong . . ."

The wolf huffed.

"Maybe," Firekeeper continued giving him a hug, "maybe Queen Valora just watching the wedding like others. Maybe she not know killers is there. Maybe, though, she know and wait to find if her den is empty and waiting for her to come back."

Derian drummed his fingers on the table.

"No one knows who sent those slaves," he said, "but it does stand to reason that if certain parties sent them they wouldn't have been content just to create chaos and then step back. Now some might have—Stonehold, maybe, or even Waterland. I understand that Waterland is wondering if the current shift in power means that Bright Bay isn't going to be able to rival them in naval power anymore. They might have wanted to make certain that would be so.

"And maybe," he continued, "Queen Valora decided to take advantage of having all her enemies in one place to make a strike. Even if no one was killed, she'd have made them nervous and nervous people make mistakes."

He made a sweeping gesture toward the window through which the retreating parties of former guests were still visible.

"Look at that. Think of the rumors they'll spread, of the doubt and fear and uncertainty." He rubbed his eyes. "My dad collects rumors, you know, from the travelers who hire horses and carriages from his stables. Rumors do a lot more than people think. Given time, they might even end up doing as much harm as if the prince and princess had really been killed."

Firekeeper nodded. "So I think, though only not so much. What should we do? Do we keep this, just us three, or do we tell someone?"

Derian felt quite acutely how young he was and a certain unfair desire to lay this responsibility on older shoulders.

"King Tedric," he said, "doesn't leave for Hawk Haven until tomorrow or the day after. He wanted to make certain that he could honestly report that Sapphire was out of danger. Let me see if I can get an appointment with him.

"It might not be possible," he cautioned, when Firekeeper

leapt to her feet in sudden enthusiasm for his plan. "I only said I'd try."

But three hours later, Derian, Firekeeper, and Blind Seer were admitted into the king's presence.

The king wasn't alone, but then neither of the kings, nor the queens, nor any of the princes or princesses had been alone since the assassins' attack. Now that the first shock of that attack was over, Derian had heard there was some grumbling from the younger parties, but he doubted that there would ever be any from King Tedric.

At seventy-five, the old king had given the last forty-seven years of his life to ruling the kingdom he had inherited from his father, King Chalmer. Reportedly once imperious and even arrogant, Tedric had changed with the years—not softened, but mellowed, and like an aged wood, he was stronger for the seasoning.

Derian was this king's youngest counselor and though he had grown somewhat comfortable with attending large meetings and even speaking out when needed, he was still acutely aware whenever he met with the king in smaller gatherings that he was young enough to be the great man's grandson.

Rising from his deep bow, Derian gave a briefer but still polite bow to the king's guard, Sir Dirkin Eastbranch, and took the seat the king indicated to him. Firekeeper sat, as was her custom, on the floor beside Blind Seer. The wolf did not lounge as he had in Derian's room, but sat bolt upright, so his head was far higher than the woman's.

It said much about both the king and his guard that neither showed even a reflex trace of nervousness at the wolf's presence.

"Well, Derian Carter," the king said, coming to the point without any waste of time. "What is this you felt so urgently that I needed to hear about?"

If there was the faintest of twinkles in the pale brown of Tedric's washed-out eyes, Derian felt comforted by it rather than threatened.

"Well, Your Majesty, Firekeeper came to me with this story . . ."

As concisely as possible he told the tale as Firekeeper had him, adding the information he had garnered from his own questions. Out of fairness to Firekeeper, he spoke not one word to protect himself from accusations of being too credulous, but spoke as if he believed—as he realized that he did—both that she could understand the wolf and that the wolf could read the winds as humans read print.

When he finished his report, the king said mildly, "Well, that's interesting indeed. I wonder . . ."

Closing his eyes, he sat silently mulling over the information for so long that even Derian, who respected him with something close to awe, thought he might have fallen asleep. At last, the king opened his eyes and said:

"If Valora was behind the attack on Sapphire and Shad then she must be sorely disappointed. Nor do I find it surprising that Duke Half-Moon, her representative, was among the first to take his leave. Still, as pleasant as it might be, we cannot take her mere presence in the vicinity as proof of guilt. We can stand warned, but we cannot act, not without risking war."

When Derian glanced at Firekeeper, he found the wolf-woman's expression unreadable.

"We could not," King Tedric continued, speaking directly to Firekeeper, "even if our witness was more prominent than one keen-nosed wolf. For all we know, this is precisely what whoever sent the assassins was hoping for—that we would accuse Valora and that she could then use such accusations to trigger a war. Many of those who now stand neutral would choose her side if they felt that King Allister and myself were acting in a high-handed fashion."

Firekeeper spread her hands widely. "But what to do? We do not want to start a war, but I think Queen Valora does. What to do to stop this?"

"We keep alert," the king said, "and calm and give no reason for outcry against us. The longer we act in such a manner, the longer will those neutral parties see us as the bastions of a solid kingdom and Valora as the warmonger rather than the wronged queen seeking to return to her people."

"It seem wrong," Firekeeper said, voicing the protest Derian could not bring himself to speak, "to let her do harm and not harm back."

"True," the king said, "but my hope is that Valora—or who- ever was behind this attempt, for we have no definite proof— will harm herself."

Firekeeper looked puzzled. "How?"

King Tedric answered her with a question of his own. "Don't wolves drive the deer?"

The young woman frowned. "Yes and when they run then we catch the slow and weak."

"And sometimes," the king continued, "don't you catch those who make themselves slow and weak when they trip right over their own feet?"

Firekeeper nodded, smiling her understanding. Derian wished he felt as certain that Queen Valora could be made to trip.

Firekeeper asked, "Will you tell King Allister what we tell you?"

"In confidence," Tedric replied, "even as you have told me. I think Allister's Whyte Steel can be trusted, but we must keep this close. After all we cannot have new rumors starting that kings are now taking counsel from little girls."

Derian knew that Firekeeper would have growled if anyone else had called her such, but the king's age was so great that even she saw he had earned the right.

"We try," she said, stroking Blind Seer's fur, "Blind Seer and me, to do what we can to make you safe."

"We appreciate that," the king said, "and someday, in the ungrateful fashion of kings, we may call upon you to do even more."

Derian wondered at the force in those simple words and felt himself squaring his shoulders as if he was a soldier called to duty.

A chiming of bells made the king sigh.

"As much as I would rather prolong this visit," he said, "that announces my next appointment. Keep what you have told me to yourselves. Trust that I will pass it on where it will do the most good."

"We do, Your Majesty," Derian said.

Firekeeper nodded agreement and rose lithely to her feet. Together they bowed and took their leave. As they left, they were surprised to see Doc waiting to come in, his expression grave and a rolled piece of paper held loosely in one long-fingered hand.

"Anything wrong with your patients, Doc?" Derian asked, regretting his impulsiveness even as he spoke. If either Shad or Sapphire had taken a turn for the worse, Doc would certainly not speak of it in a public hallway.

Doc, however, smiled reassurance. "No, this time I am the patient—after a fashion. I'll see you later."

Leaving them mystified, the knight entered the royal presence. As the door shut behind him, Derian realized that Firekeeper was looking at him, clearly expecting him to clarify Doc's cryptic statement.

"I don't know what he meant," Derian said honestly, clearly disappointing not only Firekeeper but the two listening door guards as well. "But I suppose he'll tell us later."

Firekeeper shrugged. "I'm hungry. Let's get something to eat."

Beside her, Blind Seer opened his mouth to show his teeth, panting in what seemed obvious agreement.

He understands us, Derian thought, *far better than we do him. Any of us, that is*, he amended, *but Firekeeper.*

"I could use something myself," he said aloud. "Let's drop down to the servants' hall. There's usually at least bread and cheese."

Derian thought that it said something about Firekeeper's character that neither he nor she thought it at all remarkable that Lady Blysse Kestrel should go from an audience with a king to dining in the servants' hall. What Derian didn't consider was that it said something about himself as well.

VI

AT ABOUT THE SAME TIME Firekeeper and Blind Seer were heading off to see Derian, Lady Elise Archer went to call on her cousin Sapphire—and to take her turn as interior chamber guard.

There were two armed guards outside the door to the makeshift infirmary, and more patrolled the gardens outside the windows. Shad and Sapphire both had balked at having other guards inside the room, and a compromise had been reached. Someone they viewed as a friend rather than a henchman—no matter how loyal—was to stay within the room. That person was given a bell-pull with which to alert the corridor guards and instructions to raise a fuss at the least suspicion of trouble.

As with most compromises, no one was completely happy, but as everyone was less unhappy the arrangement worked out.

Elise was scheduled to relieve Prince Tavis, who had taken the early-morning shift. The young prince didn't leave immediately when she arrived, but stayed to finish the game he was playing with his brother. It was a complicated tactical game in which one side took the role of the pirates and the other that of a naval contingent sent to hunt them out. Each piece seemed to have its own values and rules for moving and attacking.

Though the board was rather pretty, and the carved and painted pieces representing the ships were absolutely darling, Elise was rather relieved that no one expected her to learn it. Sapphire, on the other hand, all but panted to have a chance. When Elise came in, she was alternating between reading the rules pamphlet and asking questions about the game in process.

After greeting all present, Elise accepted the bell-pull from Tavis, freeing him to concentrate on his game. At times the arguments over moves became rather heated—so heated that Elise, who was an only child, was startled that such furious debate could be followed by laughter and even cheers at a particularly good move by one player or another.

For her part, she pulled out her embroidery and arranged her chair to make the most of the midmorning light. After a while, Tavis left, still arguing that his brother's winning tactic had been unfair. Shad, who had been playing the pirates, laughingly told him that expecting fairness from pirates had been the downfall of far too many naval commanders.

"Elise," Sapphire said soon after Tavis had departed, "do you think you could put that sewing by and give me a hand? I think I understand how to move the pieces now, but our beds are too far apart for us to play even with the table set between them."

"But if I," Elise said, divining her thought, "came and moved your pieces for you, then the board could stay where it is."

"Exactly!" Sapphire replied, pleased.

Elise was pleased, too. The distance which the newlyweds' beds had been set had been dictated by the wishes of both the attending physicians—who wanted to make certain that their patients were not tempted into unwise actions—and by those concerned with security, who wanted to make certain that there were no narrow avenues to block any defensive actions should they prove necessary.

As with the need for someone in the room at all times, this arrangement had rather irked both Shad and Sapphire. Elise had overheard the prince saying to his father that the only thing worse than being married to a beautiful woman and being forced to delay the wedding night was being locked in a room with her day and night and not being permitted even to hold her hand.

King Allister had replied rather dryly that Shad and Sapphire *could* be put in different rooms, if that would be preferable, and Shad had quickly stopped complaining.

Elise was rather happy that her quick agreement had kept the complaints from starting again. Privately, she was in sympathy with the newlyweds, but she couldn't forget the blood-soaked carpet in the Sphere Chamber or the whiteness of Sapphire's face after she had been wounded. If prudence would prevent this happening again, so be it.

For the next hour or so, Elise obediently moved naval ships along the paths Sapphire dictated. She was even getting a feeling for the strategies involved in constructing effective search patterns when there was a knock on the door and the porter announced Lord Rory Seal, the Royal Physician.

Elise swallowed a groan as Shad politely thanked the porter and said that Lord Rory should be admitted. She couldn't help it. She didn't like the pompous nobleman. It wasn't just that she felt annoyed at how he treated Sir Jared, it was that even to someone with her limited training in the healing arts he was so obviously incompetent.

Perhaps, Elise admitted to herself, barely competent would be a fairer description. Lord Rory knew enough to act the physician, but Elise thanked her patron Lynx that Sir Jared, not Lord Rory, had been the first on the scene when the assassins had attacked.

Superficially, Lord Rory looked exactly as a trusted family doctor should. A man in his middle forties, he was tall enough to possess an aura of command, but not so tall as to be intimidating. His build was precisely right, hinting at an athletic youth maintained into his mid-years, but without some frantic attempt to pass for younger than he was. In repose, his face bore lines that hinted at deep thought—though Elise preferred to believe that they indicated a need for spectacles. His hair was heavily, but attractively, touched with silver. He wore no beard.

Elise couldn't help but notice that the leather bag in which Lord Rory carried his physician's tools was unscarred and showed no sign of having been through weather. Equally, the tools within were perfectly kept—and hardly used. Moreover, they lacked the variety and personalization she had seen in

Doc's bag, the sense of items added as they were discovered, tested, and found useful.

All in all, Elise didn't like Rory Seal a bit, but though she would have been happy to retreat to her embroidery, a sense of responsibility acquired with her field training kept her nearby. It would have been wrong to leave Sapphire and Shad at the Royal Physician's clumsy mercy.

"Well, how are you two lovebirds?" Lord Rory said heartily, clearly believing that he was privileged beyond formalities—at least in private. Elise had noted, again to his detriment, that when kings or queens were present, he was correct enough that a ruder person than herself might have said he was groveling.

"My wound is nearly healed," Sapphire replied bluntly, "and I grow tired of staying in bed."

Shad, who had, as Doc had predicted, actually had taken more damage from the poison introduced into his system than had been initially obvious, said much the same.

Lord Rory laughed in his bluff and hearty manner.

"Now it's good to hear you speaking that way, but," and here he paused to twinkle in what Elise found a nauseating manner, "that's for wiser heads to decide."

Sapphire, who had been wounded before in battle, clearly found this condescension infuriating but she held her temper as befitted the heir to two thrones. Shad, perhaps because longer experience had inured him to the man, did not seem offended. When requested, he showed becoming meekness as he extended his wrist so that his pulse could be taken.

Shad may, Elise thought, swallowing a giggle, *be the perfect husband for Sapphire. His patience has been tested by far more trying people.*

Coming closer, Elise affected an air of maidenly modesty when the time came for Lord Rory to inspect Sapphire's vital signs and the healing wound. He had shown his inexperience before, becoming quite embarrassed when opening the princess's gown to check the slice along her side and into her breast.

Elise spared him the worst, opening the buttons on the gown

and parting the fabric just wide enough to permit him to see the cut. It was healing neatly, helped along by Doc's talent so that the stitches could probably be removed soon.

Lord Rory, however, barely glanced at the cut, his flushed face and nervous glances in Shad's direction making quite clear that he feared the prince's ire for taking such liberties, especially with his yet unbedded bride.

This time Sapphire showed no mercy.

"How are the stitches, Lord Rory?" she asked, her query forcing him to take a longer look and even to touch the healing flesh to either side.

"They are holding nicely," Lord Rory replied hastily. "Very nicely."

"And when shall they come out?" Sapphire pressed. "I've had such procedures before and found that when they feel this way they are usually ready to be removed. Perhaps they should be taken out now. Lady Elise has assisted with such many times before."

Lord Rory stood up and frowned a fatherly frown that held just a hint of a condescending smile.

"Now, young lady, it is not your place to dictate such important medical decisions. Nor should you put such burdens on your pretty cousin."

Elise replied dryly, "I assure you, it would be no burden at all. As Sapphire said, I have assisted in far more onerous operations."

Sapphire continued pushing her point, speaking demurely, those dangerous blue eyes held downcast and modest.

"Indeed, Lord Rory, I am eager to have the stitches removed. They are a barrier to my doing my duty to husband and kingdom . . ."

A choked-off gurgle of laughter from Shad almost interrupted her.

"And a princess must not be prevented from doing her duty to her land," Sapphire concluded with amazing steadiness.

Elise admired how Sapphire managed to look both innocent and powerfully seductive as she peered up at the physician through her thick, blue-black lashes.

Lord Rory colored to the silver hair at his temples.

"I do not . . ." He stopped and began again. "I shall take the matter under consideration," he replied.

Then, packing the few items from his bag with almost indecent haste, Lord Rory took his leave.

Once the door was firmly closed, the three let their laughter roll forth.

"You had him scared, darling," Shad said admiringly.

"You did," Elise agreed. "I thought he was going to admit that he didn't know how to tell when stitches should be removed."

"I doubt he does," Shad said, somewhat more soberly. "His position is purely hereditary and I think he has taken advantage of the fact that neither my grandfather in his elder years nor my cousin Valora in her younger ever put themselves in direct danger of injury in battle to avoid learning a surgeon's skills. He has drawn a stipend from the court for feeling the wrists of the queen and her husband a few times a year and praising them (and by inference himself) for their remarkable good health."

"How," Elise asked, "did his family ever get the position if they have no interest in the healing arts?"

Shad sighed. "You must have noticed that the court of Bright Bay is far more enamored of titles than is your homeland."

Elise nodded. Queen Zorana, the founder of Hawk Haven, had been so adverse to titles that she had restricted them, by law, to the barest minimum. Superficially, Bright Bay had appeared to do the same, but during Elise's sojourn in the castle at Silver Whale Cove she had seen that this was not the case.

"I did notice," she said, trying to stay polite though she had inherited a prejudice against such "unzoranic nonsense," as King Tedric called such titles. "I've met the Warmer of the Shoes, the Keeper of the Keys, and the Holder of the Chalice, along with a few others that escape me now."

"Those type of titles started with King Gustin I," Shad explained. "He was torn between wanting to be able to claim—as your Queen Zorana did—that our kingdom was starting afresh after Old Country domination. At the same time, I think he was more vain than she was."

"Differently vain," Sapphire said with what Elise thought amazing fairness given that her cousin had usually wanted herself and whatever she could claim as her own to be the unquestioned first and best. "From what I've heard, Queen Zorana had her share of vanity as well."

"Whatever the case," Shad said, acknowledging the interruption with an affectionate smile, "Gustin Sailor decided that he could have it both ways. He simplified the landholder titles in a way not all that different from Queen Zorana, but he also added a slew of *new* titles. Some of these he granted to himself, like Protector of the Weak—which he claimed was forced on him by some of the common folk. Other titles were given to those who had served him particularly well."

"Like knighthoods in Hawk Haven?" Elise said.

"Pretty much," Shad agreed, "but the difference was that while your knighthoods are nonhereditary, lots of the titles that Gustin I invented were hereditary. Apparently, Lord Rory's grandsire, the first Royal Physician, had the healing talent, just as Sir Jared does. The talent, however, did not pass to his children; nor, apparently, has it passed to his grandchildren. To make matters worse, even if it had, the title was worded in such a fashion so that it passed to the original man's *heir*, not to a logical successor. So even if there had been a member of the family with the talent—I think there was a niece who would have been better qualified than his heir was—the title bypassed the person with it and was handed down as if it was a sack of gold coins."

"That doesn't seem very smart," Elise said, trying to be polite, "but I guess it wasn't that different from what King Chalmer did when he gave the Great Houses their emblems and names."

"Gustin the First wasn't smart in a lot of ways," Shad agreed bluntly. "What he was was decisive, charismatic, and clever—but you can be clever without being smart. He saw the titles as a way of rewarding those who had served him well, and of binding them and their families more closely to him. I don't think he worried much about the consequences that might crop up a hundred years later."

"Like," Sapphire said with a disdainful sniff, "having the royal family's health overseen by a complete incompetent."

The porter's knock wasn't completely unexpected. Sir Jared also liked to make a morning check on his patients, but he waited until Lord Rory had come and had been given ample time to depart lest there be unpleasantness. Unlike Lord Rory, Sir Jared was warmly—if peevishly—greeted by the bedridden couple.

Elise found herself wishing that Sapphire reserved for Doc a trace of that courtesy she accorded to Lord Rory. Then she scoffed at herself.

Silly! Sapphire's only courteous to Lord Rory because she can't stand him. Her relaxed—if rude—way with Doc is her way of saying that she trusts him.

As for herself, Elise found herself unable to banter along with the others, who were describing—in increasingly colorful language—the agonies of their "imprisonment." She stood by and assisted the physician with his examinations, writing down pulse rates and other such figures, but she found herself suddenly without words. It troubled her, for she did not wish to seem either cold or haughty, but somehow the very ease with which Sir Jared accepted her help left her feeling out of place.

Elise distracted herself by listening to Sapphire's latest turn.

"Please, Doc," the princess was pleading, her tones theatrical, "release me from these silken bonds you have placed in my flesh, for they keep me from my new-made husband's side."

Sir Jared allowed himself a brief smile, gone almost as it formed, and turned from his inspection of Shad's wound.

"Your Highness would not wish to leak blood and pus onto that selfsame spouse, now would you? Trust me, had we pressed the wound too swiftly, that, rather than kisses, would have been what you would have showered upon him."

Sapphire wrinkled up her nose in distaste at this rather ugly image, then leaned back against her pillows.

"Honestly, Sir Jared. The wound feels so much better. Shad

turned and let me look at his wound and it isn't even in the least bit angry-looking anymore. If we're kept like this much longer, I'll start thinking there's some conspiracy."

Sir Jared nodded. "Well, we can't have that. Let me have a look at you."

Sapphire opened the front of her gown herself, folding back the fabric matter-of-factly. Elise had to remind herself that her cousin was a soldier to keep herself from thinking Sapphire unduly immodest.

"There!" Sapphire said triumphantly. "Pink and clean and not a hint of soreness. Press harder if you'd like," she prompted. "I won't wince."

"I'd prefer if you would if there is need," Jared said sternly. "At the least suspicion that you're hiding anything from me, I'd wait. The stitches won't be in danger of becoming ingrown for days yet."

Sapphire nodded. "I'm being honest with you. Do you think I'm such an idiot as to lie to my doctor?"

"It's been done," Doc said mildly. "However, my inspection agrees with your statements. The wound is clean of infection and knitting nicely. I can clip out the stitches and report to King Tedric that I think you're ready for action—indoor action, no riding or sailing or such for several days yet. You've lost lots of blood and your body will have robbed muscle to rebuild it."

From his bed Shad asked, "And me, Doctor?"

Sir Jared grinned. "I would have given *you* a clean bill of health several days ago, but I'm not your doctor, nor did I care to challenge Lord Rory. I thought my patient would heal better in congenial company."

Prince Shad looked momentarily angry; then he had the good grace to laugh.

"Will you pass on your recommendations, Sir Jared? I'm certain that Lord Rory can be made to think that they're his own if my mother goes to work on him."

"Very well, Prince Shad. I'll do my best."

Doc turned to Elise.

"Would you assist me in freeing your cousin, Lady Elise?"

Elise longed to say something witty, something like, "If a bold knight like you needs a mere maiden's aid, then gladly, sir," but cleverness escaped her.

"I'd be happy to," she said, and fancied that she sounded stiff and formal.

But as always all awkwardness vanished once they were at work. Elise handed Doc scissors and tweezers, holding everything steady when Sapphire—who predictably refused anything to dull the slight pain of the removal—jumped at the tugging.

Sir Jared distracted his patient by telling a funny story; then Shad leapt in with a sea tale about two men in a small sailboat with an overactive boom. The punch line was predictable, but set them all laughing nonetheless.

Sapphire inspected the healing incision with the help of a small hand mirror. Then she said in the tones of someone who is trying out a plan for the first time,

"Elise, what do you think King Tedric would do if I asked him to make Sir Jared Hawk Haven's Royal Physician? I've been thinking that if we did that and if we acted as if the title had been in place—just that no one had thought to mention it to Lord Rory—that would smooth out these matters of precedence rather nicely."

"Isn't there already a person who holds that post?" Elise asked. "I'm certain I've met him."

"There is," Sir Jared said. "It's a job, not a title, and the man who holds it is very good. He's probably responsible for King Tedric and Queen Elexa being as healthy as they are. The only reason he isn't on this trip is that he strained a shoulder in a riding accident shortly before their departure and agreed to stay behind because he could ask me to take over for him."

"I see," Sapphire said thoughtfully. "Let me think a moment."

After slightly more than a moment she said, "Still, there should be something we can do. Let me write a note to King Tedric explaining Doc's difficulty."

"I really don't have any difficulties with Lord Rory," Jared protested. "I simply avoid him when possible and humor him when necessary."

Sapphire looked annoyed.

"You shouldn't need to," she said bluntly, "not with your talent and your training. Elise, could you reach me writing materials?"

Elise did so, aware of her own mixed emotions on the matter. On the one hand, she agreed with Doc that he could deal with Lord Rory, title or not. On the other, she would like to see him recognized for what he could do. After all, King Tedric's physician might not have enough time to deal with all the members of the newly expanded royal family—especially if Sapphire and Shad got down to the business of producing heirs.

Although he never had spoken of it to her, Elise had the feeling that without Earl Kestrel's patronage, Sir Jared would lead a rather hand-to-mouth existence. Knighthoods were nice, but as a younger son of a small landholding family, he could expect little or nothing in the way of inheritance. Official patronage by the royal family would practically guarantee him a thriving medical practice.

While Elise was musing thus, Sapphire finished her letter. After sanding the wet ink and shaking the paper, she leaned over to slide the damp missive over to Shad.

"What do you think?"

Elise was impressed that Sapphire would bother to consult anyone—another change from the headstrong young woman she had known all her life. How much of that arrogance might have been Lady Melina's influence or, conversely, how much of Sapphire's new tact might be due to King Tedric?

Perhaps most importantly, how lasting would the changes be? Once the thrill of her new titles and marriage had worn off, Sapphire could quite easily lapse back into her former manner.

"Clear, concise, and well thought out," Shad said, setting the letter down on the table. "What King Tedric's reply will be, however, I cannot say."

"Nor I," Sapphire said, blowing lightly on the letter to make certain that it was reasonably dry before folding and sealing it. "Now, Sir Jared, see if you can get an appointment to deliver this to King Tedric in person. If you cannot, at least make certain that it is delivered to him."

Sir Jared dipped a bow that, to Elise's eyes, was at least a trifle mocking.

"As Your Highness commands," he said. "Perhaps I should take my leave immediately so as to better effect your wishes."

Sapphire arched an eyebrow slightly, as if not entirely certain whether or not she was being teased.

As Doc took his bag in one hand and the letter in the other, Shad said, "And Sir Jared, you *will* use your influence wherever possible to get me a clean bill of health?"

"I promise," Doc said, and with a bow to Elise and another to Sapphire, he departed.

"You were pretty quiet, Elise," Sapphire said. "Don't you like Sir Jared? I think he's quite fine—interesting, intelligent, even handsome if you like that type."

Elise managed a smile. "I like him fine, too, cousin. I just didn't have anything to say."

And, she added to herself, *I'd better practice finding things to say unless I want to chase him off completely. After all, once we leave this place how often are our paths likely to cross again? I'd hate to lose a friend just because I think I might like him a bit more than just as a friend.*

Admitting this to herself, for the first time she wondered what her parents would say if a penniless man of no title came courting her. Discouragement flooded her breast as she realized that no matter her own wishes in the matter her father, the baron, would probably show Sir Jared the door.

THE NEXT DAY, Firekeeper and Blind Seer were granted permission to go for a long run through the scrub forest bordering one edge of Silver Whale Cove—the actual cove rather than the city that bore the same name.

The water table here was quite high, enough so that even in the driest weather the ground a few feet under the surface was damp and water tended to collect in shallow depressions.

However, slightly inland there was a point of higher ground, uncontaminated by the brackish water of the bay. Here the castle had been built, possibly shored up by some of the same Old Country sorcery that had once lit its interior. In the vicinity of the castle and the fine natural harbor, a city had grown up, but there was still enough open land that no effort had been made to drain the nearby scrub forest. Strong winds off the waters kept disease bearing insects to a minimum and the tides washed the pools and puddles so that only under the worst conditions did the damp area bear fever.

By tradition, the forest belonged to the castle and only those with permission hunted for waterfowl and small game along its banks or under its trees. True, children did sneak away to play there, drawn into its shadow-haunted reaches and mysterious pools as children have always been drawn by places unused by their elders—as places that they can claim as their own.

Firekeeper found the scrub forest quite fascinating. She had never been near a land ruled by the tides, and the marks they left even away from the shore were intriguing. She lost one of the boots Derian had insisted she wear when she stepped in a sinkhole, and gleefully threw the other away. True, the ground was cold, but she was accustomed to being physically uncomfortable in some fashion. Only recently had she been otherwise more often than not.

Blind Seer also enjoyed the chance to get out of the castle grounds and stretch. He ran circles around his two-legged companion, darting off after interesting scents, starting rabbits and chasing them for the fun of watching their panicked flight. He didn't kill any, however, for he'd been kept well fed— even overfed—by a castle staff terrified of the consequences if the giant wolf should feel even the least bit hungry.

Together they explored, Firekeeper pausing to admire the

iridescent interiors of shells vacated by the mussels that clung to the rocks along the shore, Blind Seer rolling in a particularly odoriferous fish so long dead that its species could only be guessed at. They were crouched on the edge of a tide pool—Firekeeper poking at something that snapped at them with claws from behind a cluster of small rocks, Blind Seer barking in excitement—when a shrill screech interrupted their play.

An enormous peregrine falcon—as large as an eagle and thus as oversized for its species as Blind Seer was for his—stooped from above and came plummeting down from the clear autumn skies. Inches above the waters, it caught itself, banked its wings, and lifted. Flapping strongly but effortlessly, the peregrine rose, causing ripples like the kisses of a flirtatious wind to distort the surface of the tide pool. Then it came to a perch on the outthrust branch of an oak that had been half-killed by the proximity of brackish waters.

Folding its wings neatly, the peregrine commented sardonically, "Well, the two of you haven't changed much. Still mad. Well, all wolves are mad and humans who think themselves wolves are probably twice mad."

She was a magnificent falcon, even as a representative of a species that many humans—as Firekeeper had learned—regarded as the most handsome of all the falcons. Her compact body was feathered a deep blue-grey, while her head was capped in plumage the color of slate. White feathers along her throat and underbody provided contrast, while darker bars across the white added dimension. Her eyes were dark brown, rimmed with gold.

"Elation!" Firekeeper cried, the greeting echoing across the waters like a wolf's howl so that those who heard it shivered at hearing such a sound at midday. "Elation, you have returned!"

Pleased, the peregrine ruffled her feathers and preened.

"Well, you didn't think I'd gone forever, did you?"

"We didn't know what to think," Firekeeper admitted. "Derian said that one day you simply flew away. I knew," she said in the tones of one who is verging onto unfamiliar grounds, "that many of the winged folk migrated. I thought perhaps that impulse had seized you."

Elation chuffed. "We Royal Falcons are not as bound by such things as our cousins are. True, we often have the sense to take passage to better climates rather than winter where food will be scarce and conditions hardly pleasant, but we can overcome the impulse."

"Oh."

"So where were you?" asked Blind Seer. "You said nothing to us of leaving."

"I am not," the falcon snapped, "required to report to you."

Blind Seer lolled out his tongue in a wolfish laugh. "Never said that you were. You're touchy today. Gone short of food?"

"I wouldn't say no to a rabbit or so," the falcon admitted. "Harvested fields offer less variety in hunting than I could wish."

"Mice," the wolf sniffed in understanding. "If my mere presence hasn't scared all the game to earth, there are plenty of fat rabbits in the woods."

"I'd prefer duck," Elation said, "and the ones my coming startled should have settled to the water again by now. Bide a moment."

Firekeeper found a sunny patch and made herself comfortable against Blind Seer's flank. In the near distance there was the sound of squawking ducks, the dull thunder of many pairs of wings rapidly taking flight. Then the peregrine returned, a fat green-headed male mallard held strongly in her talons.

"They're complacent here," she said, ripping into it with a shower of feathers and gutting the body with a single skilled tear. "A pity that I won't have a chance to teach them due prudence."

"You're leaving again soon?" Firekeeper asked.

Elation lifted a bloody head from her meal. "We all are. I've come to take you home."

"Home?" Firekeeper asked, feeling an odd mixture of excitement and dismay. "Is all well with our pack? What are you talking about?"

"And since when," Blind Seer asked with acuity, "have the wingéd folk run errands for the wolves?"

Elation gulped down the duck's liver in a single swallow. "I'll tell while I feed because I see you're confused. I'm not running errands for the wolves, nor is there anything wrong with your pack. By home I meant to the lands west of the Iron Mountains, the lands where humans rarely go."

"Eat first," Firekeeper said with a wolf's courtesy, because no wolf ever waits a meal. "A tale that has waited this long can wait until you have fed."

Still, though the peregrine reduced the duck to feathers and bones—and not overmuch of the latter—in very little time, the wolf-woman found the wait for her tale very long indeed.

"Soon after the war ended," Elation began, "I went with Derian back to Eagle's Nest. His family was very impressed with me, almost as much as they were with the counselor's ring he had received from King Tedric. Although I think Derian would have enjoyed having more time at home, soon he had to travel to Bright Bay for the wedding. I went with him, the finest member of the noble entourage that included Earl Kestrel and Earle Kite."

"We know all of this," Firekeeper interrupted, impatient with the falcon's self-aggrandizement. "Why did you go west?"

Elation ruffled her feathers, but otherwise did not acknowledge the interruption.

"We were within a day's ride of the castle at Silver Whale Cove when, to my great surprise, I was hailed by one who spoke my language. I had been so long gone from civilized lands that I had practically forgotten that any but you and Blind Seer could speak to me."

"Birdbrain," muttered the wolf, and maybe the falcon didn't hear. Certainly she didn't comment.

"The speaker was a kestrel of the Royal kind. Had he seen him, Norvin Norwood would surely have done anything to add him to his aeries."

Firekeeper growled softly, but Elation would not be hurried.

"The kestrel—one Bee Biter—told me that rumor had come

to the Royal Beasts of a great battle between hosts of humans.
He asked me if I knew of any such battle. I said that I did,
that I had witnessed it, and that I knew the reasons for its
being joined at that place and at that time.

"Then Bee Biter charged me—using secret words known
only to the wingéd folk—to come to make my report. I could
no more have disobeyed and maintained my stature among my
people than I could have eaten grain. Without any delay, I
flew west, letting Derian see me depart. I was sorry to cause
him worry, but I could not go against the charge laid upon me
by the kestrel."

"Why," Firekeeper asked, "didn't you stop in Hope and tell
me where you were going?"

"I accompanied you east," the peregrine replied haughtily,
"as an agent of my people. I owed you no report.

"Also," Elation added after a moment, perhaps thinking she
had sounded unduly harsh, "the kestrel set us a path due west
and I did not wish to anger him by diverting north on the
chance that I might find you—after all, you might have already have left Hope for Silver Whale Cove."

"True," Firekeeper admitted.

"We crossed the Iron Mountains with a speed and directness
which I must admit I found welcome after months shackled
to human pace. Once across, we went to a place I don't believe
you have ever seen—the Brooding Cliffs, where many generations of falcons have fostered their young.

"Once there, I found that the Mothers of many aeries had
gathered. In addition to the raptors, there were speakers for
some of our corvid kin—the ravens and crows. There was
even an owl or two. However, I soon realized that something
greater than my coming must have caused this gathering."

Something in the peregrine's posture revealed the falcon's
wounded vanity. Firekeeper smothered a chuckle, eager to
reach the part of the story that would pertain to Blind Seer
and herself.

"I told my story," Elation continued, "and found that parts
of it had been known before me. Ravens and crows have ever
been drawn to battlefields and the Iron Mountains are not a

barrier to the wingéd folk as they are to those who are flight-less. However . . ."

Here Elation straightened, pride recovered. "The ravens and crows had not learned all of the story, nor did any know in full the intricacies of the political maneuvering that had led to King Allister's War and the eventual truce between Hawk Haven and Bright Bay.

"When I had concluded my tale, the Mothers went into conference. I believe they even sent messengers to the flightless. After much discussion and much flying to and fro, I was commanded to fly east once again, to seek you out, and to order you to come before the Royal Beasts."

Firekeeper waited for further explanation, but it seemed that none was forthcoming. Finally she asked, "But why? Surely you saw more than I did. Indeed, at first I needed you to explain to me the ways of monarchs and their vassals. Why am I needed?"

Elation looked uncomfortable. "I was told to tell you no more than I have, but out of respect for the friendship that is between us I will say a bit more. King Allister's War troubled the Mothers more than I should have thought possible. Indeed, I thought that the more impetuous among them would have flown to speak with you themselves. Some were ready to take wing when others pointed out that if humans saw so many of us, questions would be raised—questions we are not quite ready to answer."

"Questions?" asked Firekeeper.

Blind Seer raised his head from his paws. "Dearest, don't you recall the clamor that Elation and I raised when we accompanied you east? Should a flight of the rulers of the air come to visit you, surely other questions would be raised. Didn't you listen when Elation said that Earl Kestrel would have loved to take captive such a fine kestrel as Bee Biter? Such greed would be the least of the emotions that would be aroused."

Elation added, "Our tales tell how, in the years before humans came from across the seas, the Royal Beasts lived in the lands east of the Iron Mountains. Indeed, each year the Mothers warn the young hawks preparing to make their first passage about the dangers of encountering humankind.

"I myself," and here the peregrine hunched her head between her shoulders, "was once drawn out of the air and kept by a small holder in the west of Hawk Haven for an entire season before I made my escape. However, the land-bound rarely cross the mountains and, as human memory is short and history rapidly degenerates into fantasy, we have become as legend."

"But if the great birds were to come east in a group," Firekeeper replied, understanding, "then many would begin to wonder if there was truth to the fireside tales the old folks still tell."

"You understand." Elation nodded, a jerky motion that incorporated her entire body. "And now you know why you must come west if the Mothers are to question you."

"I still don't understand why they want to speak to me!" Firekeeper protested.

"Can you make the journey without knowing?" Elation asked. "If you would not do it out of friendship for me, then would you do it for those who fed you during the long years of your childhood?"

Firekeeper nodded. "I can and will, though I will still expect some explanation. I suppose these Mothers of yours want me to come at once."

"They do," Elation said, "but out of consideration for your limitations as a traveler, they have agreed to meet you on the most eastern verge of the mountains, in a place where humans rarely ever go—indeed where humans are certain not to go now that winter cold is stealing down the slopes."

"Where is this place?" Firekeeper asked.

"Almost due west of here," Elation answered, "as the falcon flies. Do you recall the rough, broken land that bordered the field upon which Allister's War was fought?"

"I do."

"Humans call those the Barren Lands, and they are well named. Nothing much grows there and few creatures live there if they have another choice. The ground becomes rougher the higher one climbs, but at the top there is an enormous lake—humans call it the Rimed Lake or Lake Rime, for the waters are often frosted, even in high summer. Among our people there is a tale that the lake is the child of a mountain that once breathed fire. This lake is the source of two rivers—the Barren, which divides Hawk Haven from Bright Bay . . ."

"I know that river," Firekeeper interrupted.

"And the Fox River, which is the border between Stonehold and Bright Bay. The Mothers will meet us on the western shores of that lake and with them will be some of the landbound. I believe your own Ones will be among them."

"That alone," Firekeeper said, suddenly homesick, "is reason enough to make the journey. Give me time to make excuses to the humans. I cannot simply disappear as you did. Some might come looking for me and if they did, there might be seen what should not be seen."

Blind Seer wuffed his agreement. "Don't forget, Firekeeper, that you must make excuses to Princess Sapphire. She had wanted you to stand with her at both of her weddings. Even if we run hotfoot each night I doubt that we could return to Eagle's Nest in time for that occasion."

"True." Firekeeper bit her lower lip thoughtfully. "Still, I shall find some way to sweeten her. Elation, will you come to the castle with us?"

"I will come," the peregrine said, "though not with you. I should prefer to excite as little comment as possible. Tell me rather how to recognize your window or Derian's and I will go there."

Firekeeper did so, though she found such descriptions difficult. She had never thought about seeing the castle from the outside as the falcon would—nor had she considered the building in any detail. In the end, the time she and Blind Seer had spent on the parapets came to her aid and she satisfied the falcon's needs.

When this was resolved, they parted, Elation to hunt, Firekeeper and Blind Seer to return to the castle.

"In any case," Firekeeper said as she rose and began trotting across the damp earth, "we shall have begun to make the humans nervous by our absence. Ah! It will be good to be out of their care and free once again. I can hardly wait to run by night and sleep by day, to eat my food without spices and drink only clean water."

"And at night," the wolf added dryly, "the ground will be damp or frosted. Your feet will grow cold and you'll tuck them under my belly fur for warmth. The water may not always be clean and so you will go thirsty. If we stay on the roads, we may be seen and hunted. If we do not, we may run afoul of farmers and herders."

"Pessimist," she said, kicking him lightly in the ribs.

"Realist," the wolf protested. "Given what I recall of the Barren Lands, even at their lowest reaches, I really think you will miss those boots."

Firekeeper scoffed and he laughed. Jogging side by side, they ran through the marshy scrub toward the castle, where candlelight was setting fireflies behind the windows.

VII

DERIAN WAS PACKING in anticipation of Earl Kestrel's departure for Hawk Haven the next day.

Though his hands moved efficiently, Derian's thoughts were far away from his present task, wondering which of several choices for future employment he should make. He was still amazed by how his market value had risen among people who wouldn't even have looked him in the face a few months before. Then a shrill screech at his window jolted him into the present.

Revelation Point Castle was equipped with glass windows—many of these relics of the days when it had belonged to some noble of the colony of Gildcrest—but no pane of glass, no matter how thick or how well set, could keep out the cry of a very large peregrine falcon, not when she was determined to be heard.

Derian leapt to his feet and flung open the window, unmindful of the faint, chill drizzle that had just begun to fall. The peregrine in all her glory swept in and took a perch on the back of a chair near the fire. It was a heavy chair, carved of solid maple and upholstered with heavy brocade fabric stuffed with horsehair, but even so she nearly toppled it. What her talons might have done to the finish could be left to the imagination, for—some might have thought by design—she had chosen the chair over which Derian had hung his outdoor coat when he had come in hours before.

"Elation!" Derian said, stroking lightly along her head and back feathers with his index finger. "Fierce Joy in Flight! I thought you'd gone forever!"

He had to swallow hard then to stop a sudden welling of emotion that was quite unmanly—there might even have been tears.

Elation purled and chuckled deep in her throat in response, and Derian felt certain that the sounds were more than meaningless expressions of contentment. As with Blind Seer, he had ample reason to think that Elation understood him far better than he did her.

"Well, I'm glad to see you, too," the young man said. "You look well fed, so I'll hazard you've been taking care of yourself as usual. Let me close the window."

He did so, noting that the drizzle was rapidly turning into steady rainfall.

"I hope that Firekeeper and Blind Seer have the sense to come in out of the rain," he said to the falcon, "but who can say with those two."

Elation flapped her wings slightly, perhaps to shake off the raindrops, but Derian couldn't help but feel that she was commenting on the incomprehensible motives of wolves.

"I was just packing," he said. "King Tedric departs tomorrow for home and Earl Kestrel is too mindful of opportunity not to leave with him. We'll go slowly, for Queen Elexa's health must be looked after. I think the king will be glad to

have the earl's entourage added to his own. Counting myself—
though I'm not certain Earl Kestrel would—we'll add four
good fighters to the company, and Valet is priceless when
matters of personal comfort are in question."

Derian kept talking, enjoying the peregrine's listening silence. "And then there is Firekeeper. She cannot be overlooked. Blind Seer will terrify the horses, and Firekeeper
herself will run off into the night, causing comment and gossip. Still, though we travel through territory that is technically
friendly, I will be happier knowing that she is there scouting
for us. Race Forester has a human perspective and that means
he trusts sometimes. I don't think Firekeeper ever trusts a
stranger."

This time the falcon did reply, a thin, peeping noise that
Derian was at a loss to interpret.

He continued packing in relative silence for a bit, but
whereas before his thoughts had been his company, now he
simply relaxed into happiness that the peregrine had returned.
Perhaps because he hadn't wanted the loss to hurt, he hadn't
let himself admit how much he had been worried about her.

City born and bred though Derian was, he had been given
ample opportunity to see how the nobles valued a good hawk.
That Elation was superlative went without saying. He had seen
the covetous glances she had attracted back when the armies
were gathered at the twin towns of Hope and Good Crossing.

For all his recent honors, Derian knew himself a commoner
and knew there were those who wouldn't think him worthy of
such a bird. That the bird had chosen him, not the other way
around, would matter not at all. Most would not believe the
truth if they were told it, and those few who did would probably not be among those who would covet another's possession.

But as real as the possibility that Elation had been interred
in some alien mews, snapping at her keeper and tearing at
jesses twined around her ankles, this had not been what Derian
truly feared. It had seemed far more likely to him that as
whimsically as the bird had taken a fancy to him, she could
grow bored. After all, she had arrived with Firekeeper, trans-

ferred her attentions to him, and now, quite possibly, some third party or interest had lured her away.

And now Elation had returned and sat drowsing by his fire, leaving the occasional line of hawk chalk to be scrubbed from his coat and his floor. Derian could not have been more content.

A thumping on his door broke his tranquility.

"Come in," he called, and the door was flung open and Firekeeper and Blind Seer romped in.

Both were bedewed with raindrops and panting hard, but they seemed to have escaped the worst of the rain. Firekeeper, Derian noted, was barefoot.

"Where are your boots, Lady Blysse?" he asked sternly.

She turned to him, all wide-eyed innocence.

"They were tugged off by the mud. The forest floor is wet and full of wet places. I stepped in one before I know what it is and away go the boot."

"Boot?"

"I could not run in just one, could I? I left the other for the creatures to chew on."

"Those boots," Derian said with a sigh, "cost what a good farmer might earn in a year. You are absolutely incorrigible."

"What that?" Firekeeper asked, honestly perplexed.

"Never mind. It wasn't a compliment."

While they had been talking, Firekeeper had been shaking off the worst of the rain from her hair and combing the damp locks into some sort of order with her spread fingers. It didn't seem to bother her that her vest and breeches were wet and, as the leather had been treated to shed water, they probably weren't too uncomfortable.

Blind Seer, fortunately, had apparently shaken off earlier, probably all over the guards in the courtyard, who would have been too scared to protest.

Derian noted that neither woman nor wolf seemed surprised to see Elation there and surmised that the falcon had sought them out first.

"Derian," Firekeeper said, sitting herself in front of the fire with Blind Seer next to her—the room promptly became suffused with the odor of damp dog—"I have a problem. Elation tell me that I am wanted back home."

"Home?" For a moment Derian was puzzled; then he understood. "You mean with the wolves?"

Firekeeper seemed pleased by his quick comprehension.

"Yes, with the wolves and . . ." She stopped, and Derian had the definite impression she was leaving something out.

"The Ones," he prompted.

She nodded. "Yes, the Ones. They wish to see me."

"Can't it wait until spring? Travel across the mountains is going to be difficult this time of year. Elation could carry a message, perhaps. It's easier for her."

The peregrine preened as if accepting his praise.

Firekeeper shook her head. "No. I am wanted now and if I not go, they may be angry. You not want me to make wolves angry, do you?"

"I don't," Derian agreed. He'd gotten used to Blind Seer, mostly by thinking of the wolf as a unique individual. The idea of an entire pack of such wolves was rather terrifying.

"Then I must go and you must help me talking."

"With the wolves?" Derian started, less than happy with this thought.

True, he'd planned to make a trip west—perhaps in the comfortably distant spring—in order to place markers on the graves of those who had been of Prince Barden's party. However, a trip when autumn would be wheeling into winter . . .

Firekeeper reassured him. "No, Fox Hair, not to the wolves, to the humans. I need to tell Sapphire I no be in wedding at Eagle's Nest. I need to tell Earl Kestrel, since he call me his ward and daughter." She sniffed slightly at this presumption. "I need to tell the king because he have been kind to me.

"I not worried about the king," she continued, "for he make no claim to me, but I worried about the earl and the princess."

Derian nodded. "As always, Firekeeper, you have put your finger on those who would be most likely to be offended. Let's see. If we see the king first and he gives his permission, the others could hardly deny it, but then they might be offended— as if you were pulling rank . . ."

He mused for a few moments. "I think I have it. You should see Princess Sapphire first, since the earl's immediate objection will be that you might offend her. When you get her permission, then you should see the earl. That way you can use the king as a reserve if either of them balk."

"Do you think they balk?" Firekeeper asked, her brow furrowed with worry.

"I think they might, initially," Derian replied honestly. "But I'll let you explain in your own words and stand by as backup."

"Be easier," Firekeeper grumbled as if to some comment Derian had not heard, "to just go, but then someone would be sent to look for me."

"Probably your humble kennel keeper," Derian said, pointing his thumb at his own chest, "with Race Forester as backup. Do us a favor and don't send us on such a chase. I know we couldn't find you if you didn't want to be found."

Firekeeper grinned agreement. "I make it easy on you then, Derian Fox Hair, even if it make it harder on me."

Although Crown Princess Sapphire and Crown Prince Shad had both been permitted out of bed, for now their freedom was restricted to the castle's main building—no stables, kennels, kitchens, storage buildings, or mews. Their guards didn't even want to let them outside the building, but Doc's insistence that fresh air and sunlight—pallid though the autumn sunlight was as it filtered through the mist from the bay—were needed for the pair's recovery to full health extended their parole to a few of the interior gardens.

However, by the time Firekeeper had told Derian her story and they had discussed their strategies, it was time to dress for dinner. After the dinner—really a formal banquet to honor the departing Hawk Haven nobles before sending them on their way—Sapphire found time to grant Firekeeper a private audience.

Shad was not with her, his time being even more in demand than hers since this was the kingdom where his father reigned. In any case, it was Shad's job to make himself visible to as many of the visitors as possible in order to quell rumors that he was ill or dying.

When Firekeeper, Blind Seer, and Derian were conducted into the crown princess's presence, the dark-haired beauty was in a mellow mood. Apparently, Derian thought, the much anticipated wedding night had been a success, nor had it hurt the proud, young woman's sense of well-being to be fawned over by the many who had much to gain by acquiring her favor.

Immediately upon their entry, Derian could tell that Firekeeper's bow—the same she offered to any but King Tedric—was not sufficiently deep and formal to please the princess. Apparently Sapphire's opinion of herself had changed over the last several days—or maybe, he thought, recalling how Sapphire had behaved during the trip from Eagle's Nest to Hope in the days before King Allister's War, maybe it was returning to where it had been before the shocks of being murderously assaulted, revolting against her mother's domination, and experiencing her first pitched battle had granted her greater perspective and humility.

And maybe, Derian added to himself, *Sapphire doesn't like that she is not the heroine of that fracas in the Sphere Chamber. If anyone stood out from the crowd, it was Firekeeper. Sapphire has never cared to have her light dimmed by another's.*

Firekeeper started speaking almost at once.

"Am glad to see you are strong again, Princess Sapphire," she said, and her tone was sincere.

Sapphire looked somewhat mollified.

"I have great favor to ask of you," Firekeeper continued. "Wish not to come to Hawk Haven and be at second wedding."

A gamut of emotions rippled across the princess's face: surprise, indignation, and, finally, something like scorn.

"I suppose," Sapphire said, her tone so expressionless as to constitute a gibe more pointed than open disapproval, "that you are afraid that there will be another attack."

"I no such afraid," Firekeeper replied without heat. "King Tedric too greatly value you to take such risk. Am sure will be careful guest-watching. Even if was assassin come," she added in admiring tones, "you should be match for all."

The little bitch is flattering her! Derian thought in astonishment. *Though why that should surprise me I don't know. Isn't all that jaw-licking, groveling, and backside-sniffing that I've seen dogs do a form of flattery? Wolves must do it too. I've let Firekeeper know that Sapphire has the potential to harm her and she's doing the equivalent of rolling over.*

Sapphire also seemed startled. Almost certainly, knowing Firekeeper possessed a fighting spirit to match her own, she had expected gibe to be answered with gibe. Faced with no return shot, the princess was forced to ask:

"Why don't you want to take part in my second wedding?"

Firekeeper pulled a sad face. Again Derian was reminded, uncomfortably, of a dog.

"I have had message from home pack. I am wished there soonest, before winter closes the mountains to my feet. If I wait until after your next wedding, which is not to be until Boar Moon has nearly turned her face, then I should not be able to go as I am called."

Sapphire hadn't been raised by a domineering mother for nothing. She understood the compelling force of family summons. Nor did she wish to lessen herself in the eyes of the silently fascinated bodyguards who stood their posts—one near the door, one near the window—by asking just how Firekeeper had received this message from home.

Or maybe. Derian thought a touch grudgingly, *she has somehow learned of Elation's return and put two and two together.*

Mollified by Firekeeper's nearly begging her permission, Sapphire's haughty mien had softened.

"I accept that you are not afraid to attend this second wedding," she said, granting the concession graciously, "but I will be sorry not to have you present. Tales of your swift Fang will have preceded you and many will be disappointed not to see you at my side."

Though you won't mind having her out of the way, will you? Derian thought.

Derian had to swallow a grin. Firekeeper was handling this very well. It wouldn't do for him to queer her pitch.

"Then I have your permission, Crown Princess?" Firekeeper asked.

"And my wishes for a swift and safe journey," Sapphire replied. She added with the complete confidence of someone who knows she is offering a prize that cannot be claimed, "If you re-cross the mountains east before the wedding is concluded, please come to Eagle's Nest. There will be a place for you among my attendants."

Firekeeper bowed, more deeply this time, acknowledging Sapphire's kindness.

"When do you leave?" Sapphire asked, formal manner gone and only common curiosity remaining.

"Tonight, if I can speak with King Tedric and Earl Kestrel before, next night if not. It is better for Blind Seer if we go by darkness."

There was nothing groveling in the wolf-woman's manner now. She stood slim and proud, her hand lightly resting on Blind Seer's back. She spoke of a journey many days' travel to the west, into mountains already feeling the first fingers of winter, as if she were going around to the corner milliner's to buy ribbons for her hat.

Sapphire studied her, a trace of her guarded attitude returning.

"Good luck then. If your feet carry you into Hawk Haven again, you have my permission to call upon me."

And, Derian thought sardonically, *you rather hope she doesn't take you up on that little invitation. Right, Princess?*

Firekeeper accepted this dismissal. Derian made his own parting bow suitable for the occasion and Sapphire's perception of his rank. King Tedric could afford to chat informally with carters' sons, secure in his place. Sapphire—at least as of yet—was not confident enough.

As Derian had predicted, neither Earl Kestrel nor King Tedric presented Firekeeper with any obstacle to her departure. True, the earl asked many questions, including some rather pointed ones regarding the likelihood of his adopted daughter's return.

"I cannot know," Firekeeper replied honestly, "until I know what I am wished for. But I have found friends I care about in these east-lands and if nothing prevents me, I will come back."

King Tedric offered Firekeeper a much more sincere invitation than Sapphire's to call on him upon her return.

"For I believe that you will come back, dear child. If we are still alive, either myself or Elexa would welcome you quite warmly."

Firekeeper smiled at him and dipped into her deep bow rather more quickly than might have been expected. Derian, rising from his own bow, saw the tears that brightened her dark brown eyes.

In the end, though Earl Kestrel—through Valet—tried to press soft boots, warm clothes, food supplies, and even the use of Patience the grey gelding on Firekeeper, the only things that the wolf-woman would take with her were a good whetstone for her Fang, a canteen that could be strapped to her belt, and a small container of salve that Doc assured her would hasten healing of any of the cuts and bruises she was certain to receive.

She already had her flint and steel and clearly considered herself well—even overly—equipped for her journey.

Derian walked Firekeeper to the castle gate and a few steps beyond, out of earshot of the guards.

"Please take the boots, Firekeeper," he said, holding out a pair and some thick socks. "I've seen the rocks at the lower reaches of the Barren Lands. During the war some of Bright Bay's scouts told tales about how sharp the rocks become higher up—sharp enough to cut thick leather."

Stubbornly, Firekeeper shook her head. "Boots rub my feet raw. Why not let rocks do what boots do?"

Derian gave up.

"Be careful, then," he said.

"Always."

Then, to Derian's astonishment, Firekeeper stood up on her

toes and kissed him lightly on the cheek. It was a completely sexless act—like a kiss from a sister—but it touched his soul. As far as he could remember, the only person he had ever known her to kiss was Blind Seer.

The wolf, in turn, gave Derian the deep bow that he had heretofore reserved for King Tedric.

"Thank you, Fox Hair," Firekeeper said softly. "Without you to nursemaid me, I could never have become human. If I live, I promise to visit you again. If I die, Elation—or one of her kin—will be sworn to bring you my Fang as word."

Before Derian could find a reply the wolf-woman had turned and begun running. It should have been impossible on such a well-traveled road, even on a misty night, but before Derian could dash away the tears that suddenly welled hot in his eyes, Firekeeper and Blind Seer had vanished.

VIII

King Allister didn't know whether he was relieved or disturbed when the last of his high-ranking guests departed Revelation Point Castle.

He sincerely liked Uncle Tedric and Aunt Elexa, but he had never stopped worrying about their safety from the moment that fast-traveling post-riders had brought him the word that the king and queen had crossed the border into Bright Bay. Queen Elexa's fragile constitution was a matter of record, but that would not have helped Bright Bay if her health had failed while she was within the boundaries of a kingdom that so recently had been not simply a political rival, but a bitter enemy.

Nor was King Tedric's health much stronger, and the assassination attempt—though apparently directed at members of Allister's own household—had not made for a relaxing visit.

Someday, Allister thought, *I will look back upon these unsettled times and smile at my fussing.*

And now that the foreigners had left, King Allister had no doubt that the internal kingdom politicking would begin in force. He'd already had numerous private requests for favors. This morning would be the first time those claims could be pressed in public.

When the Hawk Haven party had been seen off with due pomp and circumstance, Allister proceeded to the Sphere Chamber. The room was cleaned now—all but the white carpet, which had defied all attempts to remove the bloodstain.

With a glow of the same inspiration that had made her a good household manager for a duke with no duchy, Pearl had insisted that when the carpet was dry it be rolled and stored in the main treasure vault to be brought out on the anniversary of the attempt as a reminder "of the blood spilled to make this kingdom strong."

Never mind that much of the blood belonged to the assassins—the symbolism was good.

The Sphere Chamber had been remodeled into its usual business mode. Ornate carved screens divided the rounded central dais into two halves. Behind the screens, clerks and secretaries could do their tasks without impeding majesty. In front, an imposing but surprisingly comfortable throne had been placed for Allister along with several good—but definitively not throne-like—chairs for Pearl, Shad, and Sapphire should they choose to attend morning business.

Pearl would not. She had told Allister that she had her hands full doing a steward's job—in this case finding permanent replacements for the staff Valora had taken with her. Those servants hired in preparation for the wedding now wanted their positions—and wages—formalized. Those borrowed needed to be returned.

The servants from Pearl and Allister's former household could fill only so many positions at the royal castle—most were needed to maintain their former estate. Allister was not giving up the place, modest as it might seem by the family's current standard of living.

At the very least, the estate could provide an inheritance for Tavis or one of the twins. Pearl might need it as a dower house if Allister predeceased her. He had no illusions that Sapphire might prove a difficult daughter-in-law. In a worst-case scenario, he might need it as a retreat himself.

As today was the first return to business as usual since the wedding, King Allister did not expect a quiet day. Still, he was somewhat surprised at the number of people waiting in the seats fronting the dais. This would almost certainly mean his afternoon would be filled with private appointments, for not everyone would want to discuss their business in front of a crowd.

Swallowing a nostalgic sigh for those days when he could count on hours to himself for reading or riding about his lands—or even playing with the children—King Allister mounted to his throne. As he had expected, both Shad and Sapphire joined him. He was pleased they were looking so well. When he had seen them first placed in the makeshift infirmary, pale from pain and loss of blood, he had dreaded that neither would survive.

A former undersecretary of Queen Gustin IV, promoted to Chief Court Clerk because of his familiarity with Bright Bay's royal rituals, made the usual announcements and then came to the king's side.

Although Allister had no plans to dispense with the services of the woman who had been his personal secretary for many years, he thought he could have done worse than this young man. A junior scion of House Seal—something like the second son of the current duchess's youngest sister—he did not even bear a title.

His given name was Bevan, a frequent appellation in that particular house; however, he had asked the king to call him "Calico," a nickname he had been given because of several large brown birthmarks that spread unattractively over his face and hands—and for all the king knew, over other parts of his body as well. Allister admired Calico's courage in embracing his deformity rather than attempting to deny it. It spoke well for his ability to see things as they were.

Bowing to the king and his heirs with just the right degree of deference, Calico said, his tone pitched for their ears alone:

"Grand Duchess Seastar Seagleam has requested the first audience. She is not here yet, so should I move to the next order of business?"

Allister thought for a moment. He knew his aunt. She would take offense at being skipped, even if the fault was her own. Gustin III's younger sister was rather sensitive about being passed over. She might even have timed her arrival specifically in order to create a scene.

"Let us give the grand duchess a moment more. Hand me a stack of papers and send a runner you can trust to be discreet to learn if she is on her way."

They had barely begun this subterfuge when the grand duchess, accompanied by her son, Dillon, swept into the Sphere Chamber.

So she did hope to cause a scene, Allister thought. *A point to the navy, rather than the pirates.*

He perused the documents and then gestured Calico to him.

"I believe you may begin the regular order of business now," the king said, permitting his clerk to see just a hint of a smile.

Calico remained the soul of perfect decorum as he moved to the desk set to one side of the dais.

"King Allister of the Pledge," he announced in a booming voice that hinted at herald's training in his past, "is pleased to recognize the Grand Duchess Seastar Seagleam."

Seastar Seagleam was about the same age as King Tedric and, like him, she showed her years. Those years had marked her in a different fashion. Where Tedric was a bent old eagle, she possessed an upright, if stiff, posture. The grand duchess's wrinkled skin was powdered, giving it a translucent glow. Like many of her age and generation, she wore a wig, but it was not tinted to make her appear younger. She wore the white of age with a dignity that made it seem a crown.

She rose with grace rather than speed and swept up to the

dais, eschewing her usual cane of carved rosewood for her son's arm.

A good move that, the king thought. *It permits her to bring Dillon to the fore without my express permission.*

Lord Dillon Pelican—unlike Allister himself before his coronation, he bore his father's name rather than his royal-born mother's—handed his mother onto the dais and took one of the seats left empty in the front row of petitioners.

Grand Duchess Seastar had remained at Revelation Point Castle when most of the guests departed. Allister had no illusions that she had done so out of loyalty to himself or belief in his dreams. Indeed, for many years, while Gustin III had remained childless, the grand duchess had imagined that she herself or one of her sons would ascend to the throne of Bright Bay.

Valora's birth comparatively late in her father's reign had not immediately dashed Seastar's hopes. Children do die, or are awarded regents if they take the throne at too young an age.

Only when Valora had assumed the throne did Seastar swallow her dreams, and by all reports that had been a bitter draught. Now, with the restructuring of Bright Bay, her ambitions had awakened again. Her son Culver had borne the title Crown Prince—though no one but his mother had expected he had a chance for the throne. Valora was young and healthy and would certainly bear an heir. Indeed, Culver himself had done little agitating for power. He was a strong sailor and had gone from a respectable career in the navy to captaining a merchant vessel.

Allister rather liked his cousin Culver, but he was less certain about Dillon. Dillon had all his mother's ambition and little of his brother's drive. He also possessed good political sense—a potentially dangerous trait, for it meant he could see his own advantage and would be willing to be used by others.

All of this sped through Allister's thoughts in the time it took for Grand Duchess Seastar to progress to the dais and make her deep curtsy to the throne.

"Nephew," she began, and Allister knew she used the title

to remind any who might forget her relation to the throne, "in a few days' time you will be departing Bright Bay to attend Crown Prince Shad's second wedding in Hawk Haven."

She managed to say "second wedding" with an intonation that made the affair seem vaguely scandalous. From the corner of his eye, Allister saw Sapphire bristle slightly—perhaps believing herself safe since the grand duchess was turned in such a way that she could not see how her barb had hit home. Dillon was watching, though, and he would report.

I must find a tactful way to speak to Sapphire about hiding her reactions. They run too close to the surface and, whether likes or dislikes, they can be used against her—and against my son.

"That is so," Allister replied mildly.

"And when you depart, your heir apparent will depart with you."

"He must," Allister said, managing to time his words so they were not quite an interruption, "as it is his wedding."

There was a light flutter of laughter at this, enough to discommode the grand duchess for a breath's pause.

The king reflected, *Doubtless she was about to say something such as "and the Princess Sapphire will also be gone," underlining the absence of those in immediate line for the throne. I think I see where she is heading. Unhappily, she is in for a shock.*

Old hand at politics that she was, Grand Duchess Seastar regained her poise without much difficulty. She had grown accustomed to Allister's self-effacing manner when he was merely Allister Seagleam. The twenty-some days that had passed since his formal coronation had not been enough to reeducate her, but the king had no doubt she would not forget again.

"With you and your heirs away not only from the capitol but from the kingdom," the old lady continued, "the question has arisen as to who will hold the reins in your absence."

"I thank you, Grand Duchess Seastar," Allister replied, carefully not omitting *her* title, "for raising a matter that I had planned on addressing myself. In my absence, I have appointed two of Bright Bay's nobles to act as joint regents."

Seastar frowned slightly. She had heard nothing of this, but then Allister had sworn the parties concerned to absolute silence—a thing they were more than willing to do given the favor he was showing them.

"Duke Dolphin and Earle Oyster will act as regents in my place. I had thought to ask my father-in-law, Duke Oyster, to act as regent, but he begged for permission to travel to his grandson's wedding—a return of the courtesy that so many of Hawk Haven's noble houses accorded us by sending their representatives here."

That stung! Allister thought, smothering a certain boyish glee. *Aunt Seastar never offered to make the journey to Hawk Haven herself, nor even to send either Dillon or Culver. She was too eager to have them here to profit from my absence to realize that she was acting less than the great lady she wishes to be thought.*

"Duke Dolphin has graciously agreed to send his wife and heir to the festivities in his stead. Although he is not a young man, his health is unquestioned and with Earle Oyster as his deputy, he will have someone on hand should pirate trouble arise."

By common euphemism any naval trouble was assigned to pirates, though many times it had its inception in Waterland or other, more distant, sea powers. It beat declaring war.

And I expect that when good sailing weather comes again, Allister thought, *Valora's fleet will add to the number of "pirates" combing the waters.*

Grand Duchess Seastar, who had clearly meant to gracefully offer herself or her son as regent, recovered with a swiftness that did her credit.

"Your thoughtfulness in this important matter," she said with a somewhat forced smile, "is appreciated. Having heard no announcement of the regency, I had mistakenly supposed that the excitement of Crown Prince Shad's wedding had driven such relatively distant matters from your mind."

Allister gave her a gracious nod, resisting the automatic impulse to bow to her as he had all his life.

"I had intended to make the announcement tomorrow. Today was filled enough with the departure of our fellow monarchs. Still, I thank you from the depths of my heart for your concern for the safety and stability of our realm."

The grand duchess dipped a curtsy and took her leave. As Calico called the next order of business—a report from the Illustrious Commissioner who had charge of roads—King Allister mused:

Well, Aunt Seastar's going to be upset, but even so she cannot blame me. Oyster has been my firmest support from the start and Dolphin is still eager to repay Gustin's lineage for the insult Gustin III gave their house by divorcing Lady Brina. As fine as Grand Duchess Seastar's titles are, I must conciliate my Great Houses before worrying about lesser nobles.

Then he turned his full attention to the road commissioner's report. This particular commissioner was of Lobster blood, if he recalled correctly. Her house had been the most fragmented by the recent upheavals and clearly she was making certain that her new king would have no doubts where her loyalties lay—with Bright Bay, which had entrusted her with care of its central road network. If Allister was careful and courteous, he could turn that abstract loyalty into one to himself, personally.

Allister leaned forward slightly to demonstrate his attention, took a few notes, smiled at a particularly salient point.

Shad and Sapphire sat side by side, also listening. Their expressions were set but attentive, their fingers—off where they thought them hidden from sight—were discreetly intertwined.

LIKE EARL KESTREL, Baron Ivon Archer had seen a distinct advantage to departing Silver Whale Cove in order to travel with King Tedric's party. Like Earl Kestrel, he could make himself visibly useful to his monarch—a silent reminder that he had remained when others had used the threat of assassins to flee.

Elise had to swallow an unladylike grin when she thought just what Aurella Wellward might have said if her husband had tried to leave. Lady Aurella was devoted to her aunt, the queen, and had done her best on the long journey out to ease the strains of the road. Even so, Queen Elexa had been worn to—not a shadow, Elise thought, shadows were too dark—more to a thin, silvery-grey wisp of spiderweb shaped in the form of a woman.

The journey out had taken six days and Elise was willing to wager—had there been any takers—that the return trip would take at least seven. King Tedric was taking no chances with his wife's health, especially as she would need to preside at the second wedding almost as soon as they returned.

Since Silver Whale Cove was on the innermost tip of the deep bay from which the kingdom took its name, the Hawk Haven group began their journey well west of the ocean. They headed north, following roads that would eventually take them to the border between the countries. There they would cross from Bright Bay into Broadview, a thriving town built at the confluence of the Barren and Flin rivers.

Broadview and her Bright Bay sister city, Rock Fort, took advantage of the trade that came down along both rivers from the interior of Hawk Haven on its way to that kingdom's one port. There was no bridge such as spanned the Barren between the twin towns of Hope and Good Crossings farther west. Here the Barren, fed by the waters of its sister river, was too wide and too swift.

Nor had Broadview become the center for illicit trade that its western sisters were. The very width of the river made such goings-on less profitable, although far more wealth, measured in the most basic terms, went through this point.

Another factor limiting smuggling in the vicinity of Broadview was that both kingdoms maintained large garrisons in the area. Before the peace Bright Bay had often tried to take advantage of the rich cargoes shipped toward the ocean from the city. Needless to say, Hawk Haven had taken steps to prevent them from easily doing so.

Now in peace both forces remained, reassigned to the difficult tasks of taxing legal trade and of preventing the growth of illegal trade. Already entrepreneurs were establishing regular ferry service across the river. As the tricky currents were beyond even the skills of the average citizen of Bright Bay— all of whom claimed they could sail as easily as they could walk—these new businesses were doing quite well.

Elise Archer was rather pleased when she anticipated a journey of six or seven days. Although not a greatly experienced traveler, she was young enough that the hardships of the road didn't bother her greatly. Just a few moonspans before, during the negotiations that had led to King Allister's War and through the war itself, she had lived in a tent. Now, enough weeks had passed that she was rested and nostalgic about the relative freedom of those days.

Even the increasingly cool nights didn't trouble her. The pavilion she shared with her parents and Ninette was floored with thick carpets and her own cot was supplied with a generous heap of blankets. The daytime weather was a gift from the ancestors—bright and clear and relatively warm, presented, all agreed, as a reward to the elderly king and queen for their courage in making a journey to further peace.

Before their departure from Hawk Haven, Baron Archer had presented his daughter with a fine riding horse, a substitute for the gentle white palfrey that had been her more usual mount. Elise, never much of a horsewoman, had taken over that palfrey from her mother; now she passed it on to Ninette.

Elise's new mount was younger and more spirited, but not so spirited as to challenge Elise's riding skills. Instead she— the horse was a mare—was a bit of a flirt, given to tossing her head and stomping a forehoof. Taking a cue from Lady Melina Shield, who had always made certain her children's mounts were fashion accessories as well as mere transportation, Baron Archer had sought a steed who would accent his daughter's fair-haired loveliness.

Cream Delight possessed a coat of deep, shimmering gold,

but her abundant mane and high-set, flowing tail were silvery white. Her head was delicate and pretty; her gaits were easy and, even at a trot, surprisingly smooth. In short, she was the perfect mount for a young lady of quality who needed to look good almost more than she needed to travel.

To her own surprise, Elise grew fond of Cream Delight in a way she had never been of any of the other ponies and palfreys she had been given. Of course, grooms took care of routine grooming and feeding, but even when they had safely arrived at the castle at Silver Whale Cove Elise had found time to steal out to the stables with a carrot or apple. A few stolen moments stroking Cream's neck and murmuring her troubles into the mare's perked ears revitalized the young woman as did nothing else.

Elise found herself riding more often as well. During the trips to and from Hope a few moonspans before, Elise had tended to travel in the carriages or walk, only occasionally venturing out on horseback. On the journey to Silver Whale Cove, however, she had gradually found herself riding for longer and longer stretches, until by the time they arrived she could stay in the saddle for most of a day without becoming more than reasonably stiff.

On the return journey, Elise planned to do the same. She regained her seat easily and felt quite good about herself, so that she welcomed Derian Carter when he came trotting up to visit with her.

His mount, Roanne, was a showy chestnut mare whose white stockings showed off her polished copper coat as if ordered expressly for the purpose. With her developing eye for good horseflesh, Elise could tell that Roanne was a superior mount. For a moment she wondered how Derian could have afforded such a horse. Then she recalled that his family owned an extensive chain of livery stables, and that small mystery was solved.

Derian reined Roanne in alongside Cream. The two mares blew at each other, Cream submitting just slightly. Doubtless the horses had worked out matters of precedence while stabled at the castle.

"Hello!" Derian said cheerfully. "How do you like the mare?"

"She's lovely," Elise answered promptly, "and as comfortable as a chair in my mother's solar."

"I must tell my father," Derian said with a grin. "He's the one who found the mare for the baron, though I think my sister, Damita, had something to do with the final choice. Dami's developing an eye for the proper turnout to give the lady of fashion."

Elise laughed. She vaguely recalled that Derian had a sister a few years younger than himself and perhaps a brother as well. For a moment she felt a familiar flicker of loneliness. Aurella Wellward had inherited the same weakness as had her aunt, Queen Elexa, but whereas the queen—perhaps out of a sense of duty to her line—had borne three living children, Aurella had borne no other child after Elise.

In return, Aurella was in far better condition than her aunt, showing none of the signs of premature aging that plagued the queen. Elise, who loved her mother, supposed it was a fair trade, but she wished that her parents had at least adopted another child.

Apparently, the baron had considered such a course but had been dissuaded by his sister, Zorana, who had loudly proclaimed that the title their father had won should not pass to a stranger's child when she herself had four living.

Three now, Elise thought sadly, for her cousin Purcel, Zorana's eldest at fifteen, had died on the field during King Allister's War.

Derian must have noted Elise's suddenly somber mood, for he said, "If you'd prefer, Lady Elise, I can leave you to your thoughts."

"Please don't leave," she said, putting a hand out to touch his arm. "I was just remembering my cousin Purcel."

"A real loss," Derian said sincerely. "Purcel was a good horseman, as well as a good fellow. I wonder what happened to his bay hunter? It's too big a horse for little Kenre and I don't imagine that either Nydia or Deste would fancy it."

"I don't know," Elise admitted. "Aunt Zorana may have

kept it for herself. She's far more likely to go hunting than is Uncle Aksel."

"He's more the scholarly type," Derian agreed. "Well, if you find they're looking to sell the bay, suggest my parents' stable. They'll give your aunt a fair price."

They talked for a while of such general matters and eventually, to Elise's delight, Sir Jared drifted over to join them. His mount was a solid, unpretentious chestnut gelding, its coat showing a touch of red but lacking Roanne's glowing hues. The gelding was clearly an older horse, slightly past its prime, and Elise on her golden steed was uncomfortably reminded of the difference in their stations.

After bowing greeting to Elise, Sir Jared said, "I thought I'd let you two know that a halt for a light meal will be called as soon as we get around that bend. Race reports that there's a harvested field ahead whose owner is honored to let us stop. Afterwards, the king hopes to put in a few more miles before we're forced by lack of light to pitch camp."

"Thanks, Doc," Derian said. "It's a pity there are no good inns along this road. Those that are here are of the six-to-a-bed and meal-in-a-pub type. The pavilions the noble folk packed along will offer far more comfortable accommodations."

"Someday there will be better inns," Sir Jared predicted, "if the peace holds. This road will become a major trade corridor and nobles traveling between the kingdoms will be happy to pay for a pleasant place to sleep and a good hot meal."

Elise nodded. "I agree. The distance between Eagle's Nest and Silver Whale Cove by water is much greater. I suspect that the freelance boaters crowding the banks now will be replaced by some sort of regular ferry service. A bridge will always be impossible with the river so wide."

"True enough," Jared agreed.

He looked as if he was about to depart, so Elise asked quickly, "Tell me, Doc, whatever became of Sapphire's request?"

"Request?" Derian asked.

"She wanted Sir Jared made some sort of royal physician—like Lord Rory."

Sir Jared grinned at the memory.

"Well, Lady Elise, the matter has been put by for now. King Tedric said that he'd be happy to grant the princess's request, but he wants to speak with his own physician beforehand—make certain there're no hurt feelings."

"Good idea," Elise commented.

"Then," Jared continued, "King Tedric says he may still wait, consult a few people. Once our ranking families hear how many special titles and posts there are among Bright Bay's courtiers there will be agitating for parity in Hawk Haven—no matter how unzoranic that would be."

Elise grimaced. "Not everyone would be after new titles but some would be just delighted. My Aunt Zorana, for example, or Titchy Trueheart. Do you know her?"

Sir Jared nodded, "Met Lady Titchy once when she came to a large party at Cousin Norvin's city manse. Pretentious."

"I met Titchy," Elise giggled, "one spring when she invited herself to our family house to do watercolors of the gardens—my great-grandmother Farmer put in some water lilies that have become quite famous. Titchy complained night and day about the servants, and hadn't considered that there might be mosquitoes."

Derian asked, "Isn't the Archer Grant along the Barren?"

"It is," Elise replied, pointing vaguely northwest. "East of Hope and Good Crossing, but west of Broadview. Back when King Chalmer granted my grandfather his title and lands, the border was rather hotly contested—just as it was in the days when Queen Zorana laid in the Crown's claims to much of the river land. Despite the good access to water, no one particularly wanted land so susceptible to raids, so no one argued when King Chalmer gave my grandfather a nice piece."

"Who holds the land at the confluence of the Flin and Barren?" Derian asked. "Wellward?"

"Not exactly," Elise said. "It's surrounded by much Wellward land, but Broadview is a crown city. I think that Grand Duke Gadman is technically its governor, though a city council does most of the day-to-day managing. Grand Duke Gadman simply provides the final word on any major changes and collects some income.

"Even so, the system works well for everyone. Otherwise my grandfather Peregrine might have been expected to provide all the troops for Broadview's defense—and no one would like that, not the troops, not the Peregrine treasury, and not the king, since that would mean he'd need to permit the Wellwards to maintain a fairly large private army."

Sir Jared commented. "My family's lands are further north—part of the Norwood Grant. Most of the Norwood Grant borders New Kelvin along the White Water River. I suppose because Hawk Haven has never been at war with New Kelvin, the Norwoods have never worried about keeping a standing army. There's a local militia, but that's useful in several ways. It gives work for extra children of local families and provides the Kestrels with a pool of trained soldiers to draw on when the Crown calls for troops."

"Remember that the White Water's rougher than the Barren," Elise stated, tracing a map in the air with her fingertip, "though the Barren's no millpond. Along most of the White Water's length it's broken up by rocks and falls. That makes it a more effective barrier between the kingdoms."

"You *do* know your geography," Jared said admiringly.

"I like learning about strange lands and peoples," Elise admitted cheerfully. "That's one of the reasons I was so glad to make the trip into Bright Bay."

"And yet," Jared said, "Bright Bay is practically Hawk Haven when you compare their peoples and customs to ours. My family's lands are south of the White Water, in the foothills of the Iron Mountains. Even though we're not on the border, I've met New Kelvinese traders when they come to sample the year's pressings and order wine."

"I remember now!" Elise exclaimed. "Your family owns a winery."

"A new one, as such interests are judged," Jared answered, laughing at her enthusiasm, "but we sold our harvest to larger growers before our vines produced enough to turn to our own use. I've been to more than a few wine-fests."

They fell to talking of wines and economics, of the strange habits of the New Kelvinese, drifted into analyzing the customs of the plutocracy of Waterland, and touched on the current political question before drifting to speculation about what countries might lie beyond those they knew.

Neither particularly noticed when the party stopped for lunch, but munched their bread and cheese and drank their wine as they continued talking. Neither noticed when Derian drifted off to visit with Ox and Race.

Nor did either notice the sour looks that Baron Archer turned in their direction.

LEAVING REVELATION POINT CASTLE, Firekeeper and Blind Seer ran and walked, ran and walked until dawn was pinking the horizon. Several times they stopped to rest and dine—Firekeeper on fruit scavenged from the upper boughs of some well-tended trees, Blind Seer on any wild creature unfortunate enough to let him catch it.

Shortly before dawn they halted. Firekeeper caught a fish in a stream and grilled it lightly over a fire built in a circle of river rocks. Their stopping place was along the edge of a mown hayfield. Firekeeper made them a burrow in the side of one of the many towering haystacks that dotted the acreage and there they slept warm and well.

She woke stiff and with feet aching from the unaccustomed exertions, but as she had not let herself get too out of training—her run from Good Crossing to Silver Whale Cove had been only a few days before—soon her muscles loosened up and she had no trouble maintaining a tireless jog-trot.

Blind Seer, of course, was not taxed within even an iota of his strength. He had time to range widely and did so, hunting freely and bringing back a portion of his kills for Firekeeper's meals.

Elation scouted out their route, one that avoided main roads, towns, and even the larger farms. As in Hawk Haven, five generations had not been enough for the population of Bright Bay to recover from the ravages that had begun with plague and continued into war. Moreover, since the citizens of Bright Bay looked to the sea rather than the land as a source of wealth, most farmed for their own use rather than growing surplus for trade. Broad areas covered by second-growth forest were only just beginning to be reclaimed for farming or pasturage.

Between these pockets of human habitation, wilderness abounded. Had it not been for the occasional scent of wood smoke or a trail bearing the marks of horse or wagon, Firekeeper might have thought herself already west of the Iron Mountains.

This established the pattern for the remainder of their journey west. As the year was drawing into winter, the hours of darkness stretched longer and longer, giving them plenty of time to travel—for Elation was an unusual falcon, even among her kind, and had no problem flying by night.

Her preference, however, was to course ahead while there was light—either early in the morning or as evening drew near—to map out their course, and then sleep through a few of the dark hours. In this way, Firekeeper and Blind Seer were spared at least some of her sardonic commentary on the sluggish pace of the wingless.

They timed their arrival at the edge of the Barren Lands with hours of darkness to spare. The thriving towns of Hope and Good Crossing were just east of the foothills, and had they come in daylight there was a chance that they might have encountered people.

None of them had reason to fear humans. Indeed, Firekeeper would probably have been known to most—at least by reputation. However, since their destination was a secret—Firekeeper still felt a little bad about having misled Derian—they had no wish to be seen.

"Wisest," Elation said as they rested before beginning the climb, "if you follow the canyon cut by the Barren River. As I told you, the river has its birthplace in the mountain lake and so you will not be taken too far astray."

Firekeeper frowned. She had seen something of river canyons during her migrations with the wolves and knew that sometimes even the cleverest pair of feet could not find purchase. Sometimes the water had risen to cover footholds; other times it had worn everything smooth.

She expressed her concern to Elation, but the peregrine was confident.

"Surely if you have trouble you can take to the waters for a spell. The great wolves don't fear getting wet, do they?"

Firekeeper still had her doubts, but permitted herself to be convinced. Blind Seer, confident in his young strength—he was only rising four and despite his inborn wisdom had seen much less than had Firekeeper—was unconcerned.

"We ground travelers must try to gain height as we travel," Firekeeper reminded bird and wolf. "Or else we may find ourselves at the foot of some great fall with a sheer cliff blocking our way."

They entered the canyon and moved west for the remainder of that night's hours of darkness. However, after only a few hours' sleep Firekeeper punched Blind Seer awake.

"I've been thinking," she said, speaking into his ear so as not to wake the peregrine. "Elation cannot be our scout in this place. She thinks too little of obstacles that would halt us, even force us to double back. From this point until we reach the top of the Barren Lands, we travel when there is light. If the traveling is good, we can continue after dark."

The wolf grumbled some but was convinced by the mere fact that Firekeeper would go on without him. Moreover, he had already seen how the waters had sliced the sides of the canyon so that at times they had needed to jump from miniature island to miniature island rather than walking or running.

Elation, when informed of Firekeeper's decision, merely shrugged her head into her feathered shoulders in a gesture of dismissal.

"You know your limitations better than I," she said, and leapt into the air in a burst of wings to avoid Blind Seer's snap.

By the end of that day, it was apparent that Firekeeper had chosen wisely. Her keen eyes, which she relied on as the wolf did his nose, found at a distance the trails that animals had used to come down to the river for water. These provided stretches of easier going, but as most of the animals who lived in the Barren Lands were small creatures—rodents and those who preyed on them, with the occasional goat or sheep—these trails were hardly broad highways.

Moreover, the mountain wind liked the channel cut for it by the river and howled down it like some spring-maddened wolf. When the sun shone, the wind's game only made the travelers uncomfortable, but in the shadowed places ice formed wherever water had splashed, making the footing slick and treacherous.

These difficulties slowed their progress. Indeed, sometimes Firekeeper imagined that by day's end they had progressed only a little distance farther west but had instead climbed endlessly upward. Other times she could not even fancy that much progress, for they were forced to leave the river entirely, taking long detours through sharp broken rock that made Firekeeper reconsider—if only in the privacy of her thoughts—the wisdom of boots.

But after day and night, day and night, and day again, they made camp to the sound of unbroken thunder and knew that they were nearing the source of the Barren River, the lake that humans called the Rimed Lake.

The next dawn they began their final ascent and found themselves with some unexpected company. A kestrel as vibrantly blue and red as Norvin Norwood's favorite waistcoat—indeed far more brilliantly colored than any other representative of that type that Firekeeper had ever seen—fluttered down to meet them.

Even though, as with most of the Royal Beasts, this kestrel was larger than usual, he was still diminutive when compared with Elation. Indeed, Firekeeper found herself doubting that this little hawk could best even a prime sparrow—but, then, the Cousin kestrel hunted mostly insects.

"Bee Biter," Elation said, "what brings you here?"

The tiny falcon darted down and perched on a twig slightly above them. Firekeeper was reminded of a songbird rather than a hawk—but Bee Biter's hooked beak and curving talons gave lie to that fancy. Still, she supposed that the protective coloration served the kestrel well.

"I come to guide you this last way up the rock," the kestrel cried in a high, shrill voice. "I have watched and studied and will share my knowledge freely."

Elation flapped her wings, clearly affronted that the other thought his guidance superior, but Firekeeper cut in before the peregrine could speak.

"Thank you, fleet Bee Biter. We are grateful. My naked hands freeze to the rock and the spray from the waterfall chills my skin."

"Follow then!" Bee Biter shrieked, bounding into the air. "Follow!"

Unlike Elation, who must fly or soar, Bee Biter proved dexterous enough to nearly hover over them. His eye for detail was considerable and Firekeeper suspected that either he had been watching them and considering their limitations or he had watched other humans make this climb.

Time and again, the kestrel steered them away from the obvious path to one that—though more difficult—proved a better choice. Eventually, they climbed to where they could see the waterfall, and Firekeeper was amazed.

"From the sound and the mist, I had thought it close enough to touch," she exclaimed, "yet we are so far away!"

"It is like a wolf pack," Bee Biter said, fluttering a safe distance from Blind Seer, "noisy enough that one cannot judge the size."

Blind Seer, however, was too weary to take offense at this comment. Whereas the climb had been rough on Firekeeper, at least the human had hands with which to grasp. The wolf must leap from rock to rock or scrabble up paths that showered down gravel as he struggled for a foothold. Even the paws of a wolf—surprisingly skillful at bracing and balancing—were challenged by this climb. Had Firekeeper not shoved him over some blockades and dragged him over others, Blind Seer could not have come this far.

Firekeeper stroked him, rubbing beneath his chin and along his throat. She fancied he had lost some weight during these past several days, but then he'd had weight to spare. Now he was firm and strong, as a wolf in pre-snowfall form should be if he expected to survive the winter.

They resumed their climb. The sound from the great torrent of water never diminished, but the time came when they looked down at it, to where its base vanished in mist. By evening, they were on level ground, but another surprise awaited Firekeeper and Blind Seer.

"You said we were coming to a lake!" Firekeeper said accusingly to Elation. "This is no lake. It is the ocean held in the breast of the mountain!"

Elation laughed. "If you could take to the skies at midday, little wolfling, you could see the far side of the lake. Still, I admit it is a grand stretch of water and what you see before you is only one section. The waters fill two lobes of almost equal size. One spills, as you have seen, into the Barren River. There is enough left to birth the Fox and yet even when mid-summer is driest the waters recede only a little."

"I am," Firekeeper admitted, "awed and no little bit terrified. I am also exhausted. Will the Mothers forgive us if we sleep? As I recall, we are to meet them to the west of this ocean lake."

"They will forgive," Bee Biter said promptly. "Indeed, it would be best if you had light for the next challenge."

"Next?" growled Blind Seer.

"Think, wolf," the kestrel said teasingly. "Have you yet crossed the Barren River? You began your climb on her more southern bank. To go around the lake you must first cross to the northern bank."

Blind Seer shook, more in dismay than because he was wet, though droplets did scatter from his thick coat.

"True enough, bug-eater. At least the ground is softer here than below."

Elation shrieked laughter, perhaps pleased that the wolf had offered the insult she had not dared. Then she spoke:

"I will hunt for you land-bound. Lick your paws and soak your feet. Build a fire and rest. You have done a great thing for two who have no wings and only six legs between you."

Wolf and woman were too weary to answer to whatever insults might be implied. Glad of a chance to rest where the ground was level and dry, they stretched out on the carpet of dried grass for a brief nap.

Eventually, Firekeeper rose and found kindling among the driftwood washed along the pebbly shore. Blind Seer had eaten two rabbits—head, hide, and entrails—by the time her fire was ready for cooking her own meal, but she was glad of the blaze's warmth as much as its use in preparing food. With full darkness, the lakeside had grown cold.

When she slept, she curled between the fire and Blind Seer. As the wolf had predicted, she tucked her bare feet beneath his belly fur for warmth.

IX

EVEN WHEN THEY DID SO, Allister had known that he and Uncle Tedric had been pushing the limits of probability when they had set the date for the second wedding for a mere fifteen days after the first. Still, there had been little choice in the matter.

Boar Moon shone down on late autumn, a time when the early harvest had already been gathered and most farmers were turning their energies to preparing for the first snowfalls. In the northern parts of Hawk Haven, he had heard, there would be snow before the moon finished waning. Bright Bay was enough farther south and her climate was so influenced by the great bay at her heart that winter took a bit longer growing severe, but once the cold set in it always seemed reluctant to let go.

The first wedding had taken place on the twenty-second day of Lynx Moon, about as soon after King Allister's coronation as was reasonable, given the distances some of the guests were required to travel. The second wedding, therefore, could not be scheduled any sooner than the ninth day of Boar Moon.

After the assassination attempt, Allister and King Tedric had discussed delaying the wedding a few more days, but they had decided against it. Already they were tempting the forces that ruled wind and rain; to delay further would tempt cold as well. Moreover, Hawk Haven was farther north. The capital, at Eagle's Nest, lay somewhat closer to the mountains.

Yet if they did not hold the wedding in early Boar Moon, it must be delayed until winter had released its grip on the land and the worst of spring's rains were past—late Horse Moon or even Puma Moon.

True, a hardy group might actually travel more swiftly once the snow was on the ground and wheels could be exchanged for sled runners, but it would take a deep freeze indeed to ice over the Barren, and King Allister had no wish to trust his loved ones to a semifrozen river rife with ice floes.

Moreover, much as he loved her, he was the first to admit—perhaps second after Pearl herself—that his wife was not a hardy traveler. Women Pearl's age still commanded ships or rode to battle—she was just past forty, after all—but Pearl Oyster was not of that type. She was a settled noblewoman who never rode if there was a carriage to hand, had never sailed for herself since her sons had grown eager to take the lines, and rejoiced in a well-managed household.

The twins were still slim girl-children, as light and delicate as the fish and flower for which they were named. Minnow and Anemone might start out finding a multiday sleigh trip exciting. (Even with perfect conditions, they couldn't hope to cover the necessary distance in less than four days.) By the end they would be shivering and miserable, their noses bright red and running, hardly the perfect appearance for maiden wedding attendants.

But as much as King Allister loved his family—and he did so with the open heart of an unambitious man who had never needed to dream his children into anything more than the people they were—it had not been consideration for them or their needs that had made him urge King Tedric to let the wedding remain on its scheduled day.

It had been politics.

A delay until even Horse Moon—if the roads were not sodden with mud—would give the schemers half a year to plan and plot. Rumors would be spread that the wedding had been delayed because the truce was weakening, because Shad and Sapphire had grown to hate each other, because one or both were ill.

In winter, rumors spread with the speed of a skater across the ice and grew around firesides like exotic plants in a New Kelvinese hothouse. Half a year of rumors could destroy his reign more neatly than an assassin's dagger. Best instead that they go ahead and finish the formalities.

Shad and Sapphire would winter in Hawk Haven as planned—King Tedric's age and health made it unwise for his heirs to be too far away when they might be needed. In return, several of the younger members of Hawk Haven's court would winter in Bright Bay. Allister knew that Sapphire was hoping that one or more of her younger sisters would be among that number, but Lady Melina's recent behavior made that uncertain.

Our young guests won't be hostages, Allister thought with grim humor, *not really, not quite, but that won't stop those who think the worst of rulers from seeing them as such.*

So it was that on the second day of Boar Moon, King Allister and a fairly sizable entourage prepared to depart from Revelation Point Castle. In the back of his mind, Allister was aware that King Tedric and his party would not yet have arrived home—and that they would not until just a few days before their guests.

Since the trip out from Eagle's Nest had taken King Tedric's party six days, Allister had hoped that his group—which after all contained no invalids—could do it in less.

One look at the long train of horses and carriages, baggage wagons and overburdened mules quenched that hope. Allister had not been king long enough to feel he could do as he desired—stride down that line like a captain inspecting his officers and strip those traveling with him down to bare essentials.

Don't forget, Allister, he told himself, *that they are making a brave venture into enemy territory. They'll want to make a good show, put on their best finery for our new allies. Don't ruin their pride.*

Shad, still holding his left shoulder somewhat stiffly, rode up beside Allister.

"Don't worry, Father," he said, his words for the king alone. "We'll make it there no later than the evening of the seventh. Sapphire and I have discussed tactics, and have decided that we'll ride to the point, keeping up the pace and shaming those who would go too easy."

Allister chuckled.

"You can do that where I can't," he admitted. "You're still touched with the glamour of your newlywed state."

"And what better way," the prince added, showing that he too had been thinking of how vulnerable their position was, "to quell any rumors that Sapphire and I might not like either each other or this arranged marriage than to be urging everyone on?"

"You're a good son," Allister said almost complacently.

"And Sapphire is a fine wife!" Shad nearly glowed in his enthusiasm.

Allister followed the direction of Shad's gaze and saw his new daughter-in-law swinging into her horse's saddle. Gone was the elegant bride, gone the pale invalid. Here was the warrior whose appearance had enchanted the troops fighting before the walls of Good Crossing. Today she didn't wear armor or sword, only a hunting knife at her belt, but her steed was the mighty Blue she had ridden into war.

The Blue was actually a pale grey, but Lady Melina's desire

that her children be clad and accoutered in keeping with the theme of their names had extended to horses. If there were no blue horses, then one must be created—in this case, by means of dye.

When the Blue had been relocated some days after the final battle of King Allister's War—he had fled during a particularly bad press—Sapphire had reclaimed him, treated his wounds, and then permitted her mount to go back to his former color. To her evident delight, the Blue's mane and tail turned out to be a smoky blue-grey, quite striking against his paler coat—and an ample reminder of his former gaudy glory.

"Lead on, son," Allister said. "Gather up your lady and tell whoever Whyte has assigned to point guard that we're to get under way. There's no better way to convince the stragglers to stop straggling than to give them no choice."

Shad trotted his own mount—a dark bay with off stockings white almost to the knee—to join Sapphire. Allister accepted a hand up into the carriage that had been prepared for him. Later, he would ride up and down the line, visiting with his companions and consolidating his reign a bit more. However, he had agreed with Whyte Steel's recommendation that to begin the journey in that fashion would be to invite trouble.

And not just from assassins—if any are about, Allister thought. *Too many would press for the honor of riding in my vicinity. The main roads of Silver Whale Cove are wide, but we'd bottleneck them just the same.*

For the first several days of their journey the weather remained clement and the king kept to his resolve to mix with his entourage as much as possible. The autumn air was crisp and his mount—a sorrel with the undignified name of Hot Toddy—was smooth-gaited at both walk and trot. Toddy's canter was like flying, but Allister rarely had the excuse to press the horse that fast.

Instead he rode at easy pace, always dogged by one or more riders—even if his own court had not taken advantage of the king's availability, Whyte Steel would not have left him unprotected. Nor were the members of his own entourage the only ones who sought to get close. The passage of the royal group from Hawk Haven had not quelled the enthusiasm of those who lived anywhere at all near the road for spectacle.

So many people crowded the verges, especially whenever the group passed near a town or village, that Allister idly wondered who precisely was left to get in the harvest. If the baskets of hand-polished apples and other fresh goods—from pastries to eggs—they were offered were any indication, it had been a good harvest, despite the fighting farther west.

They were forced to turn away many of the gifts, or no people, only groceries, would have arrived in Hawk Haven for the wedding. Still, at night when the temperatures dropped, Allister found himself glad for a mug of hot cider to warm his insides.

The day after they crossed the Barren at Rock Fort and left Broadview behind them, the weather turned ugly. Rain washed down in torrents, turning the packed road sticky with mud. The sailors among them pulled out foul-weather gear and rode on as if this were nothing more than a squall at sea. Sea chanties were bellowed out to answer the force of the wind until even the horses seemed encouraged.

Uncle Tedric should be home by now, Allister thought as he guided Hot Toddy around the puddles. He'd long ago left the singing to those with better voices and fallen to daydreaming about what awaited them in a day or two more. *And there will be fires blazing in all the hearths and thick quilts on the beds.*

That evening, when they made camp in a farmer's barns, Whyte Steel reported to the king that the people much admired his fortitude and noble bearing against the elements.

"They're saying that you contemplate great matters of state," the guard captain said, "and so ride as if through a soft spring day."

Allister laughed. Truly the mystique and aura of a king held a unique power if it could make people believe such nonsense.

"Don't tell them, Whyte," he said, still laughing. "I'm just sealing my lips to keep from drinking rain by the gallon."

"I won't," Whyte replied with frightening sincerity. "I most certainly will not."

❀

WALNUT ENDBROOK HATED HIS GIVEN NAME. He'd never gotten straight just why his mother had saddled him with it. Whenever he'd asked he'd never gotten the same story twice in a row.

The worst times were when she just giggled. Other times she offered him a fanciful tale by way of explanation: walnuts had been her favorite food when she was pregnant with him or he'd been conceived under a walnut tree or his wrinkled infant face had reminded her of a nutmeat.

Walnut couldn't ask his father, because his mother wasn't precisely sure who *was* his father. That lucky gentleman had gotten away from Honey Endbrook long before Walnut had been born, maybe even before he'd been conceived. There had been other men since. Many others.

Before he was eight, Walnut had beaten bloody anyone who dared call him "Walnut." On children he used his fists. Adults he bit or kicked. "Waln"—never "Nut"—became an acceptable diminutive. He would have preferred to adopt some other name entirely, but though lots of people were nicknamed as they grew older no one ever renamed him—not even a common nickname like "Tiny" or "Salty." Perversely, the hated name remained with him as stubbornly as walnut-rind stain remained on the hands.

Waln left his mother's home on Dog Island shortly after his eleventh birthday, sailing out as cabin boy on a merchant ship. When he returned, three years later, Honey Endbrook had vanished. No one seemed to know where she had gone or even whether she was living or dead. Far too many people in his old hometown called him "Walnut," though. Waln left, the money he had meant to give his mother as proof of his new worth heavy in his pockets.

He used the better part of three years' wages to buy into a cargo; the profits from that venture bought him a share in a ship. By the time he was twenty, he was co-owner. By the time he was twenty-five, he owned the vessel and another beside. By the time Waln turned thirty, he let others risk storm and pirates. While he waited for his ships to come in, he established a clearinghouse for various goods on Thunder Island.

Waln was forty and wealthy when the news came that the Isles had just become a kingdom of their own. He had grown into a big man, somewhat fleshy but not in the least fat. Just a few years before, his light brown hair had started retreating from his forehead and thinning at the top, but he accepted this change philosophically. A peaked-brim sailor's hat hid the deficiency as well as protecting his fair skin from burning.

He was wearing that hat, squinting out from under the brim's shadow in a way that had become habitual, while he listened to the news that had come via fast ship to Thunder Island Harbor. The royal governor appointed by Bright Bay was to be replaced by Queen Gustin IV—now to be known as Queen Valora—as their monarch.

Waln Endbrook was a well-known man on Thunder Island. In addition to his warehouses along the docks, he owned a fine estate on the coveted high ground above the harbor. He could have stood for town major and found no one willing to stand against him, but politics would have cut into time for making money.

He had married the daughter of one of his early partners soon after giving up the sea full-time, and now had two daughters about whom he was quite silly and a three-year-old son whose current ambition was to be a pirate. Waln had finer dreams both for his children and for himself.

When the advance party for Queen Valora arrived on Thunder Island, Waln Endbrook was among those who met them at the harbor. He offered them rooms at his estate, and made himself quite useful in convincing the royal governor to peacefully accept his demotion from effective monarch of the five Great Isles and the numerous small. Waln even persuaded the governor that the man's own best interests would best be served by accepting the offered appointment as prime minister to the new queen.

Prime minister wasn't a post Waln coveted in the least. He wanted to be more than a court attendant, a flunky chained down by custom and duty. He wanted to be invaluable.

Queen Valora recognized Waln's abilities as soon as he brought himself to her attention. Her first award to him was the title "lord"—with hints that he might be promoted to baron or even duke when she had decided how to reassign territories within her new holdings. Intellectually, Waln knew that a title and a promise cost Queen Valora nothing, but he was pleased nonetheless.

Lord Waln's first major duty for his new queen was diplomatic and quite dangerous. About the time that Bright Bay was preparing for the marriage of Crown Prince Shad to Crown Princess Sapphire, Waln sailed north on a fast, light ship. In the dead of night, he debarked at First Harbor, Waterland's capital.

Waterland had not yet decided the status of the newly made kingdom of the Isles, but in this well-watered land wealth was the supreme ruler. One of Waln's trade contacts could be trusted to stay bought, and she arranged for him to travel west, to cross the Sword of Kelvin Mountains, and finally to reach Dragon's Breath, the capital city of New Kelvin.

The tales Waln brought back from that trip—of houses made of glass and crystal, of veiled women wearing silk and gold to the market, of horses wearing helmets designed to make them look like strange beasts from forgotten legends—would make him popular around any fireside, even among a sailing people who pretended to be jaded beyond any wonder. Yet the first tale that Waln told after returning from that journey was one of failure.

The New Kelvinese rulers would not meet with him—not even when he presented his credentials as ambassador for the Queen of the Isles. He thought he had caught a glimmer of interest in the eyes that gazed out at him from the fantastically dyed and painted features of the official who interviewed him, but he couldn't be sure.

Only when Waln whispered a hint about what business had brought him so far and through such hardships at a time of year when many travelers stayed close to home was Waln certain of the interest. Even the official merely recited in cadences that turned his accented speech into strange poetry:

"You speak of sorcery, Ambassador, but you have no taste of that sacred art about you. We can no more speak of sorcery with you than we could discuss color with one blind from birth. Return only with one who has eyes to see those arcane hues, return only if you bear with you that which you wish to discuss. Otherwise, cross not our threshold again. Be warned. The penalties for disobedience would make you welcome death."

No matter how he blustered, bribed, or even—just once—bullied, Lord Waln could get no better answer. He returned to Thunder Island to report his defeat and found Queen Valora in a curiously cheerful mood.

Queen Valora was a lovely woman, neither tall nor short, but some feminine compromise of the two that permitted her to be both slender and strong. More than one figurehead had been carved with her upper torso as inspiration, but although buxom, Valora was not in the least bovine. Her aristocratic features were framed by golden hair just touched with a warm glow, like the first touches of a glorious sunset. Eyes the clear blue of the sea saw deep into a man and then right through him.

Seated next to his queen at a council table, Lord Waln felt his height and strength transformed into awkward bulk. His expensive clothing—including a waistcoat cut from a New Kelvinese brocade purchased in one of their markets and of an ornate beauty never before seen on the Isles—became the mere gauds adorning a rusty feathered crow.

In short, Valora's heritage as a daughter of monarchs reduced Walnut Endbrook to what he had never ceased to be deep inside—a prostitute's child who had never known his father and whose mother was perhaps an even greater mystery.

Queen Valora listened to Lord Waln's report with perfect composure. They were alone—even her secretary and bodyguards had been told to wait outside. When Waln finished, the queen touched his hand lightly, a gentle caress that made his weathered skill tingle.

"You tried, Waln," she said gently, "and made a long journey with gull-wing speed. You are to be commended."

"But I failed you, Your Majesty!" Waln heard the plea in his own voice and wondered briefly at his own desire for this woman's approval.

"Failed? No, you brought us back information. We now know that the New Kelvinese will treat with us—only on certain terms, but that is better than nothing."

"Those terms, Your Majesty!" Waln shook his head. "They might as well have said 'Bring us a dragon's egg and a griffin's heart.' Where can we find a sorcerer? None have been known for a hundred years!"

The queen snorted softly. "The New Kelvinese think otherwise. Didn't they as much as claim themselves knowledgeable about those lost arts?"

Waln nodded reluctant agreement.

"And if a skilled trader like yourself says that he thinks there was a glimmer of interest, then I'll believe him."

"They paint their faces so strangely," Waln reminded her. "I could have been mistaken."

"I think not. Leaving out poetry and pomp, I see two terms have been set. You must return with someone skilled in sorcery and with the artifacts we wish to be taught to use. Simple as dragging a seine, Ambassador."

Waln sipped from his wine—a dry white from Stonehold, part of a shipload of interesting and valuable gifts that strange nation had sent to Queen Valora shortly after her arrival.

"I don't see that we have a choice," the queen continued. "King Allister has made no move to retake those royal treasures, but as soon as spring brings safer sailing, we may find ourselves pressed—if not by Cousin Allister, then by the Waterlanders or even by old King Tedric. Too many people know those artifacts exist. If we cannot use them to our advantage, we will lose them.

"And," she continued, emphasizing her point with a stab of

one long-nailed fingertip, "if we do not learn to use them, then someone else will. And then . . ."

Her blue eyes became stormy. Waln was reminded of gossip prevalent in Thunderhead, the recently anointed capital city of the Isles, gossip that said that Queen Valora had paid for assassins to kill the royal families of both Bright Bay and Hawk Haven.

The tap of Waln setting down his wineglass shook the queen from whatever angry reverie into which she had descended.

"We know of one skilled in sorcery," Queen Valora said. "At least, she claims to be skilled in sorcery. You must convince her to accompany you to Dragon's Breath. Prepare to sail on the next advantageous tide."

"And where shall I tell my ship's captain to sail?" Waln asked. He felt a fleeting regret that he would not have more time with his family, but soothed himself with the thought that he was acting in their own best interests.

"To Port Haven in Hawk Haven," the queen replied. "From there you will ride west to Eagle's Nest and attach yourself to the diplomatic party I have sent to attend this ridiculous second wedding. No one will notice one more member more or less. Do not make a secret of your wealth or status in the Isles, but I think it would be best if you didn't mention your recent trip into New Kelvin."

Waln surrendered his pride. "Your Majesty, I beg you, tell me who am I to seek when I get to Hawk Haven?"

The queen smiled slowly, reminding Waln uncomfortably of a shark.

"Her name is Lady Melina Shield. She is the mother of Crown Princess Sapphire."

Waln remembered that the princess's mother had caused quite a scandal by failing to attend the Bright Bay wedding—claiming as thin excuse to be in mourning over her husband. She could not so easily avoid attending this domestic affair.

"One of Lady Melina's brothers," Valora continued, "was Prince Newell, the widower of King Tedric's late daughter Lovella. Newell was friendly to my court."

Waln knew why his queen used the past tense to refer to the prince and did not interrupt.

"Lady Melina's own actions make me think she might be amenable to accompanying you to New Kelvin," Valora mused. "I wish you to sound her out. If my guess about her character is correct, convince her to accompany you to New Kelvin."

"Yes, Your Majesty," Waln said, swallowing a superstitious dread of sorcery, the Old World's shadow over the New.

"Now," the queen said, "we must work out the details: what you can offer Lady Melina, what securities we must demand, how we may preserve the artifacts from those who will be more than ready to grab them from you."

She opened a box and took out paper, pen, and a flask of purple ink.

"Then there will be some letters to write . . ."

Her next words sealed his devotion.

"And since I must steal you from your lovely wife and children, I will beg them to call on me while you are away. I have so few friends here in these Isles. I fear I neglected these lands, even when I was their queen. Your fair lady can advise me on how to repair my errors. Do you think she would, Baron?"

The newly made Baron Waln Endbrook could only nod, marveling over his good fortune.

WITHOUT FIREKEEPER TO LOOK AFTER, Derian was free to rejoin his family immediately upon his return to Eagle's Nest. True, Earl Kestrel had offered him a room at the Kestrel manse, but Derian politely declined.

"I am eager to see my family," he told the earl, and Norvin Norwood dismissed him graciously.

"Call on me any time over the next few days," the earl said

at parting. "I will be staying in the capital until after Princess Sapphire's wedding."

Derian promised that he would and, after saying good-bye to his friends in the earl's entourage, he took his leave. He'd said his farewells to Elise when they were approaching the city, having noticed that Baron Archer was not overly fond of his daughter's familiarity with the unmarried—and less than perfectly eligible—young men in the group.

Elise, too, had invited him to call. Her family owned a nice house with fine gardens in Eagle's Nest—a gift from the Wellwards to Aurella when she made her marriage to Baron Archer. Derian did not plan to call, but neither did he refuse. He preferred to keep his options open.

But for now, Derian's thoughts were far from the manses of the noble folk. His family's main stables were not far from the east gate of Eagle's Nest.

"Gate" was an accurate term only in the loosest sense of the word. The city of Eagle's Nest had long ago outgrown the sturdy stone walls that had surrounded the original city—though those walls were maintained by order of the Crown and by law no home or business could be constructed in such a way as to impede their effectiveness.

However, land within the walls could be expensive and horses required ample space if they were to be well kept. Therefore, the Carter livery stables—the business had long ago grown beyond mere hauling—were outside the walls.

Roanne broke into a brisk trot of her own accord when she realized where they were heading. Indeed, Derian had to hold her back from breaking into a canter. Six days of leisurely travel along decent roads had not tired the spirited chestnut even a bit. In very little time, Derian caught sight of the familiar stables and outbuildings.

Unexpected tears clouded his vision, so that it was a good thing that Roanne knew her way. She came to a halt, blowing slightly—more from excitement than from anything else—in front of the handsome building from which Colby Carter directed operations.

The building was wood-framed, painted white with lucky

red trim around the door and window frames. A prancing horse stepping high was painted within a circle and hung from a signpost over the door.

As always, Derian admired it. Roanne had been the model, and last winter they had officially changed the business's name from the simple "Carter's Services" to "Prancing Steed Stables."

Colby Carter was out the door to greet his son as soon as Derian was out of the saddle.

"Outriders and gossips have been coming through all day," he said, hesitating between pumping Derian's hand and hugging the young man and settling for doing both. "King Tedric's return is big news. I'm glad you're home safe."

Colby had just finished this speech—a remarkably long one for him, though when need arose he could talk the near hind leg off a donkey and make decent inroads on the remaining limbs—when a stocky whirlwind blew up.

"Brock!" Derian said, grabbing his brother around the waist and swinging him in the air. The eight-year-old laughed gleefully.

"Did you bring me anything, Deri?"

"Maybe," Derian teased. In fact, one of his few independent ventures into the town of Silver Whale Cove had been to buy gifts for his family members.

"I'll get your saddlebags," Brock offered.

"Better not," Derian said. "They're heavy. Dad, where can I stable Roanne?"

"Try Number Three barn. I told them to have a loose box ready for you there. She'll be between Brock's pony and old Hauler, so Roanne won't need to show off to everyone just how important she is."

Derian got the impression that his father was pleased that Derian himself hadn't tried to show how important *he* was. After all, a man must wonder how a son who has been consorting with nobles will act when he comes home again.

Well, I may have been consorting, Derian thought as he led Roanne to the indicated building, *but most of the time I'm just some sort of glorified servant.*

Fleetingly, he thought of Firekeeper, of the look she had given him right before she left. Then he turned his attention to the boy trotting along at his side. He could do nothing for the wolf-woman; better to attend to those for whom he *could* do something.

After stabling Roanne and admiring Brock's new saddle, Derian returned to where Colby waited beneath the sign of the prancing horse. All around him there was activity: grooms walked horses, stablehands wheeled loads of manure or hay, drivers worked over rigs to have them ready when called for. Some of these last were simple wagons, others carriages elaborate enough to suit the most fussy noble.

"You've a good many people working for you now, Dad," Derian commented. "How many?"

"Two dozen or so, if you don't count the drivers and the folks at the warehouse," Colby replied a touch complacently. "Planning on throwing up a new stable out by Number Two. Land inside the walls is getting so expensive that there's a profit to be made selling it, so we're getting more boarders."

"Sounds good," Derian replied, "for us."

Colby nodded. "I think the trend will continue. Some of the nobles are buying up a house or two, tearing them down and converting the lot into a mini-estate with pleasure gardens."

Derian thought of the family home that was securely within the walls.

"You and Mother aren't . . ."

"No," Colby chuckled. "Home's safe. We may be buying some acreage by the Flin and shifting some of the horses there."

"A second livery stable?"

"That's right. Mostly for boarding now that the nobles are learning the pleasures of having someone else take on the flies."

While Derian was still chuckling over his father's joke, Colby was shouldering into his coat.

"Toad!" he called.

An older man Derian had known for years came out of one

of the wagon sheds in answer to the summons. He beamed when he saw Derian and offered his hand.

"Welcome back, Derian! Good to see you! When you've settled in you must come and tell about the princess's wedding. You were a guest, weren't you?"

Derian shrugged. "As a trusted servant might be."

"But you saw the ceremony with your own eyes and . . ." Toad paused, eyes shining. "And what followed. The tales the post-riders brought back could hardly be believed. We heard that . . ."

Colby interrupted, bluntly but not rudely.

"There's enough time for that later, Toad. Derian hasn't yet seen his mother or sister. I'm going up to the house with him and Brock. If there's anything you can't handle, send up a runner."

"There's just a few carriages to go out and a few mounts to come in." Toad's grin didn't fade as he contemplated the evening's work. "I'll try to leave you a quiet night at home, Colby. Good night, Derian. Night, Brock."

Father and sons left the stables and walked slowly up a gradual slope into the more densely populated parts of the city. Brock, burdened by one of Derian's saddlebags—which he had insisted on carrying over his brother's protests—trudged happily along, trying to get a peek at what was inside. Colby and Derian talked easily about nothing at all.

Derian had lived in Eagle's Nest all his life. Its sounds and smells were as familiar and as little considered as the pulse in his wrist, but moons had waxed and waned since he had walked these streets in this easy manner.

Surrounded by ordinary things made precious by homecoming, Derian found himself relaxing as he had not since before his parents had decided that their eldest son's attendance should be a condition of permitting Earl Kestrel to rent the mounts for his expedition west. Now the expedition was over, the matter of the king's successor settled, and Derian wanted to believe his life was back to normal.

The heavy thud of the ruby ring he wore on a chain around

his neck warned him that, as much as he might wish it, there was no going backward.

Vernita and Damita Carter greeted them at the front door of the big brick house that had been in their family for several generations. Derian grinned and threw open his arms to both mother and sister.

Fleet-footed Horse! Derian thought joyfully as he hugged them to him. *It's good to be home!*

X

WHEN FIREKEEPER AWOKE THE NEXT DAWN, there was frost on the grass and the lake waters nearest to her were rimed with ice. She, however, was quite comfortable—reluctant indeed to leave her warm nest against Blind Seer's flank.

Embers from her fire still glowed. She vaguely recalled waking just enough to add a bit of wood, but the stack she had made the night before was almost gone. Had she used that much wood?

Answering the question written on the wolf-woman's thought-wrinkled brow, Elation swooped down from her perch in a nearby tree and picked up one of the chunks of wood as lightly as if it had been a rabbit. With artistic control, the peregrine dropped it onto the embers, fanning them into a blaze with the wind beneath her wings. Young flames licked the dry wood and caught easily.

"So I nursemaided you through the night," Elation squawked. "Bee Biter has flown ahead to tell the others of your coming. When will you be ready to begin?"

Blind Seer rose and stretched. Without his blanketing warmth, Firekeeper was happy enough to leap to her feet and jog in place to get her blood running.

"Food," she hinted, whining in the fashion of a very small pup, "would be welcome if the great lady of the air could bring me some. I am as hollow as a bear-stripped bee tree."

"I have anticipated your need," Elation replied, not quite boasting, "and your breakfast hangs in the tree."

Breakfast proved to be another rabbit. Firekeeper skinned and gutted it, tossing the offal to Blind Seer, who snapped it down in a single gulp before racing off to find himself something more substantial.

Doubtless Earl Kestrel would not have found fire-seared rabbit a suitable repast for his adopted daughter, but Firekeeper was well satisfied. The sky had not lost dawn's pink before she was fed, washed, and ready to go.

"Below," she said, admiring the view east from their vantage, "the clouds are like sheep on a well-chewed pasture. Here the sun is bright and warming."

She blew her breath before her, laughing at the white puff it made in the chill air.

Crossing the Barren River proved to be a matter of leaping from rock to rock. It was not an easy task. Many of the rocks had not yet been smoothed by the action of the waters; some rocked, though they had seemed firm to the test. Both wolf and woman were splashed by the icy waters rushing through the narrow channels between the rocks, but neither quite fell in.

On the other side, they shook themselves as dry as possible. Privately, Firekeeper missed just a bit the thick towels she had used at the castle. As she dried off, she noticed that the water beaded on the oiled leather of her breeches and vest. Her skin, by contrast, beaded from cold where the water had splashed it.

A fair enough trade, Firekeeper thought, enjoying the whimsy of the image.

Once she was as dry as she could get within her limited means, Firekeeper fell into the easy jog of a traveling wolf. Giving his coat one more great shake, Blind Seer dashed away from the ensuing shower of spray.

As they ran, they set their course somewhat away from the

shore of the lake, for the footing near the water varied, inviting a twisted ankle or trapped paw. Here there was dark, glittering sand ground from the rock, there heaps of brambles or branches tossed up by the waters.

Everywhere there were chunks of basalt. Many of these were deceptively rounded and smooth, but Firekeeper had learned that their bubbled edges chewed into skin like small teeth. Where the rock had more recently broken, it was often straight-edged and sharp.

Farther from the lakeshore, however, there was mountain meadow and beyond that forest. Running felt good after the past several days of creeping and climbing. The kinks in the wolf-woman's muscles smoothed out and the dry grass underfoot felt like a carpet after the sharp stones of the Barren River Canyon.

Wolf-like, she didn't brood about the inevitable descent. That would be dealt with in its time. Nor did she brood about the summons from the Royal Beasts. Elation had assured her that if they pushed on past dark they could round the lake before the next dawn. Pushing forward, therefore, was what the wolf-woman concentrated on. The answers would come of themselves and time.

Several times they stopped to rest and nap. Firekeeper ate only lightly, accepting what Elation brought her with humble groveling. Elation's finds were worth the thanks, indeed.

Although the peregrine herself ate nothing but flesh—and that preferably not only warm but still pulsing with the life of the creature that had grown it—Elation had made herself a scholar of human tastes. Twice she brought chunks of honeycomb, clotted with crystallized sugar. Once she brought a tattered bunch of wild grapes, tart and juicy. Nuts were awkward for the falcon to carry, but after Firekeeper cobbled her a sack from a still damp rabbit hide, the falcon brought them in such quantity that Firekeeper found herself wondering what squirrel would starve that winter.

The wolf-woman spared little sympathy for the squirrel, but cracked the nutshells in her fist or between her jaws as she ran.

Day dimmed into dusk. The night sky darkened and then gleamed with hard, white stars. The moon rose, thin now, but fattening. At last a shifting wind brought Firekeeper the scents of many beasts gathered together. From the depths of the forest, a pale white form bounded to meet them at the tree line's edge.

"Mother!" Firekeeper howled in delight.

She rolled on the ground at the silver wolf's feet, rubbing her head against the she-wolf's jaw and whining in an ingratiating fashion. The wolf gaped open her jaws in a fashion a human would have found alarming. No food came forth, but Firekeeper, who had often been fed this way, reached inside the fanged jaws and touched the lolling tongue.

"Mother," she repeated, more quietly.

The she-wolf licked her, then licked Blind Seer, who rubbed against the silver wolf, almost knocking her off her feet with the force of his greeting.

"You've grown," said the One Female approvingly, "as has Little Two-legs. The hunting is good east of the mountains?"

Blind Seer gave a short barking laugh. "It could be. Not only are there deer and elk and rabbits, but the humans keep creatures they make stupid so that they can control them. Horses are not bad—some of them have spirit—but sheep and chickens beg to be eaten. What threat is a cow, especially when she has had her horns sawn off, or a bull once he's been gelded?"

"You hunted such?" The One Female's tone mixed curiosity and a certain degree of disgust—or maybe envy.

"No," Blind Seer drawled. "Instead, humans trembling in fear of my size and power carried already killed meat to me on sheets of beaten metal. I grew fat without effort—and would have grown fatter but for the need to watch over sweet Firekeeper."

Firekeeper snorted and punched the blue-eyed wolf in the shoulder. She glanced from side to side, sniffing the air.

"Is the One Male with you, Mother?"

"No. He remained to mind the pack. The puppies are growing both bold and stupid. We did not dare leave them with only the lesser wolves to discipline them."

The next moments passed as the One Female brought them up to date on the status of their pack—a fairly large one, as the hunting in their territory was good and the Ones wise leaders. A yearling had broken his back in a fall. A two-year-old had dispersed and was reported to be hunting with a single male to the northwest. Two of last spring's puppies had died: one of a fever or some poison, another from tangling too boldly with an elk.

"Elk do have horns—or rather antlers," the One Female commented mildly, "and none of his birth siblings will forget that lesson."

Firekeeper nodded somberly. She had experienced such losses before. A Royal Wolf pack did not produce pups every year as did the Cousins, but if its size diminished, the answering urge replied. In all her life with the wolves, she could only recall two years—and one of those dimly—that there had not been pups in the spring, and never once had every member of a litter survived into the following spring.

"Others wait," the One Female said, turning the conversation away from family matters, "to meet you and speak with you. Would you rest first?"

Firekeeper considered. "What do you advise?"

"Cry sleep," the One Female said promptly. "Bee Biter reported when you began this day's run. None will doubt that you are tired."

"I am, most honestly," Firekeeper admitted, smothering a yawn behind her hand.

"Then rest," the One Female said. "If you need food, I will hunt for you. Best that you face these questioners with a clear mind and full belly."

Blind Seer growled as at a faintly scented danger.

"Mother, they don't intend to harm Firekeeper, do they? I must warn you, if they have summoned her so far only to hurt her, I will spill their blood and all of mine if that is what is needed to defend her."

The One Female nipped him lightly on his left ear.

"Foolish pup! Do you think I would have nurtured Little Two-legs only to give her to enemies when she finally learned to hunt on her own? No, they don't intend to harm her, but they are worried, and worried creatures have tempers sharper than a winter thorn tree."

Blind Seer relaxed, content with his mother's reassurance.

"Still, I believe I will not leave Firekeeper's side."

"Sleep hungry then," the One Female said, approval in the slow wag of her tail, "and sleep lightly."

Elation, waiting unheeded all this time in a tree above their heads, called down:

"I will tell them that Firekeeper will be rested when next dusk comes. You wolves sleep well."

"You've made a friend of that bird," the One Female said after Elation had flown off. "A good thing. Perhaps you should make other friends among her kind. It would be useful."

"Why, Mother?" Firekeeper asked.

No answer came. Instead, the she-wolf curled herself into a ball, making a nest for herself among the dead leaves at the base of a tree.

Firekeeper stared at the One Female for a long moment. Then she shrugged acceptance of her silence.

Going to the lakeside to wash and drink, the wolf-woman was aware of shadowy figures bulking large against the trees a short distance away. From them she caught wisps of scents that should not be blended. These watchers did not trouble her, nor did she greet them.

Rejoining the wolves, Firekeeper rested herself against Blind Seer's side. Even though she lay cradled between the wolves' great bodies she felt cold, chilled from within by apprehension of what the dawn would bring.

Her fears followed her into sleep.

The wedding. Assassins surge out of the gathered throng. Firekeeper's heart squeezes tight in her chest, tighter than the gown that tangles her feet as she tries to move.

Move she must. Blind Seer's warning echoes in her ears. To fail would be to fail not these kings and queens, not these nobles and diplomats, but to fail him—he who has trusted her to hear his cry and be his hands and feet.

"She must live. Someday we will have a need of her."

The Sphere Chamber is transformed, become King Tedric's field pavilion. Once again, Firekeeper circles round and round, her blood trailing only slightly behind her. Prince Newell laughs mockingly. Then he is dead.

Firekeeper wants to rest, but the assassins are near. They want Sapphire and Shad. She alone stands between them. "Someday we will have a need of her." They must live. Someone has a need of them.

She raises her head, claws through the fog that enshrouds her mind, focuses on the assassins. For a moment, their features become clear.

She knows them. They are her friends.

KING ALLISTER FOUND HIS ENTOURAGE'S RECEPTION at Eagle's Nest handled so smoothly that no one would have guessed that the master of the castle had been on the road himself until a few days before.

Of course, he thought, *Uncle Tedric and Aunt Elexa have been living here much longer than we have in our new home, and all their key staff didn't get carried off by the previous tenants.*

Allister and his family—including Princess Sapphire—were given rooms in a tower that offered among its amenities private access to the castle's grounds.

Sapphire commented with a strange, sharp laugh that this was the same tower in which Earl Kestrel and his party had been housed over the time when King Tedric had been inspecting Lady Blysse Norwood. In those days, Firekeeper and Blind Seer had been much less familiar with human customs, and easy access to the outdoors had been something of a necessity.

Most of those members of Hawk Haven's nobility who would usually take rooms at the castle had found places to stay in the city or surrounding countryside. As the six Great Houses were becoming closely intermarried, it was not difficult for anyone who was anyone to find someone from whom hospitality could be claimed.

Most—but not all. Both Grand Duke Gadman and Grand Duchess Rosene—King Tedric's younger brother and sister— retained their accustomed suites.

"All the better to see you, my dear," Allister thought, remembering Aunt Rosene's greeting.

There had been something fierce and even threatening about both Gadman and Rosene—a ferocity tinged with bitterness. Gadman's attitude might have been slightly less so, but then he had seen one of his candidates for the place of heir apparent to the throne win the race—Sapphire was his granddaughter through his son, the recently deceased Lord Rolfston Redbriar.

That Rolfston had apparently been a disappointment to both his father and to his wife, Lady Melina Shield, and that Sapphire had so clearly allied herself with the king, her new father by law and a replacement for the lost Rolfston in fact, probably made the Grand Duke's apparent victory rather bitter.

And probably made him resentful of me as well, Allister mused with an honesty that his own politically charged childhood had given him. *Sapphire will reign after me and so she grants to me a certain degree of deference—deference that doubtless Uncle Gadman thinks should be his alone.*

But contracts between the two newly allied families were not all charged with political overtones. At the banquet held the afternoon following their arrival, Prince Tavis rekindled his tentative friendship with young Nydia Trueheart, the elder daughter of Lady Zorana Archer.

It warmed Allister that their friendship was based on a shared enthusiasm for some of the classic New Kelvinese poets. He liked thinking that his younger son might have at least one friend here in Hawk Haven who thought of him primarily as a person and only secondarily as a prince.

Allister snorted through his nose in derisive self-condemnation.

Nydia is only what—twelve? thirteen?—but her mother is ambitious for her children and will probably contaminate even that innocent friendship.

He said as much to Pearl during the relative privacy of a pair dance during the informal ball that followed the banquet.

"I think," Pearl said a touch sharply, "you may do Lady Zorana an unkindness. There is nothing wrong with a mother wanting the best for her children, and what is more useless than a surplus child of noble heritage but possessed of no title or lands? Lady Zorana's brother, Ivon, will inherit the barony their father won; her husband is, like herself, a younger child with minimal prospects."

Allister nodded, twirled his queen away from him, exchanged her for another partner. When the movements of the dance brought her back into his arms again, he had his reply ready.

"All the more her duty then to see that her children have training for later life," he said. "My father did so for me and there could have been no more useless noble-born child than myself."

"Zorana did her best for her eldest," Pearl reminded him, strong disapproval in her softly spoken words, though her expression remained tranquil. "And now Purcel—a boy our Tavis's age, remember—lies dead beneath the ground outside of Hope, dead fighting a war in which he hoped to serve his king and win honor for his family."

Allister used an intricate series of hand changes to mask an apologetic kiss.

"I will remember that sacrifice, and that many others paid the price for our dancing here in what was once the stronghold of our enemies."

Pearl softened. "And I will remember that many here will see our unmarried three—young as they are—as prizes to be won."

Sometime later King Allister noted that Sir Jared Surcliffe, who had been dancing with Lady Elise Archer, now stood near one of the refreshment tables, a glass of wine held loosely between his long surgeon's fingers, a dreamy expression on his face.

Remembering his promise to Shad and Sapphire that he would accord Sir Jared at least the recognition of his evident favor, if not the position the princess thought he deserved, the king made his way to the younger man's side.

Sir Jared came out of his reverie with a start, dipped a bow that was sincere if not polished, and asked how he might serve the king.

"I thought I'd request your professional opinion as to how Shad and Sapphire look," Allister said, gesturing for Sir Jared to be at ease. "They insisted on riding most of the way here from Silver Whale Cove, even when the weather got ugly and wiser heads sought a space in the carriages."

"I don't think their exertions did them any harm," Sir Jared replied promptly. "They're young and possess the resilience of youth. Mind, I wouldn't recommend a continuation of the punishment they've been giving themselves. Both were wounded during the war and Sapphire was injured shortly before that as well."

The healer's voice dropped so that among the eddying tide of those who hovered hoping for the king's notice—or even among the closer circle that assured him a measure of breathing space—only Whyte Steel might have overheard his words.

"Yet, Your Majesty, I would advise you to find someone who shares my talent and make some excuse for keeping him or her close to the heirs. They would not have healed so swiftly—and thus so cleanly—without the aid I was pleased to give them. If they continue to insist on leading by example there will be other injuries and I cannot always be near to hasten their mending."

King Allister replied without thinking, "Would you like a post as their physician?"

Only as Sir Jared's eyes widened in surprise did Allister realize that he had forgotten his new power. He had spoken as he would as master of his own former estate, one man offering another employment—not as a king bestowing honors and likely to be offended if the other refused. He hastened to add:

"Feel free to decline if you so desire, Sir Jared. I realize you have other commitments."

Sir Jared bowed. "My commitments are mostly to my cousin, Earl Kestrel, and I believe he would release me. Certainly your offer is tempting."

His gaze flickered for the briefest instant to where Lady Elise now danced with a scion of Duke Kite—a youth several years her junior and clearly enchanted with his lovely partner.

Allister Seagleam was no fool. He had noted the rapport between Elise and Jared, had realized, too, that such a match was probably impossible. Earl Kestrel called Sir Jared "cousin," but the relationship was one of several removes— an indication of the earl's regard for the younger man rather than close kinship.

Baron Archer, like his sister Zorana, was only too aware of the tenuous nature of his family's power. He would wish his only daughter's marriage to serve future generations of Archers.

Suddenly, Allister thought he might understand why Sapphire had pressed both him and Uncle Tedric to grant Sir Jared some greater degree of recognition and he liked his new daughter-in-law all the more for this indication of her compassion for the impossible romance.

"Think on my offer," King Allister pressed the knight, "but know that you will be welcome in my court whatever your answer may be."

Too many others had claims on his time for the king to extend the audience. He accepted Sir Jared's thanks and turned to smile upon Duchess Trueheart.

"Grace," he said, claiming her as a friend, since she had served under his command during the recent war. "I heard that you had not yet arrived."

The young duchess—a mere twenty-four and new to her title—smiled. She kept her composure at the king's friendly address, but from the way her eyes sparkled, she appreciated his including her among his intimates—and how the inclusion would raise her in the eyes of her doubters.

"We hit bad weather on the way in, Your Majesty," she said. "May I have the honor of presenting my husband, Alin, and our son, Baxter?"

King Allister turned to do so, accepting the man's bow, and kissing the infant's cheek.

And so we go, he thought wryly. *Passing on the aura of kingship, playing the game, cementing alliances.*

Just beyond him, the dancers swirled and eddied. Lady Elise went by, this time looking less than happy in the arms of Jet Shield, the crown princess's brother, and once Elise's betrothed.

So we all dance, Allister thought, *whether to music or to other, more subtle, less pleasant tunes.*

BARON ENDBROOK HADN'T THOUGHT he'd be nervous. After all, he was an important man on Thunder Island and an internationally known shipping magnate—not to mention a baron, and a chosen member of the diplomatic contingent from the Isles. He decided that the last factor must be why he was nervous. Hawk Haven and Bright Bay had intertwined fingers and heirs and so made peace—a peace that looked as if it stood a chance of lasting, not like previous truces that merely had been intermissions in an ongoing conflict.

This time there was a new and important reason for both Bright Bay and Hawk Haven to keep the peace. They had made enemies in common and he, Baron Endbrook, was a representative of one of those enemies. An undeclared enemy, true, but one nonetheless.

They'd have done better to kill Queen Valora, Waln thought dispassionately, remembering the suppressed fury in his queen's deep blue eyes. *But then others would have taken up her cause.*

Baron Endbrook wasn't politically sophisticated enough to frame the thought that a dead martyr—especially a martyr who was a young and lovely woman—could be far more dangerous than most living foes, but the idea lurked around the edges of his mind, trying to take form.

It had almost done so when a subtle shift in the murmur of conversation caught Waln's attention. The orchestra continued to play, the dancers to face off and form their elaborate patterns, but somehow the dynamics in the crowded hall had shifted.

Taking his cue from those around him, Waln glanced toward the high arched doorway into the hall. When he perceived who it was whose entry had caused the shift in mood his heart skipped a beat. There *she* was, the woman he had come so far to see: Lady Melina Shield.

Waln had glimpsed her earlier, an honored guest at the banquet King Tedric had laid on to welcome the visitors, but at that event, as was only appropriate for a close relative of the bride, Lady Melina had been seated at one of the head tables. The delegation from the Isles, though accorded every courtesy, had not been overly close to those august seats.

Then, as now, Lady Melina had been escorted by her son and heir apparent, Jet Shield. Jet was a young man in his early twenties, so impressively handsome that Baron Endbrook did not doubt that he had but to smile and the girls would fling themselves at his feet. Despite Jet's elegant appearance—midnight black hair, glittering onyx eyes, a sensuous yet somehow brooding mouth—there was nothing effete about Jet Shield. From the thickness of his dark brows to the firmness of his tread, Jet was as male as a tomcat, though far more polished.

Baron Endbrook moved to where he could get his first close look at Lady Melina. Pride suffused the lady's bearing, pride and an alertness that said she knew that people talked about her—and that sometimes, out of fear, they whispered.

Lady Melina's skin was pale and somewhat translucent. There were circles under her eyes, yet these caused her to appear tragic rather than haggard, as they might have a lesser woman. Otherwise, Lady Melina was so smothered under veils and black velvet that nothing could be guessed of her figure or even her age.

Mother and son were clad entirely in black: gleaming rooks amid the brilliant rainbow that surrounded them. From what Baron Endbrook had heard, Jet always dressed in black, thus keeping theme—as all of Lady Melina's children did—with his given name. Proof of this rumor was the diadem he wore even now, a thick band of gold set in the center with an intricately carved piece of jet.

Lady Melina's reasons for choosing to wear black were more obscure. Some said her choice was out of grief for her late husband or—this last was usually whispered—for her brother, Newell, the traitor. However, black was not universally recognized as symbolizing mourning. White would have done as well if that was her desire.

I'd bet half the cargo from any ship in my fleet, Waln thought sardonically, *that the lady's real reason for choosing that color was that she knew it would make her the center of all eyes, even with two monarchs and their spouses for competition.*

He sought a glimpse of the famous necklace of enchanted gemstones Lady Melina was reported to wear at all times. Rumor said that the necklace held five stones—one stone each to bind the souls of each of her five children. Some said that now the necklace held only four—that the blue stone that had represented Sapphire was gone, vanished even as its mate had vanished from the diadem about the princess's brow.

Tonight, however, Lady Melina's necklace was not in sight, though Waln fancied that something did bulk beneath the neckline of her gown.

From his studying of the packet he had found waiting for him in his ship's cabin, Waln knew that Lady Melina Shield was the youngest child and only daughter of the late Pola, Duchess Gyrfalcon. As a much petted and long-awaited daughter, she had been given a large dowry on the occasion of her marriage to Rolfston Redbriar, a fact that—if Queen Valora's spies were to be believed—had not set too well with those three brothers who stood no more chance than she of inheriting the duchy.

Whether or not the marriage that had occasioned such generosity had been a good one remained a matter of debate. Some said that the marriage had been happy, that Lord Rolfston had been content to be ruled by his wife. Others said that he chafed, maintained a series of common-born mistresses, and longed for personal recognition, but that he feared his wife too much to openly challenge her authority.

Happy or not, the marriage had produced five children, each named for a gemstone: Sapphire, Jet, Opal, Ruby, and Citrine. Jet had been the only son and—most agreed—his mother's favorite. Sapphire had been too headstrong, too aware of her own power as heir apparent to the family's generous holdings.

Now, however, Waln mused, *Sapphire is King Tedric's daughter by law and Melina's favorite will take over—that is, he'll haul the load but she'll touch the reins or the whip. Nor, if her forbidding their attending Sapphire's Bright Bay wedding is any indication, has the lady given up plans to run her younger daughters' lives.*

Speaking to Lady Melina here would be too public for his purposes, but there were ways he could contact her, even in this press, without being any the wiser.

Waln waited until Lady Melina condescended to join one of the long pattern dances. Then he hastened to find a partner of his own, pleased that the nearest available was a pretty enough fair-haired minx.

When Lady Melina had marched her own partner to the head of the line, Waln guided his partner to a space farther down, carefully counting so that—if the form of the dance was the same here as in the Isles—before the dance ended he would tread a measure or two with Lady Melina.

Then, making as if to tighten the buckle on his shoe, he transferred into his shirt cuff the short note he had written earlier in the privacy of his room.

"Lady Melina," it said, *"I have a proposition that should interest you greatly, but we must speak of it only in the greatest possible privacy. Suggest where we may meet."*

Baron Endbrook left the note unsigned. After all, Lady Melina would surely discover the sender's identity.

Quivering with equal parts anticipation and apprehension, Waln concentrated on the dance. The steps were not too different from what he had learned on the Isles, though he rapidly discovered that his more boisterous execution of some of the moves was considered a bit "country."

A kind young fellow muttered a few hints to him as they passed in one set and by the time Waln's segment of the line had intersected with Lady Melina's, Waln fancied that he was dancing as well as any—and better than many. Wine and sweet hard cider had been freely available and some of the dancers had not sweated their indulgence from their systems.

Partnered at last with Lady Melina, Waln deftly slid his note inside the palm of her black, lace-trimmed gloves. With a nod and a smile, he exchanged the lady for his own partner, whom he promptly marched away under an archway of interlocking hands and into the next set.

The music ended before his set intersected again with Lady Melina's. Rather than make himself conspicuous, Waln thanked the pretty blonde and offered his services to another, somewhat older, lady. After two more dances—changing partners each time—he felt a breather was in order. He thanked his most recent partner, handed her graciously to another dancer, and went to find himself something to drink and a bit of wall to lean against—the chairs were reserved for the ladies.

Waln was finding the hard cider a trace too sweet for his tastes when Lady Melina happened to stroll by. She was fanning herself gently while talking to a man Waln recognized as her second-eldest brother, Lord Rein.

So intent was the lady on her conversation that she accidentally trod upon the hem of her gown. She stumbled and her brother caught her up, but as she recovered her balance her fan dropped from her hand. Waln bent to pick it up for her and discovered—not at all to his surprise—a slip of paper tucked into the base.

Extracting this, Waln returned the fan to its owner, inquired after her well-being, and, after hearing her laugh lightly at her own clumsiness, excused himself. He traded the cider for a glass of white wine whose sharp dry flavor cut the sweet fug in his mouth and seemed to clear his head as well.

He was cornered by a plump energetic woman wearing a brooch bearing the silver heart of House Merlin. She proved to be a minor functionary of that house, very interested in trade possibilities between the Isles and Hawk Haven. They discussed possible markets for a time and Waln found her well informed as to the needs of the island communities—enough so that he did not need to feign interest.

After this lady departed—having exchanged contact information with him so that they might do further business—Waln took advantage of tucking her card away to glance at Lady Melina's note. It was brief, scrawled on the back of someone else's calling card.

"My room in the castle. Tonight. Two hours past midnight."

Baron Endbrook spent much of the intervening time by becoming a veritable hurricane on the dance floor. He was helped in this by the fact that this ball was fairly informal. That is, only the sticklers for form—or the extremely popular—kept dance cards. There were plenty of women available and eager to dance. He even found himself a commodity—the exotic sailor from the Isles—and had to stop himself from accentuating the roll in his walk.

Dancing continued until well after midnight. When the exhausted orchestra began to falter, Waln was surprised and astonished to discover that there were those among the honored guests quite interested in taking the musicians' places. The substitute musicians were less polished but more enthusiastic and the dancers took on an ebullience wherein Waln's "country" steps were not out of place.

He excused himself before the appointed time for his rendezvous. With a question here and a question there he had learned how to find Lady Melina's room.

After finding a corner where he could tidy himself, Waln made his stealthy way up a flight of stairs. He counted crosshalls and landmarks and upon arrival found that stealth had been unnecessary. The corridor was empty even of servants.

Apparently, all those who were awake were enjoying the ball.

I suppose it makes sense, Waln thought, raising his hand to tap on the door. *I doubt that the elderly king entertains on this scale very often.*

The door opened to his touch and he found himself entering a single room made up as a bedchamber. Some of his astonishment must have shown, for Lady Melina's first words were "We castle residents are very tightly packed. The suite I would usually command is given over, I believe, to the contingent from the Shark Barony. My maid is sleeping belowstairs, my children are in town staying with their Redbriar relations. You and I are quite alone."

Waln collected himself with some difficulty. Lady Melina had all but purred those last few words, sending an unexpected thrill through him.

Easy, Waln, remember that she's a sorceress, he cautioned himself, and found that the thought chilled him as iced water might.

Freed from the veil she had worn in public, Lady Melina proved to be fair-haired, though even candlelight revealed the silver intermixed with the fading blond. Although she was a small woman—Waln was surprised to learn just how small now that they stood close—she exuded confidence.

The notorious gemstone necklace was visible now as well—surely for his benefit, for she could have continued to conceal it beneath her dress. He noted that there were indeed five stones. If Sapphire had rejected her ornament, Melina had retained her own.

Waln dismissed fascinating speculation as to what effect Melina's silent claim to continued domination over her daughter might have on Princess Sapphire's reign as the crown princess established herself in her new role in Hawk Haven. His business was with Melina alone—and for her own qualities, not for her relation to the princess.

Lady Melina directed Waln to take a seat on one of two chairs she had drawn up a short distance from the bedstead. The bed's curtains were mostly drawn—as if to reject any invitation to dalliance—but were open enough that Waln could see that no one hid behind their shelter.

In any case, he reassured himself, *even in a small room like this she could hide someone beneath the bed or in a clothes chest if she wished to violate my request for privacy. Here is when I must begin thinking of her as a potential partner.*

"I am," he said, "meeting with you at the request of a powerful personage."

"Queen Valora," Lady Melina said, something of a decisive snap in her tone. "Unless you wish to deny that very obvious deduction."

"No," Waln said slowly, "I do not. Very well. I am here as a representative of Her Majesty. Recently she has inherited some quite interesting objects. It is her belief that you could be of use in learning their true use and value."

"Inherited," Lady Melina interrupted. "If these objects are what I think they may be, some might say that 'stolen' is a better description for how she acquired them."

"As you wish," Waln said, bowing his head slightly.

He'd learned long ago that the best way to deal with people who wished to show how wise and knowledgeable they were was to let them talk. He'd also learned that nothing was to be gained by arguing with someone you needed.

"Three enchanted objects—the very knowledge of their existence enough to trigger a war," Lady Melina mused. "There have been those who have said that Queen Valora was an idiot to take them from Revelation Point Castle."

Again Waln let the gibe pass, but he added the insult to his queen to the rapidly growing list of those things he would not forget.

"No doubt," he replied mildly, "Her Majesty felt differently."

"As is shown by her taking them." Lady Melina tossed her head, her hair silvery in the candlelight. "Now she wishes me to show her how to use them."

Waln permitted himself to show some surprise. If Lady Melina were more skillful, she would taunt less frequently. As it was, the acid of her tongue was losing its sharpness. He merely anticipated it and schooled his reactions to play her moods as he wished. Sorceress or not, she was no master politician.

"Could you?" he asked, allowing an eager tremor to enter his voice.

"Not without seeing them," Lady Melina replied, suddenly reasonable. "And even then, the unraveling of their secrets might take time."

"True," Waln said, dropping a card on the table, "so the New Kelvinese said when they were consulted."

"New Kelvinese?"

Lady Melina was either genuinely astonished or far more skilled at dissembling than Waln would have guessed.

"New Kelvinese," she repeated. "You took the objects to *them*?"

"Not quite."

Briefly and directly, Waln summarized his visit to Dragon's Breath—all but the final command that he return with someone skilled in magic or not at all. This portion of his approach was according to Queen Valora's express command. He would probably have held more information back until he had sounded Melina out in greater depth.

The queen, however, must have recognized some element of personality in the materials in Melina's dossier that he had not. When Waln finished speaking, the sorceress's eyes were alight with interest, even with eagerness.

"New Kelvin," she said, her voice a reverent whisper. "Dragon's Breath. I was only there once, when I was but fifteen. I spent two weeks . . ."

She stopped, pulling herself from her reminiscences with a visible jerk.

"I envy you," she said, her tones parlor-proper again. "Much. The New Kelvinese have retained a reverence for the past that was lost in this country. There was no burning of books, no rooting out of sorcerous objects as there was here."

"I saw their reverence for the past," Waln said, seeing his line now and praising his queen's insight.

He, too, had read the reference to that long-ago trip but had failed to deduce that it might be a romantic memory for Lady Melina. Waln went on, recalling the buildings he had seen, the strange rituals he had glimpsed.

Waln did not mention that he had thought that an honest desire for preservation could be carried too far. If the New Kelvinese retained some of their founders' enchantments and sorceries, these were not readily available. More than one building had been smokily lit by torch or candlelight rather than having a window or two knocked in revered walls. City streets had often been far too narrow—as if constructed to bear lighter or different traffic.

Although he found Lady Melina an avid audience for his traveler's tales, Baron Endbrook was too canny to talk for long. While Lady Melina was still smiling gently in the glow of her memories, he flashed his lure once more.

"Sadly, I failed to come to any sort of meeting of the minds with the New Kelvinese with whom I met. When they spoke of magical matters, they used words that could not be translated, either by the skilled merchant I had hired or their own people. It was as if they spoke of color to a man blind from birth," he concluded, turning the New Kelvinese's insult to his own use.

"My queen," he said, "immediately deduced that what we needed was one who might not be blind to those colors."

That was as far as he was willing to go in mentioning Lady Melina's reputation for sorcery. In Hawk Haven—and most other countries he knew—sorcery was still considered a foul art.

What the New Kelvinese might or might not do with magic was made acceptable simply by regarding their interest as not in sorcery as such. If some mad antiquarians dabbled in such arts this was simply part and parcel of the national fanaticism for old things. That New Kelvin had remained a small nation, unthreatening to any and all, had made this mental reservation an easy one to maintain.

That New Kelvin is the only place we know that supplies silks and some of the more exotic drugs doesn't hurt either, Waln thought cynically.

Lady Melina fingered the stones in her necklace.

"I have made something of a study of color," she said, "and might be interested in turning that knowledge to your queen's benefit. Indeed, why go so far as Dragon's Breath? Winter is coming and the Sword of Kelvin Mountains make a formidable barrier in the colder months. Why not let me study these objects here—or even in Her Majesty's domain?"

Waln had been expecting something like this. Queen Valora did not want Lady Melina given time and leisure to toy with the enchanted artifacts. Nor did the queen believe that Lady Melina had the ability to unlock their secrets without help.

"Not," the queen had said, "that I doubt she has made some study of the arcane arts, but compared to Hawk Haven, Bright Bay was positively open-minded on the subject of magic. Lady Melina may have stumbled on a text or two, even studied with some knowledgeable elder now gone to the ancestors. In time, she might even unravel the secrets, but I don't *have* time. If I am to make my new kingdom more than a playing piece on someone else's board—or worse, see it become a prize of Waterland—I must have power of my own. Real power—not just the threat of power."

Waln had agreed. The more he listened to Queen Valora the more he realized how vulnerable the Isles were. True, a good part of the fleet had followed the queen, but without the stands of timber from the mainland, without the metals, without the dozens of things the island shipping industry had taken for granted, they were doomed.

"I cannot permit you to do so," Waln replied bluntly to Lady Melina's request. "My queen's orders forbid such. What I can offer is a chance for you to come with me to New Kelvin— to be my translator in this language of color."

I don't need to tell her now—or ever—that bringing such a translator was a condition of New Kelvinese cooperation.

"And why," Lady Melina said, her slow smile showing that she had deduced at least some of the reasons for Queen Valora's refusal, "does your queen trust me?"

Again Waln was blunt.

"She does not, Lady Melina. If you were to join me on this

expedition, she must have hostages against your good faith."

Lady Melina's laugh was as rough as a puma's purr.

"I like you, Baron Endbrook. You are a sailor without a drop of artifice."

If you wish to think so, he thought, swallowing a silent chuckle, *I am pleased to have you do so.*

"Hostage against my good faith," Lady Melina repeated. "What might this be?"

"You have children," Baron Endbrook said, feeling a momentary pang as he thought of his own little girls.

"I do," she said, "four, now that the king has taken one. Jet cannot be spared his new responsibilities. Sapphire wants her sisters as hostages to winter in Bright Bay. I might be able to spare you one, though."

Baron Endbrook managed not to look disapproving at Melina's cavalier disposal of her young, remembering that it was not uncommon for the members of the Great Houses to trade children for entire seasons in order to foster friendship between their families. Probably Lady Melina thought of this arrangement as nothing more than a rather peculiar form of such fostering.

"And there must be some guarantee in the form of something you value."

For the first time, Lady Melina showed a flash of maternal fury.

"As if I do not value my children! Think again, Baron Endbrook. I value them highly. They are my greatest wealth and immortality—and all that remains to me of Rolfston."

Her sorrow on this last point seemed genuine, but Waln had his orders.

"I am sorry, my lady, but we will be entrusting you with access to three irreplaceable artifacts of great value. It is only reasonable that you give into our keeping something that you find equally valuable."

"And that is?"

"Your necklace."

Lady Melina pealed with laughter, the sound coming from

her in shrieking waves and continuing until tears ran down her cheeks.

"My necklace?"

Waln felt puzzled and uncomfortable. He had expected fury, refusal, counteroffers—anything but this hysterical howling.

"Yes, my lady. Your necklace and at least one of your children to be kept in secret and sacred trust until we return."

Lady Melina wiped the tears from her face, first with her sleeve and then with a dainty linen handkerchief.

"And what do I get for all of this?"

"A chance to gain knowledge," Waln said, "monies from Her Majesty's treasury, and favored trading status between your personal house—and your Great House, if you wish—and the Isles."

"And," Lady Melina said, hysteria vanishing to be replaced by studied menace, "one of the three artifacts for myself."

Waln had expected this; so had Queen Valora. He did not pause in his reply. Lady Melina would have had to be a complete idiot to think that they would not have been prepared for this demand. He was ready to believe her insane, but never would he mistake her emotional extremes for idiocy.

"One of the artifacts," he said, "but that one of Her Majesty's choosing. You cannot expect us to give to you something that might destroy us."

"And if these artifacts cannot be used except by one who can see these colors?"

"Then perhaps," Waln said, "you might find yourself offered a place at the queen's side."

"I might enjoy that," Melina said, "and might need such sanctuary if my holiday with you is misinterpreted by my homeland."

"That could be arranged, but we plan to take care that none but those who must know have any idea of where you are going. It will not hurt that winter will slow communications."

"Or," Melina added with a sly grin, "that I have been something of a recluse."

Some haggling remained as to the payment Lady Melina could expect—and how much in advance. They also settled on her youngest daughter, Citrine, as the least likely to be missed and most tractable.

Baron Endbrook departed Lady Melina's chamber weary to blood and bone but curiously exhilarated. The wedding festivities must pass and certain other arrangements be made, but it was done.

It was done.

XI

DERIAN HAD NOT BEEN INVITED to attend either the banquet or the ball the day before the wedding, but he did not feel slighted. Those grand events were mostly for the guests who had traveled a fair distance to attend the wedding. He was at home.

Home, however, was not proving as relaxed and comfortable a place as he might have wished. It wasn't that his parents didn't make a big fuss over his achievements. It was precisely that they *did*.

"Deri," his mother said to him one evening after dinner a few days following his return home, "your father and I need to speak with you—in private. Shall we use my office?"

Despite her framing the last as a question, Derian knew an order when he heard one. So did Brock. The little boy looked wickedly delighted.

"Oh! Derian's in trouble! Derian's in trouble! If he's smart he'll run on the double!"

Brock's impromptu rhyming—amusing only when it wasn't directed at you—was cut short by a barked command from Colby Carter.

"Enough, Brock! Obviously, you're overtired. To bed with you, my lad, and don't spare the soap when washing. Damita . . ." This last was directed toward the thirteen-year-old, who was looking on with an expression of pleased superiority. ". . . make certain Brock washes above his cuffs and around the back of his neck."

"Yes, Father." Damita looked delighted to have an excuse to boss her younger brother.

"But, Father!" Brock began with the faintest hint of a whine. "I'm not . . ."

"Tired or not," Colby cut in, "it's bed for you. Any more arguments and I'll ban you from the stables tomorrow."

Brock swallowed his protests immediately. The next day promised to be busy and exciting. Numerous noble visitors to the city—and even better, in Brock's opinion, their horses— were expected to arrive.

Other important people had rented carriages to take them to the castle for the introductory banquet or had ordered that the vehicles and teams they kept at Prancing Steed Stables be polished and prepared for use. Brock had been anticipating a day of running hither and yon, making himself "useful." Being banned from the stables would mean remaining at home and doing his lessons under his mother's critical supervision.

Derian sympathized with the boy, his momentary annoyance at being teased vanishing. At that moment, he wouldn't have minded being sent to bed himself. He'd spent the last few days working over at the stables, and his muscles ached from the unaccustomed labor involved in mucking out stall after stall.

Today had been particularly busy because, in addition to all the other traffic, Steward Silver had sent all the castle's over-flow to Prancing Steed Stables. Derian knew this was meant as a compliment to him—one of the small benefits of being a king's counselor—but after the huge train from Bright Bay arrived, late and muddy from bad weather on the road, he would have been just as happy to have seen the business go elsewhere and go home to the fresh bread and bean soup he knew Cook had planned for that night's dinner.

Whenever Derian closed his eyes, all he could see were hooves needing to be cleaned, and every flank and mane he'd groomed that day—not to mention other, less lovely stuff.

Derian's eyes had drifted closed while Colby scolded Brock,

but he was thrust from the edges of drowsiness by the heat of a mug of cider pressed into his hands.

Vernita stood over him, the amusement in her expression tinged with severity.

"Shall we go to my office?" she said.

Vernita Carter had been considered one of the great beauties of her day, and even after bearing three children she retained a certain elegance. With his increased knowledge—gained largely from conversations with Ninette—of the arts gentle-born women used to maintain and enhance their own appearances, Derian thought that his mother could still put any woman her age to shame if she cared.

But Vernita Carter didn't care—at least not on a day-to-day basis. She had passed over several quite interesting proposals of marriage to accept one from Colby Carter. Together they had built the small carting business he had taken over from his parents into a concern with stables in most of the major towns and villages of Hawk Haven.

Colby's parents now lived in semiretirement in Port Haven, managing the stables there with Colby's younger sister. Vernita's mother—her father had died some years ago—managed the stables in Broadview. Numerous other relatives benefitted from various aspects of the business—either as independent affiliates or as direct employees. And Derian stood to inherit the entire operation someday.

I'm glad, Derian thought as he settled into a chair in his mother's office and looked at the neat stacks of contracts and other documents on the tables and desks, *that I won't be expected to take over for a long while yet. I don't know half of what is involved in something this complicated. I know a good horse and how to avoid the obvious swindles, but I'm glad that I won't be in charge for a long, long time.*

It never occurred to him until his parents brought up the subject that he might not take over at all.

"It's not," Colby hastened to say, "that we'd be disinheriting you, son, not at all. Simply put, you have prospects that your younger brother and sister do not."

Derian frowned. "Prospects?"

Vernita looked impatient.

"Derian, you're smarter than this. Think! Your nineteenth birthday is next week. Already you have been made a king's counselor."

"The king is old!" Derian protested. "Sapphire doesn't think much of me—doesn't think anything of me as far as I know."

"Nonsense," Vernita snapped. "Son, think about what you just did. You said 'Sapphire,' speaking of the crown princess by her first name not with irreverence, but with the casualness of close contact."

"I'd *never*," Derian said, "speak so to her face."

"Of course not. You're not a fool, but you might to someone else—say Lady Archer—and, more importantly, Lady Archer would not think you were taking liberties."

"Lady Elise," Derian said, "has her head on straight. She doesn't go for false pomp."

"But don't you see, Derian," Vernita persisted. "You know her well enough to know that. Many of the nobles of your generation are not strangers to you. The nobles belonging to your father and my generation know that King Tedric selected you as a counselor. Whether or not the crown princess also selects you doesn't matter right now. You can use that favor to find yourself other patrons. Then, even if the crown princess does not offer you the counselor's ring, you will benefit."

"And," Colby added weightily, "your brother and sister will be secure.

"I don't know," Colby continued, stretching his legs out toward the hearth, and speaking with the deliberation of a man who preferred not to make speeches, "if you realize how much business your connections brought to us these last few days. We don't have a spare stall. I sent business to Tolken Farrier and his sister—and they're paying me for the privilege. We'll make the price of the new buildings in just this next week."

Vernita ruffled through a stack of papers until she came up with one on which she'd drawn columns.

"This is my estimate of how much business we would have taken in without your connections," she said. "I based my figures on how we've done during major festivals these last five years."

"And the important thing is," Colby added as Derian scanned the columns, "that if we do a good job for these people—as we will—many of them will return to our stables again and again. They'll seek out our affiliates in other towns."

"All because of me?" Derian asked hesitantly.

"Not quite," Vernita replied kindly, "but because of you, we were given the chance to show our services to these people. You gave us exposure that otherwise would have taken us years to gain through word of mouth."

Derian stared at the figures on the sheet of paper. His mother had drummed enough mathematics into him that he could see the sense in them.

"Then what do you want me to do?" he asked, setting the paper down and wrapping his fingers around his mug of cider.

"Take one of the positions you have been offered," Vernita said. "Earl Kestrel's continued patronage would be useful. He'll be Duke Kestrel before too long. The duchess's health is good, but her years are against her. His son, Lord Kestrel, is about your age and if you make a good impression with him, you will be secure for life."

Vernita rose and stirred the fire. "That's one course, a good, safe one. However, you could take a position with someone else for a time. Didn't you say that Earle Peregrine spoke with you?"

"Her steward did," Derian admitted, "though the nature of the post was unclear."

"And you said that one of Bright Bay's nobles had spoken with you," Colby prompted.

"Not directly," Derian said, "but one of Duke Oyster's people did mention that they will be needing someone to act as liaison between the kingdoms, smoothing the way for reunification."

He regretted the cheerful boasting he'd done immediately after his return home. His parents had taken that information in a direction he hadn't considered.

"Oyster," Vernita said, "that's Queen Pearl's birth house, correct?"

"Yes, ma'am," Derian said.

"And the firmest supporter of King Allister," she added.

"Yes, ma'am."

"I saw," Colby added relentlessly, "how many of the Bright Bay people knew you by sight and greeted you warmly. You have obviously made the type of impression we had hoped our son would make."

Derian groaned. Setting down the now empty mug, he thrust his face into his hands.

"I need to think," he said, hearing to his dismay a wail not unlike Brock's in his voice. "I'd never considered any of this. I knew you wanted me to make connections, but I always thought I'd simply make a decent marriage and come home again. This . . ."

He trailed off and was both comforted and embarrassed to feel his mother patting his arm.

"There, there, Deri," his mother crooned. "I know it is a great deal to take in."

"And never," Colby said, "think we're throwing you out, but we have hopes for you beyond mucking stalls."

Derian nodded weakly. "I know."

That night his dreams were not restful and late the next afternoon when the worst of the rush was over—for the guests were all gone to the banquet—he asked his father to be excused.

Colby agreed so readily that Derian knew he felt a bit guilty about the pressure they'd put on him.

Derian pulled a knitted wool cap over his hair and hunched himself into a barn coat. Then he went out to walk the streets of the city that had always been his home—and that he had always believed would continue to be so.

The sky was clear, as if the rain that had so carefully muddied the roads for King Allister's entourage now regretted its work and was striving to make amends by shining with almost summertime brightness.

Is it lucky or unlucky for the bride if it rains on her wedding day? Derian mused. *I never can remember. Looks as if to-morrow will be bright enough.*

Passing through the gates into the walled section of town, he walked along some of the trade streets, glancing at the wares laid out on display. Along Weaver's Row doors stood open so that the workers at their looms could enjoy the pleasant daylight. Derian exchanged casual greetings here and there, enjoying the friendliness.

Turning along Blacksmith's Way, Derian noted that the last of the active smithies was gone, moved outside the walls because of the neighbors' complaints about the noise and smoke. There were shops here instead, some selling ironwork but others selling a mixture of goods. Many of the shops had been converted completely to residences—though many of the shopkeepers had always lived above their shops.

I recall Tannery Row has gone much the same way, Derian thought, *despite the guild's complaints. Still, the air is kept fresher with the smellier trades outsides.*

He was heading for the Market Square when he heard a dull, almost monotone, but somehow musical sound: the plunk-plunking of someone alternately plucking and strumming on a fat-bodied guitar.

Derian's head snapped up like Roanne smelling hot oat mash. This was a sound he hadn't heard in far too long, the sound of a street musician absorbed in his woes. That the same instrument could be played far more dexterously—made to ripple and sing like a laughing brook or trip through all the dances ever danced—didn't matter to Derian.

This was a music engendered in the dark reaches of the heart and soul. It took its rhythms from the slow beating of the pulse and the dragging of reluctant breath. It had never set the pace for sailors at sea or for farmers bringing in the harvest. It was city music, introspective and forlorn.

In short, it fit Derian's mood perfectly.

He found the musician seated cross-legged on a low bench outside a tavern that had closed for the slow hours of the afternoon. A depressed-looking dog, lean and black with drooping ears and large brown eyes, lay with its head on the man's well-traveled boots. It raised its head as Derian came close, then lowered it with an audible sigh.

The musician didn't look up as Derian approached. He was a scraggly fellow with hair of an indifferent brown pulled back into a loose queue. He was neither bearded or clean-shaven but rather looked as if he'd forgotten which style he preferred and had settled for something halfway between. The clothes he wore were grubby with street grime and mud, but not greasy.

His guitar, however, was spotless, rubbed to such a shine that Derian fancied he could catch the scent of the polishing oil. An empty tin cup rested by the musician's feet with a worn token set in the bottom as a hint to potential patrons.

Derian leaned against a wall, thrust his hands into his pockets, and listened. After several minutes, as if at last realizing he had an audience, the man started to sing. His voice was rough and slightly cracked but like his plunking on the guitar oddly melodious.

Unlike most of those who sang for their supper, this man didn't launch into a tale of heroism or popular legend. Instead he began:

> She left me in summer, when the sun was bright
> But without her lov'n, I was cold as winter night.
> I forgot how to smile, forgot how to frown.
> My heart she had frozen, like snow on the ground.

The musician moved his lament into autumn, when the abandoned lover couldn't see the beauty in the colors of the trees or smell the rich scents of the harvest. Only beer gave him some comfort but left him:

> Wish'n I was dead, with a pain in my heart
> and an ache in my head.

By winter the musician was warming to his theme, growing more passionate as he crooned about the beauty of ice and the softness of snow, the embrace of sleet and the glitter of cold.

Derian tossed a couple of tokens into the musician's cup and turned away before the song could pass through spring and return to summer. He didn't want to know if the unknown subject found redemption or some chillier and more permanent peace.

As he continued his way to the Market Square, Derian hummed the infectious lament to himself.

You can't call it a tune really or even a melody, but it's music nonetheless, he was thinking when a voice called out his name.

"Derian!"

The voice was female, robust, and terribly familiar. Derian looked up from his contemplation of his boot toes and saw a rounded figure swathed in cloak and shawl, a basket over her arm, waving to him from across the Square. There was no market today, so nothing impeded his getting a clear look at her: Heather the baker's daughter, the girl he had been walking with before he'd been hired by Earl Kestrel.

"Heather," he said, bending to bestow a chaste kiss on the round, red cheek she held up for his salute. "How are you?"

She smiled up at him, her bright smile tinged with something wicked.

"Well enough, Merry Deri." Her smile became arch. "I'm betrothed now, or will be as good as, by the end of next moonspan."

Derian recalled that like him Heather had been a cold-weather baby. She'd be nineteen next month and old enough for a completely respectable betrothal. The fact that they both were on the verge of legal adulthood had added a certain very interesting tension to their strolls—and to the occasional visits to her father's flour shed or to some infrequently used barn.

As Heather gossiped amicably about their mutual acquaintances, Derian recalled their time together. Heather hadn't been a tease, not quite, for she'd made clear that a public promise of marriage was her price for letting him get any farther than the inside of her well-rounded blouse.

Derian might have given her that price, too, but he was a bit more experienced than Heather imagined—or she wouldn't have risked tempting him. There had been a girl or two who worked around the stables who hadn't been adverse to a roll in the hay with the boss's son. Their willingness had kept him less than desperate and so free.

"You know, Deri," Heather was saying, a change in her tone bringing him back to the present. "I liked you quite a lot. I cried myself to sleep at night for weeks when you rode off west with Earl Kestrel. Cried and cried."

"I'm sorry," he said awkwardly.

"I thought you'd get eaten by a bear or something," she continued, shifting her basket from arm to arm.

Derian politely took it from her. It was heavy with fresh-baked loaves, wrapped against the chill.

"Can I walk you wherever you're going?" he asked.

"I'm delivering these to the Archer Manse," she said. "I'd be glad for the company."

Elise's house, Derian thought. *And I have an invitation to call.*

He resolved to keep his hat pulled well down over his hair and slouched a bit, shuffling his feet against the cobbles.

"My father," Heather said, "told me that you'd come back alive, but you'd never come back to me. He was right enough."

"You," Derian said indignantly, "refused to see me when I called!"

"I did," she sniffed. "I wasn't going to cheapen myself walking out with a fellow who was living with another woman—seeing her stark naked by all accounts."

Derian shrugged. That had been true enough. He hadn't really been living with Firekeeper, but he'd seen her naked often and had found it embarrassing rather than stimulating.

Still, he didn't bother to defend himself. He had no desire to resume his relationship with Heather—or to anger her almost-betrothed. Heather wouldn't be above teasing her fellow with the threat of a rival, just to make sure that her sweetheart cared.

"Father said," Heather prattled on, "that if I waited for you it would be just like it had been for him and your mother."

"My mother!" Derian was astonished.

"Sure." Heather was delighted at having information he lacked. "Didn't you know that they were sweethearts? Daddy still says that she was the prettiest girl he'd ever seen. Makes Mother right annoyed at him, but it slips out from time to time, especially when he's had a cup too many."

"My mother and your father?" Derian repeated more calmly. "Really?"

"Sure, back when they were younger than we are now, seventeen, maybe," Heather said with the loftiness of her almost nineteen years. "You mother had bigger dreams than being a baker's wife, though. She dumped Daddy when he got serious about her and eventually married Colby Carter. Guess she was right about *his* prospects. They've made a real business out of just a few carts."

Heather sighed. "And my father is still baking bread and so that's what my husband will do, too. I'll be baking babies in *my* oven and delivering loaves."

"There are worse things," Derian offered awkwardly.

Heather gave him a defiant smile, but there was something ugly beneath the grin.

"Lots worse, like being a boot-lick for the nobility or a kennel keeper for a naked girl who eats raw meat. At least *my* husband will be his own man."

She tugged her basket from his arm and tore off down the street. Derian stared after her, too astonished to be angry or even hurt. That would come later.

Distantly, he thought he could hear the guitarist plunk-plunking away.

She left me in winter . . .

MORNING CAME EARLY this high on the shore of Lake Rime, for there were no mountains in the east to block the sunrise, but Firekeeper awoke even earlier than the sun. The wolves uncurled from sleep at her motion and there was no need for speech among the three.

Together they slipped into the woods and hunted, bringing down a young buck too stupid to be allowed to breed since he had stayed in the vicinity of what even Firekeeper's nose told her was an improbable and even contradictory host of scents.

She used flint and steel to strike sparks for a fire, and lightly grilled a steak cut thin.

"Mother," she asked the One Female, "who taught me to cook my food?"

The One Female looked up from gnawing on a thighbone. There was a sharp crack as she broke it to expose the marrow within. Her silvery fur was all over blood, not only muzzle and throat, but chest as well.

"You have done so for as long as I have known you. Isn't such practice the human way?"

Firekeeper sensed an evasion, but didn't press. She had held her question until the wolves had reached what humans might call dessert, knowing far better than to distract a feeding wolf.

By the time the thighbone was cleaned, her own meat was broiled to her satisfaction and she kept her silence while chewing on thin slices of the hot, rare venison. It was tough, but not impossibly so, for the buck had not yet lost all of summer's fat.

By the time Firekeeper had finished eating, the sky as glimpsed through the interlaced tree branches was streaked with pink and yellow. The wolves were willing to let the crows and jays pick at what remained of the buck. In truth there was not much. Several days of dining on rabbits had given Blind Seer an appetite for a solid meal.

"Wash," the One Female ordered. "The others will be waiting impatiently."

Firekeeper asked, "Mother, are we then important that they must wait on our pleasure?"

"We are," the One Female replied, "no more important, but no less, thus they can no more order us about than we can them. We do them the courtesy of joining them, they of waiting until we are fed."

"It is unwise," Blind Seer quoted unexpectedly from the store of proverbs the wolves used for teaching pups, "to talk with a hungry wolf."

Firekeeper nodded and loped beside the silver wolf and the grey to where the waters of Rimed Lake waited still and shining in the dawn light. The wolves waded in directly, snapping at the thin shell of ice and drinking in great gulps of the chill water.

Hesitating only to strip her clothing from her, Firekeeper stacked the pieces, placing her Fang on top where she could easily reach it. Water would do no kindnesses to the tanned leather of her vest and breeches, and even the fine blade that had once belonged to Prince Barden was not immune to rust.

As she stood poised for the plunge, she caught a glimpse of her reflection in a side pool that had returned to tranquility after the wolves' games.

Her hair, grown longer since she left the wilds to live among humans, was matted and poking out at odd angles—no wonder, since she had neither combed nor brushed it since leaving Revelation Point Castle, but only made certain that the longer ends remained pulled back into a queue.

She had lost weight as well, though she was far from the slat-sided waif who had first crept out of the forest to speak with Derian. The small, rounded breasts that had developed after she had begun to eat more regularly remained, as did a certain healthy sleekness.

Nothing but great magic would alter the scars that stitched her hide, nor did she particularly desire them gone. They were the price she paid for being a hairless wolf. More would she have preferred fur and fangs and four strong legs and a voice that could howl across the void to shake the moon in her dance.

A buffet of icy wind across her naked body interrupted this momentary introspection. Firekeeper dove into the clear waters of the lake, cutting the surface as cleanly as did the waterfowl from whom she had learned the maneuver.

Ignoring the cold was impossible, so she accepted it without dreaming of hot baths as a human might. Instead she grasped handfuls of black sand from the lake bottom and used them to scrub the blood and trail grime from her hide.

Despite vigorous finger combing, Firekeeper could do nothing about the knots and snarls in her hair, so after she had shaken and danced herself warm and fairly dry, she dressed, noting woefully that all her garments could use a good cleaning.

Then she used the Fang to crop her hair short once more. The blade bore a keener edge than even the razor Derian used to shave and she honed it frequently, thus managing a neater end result than ever before. She cropped the hair shortest near her face, allowing herself to retain some longer strands near the back, which she gathered into a defiant little tail with a piece of faded black ribbon.

Blind Seer lolled on the sand near her, chewing a burr from between his toes and chuckling at her efforts.

"Even a wolf may have her vanity," Firekeeper said, booting him in the ribs with one bare foot. "If this little tail becomes too much trouble, I can chop it short as fast as I could remove your obnoxious bush."

Blind Seer stopped laughing and beat his tail on the ground, hearing the threat in the words. The wolf-woman accepted his apology and knelt to kiss him on the black leather of his nose.

"Mother has gone to see if the others await," she said. "We should not make her call us to her like idiot pups who have been hunting crickets and so risk missing the meat."

Rising and shaking the sand from his still damp fur, Blind Seer said softly:

"And remember, I am with you, not with anyone else, not even with the One Female. If any or all press you beyond endurance, I will guard your back."

Firekeeper buried her hand in his neck ruff for a moment in thanks, but said nothing more. Only Blind Seer knew the comfort she took in his steady, fierce support and he, in turn, was oddly comforted by that knowledge.

Despite the conflicting mixture of odors she had scented since their arrival the night before, somehow Firekeeper had expected the gathering to be largely one of birds. Doubtless this was because Bee Biter had been the messenger to bring back Elation and because of Elation's own story of how she had been questioned by the Mothers. Therefore, Firekeeper had to conceal her astonishment when she saw the group that awaited her.

There was a puma lounging with lazy, golden-furred insolence on a shelf of rock that just happened to catch the best of the morning sun. An autumn-fat brown bear leaned against the lower portions of that same rock, little eyes actively denying its physical somnolence. A red fox sat conversing with a jay.

Nor was the jay the only bird present. Elation perched on a branch beside another peregrine; a kite swept out of the sky to land on the rock just above the puma. Bee Biter claimed a sweeping oak limb all for himself. A gyrfalcon hunched her shoulders next to an apparently half-asleep owl. Like large and small versions of the same bird, a raven perched next to a crow.

But it was the buck elk carefully keeping his massive rack from tangling in the tree branches and the white-tailed doe who surprised Firekeeper the most by their presence.

Once or twice a winter the young wolves might run races against the more arrogant of the elk, but to see these two food animals standing without apparent fear among the carnivores brought home the importance of this meeting. She wondered who else might be watching more privately from the concealment of the underbrush.

No names were exchanged, no introductions made. Each of these creatures was so clearly present as a representative for their kind among the Royal Beasts that such flourishes as personal designations were superfluous. The elk was clearly all Elk, even as at times King Tedric spoke as the voice of Hawk Haven.

The raven proved to be the director of this meeting, and Firekeeper was reminded of human posturing when he flared out the long feathers on his legs and neck as he landed on the dried grass in the center of the circle. He strutted a few paces and then, without the preamble a human would have given, squawked at Firekeeper:

"Human, can you confirm the tales told by one peregrine Elation that among your kind has again surfaced the shadow of magic?"

"Among the humans of the lowlands," Firekeeper replied carefully, "such has been rumored, but I have seen nothing that could be confirmed as such."

She thought of Lady Melina's necklace and the magical control it seemed she wielded over her children but chose not to volunteer that information.

I didn't see her use it, the wolf-woman comforted herself, *and didn't Hazel Healer say that the power could have been some other thing she called trance induction rather than true magic?*

The raven strode a step or two, fanning out his head feathers so that he now appeared to have ears or little horns off the top of his head. Although, like all the Royal Beasts present, the raven tended to be larger than the average of his kind, still he remained a bird on the ground and Firekeeper was not intimidated.

"Human," the raven began, and this time Firekeeper interrupted.

"I can understand," she said dryly, "that the question of whether I am human, as is my shape, or wolf, as is my heart and upbringing, could be a matter of long and useless debate, but, since there appears to be an antagonism to humans in the thread of your questions, I would prefer you address me by my given name. I am Firekeeper and I demand that you not forget it."

There was a murmur at this speech, punctuated by a dry cough of laughter from the puma. The raven flattened his feathers, raised them, then settled.

"Firekeeper," he began again, "although you did not see

anything that you could confirm as magic, is it your best estimate—taking the scent from the wind as it were—that the humans believe that the kingdom of Bright Bay was possessed of objects that they think are ensorcelled?"

"Yes," Firekeeper replied. "Elation may not have known to tell you, but those very items of which you speak are no longer in the keeping of Bright Bay, but have been taken away by the woman called Valora, who is now Queen of the Isles."

This caused a hubbub, including a few queries shrieked at Elation who denied any desire to deceive. The peregrine's indignant denials were honest as far as they went. Since she had never reached Revelation Point Castle, the peregrine had not learned of Queen Valora's theft until after her meeting with the Mothers.

Firekeeper and Blind Seer had confided in Elation later, during their journey west, and all three had agreed that it was best if Firekeeper presented that report—evidence of her good faith toward whatever the Royal Beasts intended.

After the initial astonishment had passed, Firekeeper reported on the circumstances leading up to Queen Valora's departure for the Isles with the supposedly enchanted objects, speaking with an ease and fluency that would have astonished her human friends, who were accustomed to her more halting command of a language that—to her memory at least—she had not spoken until slightly over half a year earlier.

When she had concluded, a boar with gleaming white tusks, who had arrived during the early stages of the meeting, grunted:

"This tale troubles me. Such care to steal speaks of desire to use. One does not go to the work of grubbing up roots merely to leave them rot."

"Nor," agreed the jay, "does such passivity mate with what we have observed of this Queen Valora."

"We are agreed then," the raven said, "to continue the course of action we settled upon when first the peregrine Elation brought her report?"

Assent sounded all around, no less enthusiastically in the howling of the One Female than in the bugling of the elk.

Even the white-tailed doe, wide eyes reflecting concerns that Firekeeper could only guess at, stomped a forehoof firmly thrice.

"Human Firekeeper," the raven said, sleeking his feathers then ruffling them again, "we have called you here not only to add your report to that of the peregrine Elation, but so that we might set a charge upon you."

Firekeeper frowned and would have spoken, but to her surprise the One Female nipped at her arm, warning her to silence.

"We want you," the raven continued, "to find these three objects and steal them from their current possessor. Bring them to us and we in our turn shall make certain that they are never again used."

Firekeeper spoke, heedless of the snap of her mother's fangs against her bare skin.

"Steal them?" she asked, her voice high and clear with amazement. "For you? What use do the Royal Beasts have for things made by humans, for humans?"

From seeming sleep the bear said in a voice thick with honey, "Because they were made by humans, for humans—that is why we want them. You are a naked wolf. I accept the evidence of my ears even though it violates the evidence of my nose. Surely you know that nakedness is a human's greatest strength."

Firekeeper stared at him.

"I cannot solve your riddle, wise bear."

But the bear appeared to have drifted off to sleep again and it was the fox who replied.

"Because I am smaller than a wolf, I must dig hiding places through all my territory. Humans are even weaker than I and so they make dens out of the bones of the earth and the flesh of the trees. They make fangs from metal and from stone. They wear our skins—or those of our Cousins—lest they freeze."

Firekeeper nodded slowly. "I begin to understand. And these objects—what are they? I have heard humans speak of the old magic as a thing to fear, but I lack the knowledge to sort the stories a bard sings from the truth."

"We owe the wolf cub a tale," the puma drawled from his rock. "I will begin."

Firekeeper sat, leaned back against Blind Seer, and opened both ears and heart to listen.

XII

"FIRST OF ALL, LITTLE WOLFLING," the puma began in a voice like velvet, "even the humans know themselves strangers to this land. They call it the New World or the New Countries, as if they had created it by stumbling upon it, but like all lands this one has been here since the oceans suffered portions of the earth to rise above them.

"You may have also heard their tales of how these lands were uninhabited, ripe for settlement, eager for the axe and the plow. This is not true. We Royal Beasts lived here and our tales say we have always lived here, though our tales may miss some fragment of the truth.

"Suffice to say that we lived here long before the coming of the humans. Were it not for the tales the wingéd folk brought back from their migrations, we might have thought that there were no other peoples than those we already knew."

Firekeeper, who had been living and breathing politics since her departure with Earl Kestrel the previous spring, thought she detected a ripple of uneasiness on the part of some of the Beasts. The doe folded back her ears and the boar grunted to himself, but no one challenged the puma, so he continued his tale unchecked.

"When the humans first landed their boats on these shores it was at a place far from here. Some of our kind went to meet with them and indeed for a time the humans behaved as visitors in our land. They agreed to the limits we set and we even made treaties after the human fashion."

The bear shook himself and muttered sleepily, "They had not the wit to read the warnings in claw-marked trees or the noses to scent other kinds of markings."

"Nor," the puma continued, "did they seem able to share the land with others. I have my territory, but it is the territory of the wolves as well, and of birds and even of fish. Sometimes we challenge each other, but when a challenge is ended and a particular conflict solved, we go back to sharing. Humans cannot even share land with each other—and never with those they fear."

The doe spoke, taking up the thread of the tale with an enigmatic glance at the puma.

"And so, Firekeeper, the time came that the humans exceeded the amount of land the Royal Beasts had permitted them. More humans came across the oceans, wanting still more land. Some of the Beasts fought—challenging the human right to claim our territories as their own. And then we learned that they had claws sharper than the puma's, armies larger than packs of wolves. Lastly, we learned that these seemingly naked creatures had weapons more terrible than any we had been born to—the power of what humans now call Old Country magic."

"When first the humans came," the One Female said—her storytelling recalled to Firekeeper the many stories she had heard in her childhood—"they were mostly sailors and merchants and farmers. Later, as the colonies grew and were founded by many nations of the Old Country, the humans began to contest among themselves. Clearing away trees a hundred and more years old is great labor. A beaver enjoys damming streams, but digging courses to carry water to fields would defy the most optimistic mole. You have seen the dens humans build, the trails they cut . . . None of this happens easily. Soon the newcomers thought that it would be more efficient to take the first comers' lands from them—as a bear might steal a young wolf's kill."

The bear opened both eyes and reared in astonished protest.

The raven squawked, enjoying his role as meeting head, flapping wings that spanned nearly Firekeeper's full height when spread.

When the bear had halted—already halfway across the ground to the One Female—the raven said:

"Tell your tale, wolf, but remember that you are not speaking before your pack. Keep insults to yourself."

Firekeeper was astonished when the One Female abased herself, pressing her belly to the ground and whining.

"I did forget my manners," she said, "speaking as I was to one of my pups."

The bear collapsed back as if deciding against the effort to rise, but Firekeeper could tell that there was bad blood between this creature and her mother. At the folding of the raven's wings, the One Female continued the tale:

"When the humans first fought those Beasts who challenged their right to claim territory, they fought mostly with their false fangs and claws. Worst were the arrows, for they came from a distance and often from secret. Still, we held our own against even these. The wingéd folk especially learned to spot the archers, and how to spoil both their hiding and their aim."

Judging from how the gathered raptors shifted from foot to foot and admired their talons or honed their curved beaks against branches, the wingéd folk had spoiled more than those long-ago archers' aim.

"When the humans began to fight each other, however, a new and terrible force entered our land, and with its coming we learned to feel true terror of humanity. No longer did they seem naked creatures, but more akin to a poisonous insect that seems small and weak, but injects fire and sometimes death into its bite."

The elk—who had been digging furrows in the soft forest duff with his spreading rack—now took up the tale, his telling recalling the wind moaning through bare tree branches in the dead of winter.

"We had long known that humans possessed magic. Indeed, that was one reason we had treated with them as equals rather than dismissing them as Cousins, for one of the things that separates the Royal Beasts from the lesser Cousins are the magical gifts that occur from time to time.

"Among the first humans to come there had been those who could communicate with us—not as freely as you do, Fire-keeper, but in a halting fashion. Almost every ship that had made the long voyage across the oceans had carried someone who could whistle up a wind. Early in our meetings, their healers used their talents for our good rather than reserving them for their people alone.

"But when the humans began to war among themselves, there came from the Old Country those who were gifted beyond some talent. These sorcerers came in many varieties, but one and all they possessed an ability we did not have—the ability to channel power in multiple ways, not merely one, as with a talent. Through rotes and rituals, they shaped the magical force. The greatest among them not only used these spells, they could enchant objects so that the least talented among them became suddenly sorcerous."

The kite spoke from her high perch.

"At first they directed these powers against each other, but when they had resolved their wars, the sorcerers acted against us. No talon is so sharp as to cut fire that explodes out of empty air, no bite tears so deeply as to seize lightning from the skies. And our tales tell of other things—of magics that warned of our approach so that even the stealthiest were detected, of invisible shields that wrapped the humans' limbs so that they were unbiteable.

"Eventually, solemn counsel was held among the Royal Beasts. There was much land east of the Iron Mountains, so much that the humans would be many years filling the space. We resolved to flee—flock and pack and herd—to make those mountains our stronghold.

"We had learned that iron weakened the sorcerers' power, though it did not appreciably weaken the abilities of those with inborn talents. We had noticed that the sorcerers were reluctant to chase us into the mountains and wondered if the very iron ore so plentiful in some of the mountains' rock caused them discomfort. And we had learned that humans were lazy. Surely they would not pursue us if there was no need and room enough east of the Iron Mountains for them to spread."

In a sharp voice, like but unlike the barking of a dog, the vixen spoke on, "It was a well-thought-out plan, yet not all the Royal Beasts chose to abide by the decision of the council and no one forced them to do so.

"Initially, those who remained behind found it easier to hide themselves, for they were few and more careful not to confront the humans. Even so, within a few generations none of the larger Royal-kind remained alive east of the Iron Mountains. Some of the wingéd folk did go east, but these did not do so out of stubbornness or stupidity. They went—even as the peregrine Elation has so recently done—to spy out human doings.

"As Royal-kind passed into human legend, any humans who might chance upon an unusually large hawk or an especially brilliant jay dismissed the evidence of their own eyes—an easy thing to do, for it is hard to judge the true size of a flying creature."

The sun had risen high during the deliberations and the tale-telling that followed. When the fox paused and a crow was about to take up the telling, the kestrel Bee Biter interrupted:

"Much time has passed and I am hungry, yet I would not miss the smallest part of this story, for it is rare to hear it told in full. Let us pause and hunt . . . and graze," he added with a glance at the herbivores among the gathering. "I suspect that Firekeeper would like time to think on all she has heard."

The raven glanced around the circle and saw that many were in agreement with the kestrel.

"Then we shall adjourn," he squawked, "until evening time brings the sun low."

The Royal Beasts melted into the forest or soared into the air until Firekeeper stood alone but for Blind Seer and Elation, looking around in wonder at what had been a crowded glade.

❀

ELISE AWOKE on the morning of the wedding day oppressed by a feeling of nightmare.

She shifted into a sitting position within her curtained bed, burying her hands deeply in her golden hair and pushing her fingers against her scalp as if in that way to banish a vague sense of wrongness. All she succeeded in doing was bringing it into focus.

The ball the evening before . . . Accepting an offer to dance from the large man with the roll to his walk and the Islander accent. Prancing up and down the line, trying to be polite to her partner, yet acutely aware that Sir Jared danced a few couples away, that his set would intersect with hers.

Glancing toward Sir Jared during one exchange and seeing what she intuitively knew she was not meant to see: Her partner, Baron Endbrook, tucking something into Lady Melina Shield's glove. The movement had been smoothly done, so neatly managed that it could have been a part of the dance. Indeed, flirtation was a recognized element of the fun.

But Elise felt certain that Baron Endbrook had not been flirting with Lady Melina. He had made no effort to seek her out before this; after the dance ended he made no effort to ask her to dance.

Guardedly, not certain why she was so suspicious, Elise had kept an eye on the two, helped by the fact that Baron Endbrook was quite tall and that Lady Melina, clad as she was all in black, made her soft-footed and mostly silent way among the more gaily clothed guests like a black cat in a cage of songbirds.

Elise had nearly given up her vigil when she saw that Lady Melina's course as she strolled about the room on arm of one of her brothers would take her quite close to Baron Endbrook. As they had stayed almost conspicuously apart since the note was passed, this seemed significant.

When Lady Melina had dropped her fan where Baron Endbrook could retrieve it for her, Elise nearly cheered with delight. This was too much to be insignificant. She couldn't tell for certain if Baron Endbrook removed anything from the fan before returning it to the lady, but he certainly had the opportunity.

Lady Melina had departed soon thereafter and Baron Endbrook invited a new partner to dance. He was still dancing when Elise's parents suggested that the family depart for home and Elise was forced to give up her vigil.

Yet once she was out in the family carriage, Elise had found herself doubting that she had actually seen anything important. Perhaps Baron Endbrook truly *had* been flirting with Lady Melina.

Lady Melina was not an unattractive woman for the mother of five, and she was now widowed. Her family connections were irreproachable—if one could leave out her traitor brother, and such a brother might make her more interesting to an Islander. If Baron Endbrook was unmarried, he might wish to raise his status by wedding her.

A casual question to Lady Aurella—easily enough asked, as all were gossiping about the other guests—had brought Elise the information that Baron Endbrook was indeed married and the father of three. That ruled out a marriage alliance, unless he intended a divorce, or was thinking about a marriage for his children rather than himself . . .

Elise had bit her lower lip in frustration, glad that the darkness within the carriage granted her a measure of privacy. She longed to ask what her mother thought, but that would mean explaining just why Elise had such a great dislike of Lady Melina—a thing Elise had sworn to keep secret.

Nor could she confide in Ninette. The events of last summer had left her lady companion no less afraid of the reputed sorceress.

At that moment, more than ever, Elise had wished for the freedom of the military camp. If only she could talk with Firekeeper or Derian or Doc! Firekeeper, however, was gone, apparently in answer to a summons from the wolves—an odd thought Elise shied from thinking about too much, for it threatened her sense of the natural order of things.

Then Elise had felt happier when she recalled that both Derian and Doc would be attending the wedding. They were not in the wedding party, but surely she could speak to them at the reception, alert them to her suspicions—vague as they were—and ask them to help her keep an eye on Lady Melina.

Now, with the coming of morning, anticipation chased away the nightmare. Elise swung her long legs to the cold floor, grateful for the fire already burning on the hearth.

She rung for her maid, eager to start dressing, as if preparing for the event could make it come the sooner.

KING ALLISTER STOOD thinking about the arrangements that had been made for wedding security, fidgeting slightly as his body servant brushed his trousers and put a final polish on his boots. In the next room he could hear Pearl talking to the twins as they prepared for the wedding—an intricate waltz involving not only the three participants but what seemed to be a small army of maids and seamstresses.

The little girls were caught up in an emotional whirl that was half-fear, half-excitement. They had spent all morning the day before being fitted for their new gowns, had attended the banquet, and then had insisted on attending much of the ball. Consequently, they were now overtired and edgy.

They were also nervous about how they would measure up when compared with the—to them—sophisticated Shield sisters. Citrine was close enough to their own age not to worry them much. She was also a sweet child. Ruby and Opal, however, awed them from the heights of fourteen and seventeen years.

It didn't help matters that only the previous afternoon Lady Melina had finally given her word that Ruby and Opal would winter in Revelation Point Castle along with—at their mother Zorana's insistence—their cousins Deste and Nydia Trueheart.

Allister didn't quite understand why Minnow and Anemone were so anxious about processing in company with the three

Shield sisters. After all, the twins could claim experience the others could not.

Pearl had laughed indulgently when he asked her what was the source of the problem.

"Minnow and Anemone knew then that no one would compare them to Lady Elise—she's a young lady of eighteen while they are only twelve. Lady Blysse is closer to their age but still enough older to be in another class."

"And," Allister had chuckled, "she is Lady Blysse. But," he added, remembering, "though Ruby is just a couple years older than our girls, Opal is nearly the same age as Elise."

"True." Pearl sighed. "Age is only part of the problem. Lady Elise is as unaffected as one could hope—especially given that she is heir apparent to a barony. Oh, she has her flighty moments, but most of the time, she's a reasonable girl. Probably that same frequent access to the king's castle that her cousins twit her about gave Elise a realistic sense of her own importance.

"Opal and Ruby, however, are quite affected. They are polished dancers and trained courtiers. Their mother made certain that if they couldn't haunt their great-uncle's castle, they would be frequent guests at the Gyrfalcon ducal residence. They at least pretend to a solid sense of their own importance—so much so that the pretense has become a part of them."

"Snobs," Allister said.

"Snobs," Pearl agreed, "without a real reason to be snobbish. All their claim to importance rests on relationships—and perhaps a touch of the not completely wholesome aura that clings to their mother."

After hearing this, Allister resolved to make a great fuss over the twins when they emerged from the ladies' bower and, indeed, it was not difficult to do so.

Although originally, the bridal party was to wear the same gowns to both weddings, the assassination attempt had made this impossible. Sapphire's gown had been completely ruined, as had Lady Elise's. Even the twins' gowns had been spattered with blood.

This led to a difficulty, for the augmented bridal party already had gowns made to match that made for Lady Elise. Fast post-riders had confirmed that enough of the expensive material remained to make a new gown on a similar pattern for Elise, but not for the twins—even if wearing Hawk Haven's colors would have been appropriate.

There simply had not been sufficient of the gold-hued silk for the underdress left to duplicate the twins' original gowns; the material had been imported from New Kelvin by Valora when she was still Gustin IV and forgotten when she had departed. Nor would the strongly patterned green brocade look as elegant without the gold silk to balance it.

Pearl had gone into conference with her favorite dressmaker and they had worked out a compromise. The underdress was to be made of a pale yellow fabric onto which were appliquéd wherever the underdress would show fantastical sea creatures cut from the original gold silk. With something to balance the sea-green brocade, the rest of the bolt could be put to use— although Allister understood that it had taken some clever cutting on the part of the seamstresses to eke out enough fabric.

"I like these dresses so much better," he said, beaming at the girls. "The softer yellow brings out the roses in your cheeks."

Minnow tried to maintain her dignity, spinning so he could see the whimsical creatures decorating the undercoat. Anemone was less concerned about such things. She hugged him, causing his body servant to swallow a sigh as she crushed the king's own elegant attire.

Pearl joined them last, allowing the girls an uninterrupted moment with their father while her maid carefully set her crown in place among her elegantly styled tresses.

Although her gown had been ruined as well, Pearl, at least, had not needed to match anyone. A court gown from her existing wardrobe sufficed, but determined not to have Bright Bay look poor in Hawk Haven's eyes, the queen had spent much of the journey out stitching tiny pearls onto the chosen gown's bodice and skirt. Her hours of labor in the jolting carriage had resulted in a shimmering confection of white over rose that enhanced her own warm coloring.

Allister felt unreasonably proud of his family—unreasonable because he knew better than anyone that gem-encrusted gowns and crowns did not make queens and princesses, but proud because these honors were gracing his women.

A bell chiming summons as his valet set his own crown in place saved the king from saying anything embarrassingly sentimental.

The large hall in which the wedding was to be held was a solid stone-walled room without any of the sorcerous embellishments that graced the Sphere Chamber in Revelation Point Castle. Nor were the stone walls warmed by tapestries as might have been expected. King Tedric had confided to Allister that Sir Dirkin Eastbranch had insisted on stripping away anything beneath which an assassin might hide.

Steward Silver had used holly and ivy, the former bright with scarlet berries, to soften the bare stone, but even so the long room held nothing that could match the magical trapped-within-a-pearl mood of the Sphere Chamber.

Perhaps all for the good, Allister reflected. *There is a security and comfort in solid stone.*

Shortly before the ceremony began, the guests filed in. Each had been checked for weapons. Not even the most highly ranked had been permitted attendants. Therefore the mood was tense with suppressed indignation and excitement.

When the orchestra began to play a stately march, the musicians didn't sound as polished as they should. King Allister knew that this was because their membership was heavily salted with soldiers loyal to the king. Last night's musicians had been—at least early on—professionals, but at that occasion the waiters and serving maids had been drawn from Hawk Haven's military.

King Tedric wasn't taking any more chances than he must.

When Sapphire processed in, following the long train of her attendants, the bride proved lovely. She wore a dress that had been given to her by her grandmother the duchess and that some whispered had belonged to Queen Zorana the Great.

The groom wore his second-best naval uniform.

And despite all the preparations and worries—or perhaps because of them—the wedding proceeded without incident. This time the amulet bag was sewn shut without disturbance, the witnesses cried their acclaim without any scream of horror breaking the joyful accord.

Prince Shad and Princess Sapphire were wed before representatives of their assembled peoples.

And now, thought King Allister, *I hope and pray that they will indeed live happily ever after—both for their own sakes and for the peace they can bring to our kingdoms.*

DERIAN FELT DISTINCTLY out of place at the wedding reception—all the more so when he saw Ox standing solemn guard at one of the doorways, Valet circulating with smooth grace offering wine to the guests, Race puffing away on his flute in the second row of the orchestra.

That's where I belong, he thought, *with the trusted servants, guarding and supporting, but not out here pretending to be a person in my own right. I wish I could run off like Firekeeper did.*

He felt terribly awkward when Lady Elise came gliding toward him in her beautiful gown, but the anxious expression in her wide sea-green eyes set him paradoxically at his ease.

"Derian," she said in hurried tones so soft as to be almost a whisper, "I must . . . I need . . . Can we talk?"

For a horrible moment, Derian thought that as once before Elise had suffered an enchantment that restricted her ability to speak freely. The young woman must have intuited his concern, for she managed a wry smile.

"No, I *can* talk—I'm just . . . well . . . worried and I'm not sure that this is the place to talk, but I need . . ." She grabbed him on one forearm. "Come and walk with me in the garden.

It will be cold outside, but no one should miss me for a few minutes."

Derian grinned. "And no one will be looking for me at all."

Elise looked embarrassed.

"I didn't mean it that way," she said indignantly. "Simply put, your parents aren't here wanting you to dance with this important person or say something flattering to that important person."

Derian opened a door that—from last summer's sojourn in the castle—he knew led into a side garden.

The man guarding that particular door looked surprised that anyone would want to go out into the chilly afternoon, but he schooled his expression to polite neutrality. His job was to keep intruders out, not to monitor the guests' behavior, unless that behavior seemed to promise violence.

"No," Derian said to Elise as they stepped out into the late-autumn sunlight. "My parents are at home *hoping* that I'm talking to this important person and asking that important person to dance—but it's all right if I leave the party since I'm with you. They count you in the list of those who are pretty important."

Elise laughed, relieved to be teased.

"Walk with me. We can pretend to be looking at frost-frozen roses or ornamental kale or something."

Obediently, Derian took her arm. Elise was shivering slightly, but that might be from nerves. The fabric of her dress, as he knew from inspecting Firekeeper's similar garment, was quite heavy.

"Last night . . ."

Elise began her tale without further prologue and with a conciseness that was not typical of her. She told Derian how Baron Endbrook had slipped a note to Lady Melina, how Lady Melina had responded, about Elise's own suspicions.

"The worst thing of all," Elise concluded, "is that I don't know if I'm simply unwilling to trust the woman, and so I am spinning shawls out of fog and moon dust. It's just that after what we learned last autumn . . ."

Derian nodded his comprehension.

"We know that Lady Melina is capable of inflicting both pain and humiliation to achieve her ends," he said bluntly. "Next to that, what's a little political game-playing? The Isles aren't actually our enemies, really, just less than perfectly friendly neighbors."

Elise sighed.

"What should we do?" she asked, steering him back toward the door.

Derian frowned. "Off the cuff, I'd say we should see where both Lady Melina and Baron Endbrook go when the festivities are over. That won't be easy, but it won't be impossible. Almost everyone is stabling something or other with my parents' stable—or through people we've contracted with. I can use that for checking. And you can talk to Citrine—cautiously, of course."

"Citrine?" Elise was puzzled, clearly wondering why he would suggest involving an eight-year-old.

"Rumor says," Derian smiled a touch slyly, "that Ruby and Opal are going to winter at Revelation Point Castle but that Citrine is not. Presumably, she is staying with her mother and so will have an idea of Lady Melina's plans."

Elise showed her astonishment.

"How could you know that already? It was only announced yesterday afternoon!"

"Jet Shield looked into having a family sled reupholstered—or more specifically, he sent a servant to do so," Derian replied a trace smugly. "The servant explained that the young ladies were going south for the winter, but that their mother wanted them to have their own light flyer for attending parties and such."

"Amazing!"

The guard held the door for them. Elise smiled her thanks. Derian nodded and, when he was almost past, winked slyly at the man. After all, the obvious reason for going walking with a pretty girl *wasn't* to discuss intrigue and conspiracy.

Derian escorted Elise to the hall where Baron Archer was—without making it too obvious—clearly looking for his daughter.

"You're wanted," Derian said, releasing his light hold on Elise's arm. "I see that dance cards are coming out. Doubtless your father wishes you to make yourself available to dance with some of those important people you mentioned."

Elise looked as if she was tempted to stick her tongue out at him, but all she said in parting was:

"Tell Doc. He's smart and . . ."

And, Derian thought without rancor as he watched Elise take her father's arm and give him a winning smile, *you like him in a way you don't like me, but that's just fine. I'm happy to have you as a friend.*

He felt infinitely cheered, no longer out of place—not because, he realized to his amazement, someone had given him a job, but because Elise had reminded him that he was at this function because some people valued him for himself.

Whistling would have been out of place, but Derian nearly did so as he strolled along the edge of what would become a dance floor but was now thronged with the mingling guests.

Here and there women were fluttering elegantly printed dance cards threaded on satin ribbons. To be invited to this wedding at all, one needed to have some political or social connections, but being noble-born didn't make all women pretty or young or popular. Many of those would be worried that their cards would remain empty, but for a token dance from some generous relative.

Derian liked to dance and he had no lady or patron to flatter. After watching the ebb and flow for a moment, he checked his own card for the names of some of the earlier dances. Then he walked up to a rather plain woman in Merlin colors and bowed deeply.

"If I could have the honor, Lady," he said, "I was hoping you might have the Prancing Dapple open on your card. My name is Derian Carter. I have the honor to be a counselor to King Tedric."

The woman looked pleased to have been noticed, but she colored slightly. Derian had noted similar responses in much more humble settings. He guessed that her card was completely empty and that she was embarrassed to have him see that he was the first to ask her to dance.

He glanced away, signaled a waiter, and accepted two cups of punch. Taking this reprieve, the woman looked up from marking his name on her discreetly shielded card.

Handing her one of the punch cups, Derian pulled his own card from the pocket of his waistcoat.

"If I might have the honor of your name . . ."

He sketched it in—she proved to be a lesser scion of House Merlin, much as Doc was of House Kestrel. Then Derian bowed and thanked the woman in advance for the promised pleasure. Now that the preliminaries had started, Derian began enjoying himself.

As he cast around for another suitable partner, Derian felt a fleeting sorrow for Firekeeper. The wolf-woman did love to dance and here she was missing another ball. He hoped that wherever she was, she was happy and at least reasonably warm.

The rest of the reception flew by on—for him quite literally—dancing feet. He found that many ladies of title and prestige, including to his astonishment the elderly Duchess Kestrel and a giggling Princess Anemone, were quite pleased to hint that they would like a dance with him. Apparently his reputation as a dancer had proceeded him, quite possibly from the Bridgeton Ball that had provided the opening skirmishes of King Allister's War.

Derian was glad when Earl Kestrel offered him a ride home on the box of the Kestrel carriage. His feet were so tired that he would have limped if he had made the long walk home alone—not that the drivers of any of the dozen or more carriages hired from his parents' stables would have let him do so.

After a long afternoon that had begun with the wedding, moved into the reception, the first set of dances, a light supper, and then a second set of dancing, Derian was astonished upon arriving home to realize that the hour was not unduly late. Winter darkness combined with physical weariness had conspired to fool him into believing it at least midnight.

Coming into the house, he found his parents and Damita awake, playing cards by lanternlight.

"Tell us," Dami demanded, setting down what was clearly a winning hand, "all about it."

And he did, talking even while he eased off his boots and put his feet in the shallow pan of warm water that miraculously appeared. He was aware of Cook and the housemaid listening from the shadowy kitchen door, that old Toad, who had retired from driving and now helped with the household's heavier chores and around the stables, had emerged from his attic room and was listening at the top of the stairs.

Cook brought out hot peachy and thin wafer cookies to prompt Derian when he flagged and Vernita invited the servants to join the family circle. Brock woke about then and curled sleepily on the hearth rug, waking only fully to ask yet another question.

Derian did his best not to leave anything out, to describe the gowns, the uniforms, the jewels. He told of every dainty served, answered questions about the wines (very good, but not excellent) and whether the gentlemen had worn swords (no). He listed every dance he'd danced and with whom, and by the end of his recital, his throat was hoarse but his tiredness had vanished, replaced by a curious light-headedness.

The only thing he didn't share was what Elise had confided in him, but no one would have expected that from him—not even Cook, who was the most accomplished gossip in the marketplace.

When Derian finished, the hour was truly late, for the telling had taken nearly as long as the doing. Derian padded up to his room in his stocking feet and was just undressed and under the covers when there was a tap on his door, and Vernita entered. She sat on the edge of his bed as if for all the world he was still Brock's age.

"I just wanted you to know, Derian, that if running a stable or breeding blood horses is what you want, well that's fine with me and your father. We spoke seriously to you the other day about the possibilities open for your future, but never think we'd disown you or be disappointed if you chose another way."

She bent and kissed his forehead.

"We're proud of you, son."

For a moment, Derian didn't trust himself to speak. When he found his voice, he said a bit rustily, "I love you, too, Mother."

He thought about asking her about what Heather had said, about the baker and about lost romances, but by the time his tired brain could frame the questions, he had fallen sound asleep.

XIII

WHEN THE GLADE FILLED once again with the graceful and impressive figures of the Royal Beasts, the sky still held faint light, but the interwoven branches of the overarching trees sufficiently dampened the reddish glow so that it was as if shadows rather than substance kept company therein.

The first to pick up the tale was a Beast that Firekeeper had not noticed earlier in the day, a boar raccoon so burly and powerful that he might have been taken for a small bear. In the direct fashion of the Beasts, he did not waste breath on preamble, but took up the account precisely where the vixen had left off.

"And so we traded land for security and once we were gone from their ken, the humans preferred to forget our existence. A few adventurous types made forays into the mountains and occasionally beyond, coming after furs and such other things as humans treasure. Royal policy remained avoidance rather than confrontation, so those humans who returned told of thick forests, of untamed lands, of clear streams, but never of our kind."

The raccoon paused then and in the dim light Firekeeper, who knew how to see in the dark far better than did a human, could see him twisting and intertwining his dexterous black fingers as if undecided how best to continue.

Glancing about the glade, she saw signs of the same indecision and wondered at it. Before she could whisper a question into the One Female's ear, the puma gave an arrogant stretch and snapped his long, tawny tail against the rock.

"Much time passed," the puma said with a growling purr. "How much, we cannot say precisely, for Beasts do not record time as humans do. Moreover, our lives—though long by comparison with those of the Cousins—are often shorter than those of humans. We think of time in terms of seasons—the summer when the deer ran as fat and thick as blackberries in a thicket or the winter when the cold was so severe that even the water in the deepest lakes and fastest running rivers froze.

"Suffice to say that much time passed. We never forgot humans, but some of our fear abated, for they seemed content to stay east of the Iron Mountains and to fight among themselves rather than trouble us. We told our cubs and pups, fawns, piglets, and fledglings enough to keep them cautious, listened when the wingéd folk brought happy news of war or sorrowful news of wide-sailed ships, and returned to our ways.

"Then came the day a raven—or was it a crow?—brought a curious tale."

"It was a raven," said the raven, interrupting without fear of the long claws that suddenly unsheathed from the puma's paws and scraped against the rock. "And this part of the tale is mine."

The enormous black bird fluffed out the feathers on his legs and neck, made a seeming of ears grow upon his head, and strutted up and down in front of Firekeeper—a clownish yet somehow also frightening sight.

"The tale the raven brought was one of death," the raven croaked in a voice so ancient and hoarse that Firekeeper found herself convinced that *this* was the very raven who had borne the tale. "Death, but not from war, not from age, not even from murder or from intrigue. This was death from sickness—a sickness that spread with the speed of breath or touch, a sickness that caused the victim to burn from within not so much with fever but as if a secret fire that fed on the human spirit had been kindled within."

"We ravens watched freely and openly, for the deaths were so frequent and so plentiful that there was not a town or village, castle or cottage that lacked its flock of carrion eaters. Any who saw us glimpsed in our vast wingspans and triumphant swagger omens of their own deaths.

"Now you may ask," the raven said, turning a bright, beady eye on the listening wolf-woman, "were we not risking the wrath of the sorcerers? Initially, we were indeed chary of these, but some moonspans of watching taught us a great and wonderful thing. Those who burned fastest and brightest and who never ever recovered from the plague were those who practiced sorcery. From the merest apprentice to the mightiest wizard, they died.

"The talented fared somewhat better, but among these too—as far as we could tell—not a one escaped the sickness. Some of these, however, did mend. Nor did those without any hint of magical gift escape the plague, but among them it was more likely to leave behind battered, broken, and shaken souls who—if they escaped further illness, starvation, or murder at the hands of the wild ones who, seeing death all around, forgot law—then they might live."

The One Female rubbed her muzzle against Firekeeper's arm, for the feral woman had started to tremble at this cool account of chaos.

Firekeeper understood now why the humans always spoke of the plague in hushed voices and hurried on to other subjects. Even as a thing many more than a hundred years gone, it was terrible to contemplate.

She suspected, too, why there was so little magical talent among the Great Houses of Hawk Haven and—as far as she knew—Bright Bay and elsewhere. The plague had killed those with sorcery, weakened those with a trace of talent, and left those without either to rise to power.

Fleetingly, she wondered if Zorana the Great, so revered in Hawk Haven, had been among those the Royal Beasts termed the "wild ones," the forgetters of law, but further speculation on this must wait, for a crow had taken up the tale from the raven.

It cawed loudly as if realizing that Firekeeper's attention had fled, and said:

"Seeing how the Fire Plague touched those with talent, we feared for ourselves and our own, since—as you know—talents occur among Royal Kind. But these fears proved rootless. Even those among the ravens and crows who had dined on the flesh of sorcerers killed by the plague—a thing we did with enthusiasm and glee before we realized there might be danger of contagion—even these remained firm and fit and healthy.

"After much time, the Fire Plague burned itself to ashes and was no more seen, but by then the world had been transformed. The population of humans in this land had been reduced to a quarter of its former size—not all by plague, but by the attendant menaces the raven has already mentioned as well. There were no sorcerers remaining in the land and an aversion to sorcery in any form—extending in some places to even the relatively innocent talents—had become universal among humanity.

"Moreover, the Old Country rulers who had once dominated these colonies fled early in the plague cycle. Perhaps they hoped for healing in their homelands—for by all reports the use of magic there was so prevalent as to make what we saw here seem nothing. If so, they were disappointed, for the Fire Plague had burned more fiercely in those lands.

"However, we crows believe that they fled because many of them had been cruel and contemptuous rulers, and they feared the retribution of their subject peoples even more than they feared the plague. Those foreign-born who remained were more likely to die, though whether this was because they possessed more latent magic or whether they were simply less hearty, having had others to perform all labor for them, is a matter we never have resolved."

"Or," muttered the bear, "cared to resolve. It was enough to have them gone."

A jay took up the narrative as if the bear's interruption had been intended.

"Indeed, we cared not a dry berry husk. Other questions were raised at our councils—practically from the moment that we realized the extent of the plague and what it was likely to do to our onetime enemies.

"The foremost of these questions was whether we should finish what the plague had begun. Should we wipe humans from the face of the land? There was much contention on this point, but in the end the lesson of the songbirds was recalled and the council decided to let humans live as they had lived before—with one exception.

"One of the things that had made sorcery so terrible to us was that its power could be separated from its creator. We decided that these objects of power could not be left in human hands, that we would steal them, one and all, and . . ."

There was a slight awkward pause, and once again Fire-keeper felt that something was being held back.

"And," chattered on the jay with perhaps a trace too much haste, "so keep them from being used against us in the future when humans might have forgotten their fear of sorcery. We were helped in this course by the humans themselves. Many a sorcerer's stronghold was burnt from the library outward, many a wand or staff was tossed into the flames. Still, there was work for us to do."

The One Female spoke. "Nor did we larger creatures leave all the thieving to the jays and crows and ravens. Royal Wolf packs crossed the mountains for the first time in living memory. We hunted down those bandits who had taken booty from their dead masters and when the bandits were dead themselves our wingéd allies bore away the spoils. Pumas hung from tree limbs and screamed from crags so that horses fled in terror. Herds of elk blockaded armies, braving arrows and spears to hold them. Clever-fingered raccoons and sly foxes slipped into camps and cottages, and removed artifacts tied into bags and boxes.

"Doubtless we took things that were not sorcerous in nature, for it was then a rare talent among us to be able to scent magic. Doubtless innocent books were consigned to flames, but we wished to be thorough.

"Even then," the One Female contined, "we had heard rumors of what Gustin Sailor possessed, but he had fled to a stronghold and always had an army about him. Since his contention with his former allies was over those very objects, Gustin Sailor took care never to let them leave his keeping, for he could not trust that Zorana Shield might not force or bribe someone to steal the enchanted artifacts from him."

"When," added the doe almost kindly, "the Royal Beasts saw no indication of magic being used by this first Gustin or the Gustins who followed him or indeed by any in his court or household, we thought the rumors were as dry grass: filling, but without solid sustenance. We thought that he—as had many of our own—might have been fooled by a certain shine or elegance in crafting into believing that such an ornate thing must be sorcerous."

"And," asked Firekeeper, "do you know otherwise now?"

The doe said honestly, "We do not, but we fear lest there be truth in the tales. Queen Valora—according to our spies— is an angry woman, one who would unleash a rabid dog even at the risk of being bitten herself. She has never seen the Fire Plague, has only a faint dread of magic. Now, like the sorcerers of old, she may see only a means to power, to domination of those who bested her, and to rulership."

"Your spies?" Firekeeper asked.

"The wingéd folk," screeched an eagle with pride, "have not let humans go completely unobserved. We resist being taken captive—though this has happened from time to time— but as you have already been told, we continue to watch. During this last war our spies knew where Queen Gustin IV lurked, letting others fight her battles, and we knew the fury she concealed at being stripped of her place."

Without much hope, Firekeeper said, "Cannot your own

agents steal these objects? I cannot cross the ocean without being noticed, nor can I walk into the queen's stronghold. What about the clever-fingered raccoons or the sly foxes or those famous thieves—the ravens and crows?"

Murmurs rose at this protest and Firekeeper realized that some of the Royal Beasts were no more pleased by her possible involvement than she was herself. Murmurs became roars and screeches, howls and hoots and growls.

Perceiving that the council had degenerated into unredeemable argument, the raven adjourned the meeting again, this time until midmorning, so as to permit time for sleeping and hunting.

Shortly before dawn, when she had fed and run and chased some of the fear from her soul, Firekeeper curled herself for sleep between the warm bodies of the One Female and Blind Seer.

The blue-eyed wolf, who had listened to all that had been said but had held his tongue as was proper for a young wolf in the company of his elders, now asked his first question:

"Mother, what is the lesson of the songbirds?"

"Hush," the One Female said, lifting her silver-furred head and scanning the forest with amber eyes. "This is not the time or place for *that* tale. Ask another night and I may tell you, though in truth it belongs to the lore of the Ones."

Wolf-obedient, Blind Seer submitted to her wisdom— knowing as always that it was backed up by the threat of her fangs.

Firekeeper wondered some as she drifted off to sleep, but her mind was so full of new thoughts that she could not hold another.

WINTER OR NOT, the royal contingent from Bright Bay did not leave Eagle's Nest the moment the wedding celebrations were concluded. Indeed, the weather took one of those turns toward bright days and sunshine that often happen in early winter, the type of weather that causes the optimists to predict a mild winter and the pessimists to grumble about threats of summer drought.

Instead, there followed a whirl of parties, receptions, balls, and banquets that would be talked about for years to come. Everyone was giddy with the promise of peace after a century of intermittent war—or at least everyone acted as if this was so.

Certainly there were those among the dancers and diners who must be less than happy with the changes that had been made and changes that were to come, but these had the sense to keep their mouths shut. Most of these, in fact, were more interested in finding out how they could best benefit from the new order—if new order there was to be—without sacrificing the prerogatives they had claimed under the old.

As a member of the official diplomatic contingent accompanying Duke Marek of Half-Moon Island, Baron Endbrook was invited practically everywhere. He used his time well, mostly making business contacts for his shipping fleet, for he found many of Hawk Haven's noble-born were almost pathetically enchanted with the sea, as is so often the case when a thing is alien and strange.

However, Waln also found opportunity to speak with the diplomats from New Kelvin. Even in their homeland, the New Kelvinese's peculiar manner of dress and facial ornamentation—which was echoed to greater or lesser degree through all levels of society—had been astonishing. Here in Hawk Haven, where even a lady's cosmetics were styled to look as natural as possible, the New Kelvinese seemed to belong to another race.

And that may be their intention, the baron thought, *given their damned superior attitude—though if that was the case, they wouldn't bother with the stuff at home, would they?*

The custom followed by both men and women of the New Kelvinese upper classes—at least Waln thought they were the upper classes—of shaving the hair at the front of their heads, back to just before the tops of their ears, and wearing the hair long behind conferred a curious androgyny.

This androgynous appearance was assisted by the ornate, floor-length robes the New Kelvinese wore. These gorgeous garments were usually silk and often heavily embroidered. However, the weight of the fabric and the cut of the robe masked all but the most obvious physical cues to gender.

The New Kelvinese diplomats—there were three in the group—all affected a mincing gait, rather as if their curly-tipped shoes were too tight. It should have looked funny, but instead conferred a peculiar dignity—something like the stiltedly deliberate walk of a praying mantis.

Happily for Waln, the New Kelvinese were known throughout the region as purveyors of goods that could be found nowhere else. Best known, of course, were their silks and carpets, but they also sold herbs and powders. Some of these were medicinal, but others seemed to serve no purpose but to induce strange dreams and visions. And then there was their glass—a difficult item to ship, but worth the effort for its fine, clear colors.

Since Duke Marek had styled Waln as the Isle's Minister for Trade, the baron's frequent conversations with the New Kelvinese excited no comment. During these meetings, they promised him accommodations upon his arrival, gave him maps with the best routes to Dragon's Breath from Hawk Haven marked out, and smiled darkly when he refused to name who he was bringing with him.

Of course the bastards know, Waln thought in annoyance. *They couldn't fail to know—as Queen Valora herself said, there simply aren't many who are willing to claim knowledge of the sorcerous arts.*

Momentarily, a suspicion flickered into his mind that this entire intrigue was a charade to get him to escort Lady Melina to New Kelvin. He dismissed the idea as idiotic. If the New Kelvinese wanted her to come, all they needed to do was invite her. Her fervent interest in their land and its secrets had been obvious.

To comfort himself, Waln Endbrook dreamed of a dukedom. He'd settle for Dog Island, where he had been born, and if any there thought to call him "Walnut" . . .

He smirked as he thought about the things he could do with a title and a queen behind him.

❦

ELISE COULDN'T DECIDE whether the huge stack of invitations that arrived by every post, as well as by hand, was a welcome or unwelcome distraction from the darker concerns haunting her.

Some were very welcome, such as the one from Duchess Kestrel, for Elise could be fairly certain that both Derian and Jared would be present at that gathering.

Another one that she welcomed was from Jet Shield on behalf of his mother and himself. Elise knew that her parents were astonished that Elise accepted, for she had avoided Jet as much as possible since their engagement had been broken and she couldn't help but feel a bit guilty when Aurella patted her hand approvingly.

"I really had thought," Aurella said, "that we would need to drag you there and that then you would make excuses to leave as soon as possible."

Elise colored and looked at the tips of her shoes.

"Mother, I was an idiot about Jet—I know that now and I'm determined not to make another mistake. Like him or not—and I don't—Jet is the crown princess's brother. Never mind that Sapphire is technically King Tedric's daughter now. No one is going to forget her birth family—just like there are those who will never believe that Lady Blysse is not his granddaughter."

Aurella patted Elise's hand. "I'm proud of you. You've grown a great deal wiser about such things than you were last summer."

"I've learned at a hard school," Elise replied a trace bitterly, "and had a good teacher in your example. You've never forgotten that Queen Elexa is your aunt and our family has benefitted from that."

"It doesn't hurt," Aurella replied mildly, "that I like Aunt Elexa, but, yes, I've been aware all my life that if I was to give my children—my child—any advantages I should cultivate that relationship."

The sorrow that touched Aurella's delicate features when she mentioned "children"—a reference to Elise's stillborn siblings—made Elise hold her tongue when her mother moved the conversation to a less pleasant topic.

"Elise, on the matter of attachments," Aurella dipped her needle through her embroidery canvas as she spoke, "your father and I have been concerned that you are forming another."

Elise swallowed hard, knowing what lecture was about to come.

"Sir Jared," Aurella said, as if unaware that the name on her lips sent an odd mixture of defiance and joy through Elise, "is by all accounts a good, brave, and intelligent man. He is well connected by birth and seems to have won the favor of both of the heirs apparent. Moreover, the talent with which he is blessed seems to say that he has found favor with his ancestors."

Her needle dipped and rose as relentlessly her analysis continued:

"However, Sir Jared is landless and without immediate prospects in that direction. The Surcliffes hold poor land and though they are gaining some reputation for their wines, they show no sign of becoming anything but a solid trade family.

"In short," Aurella looked up and met her daughter's eyes, "he is not the man we would wish you to marry."

Elise rubbed her hands across her face and said in tones not convincing even to herself, "I never said I wanted to marry him," and then even more defiantly, "and he has never even hinted at such thoughts."

"He wouldn't," Aurella said, needle rising and falling once more. "He is a gentleman in the truest sense of the word. He knows your station is above his own and would never insult you by suggesting a liaison. You would need to be the one to propose and even then you would probably meet resistance."

Elise started. It had never occurred to her that Jared wouldn't offer for her. She had even daydreamed something along those lines: *"My love, I have nothing to offer you but my heart and adoration. Even so, I beg you for permission to ask your father for your hand . . ."*

Her indignant snort was for her own idiocy, but Aurella— quite reasonably—took it as meant for herself.

"Your father and I are all too aware of how little a barony may come to be in the new kingdom of Bright Haven—a project we support with all our faith. The land your father inherited from his father has been borderland. Were it not that the Barren runs rough, we would have seen much fighting there. Even so, you have seen the graveyard."

Recovering herself, Elise nodded.

"Peace means that our lands—rather than being on the edge of a contested river—will be in the middle of a prosperous kingdom. We have already begun to toy with the idea of canals to bypass the roughest reaches, but such would take money beyond our small treasury. Agreements could be reached with our neighbors to expand the canals into a great network. Indeed, we are fortunate that much of the land is held by the Crown, which should favor such development, for it would increase their revenues from what are now tenant farms."

Caught in this vision for the future, Aurella forgot her embroidery. Her hands sketched maps in the air and she seemed quite the girl.

"My father might grant us some funds in return for a promise of return to House Peregrine, but a far surer source of support would be one made through a marriage alliance on the part of the future heir of House Archer."

"Me," Elise said flatly.

"You," Aurella agreed. "Arranged marriages are not bad things. Your father has been good to me, even when it became clear that I could only bear him one child. The Archer Barony has prospered—as you yourself have seen—from its ties not only to House Peregrine, but to the royal family."

"And now it's my turn," Elise said.

"You need to consider what you would be giving up if you married a relatively penniless man," Aurella said. "This barony will be your responsibility. Even if your father and I manage to build the canals, you will need to upkeep them. Consider the importance of an alliance. Earl Kestrel may favor his cousin, but he has children of his own, and what of his treasury can be spared from the duchy will go to support them and their projects."

Elise bit her lip. Responsibility to her land had been drummed into her from as long as she could remember. Her father had walked her barefoot through the newly plowed fields, boated with her on the little streams, introduced her to all their tenant farmers, and made her attend every possible naming, wedding, and betrothal.

The Archer Barony was not poor, but it was not as prosperous as lands managed by those with greater resources. Could she ignore the needs of her tenants merely because she found it easy to talk to Jared?

"I understand, Mother," Elise said at last. "I really do."

"One more thing," her mother said. "Your options are not limited to Hawk Haven any longer. Bright Bay has its Great Houses and these often lack land, for their wealth has come from the sea. There will be many a house happy to ally with a landed house—even of lesser rank—and to shower their monies into its development.

"I am very glad that you have agreed to go to so many of the social events surrounding the royal wedding. While you are there, I want you to get to know as many of the people here from Bright Bay as possible. It could well be to our advantage."

Elise tried to smile.

"I'll do that, Mother," she promised.

Later that day, between a card party and a dinner, she stole into the small room where their family shrine hung. It was a duplicate of the one at home. The ancestral masks hung on the sides. The back was decorated with an ornate and detailed map of their lands. Elise studied that map for a long time, filling in from memory the faces of the tenants, the sound of the Barren as it rushed over rocks, the silence of the graveyard.

That last stayed with her. Those who were buried there—including her grandfather Purcel—had given so much for Hawk Haven and for the Archer family.

Could she give less?

XIV

DERIAN FOUND THE DAYS subsequent to the royal wedding pleasant ones. The weather was an ancestral blessing, making working at the stables a joy—sunny enough to feel warm, cool enough that there were no flies.

Waking in his own room with the bottle window and his initials carved into the doorframe seemed nicer than being waited on by servants in any of the castles in which he'd stayed. The smell of burnt sugar as Cook sprinkled the breakfast bread, the sound of his mother and Damita arguing about the appropriateness of her current outfit, even Brock bursting in to show Derian the progress of his latest effort at wood-carving were better than plush tapestries and vintage wines.

Derian came to a tentative peace with his parents' expectations. This was not out of any nobility in his own soul, but because he realized that he was indeed a different person than the young man who had ventured out with Earl Kestrel the previous spring and that he now had very different options open to him. The young man he had been the spring before had been full of prickly pride and quick to take offense—even if that offense had remained unvoiced—at slights real and imagined.

Firekeeper had been a large part of the change, Derian

mused. While he had been teaching her, she had been teaching him.

The wolf-woman's fierce loyalty to those who deserved her respect, her open scorn for those she despised might not be safe reactions, but they were honest. Derian now found that he sometimes tried to examine issues as she might and chuckled to himself as he imagined himself trying to explain to her why he resisted taking on a job with some noble patron.

Derian: "I have my place here at home with my family. Why should I go elsewhere?"

Firekeeper: "Young wolves have pack, but still they disperse."

Derian (stubbornly): "But, why should I? I have everything I need here."

Firekeeper: "And you need nothing else? You no get things from going elsewhere?"

Derian (exasperated): "Of course I have." (Thinks, almost guiltily, of the ruby counselor's ring glowing with soft fire in his family's shrine.)

Firekeeper: "Wolves have sharp fangs and thick fur. I have neither so I use these." (Gestures to clothing and to belt knife.) "I think not dispersing be like me biting with dull human teeth—I can if I must, but it is stupid if can have knife."

Derian (thinking aloud): "And the things I can learn, the people I can meet—not to mention the tokens I can earn—those are all like knives. If I stay here, I'm biting the challenges of the future with dull human teeth when I could have had knives."

Firekeeper (looking slightly puzzled as she often does when confronting a long speech): "Yes. In human world there is not just One Male, One Female—there are many who are Ones. It isn't reasonable, but it is so. If you would be a wolf among rabbits, you need to have fangs."

Derian, who had been currying the sorrel riding horse belonging to King Allister as he framed this mental dialogue, laughed to himself with such gusto that the horse's ears flicked back as if asking what the joke might be.

Firekeeper might say what Derian had just imagined; she

might also say that if Derian could rule his pack, why did he want to be a lesser wolf elsewhere?

"The point is," Derian said, continuing his mental dialogue, *"I don't rule 'my pack'—not yet and not for a long time if the ancestors are kind and can do without my parents for a while. That being the case, what I'm really saying when I say I want to stay here and work with the family business is that I want to stay a child. And while that might be nice for a while, I'd hate myself before long."*

Having reached this temporary truce with himself, Derian dove with true enthusiasm into both his work for his family and his private project for Elise. He confided some of the details of the latter to his father, knowing that Colby had learned so much from other people's gossip that he eschewed the vice himself.

"What I'm trying to learn, Father," Derian said one morning as they walked out to the stables, "is if this man, Waln—or any of his associates—is making plans for an unannounced journey. How do you think I can find out without being obvious?"

Colby scratched his head, a gesture he had affected for so many years in his self-appointed role of simple stable man that it had become habit.

"Well, he hasn't made arrangements with me, son," Colby replied, "though the horses the diplomats from the Isles rode here from Bright Bay are in our stables, but then, if Baron Waln is involved in skulduggery he might not want to work through us—you being connected to the Crown and all. Yet he's not local and the Horse Fair won't be until the spring."

That was a long speech for Colby Carter and he fell silent as they continued on through a more crowded portion of the streets. When they had passed through the wall and were in more open country again, Colby said:

"Your man'll want to hire and, even if the lady you mentioned is involved, he won't want any trace of her involvement. That rules out using her family's mounts."

Derian offered his own partly formed plan. "I'd thought to

check the other livery stables, but I hadn't worked out how to ask without making clear what I was doing."

Colby brightened. "Tell them you're asking because the same gent came asking us and we think he's trying to undercut local business and tie up resources. He's a foreigner and we can use that to our advantages. Don't be too coy—be indignant."

Grinning, Derian slapped his father on the shoulder.

"That's the very thing!"

He went to it that very day, using the excuse of going around to the various stables to collect Prancing Steed Stables' portion of the stabling fees so that his visit would seem even less obvious.

Luck wasn't with him on his first few stops. Happily, neither was the resentment he had thought he might meet in his role as fee collector. The flush of business at what should have been the beginning of the slow season—combined with the fact that gentle-born patrons stood for a higher tariff than did the merchants who usually would have provided the bulk of trade—made for good humor all around.

This continued as Derian passed on to the smaller stables and carting establishments. For these he could not use the excuse of collecting the Prancing Steed's share, but he'd worked out a ruse involving asking after their available space and resources—implying but never promising that the Carters might be bringing business their way.

And I'm not precisely lying, Derian comforted himself, *for if the plans Mother and Father have for expanding our business into Bright Bay come through, we will indeed need extra hands.*

He ended each spiel with a variation on the same theme.

"We've heard—and in fact my mother intends to bring the matter before the guild next meeting—that some of our foreign guests don't understand fair trade. There's one fellow—and I won't name names, just say that he's a big man from across the water—who's been going around promising his business to several stables. The word is that he's getting the best price he can by offering a solid commitment, but . . ."

And here Derian let his voice drop. "The thing I've heard is that he's offered that commitment to more than one stable!"

Eventually, Derian got the information he needed and as he pieced together the picture his respect for Baron Waln rose a notch.

Waln had indeed made contracts with several stables, but never for more than two animals. In this way he had acquired three good horses—these trained for either riding or hauling, a brace of pack mules, and a light wagon that converted with comparative ease to sleigh runners.

Along with the last Waln had contracted for a driver, the promise being that the man would be paid for a round trip in advance and if he proved satisfactory he'd be given the wagon in the bargain.

Smart, Derian thought admiringly, *for he's buying the man's loyalty as well as his services and since Baron Endbrook doubtless plans to return to the Isles, he won't care to ship the sleigh home.*

To each of these businesses—whether the owners expressed indignation or the sly satisfaction of those who felt they had a good deal done and to perdition with anyone else—Derian suggested that they keep their part of the bargain and let the unnamed foreigner break the deal. Then the guild could step in and take punitive action.

The various guilds spread their influence throughout both Hawk Haven and Bright Bay. Since the Isles had been until recently a part of Bright Bay, they also fell under standard guild rules and regulations. At times of all but full-fledged war, the guilds had actually served as a form of international government, maintaining standards between the two nations.

No one expected them to do otherwise now that the labeling on the map had changed. A carter, therefore, could expect that a broken contract would be avenged.

Derian finished his rounds with a firm sense of pleasure at a job well done.

The information he had gathered confirmed Elise's guess that Baron Endbrook—and quite possibly Lady Melina—

planned a journey somewhere other than back home to the Isles. The question remained—where?

Derian studied a mental map of the region, working out possibilities.

At this time of year, the southern reaches of Hawk Haven—in which Port Haven itself lay—might or might not see snow. A wagon capable of sleigh conversion would be overkill—especially since the post road between the capital and the port boasted several establishments where a wagon could be traded for a sleigh if the weather turned ugly.

In any case, Derian had already learned from his father that the diplomatic contingent from the Isles had arranged to hire riding horses and a baggage wagon all the way to Port Haven. Therefore, Waln wasn't making those arrangements—not that Derian had really thought he was.

In the northern sections of Hawk Haven, however, as the post-riders already reported, snowfall was becoming regular. A sleigh-convertible wagon would be a good idea, since it would be difficult to say in what condition the roads might be.

Derian reported his findings to Elise and Doc during a quiet moment at the Kestrel ball, the only one of the numerous post-wedding festivities to which he had been invited. The trio had retired to a private room that Doc, as a resident guest of the household, secured for them.

As Derian talked, he noticed that Elise seemed tense and unnaturally stiff, especially when she greeted Doc. Inwardly he sighed, sensing yet another development in that undeclared romantic drama.

Derian finished his report by saying, "I plan to find that wagon driver if I can. His name is Orin Driver, called Fox since his father has the same name but belongs to the Hummingbird Society. Fox is a bit of a scoundrel—as might be expected of someone who'd take a job which anyone could guess must be a bit shady. Still, I may be able to get him a touch drunk and learn the route they're taking."

Doc nodded his approval.

"Good. Now, I think you're right in guessing that Waln is

planning on taking a trip north. If we rule out a meeting with someone in Hawk Haven, he's going either into New Kelvin or Waterland. Waterland is a possibility, but not my favorite."

"Why rule out Hawk Haven?" Derian asked.

"Because he could meet almost anyone in Hawk Haven more easily and with less fuss here in Eagle's Nest. The royal wedding itself is excuse enough for a journey here."

"I'll buy that," Derian said, "so you prefer New Kelvin."

"I do, but let's rule out Waterland first." Doc gestured as if he was writing. "Rather like diagnosis of an illness, don't you see? We rule out the less likely and then we have a better idea what is likely. Then we can find a way to treat the illness."

The knight glanced at Elise and the young woman managed a tepid smile.

"Right," Doc continued. "Now, Waterland certainly seems a possibility. One, the assassins who attacked at the first wedding were from Waterland. Two, Waterland has been—until recent events—an enemy of Bright Bay and an ally of Hawk Haven. It is still unclear what new alliances they might find profitable. It could be that Baron Endbrook is going there to plead his country's case."

Elise stopped looking wan and tense long enough to protest, "But the Isles have long sheltered pirates and privateers! Waterland wouldn't make an alliance with them!"

Doc grinned. "They would if those same pirates and privateers could be turned against Bright Bay's shipping rather than Waterland's. Remember, Waterland traditionally chooses the course that leads to the greatest financial profit."

"That is true," she admitted, relaxing now that they were discussing international relations—one of her favorite subjects.

Doc continued his diagnosis.

"Both of these reasons can explain why Waln might go to Waterland, but we are left with several reasons to discount them. One, as an Islander, he would probably choose to go by sea."

"Even at this time of year?" Derian asked, with a landsman's distrust of ocean tempers.

"I think so, but," Doc said, showing a trace uncertainty, "I could be wrong. My second reason is stronger. What advantage would he gain in taking Lady Melina to Waterland?"

"None that I can see," Elise said, "but there *would* be a possible advantage in taking her to New Kelvin. She is known to have great interest in things sorcerous and they nearly worship the old ways."

"Just my thought, Lady," Doc said enthusiastically. "Moreover, the waistcoat Baron Endbrook wore to the wedding was made of intricately figured New Kelvinese silk—a kind they do not usually export but that is sold in markets in Dragon's Breath. I have seen the like on traders coming from New Kelvin to wine-fests."

"That's a slim thing on which to base a judgment," Derian protested.

"True," Doc said, "but I do find it interesting that—as far as I can tell—Baron Endbrook is pretending relative ignorance of New Kelvin."

"That *is* interesting," Elise mused, "and combined with his interest in Lady Melina . . ."

"It may just mark his destination," Derian interrupted, forgetting protocol in his eagerness. "It fits nicely in with the convertible wagon I mentioned earlier. New Kelvin is north and west of here. The likelihood of snow will be greater."

"Crossing the White Water River from Hawk Haven is one way into New Kelvin," Doc added. "It still isn't precisely simple, but there are recognized crossings."

"I hadn't realized," Derian said uneasily, "that we were so vulnerable on that border."

"Oh, we're not," Elise said distractedly, speaking like one whose thoughts are mostly elsewhere. "The White Water has cut deep canyons and the ice is broken by rocks that make for treacherous spots that freeze and thaw unpredictably. Still, as Sir Jared says, there are ferry points and much of our trade with New Kelvin crosses during the winter months."

"Thank you, m'lady," Derian said.

He tried to sound flippant—afraid her serious mood would return—but genuine respect crept into his voice. After all,

Elise's own lands were all the way across Hawk Haven from the White Water. Who would ever have guessed she'd know so much about distant lands?

Elise smiled and seemed to come back to the present moment.

"I enjoy such things, Derian. Now, I rather agree with Sir Jared that New Kelvin seems more likely than Waterland—especially if Lady Melina is involved. I seem to recall my mother saying that she—Lady Melina—went there when she was about my age and talked about the journey for a long time after."

"A return trip in itself, then," Derian said excitedly, "might be reason enough for her to link up with the baron."

"True," Elise said slowly. "Lady Melina and Lord Rolfston's family has never had as much money as the gems and fancy horses might seem to indicate. I heard rumor that the estate Jet is taking over carries a good deal of debt.

"But," Elise continued after a moment, "a pleasure trip would not be reason for the baron being so secretive—unless he fears his wife learning and social scandal. I'm afraid I will continue to think the worst of Lady Melina."

Doc nodded gravely. "A wise thing to do. However, the fact that we can all think of reasons why Lady Melina might legitimately travel with Baron Endbrook, and the fact that neither New Kelvin nor the Isles are our declared enemies . . ."

"Remember, the New Kelvinese got plenty pissy when we went to Bright Bay's aid against Stonehold," Derian reminded him.

"But they never declared war nor sent aid to our enemies," Doc said.

"At least," he added, "that I know."

He glanced at Elise as he said this and the young woman shook her head.

"No, not that I have heard either. Am I correct in thinking that you feel, Sir Jared, that the evidence we have to support our suspicions is, as of yet, fairly flimsy?"

She didn't sound affronted—as she would have had the

right to do, given that she was the one who had started suspecting Baron Endbrook—merely interested.

"Not at all, Lady Elise," Doc replied levelly, "simply that we have knowledge of Lady Melina's character that most do not and since we are sworn not to share that knowledge we are in something of a bind."

"I agree with you," Elise said. "That's why I spoke with the two of you rather than my parents. My mother may not particularly like Lady Melina, but she thinks of her as a charlatan. As far as I know, my father doesn't consider Lady Melina much at all—except as sister to a traitor and another failed competitor for the throne."

"Faint praise," Derian said, needling her deliberately, "for your confidants, eh?"

Elise colored and seemed for a moment the same lovely and uncomplicated girl he had mooned over for a time the previous summer. Then a certain gravity settled on her features once more.

"I trust you," she said firmly, "both of you, like the brothers I never had. Is that praise enough?"

Derian grinned. "Better."

"We can't stay closeted here much longer without causing comment," Elise said. "What do we do to get more evidence?"

"I'll do what I can to make acquaintances among the New Kelvinese diplomats," Doc offered. "It isn't easy. I know because I've already tried—I'm honestly interested in their herb lore. Still, since some of their trade is medically related, I have an excuse to keep pressing. I won't ask anything direct about this matter, but I hope to learn a thing or two that will make it easier for us if—Eagle spread her wings against it—we need to cross the border after Baron Endbrook."

Casting a glance toward where Ninette—now fully and somewhat unhappily in her mistress's confidence—was keeping an eye out for anyone who might chance upon them, Elise spoke:

"I've had little chance to speak with Citrine as of yet. Her mother is keeping her away from even her usual playmates like little Kenre Trueheart. Tomorrow night, however, there is a dinner and small dance at the Shield/Redbriar home. I'm certain I'll be able to talk with her there. Now, I must go."

Gifting each with a small smile and a gracious curtsy, Elise left them with such promptness that her departure could have seemed flight.

After watching her out of sight Doc turned to Derian.

"My cousin asked me to speak with you informally about the post he offered you for this winter. He'll be heading to Kestrel lands in a few days and hopes that you'll accept and travel with us."

Derian nodded. "I've been considering it seriously. It's certainly an attractive offer and one that would permit me to see Firekeeper again—if she ever comes back."

"*When* she does," Doc said firmly. "You say she promised you that she would visit you again. Surely she would be more comfortable on the Kestrel Grant. Part of the North Woods are still wild and there would be good hunting for Blind Seer."

"She might not come back at all this winter," Derian said.

"But the earl has offered you a post as riding instructor to his children and as advisor on his stable," Doc reminded him. "It's not makework. Duchess Kestrel let the stable slide for a time and Norvin had other projects with which to occupy himself."

"That's true," Derian admitted. "Otherwise he wouldn't have needed to hire mounts from my parents when he set out west."

"Exactly," Doc said. "Do come out. You'll have friends there, which is more than you can say in any of the other places you've been offered posts."

Derian nodded. "And I'd see another part of the kingdom. I've only been out that way once or twice and then usually in the summer. We have one stable—an affiliate with a relative of my mother's—and they don't need much managing."

"Did you know," Doc asked with an abruptness that Derian realized was part shyness, "that the earl has also asked Elise to spend some time this winter with his household? He has two sons, both of whom are within a few years of Elise's age. The elder—Edlin—will be heir."

"Matchmaking?"

"I expect so," Doc said. For the first time in their acquaintance, Derian saw the desperate sorrow that underlay Doc's undeclared devotion to Elise. "It would be a good match. Their holdings are on opposite sides of the kingdom, true, but that could be seen as spreading influence, rather than concentrating it in the north."

"Has Elise accepted?" Derian asked.

"Not yet. Nor has she declined."

Doc's expression became wry.

"As with you, Derian, the earl has hinted to Elise that her presence would be a comfort to Lady Blysse should she return from the wilds."

Derian couldn't help but chuckle. "He plays people as Race plays the flute—knowing just the right stops."

"Why then," Jared said abruptly, "would he then also ask me to make myself free of his home this winter? He's no fool—he must know that I . . . care for the young woman. Nor is he cruel. Do you think he might . . ."

"Hope you could win her?" Derian shrugged. "Now, that's an interesting thought."

"Maybe," Doc added bitterly, as if the thought had just come to him, "he uses me as bait to get her there."

"Right now," Derian said bluntly, "your presence might not be an advantage. She seems uncertain of herself."

Doc hit the table with his fist.

"If only I had something to offer her!"

Derian thought he had nothing to say, but found his tongue working anyhow.

"I'll come out this winter," he promised. "Even if Elise does not, you'll be glad for a friend and so," he added, knowing it was true, "will I."

Jared reached out and gripped Derian's hand in wordless thanks.

"In any case," Doc added, "other interests seem to be pressing north. Perhaps it is just as well that we have an excuse to head that way, with or without the lady."

Derian thought from the touch of desperate hope in his

friend's eyes that Jared Surcliffe would much prefer "with" to "without."

❦

WHEN THE CONVOCATION OF THE ROYAL BEASTS reformed in the middle of the next morning, early comments from bear and boar to the general company caused Firekeeper to think that some negotiating among various groups had been going on.

She was certain of this when the puma—who had been fervent in his avocation of her acting as the Beasts' agent—rose languid and golden in the morning sunlight, stretched, and addressed the convocation in general.

"The wolf pup with human form has asked most reasonably why we ourselves did not go after these enchanted objects. I here request that honorable battle-bird, the raven, to speak for his kind."

The raven flapped his wings once, setting up a miniature storm of leaf mold and dust, then croaked:

"I speak for all my kin on this matter—the ravens, crows, and jays. Simply put, we are clever of beak and talon, sharp of eye, and swift of flight, but never have we possessed the means for opening locks or of gaining access to rooms closed and barred against even human access."

"And," squawked a jay, lest any miss the point, "it is supremely unlikely that Queen Valora keeps her treasures on display on her dressing table—or that many windows would be conveniently open in wintertime."

Then the puma said, "But you agree that this stealing is essential—that it must be done?"

The raven spoke, "Again, for all my kin, I say yes."

Next the puma put the same questions to the hawks and eagles and received a similar reply. Then he turned his inquiry to the raccoons and foxes. Their reply was as the wingéd folks' had been—that against human buildings, locks and keys, even their nimble paws and legendary slyness could not avail.

The puma licked one of his forepaws in a thoughtful manner and continued—and there was such predatory power about him that even the largest and fiercest of the Beasts did not question his sudden domination of the discussion.

"So we admit we have a need and a desire, but not the means to gain what we want. The human-shaped wolfling, though, she would not be baffled by doors and locks. Her hands are made for the undoing of these."

Firekeeper, who had kept silent to this point as if mesmerized, now gave tongue.

"I cannot cross the oceans—nor can I walk unheeded among humans. You seem to think that they are indistinguishable from each other, but I tell you, among them I stand out as a white crow among the black."

And here a huge, knife-winged gull—a bird Firekeeper was certain had not been among their company the day before—spoke from where he squatted on a rock near the puma—

"And if I told you, Firekeeper, that no crossing of the ocean was needed? Then would you take on this hunt?"

"I might," she replied cautiously, "be more inclined."

"Then know that on the day when the two human kingdoms celebrated their alliance through the marriage of their heirs—"

(Fleetingly, Firekeeper realized how her experience of human culture had shaped her thoughts. Before that time, she would have heard what the seagull said as something like "when the two rival territories joined through the mating of their young.")

"—then did Queen Valora leave her new capital upon a fleet ship and sail to Silver Whale Cove, and there stare longingly at Revelation Point Castle, as might a young gull when a whaling vessel has hauled alongside a dead deep dweller but not yet cut through the hide into the succulent flesh.

"In her arms, against the fullness of her bosom, she held a metal box. Never, through all the long vigil, did she release it, though her husband, King Harwill, offered more than once to spare her. And when the news was brought to her by a ship even more fleet than her own—though not constructed for sailing on deep water . . ."

The puma growled, "Stay to the point, fish-eater."

"She carried the box below with her," the gull said hastily, glancing at the claws the tawny cat idly bared. "Yet that very box . . ."

And here the gull's squawk rose with triumphant smugness. "That very box was seen by one of my kin—seen as it was encased in a larger box of wood, well padded within, and its true cargo disguised with an abundance of dried fish. This box was put upon a ship for the mainland, a ship that carried one of the queen's underlings. The underling went on to Eagle's Nest—as the humans so . . ."

A dry cough from the puma halted the gull's commentary in midcry.

"The box remains in a storehouse in Port Haven, doubtless to be called for when the underling has built a nest for it. So the items we wish rest on the mainland, little wolf, beyond our beaks and claws, but not—we believe—beyond your fingers."

"Likely," Firekeeper protested, "this servant of Valora will have moved the box long before I can come to that place. Have you forgotten that I lack wings? The journey to Port Haven—a city to which I have never been—will take me hands of days."

"We have not forgotten," the gull said, a trace disdainfully. "And one of my kin now watches the place where the box was put. She knows the look of the big box, the look of the small, and the look of the man who brought it there. If it is taken away, she is to follow."

"And steal?" asked the raccoon—who had been among those most adamantly against Firekeeper's involvement in the theft.

"And steal," the gull replied, "but we fear that she will not be given the chance."

The argument that followed this reply gave Firekeeper a chance to marshal her thoughts. The task did seem more possible now, but still she could not help but recall how she was the white crow when in human company. Her newly cropped hair would not help the situation, either, for all women in both Bright Bay and Hawk Haven wore their hair long—augmenting its length with falls and twists of purchased hair if needed or even resorting to wigs.

Firekeeper had worn a wig once—back during the days when Derian was teaching her in West Keep—and had found the thing smothering and given to slipping into her eyes. Surely she could not chase after this box so encumbered.

Eventually, with much squawking from the raven, and the intervention of the elk in a squabble threatening violence between the raccoon and the fox, the Royal Beasts resumed their convocation.

The elk now took up the matter:

"Speed is indeed important," he said, his voice seeming too high to emanate from his great chest, "and I am prepared to humble myself to its cause. Firekeeper, among the humans did you learn to ride their horses?"

"Poorly," she admitted, but her admission was shaded with pride. "They feared having a wolf astride their backs so only the most mild would carry me."

"I would more fear a puma than a wolf," the elk said thoughtfully, "if it was a matter of backs. Therefore, myself and one of my brothers will carry you from the shores of Lake Rime northward. Much of the journey will be through mountain lands, but we know passes and hidden valleys and can so go swiftly."

Firekeeper did not much care for this assumption that her participation had been agreed upon, but she was so awed by the elk's offer that she was temporarily rendered mute.

"And," said the Mother Kestrel, "several of the wingéd folk—corvid kin and raptors both—will risk the crossing of the Iron Mountains ahead of you. We will be your far-flung eyes and ears so that you do not chase down this box only to learn you have been tracking echoes."

"And we wolves," said the One Female, "will cross the mountains with you, hunting for you and breaking trail through the snow so that you may travel with speed and safety."

This last offer, though simpler than the others, made the greatest impression on Firekeeper. For all of her life she had listened to the teaching tales of the Ones. Every spring, every winter, every autumn, every summer there was a new tale to caution against crossing the Iron Mountains and venturing into those dangerous lands.

That all her home pack—her mother and father and brothers and sisters—would risk that crossing to assure her speedy journey made Firekeeper realize how seriously the wolves viewed this matter of enchanted objects.

It had been on her tongue to ask what gain was there to be had for her if she did this dangerous thing. Now she realized how human that thought was. Wolves might tear the very meat out of a pack mate's mouth, but they did not deny the weak the bones.

Here she was thinking not like one of a pack, but like some mad creature who had forgotten that no matter how flush was summer's hunting only the joined strength of the pack carried the wolf through the coldest freeze.

"I see," Firekeeper replied lightly, "that we have fine winter hunting here. I can do my part in bringing down the game. When do we leave?"

There was no applause as there might have been in a human council when the champion took up the gauntlet, but the stillness that held for a long moment was as resounding.

Then the raven angled his head to look at the sun.

"We have spent the best part of the sunlight in chatter," he said, "and the elks travel best by day."

"Still," the elk snorted, "we should travel while there is light. I say we should not wait."

In reply, Firekeeper rose and the One Female and Blind Seer rose with her. The peregrine Elation took to the air, calling back:

"I tell your pack that you come, ground runners!"

"And, too, you might find a meal waiting at this day's end trail," the puma purred, vanishing with a flick of his tail.

The gull surged into the air with a heavy, awkward beating of his wings, heading east—presumably to brief the watchers as to the result of this meeting. Firekeeper hoped that Lake Rime had surrendered several sleepy fish to his belly.

Her own was feeling a bit empty, for she had dined early and the morning had been long; she was not ungrateful when the bear lumbered over and thrust a sticky and somewhat dirty chunk of honeycomb at her.

She thanked the bear and turned to the elk, who was just finishing a slightly heated discussion about best routes with the One Female and a jay.

"If you go near that rock," she said to the herbivore, who looked quite enormous up close, "I think I can get onto your back with the least trouble for both of us."

The elk acceded, though something about the way he shuddered his skin made Firekeeper think that he was not nearly as relaxed about the idea of carrying her—or traveling in the company of wolves—as he had pretended.

At first, they walked, each learning how to balance against the other. Firekeeper found that she must grip hard with her knees and wished for something to hold on to. The elk's antlers were well out of reach as he leaned forward into the motion of his walk. She had a premonition that she would ache later and hoped that her body wouldn't fail her.

A broad game trail led from Lake Rime into the forested mountains, and for that day they kept to it. Since there had been no heavy snow for some time, the elk found an easy road. He broke into a gait similar to a canter, an easy lope that ate the miles as did a wolf's trot. Blind Seer and the One Female kept pace easily and Firekeeper found herself wondering if perhaps she could have done as well running on her own two feet.

She banished that thought the next day. They'd made camp at dusk, the elk finding good browsing and the wolves dining on a young deer they found draped over a tree branch and reeking of puma.

At dawn they set out again, and when the first elk grew tired another buck of similar magnificence met them to accept the human burden. Firekeeper would have been more than willing to rest at this juncture—indeed, traveling on her own she must have done so, for the cold ground, partly frozen in places, would have punished her bare feet to aching soreness.

The wolves kept the pace set by the elk, jogging steadily along, but then each of them were in fine shape. The One Female was the best her pack had to offer—as she must be to hold her place. Blind Seer was toned from his journey west with Firekeeper and still possessed ample ready fat from the easy seasons among the humans.

As had happened so many times in her life, Firekeeper—who had grown confident of her strength and woodcraft while among the humans—had to reassess her abilities in light of those born to the Beasts with whom she lived. As always, she found herself pathetically weak in comparison.

Over and over again, as the journey stretched interminably on and she gripped the elk's flanks with aching legs, she reminded herself: *They need you. Remember—they need you.*

That thought was small enough comfort.

XV

ELISE FELT LIKE A PERFECT BEAST for how she had avoided Doc at the Kestrel ball, but her conversation with Lady Aurella was too fresh in her mind for her to encourage him, even to the extent of accepting a dance.

The following day brought the Redbriar/Shield fete. The intricate unwritten rules of precedence had decreed that it must be scheduled later than those events held by the Great Houses—that is, if the family hoped for any guests to be available to attend. Yet, the very fact that King Allister and his family delayed their departure for Silver Whale Cove to attend gave the gathering a social importance beyond what it would usually command.

The cynics said that this was simply because King Allister wished Ruby and Opal to travel in company with his own party and that they could hardly be expected to depart before their own family's entertainment.

The less—or perhaps more—cynical said that this delay was King Allister's way of acknowledging his daughter-in-law's birth family and that acknowledgment conferred a rise in status to a house that was—factually assessed—neither a Great House nor a lesser.

Rumor was rife that Crown Princess Sapphire was agitating King Tedric to make her brother Jet a baron and confer title of "lady" upon her younger sisters.

Elise had her doubts about this last. She knew too well the rivalry between Sapphire and Jet—a rivalry that had come to a head with Sapphire's appointment as King Tedric's heir apparent.

That Lady Melina might be agitating the king, her uncle, or her birth daughter the crown princess to grant these titles, Elise could well believe. Thus she was rather surprised, upon her arrival at the fete with her parents, to find Lady Melina effacing herself in favor of her handsome son.

It was Jet who stood at the door greeting his guests as they arrived, not—as any who knew her would have expected—Lady Melina. Nor was Lady Melina readily evident in any of the more public rooms.

Jet reported—claiming Elise for a dance to do so—that his mother's spirit was quite broken by recent events.

"My father's death," the dark-haired young gentleman said, looking sorrowful, "was a greater blow to her than anyone imagined. Mother says the absence of his presence is like having a wall of the house blown away in a sudden storm."

Elise, who knew that Lady Melina had barely spoken to her husband and had frequently refused him her bed—this last being common gossip in the war camp last autumn—took this piteous description with a grain of salt. Certainly Lady Melina *wanted* everyone to believe her in deep mourning. The question was why?

If Lady Melina's behavior was nearly impossible, finding an opportunity to speak with Citrine was easier than Elise had dared hope. The eight-year-old could hardly compete for attention or dance partners with her older sisters and was almost pathetically glad to have Elise visit with her.

"I wanted so much," Citrine confided in Elise as they took seats at a little table off the dance floor, shielded from notice but where they could watch the dancers, "to go to Bright Bay with my sisters, but Mother said I was too young."

"Maybe your mother needs your presence to comfort her in her loss," Elise said, curious if Citrine would agree with what Jet had said.

Citrine shook her head angrily, her round eyes flooding with indignant tears.

"*Mother* doesn't care!"

The little girl almost stammered in her anger and frustration. Then she trembled and her fingers drifted unconsciously to the cognac-dark facets of the citrine imbedded in the band encircling her brow.

"Not about Father, at least," she said more softly. "I heard her say to Nanny—I was under the bed looking for my doll— that she was glad to have him gone."

"Glad?" Elise blurted, horrified that an eight-year-old should overhear such things.

"She used some other word." Citrine waved this minor point aside with a gesture of one plump hand. "But from her voice I could tell she was glad. They'd quarreled, you know, about Sapphire."

"I'm not surprised," Elise said. "After Sapphire lost her gemstone headpiece?"

"Yeah."

Elise was tempted to press for more detail, but realized that she would only be pumping the child for old gossip.

"So, why do you think your mother doesn't want you near for comfort?" Elise asked, feeling unpleasantly filthy as she grubbed in what was clearly a fresh wound. "Sometimes we don't give our parents enough credit for being weak."

If Elise hadn't been Citrine's self-appointed favorite cousin, the little girl might have merely snorted and refused to answer. Even so, the look of scorn Citrine turned on the older girl was withering.

"If Mother needs me, then why is she sending me to some people in the east—people I don't even know?"

"East?" Elise said, puzzled. "Winter at the seaside?"

"Just about," Citrine said sulkily. "And Mother won't be there and I won't know anyone."

Elise didn't like herself an iota more for continuing to cause her little cousin pain—all the more so because if Citrine hadn't been fond of her Elise doubted that she would have talked even this much. Plump she might be, a mere eight-year-old she might be, but Citrine shared a certain dignity with her eldest sister, Sapphire, a dignity that Ruby and Opal both lacked.

Therefore Elise didn't belittle Citrine by asking her if she was sure of her facts. Nor did she offer her platitudes. Instead she asked, with adult directness:

"Do you know why she's sending you there?"

Citrine shook her head, and for the first time Elise realized that an undefined dread underlay the child's defiance.

"No," Citrine whispered. "I don't. Ever since Sapphire stopped wearing her circlet, Mother hasn't liked to let us too far away. Then all of a sudden, the day of the wedding when I was asking again if I could go to Bright Bay with Ruby and Opal, she looked at me—right *at* me—and told me that no I couldn't, to stop whining like a baby, and that I was going somewhere else for the winter where I could do her more good."

"That's what she said?" Elise asked. "Where you could do her more good?"

"That's it," Citrine said. "And I am. You don't cross Mother, not when she gets *that* look."

Her voice, which had risen slightly as she narrated the events of this peculiar exile, now dropped again.

"You were lucky, you know, not to marry Jet." Citrine's

eyes teared up suddenly. "But I'm sorry you're not going to be my sister after all."

That pitiful confession broke Elise completely. Forgetful of her gown, forgetful of not wanting to attract attention to this little conference, she gathered Citrine into her lap and hugged her.

"You can still be my sister," she whispered fiercely in the little girl's ear, "maybe not by law, but in my heart. I never had a sister, but I'd be glad to have you."

For some reason, this set them both crying. Elise felt the rounded hardness of the gemstone fastened to Citrine's brow pressing against her breast and resolved to someday free Citrine—just as Sapphire had been freed—from her mother's domination.

Citrine's sudden storm of tears vanished as quickly as it had arisen and her round face was sunny.

"Thanks, Elise," she said. "I'm sorry I was such a baby. I've been so scared and nobody wants to talk to me."

"That's what big sisters are for," Elise assured her. "Talking to."

"Not mine," Citrine said with characteristic bluntness. "At least not the other ones. I'm just the baby nuisance to them."

Unwilling to stir up another storm, Elise settled for hugging her.

"When do you leave for the seaside?"

"Tomorrow or the day after," Citrine replied. "I've only stayed this long because Mother thought I should be seen at the party."

Once again, the little girl was clearly echoing her mother's words, but without Elise's broader knowledge of the intrigue in which Lady Melina might be involved they did not trouble her. To Elise, however, that "should be seen" had a distinctly ominous ring. She put her worries from her with an effort.

"Well, then," Elise said brightly, "you should indeed be seen. Come with me and we'll wash that smudge off your nose and then we'll see if we can't find a pair of gallant souls who want to dance."

Citrine glowed and put her fingers confidently in Elise's

hand. As they went on their quest for partners, Elise found herself wishing that she had a brother for Citrine to marry. Then she chuckled to herself:

There you go, arranging other people's lives in the same fashion you yourself have been resisting. Maybe Citrine wouldn't want *to marry your brother—if you had one—or maybe he wouldn't want to marry her!*

Still, though she laughed the thought away, Elise felt vaguely awkward, understanding for the first time from her heart—rather than merely from lessons in etiquette and procedure—how and why her parents might want to arrange their only daughter's life.

It was not comfortable to realize that their interests might be directed toward insuring Elise's own happiness, rather than merely working toward their own gain. And this realization made it even harder for Elise to resist their desires.

With Citrine trying hard to walk in a dignified fashion beside her—but nonetheless bouncing just a bit—Elise made her way to where two young scions of Bright Bay's nobility stood sipping punch and studying the dancers.

"I understand," Elise said, smiling, "that the next dance is Clover in Springtime. My cousin and I thought you might not know it and would enjoy showing you the steps."

Both of the young men—boys really would be a fairer term—colored while still managing to look quite pleased.

"We'd be honored," said the elder of the two—a youth of perhaps fifteen. "We've seen it danced at a few other events here in Eagle's Nest, but it isn't done in Bright Bay."

"Though," his friend said with an almost scholarly thoughtfulness, surprising in one who couldn't be more than thirteen, "it does resemble the dance we call Dolphin Pod—at least in some steps and the general cadence of the music."

Conversation came easily as—after introducing themselves—Elise and Citrine showed the young men what they would need to know to comport themselves with sufficient skill. When the current dance ended and the two couples proceeded out onto the floor, Elise glimpsed an expression of proud satisfaction on her father's face before Baron Archer returned to his conversation with another of the foreign guests.

Not all our victories are won on the battlefield, Elise thought as the music began and she subtly steered her partner through the first steps. *The most important ones may be won in places like this.*

Elise's satisfaction at this thought, however, was muted by a glimpse of Lady Melina entering the room, attended by a small entourage of men—Baron Endbrook of the Isles among them. Elise concealed a shiver, thinking that Lady Melina was far more skilled than she at manipulating the social battlefield and wondering what victories the older woman might have already achieved.

BARON ENDBROOK HAD STOPPED feeling in the least bit nervous. Arranging for horses, driver, and wagon had been so much like tasks he had performed dozens of times before in the course of his varied shipping ventures that the entire realm of international intrigue was beginning to seem simply like another business deal.

Indeed, why shouldn't international politics be conducted so? Wasn't the principle much the same? Queen Valora, Lady Melina, the New Kelvinese—even himself—each wanted something, each had something to trade. In the end, with a bit of give-and-take, a touch of compromise, everyone should be more or less satisfied.

Even the element of secrecy wasn't unfamiliar. Too many good trades could be queered if the information got out too soon. Most of the deals that had made Waln's fortune had been conducted in secret.

The day following the Redbriar/Shield fete, Baron End-brook joined Duke Marek and his diplomatic entourage in departing for Port Haven. Although he had not *said* he was leaving the mainland, it was to Baron Endbrook's taste that most think he was gone. In this way he would avoid the complications of continued social and business invitations. He'd been surprised at how eager Hawk Haven's monied elements had been to talk the possibilities of seaborne trade. They might have been from Waterland rather than genteel, nearly land-locked Hawk Haven.

There was a good, straight road between Hawk Haven's one port and her capital city. After the Isles diplomatic party had ridden a few hours out from the capital, Waln changed to a fresh horse and picked up his pace. He had many reasons to get to the port before the others, and his companions—knowing the queen's favor was upon the baron—asked no questions.

Waln's first task upon arriving in Port Haven would be to finalize arrangements for Citrine Shield's captivity. After some rather heated argument with Lady Melina, Waln had agreed that the little girl would not be taken to the Isles—her mother had expressed reasonable enough concern regarding the late-autumn storms.

What Lady Melina did not know, nor did Waln feel she needed to know, was that Baron Endbrook had never intended to take Citrine across the waters. It would actually be more difficult to hide her on the Isles rather than in her native land. Instead, he had arranged to stow her in an isolated tower—a failed lighthouse in the swamps north of Port Haven near the Waterland border and more accessible from the ocean than from the land.

The tower might have failed as a lighthouse, but it had succeeded admirably as a drop point for smuggled goods going into Waterland across the swamps. Hawk Haven was traditionally weak at sea, so it could not effectively prevent traffic in those tricky waters. Waterland, in her turn, risked violation of its alliance with Hawk Haven if it was too blatant in its fleet's attacks in the neighboring waters.

The swamps made an effective barrier by land, though when Princess Lovella had been alive, she had trained some of her elite forces in the area and had nearly vanquished the smugglers for a time. But Lovella was dead these two or more years and no one else had cared to take up the challenge—especially since the pirates scrupulously left Port Haven alone and concentrated their force on Bright Bay and, when necessary, Waterland.

Therefore, the tower had become a pirate stronghold: a mainland base for those who raided the waters in the region and a point from which they could disperse at least some of their goods without fear of retaliation—and without paying the high prices charged by go-betweens ashore.

The swamp dwellers had long learned to avoid Smuggler's Light, as it had come to be called, no matter what they heard or saw in its vicinity, so Citrine should be quite secure.

That the smuggled goods included slaves was all to Waln's taste. Should Lady Melina betray him, Citrine could vanish into the Waterland markets none the wiser. That her mind might be damaged by numbing drugs or her tongue cut to keep her from telling who she was certainly was a pity, but if her mother kept her word, Citrine would be safe as a clam in its shell.

Baron Endbrook had made certain that Lady Melina knew what her daughter was risking as an added assurance that Citrine would indeed prove bond against her mother's treachery. He thought he owed the little girl at least that much consideration.

Perhaps there would be some in Hawk Haven who would be surprised to learn that a respectable merchant had contacts with pirates and smugglers, but none would be in Bright Bay. It had long been a problem for the Bright Bay navy that some otherwise respectable Islanders worked with the pirates— sometimes merely by hiding them, other times by shipping stolen goods under legitimate seal, still other times by joining in the occasional sea battle on the side of the pirates.

The Islanders justified this as insurance against pirate actions directed toward their own vessels—a form of patriotism—for it meant that the pirates chose to prey on mainlanders instead.

In addition to arranging for Citrine's incarceration, Baron Endbrook must also retrieve the precious artifacts he had stored in a secure warehouse in Port Haven. The warehouse owner's register showed that he was holding a crate of dried fish. If he believed that there was anything more within the crate, he had been paid to look the other way. However, if despite that payment he *had* looked, he would have discovered a couple of casks of very expensive, highly tariffed wine from a land south of Stonehold. The box with the enchanted objects was within one of these casks, hidden in a secret compartment around which liquid sloshed quite convincingly.

Waln had checked and found that each of the three artifacts was packaged separately, each so securely that the contents did not rattle. As the largest of the boxes was only about the length of his shoe—though much flatter—Waln had arranged to stow the boxes in a sturdy leather bag with straps that permitted him to carry his burden over his shoulder or across his back.

After the boxes were in his saddlebags, Waln planned to proceed north and west—roughly parallel to the swamps. There he would rendezvous with Lady Melina and receive her securities. After these were delivered to their hiding places it would be a simple enough matter to make their way into New Kelvin.

Baron Endbrook was pleased with his arrangements, very pleased. At the close of his most recent letter to Oralia, he had asked his wife what colors of silk she would like for her new gowns and which shades she thought would best suit the girls. He himself would choose the colors for his son.

After all, his family must be well attired when the queen invited them to court.

IN THE MIDDLE OF THEIR SECOND DAY of travel Blind Seer slunk up to Firekeeper. The small group had paused in order to let the elk find something to drink and to enable Firekeeper to eat a quick mouthful of cold rabbit and waxy honey.

The feral woman was appalled by the fashion in which the blue-eyed wolf hung his head and by the droop of his tail. For a moment she thought that the One Female must have been reprimanding him; she saw no blood nor even a damp saliva trail on his thick grey fur, so that guess must be wrong.

"What makes your tail droop, dear heart?" she asked, dropping to her knees beside the wolf.

"I must tell you something that makes me sorrowful," Blind Seer replied.

Firekeeper's heart raced with fear. Surely the One Female had not forbidden him to accompany her back into the human lands. True, he did attract attention—attention that she now understood that the Royal Beasts had avoided for many years—but he had been seen, he was known! Concealment at this late date would be like digging after the rabbit once it had bolted out a back tunnel from its burrow.

"Tell" was all she could manage to say, and her tone was unwontedly severe.

"I have lied to you, sweet Firekeeper," the blue-eyed wolf confessed, raising his head so that their gazes must meet.

Normally, Firekeeper would have been horrified, for her faith in the basic honesty of wolf-kind—except perhaps when it came to confessing where they had stashed some hoarded bit of food—was a belief so deep that she did not even think of it as a belief but instead as Truth.

Now, however, she was so relieved that he didn't plan to leave her that she laughed lightly and punched him in the shoulder.

"Tell me, two-tongued wonder. Tell me of this lie! Have you been too much among humans and so have learned their ways?"

"It was a wolf who taught me to lie," Blind Seer said, something in his folded ears and raised hackles showing that he, too, had been shocked by this violation of Truth. "When first I decided to run east with you and see what lay across the mountains, the One Male came to me."

"He came?" Firekeeper said. "I never knew!"

"He came one of those long afternoons when you believed

me asleep and you sat in the human camp learning of their ways. He told me not to tell you of his coming, for he feared a weakening of your resolution. For the same reason, none of our family came to see you off on your journey."

"I wondered at that," Firekeeper admitted, "afterwards, but thought that the pups were so tiny that the pack could not range far."

"My lie," Blind Seer continued, dragging them back to the subject with an almost physical effort, "made you a liar, too, though unknowing, and will force you to continue as one all-knowing."

"For you, dear one, anything," Firekeeper promised. "Now spit out this lie lest it poison you like rotted meat unvomited."

"Before I left with you for the lands east of the Iron Mountains," Blind Seer said, "the One Male came to me and told me thus:

" 'Son,' he said, 'when you go east, you may see those who are of Royal-kind—wingéd folk mostly, but perhaps some others. I bind you to never speak of them to Little Two-legs. She is too young and faces too many challenges to her ideas of the world to be confronted with this as well. Let her believe that the only creatures of our kind who dwell east of the Iron Mountains are those who travel with her—you and the falcon Elation.'

"I agreed readily, nor was it a difficult vow to keep. Even I saw few that I could feel certain were of Royal-kind and these never spoke to me. But on the day that Sapphire and Shad were first wed and I stood on the parapet outside our room longing to be with you and see you in your glory, a gull flew up to me.

"In a few words he told me how Queen Valora and some of her trusted allies waited in the bay, waited in hope that a coup attempt would succeed. The gull suggested that I warn you of their presence, that I put you on your guard. When I asked how I should do this without telling you how I knew—when later you asked as you surely must—the gull pecked me on my nose and said:

" 'I suggest you claim to have scented the queen. Humans

are nose-dead and the child'—by which the gull meant you—
'is credulous regarding the power of wolves.' I protested, but
could not think of any better solution. Moreover, I felt I must
warn you lest your death come from my failure."

He finished and his great head hung so low that it touched
the ground. Firekeeper seized it and pressed it to her heart.

"I forgive you your lie, dearest. You were trapped between
honorable obligations."

She laughed, still light-headed from her relief.

"And I was not so credulous as the gull believed—I simply
thought you the best at scenting distant odors of any wolf ever
born."

Blind Seer shook his head from her hold and licked her
cheek. They rolled together in play, as if for a moment both
were puppies again. Too soon did the One Female summon
them, and Firekeeper hauled herself onto the elk's back once
more.

Her muscles seemed to ache less; however, a new uneasiness had entered her thoughts following Blind Seer's tale. If
the wolves had lied to her—even if merely by omission—what
about those other interesting gaps in the various stories she
had heard during the last few days, what about the times the
teller had paused and then hurried on?

Firekeeper might have agreed to do as the Royal Beasts
commanded her, but in the silent depths of her heart she was
uncertain. She remembered what King Tedric and King Allister had said about the risk of war if Queen Valora felt herself
threatened. Firekeeper didn't know if she could face the bru-
tality of another war—especially since this time she would
know herself its creator.

Caught within a mesh woven of old fears and new, she was
relieved when Blind Seer reminded the One Female of her
promise to tell the story of the songbirds. Perhaps the defiant
note in his request came from similar uneasiness or, perhaps,
his conscience now clear, he simply wanted entertainment for
the way. Whatever the reason, when the One Female tried to
put off the tale, the blue-eyed wolf pressed.

"You said we might hear, Mother."

The One Female ran on, as mute as the day's old snow.

The elk, surprisingly, forced the issue.

"Let the little ones hear the story of the songbirds," he said, "for it is a part of our history they should know—an ugly tale, but no less useful for that. They are your pups, so I will give you precedence in their teaching, but if you refuse, I shall tell them."

The One Female snarled so that all her fangs showed and her hackles were stiff along her neck, but though Firekeeper felt the elk tense for flight, the she-wolf did not spring.

"Very well," the One Female conceded. "I am fairly trapped between a swift river and a raging fire. I will teach my pups, though among our people such stories are not told to any but the Ones."

"And are these not," the elk said with a mildness that bespoke a desire to save face for the wolf, "these two as Ones when they venture east alone? Surely they will have no pack heads to guide them. If we do not give them wisdom, we are dooming them to failure."

The she-wolf's hackles relaxed and her expression became thoughtful.

"I had not considered that point. To our pack, Little Two-legs has been our pup forever, but you are right, Steady Runner. I owe these two a teaching and suspect I resist because the tale does no credit to any of our kind."

Without further delay, the One Female began:

"Long ago, so long ago that even the fixed stars have moved since those days, the Royal Beasts were the rulers of this land—even into the reaches beyond the broad river to the west and to the ocean beyond it. Through the wingéd folk and the water folk we sent out embassies to other places and were regarded as great among the powers of the earth.

"But great powers must sometimes fight to keep their greatness and so the Royal Beasts fought. Those wars are not part of this tale, however. Suffice to say that because of the fighting certain of our kind became very important—among them the raptors of the air and the hunting beasts of the land.

"Now, in those days, there were Royal-kind such as are not

seen in these lands today. These were the songbirds and the smaller game animals. Like all others of Royal-kind, they were gifted with somewhat greater size, somewhat longer lives, and occasional magical talents.

"The hunters among the Royal Beasts considered these fair game, fair but difficult to catch. Usually, hunting Cousin-kind was a better return on effort.

"But in those long-ago days, the hunting beasts of air and land became arrogant. They said to each other: 'Why should we make our meals mostly on those creatures of Cousin blood? They are smaller and less filling. Nor does hunting them hone our skills as they must be honed for us to serve as the warriors for our land. The Royal deer, elk, rabbits, and squirrels—as well as the song and game birds—were clearly created for our meals.'

"They spoke thus only to each other and soon the idea spread. At first, the songbirds and herbivores were none the wiser—accepting their losses as part of the natural order. However, eventually the bears and raccoons and other such who ate both meat and plants learned of the concerted effort being made to exclusively hunt Royal-kind. They became uneasy, for they did not know whether they would be grouped with the prey or the predators.

"Thus these in-betweens spoke to the herbivores and the songbirds and the game birds, and these were horrified to learn that they were now being sought out as prey rather than falling to the hunter as in the normal course of things. In fact, in the flurry to hunt only Royal-kind, many of the Cousins were slain and left to rot as not fine enough for Royal stomachs.

"The songbirds protested both this abuse and the waste, but to no avail.

" 'What use in a songbirds?' gibed the raptors. 'What use is a grouse or rabbit?' laughed the wolves and pumas. 'We shall eat them and grow fat and—well—if some escape, all for the good for that means more interesting hunting in the future.' "

The One Female fell silent, using as an excuse for her silence the fact that the terrain they were crossing—a pass between two low mountains—was steep and that she and Blind Seer must break a path in the snow so that the elk could follow with greater ease.

Firekeeper, however, could see the silver wolf's embarrassment at reporting this ancient folly. However, when they were through the worst of the snow and into better land, the One Female conquered her embarrassment and resumed:

"In time spring passed into summer and around the seasons until spring again, but this spring brought with it hordes of insects. There were little ones of the air that bit noses and swarmed in eyes; there were fat grasshoppers who stripped the land of grass and the trees of leaves.

"Needless to say, without sufficient grazing and browsing, the deer and elk and other game animals grew thin. Even fish became difficult to catch, for the starving herbivores had stripped the riverbanks of every growing thing. Thus, when the rains beat down their water they flayed the soil from the banks, turning the swiftly flowing streams to mud torrents, and choking the creatures who lived within them.

" 'What use is a songbird?' sang the few surviving songbirds. 'What use a grouse or a rabbit?' And the wolves grown lean and hungry, the pumas grooming tatty fur over jutting ribs, listened to the song and were humbled.

"As a token of their change of heart—their admission of the waste and destruction they had permitted—the Royal hunters ceased hunting the Royal songbirds and game birds and the land-bound herbivores though they were starving for a good feed."

Firekeeper felt as much as heard the indignant snort of the elk who carried her. The One Female must have as well, for she moderated her fierce enthusiasm for this particular element in her account.

"Yet," the One Female went on with an unreadable glance toward the elk, "this admission of wrongdoing was not sufficient—still the hunters must be punished.

"The surviving songbirds—made fat on grasshoppers and other insects or on grass seed too small for others to find—guided flocks of their Cousin-folk to sheltered places where the raptors could not see them. The rabbits fortified their Cousins' burrows with clever twisting and turning. The grouse and other ground birds played decoy for their less clever kin—and often led the exhausted hunters on a meatless chase. The elk and deer hid their Cousin-folk in their own secret yards. So it seemed that the Royal hunters must all starve."

The elk muttered, "Fair enough, for—as our senior cows tell this part of the story—we were starving alongside our tormentors though we were guiltless. Realizing that the wolves and pumas would slay the weakest and so survive while we still died, we struggled to punish those who had violated ancient custom and brought this doom upon guilty and innocent alike."

To Firekeeper's surprise, the One Female did not growl at this interruption or take offense at this criticism. Instead, she gave a single low wag of her well-furred tail in acknowledgment of the other's point of view.

"I did say," the One Female said, "that we hate this tale."

The elk bugled shrilly in laughter. "But you tell it well, with only the least flavoring of self-pity. Speak on, she-wolf, you are almost come to an end."

"Even the carrion vanished," the One Female continued, "gobbled up at a fantastic rate by the crows and ravens and jays, for corvid kin had sided with the seed-and bug-eating members of the wingéd folk, turning away from those of us who had long permitted them to share our hunting.

"The bears and raccoons and wild pigs helped drive us from even these poor meals—for less restricted in what they could eat they were stronger than we—and they stood us off when we would have sacrificed eyes and ears to the beaks of the corvid kin in return for a mouthful of rotting meat.

"And when the starving was nearly complete, when the ribs of every wolf stood out like tree branches in winter, when the pumas lacked the strength to groom even the paws they rested their heavy heads upon, when the foxes considered their own fleas fine dining, then an embassy came to the eaters of meat, an embassy of those we had in our arrogance taken to be our rightful prey.

"A fat robin sat upon a tree branch and whistled, 'What use a songbird?' A wolf replied, 'We have ceased to hunt the Royal Beasts. We are humbled to death. What do you want?'

" 'A promise,' said the robin, 'that you will never do this again, that you will teach your children of your folly.'

"The wolf, speaking for all the hunters, said, 'We gladly give this promise. From this day forth, no Royal Beast will be preferred game, but will only be hunted as before—when made vulnerable by the course of life.'

"The robin bobbed acceptance, but was not yet content. 'And we demand an apology from all of you for thinking that simply because you could slay our enemies you had earned the right to view any living thing as your enemy. We want an apology for the wasted lives—both kin and Cousin—that were spent in your pride.'

"Again the wolf agreed, adding, 'We have learned that it is pure madness to kill without eating. How often have we longed for those Cousin-kind we slew without eating. We beg forgiveness and ask to be allowed to eat once more. If you wish, we shall forgo Royal-kind completely and dine only on Cousins.'

"The robin sang a merry note. 'What use a hunter? We, too, are hunters—though you mocked our insect prey as puppy game until you were starving. Even those who eat the growing things are hunters, for without them the trees would be choked by their own saplings and the grass by its older growth. Hunt as before, hunt warily and well—and always eat what you kill.' "

Here the One Female stopped her story and glanced at the elk. Firekeeper could tell from the set of the wolf's ears that she was uncomfortable and her tones when she addressed the elk held traces of a puppy whine.

"Great elk," the One Female said, "this next part of the tale has always troubled me for it seems more a hunter's fantasy than any possible reality."

"Tell the story," commanded the elk, "as you learned it when you rose to strength."

Even with this assurance, the One Female seemed unhappy as she continued:

"As my first mate told me the tale when I had beaten all comers and become the One, at this point the robin flew down from the tree and offered her fat breast to the fox. A deer and an elk leapt from a high place, breaking their own necks and backs, and thus there was food for the wolves and pumas. Even the timid rabbits and foolish ground birds bent head and necks to the hunters' fangs. In this way the hunters were given strength to hunt again and returned to the chase—though never again did they turn exclusively to Royal-kind as their prey."

Firekeeper gasped at this incredible conclusion to the tale. She understood why the One Female believed it fancy, but the elk running beneath her did not gainsay the account.

"So it is told among my people," the elk said, "with slight variation of detail and emphasis. For we are told that the robin's lesson—the lesson of the songbirds—was for all Royal-kind. Though our lives are precious to us, still the tradition of sacrifice is in our blood. When the hunters come, we put our young in the center of the herd and defend them. When all must run, the weakest know that their falling back preserves the herd. This tradition is not so different than that of the hunters."

The elk snorted and bounded over a place half-ice, half-mud, before continuing.

"For the lesson of the songbirds is for us as well. If our numbers grow too great, we will become as the insects that stripped the land of all growing things. Every year when the tale is related some little calf asks why Royal-kind gave of itself rather than herding forth some Cousins to die instead—if indeed . . ."

Here the elk chuckled. "If indeed that calf thinks the hunters should have been preserved at all. And we tell the calves that had we let the hunters continue to starve—or had preserved them at the cost of Cousin-kind—then we would have shown that we had not learned the lesson so dearly taught."

The One Female replied slowly, "I almost understand."

"You understand," the elk said, "else Little Two-legs here

262 / Jane Lindskold

astride me would have died long ago. Surely some of your own went hungry to feed her. It is not so great a step from that sacrifice to the other."

But the she-wolf was not certain and the elk read this in the angle of her tail and the tilt of her ears.

"Think this then, silver wolf. The story begins with the hunting beasts protecting our lands from those who would take them from us. Many are said to have died in those battles and you have no trouble accepting the truth of that part of the story. How does that dying differ from the other?"

Blind Seer protested, "In a fight the blood is hot!"

"I tell you, young wolf," the elk replied, "the blood of those who gave their lives to feed the hunters was hot as well, for fear makes the heart pump, even as does fury."

They were all silent, thinking about this for a time. Then the One Female said to Blind Seer:

"Now you and Little Two-legs know the story of the songbirds. May you be well served for your curiosity."

Firekeeper puzzled over this; then at last she asked:

"But, Mother, what happened to the songbirds? According to this tale, they lived and even prospered, yet I have never seen a Royal robin or other singer. Royal rabbits and such are simply joking excuses for failed hunting. Many times have I heard a pack mate swear, 'That one must have been Royal, else it could not have escaped me.' "

The One Female sighed, "We live in borderlands, upon the fringes of which those battles so long ago were fought. No one sees the smaller beasts here, but it is said that they can still be found in the deeper lands, farther from the ocean, nearer to the great wide river."

"My people," the elk added unexpectedly, "say that the songbirds left this land for it had been made sorrowful by memory of the carnage. Flying far away, they found new nesting lands where they never again had to fear a breaking of the truce. In the loneliest part of winter, our young bulls bellow long, low songs describing islands full of singing birds whose every note is ripe with wisdom."

"Who knows which is the truth?" the One Female said.

"Maybe I will learn the truth someday," Firekeeper said, "for it is in my thoughts that I shall travel far before I dig a den for myself."

"Come and tell us tales of your journeying," the elk requested a trace wistfully.

"We shall."

And that promise came from Blind Seer.

XVI

KING ALLISTER AND HIS PARTY began their return journey to Silver Whale Cove on the fourteenth day of Boar Moon. Without Sapphire and Shad dispensing cheer among their fellow travelers, the group seemed much smaller, although in fact it was larger by the addition of four young ladies and their various attendants.

The young ladies were Deste and Nydia Trueheart, the daughters of Lady Zorana Archer and Lord Aksel Trueheart, and Ruby and Opal Shield, daughters of Lady Melina Shield and the late Lord Rolfston Redbriar. In point of fact and order, only the latter two had been specifically invited, but when Lady Zorana—a forceful woman not above trading on her close kinship to King Tedric to get what she wanted—chose to assume that her daughters were included in the invitation, King Allister had accepted them without protest.

Pearl's reminder of the son Zorana had so recently lost certainly played a part in softening the king's heart. He hoped that Pearl wouldn't regret her sympathy, for managing the young ladies would fall much into her sphere.

Allister had narrowly escaped taking along a handful of other young people—scions of various Great Houses—but had been saved from this influx by a rumor which suggested that the girls were not so much guests as hostages for the safety and good treatment of Prince Shad in his new home.

This was ridiculous, but as the rumor served Allister, he didn't particularly mind. In fact, the giggles and gossip coming from the carriages had been a nice balance to the emptiness he felt when they took their departure, leaving Shad behind in Eagle's Nest.

The odd thing was that this was hardly the first time that Shad had been away from his family. Indeed, over the past several years Shad had served in Bright Bay's navy and, had the ancestors not chosen to make Allister king, Shad would have spent the greater part of the next several years—if not decades—at sea, coming home at last to whatever estate was his inheritance.

But this time, Allister thought, *Shad is going from us not merely into unfamiliar waters, but into a way of life none of us can imagine. Now he must learn to reign—not simply to command—and he must learn to be a married man, not simply a promising youth. I wonder if I'm feeling the first touch of old age's frost.*

Allister laughed at the idea. In truth, he had rarely felt more alive or more anticipation for what the future would bring. The trip to Hawk Haven had solidified his relations with some of those members of his court about whom he had felt uncertain. In an unfamiliar place, surrounded by people for whom strange customs and accents were familiar, the guests from Bright Bay had formed a tenuous bond that their king looked forward to twisting into a stronger rope.

Allister was not so naive as to think that the trip had been enough to win over those who were inclined to be his enemies—not in the least—but he was certain that he had progressed in forming alliances with those whose feelings were more neutral.

Reports from the two regents he had left governing in his stead at the capital were promising. Grand Duchess Seastar was taking advantage of his absence to promote her sons, but not to the point of encouraging treason. Mostly she seemed interested in having Culver made an admiral and Dillon being promoted to some important but not too onerous position at court.

Earle Oyster, who had taken charge over investigating the assassination attempt in the absence of both the king and Whyte Steel, reported (in cipher!) that she had run into nothing but dead ends. She apologized to her brother-in-law for her failure and begged his permission to continue. As of yet, Opulence Rosen was not agitating to return home to Waterland and she still hoped to learn something from him or his correspondence.

Let her keep trying, Allister thought. *There is nothing to be lost by appearing firm, but I suspect that the Opulence knows no more than anyone else and that no one will be foolish enough to write anything incriminating.*

Really, given that no one irreplaceable had been killed and that Shad and Sapphire had become heroes in the eyes of the public, Allister could almost be grateful to whoever had attempted the assassination. It didn't hurt to have one's heirs popular with those who would be ruled by them. Not only did their popularity solidify the future, but it strengthened the present reign as well—at least until the heirs apparent grew ambitious for the throne. Shad and Sapphire would have plenty to keep them busy, so that they should not be in a hurry for more responsibility.

King Allister chuckled softly to himself, thinking that had not there been so much blood and the injuries to both Shad and Sapphire *and* the slain guards, his political adversaries might have thought the entire thing a put-up job on the part of the king. All the tales being told and ballads being sung would nicely keep both Shad and Sapphire vivid in the public imagination, even when their duties carried them off into Hawk Haven.

Some of the king's cheery mood left him as he thought of the guards who had died, those men in their shining dress armor, so proud to have been chosen to attend upon the royal family. Death in the line of duty had been common enough of late—King Allister's War had seen to that—but even so the king should invent some posthumous award to recognize this particular sacrifice on this unusual battlefield.

Such an award would provide incentive to those guards who—as they had every day since the assassination attempt—continued to put themselves between their king and possible disaster. Since Allister had refused to be locked in a carriage, feeling that this would simply mean that their undeclared enemy had won a smaller victory, the guards had a difficult task indeed. Still, a king who hid in fear soon became no king at all.

Allister nudged Hot Toddy with his heels and the sorrel trotted up toward the middle of the line, where Queen Pearl rode in a carriage with her ladies. On the way, he passed Nydia Trueheart—now her family's heir apparent—and Prince Tavis riding side by side, engrossed in a competition to discover who could recite from memory more lines out of the canon of some New Kelvinese poet.

The rhythmic syllables—never mind that they were in a language Allister didn't understand—provided a completely nonmartial counterpoint to the thudding of horse hooves on the dirt road and jingling of harness leathers.

Life seemed very pleasant indeed. Even the weather changing to rain the next day, transforming the roads to mud couldn't alter Allister's sense of deep contentment. The weddings were over, the coronation concluded. Now he could get onto challenges he understood without ceremony to fetter his energy.

Swinging down from the saddle, Allister hummed softly as he helped shove yet another wagon out of a patch of sticky mud. Discovering Tavis behind him, placing his own shoulder against the wagon's side while still reciting poetry to a laughing Nydia, only added to the music in the king's heart.

ON THE DAY FOLLOWING King Allister's departure, in those dusky moments that are neither evening nor yet night, that time when stars can be seen but the sky itself is bluish rather than black, a curious thing might have been glimpsed in the semi-wild gardens back of Eagle's Nest Castle.

A figure, slim and graceful, so soundless that it might have been taken for a shadow had there been anything present to cast such a shadow, mounted the wall that separated the wilder gardens from the exquisitely tended ones within.

In the days when Eagle's Nest had been merely the name for a castle, rather than that of the town sprawled about the castle's feet, the dwellers in the castle had claimed for themselves not only the gardens within the walls, but the space surrounding those walls.

As the castle itself stood on a high bluff overlooking the Flin River, and as the owners of the castle were both martial and magical in nature, no one felt inclined to protest. Even years later, when the castle had been captured by she who would become known as Queen Zorana the Great, the claim on the surrounding lands had been maintained.

In more recent years, indeed, since the reign of King Tedric (long though that had been), the city had grown up close to the eastern walls of the castle. A wide, open field was still maintained there, but it was used often as a gathering place when the king addressed his people or as an arena for public spectacles such as circuses, tilting matches, and important executions.

The area west of the castle, however—the high ground along the bluff—had remained in the keeping of the castle. No herds or flocks were grazed there, excepting a few dairy cows and goats kept for the convenience of the castle's occupants. No crops were grown there—even the castle's kitchen gardens were within the walls.

Sometimes small parties hunted in this wilder zone—mostly with hawks, for larger game found its way onto the bluff only rarely now that the surrounding regions were so well farmed and tended. Mostly it was left to itself but for occasional inspections by intelligent and sharp-eyed soldiers who came to cut back trees that might be felled to bridge the ravines that separated the bluff from the lower lands.

Yet it was from this wild garden that the shadowy figure emerged. Nor did the stone wall—quite high and topped with iron spikes—give it pause. It slipped between the spikes and dropped lightly to the ground. Moments later, had any been listening, they would have heard the thunk of a bolt being shot back, a faint squeak as the hinges of a little-used gate swung open.

Now a second shadow, more massy than the first but lower to the ground, joined the first. After it had passed in, the gate was closed and, if ears could be believed, the bolt slid home.

The shadows were lost in the gathering darkness.

FIREKEEPER HAD BEEN PUZZLED about where to go when she returned to Eagle's Nest—for Eagle's Nest was where she hoped to find friends to help her in the duty imposed on her by the Royal Beasts.

Wolf-like, she wanted the support of a pack, but that was not her only reason for coming here first rather than hurrying down to the warehouse in Port Haven where the enchanted objects might still be found. Firekeeper knew too well her weakness regarding human ways and means. If she was to be better than a raccoon or fox at this theft, she needed human knowledge.

Although she had lived in Eagle's Nest for some time, Firekeeper knew little of the city. At King Tedric's request, she had resided at the castle and had been glad enough for the invitation to do so. The city contained more humans than her mind had been prepared to accept. In the castle's grounds, amid its smaller population, she could adjust to the idea that she was not the only human on the earth.

So to the castle she had returned, making her way with ease across ravines that would have barred armies—partly because no one sought to actively prevent her, partly because she could find footholds and handholds where most could not.

Blind Seer had experienced some difficulty in the climb, but Firekeeper had anticipated this. A farmhouse had provided a coil of light but strong rope. Now understanding something of human customs of payment, Firekeeper had left a trio of freshly killed rabbits in its stead. This rope, knotted into a rough harness, had provided the means for hauling the wolf across the deepest divides.

But Blind Seer, too, had learned something in his journeys. Climbing up the Barren River Canyon had given him perfect skill in judging just how far he might jump, just how high he could leap. Thus, they only needed to resort to the harness a few times.

Once within the castle grounds, Firekeeper made not for the towering fortress in which the king resided, but for the low-walled kitchen gardens. As these walls were meant mostly to hide the mundane herb and vegetable gardens from the sight of those who would walk among the roses or through the intricate knot gardens, their gates were not locked.

Firekeeper knew the kitchen gardens well—having frequented them the summer before King Allister's War—and now she made her way through the mazes of walls and buildings to where a small cottage nestled among gnarled fruit trees. These were bare now, picked clean of even the withered leavings of the harvest, but Firekeeper had seen them bent beneath their bounty and welcomed them like old friends.

Most of the cottage's windows were shuttered against the cold, but a small one near the front door remained open, though curtains were drawn against the glass within. Through this translucent aperture, Firekeeper glimpsed the warm reddish light of a fire not yet banked to coals.

She lifted the knocker—a clever thing shaped like a hummingbird nestled in a flower—and rapped several times, enjoying the sound as the bird fell against the wide-spread petals of the bronze blossom.

Her sharp hearing caught the sound of a chair being pushed back from a table, the sound of footsteps assisted by a cane. Then she saw the curtain pushed back from the window as the occupant sought to see who waited without. Some bit of mischief made her stand away from the window, but the door was opened nonetheless and a strong though aged voice began:

"Robyn! How many times have I told you . . ."

The remonstrance, delivered with firmness but not anger, cut off in midphrase. The cottage's occupant, a rather bent woman with a face like a withered apple haloed in wispy white hair, said instead:

"Dan . . . Firekeeper! Out in the cold and snow, and with bare feet and head! Come in, child, and warm yourself by the fire."

Firekeeper obeyed, for though there had been little snow since she left the mountains, the stone flags of the path were like ice. The air temperature without was not unbearable for one who had been climbing walls and the like, but it was brisk when one stopped.

Blind Seer paused at the threshold as if uncertain that the invitation included him, but the old woman waved him in as well.

"Come in, come in!" she said to the wolf, glancing up and around and into the tree branches, "and the falcon, too, if she's with you."

"Elation is not," Firekeeper said. "She has gone to look about, maybe for Derian."

"She'll find him at his parents' house, I believe," the old woman said, leading them into the cottage's central room and clearing her dinner dishes from a table by the fire as she continued, "Though not for much longer. Derian takes service with Earl Kestrel this winter, teaching riding and helping assess the stables."

"You have seen him?" Firekeeper asked.

"He visited, dearie," came the reply as the old woman moved the teapot over the fire to heat, "a few days after the wedding. Timin had some small business with Prancing Steed Stables and Derian chose to run the errand."

She turned and held open her arms.

"Now give this old lady a hug and tell her where you have been and what you've been up to."

Gladly, Firekeeper hugged her. Holly Gardener had become her friend at a time when the feral woman knew few she trusted to value her for herself, rather than out of any hope of personal gain. Holly was no noblewoman; her family's place as the castle's gardeners was secure. Thus she had accepted Firekeeper simply as a girl who wanted to learn gardening.

The former head gardener for the castle, Holly had retired some years before, passing the job on to her son, Timin. Both mother and son possessed the Green Thumb, a talent that assured that these walled gardens would produce more and better fruit and flowers than could be expected under even the best of ordinary care.

From Holly, Firekeeper had learned something of the mysteries involved in growing rather than hunting one's food, and familiarity had not diminished the high respect she felt for the old woman's knowledge.

Once she had released Holly from an enthusiastic embrace, Firekeeper nestled on the hearth rug and leaned back against Blind Seer, who lay watching the flames through slit eyes.

"I been up to mountains west," she said in answer to Holly's question. As she framed the sentence, she was vaguely aware that her grammar had suffered from disuse.

"So Derian told me," Holly replied. "He said that your folks needed you."

Firekeeper smiled, pleased at how Derian had related what to most would be rather odd information.

"They did," she said.

"And are they well?"

"All well enough." Firekeeper couldn't talk about the council of the Royal Beasts, but she saw no reason for not talking about her own pack. "One new pup not lived through spring—fell into runoff creek and drowned. Another pup died in fall when it not see an angry snake, but other young are well. The Whiner is no longer scrawny, but grows into a fine she-wolf."

Blind Seer thumped his tail in agreement. He'd been completely surprised by the improvement in his younger sister. When they'd left, it had been anyone's bet whether the yearling would make it through another summer.

"One other—Blind Seer's older brother by one litter—has come back from travels, but should go out again. The pack is strong and Mother says that no pups this year to raise the little ones stronger."

Holly, accustomed to Firekeeper's somewhat peculiar sentence structure—and probably the only person to whom Firekeeper had talked about the family she had left behind—followed this fairly well.

"You look well, too, dearie," Holly said. "Was your family proud of you?"

"Very," Firekeeper said a trace complacently.

Holly handed the wolf-woman a cup of rose-hip tea and took another for herself.

"And now?"

Firekeeper reflected that when she desired to do so Holly could go after information as if she were digging for potatoes—directly, but without a bruise or scrape left in passing. It was a different form of tact than the misdirection common in the court, and the wolf-woman rather liked it.

"Now," Firekeeper said, "I find Derian. You say he go to Earl Kestrel this winter?"

"That's what he told me."

Firekeeper frowned. Elation was actually not seeking Derian—she was trying to find out whether the stolen artifacts were still warehoused in Port Haven. If they were, having Derian scheduled to go west and north to Norwood lands, rather than east and south to the coastal city, would be difficult.

She shrugged the thought away. There was nothing she could do to change that now.

"I find Derian," the wolf-woman repeated, "but I have problem in that I not know *how* to find Derian and I think that Blind Seer not be welcome in the city."

"True," Holly replied, adding a dollop more honey to her tea. "Honestly, child, you wouldn't be very welcome either. Have you taken a look at yourself?"

"Not but in water," Firekeeper admitted, "and then not long or hard."

"I thought not," Holly tutted. "You're a mess."

Firekeeper was indignant.

"I washed!"

"I'm sure you did," Holly agreed, "but dipping into a stream here and there, and scrubbing off the worst of the mess does not a proper grooming make."

"She's right," Blind Seer commented. *"Now that I see you in human company, you look positively molting."*

Firekeeper hit him, but the wolf continued to snigger.

Holly accepted this incomprehensible act on the young woman's part with the calm of one who had seen the like before.

"Happily," the old woman continued, "this cottage has some amenities. I insisted on them when I gave Timin the Head Gardener's house."

"Amenities?" Firekeeper asked.

"In this case," Holly replied, "that means a tin tub, a kettle big enough to heat water in, and plenty of soap. Hop to and we'll get you set. You can wear one of my dresses, and I'll see if anything can be done about those leathers. If you're good and quick, I believe there is an apple pie somewhere about and some mutton stew."

Firekeeper sighed. A hot bath would feel good, but somehow she felt as if she would be washing off more than travel dirt in the water. Still, Holly was right. She couldn't stay as she was and not cause embarrassment or worse for her human friends.

Jumping to her feet, she went to pump water into the kettle.

FIREKEEPER SLEPT ON THE HEARTH RUG in front of the fire and had to admit—even if only to herself—that the blanket Holly gave her to put over herself felt good.

When morning came, Holly offered her use of one of Holly's own gardening dresses.

"It isn't very big," she admitted, "but then neither are you, though I think you've grown since I saw you last."

Firekeeper, her mouth full of bread and honey, nodded. She knew she had, mostly from needing to have her clothing altered.

"My other clothes?" she asked.

"I haven't had a chance to see if I can get them cleaned and mended."

There was a stubbornness in the old lady's expression that made Firekeeper think that she wasn't likely to see *that* particular set of vest and breeches again. She accepted the use of a dress—a rather shapeless smock of brown homespun that hung to midcalf on her—but none of Holly's shoes would come close to fitting the wolf-woman.

"That fine," Firekeeper said. "I have gone without for long."

After Firekeeper was dressed and fed, and Holly had given up on trying to make some order out of her knife-cut hair, they headed for town.

"I *do* wish you'd wear a bonnet," Holly sighed, but Firekeeper flatly refused. She was beginning to think that hats—like shoes—probably had their place, but she couldn't see how this was one of them.

Holly had come up with a simple solution to the problem of Blind Seer.

"Put him on a leash," she said. "I still find it astonishing what people will accept if they think it is under control."

Firekeeper took the old woman's advice. While Blind Seer wasn't absolutely thrilled with the collar and leash they rigged for him, he was willing to accept the arrangement.

The gardens were nearly empty when they crossed to the unobtrusive gate used by the staff. There was no need, now that the hard frost had killed most of the annuals, for the garden staff to get out early to tend to anything.

The guard at the gate started from drowsy contemplation of the steam rising from his mug of tea when he saw the two women and the wolf approaching.

"Good morning, Goody Holly!" he said, doing his best to hide his surprise. "And good morning, Lady Blysse."

Firekeeper nodded gravely. She knew the man slightly—he had been among those who had fought in King Allister's War.

"Good morning, Rush," she said. "Is your leg better?"

"Healing, healing," he replied, obviously pleased that she had remembered. "And your injuries?"

"All well," she said.

Holly snorted at this. The evening before, when bathing Firekeeper, she had said a great deal about people who would let a "mere slip of a girl go running about with scars like that hardly mended."

Firekeeper had let the criticism pass. She took a curious pleasure in the way the old lady fussed over her—perhaps because all Holly *could* do was fuss. It might have been different if Holly had possessed the power to stop Firekeeper from doing what she wished.

Rush didn't ask any questions, having become, like most of those who served with King Tedric's forces, accustomed to the wolf-woman's odd comings and goings. Giving the trio a hearty wish for a good day, he sent them on.

"And," Holly said as soon as they were descending the road from the castle, "he'll be telling what he saw to the next person who uses the gate—if he doesn't abandon his post to pass on the word. I hope you had no reason for wanting your coming kept secret."

"None," Firekeeper said.

She didn't feel much like talking. Although she had grown more accustomed to human cities and towns, Eagle's Nest remained the largest she had visited. The towering two- and three-story buildings made her feel shut in. The streets thronged—at least to her way of thinking—with foot traffic filled her with a desire to bolt.

Blind Seer didn't like it any better than she did and hung close to her side, growling or whimpering occasional rude comments.

Holly guided them through streets too narrow for any but foot traffic—knowing that Blind Seer would cause the most panic if he was encountered by horses or oxen. Firekeeper thought that the old gardener was enjoying this small adventure quite a bit. Even though Holly leaned heavily on her cane, her steps were steady and brisk.

When they reached the corner on which the Carter family's house stood, Holly had Firekeeper and Blind Seer wait in an alley along the back of the gardens while she went and rang the bell.

"Derian might not be in," she explained, "and there's no need to cause a fuss."

Firekeeper hunkered down and waited, her head against Blind Seer's flank. From the other side of the white-painted fence she could hear chickens fussing. Doubtless they'd somehow become aware of the wolf and were just smart enough to be afraid.

"They probably think you the biggest fox ever," she said, trying to lighten both of their moods.

Blind Seer, who had dined lightly on the remnants of the mutton stew, only growled.

Derian's familiar voice called out from the back door of the house.

"Come on in, you two!" he said. "We've warned the cat and the cook."

They emerged from the alley to find Derian unlatching the side gate, a welcoming grin lighting his face. He was dressed in working clothes: rough trousers, a smock, and scuffed boots—all smelling strongly of horse. His red hair was drawn back with a leather thong rather than the black ribbon he had worn at court. All in all, he was a comforting sight.

Firekeeper saw Derian's grin broaden at her attire. Then he frowned slightly as he looked at her hair.

"You've chopped off your hair again," he said sternly.

"Had to," she replied. "It got in my eyes."

"And just when I had you passing in company," he said, but there was laughter in his voice. "Come inside. I want you to meet my mother and my sister. Father and Brock have already gone to the stables, but I stayed here to help old Toad with shifting some timber."

"Good thing," Firekeeper said.

She felt suddenly shy. Derian had told her about both Vernita and Damita, speaking of them with great fondness. For a moment, she wished she had done as Holly wished and found more suitable attire. Then she straightened and followed Derian into the house.

They entered through a broad, bright room smelling of bread. She remembered how Holly's loaf had been brought to her by her grandson, Robyn, and the numerous busy bakeries they had passed on their way through town. It seemed to her that Derian's family must be fairly well off if they possessed their own ovens.

A stout woman with greying brown hair, her blue-flowered dress covered by a full apron, curtsied stiffly as they came through.

"Cook," Derian said with easy courtesy, "this is my friend, Blysse Norwood. Firekeeper, this is Evie, our cook and house-keeper—our family's Steward Silver."

Firekeeper, who greatly respected Steward Silver, gave Evie Cook a deep curtsy. Cook suddenly dimpled.

"Pleased to meet you, Lady Blysse."

They passed through the kitchen to a front room that nearly matched the kitchen in size. A long table stood at one end; comfortable chairs were clustered at the other. A fire burned merrily in a tall stone fireplace, adding its light to what poured through a multipaned window that looked out into the street.

A tall, elegantly graceful woman rose as they came in, gesturing for the girl next to her to do the same. Both mother and daughter shared Derian's red hair. Vernita's showed some threads of silver, but Damita's was as bright as polished copper. The three woman curtsied all at once and somehow this broke the solemn mood.

Vernita smiled at Firekeeper.

"We've heard much about you, Lady Blysse. Please, make yourself comfortable."

Damita, her gaze on Blind Seer—though in fascination rather than fear—nodded.

"I about you too," Firekeeper managed.

Holly, seated in a chair near the hearth, chuckled.

"Our girl here isn't at her best for talking until she gets to know you," she explained. "I recall when she first started haunting my gardens. She'd climb up on the wall and stare down at my digging, looking for all the world like an over-sized cat."

Firekeeper, remembering from some vague lesson in etiquette that the others would not sit unless she did so first, plopped down near Holly's feet.

Damita's eyes widened. Firekeeper saw Vernita nudge her daughter covertly, so covertly that the wolf-woman probably wouldn't have even noticed if she hadn't been on the receiving end of similar nudges so many times.

"May I offer you refreshment, Lady Blysse?" Damita said quickly, red flooding her cheeks.

"Am thirsty," Firekeeper replied, "and, please, am Firekeeper to Derian's family—not Lady Blysse."

Damita smiled and headed into the kitchen, emerging again so quickly with a tray of tea, cookies, and sliced bread that Evie Cook must have had it ready and waiting.

Passing out refreshments took the rest of the awkwardness from the meeting, especially after Firekeeper had fed Blind Seer several slices of bread.

"He's so dainty!" Damita exclaimed.

"Sometimes," Firekeeper agreed.

"You wouldn't think so," Derian laughed, "if you'd ever seen him go after a hunk of raw meat. Hard to say who was sloppier when I met them—Blind Seer or Firekeeper."

Vernita gave her son a disapproving glance, so Firekeeper came to the rescue.

"Is true," she admitted. "Derian have much trouble with me."

They chatted until the tea and cookies were gone; then Holly said that she really must return to the castle. Firekeeper turned then to Derian and—under the cover of Vernita's polite parting requests that Holly feel free to visit again and Holly's return invitation for mother and daughter to call on her at the castle gardens—spoke urgently:

"Can we talk?"

Derian nodded, looking quite serious.

"I have things to tell you, too. Why don't we walk Holly back to the castle and then find some privacy?"

"Blind Seer?"

Derian shrugged. "The leash is a good idea. Anyhow, it's about time the people of this city got used to him. You *are*

Earl Kestrel's adopted daughter, and that gives you some privileges."

Firekeeper took the young man's word for it. After taking their leave of Derian's mother and sister, and complimenting Evie Cook on her excellent cookies, the three humans and the wolf made their way back up toward the castle. The streets were more crowded now and Holly moved more slowly as they mounted the hill to the castle.

Derian frowned, snapped his fingers, and then signaled to a youth pulling a light cart. Apparently, it had until recently held a load of root vegetables, for their earthy smell—and a dusting of dry soil—remained.

"Want to earn a bit extra this morning?" Derian asked the youth.

The youth—probably about thirteen, but well muscled—nodded, tow-colored hair shaking into his eyes from a loosely tied queue.

"If the work is honest."

"Give the grandmother here a lift to the castle in your cart. I'll help pull if the weight's too much for you."

The youth bridled. "I hauled this full of carrots and taters this morning two loads already. She doesn't look as if she weighs more than a bird. I can haul her, the chit, and her dog without *your* help."

"Easy, brother," Derian said, lapsing into an accent similar to the young man's. "I wasn't faulting you. Here's a Kestrel token. Make the ride smooth and you'll have another."

The bargain was struck, though Holly protested that she didn't need a ride. Derian only shook his head and helped her into the cart, spreading a bit of sacking for her to sit upon.

"You've dressed and fed the earl's daughter," he said. "He'd beat me if I didn't take care of you."

Firekeeper realized that this was meant as much as a brag for the listening youth as to reassure Holly, and swallowed a smile. Apparently, Derian had not liked hearing herself described as a "chit" and had decided to give the youth something to think about.

They saw Holly to the castle gate, but didn't pass through

themselves lest someone delay them. The old gardener gave them each a kiss on the cheek and made them promise to visit again before they left the city.

The youth with the cart had pulled hard and well, refusing help even on the steepest parts of the road. As Derian gave the boy the rest of his pay, he added:

"And if you're looking for more work, stop out at Prancing Steed Stables and ask for Colby. Tell him Derian referred you and will testify that you're a hard worker."

The youth bobbed respectful thanks—though without a trace of groveling—and hurried down the road.

Firekeeper, Derian, and Blind Seer veered off the road short of the city and headed toward the banks of the Flin. Upstream of the city, the river's waters ran sweet and clear. The royal family owned the land and kept it open for reasons of defense, but as the castle had not been besieged since the time of Queen Zorana the Great the broad strip of river meadow had effectively become a public park.

Given the briskness of the late-autumn morning, Derian, Firekeeper, and Blind Seer had the broad strip to themselves. Market day had passed, so even the merchants who paid a small fee to camp along the river were not about.

Blind Seer cut loose from the two humans almost as soon as they were off the road.

"Rabbits?" Derian asked.

"And maybe just too many people," Firekeeper said. "He no like the leash, even though I promise not to hold him if he want to fight."

"Good thing that the people who were staring at you on the streets didn't know that," Derian commented dryly. "Now, who first?"

"My news is easy," Firekeeper shrugged, "to tell if not to do."

"Oh?"

"They call me because they hear of the magical objects," Firekeeper replied.

"From watching the battle," she added, seeing Derian's expression of surprise, "the ravens and crows—not wolves."

Derian nodded slowly. He knew Elation. It wasn't too great a leap for him to imagine crows and ravens of similar ilk.

"And," Firekeeper continued, "they not like having those objects out and want me to steal them. They not understand how this not be easy, even with the objects not on the Islés."

"Not?" Derian said, his brain whirling at the implications of wolves and crows and ravens meeting to discuss what and what not humans should be permitted to do. He seized on something he thought he *did* understand. "Back up a little. The magical artifacts are not with Queen Valora on the Isles?"

"They not."

"But . . ."

"Wait and I tell."

Firekeeper told Derian what the gull had reported to the conclave of the Royal Beasts. The telling took a while, for she had to keep stopping to clarify whenever Derian's puzzled expression told her that she had skipped too much—usually some apparently minor point she took for granted because of her upbringing.

By the time she finished she had a feeling that Derian now knew—or could deduce—more about the inquisitiveness of the Royal Beasts than perhaps those creatures would think was wise.

Derian, however, ignored that aspect of her story, worried about a more immediate problem.

"Damn, Firekeeper! What you just told me fits all too well with what I've been waiting to tell *you*," he said.

Pacing back and forth over the stubble, Firekeeper listened as Derian told her how Elise suspected that Lady Melina was intriguing with Baron Endbrook, how Baron Endbrook had made arrangements to travel by land—and their suspicions that the pair intended to go into New Kelvin.

"Doc thought that what connected the two might be magic," Derian said. "I wondered, but now I'm sure he was right. They're going to do something with those cursed magical objects."

He kicked hard at a water-polished branch. Firekeeper had

heard enough campfire tales by now to have an idea of the horrors her friend might be imagining.

"Elation go to Port Haven," Firekeeper offered in an effort to relieve Derian's worries, "to see if objects still there."

"I'll bet they're not," Derian said, driving his fist into his palm. "Baron Endbrook left Eagle's Nest several days ago—early the morning after Lady Melina's party. I was able to learn that he'd made arrangements to trade horses at posthouses along the way, so if he's willing to have a punishing ride, he could be collecting the artifacts even now."

Firekeeper frowned. "If he does, there will be a watcher to follow him, but a watcher is not a thief."

"And," Derian added, "if the watcher doesn't have anyone to relay information to, then no one will know just where Baron Endbrook has gone."

"True," Firekeeper admitted. There were shortcomings to the surveillance net set up by the Royal Beasts—largely created by the fact that it had been put together to collect information, but not to enable anyone to act on it.

"If only," Derian said, "you knew how to write and had sent Elation ahead with a note! We might have stopped him or delayed him or at least followed him!"

Firekeeper bristled, all the more defensive because she had been thinking along similar lines.

"If I do this, how I know you be of a shape of mind to believe me? Without Elise seeing what she seed . . ."

"Saw," Derian corrected automatically.

"Would you be so ready to believe me when I say that those things are not on Isles?"

Derian shook his head. "From you, Firekeeper, I find it easier to believe the impossible than not."

"Wolves can lie," Firekeeper said, remembering what Blind Seer had told her.

"Oh, I don't doubt that," Derian said with a breeziness that Firekeeper suspected was assumed, "but you're so incredible all in yourself that I just try to see the world as you do. It's a twisted view, but it's easier than trying to stuff everything you say and do into the world as I was taught to see it."

Firekeeper didn't understand all of Derian's words, but she understood the sincerity of his tone.

"Write or no," she said, "is too late. We must wait for Elation. No use running after this man Waln and finding him gone. Maybe we tell Elise and Doc what I know and see if they think what you think."

"Sounds good," Derian replied. "Now, where do you want to stay while we wait for Elation?"

Firekeeper had been considering this matter on and off since she had left her wolf pack in the eastern foothills of the Iron Mountains.

"If Earl Kestrel is here, then his daughter Blysse should go to him," she said.

"Not a bad idea," Derian agreed. "He's used to you and Blind Seer—at least as much as anyone is."

"And," Firekeeper added, brushing at Holly's dress, which had picked up twigs and bits of bracken in its rough weave as they had walked along the Flin's bank, "I fit into his trousers."

XVII

ELATION'S REPORT, UPON THE FALCON'S RE-
turn to Eagle's Nest was not encouraging.

That is, Derian thought, *if we all believe that Firekeeper is actually translating.*

The difficulty with that excuse was that Derian knew that the three of them—Doc, Elise, and himself—did believe. As Derian had said to Firekeeper two days earlier, it was easier to believe than not.

And that makes the three of us—four if you count Firekeeper—mad as a kitten in a catnip patch, at least as far as most of our circle of acquaintances would judge us.

"A gull," Firekeeper reported, "was there when Elation

come to Port Haven, but Waln had come and gone. A crow followed him, but the gull had heard nothing back from the crow."

"Which direction did he go?" Derian asked.

"North," Firekeeper replied, "on the back of a horse with his saddlebags more full."

"And that's the last any have seen of him?" Doc asked.

"The last the gull have," Firekeeper said. "Certainly the crow—unless blinded—continues to see him even now."

A certain twinkle in her dark eyes made clear she was trying to lighten the mood.

Elise rose from the chair where she had been sitting doing fancy work when they had called on her so that she could hear Elation's report firsthand. Her embroidery hoop slid to the floor unheeded, nor did she notice when Doc picked it up and set it on a delicate three-legged table.

"And I cannot learn anything about where Citrine might have gone," Elise said, beginning to pace. "She left Eagle's Nest with her mother two days after the family fete. Although it was generally assumed that they went to some of the family's country holdings, I've found excuse to write and the post-rider brought back my letter undelivered."

"Citrine did tell you though," Derian said, recalling Elise's report the day following the Redbriar/Shield fete, "that her mother planned to take her to the shore. Isn't that correct?"

" 'East to the seaside,' " Elise replied, quoting the little girl as best she could, "to stay with some friends of her mother's she didn't know."

Firekeeper growled—a distinctly bestial sound, not the human facsimile. Derian wasn't surprised. Citrine, along with her slightly younger cousin Kenre Trueheart, had been the first friends the wolf-woman had made at Eagle's Nest.

"Easy," he said to the wolf-woman, patting her arm. "Lady Melina won't let her daughter come to harm."

"Hah!" was Firekeeper's unbelieving retort.

Derian's feelings weren't hurt. He had to admit that he didn't believe his own reassurance, but he kept that doubt to himself.

"If Ruby or Opal were here," Elise continued, pacing back and forth with a steady, restless tread, "then I would certainly be able to pry something out of one of them, but they've gone to Bright Bay."

"And Jet?"

Doc asked the question Derian had wanted to ask but hadn't dared, recalling too well Elise's former infatuation with the handsome young man.

"Jet?" Elise frowned. "I don't think he'd tell me anything and if he got suspicious he'd be certain to report to his mother."

"Do you think he knows how to contact Lady Melina?" Derian asked.

Elise spread her hands in a pretty gesture of frustration.

"I don't know, but I don't think we can take the risk that he can. Our best hope is that the crow Firekeeper mentioned will somehow get a message to someone who can contact Firekeeper."

Firekeeper nodded. "I ask a kite with broad, fast wings to go to the gull at the shore and then to find us here if there is news from the crow. When we leave here a raven will watch and send the kite after us."

"I'm fascinated," Doc said. "Is this usual behavior?"

Firekeeper snorted. "Not one bit! The corvid kin mock and tease the raptor kind, but for this, for fear of the sorcery coming to power, they will give up ancient rivalries for a time."

Elation squawked and ruffled her feathers in something that looked remarkably like agreement.

"North," Derian said, seizing on something solid. "The report is that Waln went north. That confirms our guesses."

"And the wagon and horses that he arranged for?" Doc asked.

"No confirmed report beyond a day from the city, but one of our regular drivers told me that he passed what could have been that rig on the road heading north."

"Very well," Elise said, ticking points off her fingers rather like her father the baron organizing his archers for battle. "Let us assume then that Baron Endbrook and Lady Melina departed separately to minimize comment. Let us further assume that Baron Endbrook—who had a full day's head start, remember—went to Port Haven while Lady Melina took Citrine to these 'friends.' "

Firekeeper, who had been studying the map of Hawk Haven, now looked up with a frown. She still had trouble thinking of lines on a map as honestly representative of places.

"This 'seaside'—it means what it say? I mean, it means at the side of the sea?"

"That's right," Derian said.

"On this," Firekeeper gestured at the map, "I can cover Hawk Haven seaside with my thumbnail—it is a little place between river and river."

She pointed at the Barren to the south and the White Water to the north.

"Why would Lady Melina leave her there? Is it because it is close to the sea and this Waln come from over sea?"

"Possible," Doc said thoughtfully, "but you must remember, Firekeeper, that a good many people live in that thumbnail space. None of us are precisely good friends with Lady Melina and it is quite possible that she simply wanted her daughter to have a new experience. In fact . . ."

Doc's face lit as if illuminated from within by a new idea.

"In fact, who is to say that Lady Melina isn't bringing Citrine with her to New Kelvin?"

"Citrine said nothing about going there," Elise replied dubiously. "She was rather upset about this seaside trip."

"True." Doc's words tumbled over each other in his hurry to get them out: "But if Lady Melina didn't want her own going to New Kelvin to be known at large she wouldn't tell Citrine precisely where they were going. She might even lie to her so that if anyone *did* question Citrine about her—or her mother's—plans, the little girl wouldn't be able to give the game away."

"It does make sense," Elise said slowly, her worried expression lightening. "And it's not at all unlikely that Lady Melina would want her daughter to have a chance to see New Kelvin, given that she herself remembered her own trip there so fondly. It makes perfect sense, when you think of it that way."

She beamed at Doc.

"And I'd been so worried about Citrine!"

Doc flushed from his recently grown beard to his eyebrows.

Derian spoke up quickly lest Elise have a chance to remember that she had been treating Doc like a piece of particularly useful furniture—something you didn't abuse, but you didn't really notice either.

"Good," he said heartily. "Then we will assume Citrine is with her mother. Now, to take up Elise's reconstruction of events. After Baron Endbrook does his business in Port Haven, presumably he will join up with Lady Melina—and Citrine— at some inn. That's where they'll also meet up with the hired wagon and horses."

"Sounds reasonable," Doc said. "It even makes more sense now that Waln opted for a wagon rather than horses. Citrine's too small to make that long a ride astride a horse, and a pony would tire out."

"And be noticeable," Elise added. "A rider or two alongside a wagon could be almost anyone, but a little girl on a pony . . ."

"Little girl with citrine on forehead," Firekeeper added, indicating where Citrine, like all her mother's children except for Sapphire, wore a sparkling gemstone.

"Yes," Elise nodded. "Even if Citrine wore a hat or scarf, it could slip. Better have her wrapped in furs or blankets in the wagon with the luggage."

"If they don't want to be noticed going into New Kelvin," Derian added practically, "they'll pose as merchants. As you noted, Elise, this is a good time of year for trade with New Kelvin. I didn't think to check if Waln also arranged for cargo."

"We'll assume for our purposes," Doc said, "that he did or that he has plans to pick up something along the way. I didn't have much luck with the New Kelvinese before they left for home—they're a closemouthed lot, or at least those I met here were. Still, I did have a couple of decent chats with a younger fellow—hardly more than a servant. I got the impression that he had encountered Baron Endbrook before this, but he didn't want me to know.

"Mind," the knight added hastily, "I may have been seeing what I wanted to see. At the very least, I did pick up some trivia about the customs of the country that could come in handy."

"So you think that we might need to pursue this into New Kelvin?" Elise said slowly.

"Yes," Doc said bluntly, and Derian nodded his agreement.

"I go," Firekeeper said, tracing her finger along the map of the New Kelvinese border. "I go wherever and however far I must to steal those three things."

The wolf-woman looked at them all, her dark eyes serious and her expression quite worried.

"I promised."

❦

AFTER HER GUESTS HAD LEFT, Elise attempted to return to her embroidery, but her thoughts kept wandering and twice she tore out stitches before giving up entirely. Idly, she rolled the hoop between her hands, feeling the flexible wood bounce lightly like carriage wheels against a road.

Finally, she admitted to herself what she had been struggling to deny: she didn't want to be left out of this venture.

True, Firekeeper had returned from her journey with orders that made this matter her own. True, Elise's alertness had served them well, enabling them to deduce not only who had the artifacts, but where they might be being taken.

Surely this was better than the vague information which otherwise would have been all that Firekeeper had to act upon.

I've been useful, Elise reminded herself sternly. *I've done my part. I have other duties now.*

Foremost among those duties was choosing which of her winter guestings she would accept. She had made winter visits before—they were a common way to liven cold-weather dull-ness—but never before had she received so many invitations.

Elise took the heap of handwritten cards from where she had wedged them into her embroidery basket. There were the usual ones from her Wellward relatives, invitations to stay for a moonspan or more. Each of Hawk Haven's other Great Houses—or one of their cadet branches—had also invited her to stay: for a week or a fortnight, for a house party culminating in a dance or masquerade.

Elise couldn't help noticing that most of these invitations mentioned in passing some son or nephew who would be a companion for her.

There was even an invitation from Sapphire asking Elise if she wanted to come stay at the castle. That one was tempting, because—as far as Elise could tell—it offered no attempt at matchmaking.

Despite Lady Aurella's hopes, there were fewer invitations from Bright Bay. Doubtless the nobles there were still trying to figure out what alliances offered the greatest advantages. Still, there was one from a Duchess Seal and—no surprise—the duchess mentioned having a houseful of young sons *and* nephews who would be happy to keep the winter days from growing dull for their foreign guest.

Elise sighed, blowing out her breath with such force that a stray tendril of her fair hair fluttered as in a gale.

In most cases, the invitation from the crown princess would have had unquestioned precedence, but Elise thought that she could manage to appease Sapphire with a shorter visit. How-ever, to do so without hurting her feelings—Sapphire had al-ways been quick to perceive insult—Elise should have her destination picked out and some good excuse for going there.

Once again she spread out the invitations, sorting them by what claim they had on her. As much as she would enjoy visiting her Wellward kin, they must be given lower priority. She was well known to them and they to her. That she might still end up marrying some lesser Peregrine was possible, but, as Lady Aurella had indicated, the Archers already had a blood tie to that house.

Elise considered the others, sliding them back and forth on a polished tabletop in a fashion that reminded her of Sapphire and Shad playing the pirate game.

This, too, calls for strategy, Elise thought, grinning to herself at the comparison. She must share it with her mother at dinner.

At last she had reduced the pile to two or three in addition to Sapphire's elegantly written card. Duchess Seal certainly had a claim and Elise thought that she couldn't quite ignore the one from Lord Polr, Duke Gyrfalcon's second brother.

The Shields were still rebalancing the scales—honored by having a granddaughter of the house chosen as crown princess, shamed by having a son of the house a proven traitor. For those reasons, they might offer some advantageous alliance or even business deal.

Then there was . . .

Elise set Lord Polr's card, which she had been about to reread, aside and reached for one that had sat in its own pile of one at the table's edge since the sorting had begun. It was from Duchess Kestrel and invited Elise to travel to the Norwood Grant with the Kestrel family when they returned home.

During their recent visit, Elise had learned that Derian would be among the Kestrel party, as would Doc and Firekeeper. The duchess's invitation was open-ended—a routine courtesy with winter coming on.

And I could go with them, Elise thought, *and miss nothing. Nor does it hurt that Earl Kestrel's eldest son, Edlin, is a few years older than me or that his next, Tait, is just a bit younger. That should satisfy my mother and father.*

She remembered an earlier visit some years before when she had been about eight. She'd torn about the gardens and fields with Edlin and Tait as if she were as wild as Firekeeper.

My hair was in plaits down my back, she remembered fondly, *and Edlin kept tugging at them. I kicked him in the ankle and he limped for two days. His father wouldn't let Doc . . .*

Doc—or Sir Jared—had been neither healer nor knight then, merely a beardless youth of fourteen or fifteen with dark hair and the Norwood nose. He'd been showing traces of his talent then, but Earl Kestrel had bluntly refused to let him use it for Edlin's benefit.

"You say it isn't broken, Jared?" the earl had said. *"Then let Edlin learn the consequences of his actions. It's not too early, not if he's already being bruised for them."*

And young Jared had solemnly agreed, but he'd bound up Edlin's ankle, then taken them all fishing so his young cousin could take the weight off the injured member and cool the bruise in the water in which they dangled their lines.

Elise was pulled from her memories by the sound of the solar door opening. She looked up to see her mother entering, her footsteps noiseless on the thick carpets thrown down to guard against the chill from the stone floors.

Lady Aurella smiled when she saw what her daughter had been doing.

"I remember those days," she said with a light laugh. "My sisters and cousins and I would count our invitations and lord them over each other as if we'd actually done wonderful by receiving them. Have you decided where you wish to go?"

Elise hedged for time.

"I must visit with Sapphire at least for a day or so, or her feelings will be hurt," she began.

"Wise," her mother agreed, taking a seat where the light was good and opening her own embroidery basket.

Elise noted that Lady Aurella had also chosen a place from which she could not see which cards her daughter had selected. There was a measure of courtesy and restraint in this that Elise appreciated.

Doubtless Aunt Zorana would sweep over here and run her fingers through the cards, pointing out which important ones I had overlooked.

"But you will not winter with the crown princess?" Lady Aurella asked, needle dipping and rising.

"I think not," Elise replied. "Sapphire will be busier than she knew when she wrote this out. I remember something of court routine. She's forgetting that her days will not be the usual idles of winter."

"Perhaps so," Lady Aurella agreed. "If you make good excuse, she will forgive you not offering to give her a longer visit."

"Just what I was thinking."

Elise paused, wondering if she should move directly to Duchess Kestrel's invitation or lead up to it through some of the other candidates. The latter tactic *would* give her opportunity to read her mother's expression. She was about to begin when Lady Aurella stole a march on her.

"I understand from the butler that you had visitors this afternoon: Lady Blysse, Sir Jared, and Counselor Derian. Did they call to bid you farewell before returning north? I understand that Duchess Kestrel is beginning to be concerned that the weather will turn and make their journey unpleasant."

"Not quite," Elise said, unwilling to lie.

"Then did they come to plead with you to come to Norwood with them?"

There was a teasing note in Aurella's voice that made Elise suddenly angry.

"No, they didn't!"

"Ah."

There was a wealth of sympathy and understanding in the single syllable that made Elise even angrier. She kept her temper, however, as befitted a lady.

"Too courteous, no doubt," Elise managed, "or perhaps embarrassed. Duchess Kestrel does mention in her note that Lady Blysse stands to have a lonely winter. Doubtless they didn't wish to pressure me to come and keep her company."

"Doubtless."

Lady Aurella's tone was unreadable.

"I'd like to go, though," Elise admitted. "I have good memories of visits to the Norwood Grant."

"Summer visits," her mother reminded her. "Winter gets bitter in the North Woods."

"True, but Lady Blysse is a friend."

Silence punctuated by the rise and fall of the needle.

"And I don't feel ready to contract a marriage yet."

The words, sneaking out from some quiet parlor in her soul,

startled Elise even more than they did her mother.

"You don't?" Lady Aurella said, raising her elegant eyebrows. "You were ready enough last summer."

"I think that's why I'm not ready now," Elise replied. "I'm not nursing a broken heart, Mother, honestly I'm not, but I can't bear the idea of spending the next several moons making courting conversation and all the rest."

"You'll need to be polite on the Kestrel estate," Aurella said. "You're no longer a child of eight who can kick her host."

"You remember that too!"

Aurella laughed. "Your father and I were terrified you'd crippled the heir apparent to a Great House."

"Apparent, apparent," Elise said, remembering an old jest they'd used to taunt Edlin when he got too full of his own barely understood importance.

"And," Aurella said, sharing Elise's smile, "Edlin and Tait are both potential matches for you."

"Edlin," Elise said, "has lands coming to him through his grandmother and father, but you're right, a separate tie to our barony—given how far apart we are—would benefit us both."

"And I think you were once fond of Edlin," her mother prompted.

"True, but, Mother, I meant what I said. I'm not ready to contract a marriage: not to Edlin or Tait or Jared."

The last name slid out but once spoken could not be ignored.

"No?"

"No. I'm hardly an old maid yet. I won't reach my majority for moonspans yet. I promise to consider any Kestrel offer, but I think I'd like to wait until I have a better idea of our needs."

"Our?"

"The Barony of Archer."

Aurella studied her daughter for a long moment. At last she nodded.

"Go to Norwood then, Elise, with my blessings. I'll make your father understand that this is best."

Elise ran her fingers across the piles of invitations.

"But what about these? What about the other possibilities? There's an invitation here from Duchess Seal of Bright Bay and another from Lord Polr that might as well be from Duke Gyrfalcon."

Aurella shook her head slowly. "Those don't matter if your mind is made up not to contract a marriage. Indeed, it might be dangerous for you to go to them under what might be construed as false pretenses. Not every good match will be made this winter—though many will be. If you're thinking of the barony, we must not sell it cheap."

"I'm thinking," Elise admitted honestly, "about me."

"And someday you will be the barony," Aurella replied, "so it is much the same. Duchess Kestrel's invitation has an advantage over the others in that it asks you to come as a companion for her adopted granddaughter as much as for any other reason. You won't be misrepresenting either yourself or our house."

Elise nodded, thought fleetingly of enchanted artifacts, of New Kelvin, of the excitement to come.

"I suppose not," she said. "I do wish to keep Firekeeper—I mean Lady Blysse—company. She may run wild."

Actually, she thought, *I'll be more surprised if she doesn't.*

"Very good, then. Write out your reply and we'll have a runner bring it to the Kestrel Manse the moment the ink is blotted. Duchess Kestrel will want to send news ahead so that your suite can be readied."

Elise found a sheet of heavy paper embossed with the Archer coat of arms and bordered with a light tracery of scarlet and gold.

As she began to write her acceptance, she heard her mother speaking on, her tones those of one thinking aloud.

"You will take Ninette, of course, and your winter mantle will need mending. I noticed that the hem had been trodden upon. And you'll need to write Sapphire as soon as that letter is completed. It may be difficult . . ."

Elise wrote the necessary missives, hearing only half of

what Lady Aurella said, for her own excited heart beat a drum in her ears.

🕸️

BARON ENDBROOK MADE GOOD TIME to Port Haven and better to the large post-house where he had arranged to meet Lady Melina and her daughter. Despite stopping along the road to stash Lady Melina's gemstone necklace where he alone could find it again, he arrived just as the setting sun was stroking the skies with orange and red.

Good travel weather for the morrow, he thought idly.

As he swung from his saddle, it seemed to Waln that the saddlebags containing the satchel with the three magical artifacts bulged unnaturally large, though to outside appearances—and indeed even to casual inspection—it was no more extraordinary than its mate. Still, he stood between it and the windows of the inn as he stretched out the kinks from his back and legs. He was more sailor than rider, but these last few weeks had prepared him well for the long ride to come.

Baron Endbrook's paranoia regarding the treasures was not helped when a large crow swooped down and began tugging at the straps as if trying to untie the bag. Doubtless it was merely the polished buckle catching the late-afternoon sunlight that had attracted the dumb beast, but nevertheless he felt a chill.

The horse that Waln had ridden was a hired mount and the baron turned it over to the stablehand without a second glance. The precious saddlebags, however, he carried himself, biting back a sharp rebuke when a porter moved to perform the routine courtesy of unstrapping it for him.

If the porter noticed Waln's anxiety, he surely dismissed it as a usual caution. There must be many travelers who worried about strangers handling their baggage.

As Waln was slinging the heavy bags over his arm, he heard a throat being cleared off to one side. He glanced that way and saw Orin—better known as Fox—Driver leaning against a shed.

"Hello, Driver," Waln said with affected heartiness but genuine relief. "Good to see you reached here safely."

"Roads are firm and dry," Fox Driver replied, coming a few steps closer, "and the horses in good fettle."

"And our cargo?"

"Riding light," Fox reported laconically. "I'm cozy as can be in a room over the wagon sheds so's I can keep an eye on it."

"Good."

The cargo itself wasn't worth much—not when compared with what Waln carried in his saddlebags—but the baron had decided that it must be of good enough quality to justify a trip north. Therefore he'd done some shopping and, before leaving Eagle's Nest, Fox Driver had picked up several crates of mixed trade goods. Nothing in the load was too heavy—Waln hadn't wanted to slow them overmuch nor tire the horses—but the cargo was costly enough that if Driver hadn't taken precautions with it, some might have wondered.

"You're warm enough?" Waln asked, stamping his feet, which were chilling as the cold seeped up through the thin soles of his riding boots.

"Warm enough and I've arranged for mulled wine to ease the frost in my bones."

Waln cursed inwardly, but said nothing. Fox Driver seemed sober enough to not have forgotten discretion.

"Then I'll let you go back where it's warm," Waln said. "Is my 'sister' here?"

He and Lady Melina had decided that traveling as brother and sister suited them better than posing as husband and wife. It permitted them both a degree of distance that would have attracted attention between spouses, and their story that they hadn't seen much of each other these last few years allowed for any discrepancies in what they might say.

"She's here and inside with your niece," Fox replied with a sardonic grin.

Waln hadn't told Fox who Lady Melina was, but it was

possible the man might have guessed. Even if he had not, the secrecy to which Waln had sworn Driver regarding what elements of his plans he had been forced to tell the man would have made Driver certain something illicit was going on.

Hopefully, he just thinks I'm running off with someone else's wife, Waln thought.

Then he bid Driver a good rest, reminding him that they would depart early the next morning.

Lady Melina waited for Baron Endbrook within the hostelry. She had claimed a table in a corner and sat knitting in the light that came through the leaded panes.

As they had agreed in one of their planning sessions—these few enough and filled with tremendous anxiety for Waln— Lady Melina was dressed after the fashion of a woman with some means but with no particular claim to wealth or title. In her long wool traveling dress, thick shawl, and close-fitting cap, Lady Melina Shield was transformed into the very picture of a prosperous farm owner.

And what else is she, after all? Baron Endbrook thought, bowing the slight amount that would be courteous from brother to sister, trying to quell the uneasiness he often felt in this formidable woman's presence. *So her mother was a duchess and her brother is a duke, but what is she herself?*

His internal remonstrances failed to buck him up satisfactorily, for Lady Melina's very purpose for being here was an unceasing reminder that the woman was more than she seemed.

Citrine sat beside her mother, hands in fingerless gloves clasped around a mug of some steaming beverage. As Waln took his seat, he caught a whiff of good cider and ordered a mug for himself.

"Just the thing to take off the chill," he said, when greetings were completed.

Citrine smiled shyly at him. Like her mother she wore a traveling dress lapped jacket-style, side to side, to better hold her heat. Her honey-gold hair was covered completely by a ruffled cap of a type not uncommon in the country, though somewhat out of fashion in the towns.

The cap suited Citrine, though, emphasizing the pert round-ness of her face while incidentally concealing the citrine-embellished band that Waln did not doubt still encircled her brow.

That band could well be a giveaway as to who she is, Waln thought. *I wonder if Lady Melina would agree to remove it lest gossip start about just who is the "guest" the smugglers are keeping.*

He decided not to make the request. Descriptions of the sorceress's fury when her eldest daughter ceased to wear her sapphire band were legion—for the ballad singers in the taverns and inns he had stayed in along the road were taking advantage of the royal wedding to regale their audiences with stories of the warrior princess and her noble spouse.

Baron Endbrook wondered if some policy maker in King Tedric's court had put out the word that the singers should make clear that the princess was no longer under her mother's control. That was possible, but it was equally probable that the minstrels simply knew a good story when they heard it.

Fear of the magical arts and of those who used them to control their vassals were a long-standing tradition—and was why Waln himself was being so careful to hide from any but his accomplice the real reason for his journey.

Dragging the saddlebags under the table where he could prison them between his knees, Waln accepted the mug of cider a pigeon-chested serving woman brought to him.

"Your sister," the woman added, "ordered soup and joint, bread and cheese, and a savory to follow. Do you wish to add anything?"

"What's the soup?" he asked.

"Bean and bacon," she said, "and thick enough for a meal itself."

"Sounds wonderful," Waln said. He didn't bother to ask about his room, knowing that Melina, in her role as his sister, would have arranged for it. "Just a mug of ale with the meal then."

The serving woman nodded. "This year's brewing won at the local harvest-fest. You'll be pleased."

She swept off with such self-importance that Waln promoted her from servant to owner. Citrine was staring at him with such wide eyes that he felt uncomfortable and turned his attention to her placidly knitting mother.

"Gloves?" he asked.

"That's right," Lady Melina replied with a brief smile. "I expect to be grateful for extra pairs before this winter is ended."

"True enough," he said.

"Uncle?" Citrine interrupted with a sudden burst of familiarity. "Let me come with you!"

Waln shook his head, but he felt an unexpected lump in his throat. Citrine wasn't far apart in age from his own girls and denying her reminded him of their tears when his last homecoming had been cut short almost before it had begun.

"I'm sorry, sweet," he said, "but this isn't traveling weather for a little thing like you. You'll like where you're staying."

Citrine pouted slightly, but she didn't complain further. The rapid glance she cast in her mother's direction held enough apprehension that Waln realized that this had been the last feint in an ongoing battle and that Citrine had risked punishment to defy her mother's wishes.

Their conversation over dinner was casual, mostly about the various journeys to this point. After dinner, they retired early in anticipation of the morning's departure.

Shortly after dawn, fortified by an astonishingly substantial oat porridge, they took to the road. Waln was pleased with the quality of the horses he had purchased, and the wagon moved as smoothly as could be hoped.

Lady Melina had decided against bringing any servants for either herself or her daughter, so Fox Driver was their only attendant. He drove with the reins lightly in his hands, half-dozing once the horses worked off their early energy. Citrine sat in a padded nest among the crates, well protected from the cold, and played some game with her dolls.

After leaving the post-house, they traveled north for a ways, then bore east. This route forced them to retrace some distance and to leave the best roads, but was necessary in order to go toward the swamps rather than into Port Haven.

The post-house that had served as their rendezvous point the evening before had been chosen since it was about a day from their eventual destination. No mishaps delayed them, and by late afternoon Waln imagined that a certain dampness in the air proclaimed their proximity to the swamps. By evening they had come to a house Waln had visited but the day before.

It stood back from the road atop a hill that the tired horses labored to climb. Nor was it the most inviting of destinations. Although built after the fashion of many a farmhouse—peaked roof, wooden siding, and square windows—it looked ominous in the twilight.

The paint was peeling, and dried leaves swirled in gusts of wind beneath bare poplars. Summer's flowers stood stark and twisted where the frost had killed them, and the hedges bordering the reaped fields were untrimmed; the shoots of summer growth rattled in the wind. Shutters were sealed so tightly over the windows that not one glimmer of light shone out. Only the sluggish smoke from the chimney testified that anyone was in residence—the word "home" could never be applied to such a dwelling.

As Waln's party slowed, a pack of brown-and-white hounds loped toward them, seemingly out of nowhere baying a fierce mixture of defiance and warning. Coming as it seemed from out of the gathering dusk, the hounds seemed supernatural rather than the rather ordinary dogs they were.

Citrine squealed in shock and fear. Normally laconic Fox Driver hastily drew his feet back onto the running board. Even the horses, tired as they were from a long day's haul, stamped their hooves.

Lady Melina remained as calm as could be, circling her giddy mare away from the hounds with a firm hand on the rein.

Waln, having the advantage of the rest, and knowing that they were watched from within, forced his own mount to the door of the house. Leaning from the saddle, he rapped on it with the base of his riding crop.

"Rain riders," he called, speaking the prearranged phrase loudly, "seeking shelter for the night."

"Tonight is wet," replied a muffled voice from within.

The words were incongruous, for though the gathering night was cold, the sky was clear as could be. Waln heard a bolt being shot back, though the door did not yet open.

"Wet indeed," Waln agreed, offering the countersign, "though I can see the stars."

The door opened promptly then and several hooded figures hurried out. Two took charge of the wagon and of Driver, another of Citrine. A fourth helped Lady Melina from her saddle, then stood by while Baron Endbrook removed his saddlebags.

"I have all I need in these," Waln told to the shadowy face beneath the hood. "You'll find the ladies' overnight bag at the back of the wagon."

"We'll bring it in," a male voice replied, "once the mounts are under cover."

Transfer of horses and wagon was accomplished in so little time that Waln had no doubt this routine—or some form of it—was a familiar drill. He did not delay his own steps, but walked through the front door into the seeming farmhouse.

"We've brought the girl," he said once the door was firmly closed behind him, "and plan to leave in the early morning."

Citrine, thinking that this was where she was to winter, burst into sudden panicked tears. Waln felt the purest hypocrite as he patted her head.

Poor little thing, he thought. *I wonder how she'll feel when she sees Smuggler's Light?*

The man Waln had addressed had shoved his hood back as soon as they were inside. He was a tall, lank figure whose clothing hung loosely from his bony frame. His features were simply but efficiently concealed behind a kerchief tied over the bridge of his nose and hanging over his lower face.

Catching sight of him, Citrine's tears turned to howls of terror.

The wind howled in return, shaking the wooden farmhouse and banging at the fastened shutters as if trying to get inside.

"How nice," Lady Melina said politely to their host, "to be inside out of the rain."

BOOK

TWO

XVIII

BY THE NIGHT OF THE TWENTY-SIXTH OF BOAR moon, Baron Endbrook and Lady Melina were a half-day's ride from Plum Orchard, the town on the White Water River from which they planned to cross over into New Kelvin.

Their route had been fairly direct once they left the rendezvous with the smugglers. They had joined up with a road that led between Plum Orchard and the royal post-road. Since Plum Orchard was the major crossing point between the nations—the others, farther west, were less convenient to Port Haven—the road was well maintained, and despite the wagon's slower pace they made reasonable time.

The weather was flowing in that mysterious and subtle transition which carries autumn into winter. Most of the trees were leafless and those that still bore foliage sported rags of greyish brown rather than the flamboyant scarlets, yellows, and oranges that represent the vegetable world's last desperate declaration of life. The days that were not overcast hosted a sharp, biting wind beneath a clear blue sky that made Waln wish for the dull grey days—even with their threat of rain.

Now that their party was reduced to three, Baron Endbrook became more intimately acquainted with Lady Melina. Although she maintained all of her ladylike airs with Fox, she softened toward Waln. Several times a day she mounted the serviceable dapple grey Waln had purchased for her and rode alongside him. At these times she would chat lightly and pleasantly, telling tales of her childhood or the court. Despite the subject matter, Waln felt she was talking with him as equal to equal. A time or two he even thought she might be flirting with him.

When she did not ride, Lady Melina retired to the back of the wagon, where, seated on a heap of bedding that did something to absorb the jolts of the road, she buried her attention in several books she had packed along from Eagle's Nest.

When she took up these studies she was so absorbed in her own world that she noticed nothing else. Several times Fox Driver had needed to warn her to get into cover when rain began to fall—a thing he never failed to do after she had viciously scolded him when a few raindrops plopped onto the printed pages.

Before too many days had passed, Waln learned that Lady Melina's books—which at first he had superstitiously shied away from as potential treatises on magic—were nothing so exotic. They were merely writings on New Kelvinese language and culture.

New Kelvin had not been colonized by the same Old Country that had founded Gildcrest—the original colony of which Bright Bay and Hawk Haven were halves and the Isles a sprig. Waln supposed, given their destination's name, that the founding nation must have been named Kelvin.

Whatever the truth of that matter, the language spoken by the New Kelvinese was quite peculiar. Waln had learned enough to respond to common greetings, to offer thanks, and to ask very simple directions, but even this sparse knowledge had been enough to convince him that he did not care to invest more of his time in that direction.

New Kelvinese was full of round sounds ending in "a" or "o," of drippingly liquid polysyllables, and sharply accented phrases. It was—so he had been told—a language that turned even the simplest request into poetry, a language filled with idiom and allusion, not a language that was inviting to a plain-spoken merchant sailor like himself.

Lady Melina, however, seemed obsessed with it. When she wasn't poring over her texts, memorizing rules of grammar and form, she was laboring over volumes of poetry or drama. Even on horseback she did not abandon her studies. Several times when Waln had ridden up alongside her, he had heard her chanting rhythmic phrases. When questioned, Lady Melina had explained that these were parts of poems.

A few she had recited for him in all their musical fullness, but when he had asked her to translate she had refused with a giggle that was definitely coquettish.

Apparently, Lady Melina told him, a common entertainment among the better classes of New Kelvinese was poetry recitation. Another was a game that involved one person reciting a line from a poem or play—and not necessarily from the opening—and then challenging the rest of the group to continue the piece from that point.

For Baron Endbrook, whose idea of a pleasant social occasion involved dancing or perhaps drinking and telling sea stories, this sounded impossibly dull. Lady Melina, however, seemed to be looking forward to joining in on at least some of these socials.

He wondered—after a particularly long recitation after which she colored and glanced up at him through her lashes— if she was contemplating other entertainments as well. He found himself restlessly anticipating the day when they would have some privacy from Fox. He had married Oralia after he had given up a sailor's life, and his mother's profession had made him feel nothing but revulsion for those women who sold themselves.

Lady Melina was different from these. She was a born noblewoman—not one newly promoted to title, like his wife. Though he despised himself as a snob, Waln realized that Lady Melina's rank drew him almost as much as her personal charms. And he realized with a mixture of guilt and almost painful desire that she could tempt him into infidelity where no other woman could.

Occasionally, Lady Melina put her grammars aside and studied instead a book illustrated with colored woodblock prints of some of the designs the author/artist—a silk merchant from Eagle's Nest—had observed in his travels. The author also offered his conjectures as to the significance of the designs and of the manner (painted or tattooed) that they were applied.

Discovering her fascination with these, Baron Endbrook spent an evening or two looking at the paintings with Lady Melina while she peppered him with questions regarding which designs he himself had seen. Since his hosts had seemed one chaotic swirl of color, Waln was less helpful than she had hoped, but under her persistent questioning he was able to remember enough to satisfy her.

"If the author is correct in his conjectures," Lady Melina said, almost reverently shutting the book after one of these sessions, "and you are correct in your remembering," she added with what he took for affectionate severity, "then it is likely that those who interviewed you were representatives of the same group, but whether that group corresponds more closely to one of our Great Houses or to a Society is uncertain. The author has failed to ascertain even such a basic point."

"How," asked Waln, "do you figure that they are all members of the same group?"

"Several times you have mentioned the use of a tight spiral design," she said, sketching the representative pattern on the back of his hand with the tip of one finger. "This seems to be one of the signature designs. Significant, too, is the predominance of the color orange in the paint near the eyes."

Waln nodded, only partly convinced and very distracted.

"There's an awful lot of color all of them seem to wear," he cautioned.

"And doubtless it seems applied without rhyme or reason to the untutored eye," she replied severely, "but my sources indicate that to the knowledgeable they are as distinct as, say, types of ships would be to a sailor."

Waln didn't care to argue, that not being his job. Nor did he wish to alienate Lady Melina, not when they were growing so comfortable together, not when they were nearing a town where they might stay at an inn with the luxury of private rooms.

No. Most certainly he did not wish to alienate her now.

❧

HIS PARENTS HAD NAMED HIM GRATEFUL PEACE —
perhaps their wistful ensorcellment that he might be a quiet
child. Their previous three, he learned when he grew older,
had all been loud, screaming infants who refused to sleep
through the night.

Whether or not the ensorcellment had taken, Peace, as he
had been more usually called—though his eldest sister tor-
mented him with the name Grey Pee—had indeed been a quiet
child. Bookish and solemn, he had roamed through his earliest
childhood in a nearsighted haze.

When Peace was five, his father had been promoted to full
scribe at the Scriptorium. This new prosperity had meant that
he could at last afford a pair of spectacles for his youngest
son. These precious ground-glass lenses had revealed miracles
to the boy. For the first time he saw mountaintops and the
intricate lacework of tree branches. He reveled in the majesty
of cloud formations and the mystery of the distant horizon,
but even after they had become memory those early years left
their mark.

Grateful Peace could never forget what it had been like to
dwell within the private island of his myopia. Indeed, each
day when he put the spectacles aside for sleep he was reminded afresh. Raindrops or the sudden cold that misted his
lenses reduced his sight once more. From an early age he
resolved to become wealthy, for to slide back into the near
poverty of his childhood would mean that he might also slip
again into near blindness.

Ironically, it was his myopia that opened the way to wealth
and influence for him. The same weakness in Peace's eyes
that made the distance a blur made it possible for him to focus
closely without difficulty, nor did he suffer the headaches that
plagued others when they worked up close for overlong.

Peace's father was a scribe, his mother an illustrator—perhaps one reason they both believed so strongly in the magic of written things such as words.

Before Peace was seven they trusted him with their brushes and inks. By the time he was ten, his mother let him do his own makeup. By the time he was twelve, she was requesting he touch up his siblings' work—earning their resentment.

At the age when most children of his class were being apprenticed, Peace was already acknowledged a master in the basic crafts of writing and painting. Rumor of his skills came to the ears of the Illuminators—those revered mystics who were trusted with transcribing the treasured records of the past. His apprenticeship into their class promoted him forever beyond his family and guaranteed that he would never want for any basic need.

Grateful Peace missed his parents when he moved from their home into the many-windowed palace of the Illuminators. He did not, however, miss his siblings. They had resented how their parents favored him and had made his life such a misery of small torments that the punishments promised for the afterlife—even the fabled torture of living pictures—seemed less terrible.

When he was twenty-five, Grateful Peace was tattooed as full Illuminator. He was given apprentices of his own, servants, and a suite in the palace. At thirty, he married a pretty young woman who had been his apprentice.

Chutia was not as talented as her husband. Indeed, she had never risen above the ranks of a junior Illuminator. However, she possessed a capacity for joy and a wealth of compassion that made her company a never-ending delight.

She died when Peace was thirty-five, taking their unborn twins with her into the Enchanted Paradise. He vowed never to marry again and tattooed his vow across the bridge of his nose so that none could doubt his resolve.

As with his myopia, that tragedy proved to hold a hidden blessing. Realizing that Grateful Peace sincerely meant never to marry again, noting that while he honored his parents he barely spoke to his siblings, the Dragon Speaker—the first among the thaumaturges of New Kelvin—initiated Peace into his intimate circle, elevating him at last to one of the Dragon's Three.

Fifteen years had passed since the day Grateful Peace had added a dragon's claw to the feather and bar already permanently adorning his features. His hair, like that of his father, had politely receded, making the tedious work of shaving his front head unnecessary. What hair remained showed streaks of grey, so Peace had it bleached bone-white. His features had settled into grooves and lines but had not yet begun to sag.

Apheros, the Dragon Speaker who had appointed Peace, remained in power—they were much of an age—and showed promise of retaining his influence over his peers. In fifteen years he had given Grateful Peace many peculiar and often distasteful tasks, but none quite equaled the one before him in its potential to transform their world.

Grateful Peace had left Dragon's Breath as Dead Leaf Moon was waning and New Snow Moon not yet a sliver on the horizon. He took with him a small entourage: a groom, his body servant, a scribe, several guards. He also carried with him a resolve to connive at murder.

Had there been any chance that Queen Valora would insist on seeing the body of her ambassador, then more elaborate theatrics would have been necessary. Queen Valora, however, was far across the seas. The prevailing winds were from the north this time of year, meaning that to visit New Kelvin she would need to risk sailing against them and the greater danger of landing in countries where she was not welcome—and this assuming that she would dare leave her new domain before her rulership was firmly established.

No, eventually Queen Valora would receive a report that her ambassador and his party had been set upon by bandits—if possible the report would hint that these were ruffians out of Hawk Haven, a thing not unheard of this close to the border. All had been slain but for the baron's lady companion, and she was suffering from acute amnesia—doubtless brought on by shock and her own terrible injuries.

The beauty of the scheme was that Queen Valora would be in no position to publicly protest. To do so would be to risk that the Dragon Speaker would inform King Tedric of Hawk Haven and King Allister of the Pledge what cargo her messenger had carried.

These allied monarchs might well decide that Queen Valora's punishment for toying with sorcery would be a more permanent demotion than she had suffered at the close of King Allister's War. Even her closest relations would not dare openly support Queen Valora when they learned she had dared dabble in sorcery.

And New Kelvin? Grateful Peace's own home would be doubly safe—protected once by the artifacts they would then hold, protected twice by the fact that they alone of all the nations in the known world had never proclaimed a hypocritical aversion to sorcery. Everyone would fear that they possessed the knowledge and power to turn those artifacts against them.

Despite decades of intrigue on many levels, Grateful Peace was impressed by the intricate simplicity of the plan. Nor did he feel any particular guilt about betraying Queen Valora. He had no doubt she intended to double-cross New Kelvin— almost certainly as soon as Baron Endbrook had learned the nature of the enchanted artifacts. If not then, after she had settled the score with Bright Bay and Hawk Haven.

What *did* concern Peace was that the skeleton of this plan had come from one mind—that of Lady Melina Shield—and that she herself was at least temporarily safe from being herself put out of the way. She must suspect—if she didn't outright *know*—that the thaumaturges would not suffer her death until they had learned everything she knew about sorcery.

Peace wondered uneasily what other plans Lady Melina had in mind, what safeguards she had laid in place lest she be betrayed in turn.

THE PLUM ORCHARDS that had given their name to the town were bare now, their tall compact forms stretching toward the sky like spiky fingers lightly clasped or perhaps the bones of a fan slightly extended. They surrounded the town on three sides, connected to it by firmly packed dirt roads that were cobbled from just outside the fringes of the town into the town proper.

The sudden transition against the flat, bare land gave the town something of a pretend look, reminding Waln of the doll cities his children constructed from wooden blocks and other odds and ends.

Most of the buildings in Plum Orchard proper were constructed with rock from the river. Some houses were made of smoothly worn cobbles, but a more popular choice seemed to be jagged rock broken into chunks about the size of a healthy pumpkin and roughly mortared together. The result was surprisingly attractive, the uneven edges catching the sunlight and giving it back flecked with mica or shining from various shades of quartz.

Not many of the buildings exceeded two stories—creating the impression that higher walls would have collapsed under the sheer weight of stone. The tallest was a guard tower near the river. From chatting with innkeepers along the way, Waln had learned that the tower commanded the crossing to New Kelvin and that no one used the ferry without paying their toll to the local government.

Plum Orchard was a Crown city, technically under the administration of Grand Duchess Rosene. The elderly grand duchess, however, preferred to spend her time in the capital city and collect her rents from a distance. When she died, the city would revert to the Crown. Had King Tedric had any surviving children, one of the next generation of grand dukes or duchesses would have been granted the right to collect the rents.

Idly, Baron Endbrook wondered to whom the Crown would give this plum. He grinned at his own joke, then soured, for he had no one with whom to share it. Lady Melina would not find a mere pun amusing and while Waln was willing to chat with Fox Driver as a means to fill those long hours on the road, he had learned in his days as a sailor of the danger when a hireling thought himself too much his employer's equal.

Waln tucked the joke away in memory so he could include it in his next letter to Oralia. He planned to post one from here before they crossed into New Kelvin. Lady Melina did not seem to notice Waln's daily epistolary efforts. She certainly never wrote to anyone—not to the son who now administered her estates, nor to any of her four daughters.

Their travel had spent the first part of the day. Obtaining travel permits and declaring their trade goods would take the rest. Waln settled Lady Melina in a midclass inn called the Rocky Pink, which had come well recommended by one of his casual gossips. To his disappointment, the establishment maintained a separate wing for female travelers and, when offered, Lady Melina accepted a room there.

The two-storied inn was made of rough stone in which rose quartz predominated, doubtless the reason for the establishment's name. Floral skeletons suggested that the garden might be planted to continue the theme. Now, like everything else, it was grey and brown.

After their trade goods had been assessed by a mildly interested customs officer, Fox Driver took their equipage to a livery stable—a local branch, Baron Endbrook noted, of the Carter enterprises that had been so dominant in Eagle's Nest.

Waln himself went to pay their fees and obtain permission to make the crossing. He had practiced hiding his Islander accent behind something more neutral and on eliminating the roll from his walk. He fancied he did well enough. The woman on duty, distracted by the quarreling of two young children in a back room, hardly gave him more than a passing glance.

The next morning, Waln and Driver loaded the wagon and horses onto the ferry without the slightest difficulty. Lady Melina assisted to the extent of leading her own dapple grey and carrying the bag with her precious books.

The ferryboat was attached to a cable running between towers on each shore. However, although much of the motive power for pulling the boat across was supplied from the other side, that didn't mean their boatmen didn't have anything to do.

Huge, burly men—no women as far as Waln could tell—they fended the craft off from the rocks using long, heavy poles and lots of heated language. Even here where the White Water was considered fordable, the currents were unpredictable, the foaming waters likely to hide boulders dislodged from higher up the river's course beneath their churning surface.

Waln suddenly understood the preponderance of stone as a building material throughout the town. It must be dredged out by the ton all year round and the first crossing after the spring floods had abated must be reserved for the bravest and most skilled—or at least for the most foolhardy. But enough of the town's prosperity rested upon this fragile crossing to make the risks worthwhile.

Although Waln was a skilled saltwater sailor, he found the splash and foam intimidating, arousing long-held fears of reefs and sandbars that could tear the bottom out of a ship with a deeper draft. But the ferry's bottom was as flat as an iron, and even loaded the vessel drew very little water. Its very size granted it a measure of stability, and the bargemen were very good. They knew themselves skilled and shared with their saltwater sailing fellows the cocky pride that comes from successfully defying the elements.

When they were put ashore on the other side, Lady Melina wanted to continue immediately to Dragon's Breath. Fox Driver didn't quite dare counter her directly, but he spoke to Baron Endbrook in a voice loud enough that the baron knew it was meant to carry.

"The horses are shaken, m'lord. If we hitch them up now one would be likely to do something foolish—and a sprain or the like would delay us far longer."

"Can we," Lady Melina inquired acidly, "buy other horses?"

"What the lady suggests would take as long," Fox replied, still addressing his remarks to Waln rather than to Lady Melina, "as what I'd suggest."

"And that is?" Waln asked, wishing he weren't caught in

between Lady Melina's eagerness and the driver's sense of responsibility.

"Let these rest until noon," Fox said. Something in his tone said that he'd intended to suggest waiting until the next day, but that he didn't quite dare. "I'll take them where they can't hear the water so plain and walk the nerves out of them. Maybe give them a bit of hot mash—not enough to bring on colic, just enough to remind them that the world is filled with more pleasant things than raging waters.

"Horses," Fox added, "have too much imagination for their own good."

Waln didn't glance at Lady Melina as he gave Fox permission to do as he had suggested. He could no more insist that the horses be pushed on than he could insist that a ship sail with a cracked mast.

The baron toyed with the idea of insisting that they stay the night in town, but dismissed it. Lady Melina was not the only one eager to press on. Back on the Isles, Queen Valora was waiting for news and he doubted that his intermittent travel reports—mailed less frequently than his letters to Oralia, but still with dutiful regularity—would satisfy her.

Nothing would satisfy his queen but the news that the secrets contained in the three artifacts had been unlocked and that they were being returned to her, ready to arm her for her reconquest—or perhaps merely for her revenge.

XIX

 WITH ONE THING AND ANOTHER, Boar Moon had nearly passed into Owl Moon before the Kestrel party settled in at the Norwood estate. Had it not been for the charge laid upon her by the Royal Beasts, Firekeeper would not have minded the passage of time in the least.

For one thing, she finally got a chance to know her adoptive grandmother, Duchess Kestrel. Saedee Norwood was a nice enough woman, even if the edge of her tongue could be a bit sharp when she was displeased. However, she was canny, had been fond of hunting and woodcraft in her youth, and didn't believe in young people being idle. That meant she didn't try to keep Firekeeper from running wild. If anything, she encouraged it.

Another pleasant aspect of the trip was being reunited with Derian and Elise, neither of whom Firekeeper had spent much time with since King Allister's War had ended.

But even the wolf-woman's pleasure in her friends' company was troubled by the fact that not one of the wingéd folk had brought news regarding the whereabouts of Lady Melina and Baron Endbrook. Not even Elation's frequent scouting missions turned up any indication of where the pair might be, and Firekeeper came to accept that her prey might be lost to her—if not forever, then for longer than she'd like.

"I wish," she said to Blind Seer one afternoon shortly after their arrival at the Kestrel estate, "that birds howled. Then the crow or gull or whoever knows where those two have gone could howl us the news."

Blind Seer chewed at the edge of one forepaw pad in a philosophical manner.

"It might not do any good even if they could," he replied, "for to whom would they howl? If we howled, no Cousin could carry a complicated message. It must be the same for the wingéd folk."

"True," Firekeeper sighed, "but I cannot simply wait."

"Why not?" the wolf replied. "Waiting doesn't seem any more useless to me than chasing off after game that may not be where you seek it."

"We know," Firekeeper countered, "that they are going to New Kelvin."

"We think we know," the wolf said with slight emphasis on the word "think."

Firekeeper chewed at one knuckle in unconscious imitation

of the wolf and his paw. She was still doing so when there was an interruption.

She and Blind Seer had been relaxing in a room the wolf-woman particularly liked—a southern-facing chamber walled along most of one side in panes of glass. The forest on the other side of this glass wall had been cleared away and a lawn—sheep-mowed in the warmer months—stretched in lazy green openness. The sun kept the room moderately warm. Old carpets were heaped deeply on the floor, perfect for sprawled sunbathing.

Norwood family legend said that the glass-paned wall had been built using a remnant of the old magic. Earl Kestrel, who had traveled some in his younger days, said that the New Kelvinese still possessed nonsorcerous means for building just such a room.

Never mind which story was true. The room was open, warmer than the outdoors, and shielded from the wind. Because the humans found it chill—it lacked a fireplace—Firekeeper and Blind Seer could escape the bustle of the house party without being precisely rude.

However, several people had learned the location of this favored refuge and one of these came strolling in at that moment.

Edlin Norwood, Earl Kestrel's son and heir apparent, was a tall, slender youth, a year or so Derian's elder. His face was angular—and rather surprisingly lacked the distinctive Kestrel nose. His features were topped with a cap of black curls, for he wore his hair unfashionably short, on the excuse that otherwise it pulled from its queue and got in his eyes. Those eyes—pale grey and very similar in shade to his father's—danced rather than brooded. All in all, Edlin Norwood was a young man who thought well of the world.

Although, past his majority, and therefore entitled to be called Lord Kestrel, Edlin was more usually styled Lord Edlin, as if he were yet a boy. For Firekeeper, who longed to prove herself a competent adult in either of her worlds, Edlin's permitting himself to be so addressed was a mystery.

Firekeeper had been introduced to this new "brother"—

along with the three other Kestrel children—immediately upon her arrival. Tait, the next in line, was a short, rather chunky lad of seventeen who was caught between a boy's build and a man's. Facially, Tait more resembled his father than not, though his hair was sandy rather than dark. Toward Firekeeper he had been distant, but not unkind.

The two girls, Lillis and Agneta, were still clearly uncomfortable with their newly adopted sister. They were not so uncomfortable that Agneta—age eight—had failed to inform Blysse with cheerful self-importance that although Blysse was the elder by seven years, Agneta was actually the "big" sister because Blysse's recent adoption made her the younger within the Kestrel birth order.

Whatever his siblings' reactions, Edlin was clearly fascinated with Blysse. Whenever possible, he peppered her with questions about her childhood—questions she answered rather shortly, newly aware of the former enmity between the Royal Beasts and humankind.

Edlin, however, was not discouraged by her terseness. Nor was he intimidated by Blind Seer. Edlin *liked* dogs—one of his prides was a kennel of red-and-white spotted bird dogs, similar to Race Forester's Queenie.

In his interactions with the wolf, Edlin Norwood chose to treat Blind Seer as he would any big dog—that is, he accorded the wolf distance and respect. Edlin always held out his hand for the wolf to sniff, never stared down at him, and even sat on the floor or a low chair lest the wolf think he was attempting to dominate.

Now, breezing into the room, Edlin held out his hand to Blind Seer and then, when the wolf sniffed it politely, plopped down onto the rug. Firekeeper had learned that the courtesies Derian had taught her didn't always apply between brother and sister. Edlin, by walking in on her like this, was treating her no differently than he would Lillis or Agneta.

The wolf-woman, with her own strong sense of hierarchy—for even wolf pups fought each other until an acknowledged order was arrived upon—wasn't at all sure she liked sibling informality. However, she didn't know how to get rid of Edlin without insulting him—and she knew enough of human customs to know that insulting heirs apparent was a bad idea.

"Hi!" Edlin greeted her brightly. "I thought you'd like to know that Mother is back at last, bringing with her the rest of the house party, what?"

Firekeeper nodded, her pulse quickening a bit. The only member of the Kestrel family she hadn't met was Lady Luella Kite, the earl's wife. Race Forester had warned Derian that Lady Luella hadn't been completely delighted by her husband's adoption of Blysse—less because anything about Blysse herself offended her than because the adoption had been a Kestrel matter and the earl, caught up in his own dreams of power, had not consulted his wife until *after* he had gained the duchess's approval.

"When do I meet Lady Luella?"

"She's resting from the road now," Edlin replied a touch more seriously, "and told Father that shortly before dinner would do."

Firekeeper swallowed a groan.

"Formal dress," she said aloud. "I must see Derian."

"I say!" Edlin said quickly. "I have news for you about that, too. Grandmother thinks you're too old to have a male attendant—especially one as young as Counselor Derian."

"I have heared that," Firekeeper admitted, "from other lips. What do I do? Ask sister's maids or maybe Ninette?"

"Grandmother has someone for you," Edlin replied, "if you like her that is. She's a woman who does all sorts of things for Grandmother. Most of the lady's maids are frightened of the wolf, you see, but Wendee isn't."

"Wendee?"

"Wendee Jay," Edlin clarified, grinning as if he'd just offered Firekeeper a present.

"When," Firekeeper asked, feeling a vague despair that Edlin could talk so much and say so little, "do I meet this Wendee?"

"As soon as you want," Edlin said. "Shall I have someone bring her to you?"

Firekeeper remembered her human-style manners.

"This room cold, maybe I meet her in my room?"

"I say, that sounds great!" Edlin replied. He rose, bowed slightly to Blind Seer, and then paused. "And don't worry about Mother. She's no monster and I think she'll like you a whole lot, just like I do!"

He dashed out then. Firekeeper got to her feet and brushed off her breeches.

"He seem younger than Derian," she said at last, "but they tell me he is older by a year's turning and more."

"Edlin likes you," Blind Seer replied with a dry cough, "and from what I have seen of human males liking a female can make them frolic like puppies."

Firekeeper, thinking of the times she had caught Doc laughing overloud at a joke or humming to himself just because Elise had smiled at him, nodded.

"I don't like Edlin—not like that," she said stubbornly. "I will tell him."

"Not wise," Blind Seer warned her. "Even puppies have sharp teeth and no matter how he frolics now, Edlin Norwood is not a puppy."

Firekeeper sighed and then bolted to the stairs nearest to her room, running as if she could outrun these awkward social entanglements. Blind Seer loped behind her, nipping at her heels.

Wendee Jay was not at all what Firekeeper had expected. In her experience, lady's maids had fallen into two categories. Either they were like Ninette, Elise's companion, a genteel-appearing woman of fairly young years, or they were older women, bossy and officious, often assuming their importance among servants was equivalent to that of their mistress among her peers. In both cases, more often than not they were unmarried.

Elise had explained that a married woman could not be expected to keep the odd hours a lady's maid did. If a maid married, she either left service entirely or was reassigned to a post with a more regular schedule.

The first thing that was clear about Wendee Jay was that she was a mother, for the little girl with pale blond hair who clung around her neck when Wendee entered Firekeeper's room was obviously her daughter.

"I'm sorry I had to bring Merri along, but my mother and my older girl, who usually watch her for me, are busy helping get the banquet ready for this evening. That's where I was when Lord Edlin found me."

Firekeeper nodded, studying this woman who wasn't afraid of wolves—as she clearly wasn't, having glanced to where Blind Seer lay apparently dozing in front of the fire and then dismissed him.

Wendee was slightly taller than Firekeeper, with dark blond hair, blue eyes, and a voluptuous figure that turned her simple kitchen dress and white apron into something remarkable.

"But here I'm talking like you know me," Wendee went on, showing a touch of shyness, "because we all feel like we know you. I'm Wendee Jay. This is—as I suppose you must have guessed—my daughter Merri."

"And I am . . ." Firekeeper hesitated, knowing that here she was Lady Blysse, but feeling that someone who would be dressing her and such should call her by name. "Firekeeper, but also Lady Blysse."

"Whichever name suits the situation," Wendee said with a lack of fuss that Firekeeper immediately appreciated. "Well, Lady Blysse, Duchess Kestrel asked if I'd tend you while you're here and I will do so, if only as a favor to her. She's been good to my family. We have a cottage here on the grounds which is nice."

Seeing Wendee switch the child from hip to hip, Firekeeper remembered her manners.

"Please sit. We just keep Merri from Blind Seer. He not eat children, but not likes ears and tail pulled either."

"Who would?" Wendee replied practically. She set her daughter down next to a chair and handed her a doll from a pocket of her apron.

Once the child was settled, Firekeeper—aware that Lady Luella might summon her at any time—explained her need.

"I need someone to help me with formal attire," the wolf-woman explained. "I not do laces myself."

"Who can?" Wendee shrugged. "Laces are impossible. I like comfortable clothes myself, work smocks and such, but there are times a woman wants to look elegant and then it's laces and slippers and taking four or five times as long to get ready."

Firekeeper heaved a heavy sigh of agreement.

"Today, Earl Kestrel's wife has come and I need formal attire. Can you help?"

"In a heartbeat," Wendee promised. "First we ring for bathwater. You've been running outdoors and even in cold weather that leaves a stink."

Wendee pulled a short rhythm on the bell-rope.

"That will get hot water up here. Next we pick out what dress you should wear."

Wendee began arranging things so efficiently that Firekeeper relaxed enough to ask her new maid some questions about herself. Wendee told her that she'd been an actress before children tied her closer to home, and that—though there was nothing wrong with routine domestic work—she still preferred a job that challenged her.

Without being prompted, Wendee began talking about Lady Luella.

"She's a fair mistress, though I don't think she particularly likes her diminished importance in what is, after all, the duchess's establishment. She much preferred when she and Earl Kestrel were younger and had their own residence, but several years ago Duchess Kestrel began turning over more and more of the responsibility for running the Norwood Grant to her son. That meant living here, so she could confer more closely with her son.

"Lady Luella has never quite gotten over having to make the choice between living apart from her husband and giving up being mistress of her own estate. It's strange but, when the earl travels—as he did so much of last year—Lady Luella's taken to digging her heels in and staying behind. Says the children need to have some stability. I think she's fighting her reflection."

Firekeeper, who had been dutifully scrubbing the dirt from her feet, wondered if she'd misheard.

"What?"

"Fighting a nothing that seems like something," Wendee clarified.

Although this didn't help much, the mention of fighting brought Firekeeper's main concern to her lips.

"How I make Lady Luella not see me as a fight?" Firekeeper asked bluntly.

"Well, we'll start by putting you in this gown," Wendee said, the very fact that she didn't ask for clarification showing that she was aware of Lady Luella's resentment regarding Blysse's adoption. "Most of your stuff looks as if it was designed for court—I guess it was—but we don't want to put you in something that screams 'Kestrel.' That'll just remind Lady Luella that she's annoyed at the earl."

The gown Wendee eventually selected was one of the simpler ones Firekeeper had acquired along the way, a pretty light brown frock trimmed with a darker brown and touched with lace at wrist and throat.

"But you should wear the blue and pink beads," Wendee went on, "no need to deny the Kestrel connection. Then we'll put your hair up—is it true you trimmed it with a knife?"

Firekeeper nodded.

"Well, we can't mend that, but we'll tuck the ragged ends under a nice girlish cap, so you look a bit younger and more helpless. The knife stays, doesn't it?"

Firekeeper nodded again.

"That's what Valet warned me. Very well, since it stays, we'll belt it on nice and plain. No need to have anyone think it's a negotiable point."

In less time than Firekeeper could have imagined, she was clean, gowned, and groomed. Wendee Jay looked at her in satisfaction, then scooped up Merri, who had fallen asleep on the rug.

"Judging from the light, Lady Luella should be sending for you soon. Wait here and be prompt when someone comes for you. Remember," Wendee paused in the doorway, "she probably wants to like you, but you'll need to give her a reason why she should do so."

With those cryptic words, Wendee darted out the door. Firekeeper could hear her footsteps, light in spite of the child she carried in her arms, as she pattered away and down the nearest servants' stair.

WENDEE PROVED A PROPHET. Firekeeper had hardly time to give herself one more inspection in the glass when a tap at the door brought the expected summons.

"My lady wishes to meet with you in her parlor," the servant said, and departed with the anxious haste Firekeeper had seen so often in those who were less than comfortable around Blind Seer.

"Shall I come with you, dear heart?" the wolf asked, raising his head from his paws.

Firekeeper was about to suggest that he stay behind when she recalled what Wendee Jay had said about her Fang.

"Come," she said, "but with manners as for the One. You may not be what Wendee calls a 'negotiable point,' but there is no need for us not to show you at your best."

Blind Seer rose and shook then. Despite his fondness for sleeping near the fire, his fur was thickening into his winter coat and he looked even larger than normal. Firekeeper felt a momentary flicker of uneasiness. Had she made the right decision?

Side by side, the pair made their way to Lady Luella's rooms. When a servant admitted them in response to their knock, Firekeeper saw that the earl's wife waited for them alone.

Lady Luella Kite wore her long, straight hair loose and combed from a severe center part into two shining chestnut waves. From the strong scent of rosemary in the air, Firekeeper guessed that it had been recently washed and was—beneath the upper layers—still drying. This initial impression—founded as much in olfactory as visual impressions—was confirmed by the long loose robe the lady wore belted at her waist and the soft slippers on her tiny feet.

These feet were the only things precisely tiny about Lady

Luella. She was a woman of above average height and the four living children she had borne had sealed her figure into solid womanly curves.

The gaze she raised from her stitchery at Firekeeper's entrance was cool but not cold, and her greenish-yellow eyes met the young woman's with appraisal rather than challenge.

Firekeeper gave her best curtsy and Blind Seer stretched out his forelimbs in a bow. Lady Luella did not rise nor did she offer her hand, but her initial greeting was courteous.

"Take a seat, child, and make yourself comfortable. I apologize for my undress, but these several days on the road left me feeling more akin to a scullion than a hostess."

Firekeeper accepted the indicated seat—a fat puff printed with bright flowers—though she would have been more comfortable on the floor. Blind Seer sat beside her, careful not to get too close and shed even more silver-grey hair on the brown of Firekeeper's dress.

When Lady Luella studied her in silence, Firekeeper did not lower her gaze from the inspection, but neither did she challenge the older woman, staring her down as she might have the Whiner when that young wolf grew overly arrogant.

At last, Lady Luella spoke.

"You know how to hold your tongue, I'll give you that, Blysse. Or is it true what the rumors said last summertime—that you cannot speak at all?"

"I can speak," Firekeeper replied, choosing to ignore the insult. "Some, though not too well."

Lady Luella smiled, and Firekeeper thought that she had passed some test.

"You speak quite clearly. If your accent is harsh, what else can be expected?"

This was the first time Firekeeper had been told that she possessed an accent and the unfamiliar word puzzled her. Her habit of asking questions took over before she could stop herself.

"Accent?"

"A touch common," Lady Luella explained, "but then your tutors have been common-born, have they not?"

Firekeeper was already beginning to regret her question, but the rabbit was running and she saw no course but to chase it.

"I not know what 'accent' is," she replied.

"Accent . . ." Lady Luella looked thoughtful for a second. Then she said, "Accent is the way you say a word, the way you shape the sounds."

Firekeeper tilted her head to one side, reluctant to ask for clarification, but completely confused. Lady Luella continued, the cadence of her reply falling into the pedagogical rhythms with which Firekeeper was already familiar.

"A gentle-born person," she said, "will most often say words carefully, pronouncing all the sounds distinctly. A less gently born person will often run them together—lazy or perhaps hurriedly.

"T'morrow," Lady Luella said by means of illustration, "instead of 'tomorrow.' "

Firekeeper could hear the difference and nodded.

"And one way of saying is better?" she asked.

"Some people," Lady Luella said with smile, "think so. My mother and father were very strict on this point."

"And so you are?" Firekeeper asked.

"I try," Lady Luella looked fleetingly sad, "but since we have come to spend so much time at Norwood, I think that my children are becoming lazy. You lived at court, did you not?"

"Some," Firekeeper said, knowing from Elise's stories about her childhood that humans envied this as a wolf might another wolf tearing the liver from a fresh kill.

"Did you like it?"

"Sometimes," Firekeeper said honestly. "Others, no. It was very close and full of stone."

Lady Luella frowned slightly, but there was no anger in her expression, only the mild puzzlement that Firekeeper was accustomed to see on others' faces when the wolf-woman thought she was being perfectly clear.

"I like Norwood," Firekeeper explained. "There are more trees and fewer people."

"So you like trees better than people?"

There was challenge in the older woman's tone and a mildly malicious glee as if she had trapped Firekeeper into some misstep.

"No." Firekeeper shook her head vigorously, a trace frustrated. "I like people much—some people. I don't know all people. But sometimes too many people is . . ." She gestured wildly. "Too many."

She felt trapped by the cool eyes of Earl Kestrel's wife, a sense that somehow, despite her best efforts, she was going to offend this woman and cause trouble for herself. Desperate to avert the disaster she felt approaching, Firekeeper blurted:

"Lady Luella, I no take the meat from your cubs!"

Lady Luella looked completely astonished.

"Meat?"

"I no want anything that is your children's," Firekeeper said more slowly. "Earl Kestrel came west for a reason. He no wanted me; he wanted Prince Barden's Blysse. I know this."

Lady Luella leaned forward.

"Are you Prince Barden's Blysse?"

Firekeeper shrugged. "I don't know. King Tedric didn't say I am, so even if I am, I'm not."

Lady Luella laughed, a dry, throaty sound.

"You're more intelligent than I'd have believed. Tell me about your childhood with the wolves."

So Firekeeper did so, continuing when Lady Luella's maid—made rather nervous when she realized Blind Seer was present—arrived to style the lady's drying hair. It was the longest narration the wolf-woman had ever attempted to sustain without assistance and she was quite relieved when Lady Luella raised a finger in an imperious gesture for silence.

"Blysse, the dinner hour is approaching and, although your attire is quite appropriate, perhaps you should return to your room and ring for your maid."

Lady Luella's aristocratic lips twitched in what might have been an amused smile. "Tell her to remove the worst of the wolf hair from your gown."

Firekeeper rose from the flowered puff with a touch more alacrity than might have been perfectly polite, but she remembered her curtsy, and Blind Seer—showing his fangs in an amused grin at the maid's anxious start when he rose to his full height—gave a polite bow.

As they hurried back to Firekeeper's room, the wolf-woman couldn't help but think that as cold as was the winter wind, she rather preferred it to the frost that had never quite left the lady's smile.

FOX DRIVER WAS AS GOOD AS HIS WORD. The horses were calmed by midday, hitched, and ready to go.

For his part, Baron Endbrook employed himself inquiring after road conditions and confirming that the map he had purchased in Hawk Haven was accurate enough for his purposes.

Lady Melina was actively helpful—even eager—in these preparations for travel. She hovered near, effacing herself lest in this border town she might chance on some acquaintance from Hawk Haven. However, whenever Waln's ability to splice his dozen or so New Kelvinese words to gestures and carefully enunciated phrases in Pellish—the language of Gildcrest and thus that of Hawk Haven and Bright Bay—failed to communicate their desire, she stepped forward and acted as translator.

Often the subject of their inquiry—be it shopkeeper, hostler, or local official—was so pleased and astonished to be addressed in the language of the country that he—or she or it, Waln privately admitted that he still had trouble telling the gender of many of the heavily robed figures—would reveal a reasonable fluency in Pellish.

In this way, they learned that the roads should be clear for this day's journey, but that they should be prepared to convert the wagon to sleigh runners before continuing on the next day.

The road they would be taking to Dragon's Breath ran along the western foothills of the Sword of Kelvin Mountains and these, extending as they did in a roughly north-south line, trapped both the weather from the oceans to the east, and that blown down from the Iron Mountains (called here the Death Touch Mountains) to the west. However, though the weather promised to be unpleasant this time of year, the New Kelvinese government paid to have this important road packed and rolled, so sledding should prove both easier and swifter than hauling the wagon over rutted and muddy New Kelvinese roads had been.

As an Islander—a member of a people who, until just a few moonspans before, had simply been loosely annexed to a kingdom whose effective ability to reign had been limited by the interposing ocean—Baron Endbrook was astonished by the New Kelvinese's pride in the works of their nation.

In the Isles, one was first of all oneself—a sailor, a merchant, a fisher, a whoreson (this last flickered into his mind unbidden and was squelched immediately). Next one might be a resident of a particular island—though even that was not a reason for pride. Islanders were more likely to identify themselves by the ships they sailed upon. Belonging to Bright Bay had been an incidental matter, useful when collecting bounty on Waterlander vessels fortuitously chanced upon, but little more.

Even in Hawk Haven it had seemed to Waln that those he met identified themselves first as members of their own houses—if they were noble-born—or as members of their families, craft guilds, and Societies. Service to the larger kingdom—as in King Allister's War—was done as a matter of service to those more personal alliances.

But here in New Kelvin all the people he had spoken to—whether on this trip or his last—seemed to think of themselves as New Kelvinese first and foremost. Even the filthiest beggar on the streets of Dragon's Breath had seemed to look upon the baron's unpainted face and then to accept his charity with the condescension of one making a concession to a lesser being.

On his initial journey, Waln had thought that perhaps his assessment of the New Kelvinese character had been colored by his personal awareness of his gutter origins. Now, as time after time Lady Melina's ability to speak—even haltingly—in the language of the country opened comparative floodgates of information, Waln realized he had been right.

Perhaps the ability to speak of "color" that the New Kelvinese diplomats had desired was not only the ability to speak knowledgeably about magic, but to do so in their own language as well. Doubtless, Lady Melina's previous visit had made her aware of their bigotry, and thus was explained her dutiful—even fanatical—attention to her studies in the course of their journey.

Baron Endbrook had not made his fortune in trade without learning the value of intangibles. He immediately resolved to learn to speak New Kelvinese and acted on his resolve so promptly that by their last stop before departing—the public room of a pleasant inn where they ate a hot meal—he was making the serving wench laugh with his attempts to echo her as she told him the local names for such basic items as beer, bread, and soup.

THOUGH THE CUSTOMS OFFICER who had checked their map had been deprecating about the condition of the road immediately outside of town, Waln was pleasantly surprised at how smooth and well cared for it was. Replete with hot food and perhaps one more mug of the dark autumn beer than he should have drunk, he sat his horse and estimated that they would reach their destination—an inn accustomed to foreign travelers—by dusk if not before.

His mount, a sandy bay gelding whose feathered hocks bespoke one of the larger breeds in its ancestry, seemed to have forgotten its earlier fear and paced along, its ears perked forward in pleasant anticipation of what lay along their course.

"Ride with me, Lady," he said to Lady Melina once they were under way, "and continue my studies. I appear to have been remiss."

"I am pleased to do so," she said, trotting her dapple grey to his side.

As they rode on, Waln was encouraged to think that Lady

Melina's pleasure might have had a more personal element as well. When he finally pronounced correctly an intricate phrase, she blew him a kiss as a lady might to acknowledge her champion on the field. When he mangled a complicated honorific, she playfully leaned from her saddle to swat him lightly on the arm. Indeed, given that they were separated by the need to control their mounts, she seemed to find more than ample excuses to touch him.

When they arrived at the promised inn—named the Stone Giant, after some local legend—Lady Melina held out her arms quite automatically to be lifted from the saddle. Despite himself, Waln's blood was humming as he followed her into the Stone Giant. He was a sailor a long way from home and here was a woman who seemed to desire him, not some whore more interested in his money than his person.

As the innkeeper led the way to their rooms, Waln cleared his throat.

"I was thinking, Sister," he said, fearing that the words sounded stilted, "that we could dine in my suite tonight. There is much I would discuss with you."

"That would be fine, Brother," Lady Melina agreed with demure courtesy.

Her words were proper—even dull—but the slightly lascivious twinkle in her eyes as she smiled up at him suggested that she had guessed his ulterior motives.

Waln wondered if the porter who trudged behind them with the lady's box balanced lightly on one shoulder saw the color that flushed his cheeks. Not wishing to seem too eager for Lady Melina's company, Waln excused himself until dinner.

Leaving all his luggage but the satchel with his precious trust in his room, Waln headed downstairs again. A few words with the innkeeper—who thankfully spoke Pellish fluently—arranged for a small but elegant private banquet for two. Then Waln went out to check on their mounts and goods.

"They're all settled, Baron," Fox said, a trace of insolence—or perhaps envy—in his tone despite the respectful words. "Not even too worn. I had to fight to get stabling for them, though, some high-and-mighty from Dragon's Breath is staying here as well and his groom was puffed with his master's importance."

Fox grinned. "I diced him for spaces and we're settled now."

He gestured with a toss of his head toward a row of stalls. "Four of the best, right at the end."

"And the wagon?" Waln asked.

"That was easier," Fox said. "The high-and-mighty isn't traveling with trade goods. Ours are under cover right outside the stable. I'll be sleeping in the loft above the horses, so no one should meddle without my hearing."

"Can you find someone to help you change the wheels for runners?" Waln asked. "The innkeeper confirmed that the roads are packed snow from here to Dragon's Breath."

Fox nodded. "Easily done."

Though his pulse was beating time in his ears, Waln chatted a bit longer with Driver before returning to the inn. He strolled through the common room, catching a glimpse of a colorfully painted personage with hair the color of a bleached seashell sipping some steaming beverage at a table almost concealed in a sheltered alcove.

Waln's self-possession abandoned him when he was free of the public areas and he found himself taking the stairs two at a time, suddenly nervous that he had dallied too long. As he had ordered earlier, hot water for a bath was waiting. With a sense of anticipation he had not felt since he was courting Oralia, Waln scrubbed the trail dirt from every inch of his skin, conscious of the fact that, if all went as he hoped, he would be open to quite a private inspection.

Lady Melina was just late enough that Waln had begun to fear that the knock on the door would announce not the lady but some flunky bearing her excuse. However, she herself glided in, apologizing that she had needed to wait until a serving maid was available to lace her into her dress.

The dress was one of several she had brought along, quite suitable to her persona as a prosperous farm owner. Waln thought Lady Melina wore the simple midnight-blue wool as a queen might, her own inner dignity infusing it with grace and elegance. Her silvering hair was braided and caught up in a knot at the back of her head. Waln found himself imagining how it might look after he had set it free.

Through the four courses, while the serving maid hovered near, they talked of ordinary things: of the road, of how long it would take them to reach their destination, what price they might get for their goods, and what they might purchase for sale on their return. Using the foods on the table, Lady Melina continued to tutor Waln in New Kelvinese and more often than not, she found excuse to offer a caress that stayed just on the right side of sisterly.

Waln grew light-headed—at first, he thought, from her attentions. He knew the sensation could not be the wine, for he was no foolish boy to make himself half-drunk for courage only to fail in performance. Though he drank freely of the chilled water, his mouth remained dry and he found himself surreptitiously licking his lips to moisten them.

Another man might not have realized what had happened. Another man might have taken the symptoms he felt as mere nerves, but Baron Endbrook had not always been rich, had not always been titled. He had grown up in his mother's house and knew the little bottle she kept for dosing the occasional client whose manners were too rough or whose purse too tempting.

Even as he recognized the symptoms, Waln knew what wealth had tempted Lady Melina to this rash act. The three magical artifacts that had severed Gustin Sailor from his alliance with Zorana Shield, that had prompted Stonehold into war on the mere rumor of their existence, that had tempted Queen Valora into theft—those same three artifacts had seduced another victim.

The ardor that had fired Waln's blood froze into fear, but the baron was not some drunken sailor flush with wine and voyage pay. Making polite excuses, he departed as for the privy. Lest Lady Melina realize his suspicions, he gave her a slow wink and brushed his lips against her cheek. He only regretted that he dared not dig the satchel out from where he had hidden it, but that would not be in keeping with his role as besotted fool hurrying away only to hurry to return.

As he took the back stairs to the outdoor privy, Waln laid his plans with the deliberate care of a man who cannot trust his mind to hold more than one thought at a time. First, the privy.

He stumbled across a yard deserted because of the night's cold. Most guests would prefer the privacy of a chamber pot, but most weren't entertaining a lady in their rooms. His breath steamed in a ragged plume—his own life's banner urging him forward.

In the privy, Waln forced his finger down his throat until he vomited up the contents of his stomach. Then he decided what to do next. He had hidden the satchel well. Lady Melina would wait to see if he would return—or if whatever she had slipped into his wine had knocked him out—before beginning her search. She might even need to dismiss the maid if that worthy was still clearing away dinner. Therefore, she would be in the room for some time.

Waln rose from his knees. His mouth tasted foul, his knees were trembling, but his mind was clearing. Next he must find Fox Driver. Waln didn't doubt that he himself could subdue Lady Melina, but he would need Fox's cooperation if Lady Melina had allies—even the maid's screaming could bring unwanted attention.

He wondered if it was pure coincidence that an important person from Dragon's Breath was staying at this public inn just now. The more Waln considered, the less likely that seemed. He recalled how determined Lady Melina had been to get on the road as soon as possible. Had the rendezvous been planned?

It began to seem likely. Even if she had succeeded in stealing the enchanted artifacts, where could she go with them? She could take them into Hawk Haven, but if their secrets were as difficult to understand as Queen Valora had believed, Lady Melina might prefer to take them into New Kelvin, where those secrets might be unraveled.

Waln's head pounded as he sought to untangle this net of betrayal. He spat and focused again on his next step. He must find Fox, brief him, then return as quickly as possible to where Lady Melina was.

On shaky legs, Waln climbed up to the loft where Driver had said he would be staying. At first, he thought the other man had turned in early and was sleeping soundly. After all, sitting on a wagon box all day in the cold was fatiguing, bone-jarring work.

Only when he put his hand on the man's shoulder and found him stiff and cold did Waln suspect the truth. He turned Fox onto his back and discovered that the other's throat had been cut with neat efficiency. The blood had drained into a sodden mass that only the body heat from the horses below had kept from freezing solid in the winter night's cold.

Lady Melina might have done this. She could have come out between the time Waln had left Fox and when she arrived—a bit late—at Waln's own room. True, she had appeared clean and well groomed, but she merely could have changed her dress, tidied her hair, and dabbed on a bit of scent.

Waln didn't doubt that Fox would have let the woman close. She hadn't seemed to be flirting with the driver, but then she'd been very good about hiding her own flirtation with Waln. If she'd come to Fox, made some excuse to get him into the loft . . .

The baron shook his head angrily, realizing that even now he felt jealous. He felt no grief for Fox. The man had been a second-rate scoundrel—though a first-class driver. His death was an inconvenience, but sailors were swept overboard by storms and still the ship sailed on.

Since Lady Melina could have done this alone, perhaps she didn't have an ally. Perhaps Waln had time to catch her before she finished her search. Waln's blood pounded as he anticipated the beating he'd give her for betraying him and his queen.

Setting his hands on the sides of the loft ladder, Waln slid down as he might have between decks, trusting the strength of his arms and not bothering with the rungs. The rough wood rails splintered—not being as polished as those on a ship—

but Waln landed on the straw-strewn floor, instinctively flexing his knees.

Doubtless this saved his life, for the man standing to one side of the ladder swung at where Waln's head would have been if the baron had descended in a more conventional manner.

Waln heard the swoosh as the club passed through the air, the crack as it impacted with the wooden ladder. His latent queasiness was forgotten, washed from his blood by the fearful certainty that if he didn't make his return blow count he would die.

Waln's assailant was a New Kelvinese, a husky, bowlegged man with stylized horse heads tattooed in dull green on each cheek. This might well be the groom who had thrown dice with Fox for use of the stalls. Had he used that earlier game as an excuse to mount to the loft and get close enough to Fox to murder him?

Rising from the crouch in which he'd landed, Waln butted his head into the groom's midsection. The technique was pure gutter brawling, as was the fashion in which he brought his knee up into the other man's groin as the groom sought to keep his balance and his breath against the force of the first blow.

The groom was solidly built, with arms and chest well muscled from his trade. His strength meant nothing to the pain that ripped up from his battered privates. The breath that had been knocked from him when Waln's head impacted his solar plexus had not returned, so that his scream—or shout for help—came forth as a feeble shriek.

He made no other sound. Waln seized the club that had been meant to shatter his own head and used it on its owner. He put behind the blows the raging force of his own disgust at being so duped, his fear of what might come—and of what Queen Valora would say if he did not regain the artifacts.

Waln's first thought as the groom fell to the stable floor—his head so battered that the horse tattoos were fragments in a bloody mass—was to rush back to his room, beat aside any in his way, and seize the satchel.

A glance toward the inn showed him a blaze of lights on the second floor. A hulking figure almost concealed in shadow stood near the back door from which Waln had exited on his flight to the privy. Doubtless someone would be out momentarily to see if the groom had done his job.

During a hurricane, Waln had discovered his body could act without conscious command from his mind. So it was now. He lifted his saddle from where it rested on the partition between two stalls and dropped it onto his horse, tightening the girth almost before the horse realized what was coming. Later—if there was a later—Waln would need to smooth out the blankets and set the saddle properly, but damage to his mount was far from his greatest concern.

The bridle went on with equal speed. Then Waln led the gelding—now snorting with confusion and annoyance—from the stall. An irritated jerk at its headstall convinced it that the big man wasn't in a mood for games and it stopped fighting.

Still moving with dreamlike deliberation, Waln heaved himself into the saddle. The stable door was already open—he'd never closed it when he came to fetch Fox, doubtless how the groom had known where to look for him. Now he booted the gelding solidly in the ribs. The horse, already agitated and needing little encouragement to bolt, shot out of the stable.

The figure from the doorway came running out, waving his arms and shouting something.

"Sorry," Waln shouted, "don't speak the language."

The man paused slightly, perhaps thinking Waln was surrendering, but Waln kicked his horse again and the man flung himself to one side to avoid being knocked over.

Night was with the baron, night and the cold that had kept everyone inside who had even the slimmest excuse. There were a few shouts behind him, but Waln pressed the horse on, past the inn, out onto the road, and furiously down the way they had come earlier that day.

He risked a fall, a broken back or neck, a shattered leg for the horse. Compared with what lay behind him, these were glory and wonder and the hope of seeing the next sunrise.

XX

ELATION RETURNED THE DAY AFTER Firekeeper met with Lady Luella. The peregrine falcon's knife-edged wings cut through the flakes of a late-afternoon snow flurry like a physical embodiment of the last rays of daylight.

Firekeeper and Blind Seer were running circles in the snow, leaping to catch the large, fluffy white flakes before they could touch the dry grass of the lawn. Once again—despite Lady Luella's outspoken disapproval—the wolf-woman had discarded the boots procured for her. Though these were light things of the softest leather, shaped to her foot by a patient cobbler and lined with fur, she still claimed they made her clumsy. The woolen hose were not as bad, but she discarded them when they grew sodden.

The peregrine soared in to land upon a stone pylon set on the fringes of the garden in memory of some youthful deed of the current duchess. Settling herself, she folded her wings with a disapproving squawk.

"Mad creatures and wolves!" she cried. "Who can tell the difference?"

"Shrieking winds and the words of the wingéd folk," retorted Blind Seer. "One and the same to these ears."

Firekeeper booted him gently in the ribs.

"Perhaps that is so," she said, "but perhaps today Fierce Joy in Flight has some news for us."

"Perhaps," replied the falcon a trace sulkily, "but if my words are as empty as shrieking winds . . ."

"Then the fault lies in the listener's ears," Firekeeper responded soothingly. "Tell me your news. My ears are tuned to your cries."

"I have flown long and hard, through ugly weather," said the falcon, unwilling to be so easily pacified.

"There is ample game in these fields for so mighty a hunter," Firekeeper said, "and a warm perch for her by the fireside. Will you come inside or tell your tale here?"

Elation permitted herself to be appeased.

"I have found the crow," she said, preening lightly. "And he has told me of those he followed."

"Did he not stay with them?" Firekeeper asked, dismayed.

"He was worn to a windblown leaf from his following," Elation replied, "but he did not forsake his task until he found a replacement to take it for him. By good luck, another of the corvid kin—a raven—found him before I did. The raven has taken up the chase."

"So they are lost to us again." Firekeeper sighed, then brightened. "But what was the crow's news? What direction do the treasures go and is Lady Melina yet with them?"

"North," the falcon replied, "and, yes, she is."

FIREKEEPER HAD THOUGHT that knowing this—along with those scant details Elation had been able to add—would be enough to set them on the chase. She was dismayed to learn, upon reporting her news to Derian, that they could not set out at once.

"We will need to take our leave with care," the young man said. "Otherwise, the Kestrels are certain to send someone in search of us."

Firekeeper wanted to ask "why" as if she were merely a whining pup, but she knew enough of human custom to know that what Derian said was the merest truth. A wolf might choose to hunt alone, especially during the warm days of summer, and the rest of the pack would not comment. However, it seemed to her that all a human needed to do was step out of a room without explanation and a flood of questions and conjectures began.

"Moreover," Derian added, sounding quite stern, "while you and Blind Seer may be content running barefoot in the snow,

Doc and I will need some gear and either good riding horses or a sleigh."

Again Firekeeper swallowed an impulsive desire to protest. Hadn't her very reason for seeking out human help in this matter been a suspicion that she could not handle this matter without assistance?

"I know you want to bay down the trail," Derian said, borrowing an idiom she herself had used earlier in her report, "but what will you do when you get there? It is one thing to attack a traitor like Prince Newell, quite another to go after Baron Endbrook and Lady Melina—both of whom are outwardly blameless. The least you could hope for would be a blood feud between House Kestrel and their houses. You *could* ignite a war."

Firekeeper shivered at the latter possibility. It nested too closely to her own private fears.

"They might not know it me," she offered, knowing she was sliding out onto thin ice. "I come to them by night, go by night."

"And leave behind the prints of a small person—a small barefoot person—and an enormous wolf."

Derian laughed and Firekeeper wilted.

"Remember," the young man continued more kindly, "that there will likely be snow upon the ground and if not snow, then mud. It is not so late in the winter that the ground will have acquired rocky hardness."

"But what we do when we catch up to them?" the wolf-woman asked. "Will we not take away what they have? I have sworn to take those three things."

Derian looked more uncertain.

"I don't know yet," he admitted. "I suppose that we could take our chances and go after them disguised as bandits. Elation did say that there were only three, right?"

"Three," Firekeeper agreed. "Baron Endbrook, Lady Melina, and a man who drove the horses."

"No sign of Citrine."

"Not that the crow saw, but the crow did say that she *was*

there and that they kept her much in the wagon. She could have still been there."

"More likely," Derian said unhappily, "Citrine is with those mysterious friends at the seashore. I wish I felt confident that she was so safely placed."

"You fear," Firekeeper said. "Why?"

"Remember what I told you a long time ago," Derian said, "when you were going to challenge Earl Kestrel's right to order you about?"

"No."

Derian sighed. "You said he couldn't hurt you, not if he wanted to use you."

"Yes."

"Then I pointed out that he could hurt Blind Seer."

Firekeeper nodded reluctantly. "I forget because I no like that thinking."

"Well, I like the thoughts I have just as little," Derian admitted. "It seems to me that Baron Endbrook would want some assurance that Lady Melina would behave as he wished—after all, those artifacts are the most valuable things his queen has."

Firekeeper nodded.

"And taking Lady Melina's daughter . . ." Derian paused. "Let's put it this way. I'm worried that the 'friends' Citrine is staying with are *his* friends, not Lady Melina's."

"And if anything happens to artifacts," Firekeeper said, her brow furrowing as she worked through this very unwolfish logic, "then something happen to Citrine!"

"Precisely," Derian agreed unhappily. "So whatever we do, we can be sure that Lady Melina will be the baron's firm ally. We can't hope to turn her against him."

"I not hunt with her!" Firekeeper protested sharply.

"Not even to get the artifacts?" Derian's expression was wry. "I wonder if your Royal Beasts would approve of your selectivity."

Firekeeper, rather uncomfortably, found herself wondering the same.

❧

ELISE WAS SURPRISED, even a little dismayed, when Sir
Jared sought her company during the leisure hours after the
evening meal. To this point he had been politely formal, respecting her unspoken desire to keep some distance between
them, but the note he sent her via Ninette permitted no polite
excuse.

"Lady Elise," read his square but tidy hand, "Some news
regarding one of our common interests came by a late post. I
would share it with you. Could I call upon you in your suite
or, if that is not convenient, could you call on me?"

Initially, Elise thought that Sir Jared must have received
some medical text or an answer to one of the long letters he
had sent to Hazel Healer. Talk on such subjects had been the
extent of their conversations of late. Then, with a sense of
shame so sudden that it brought color to her cheeks, Elise
recalled the entire issue of Lady Melina's intriguing with
Baron Endbrook.

I am behaving like a girl with her first crush, she scolded
herself, *forgetting good sense and thinking myself wise. Surely
Sir Jared must have news regarding Lady Melina. Why else
would he request a private visit?*

Hastily, she scribbled a note back asking for the knight to
call on her an hour hence in her suite. Ninette would be present
to chaperon and if indeed Sir Jared wished to confer regarding
such sensitive matters there must be no risk of being overheard.

Elise wondered why Derian or Firekeeper had not been the
ones to bring her the news. On reflection, she realized that
Derian's calling on her would excite as much—or even more
among some of the guests—comment than if Sir Jared did so.

A visit from Firekeeper would not be a matter for gossip,
but the wolf-woman was still not skilled in relating compli-

cated matters. Her vocabulary, though growing, remained hardly more sophisticated than that of a five-year-old and she resisted learning new terms where she thought an already known one would serve.

And we cannot discuss political intrigue in terms of good and bad, right and wrong, Elise thought, *no matter how much we would like matters to be so simple.*

She had composed herself by the time Sir Jared arrived and welcomed him with courtesy, but kept the special warmth she felt whenever she saw him locked tightly within her breast.

Sir Jared bowed deeply before taking the seat she offered him. He bore with him a fat leather-bound tome and a slim case she recognized as the one in which he kept pressed samples of herbs that had interested him. For a moment, she thought she might have incorrectly guessed the reason for his visit, but his first words, prompted, it seemed, by her questioning glance at the book, set her right.

"I brought these so we might have an excuse for our visit," he said, "and I even dropped a passing comment to my cousin that some of his guests seemed less than pleased by our dull discussions of such serious matters as medicine and herb lore."

"So?" Elise asked, puzzled.

"So that if anyone questions our private converse Norvin will be sure to reply that we are doubtless discussing matters that we feared would seem dull to the rest of the party."

Elise smiled. "You seem a natural-born conspirator."

In return, Sir Jared made a slightly mocking half-bow.

"Rather, Lady Elise, say it is associating with Firekeeper and her friends that has given me practice in these matters."

"Firekeeper!" Elise leaned forward. "Has she news?"

"News indeed," Sir Jared said. "The falcon Elation has returned and, if we are to believe that Firekeeper can honestly translate the bird's report . . ."

"We do," Elise said dismissively.

"Then Elation's report is thus."

Momentarily, the physician squeezed his eyes shut as if at an effort of accurate remembrance. Then he continued:

"Elation says that a raven—or a crow—I get a bit muddled

as to which bird is which . . . In any case, Elation says that one of these Royal birds reports that Lady Melina and Baron Endbrook—traveling in company with a third person, a man—were heading north. The crow—I recall now, it was a crow—was fatigued from following them unceasingly from Port Haven and as soon as it found another bird of Royal-kind—that's where the raven comes in—it turned over the duty of following the pair to the raven. Elation found the crow while it was resting from its labors."

"Astonishing," Elise mused, "to find one crow—even for a falcon as gifted as Elation."

"My understanding," Sir Jared said, and the young woman could see that he was far more uncomfortable than she in accepting the reportage of birds, "is that Elation finally grasped the logic behind maps . . ."

"A thing Firekeeper has yet to do," Elise murmured, "at least with any assurance."

The knight gave a wry grin of agreement.

"Once Elation understood what the maps portrayed," he went on, "she realized that certain roads would be more likely conduits for Lady Melina and Baron Endbrook if they were indeed heading north. She then set herself to backtrack along those roads toward Port Haven. It was while doing this she found the crow."

"Amazing!" Elise exclaimed despite herself.

Sir Jared shrugged. "I suppose it makes sense. We draw our maps as if we are seeing the world as a flat thing, viewed from above. How else does a flying bird see the world?"

"Still," Elise said, "what a wonder! I suppose that Elation did not locate Baron Endbrook and Lady Melina?"

"No." Sir Jared shook his head. "Though my feeling is that she intends to set out after them come morning. She came here first to give Firekeeper this confirmation of her theories. The crow was too weary to make the flight here with any speed."

"Birds," Elise offered, only certain of her own uncertain knowledge of the race, "must eat a great deal to sustain the fire in their little bodies."

Sir Jared nodded. "Such has been my observation as well. Now, have you any thoughts about the wisest course of action to take? Firekeeper, I hardly need to tell you, was ready to charge out after Lady Melina and Baron Endbrook as soon as Elation brought the news. Derian has managed to convince her to wait, but I doubt even he can hold her long."

Elise toyed with a trailing thread of the embroidery she had been working while waiting for the knight to call. Distantly, she was aware of Ninette stirring unhappily over where she was brewing tea for their refreshment.

From the very moment that Elise had confided in her maid her own suspicions regarding Lady Melina, Ninette had been nervous and unhappy—a nervousness that had eased slightly when the journey to the North Woods and then the early days of their sojourn had passed uninterrupted. Although Lady Melina's sorceries had not touched Ninette as intimately as they had Elise, she feared them more and Elise could not dismiss her good sense.

"Short of locking Firekeeper in a room," Elise said, "I do not see how we can keep her from pursuit. Therefore, what we must do is find how to make that pursuit at least somewhat acceptable."

"You are of one mind with Derian and myself," Jared replied. "We have determined that we will accompany her. Moreover, I will ask my cousin's help in this matter."

"Earl Kestrel?"

"None other. As Lady Blysse, Firekeeper is his adopted daughter. Were she to depart without his knowledge he would be forced to look for her."

Sir Jared looked rueful. "Indeed, I am not certain that only duty would force him to do so. Beneath his gruff exterior, he is fond of the girl—as is his mother, the duchess."

"Very well," Elise said, "then the earl must be spoken with—but how much will you tell him?"

"That is one of the things about which I wished to consult with you, Lady Elise," said Jared uncomfortably. "You see, if we tell any truth at all of why Firekeeper is determined to leave the North Woods at such an unseasonable time for travel, we may be forced to tell something of your involvement in the matter."

"Why?"

The sharp question came not from Elise but from Ninette. The maid had paused in the very act of pouring tea, her posture so defensive that Elise feared she might hurl the pot at Jared.

"Ninette!"

Sir Jared held up a hand. "She asks a good question and I will give my best answer."

Looking directly at Ninette, he replied, "Because, good lady, I know my cousin well. He has a mind like a knife, and can cut through any fog of deceit if he sets his mind to it. His mother is, if anything, less easy to fool. Some light tale—we had thought to tell him Blind Seer had run off—will not divert him if he senses that truth is to be had."

"What is wrong with the tale about Blind Seer?" Ninette asked. "It seems a good one to me."

"To me as well," Sir Jared said, "and we have not discarded it entirely. The difficulty is that our route may take us into populated areas of this grant, areas where a report would easily get back to the earl that his daughter and her escort had been seen. Indeed, we may need to encourage their notice by asking questions.

"Earl Kestrel is no fool. If the wolf would run, why wouldn't it run into more wild areas? The only reason an untamed wolf—and Blind Seer is untamed for all that Firekeeper's word leashes him—would frequent human-populated areas is if it had become mad, and a mad wolf is a danger to people and to beasts."

"Mad," Ninette said thoughtfully, "or so accustomed to people that it no longer feared them. Either way, it would be a danger to those the earl has sworn to protect."

"And so," Jared said, nodding, "Earl Kestrel himself—or some of his trusted hunters—must set out in pursuit. The complications that could result are enough to horrify, even on mere contemplation."

"I think we see," Elise replied, "why this deception has its hazards."

"Derian and I had thought," Sir Jared said, "to offer the earl some version of the truth. How much and what we will say, we are as of yet uncertain. However, in telling that truth we may implicate you—though we would try not to do so. The difficulty is, as I have said, that I know how good the earl is at slicing through falsehood when he sets his mind to the task."

Something in Jared's expression made Elise suspect a youthful indiscretion uncovered and she bit back an urge to tease him. Such would be unseemly if she truly meant to discourage his affections.

"A version of the truth," she said aloud. "Very good. What version do you propose?"

Ninette brought over the tea tray, then settled into her own chair off to one side. She might efface herself, but Elise knew that neither she nor Jared would forget her presence—nor would Ninette expect them to do so.

"Well," Jared replied, "I was at the same ball where you first noticed the exchange of notes. Indeed, I was dancing in the same set."

Elise felt the slight burnings of a blush, remembering how it had been her awareness of Jared's presence—indeed her seeking his place in the set—that had caused her chance gaze to catch the first exchange.

"True," she said hastily. "So you will pretend that you were the one to see Baron Endbrook pass the note to Lady Melina. That should work. I doubt that even Earl Kestrel noted the precise order of every dance."

"Then," Jared said, "I shall simply continue as you did. My excuse for keeping watch over Lady Melina shall be that given her brother's recent treachery and her own overt mourning it seemed unlikely to me that she would encourage flirtation."

"Good," Elise said. "Very good. In this way, you need not mention our prior reasons for distrusting the lady."

"Precisely. From that point, I can say I consulted Derian—even as you did. Derian's information can be related without deception. We can leave what we learned from Citrine out of the picture . . ."

He trailed off then and Elise noted a look of extreme unhappiness cross his face.

"What is wrong?"

"I had dreaded telling you this, but Citrine may have disappeared."

In a few pithy sentences, he reported, beginning with what Firekeeper had learned from the crow: how Citrine had been with her mother, then had not been. He added Derian's suspicions—which he admitted to sharing—that Citrine was being held hostage against her mother's good behavior. When he finished, Elise's head was pounding with angry astonishment.

"If this is true," she said, keeping her voice steady with a great effort, "then Lady Melina is truly depraved!"

Then she frowned. "But will we be any better? I mean if we go after Lady Melina and succeed in retrieving those hateful artifacts we may put Citrine in danger."

"I think Firekeeper is worried about that, too," Jared admitted, "but she's given her word to retrieve those artifacts no matter what. My fear is that if something happens to Citrine, Firekeeper will make certain Lady Melina pays."

Elise shuddered. "Let's not talk about *that* right now. We need to settle the question of what to tell Earl Kestrel."

Jared nodded. He looked vaguely relieved that this particular bit of bad news was out and, at least for now, so well accepted.

Elise continued. "I think your manner of presenting the issue is perfectly sound. If Earl Kestrel somehow sees through it and my involvement arises, well, so be it. I can't stay out of it in any case."

"What do you mean, my lady?"

Sir Jared's question seemed to anticipate a similar one from Ninette, for Elise heard a stifled yelp from where her maid sat.

"I mean," Elise said deliberately, "that I am willing to offer my services in this chase. Certainly, you don't think it would be proper for Firekeeper to run about with no escort other than two young men?"

Sir Jared relaxed slightly. "We'd considered that. We're going to ask Earl Kestrel for the loan of Wendee Jay—Firekeeper's new attendant."

"I've met her. Nice woman. Several children."

Jared refused to be interrupted. "Wendee Jay was once an actress and knows the area well, including certain towns to the east I've only visited rarely. Moreover, she has traveled in New Kelvin and if, as we dread, we cannot intercept our pair before they cross into that land, Goody Wendee could be some help to us."

"As could I," Elise said fiercely. "I speak New Kelvinese. Do either you or Derian? Does this Wendee Jay speak it except for a few phrases of poetry?"

Sir Jared blinked, startled by Elise's intensity.

"I don't know. I suspect that she does, actually."

"That doesn't change the fact that neither you nor Derian know more than a few phrases of the language."

"I don't think either of us knows even that," Sir Jared admitted. "The merchants who visited my family spoke Pellish well enough to get by."

"Well, so there!" Elise said, dropping entirely the polite and measured manner of speech she had maintained and reverting for a moment to the little girl who had kicked her host.

"You do have a point, my lady," Jared admitted after a long pause. "I will raise it with the others. For now, let us keep you uninvolved. The earl will have enough to accept what with our claims of collusion between foreign powers—not to mention Firekeeper's more outlandish claims."

"Do we need to mention those at all?" Elise said, temporarily mollified.

"We must, I think," Jared replied, though from his expression Elise guessed that he would be happy if she could give him a reason he needn't do so. "How else do we justify our need to find Baron Endbrook and Lady Melina? There is no ruling against traveling to New Kelvin—not even in such company."

"True," Elise admitted. "Still, I wish we had some other excuse."

They talked for a while longer, trying to guess what Earl Kestrel's reaction would be; then Elise spoke aloud the worry that had been in the back of her thoughts, present but not completely realized.

"But what do we do when we find them?" she asked. "As you've said, there is no reason they shouldn't travel to New Kelvin. How do we stop them? What do we do if we do?"

Sir Jared looked uncomfortable. "We haven't exactly settled that part. Derian has suggested that we pose as bandits. There will only be the three of them and there will be at least four of us—and Blind Seer should cause havoc with their horses just by his presence."

Elise was momentarily shocked; then she nodded.

"That may be the only way to go about it," she admitted. "If we have no legal recourse, we must act illegally."

"My hope," Sir Jared said, "is that my cousin will give us some legitimate reason to act against them—suspicion of trading in magic is reason enough for a thorough search. If, however, we intercept them outside of the Norwood Grant then his legal right to commission us becomes rather shaky. In any case, Earl Kestrel may not wish to arouse Duke Gyrfalcon's anger. Lady Melina remains a member of that house. For Kestrel to act against her without first appealing to the head of her house could lead to some difficulties."

Elise bit her lower lip as she concentrated on recalling the rules of precedence and such that governed interactions between houses.

"Yes," she said slowly, "there could cause difficulties for House Kestrel—even if Lady Melina was intercepted on the Norwood Grant in possession of forbidden magics. In any case, I'm not certain that Baron Endbrook and Lady Melina will even come this far west."

Sir Jared shrugged. "One of the major crossings into New Kelvin *is* on the Norwood Grant. They could even choose to cross into Waterland and then traverse the Sword of Kelvin Mountains into New Kelvin. They could ford the White Water River into New Kelvin at a more easterly point. If the White

Water has frozen, they could even eschew the more legitimate crossings entirely."

"I doubt they'll go into Waterland," Elise said with certainty. "The best means for doing that would have been to take a ship out of Port Haven. Moreover, going that way would lengthen their journey considerably and involve at least some contacts in Waterland. The evidence of their equipment also testifies that they intended a land journey."

"So far, you make a good deal of sense," Sir Jared said. "What else?"

"We need to inquire whether the White Water has frozen," Elise said. "My guess it that this is too early in the year. However, the post-riders report such information—at least they do on my father's lands—so we should learn it easily enough.

"If we knew their destination," Elise continued, thinking aloud, "we could guess where they might cross, but . . ."

She glanced around, then rose and drew forth from her belongings a flat portfolio containing several maps.

"I brought these just in case," she said, unfolding a map depicting the northern extent of Hawk Haven and something of the countries beyond the White Water.

Running her finger along the sweeping curve that represented the White Water River, she frowned.

"I fear that we have little hope that they will cross in the Norwood Grant," she said. "Dragon's Breath—the capital of New Kelvin—is situated on the northwestern verge of the Sword of Kelvin Mountains. If we assume that city is their destination, then the best route would be to use one of the more eastern river crossings. As I recall, there are some good trade roads heading to Dragon's Breath.

"Even if they are not heading into Dragon's Breath," she continued, trying to anticipate Sir Jared's next question, "there are several smaller towns along those very trade roads. In any case, they would be safer from detection by Hawk Haven forces if they traveled as much as possible along the New

Kelvinese road system rather than covering the same distance in Hawk Haven."

"And we must assume," Sir Jared added, "that they will want to avoid notice in Hawk Haven. The New Kelvinese do not share our aversion to magic."

"Or to potentially traitorous members of House Gyrfalcon traveling in company with nobles from the Isles," Elise said.

Sir Jared drummed his fingers on the table with a sudden burst of pent-up energy.

"First we talk with Earl Kestrel," he said. "Then . . ."

"Head out," Elise said, "even if there has been no further report from Firekeeper's friends. There is a river road running roughly parallel to the White Water. We should head east along it, asking questions as we go. If the falcon Elation knows where we will be, she will be able to find us."

"I agree," Sir Jared said. "Certainly action of some sort will be better than asking Firekeeper to sit here with her hands folded. It is a day's journey to the White Water from here if conditions are good."

Elise noticed that he no longer questioned her participation in the venture. She wondered if he was convinced that they would need her help or merely too wise to argue until matters were settled with the earl. Suspecting the latter, she decided that she, too, could hold her tongue.

After Sir Jared took his leave, Elise refolded her map and tucked it away in her portfolio. Her lips moved as of themselves, supplying answers to Ninette's flurry of nervous questions, but her deeper mind was occupied with another thought.

Lady Aurella had never *told* Elise that she shouldn't marry Sir Jared. Indeed, she had even said that Elise herself would need to do the proposing. True, Lady Aurella had also said that the match was not one which either herself or Baron Archer would want for Elise, but she had not expressly forbidden it.

Musing over that fact, realizing that the choice still remained her own, Elise realized that this made her decision even harder than it had been before.

XXI

TERROR GAVE A STRANGE COMPLEXION to the events surrounding Waln's flight from the Stone Giant Inn. Afterward, he could never quite remember how he managed to evade his pursuers. On the other hand, small fragments remained extraordinarily vivid.

He recalled the exact pattern of bare branches and elegant, almost polished, thorns in the bramble he'd pulled to cover him when he lay in a ditch, holding his breath. He remembered listening to his pursuers thundering off after his horse—which he'd loosed as a diversion—but he could never recall just when he got to his feet and continued south.

There had come a time when he sat on a rock staring down at his boots, which he held in his hand. His feet were wrapped in scraps of fabric he'd torn from the elaborate waistcoat he'd worn to dine with Lady Melina. Judging from the mud caked upon these makeshift slippers, he must have been walking in them for some time, but he could remember neither making them nor walking in them.

All Waln could guess was that he'd decided that leaving boot tracks in the snow along the verge of the road wouldn't be a good idea. He would have liked to depart the vicinity of the road, but he wasn't certain enough of his bearings—clouds having robbed him of the guidance of the stars—to risk leaving it entirely.

Again he came to himself, at midday, to find himself buried deep inside a haystack. Oddly, Waln's first thought was that this was not the best hay—it smelled musty and slightly rotted. Only after he had formed that thought did it occur to him to wonder how he had come to be buried inside a haystack and, even, where he was. He had been too absorbed in Lady Melina's company and the promises hinted at in her smiles to notice details of the local landscape.

His skin felt damp and he guessed that he'd been sweating. Further examination of his surroundings caused him to suspect fever, for his breath—when he cautiously surfaced from the hay—was visible even though the cloud-shrouded sun was high overhead.

Waln lay buried in the hay, wondering where he was, how far he had come, how intent the pursuit might be, and a dozen other things, each thought chasing the other in a jolting circle, like a cat chasing its tail.

He must have drifted off to sleep again, for when hunger awakened him he discovered that darkness had again fallen. His thoughts were clearer now, but a trace of fever-induced whimsy made him feel rather like a mouse as he tunneled his way to the surface.

The night proved to be clear and crisp. The upper layer of hay snapped with frost as he pushed through it. There was no visible moon, but his eyes were already adjusted to what faint light there was.

His haystack stood against the side of a small animal shelter. The shelter was empty now, but smooth, rounded droppings suggested that goats had been kept here. That would explain the condition of the hay, as well as the lack of concern for its keeping. Goats were notorious for eating anything.

At that moment, Waln rather wished *he* were a goat. His meal with Lady Melina had been the night before and his excursions had burnt what little he hadn't purged from his system as a candle flame burns a moth. Although the islander carried extra flesh on his big frame—flesh his body was doubtless consuming even now—his stomach clamored its emptiness, accustomed to being filled three or four times a day whether it needed to be or not.

After assuring himself that he was alone, Waln eased himself from the haystack. He noted with idle curiosity that he was wearing his boots again. He didn't recall putting them on. The muddy pieces of waistcoat were stuffed behind his belt.

Fever mounting again as he exerted himself, Waln was

pleased to find that his unconscious self was such an organized and efficient type of person. He rather wished he could just go away again and let that other self take over. However, not knowing just how to call up that other self, he decided he'd better not chance it. He might just fall asleep in the snow and freeze.

There was a hut off to one side of the goat pen. Its door was open, swinging at a drunken angle from the upper pair of a set of leather hinges. The lower hinge was broken or had been eaten by mice or rats.

Waln picked his way over to the hut. He realized that he was tiptoeing—a ridiculous thing as he was moving across open ground. He made an effort to stop himself, but as soon as he stopped he realized he was tiptoeing again—doubtless some attempt on the part of his hidden self to be stealthy.

The hut proved to be empty. The thin dusting of snow across the floor showed only rodent tracks—tiny, eyelash-fine traceries for the feet and a long, narrow track for the tail. These converged around a large hunk of bread, apparently broken from a larger loaf and abandoned with the carelessness of plenty where it had fallen near the open door.

With no thought for the dirt or gnaw marks on the bread, Waln scooped up the bread and shoved it into his mouth. As he chewed, feeling the grit against his teeth, he squatted down on the floor, blotting up loose crumbs with the tip of one finger. These he stuffed in after the bread, disregarding the fact that he shoved in more dirt than bread. He wished he'd not scared the mouse away, his mouth watering at the image of that warm mouthful.

Clarity of thought returned just enough to make Waln feel revolted at this descent into bestiality, and with that revulsion came an awareness of his predicament.

The bread—while not precisely fresh—had not been completely stale. Nor was it the heavy black bread one would expect a goatherd to drop. This bread had been a pale honey-brown in color, the color of the rolls that had graced the dinner table he had shared the night before with Lady Melina.

Therefore, the person who had dropped it had quite possibly

been hunting for Waln. Perhaps the searcher had overlooked the haystack because both the hut and goat shed were nearer and were so much more obvious hiding places. The same late snow that had frozen the top of the haystack would have disguised any prints Waln would have left—especially if the searcher had come by when the light was poor.

Waln realized with a sudden thrill of fear how fortunate he had been—and that he dare not stay here a moment longer. The haystack might not escape a second inspection.

He did remain long enough to thoroughly search the·hut, hoping to find some provision hidden away against need. However, though he searched with all the cunning he'd gained in his streetwise youth, he went unrewarded.

Satisfying his belly with great handfuls of the cleanest snow he could find, Baron Waln Endbrook trudged out into the darkness. When the wind began to blow and snow to fall, all he felt was gratitude at the certainty that his trail would be covered.

His mind centered itself on a dream of fire, a reddish-orange glow that gradually resolved itself into the memory of a gemstone glimmering with·citrine fire upon the forehead of a little girl.

EARL KESTREL LISTENED with very few interruptions while Doc presented their case. Firekeeper wondered if this was because Doc was his cousin.

Perhaps the fact that Derian wore his counselor's ring, the ruby in it glinting in the morning sunlight, had also reminded the earl that one of them had been considered wise enough to advise a king. Then again, perhaps Norvin Norwood had merely grown so accustomed to strange happenings that he no longer questioned them.

Firekeeper didn't know which was true, but she enjoyed

trying to puzzle out the intricacies of human motivations as she might a game trail.

The earl had agreed to see them in his private study, a dark-paneled, thickly carpeted room that might have been oppressive but for the huge, multipaned window that dominated one wall. Firekeeper liked this window almost as much as the one in her favorite refuge. It was constructed in three sections that jutted out from the room in the style she had been told to call a "bay"—though as far as she could tell it bore no resemblance either to a body of water or the cry of a hound.

The individual panes were diamond-shaped and leaded into the three component panels. The beveled edges of the diamond-shaped panes caught the light in a fascinating fashion, creating random sparkles that transformed the entire construction into the heart of a gigantic crystalline gemstone.

The wolf-woman had been watching the dancing sparkles as Doc spoke, allowing her thoughts to drift. If she listened too closely she became all the more impatient to be off. She had just arrived at the conclusion that perhaps the sparkles more resembled the dancing of light on water than the cold glittering of gemstones when she heard the earl speak her name.

"So, Firekeeper," Norvin Norwood said, and his use of her wolf name seemed a good sign, "as I understand Cousin Jared, you will go after these stolen objects whether or not I give my permission."

Firekeeper met the earl's pale grey eyes.

"Yes. I give my word to a mother who is my mother before you is . . ."

"Are," Derian muttered automatically.

"Before you are my father."

Earl Kestrel stroked his beard.

"This once," he said at last, "your desire and my own run together."

Firekeeper blinked in surprise. She had expected—as had Derian and Doc—a long argument with the earl. With a slight twitching of his lips beneath his mustache that might have been a smile, the earl continued:

"Cousin Jared has presented your case very well—so well that had he not been gifted with the healing talent I might be tempted to have him train as a courtier."

"Eagle's broad wings forfend!" Doc protested, seeming honestly dismayed.

"We are faced," the earl continued without commenting on Doc's minor interruption, "with—if your report is correct, and I chose to believe that it is . . ."

"Gracious of him," Blind Seer commented dryly.

". . . the potential releasing of forces that we had all hoped were banished from our land."

Firekeeper tilted her head to one side in inquiry.

"You mean these magic things?" she asked, adding a quick "sir" at the end of her sentence when Derian gently booted her—a thing that was fairly easy to do undetected because of where she sat on the floor.

"That is so."

As the earl continued, Firekeeper could tell he was making an effort to cast his thoughts into simple words and phrases rather than the embroidered bardic turns that came so easily to him. Even had he not been the heir to the Norwood Grant, Earl Kestrel would have been in demand as a storyteller—a tendency that made him lean toward elaborate phrasing whenever he felt a great moment was upon him.

"That is so," the earl repeated. "If these objects have been brought to the mainland, it is our duty to recover them."

"My duty," Firekeeper stated bluntly, feeling it was not too early to remind him, "is to take them home."

Earl Kestrel looked momentarily uneasy, but some thought smoothed the unease from his features.

"Before they can be taken anywhere," he said, "first we must have them. We agree on that."

"Yes." The wolf-woman gave a sharp nod.

"And I will give you what aid I can," the earl said. "Cousin Jared's presentation of events has convinced me that sending out an armed body of our local militia would be counterproductive. Their authority would end at the borders of my grant. My neighbors might rightly protest to the king and then there would be awkward questions to answer. Worse, rumors that we know what we know might get back to Queen Valora or to her agents. That, above all things, we cannot risk."

Firekeeper wrapped her arms around her bent knees, content to listen since the earl was saying what she wanted to hear.

"I will make excuses to cover your departure. Cousin Jared has suggested a complication in your old wounds. I think that, given his fame as a healer, that excuse would be seen through too easily. Rather, I suggest that I say that it is Sir Jared who has been called away. You had been feeling housebound, so I agreed to let you go with him. Counselor Derian will accompany you to deal with the mounts—after all, working with my stables was one of the reasons he came here."

The earl permitted himself a small smile. "And it can go unspoken that he is also known for his ability to work with you, my dear."

The affection in that last seemed genuine so Firekeeper gave an answering smile.

"Wendee Jay, if she agrees, will be sent as your chaperon. If not, I will find some other suitable woman to accompany you so that your honor will not be besmirched."

Firekeeper wondered idly what sort of man anyone thought could take advantage of her. Judging from Blind Seer's puffs of laughter, the wolf was having similar thoughts.

"This is good," Firekeeper said, when the earl leaned back in his chair, signaling the completion of his speech. "Thank you."

They left the earl's office well satisfied. Derian went to select appropriate horses. Each of them already had their own mount, of course, but they would still need a couple of pack mules. Sir Jared went to confer with Wendee Jay. Firekeeper returned to her room to inform Elation of the results of the conference.

The falcon could have attended, but the earl had seemed reluctant to have her decorate his study's carpets with hawk chalk. In the interest of gaining Norvin Norwood's goodwill Elation had agreed to stay in Firekeeper's room, where a canvas cover had been spread beneath her perch to facilitate cleaning.

Bursting into her room filled with good news, Firekeeper was surprised to find that the peregrine was not alone. Elise sat in a chair near the window, the book spread open on her lap illuminated by the morning light as it filtered through the loose curtain of her golden blonde hair.

"So the meeting went well?" Elise asked.

"It did," Firekeeper said.

She knew that Doc—and to a lesser extent Derian—were worried about potential complications if Elise insisted on accompanying them. Not only was Elise the heir to a barony, but she was not an outdoorswoman. Riding long hours in cold weather would test her in a fashion that it would not the others.

Firekeeper, with a wolf's cruel view of survival, felt that if Elise wanted to test herself she should be permitted. If she failed, they would leave her at the nearest town or village. If she succeeded, their pack would be stronger by one.

Briefly, the wolf-woman told Elise about the meeting.

"But Sir Jared didn't mention my going," Elise replied when Firekeeper had finished. "Nor did Derian Carter."

Firekeeper shook her head.

"Do you mind if I go with you?" Elise asked.

Firekeeper hesitated. "Winter is hard even on those who are winter-hard," she replied. "Many who are summer-strong die in winter."

Elise puffed indignantly, reminding Firekeeper of a squirrel preparing to scold.

"I know that," she said fiercely, "and I still think I can handle it. There will be villages along the way."

"I not stay in villages," Firekeeper reminded her. "Blind Seer not welcome there. Also, if we are to go fast, we may need camp when we can, not stop when a nice inn is shown."

Elise frowned. "So you don't want me."

"I not say," Firekeeper replied evenly. "Only want you to know truth. Truth is sometimes cold as winter."

"And if I am willing to try that cold?"

"Then you must do as we do and tell the earl where you

go," Firekeeper said. "He look for you just as he look for us if we leave without saying."

"True."

Elise stood, looking out into the gardens as she considered what Firekeeper had said. The snow from the day before still clung here and there, evidence enough that the sun's light was not even as warming as a candle flame. Firekeeper watched the young woman, unwilling to either persuade or dissuade.

At last Elise turned away from the window.

"You said Earl Kestrel was in his study?" she asked.

"When we left," Firekeeper agreed.

"I must go see if he can give me an audience," and in a swirl of skirts, Elise was gone.

DERIAN CARTER WONDERED if he would ever learn just what Elise had said to Norvin Norwood to persuade the earl to permit his honored guest to join their insane venture.

Had Elise reminded him that she was the daughter of a baron and that someday either he or his son would need to deal with her as a near equal? Had she hinted that she might be persuaded to ally her house with his own? Or had she simply stated that she would go where she would go and that if he thought wolves were willful, he would soon learn that they were nothing to highly born ladies?

Or maybe she had argued logically, presenting to the earl as she had to Doc the advantages to the venture if she were permitted to join the company.

Derian doubted that he would ever know, but whatever tactic Elise had employed, she had employed it well, for there was no doubting that she rode in their midst. Her coat was of winter-fox fur, silvery white and lined with lamb's wool. Her gloves and boots were lined with rabbit fur, and her hat was fur both within and without. Despite these trappings, she huddled in Cream Delight's saddle, only her eyes visible above the silk scarf she had wrapped around her face, and whenever the wind blew with particular fury she shivered.

That wind had blown up from the north on the morning of their departure, on the day following their conference with Earl Kestrel. It had carried the scent of snow on its breath. As Derian had moved about the stables readying their mounts, he couldn't help but remember old Toad's predictions when Derian had announced he was going to the Norwood Grant, that winter would be early and bitter this year.

Hunching his head against the cold, Derian tried to remember the proofs: something about how many nuts the trees had borne that autumn and something else about how early the wild grape leaves had turned. The final proof had been how thickly the horses' winter coats were coming in.

Derian couldn't deny that Roanne's coat had lost some of its summertime sheen, but he couldn't swear that it was any thicker than usual. Still, he wished that Firekeeper hadn't been so determined to set out before the storm sealed them in.

She didn't seem to mind the cold. Maybe it was because she was pacing them on foot rather than riding. Certainly the exercise would be warming and the bulk of the horses acted as a windbreak, but slogging through drifts that sometimes topped her boots couldn't be precisely comfortable.

Boot tops.

Derian grinned. Those at least had been a victory. When Firekeeper had tromped down the stairs that morning she had looked frustrated but not in the least sullen. At first Derian had credited Wendee Jay with the victory in this often-fought battle. He'd been surprised to learn that Firekeeper credited him with—or blamed him for—convincing her.

"You talk of bare feetprints in the snow," she had said, holding out a foot in front of her, and glowering at the elegant work of the cobbler's art that adorned it as if it were a disfiguring boil. "I no can leave feetprints in boots. Just boot prints and everyone have those."

Up ahead, Doc—who was taking his turn on point—swiveled in his saddle and called down the line.

"We're closing on a town," he said. "Does anyone have reason to stop?"

Derian gave a slight shake of his head. One reason he'd been riding to the rear was so he could watch the horses. None of them were showing any sign of distress. He'd taped their hocks to give them some added support and the road surface was not frozen hard. Nor was the party setting too fast a pace. Doubtless none of the mounts would resist a warm stall and hot mash, but none needed it.

Elise shook her head sharply, but didn't say a word. Wendee Jay, almost as thoroughly bundled but less obviously uncomfortable, gave a laugh.

"I'd love a cup of mulled cider," she said, "but I can go on without."

Firekeeper spoke last.

"We are fine," she said, adding a trace sternly, "and the sun is young."

"Not so young," Doc said, nudging his horse into a slightly faster walk. "We're rising noon. Still, you're right. I'll divert when we get to town and buy us a flask or two of something warm. Blaze is fresh and we can catch up easily. Anyone want to stop with me?"

Elise shook her head as if knowing that Doc's eyes were on her.

Maybe, Derian thought, *she's afraid that if she ever gets into a warm taproom she'll never leave.*

Wendee Jay was either less proud or perhaps simply wiser when it came to taking an offered respite.

"I'll stop with you, Doc. I know the innkeeper. I may be able to convince him to give us a good rate on the drinks and not charge too dearly for the flasks."

When they came to the town, Doc and Wendee turned to the tavern while Elise and Derian took charge of the pack mules. The fact that these could not be asked to stand sweating under their burdens was part of the reason for keeping the band moving. Another was that even if the pack animals could stand without stiffening, they should not be pressed to a quicker pace to make up the lost time. Doc's Blaze and grey

Patience, who carried Wendee, would have lighter burdens and could be sheltered in a livery stable for the duration of their brief stop.

Firekeeper and Blind Seer had vanished when the first house came into view. Derian knew that the pair were making a wide circle of the area and would intercept the rest along the road once it left the town. Doubtless the wolf would not pass up the opportunity to hunt a bit as well. Blind Seer was keeping clear of the horses—Cream Delight in particular was taking offense at the wolf's presence, though she seemed to take some comfort from Roanne's acceptance of the massive beast. Still, the scent of fresh blood would be an incentive to fear.

Derian fancied that Firekeeper must have said something to the mules, for they were being astonishingly cooperative. Idly, he wondered why she didn't do the same with the riding horses. He must remember to ask her sometime.

When Elise spoke, her voice was stiff with disuse.

"He's humoring me, isn't he?" she asked.

"He? Who? What?" Derian replied, confused.

"Sir Jared," she clarified, and Derian realized that the rusty tone he had taken for disuse was barely subdued anger. "He's humoring me. All this talk about towns and hot drinks. He wouldn't bother if I wasn't along."

"You don't know that," Derian replied pacifically, though the same thought had crossed his mind.

"I do," Elise said. "I'm the soft one. Look at Firekeeper. She isn't even bothering with a heavy coat."

"The coat she's wearing," Derian countered, "is heavier than she has worn in all her life. She's even wearing boots."

"But no gloves, no hat. And Wendee Jay . . ." Elise sounded, if anything, more offended. "She's a grown woman— a mother! And yet she's riding along like this is a lark. I'd expect such from, say, Sapphire, but from the mother of two?"

"Wendee Jay," Derian said, feeling he was doomed even as he spoke, "spent many years riding the roads when she traveled with the theater troop. This is nothing new to her."

"So you're admitting that Sir Jared is humoring me!"

Derian threw his hands up in disgust, startling Roanne, who

punished him with a few dancing sideways steps. By the time he had the mare under control again, Derian had framed his reply.

"What if he is?" he asked, glancing over at the angry eyes just visible over the scarf. "What's wrong with that?"

"I don't want humoring." The words were fierce and implacable.

"So I shouldn't have wrapped the horses' hocks," Derian said.

"What?"

Derian took some small relief in that Elise sounded confused rather than angry.

"So I shouldn't have wrapped the horses' hocks," he repeated. "Even though they are prone to sprains and ice might cut them. I'm humoring them."

Elise didn't laugh, didn't smile (Derian had to guess at that last), but her sea-green eyes grew thoughtful, the curve of her brows softening from their scowl.

"I guess you are," she said. "But I'm not a horse. I want to be treated like everyone else."

"We are treating you in the only way possible," Derian replied. "Let me tell you about the . . ."

He paused to substitute a more polite word for the one he'd been about to use.

". . . lecture I got from Earl Kestrel when I tried to show Race Forester that I was just as tough as he was."

Elise listened without comment as Derian told his tale. He didn't exaggerate. He didn't need to—he'd been a proper young idiot trying to match skills with the best forester in Hawk Haven. When he finished speaking, Elise sighed.

"Stiff and cold?" she asked.

"As a board," Derian promised. "And I blistered the living daylights out of my feet walking in riding boots rather than having the sense to change my footwear when I knew I'd be walking."

Elise sighed again.

"I don't like being the weak sister," she admitted. "I'm not used to it, and I did so well between Bright Bay and Hawk Haven."

"Firekeeper wasn't setting the pace then," Derian said dryly. "And the weather was more clement."

Elise went on as if she hadn't heard.

"I mean I never rode or hunted like Sapphire, but I was as good—or better—at the things that mattered."

"Like dancing and writing letters," Derian said.

"Right," Elise agreed. "I know it sounds stupid here and now with the snow falling, but I've never had to think of myself as less than capable. Tell me where to begin."

"Drink Doc's posset when it comes," Derian advised her, "and wrap up against the cold. Otherwise you'll catch something and be sniffling when we need you to translate with the New Kelvinese."

"That wouldn't be much good, would it?" Elise said, and this time he was certain he saw the muscles of her face move in a smile beneath the silk. "Very well, Counselor. I'll take your advice."

❧

GRATEFUL PEACE FOUND the two-and-a-half-day sleigh ride from the Stone Giant Inn to the city of Dragon's Breath one of the most exhilarating yet wearying journeys of his life.

Travel conditions were not to blame for the contradictory state of his emotions. The sleigh runners ran smoothly over the carefully tended roads. The horses—changed at every post-station—were fresh and not yet dispirited from a long winter's hauling. Indeed, they seemed to enjoy how the chill air made the weight of their dragon caparisons negligible, to be rejoicing in the absence of flies and dust.

Nor did Peace have any complaints regarding his attendants. Even the young man who had taken over for the groom murdered by the escaped Baron Endbrook was proving quite satisfactory.

Baron Endbrook—or rather his continued absence—contributed a sizable amount to Grateful Peace's worries.

Although guards had been after Endbrook almost from the moment of his mad dash from the Stone Giant Inn, the islander had escaped and careful searching had not yet discovered him. The searchers had found his horse that first night, but Waln had been nowhere about. The man had vanished as if the legendary White Sorcerers had scooped him up onto one of their traveling clouds and flown away with him to their strongholds at the peaks of the Eversnow Mountains.

After careful consideration, Grateful Peace had not elected to remain at the Stone Giant Inn while the search for Baron Endbrook continued. His primary responsibility was to bring Lady Melina to Dragon's Breath. The execution of Endbrook and the driver had been a mere matter of housekeeping. Therefore, Peace left his guards behind—he knew he could commandeer more at the first post-house he passed on his return to the capital—expecting them to tidy up this loose end without much difficulty.

Peace had anticipated that the rider who arrived at the inn where he and Lady Melina had broken their first day's journey would report Baron Endbrook found, killed (if he had not died already of exposure), and the little matter closed. The thaumaturge had been so irritated at the rider's report of failure that he had almost sent the man out again without permitting him time for rest or a meal.

Only the knowledge that acting out of pique was as foolish as making faces at the moon had caused Grateful Peace to curb his initial frustration—that and the awareness that Waln might have been found in the intervening hours since the rider had departed to bring his report.

The report that was carried to Grateful Peace late the second night—riders could race faster than even the best sleighs, especially with frequent change of mounts—had been no more satisfactory. Peace realized that he would arrive in Dragon's Breath before the next report could catch up to him, especially if the search was forced to spread out over a greater distance and farther to the south.

But the disappearance of Baron Endbrook was not the only thing troubling Grateful Peace. Lady Melina Shield herself was responsible for both a large amount of his worry and a sizable portion of his exhilaration.

Superficially, she had been the very image of cooperation. She had given over to Grateful Peace the sealed box containing the three magical artifacts—suggesting that it not be opened until they were safely in Dragon's Breath.

Peace had agreed. Doubtless Baron Endbrook had safeguarded the artifacts in some way and Peace himself was not skilled in traps and locks or their undoing. By day the artifacts rested in a cabinet beneath the seat of the sleigh in which Grateful Peace and Lady Melina traveled. By night, he slept with them as an uncomfortable pillow.

Suspecting that Lady Melina had used her physical charms to distract Waln—the serving girl at the Stone Giant Inn had made this more certainty than suspicion—Grateful Peace had politely ignored Lady Melina's tentative overtures.

As soon as was possible—he found excuse during a discussion of his personal facial markings—Peace had explained his renunciation of any woman other than his long-lost Chutia.

His self-esteem was slightly dented when he sensed relief on Lady Melina's part at his announcement. Even a man who suspects he is being used wants to believe that the attraction is sincere.

Oddly, it was only after Lady Melina had abandoned her attempts at sexual enticement that Grateful Peace realized that he found the woman rather fascinating. Her naked face both interested and repulsed him, though she was neither beautiful nor ugly. Rather her eyes were what drew him.

From a distance these were unremarkable, a pale shade that might be blue, might be grey, fringed with blonde lashes that did nothing to make them distinctive. Seen from close up— as Grateful Peace had ample opportunity to do during their long sleigh rides each day—the irises proved to be a clear, crystalline blue, an incredibly pure yet elusive shade.

Grateful Peace found that he had to struggle not to be drawn into the depths of those pale eyes. He wanted nothing more than to stare, to find the wellspring of that hint of color. More than once he caught himself doing just that and had to jerk himself back to awareness of himself and his surroundings.

In his efforts to avoid being transformed into a gawking fool, Peace found himself responding to Lady Melina's myriad questions with rather more readiness than would be his usual wont. He found himself explaining how his name was atypical when she referred to the Dragon Speaker as Rusting Iron—a literal translation of his name into Pellish.

"No, never call him that," he said, rather shocked.

Iron was the metal antithetical to magic, and so never mentioned if at all possible. Even Apheros's name more closely meant "Eater of the Grey Metal that Turns Red." It was a very powerful name and showed that his parents had ambitions for him from birth.

"No?" she asked, all innocence.

"Names are not translated. Names are *names*."

"But you introduced yourself to me as Grateful Peace—not as Trausholo."

Peace nodded. "That is because my parents named me for a concept or a hope—my name is the idea, not the words. This is not the case with most names."

"No?"

"Well, what does your own name mean?"

Lady Melina blinked. "It's simply a pleasant sound. We have a good many of those, traditional names from the Old Country."

"It is the same with us," he said. "I am sorry that my own name led you astray, but pray, take care."

Lady Melina nodded and changed the subject. It seemed that the lady was interested in everything to do with New Kelvin. She questioned him with an avidity the thaumaturge might have found unsettling in another person.

From her, however, such interest seemed only reasonable. Was she not a reputed sorceress, though born in a land that abhorred the art? Might not New Kelvin seem a welcome refuge?

Lady Melina's comprehension of his explanations both

astonished and discomfited Grateful Peace. He was accustomed to foreigners who made no effort to understand the ways of the New Kelvinese, who stopped trying to understand as soon as they had learned what basic courtesies they must know in order to trade in silk or exotic drugs. In contrast, Lady Melina gave evidence of ample prior knowledge—far more than could be credited to her one long-ago visit.

As a man who had learned the power of information from his earliest days as an Illuminator, Grateful Peace might have been inclined to lie to Lady Melina, but he had no orders to do so. Moreover, evading a direct answer proved to be quite difficult. Lady Melina seemed to remember everything he had told her and to weigh one fact against another, rephrasing her initial question until she received a precise reply.

This tendency awoke a curious hope in Grateful Peace's most secret heart—the source of some of the excitement that coursed through him. If Lady Melina was this dogged when simply learning the customs of the land, how determined would she be when she turned that interrogating mind to unraveling the mystery of the three artifacts that now rode upon this very sleigh?

Almost unwittingly, on the third day of their journey, Peace found himself sharing his hopes with Lady Melina.

"In the treasuries of New Kelvin we have many objects that we are certain once held enchantments," he explained. "There are elegantly bejeweled weapons, globes that once lit without the need for fire, elaborately jointed statues that moved of their own accord, books that once spoke wisdom from the lips of the illuminated figures inscribed upon their pages.

"Now, however, few"—he stopped himself just short of saying "none," an admission that would have been treason—"of these objects work."

Grateful Peace went on, vaguely aware that perhaps he was saying more than he should, but feeling that this reputed sorceress needed to know all the intricacies of the situation so that she could better solve the difficulties.

"What theories, thaumaturge," asked Lady Melina, "have been arrived at to explain this problem? In Hawk Haven the lack of magic is ascribed to the farseeing efforts of Queen Zorana the Great, who had forbidden all magic, its teachings, and who ordered destroyed all vessels of enchantment. Such is not the case in your own land."

"No," Peace agreed, nodding ponderously.

The world seemed to have resolved into those two pale blue eyes. With an effort he made himself speak.

"One theory—the one most widely held—is that when the Burning Death spread over the land, the most powerful sorcerers among our revered Founders came together and placed a seal over the land, a seal meant to keep magic from functioning."

Lady Melina frowned. "Why would they do that?"

"It is a great mystery," Peace admitted. "However, some of the writings from that time seem to indicate that the Burning Death was most deadly to those who were sorcerously inclined. They may have hoped that by sealing away the magical emanations they would save their lives until a cure could be found."

"And was one?"

Peace shrugged. "We don't know. The Founders departed to the homeland and never returned. We of New Kelvin keep the faith of the old ways and will be rewarded for our perseverance upon the glorious day when the Founders come to us again."

"The plague was over a century ago!" Lady Melina protested. "Surely you don't believe they will return!"

"I do not look for that great occasion in my lifetime," Grateful Peace admitted. "Indeed, some of our philosophers believe that the Founders are waiting for us to find them, to prove ourselves worthy of joining in their wondrous magical community across the oceans."

"And you?" she asked, the note of protest replaced by mild curiosity. "What do you feel?"

"I do not see any harm in striving," Peace said. "Indeed, I see much virtue in the effort. That is why I view your arrival—and that of the things you bring with you—with such interest."

He kept his speech as controlled as possible, but the intensity of his words gave away some of his excitement.

"And why do you think that these three objects and my humble self could mean so much?" Lady Melina asked.

He was drowning in those eyes!

Grateful Peace shook himself and stared out into the sunlit snow, but even that blinding whiteness seemed to bear the imprint of two pale blue eyes.

"To understand," he said in an effort to get away from delicate subjects, "you must first understand something of the political forces in New Kelvin."

"My understanding," Lady Melina replied, and he thought he heard a trace of annoyance in her tone, "is that your nation is a monarchy with the monarch advised by a body of nobles led by the one called the Dragon Speaker."

"That is true," Peace said, "but only to a point. Your understanding is colored by your own governmental system."

"Pray," Lady Melina said, staring at him, "enlighten me."

"We are indeed a monarchy," Peace said. "Our ruler is called the Healed One. He is always a man, a direct descendent and—some believe—the reincarnation in the flesh of the last of the founding sorcerers of New Kelvin."

"I thought you said that the Founders all departed?"

"All but this one," Grateful Peace said. "He was too ill to leave with the rest and remained to give his last days to the colonists. To his own surprise, he survived, but whatever had been done to prevent the use of magic in the land kept him from employing his own sorcerous powers. He spent his last days preserving the traditions of the homeland and keeping us from falling into barbarism as was the case in so many other lands."

Belatedly, Peace realized that this final sentence had been less than tactful, but Lady Melina—though a descendant of those barbarians—chose to overlook the implied insult.

"So this Healed One is your king," she prompted. "What happens if a Healed One fails to engender a son?"

"Then we look among his relatives for a successor," Grateful Peace explained. "A search not unlike that which your own King Tedric recently undertook."

Lady Melina gave a sour little smile. Clearly the memory of that time was not a fond one.

"The Healed One must be male," Peace went on, "because of the belief that he is in some sense the reincarnation of the first Healed One."

"I understand," Lady Melina said. "So, is this the only difference from the system in Hawk Haven? If so, it is not a very big one."

Grateful Peace shook his head.

"In many ways, it is the least of our differences. You spoke of 'nobles.' In New Kelvin we have nothing resembling your hereditary Great Houses. Instead we have sodalities of enchantment. One does not enter these by birth alone. One must show talent and inclination."

Lady Melina tapped the tip of her nose with a finger.

"I have come across references to the sodalities," she said, "but I did make the mistake of equating them with our Great Houses—even though in some ways they seemed to more closely resemble our trade guilds."

Peace smiled, disproportionately pleased by this admission of ignorance. It returned to him some sense of control.

"There is a similarity," he said kindly, "for a skill in one of the magically related arts is needed to gain admission. My sodality, for example, is that of the Illuminators. Although both of my parents were artistic, neither had the level of skill to gain admission. I, however, was something of a prodigy and was admitted quite young."

Lady Melina looked impressed.

"But your title is not Illuminator," she said. "You introduced yourself to me as a thaumaturge."

"That comes later," Peace replied. "Bide a moment and I will clarify. There are thirteen sodalities—Illuminators, Lapidaries, Artificers, Stargazers, Alchemists, Beast Lorists, Songweavers, Divinators, Crystal Spinners, Herbalists, Sericulturalists, Choreographers, and Smiths. The thaumaturges are appointed from these ranks."

"And none of this is hereditary?" Lady Melina asked.

Peace shrugged. "It is to a point. Inclinations toward a skill do run in a family. Additionally, a member of a sodality has resources beyond those of the average person. Training, therefore, can be acquired for a promising but not overly talented child. My Chutia was one such. Her skill at calligraphy was technically accurate but lacked the purity of inspiration. She was more than adequate to enter a sodality, but, even had she lived, she would not have risen beyond the lower ranks."

"The sodalities, then," Lady Melina asked, "are not restricted by gender?"

"Not at all," Peace assured her. "Neither for entry nor within. The current heads of several of the sodalities are female."

"And your Dragon Speaker, how does he fit into this system?"

"The Dragon Speaker is elected from within the ranks of the thaumaturges," Grateful Peace explained. "I, personally, have no ambitions in that direction, but there are always those who do. They gather around them those who support them and once every three years an election is held."

"So your government can change every three years?" Lady Melina sounded disbelieving.

"Or more often or less," Peace replied. "Although the election is held every three years, a strong Dragon Speaker is usually confirmed. If the Dragon Speaker gives cause—for example by physical infirmity or by undertaking some course with which the majority of the thaumaturges do not agree—then he can be replaced. This happens rarely."

Yet, Peace thought, *we came close last year when the southern nations went to war. There were those who did not like Apheros's neutrality. They would have had us side with Stonehold and attempt to crush both Hawk Haven and Bright Bay between us. Then there was the matter of the enchanted objects Queen Valora was rumored to possess.*

He smiled softly at this last. Here, at least, Apheros had acted decisively. Many of the doubting thaumaturges had been swayed to his side at even the rumor that the Dragon Speaker had found a way to acquire the artifacts.

Still, there were those who found the threat of Hawk Haven

and Bright Bay reuniting into the proposed kingdom of Bright Haven reason for aggressive action before that reunion could occur. For now they would wait. The promise of active magic was a powerful one.

But the election is in two years, Grateful Peace thought, *and there could be a challenge before then. We need active magic before then. Otherwise, Apheros's government could well fall.*

He thought of the sealed box, of the mysteries it contained, of what would happen if those mysteries could not be awakened. So deeply did Peace lapse into his thoughts that he did not realize that he had stopped speaking, nor did he notice the appraising gaze of the pale blue eyes that continued to study him with silent intensity.

That gaze did not waver until the sleigh drew around a broad curve and the glittering lights of Dragon's Breath became visible against the gathering night. Then indeed did Lady Melina's gaze shift, but in the dimness Peace did not notice how hungry was the light within those crystalline eyes.

XXII

FIREKEEPER HAD BEEN AWARE that someone was following them since their first day on the road from the Kestrel estate. By the second day, she was certain—as Blind Seer had been from the start—who their shadow was.

A peculiarly wolfish element in her sense of humor kept Firekeeper from telling her companions—a waggish desire to learn if they would notice they were being pursued. It was an impulse akin to that which led a puppy to jump from hiding to pounce a littermate, a "got you that time!" sort of laughter.

That the pursuer might prove a problem never crossed her mind. Indeed, that he could track them so closely without the others ever knowing he was near only made Firekeeper raise her estimation of him.

Of course, that estimation had never been high.

Near evening on the second day after their departure from the Kestrel estate, the little band reached the town of Stilled. Snow mixed with sleet drove down slantwise, sliding into every crevice, soaking the travelers to the bone despite their winter wraps.

When she had lived with the wolves, Firekeeper had retreated to a cave on such days. If she had fuel, she huddled near a fire. If she did not and one of the wolves chose to stay with her, she huddled next to the wolf. Otherwise, she shivered. While so trapped, she usually became quite hungry, but hunting had been out of the question. Food had been the dream through which she had passed the hours.

Today the wolf-woman was not hungry, but she was learning that being icy and wet could be even more unpleasant. She was also exquisitely lonely.

Blind Seer had not quite abandoned her but, knowing that his presence would keep her from taking shelter in the town, he had made his excuses and vanished into the surrounding area. Doubtless, he had found himself a comfortable spot in some hollow, and was letting the snow settle around him, insulating him from the worst of the cold. After a while, not even the passing rabbits would know the wolf was there.

Come dawn Blind Seer would make his own river crossing and meet them on the other side.

The town of Stilled took its name from the partial dam that here quieted—or stilled—the raging torrents of the White Water River. Creation of the dam had been a major engineering feat undertaken in the time of Earl Kestrel's grandfather, but it had been worth the effort and expense. Before, trade had only come across farther east, effectively ruling the Norwood Grant out of the economic opportunities just across the border.

The dam could not stop the river's force, but it could redirect it, thus making ferry traffic possible, especially during the winter, when the river ran lowest. In the spring, passage was impossible, the torrents of snowmelt resisting any obstacle. Then the people of Stilled opened the floodgates and let the waters run through. Spring was planting time in any case, not a time for trade.

Tomorrow morning—weather permitting—Firekeeper and her companions planned to take the Stilled ferry across into New Kelvin. Blind Seer could make his way across the dam itself, trusting footholds a human would find slick indeed. In fact, the wolf had already done so, running ahead the night before their departure to test Elation's scouting and circling back to meet them along the road.

Firekeeper knew Derian had been relieved when she had reported that Blind Seer could get across the White Water on his own. The young man had been devising various plans to get the wolf across without attracting undue attention—attention that might at the least delay them and at the worst somehow reach the ears of Baron Endbrook and Lady Melina, alerting them to the possibility of pursuit.

Fox Hair worries too much, Firekeeper thought fondly. *He's like a mother wolf with too many pups for her teats and no nursemaid about.*

The image of Derian as a mother wolf amused and distracted Firekeeper so that she forgot her discomfort and was even surprised to find their saddle train coming to a halt before what was, even to her eyes, clearly an inn.

She couldn't read words painted on the sign over the door, but the picture—glimpsed whenever the wind swung the sign back into a somewhat vertical position—seemed to be of a mouse sitting on its haunches, an extraordinarily long tail twisting out behind it.

The warm orange glow through the opaque glass of a front window immediately conjured up images of firelight and comfort. As they stopped and Derian was stiffly swinging down from Roanne's saddle, the orange light was blocked by a form about the size of a human head. Moments later, the big front door was flung open.

A cloaked and hooded figure smelling of beef and roses burst forth.

"Welcome to the Long Trail Winding," it said in a contralto

bellow that carried easily over the wind. "Come in out of the cold."

"The horses and mules . . ." Derian began.

"Send 'em round the side," the innkeeper interrupted, "to the left. I've already rung so the gate will be open. We've stabling enough. No one's out on a night like this and our last big group left two days ago."

Before the innkeeper had finished her speech, Firekeeper had already stepped onto the porch. The wolf-woman's immediate impulse was to rush to the comfort indoors, but she knew Derian would not come inside until the horses and mules were settled.

Elise would be useless in this matter. Doc and Wendee might be somewhat better, but Firekeeper had reached an accommodation with these particular animals. She moved over to where Wendee was mounted on Patience and helped her down. Wendee gave her a grateful smile.

"Thanks," Wendee said. "I'm a bit stiff."

Firekeeper, who had run most of the way rather than get chilled, nodded. She knew she'd be stiff, too, if she'd sat on a plodding horse in the cold and wind.

"Get into warm," she said. "I help Derian."

Then she turned to Patience.

Move! she growled, slapping the horse on the rump.

The gelding was only too glad to move, even without its sometime rider's encouragement. Patience wasn't an equine genius, but it had scented the stables. If the mules had been inclined to argue—and Firekeeper wasn't certain that they actually were—Firekeeper's growl got them hurrying along at a brisk pace. A few even trotted.

At the stable they were met by two young men who stated that "Ma would have their heads for the soup pot" if they let guests of the inn remain uncomfortable any longer than absolutely necessary.

Derian took one look at the neat stable, grinned his thanks, and started unstrapping their baggage. Firekeeper helped him carry the few necessary bags inside.

"We can trust those fellows with the rest of the load," Derian said to her once they were outside again—the cold and damp seeming all the worse for the temporary respite in the stable. "I think the innkeeper's some sort of cousin of my mother's. My parents have an agreement with them, and I'll just make certain that the innkeeper knows who I am."

Whether whatever Derian said to the innkeeper was necessary, Firekeeper didn't know. The innkeeper—a distinctly fat woman with mouse-grey hair and a cheerful laugh—seemed delighted to have more guests. She sent hot wine to their rooms, plied them with bread and soft cheese as soon as they came down to the common room, and set before them not only the beef stew Firekeeper had scented, but a side of roast venison as well.

Some hours later when they were warm, dry, and well fed, sleet no longer rattled against the windowpanes. By the time Firekeeper had retired to the room she was to share with Elise and Wendee Jay, the stars were bright against a sky that looked like freshly brushed black velvet.

"No, you don't," Elise said, looking over from where she stood bent over, brushing her hair, the steadily repeated strokes making it look like a wheat field rippling in the wind.

"No, I don't what?" Firekeeper asked, astonished at the rebuke.

"No, you don't go running around outside of town howling for Blind Seer," Elise said. Her lips formed numbers as she counted the brush strokes.

Firekeeper, who had been thinking of doing precisely that, was offended.

"Why should I no?" she asked indignantly. "I no get lost."

"*Not* and *won't*," Elise corrected. "Because it is dark and cold out there, because you've been .chilled to the bone and you need to rest before tomorrow."

"Think of this," Wendee added soothingly from where she was hanging their damp clothes on a line the accommodating innkeeper had strung before the fire. Her hair was already tightly plaited, her flannel gown tied close to her throat. "The wolf has probably got himself nice and warm. He doesn't need you to wake him up."

Wendee's argument convinced Firekeeper to stay in. Still, as she drifted off to sleep on the pallet before the fire, looking up at the shadows the dangling laundry cast in the flickering light, she wondered how she could feel so alone though crowded into a room with two other women.

THE NEXT MORNING they passed through customs without difficulty. Doc had gone ahead and presented the official with a letter from Earl Kestrel while Derian supervised the readying of the horses and mules. The earl's letter, combined with the fact that nothing in their baggage was worth notice, sped them along without even the payment of a bribe, allowing them to commandeer nearly all of the first ferry.

Firekeeper was amused to note that their shadow had also found a place on the same ferry. He stood to one side, leaning over the railing as if fascinated by the patterns the sunlight made on the water. The hood of his traveling cloak was pulled up around his head—a bit unusual since the weather had turned fair as if apologizing for its behavior the night before—but Firekeeper didn't think her companions noticed him. They were all occupied with keeping the horses and mules calm during the crossing.

While visiting Silver Whale Cove, Firekeeper had gone out once on a rowboat, but this river crossing was quite a different matter. The ferry jolted and bounced on the rough water, making her stomach uneasy and causing her to wish that she'd elected to cross via the dam with Blind Seer.

The town on the other side of the White Water was named, in ornate New Kelvinese phrasing, the Gateway to Enchantment—typically shortened to Gateway. At the customs house, the official glanced through their gear, accepted the border tax Derian had ready, and otherwise ignored them.

In early winter, many visitors crossed into Gateway from Hawk Haven, each hoping to buy something unique, valuable, and possibly antique. Their party looked little different.

Wendee Jay had frequently visited Gateway during her days as a traveling actress and she became their guide.

"You'll find that most of the people here in Gateway will speak some of our language," she said. "In fact, most of them will speak more than they'll admit. It's to their benefit to pretend ignorance—especially when the bartering gets stiff."

As they rode from the riverside toward the town square, Firekeeper looked around the town with disinterest. The square stone buildings seemed little different than those on the other side of the river. The streets were marginally cleaner perhaps, but that was all. Elise apparently saw things differently.

"Look at the stone carvings!" she marveled aloud, reining in Cream Delight so she could study the archway that spanned the road into the square. "The work that went into this one dragon-thing alone must have taken months."

Firekeeper looked where Elise pointed. On the polished side of the arch a twisting figure had been incised into the stone. Having never seen a dragon, she had to take Elise's word for what it represented, but to her eyes it looked like nothing so much as a nest of hibernating snakes with only one head— and that head merged the characteristics of wolf, horse, and snake in what the feral woman privately thought was an improbable fashion.

"We not here to look at rocks," Firekeeper said impatiently. "Day is clear but sun not shine forever. We should move."

She knew she was being rude, but a sense of urgency was rising within her. Stormy weather the past two days had made a report from the wingéd folk impossible. Elation had gone out with the dawn to see if she could intercept a messenger.

Despite lacking a precise destination, Firekeeper felt they should press into the interior of New Kelvin. Surely such valuable things as they sought would not be kept near the border.

Wendee Jay shook her head at Firekeeper's words, her lips pursed in an expression Firekeeper recognized from when Merri became unruly.

"Before we go anywhere," Wendee said sternly, "I want to shop for a few things that may be essential when we reach the interior."

"What?" Firekeeper asked, torn between curiosity and annoyance.

Wendee looked around, saw that no one was in earshot—indeed, the New Kelvinese seemed to give them a wide berth—and continued:

"Here in Gateway our attire and lack of cosmetics will not cause comment, but further in we will stand out."

"Won't we in any case?" Doc asked.

"As a group," Wendee agreed, "but an individual scouting—or spying—may escape casual notice with the right disguise."

"Good point," Doc admitted.

Firekeeper privately agreed, but she refrained from saying so. She trusted herself to the cover of shadows, but none of the rest shared her skill.

Fleetingly she thought of their own personal shadow. He had gone off in another direction as soon as the ferry docked, but she didn't doubt he would know when they left Gateway. Five horses and two pack mules were hard to conceal. Indeed, they were less than welcome in the town center, so Derian had taken them to a stable near the north of town where they could be held until needed.

Elise and Wendee moved purposefully toward a shop whose garishly painted sign apparently advertised cosmetics. Doc walked a few steps behind them, looking for an apothecary. Firekeeper trailed somewhat sullenly in the rear.

She didn't like being wrong, nor being out of her element. Her sojourn west of the Iron Mountains had reawakened a wildness she hadn't known had been quieted by the moonspans she had spent among humans until it arose again. More than ever she resented being treated like a pup—and more than ever she was forced to admit that among humans, as among wolves, she was still little more.

At least among the wolves she had been used to that ranking. It was harder to accept when among humans. They were weaker than her, less swift and agile, absolute slugs when it came to foraging for themselves. To the speech of most of the world's creatures they were deaf and weren't even aware of their disability. Yet—and this Firekeeper hated admitting—even Elise was better prepared to function in the environment they now entered.

Fleetingly, the feral woman considered leaving Gateway and seeking out Blind Seer. The wolf would be delighted to see her, would doubtless have stories about his adventures since splitting from the main group the night before. Fire-keeper was no less able than their shadow to tell when the rest left town.

She was one foot on that trail when she seemed to hear again the debating voices of the Royal Beasts as they argued their need. They had chosen her because she was human—not wolf—because she could do things not even the clever pawed raccoons could. If she turned away now, wasn't she betraying their trust?

Firekeeper shook herself and trotted to catch up with the others. Doc had excused himself to visit an apothecary shop. Elise and Wendee were standing outside the window of the cosmetician's.

"No," Wendee was saying to Elise, "no one will think it the least bit odd if we purchase a broad selection of colors. More than one lady of Hawk Haven wears New Kelvinese cosmet-ics—though the custom is wider spread among the commoners than among the nobility. Another of Queen Zorana's influ-ences I suspect."

Elise smiled. "Perhaps so. Then let's go in. I can hardly wait!"

Firekeeper entered with them. The interior of the shop was a riot of color. Patterned silks hung on the walls. In front of these were open-backed shelves holding bottles and flat boxes, some spread wide to show the pats of color within. Polished mirrors caught the varied hues and sent them back again, tinted with silver. The floor was thickly carpeted, swallowing their footsteps so that all at once their breathing sounded loud.

Once over the threshold, it took all of Firekeeper's newly cultivated resolve not to bolt out again. The place reeked—and not with the honest odors of manure, sweat, and blood that she had learned humans found distasteful, but with heavy floral scents, melted wax, the sharp tang of alcohol, and a hundred other things she could not separate from the general melange.

Elise and Wendee sniffed appreciatively.

"It's like being inside a sachet," Elise said with a hushed laugh, "or maybe inside a whole drawer of them!"

Wendee was about to reply when a voice echoed from one corner.

"May I assist the foreign visitors?"

All three women jumped slightly as a portion of the intricately decorated wall separated itself from the rest, resolving into a short, round man. He wore a floor-length robe cut from the same silk that hung on the walls, and his face was painted in the same patterns. Even his hair was concealed under a close-fitting cap of the same material.

The effect was eerie and startling and Firekeeper—accustomed to the ways animals camouflage themselves—had no doubt that it was meant to be.

"Like magic!" gasped Wendee in tones that were convincingly astonished—unless, like Firekeeper, you had heard her use them whenever she played peekaboo with little Merri.

"Mere illusion," said the shopkeeper, sweeping them a bow. "How may I assist you?"

While Wendee and Elise tested the various preparations—smearing a bit on the back of their hands, testing them for water resistance, using a bit of unguent to remove each color in preparation for the next, Firekeeper drifted about the shop, examining everything, touching tentatively.

It *was* fascinating, she had to admit, though she wondered why the New Kelvinese needed to hide their true features in this way.

Were they trying to scare away predators after the fashion of those moths whose wings were imprinted with what seemed to be wide, staring eyes? Were they trying to look like something else, as a newborn fawn resembled nothing so much as a bit of sun-dappled duff?

She could hear the unctuous note in the shopkeeper's voice gradually moderate to one of genuine approval and interest as Wendee made her selections—though to Firekeeper one shade of scarlet or indigo or primrose yellow seemed much like the rest.

Another forest where I am a stranger, she thought with a trace of her earlier dissatisfaction. *Time to learn these trees—which have thorns and which bear fruit, and which do both.*

Wendee Jay neglected neither bartering for the best price nor proper packaging for her purchases. Despite this care, Firekeeper was pleased to see that the sun had moved only a little when they emerged.

"The next job will go more quickly," Wendee said, catching the direction of Firekeeper's gaze. "I want to buy a half-dozen or so robes. They sell them here for the tourists. I understand the prints are so basic that no one of the upper classes would be seen in them, but common and undistinguished is just what we want."

True to her word, Wendee was in and had made her purchases before Firekeeper had even finished examining the curiosities stacked on the shelves and piled on the floor. Glass was in ample evidence, mostly blown into vessels or drawn into soft-limbed forms that Elise claimed were monsters from legend. There were stone carvings, garishly painted wooden masks, and heaps of carpets that glowed with color.

"Trade goods for the tourists," Wendee sniffed when they were out on the streets. "Exotic 'antiquities'—none older than last year's workshop."

"They're lovely," Elise protested. Only the reminder of the journey ahead of them had kept her from buying gifts for her parents.

"Until you see the real thing," Wendee said. "You'll understand when we go deeper into the heartland."

"We go now?" Firekeeper asked, trying to keep a pleading whine from her voice.

"Right away," Wendee said. "There's Doc coming out of the apothecary's."

Firekeeper noted that Doc's coat pockets bulged, but she was too eager to get under way to ask questions. When they arrived at the edge of town, she found Elation waiting. The falcon did not even wait for flattery or questions.

"I found the raven. Baron Endbrook and Lady Melina crossed into New Kelvin five days ago. They traveled north on

the Dragon's Breath road until nightfall. That night, Baron Endbrook fled on horseback with nothing but the clothes on his back. The crow had caught up with them. Together, raven and crow elected to remain with Lady Melina, for Waln could not have borne the treasures away with him.

"Come daylight, Lady Melina and a white-haired New Kelvinese rode in a sleigh to the north. The crow understands some human tongue New Kelvinese–style and his understanding was that they were heading to Dragon's Breath. The raven came to find us, while the crow went on."

Firekeeper translated this as the falcon spoke. Wendee Jay looked somewhat wide-eyed. Even her awareness of the history of this venture and her observation of Firekeeper and Blind Seer had not prepared her for the reality of the situation.

The others were more inured to miracles.

Derian started tightening girths, slapping the horse's bellies when they tried to hold their breaths. The sound punctuated his words.

"I've been studying the maps and had a few words with the stablekeeper here. This road goes slightly north around the local fields, then doglegs northeast. Even with the best possible roads, we have at least four days' travel in front of us—probably more."

Firekeeper gave an impatient leap into the air.

"Then we go," she said, running a few steps down the indicated road. "We go *now*."

LEST THEIR GUEST THINK herself too important, Apheros told Grateful Peace to have her wait a full day before he would see her.

"Let her recall that she is separated from family and friends, that none may recall her to them unless we so will it," the Dragon Speaker said. "Then she will be eager to work with us with the proper humility an apprentice should show a master."

Privately, Peace didn't think such a small thing could humble Lady Melina. However, in keeping with the spirit of Apheros's command, he himself did not bring Lady Melina the message. Instead he trusted it to Kistlio, an apprentice Illuminator who had reached the top of his form without rising to mastery. Still ambitious, Kistlio now sought advancement by working as a clerk in the Speaker's offices.

As Kistlio was Peace's own nephew, he encouraged the lad and gave him advantages whenever possible—nobly refusing to hold his sister's childhood tormenting against her son.

Trusting Kistlio to do his duty, Peace walked the carpeted pathways behind the stone walls of the residence in which Lady Melina had been given a suite. There were peepholes here, perfectly concealed within the shadows of a wall carving, through which he could observe the encounter.

Lady Melina was alone when the door chime rang, her head bent over a book. She did not move to answer it at once, perhaps accustomed to servants who performed this service. The Dragon Speaker had ruled, however, that she was not to have servants for now—another of his lessons in humility.

When the chime sounded a second time, Lady Melina sighed, closed the tome, and, tucking it under her arm, crossed to the doorway.

"Who's there?" she called.

"A messenger from the most powerful and influential thaumaturge, Grateful Peace," came Kistlio's reply, slightly muted by the weight of the wooden door.

"Just a moment."

Lady Melina set the book down and went to work on the door latch. Despite himself, Peace was impressed that she did not—as would be the way with most women and many men—check her appearance. Either she was supremely confident or didn't care what kind of impression she made. Neither boded well for Apheros's intention to humble his guest.

Kistlio entered promptly when the door was opened. He was a slim youth of thirteen or so, wide-eyed and full-lipped, new enough to shaving his face and foremost head that the ritual remained a delight rather than a trial. He wore the blue-black silk robe of a clerk with poise, shaking the sleeves from his hands with the ease that transforms a routine action into grace.

He ducked his head in the slight bow that youth always grants to age, but otherwise offered no courtesy.

"I am here," he announced, the basso flatness that had disqualified him for song making even the most routine words sound portentous, "to inform you on behalf of the thaumaturge Grateful Peace that the Dragon Speaker will be unable to grace you with his presence today. He will see you tomorrow, if possible, the day after perhaps."

Lady Melina's back was to the peephole, but a provident designer had placed a long mirror near the door so that Peace was able to see in its reflections the slight look of annoyance that touched her features before she could school them into implacability.

"And what am I to do in the meantime?" she asked a trace sharply.

"Wait and prepare yourself for the great event," Kistlio suggested pedantically.

"May I leave this room?"

"I have no orders on that point, but I will remind you that the snows outside of the building are heavy."

"I see." Lady Melina turned now and paced toward the window, her steps quick and light. "Then you are suggesting I remain in these rooms."

"I make no suggestions. I only comment on the weather."

Peace smiled to himself. Kistlio could go far in the government—even though his lack of rank within a sodality barred him from a seat among the voting representatives.

"I see," Lady Melina said again. "Very well. I will wait here. My breakfast was brought to me. May I expect other meals as well?"

"I have no reason to believe not," Kistlio said.

"However, I lack basic comforts—servants, entertainment, books other than those I brought with me. May I ask you to tell the thaumaturge Grateful Peace that I would like these comforts provided?"

"You may," Kistlio agreed.

Peace grinned. Kistlio had only agreed that she might ask—he had not consented to relay the message. He wondered if Lady Melina realized the messenger's game.

"Thank you," she said after a long pause.

"I seek only to serve my masters," Kistlio replied.

Then, after performing another perfectly insulting bow, he withdrew.

Peace continued to watch, but Lady Melina proved to be supremely boring. After pouring herself the last dregs of what must be cold tea, she reopened her book. As best as Peace could tell, she was reciting lists of verbs in New Kelvinese.

Lady Melina haunted his thoughts throughout the morning. In the late afternoon, he decided that he would not be violating either the letter or the spirit of the Dragon Speaker's commands if he called on the lady. Indeed, he might learn something of her state of mind.

Her face when she opened the door ran through a gamut of emotions: pleasure, irritation, and finally mere politeness.

We wear our face paint for many reasons, Grateful Peace thought, *not in the least in that it provides us with a constant mask.*

"Good afternoon, thaumaturge," she said.

Her New Kelvinese was good but accented, making him unsure if he had imagined a slight stress on the word "afternoon."

"Good afternoon," he replied. "I have come to see if you are comfortable."

He did not apologize for his absence to this point. He owed her nothing. Nor did he step around her and into the room. If she wished to scorn him, he would leave and suggest to the Dragon Speaker that her interview be moved to some later date.

Lady Melina hesitated before replying. Finally, she said:

"I have had food brought to me, but I am rather lonely. Will you come in and speak with me? I very much enjoyed our long talks on the road from Stone Giant Inn to the capital."

Grateful Peace smiled. "I have some time before my next duty."

She ushered him to the grouping of chairs where he had seen her reading. He took a high-backed chair upholstered in red brocade, resting his hands over the carved claws on the armrests. Lady Melina returned to the small couch a short distance away where she had been seated before.

Peace expected her to begin listing complaints, but she surprised him.

"On our last day on the road," she said, "you were telling me the theories why magic does not function easily even in New Kelvin, about seals, and about the hopes you entertain for the objects I have brought with me. The artifacts are safe, aren't they?"

"Very," Peace said. "The Dragon Speaker is having their case examined for traps. At least one has been found and deactivated."

That last was a lie. The boxes were securely locked and sealed, but there was no evidence of any traps. Still, it didn't hurt for the lady to think there had been.

"I'm glad to hear they are safe." She leaned forward slightly. "Have you unsealed the individual boxes?"

"No. We are still examining them."

Lady Melina's expression became so neutral that Peace imagined her features were merely painted lines; then she animated into polite sociability once more.

"Tell me," she said, fastening her pale blue gaze on him, looking deeply into his eyes, "about your hopes for those artifacts. Doubtless I share them as well."

Peace blinked, feeling a touch light-headed. Then he tugged on his long braid—a gesture that dated back to his earliest days with pen and ink, when a more vigorous shrug might have smeared his work.

"Very well," he said. "Where did I leave off?"

"You had told me how your government was structured," she said, "about the Healed One who is your king, about the sodalities who send representatives to counsel him, and about the Dragon Speaker who is the first among these counselors. You also mentioned the theory that the Founders of New Kelvin might have placed a seal against magic over the land in an effort to halt the spread of the plague—what you called the Burning Death."

"All that," Grateful Peace said with an amused chuckle. "Well, then let me tell you a bit more. I told you that few of our magical artifacts work."

"That's right," she prompted, "because of this seal."

Something in her inflection conveyed her doubt. Momentarily angered, Peace snapped:

"You may doubt me, but let me tell you this. In all . . . most," he hastily corrected, "cases magic has failed to function within the boundaries of New Kelvin. Even those gifts your people term 'talents' are so rare as to be unknown among us. Where they do occur, the possessors tend to live near the borders of New Kelvin—near the edges of this seal."

"I am convinced," Lady Melina replied mildly. "Pray, continue."

Still somewhat angered, the thaumaturge did so.

"Some of us hold the theory that awakening the magic in those enchanted artifacts which the Founders left behind when they returned to the homeland would be very difficult unless one first found a way to deactivate the seal."

Lady Melina frowned slightly, but did not interrupt.

"However," Peace continued, "magical artifacts from *another* land—such as the three you have brought here—would not have been sealed in the same fashion."

(*Unless*, a defeatist voice from deep inside him whispered, *the sealing was placed upon the entire region the Founders held, rather than upon specific items. If that is the case, the seal will have barred magic from the land as effectively as rubbing wax into fabric causes it to repel water.*)

He shook his head as if to physically displace the doubts.

"Quite certainly not," Lady Melina agreed, "unless, of course, they were constructed in New Kelvin. Many of the texts I have consulted say that even before the plague, New

Kelvin was known for her deep and abiding interest in sorcery."

Grateful Peace hid his reaction to this disquieting notion beneath an urbane smile.

"We cannot know," he said, "until we make the attempt—an attempt I feel certain was made by King Gustin the First or one of his successors. However, their failure need not be ours. Only in New Kelvin were the libraries not burnt; only here was the old knowledge preserved."

As he prepared to relate his most secret hope, Grateful Peace's heart began beating rapidly, as if he had been running up one of the tightly coiling spiral stairs that led to the Scriptorium.

"Now," he said, pleased that his tone remained calm and academic, "if we awakened the power of the foreign artifacts might not the force of foreign magic be used to reignite the magic in our native relics?"

"I begin to understand the magnitude of your hopes," Lady Melina said softly. "You hope for not only the awakening of the magic within these three artifacts, but through them the breaking of the seal placed upon New Kelvin by your Founders."

Peace nodded eagerly, all his composure lost in contemplation of that wondrous event.

"I imagine," he said confidingly, staring deeply into those understanding blue eyes, "that the effect would be like lighting a fire from an ember. An ember in itself is not very impressive—hardly more than a greyish lump covered with ash. However, when the ember is touched to tinder its hidden heat is released and the tinder bursts into brilliant flames. These flames leap from point to point, igniting every receptive element that they touch."

Lady Melina reached forth impulsively and grasped his hand.

"And you believe I have brought the ember, while New Kelvin is filled with tinder for the fire!"

Grateful Peace beamed at her, pleased to have discovered such a kindred spirit.

Peace knew that the Dragon Speaker was an advocate of the ember/tinder theory. Many members of the rising generation, however, scoffed at it. These belonged to what Grateful Peace termed the Defeatist Party—though they viewed themselves as progressives. At first they had been little more than a nuisance, but now with Hawk Haven and Bright Bay vowing to reunite and become a power to rival any in the area, the Defeatists were winning influence.

The Defeatists had many theories to explain the lack of magic among their people—the Founders' seal was irrevocable; the Founders had drained all the magic from the land in order to fuel their escape from the Burning Death; the former enchantments left by the Founders would work only for their creators.

They held that the New Kelvinese should forget the past and work on making fresh enchantments—rather than seeking to preserve and awaken the old. Some radical elements said the New Kelvinese should forget magic entirely, and concentrate on mundane technologies. Only this split over which tactic to pursue had kept them from becoming a power to rival the current Dragon Speaker.

"What you have told me," Lady Melina said, breaking into Peace's thoughts, "makes me eager to begin. Why does the Dragon Speaker delay?"

So intimate had been their discourse that Peace almost blurted out the truth. Only years of ingrained caution prevented him from doing so.

"Apheros is a busy man," he said a trace weakly. "Not knowing the precise date of your arrival, he could not schedule an opening. I am certain he will see you tomorrow."

Lady Melina smiled and pressed Peace's hand—which only then did he realize that she still held within her own. He smoothly extracted it and rose, wanting nothing more than to escape before she could ease the truth from him.

"I, too, have duties," he said with what he hoped was a courtly—rather than chill—smile. Best to keep her happy.

"Thank you for taking the time to call on me," Lady Melina replied, rising smoothly from her seat and moving with stately grace toward the door. "So that I might better serve the purposes of the Dragon Speaker, might you arrange for me to have some more books? I have exhausted those I brought with me."

"They will be in our language," he cautioned.

"I have been studying most dutifully," she said, "and have a copy of the dictionary the Merchant's Guild supplies to those who wish to trade in New Kelvin."

He felt warmed by her almost childlike eagerness.

"I will do what I can," he promised and, indeed, after making his excuses and returning to his office his first task was arranging to have a few basic works on sorcerous theory delivered to her room along with a more comprehensive dictionary. He even arranged for a servant to attend her, at least in limited matters of attire and grooming.

After all, he justified to himself with a trace of uneasiness, *we brought her here to serve our purposes. What good do we do by keeping from her the tools she will need?*

The reasoning was quite sound. Peace wondered why he remained so uncomfortable.

XXIII

THE CONDITION OF THE PALMS of his hands and the fabric of his breeches, rather than any clear memory, testified to Waln as to the nature of his escape from New Kelvin.

Dirt had been so thoroughly ground into both—and into his knees where the breeches had become unbuckled, leaving the fabric to ride up. One stocking remained gartered. The other drooped around his boot top. The seat of his trousers was stiff with grime.

The nature of the dirt fascinated him. Sandy grit had left its mark beneath his skin, tiny black dots like amateur tattooing. There were smears of clay interspersed with sour fecal-smelling material, even small bits of chaff. From these—and smatterings of memory—he deduced that he had hidden in many an unsavory hole while making his way back to the White Water River.

Once there he had stowed away in the covered cargo section on one of the ferryboats—he remembered that in detail, including the way his stomach had growled and surged bile up his throat when he dared not pry open one of the crates holding cheeses a few inches from his nose.

He had dropped overboard when the ferryboat had been dragged onto rollers on the gravel strand at Plum Orchard—no one wanted to unload cargo in the mixture of sleet and rain that began when the ferry was halfway across, but they hadn't trusted the vessel to the unpredictable waters.

Doubtless the ugly weather had been the best friend Waln could have asked for, but at the time he had cursed the icy water that soaked him seemingly to the very core of his soul. He'd broken into a warehouse near the edge of town. It was mostly empty, thus unguarded.

Amid the relics stored within he had found a partial case of water-spoiled dried meat, a wedge of elderly cheese, and a partial barrel of sour wine. With rainwater gathered in an old bottle and the bottom of a metal box for a cook pot, he made himself a banquet. There was wood enough to burn from old packing cases and crates. At least the foul weather without meant that he did not need to worry about anyone spotting what smoke eddied out through the warehouse roof.

Though he ached for respite, Waln left before dawn the next morning. His fever had burned from him, but he could feel it lurking, waiting for an excuse to return. He hiked overland, clinging to the banks of the White Water for guidance and because something deep within him took comfort from the presence of living water.

Sometimes his fever must have returned because for long stretches he was accompanied by phantoms. Once his mother came and walked with him, mincing her way over the sand

and gravel in too-tight shoes. Waln asked her who his father was. She only laughed and vanished.

From a shack along the riverbanks Waln stole a heavy old coat and an oilcloth hat with a floppy brim. From the line outside a farmhouse he stole a pair of long workman's trousers and a smock. He regartered his stocking with a bit of string and carried those provisions he scrounged in a square of fabric bundled on the end of a stick.

His reflection, when he glimpsed it in a quiet pool at the edge of the river, was so unlike the robust Baron Endbrook that he doubted his pursuers—even if they should glimpse him across the breadth of the White Water—would know him. Bent with weariness, limping in boots never meant for so much walking, he was incarnated as the man Walnut the whore's son would have become had he never escaped to sea—a thief and beggar, weary, wounded, and alone.

Oddly, Waln's hatred did not center itself on the queen who had sent him on this mission, nor upon the woman who had betrayed him. It rooted in something he had trusted as he had never trusted either queen or lady—in the two items he had taken from Lady Melina as guarantee of her fidelity: a necklace of sparkling gemstones and a little girl with red-gold hair.

With this hatred to fire his heart, Waln tramped on long after darkness had fallen. The wisdom of both thief and bully kept him from stealing a horse, though he passed many set out to pasture when the days were fair—as the weather turned soon after his escape, as if regretting the discomfort it had caused him.

A bit of clothing or a few eggs or a chunk of bacon from a smokehouse might not be missed; if it was, it was not likely to be pursued. A horse, however, especially one strong enough to carry a man of his size, would be missed. Horse thieves were usually dealt with on the spot.

So Waln kept his stealing small, the hours of his walking long. The river proved a true guide and late one night the clear cold air carried on it the salt tang of the sea.

In order that he be able to retrieve Citrine Shield when he returned from New Kelvin, Waln had been taught the land way to Smuggler's Light. As Princess Lovella's campaign long years ago had proven, Smuggler's Light could be reached by land, but only with great care.

Happily, Waln had assumed that he would be coming to the swamp directly from New Kelvin, so the landmarks he had been given were visible as soon as the swamp was in sight. A tall cypress with a boulder at its base marked the beginning of the trail. This was apparent as soon as dawn pinked the sky, but Waln waited until daylight shone clear and bright to venture further.

Winter had stripped the deciduous trees of their leaves, but the swamp was home as well to thick growths of long-needled pines that seemed all the more dense amid the skeletons of trees and vines. Despite the chill wind that whipped at the baron, the footing remained marshy beneath his boots, the taint of salt and the warmer temperatures here to the east of New Kelvin having kept frost from the ground.

Tying a bundle containing a flitch of bacon to his belt, he converted his stick to a walking staff, testing before each step. The Isles had their share of swamp and marsh, so Waln was familiar with the tricks it could play: mudholes without apparent bottom, sand spread lightly over water, hummocks that rocked or sank when you jumped on them.

In addition to watching his footing, Waln kept alert for the trail markers. None of these were as crude as a blazoned tree or a cairn of rocks. The smugglers preferred more subtle signs. Two bird's nests in the crotch of a dead scrub oak marked one turning, a sapling "chance bent" along the ground made a long pointer. By these and other signs, Waln made his way.

He had just realized that the flat grey in the near distance was dressed stone overgrown with vines when a voice spoke to him from above:

"Name yourself and your business."

"Rain riders," Waln said, "seeking shelter from the storm."

"Come along, Baron Endbrook," the voice said. "We had not looked for you so soon and garbed so fashionably."

There was dry laughter beneath the words, holding within it mockery and menace. With a sudden seizing of his heart,

Waln Endbrook wondered if he had come to a refuge or to yet another betrayal.

❧

WINTER THUNDER WAS RUMBLING among the upper peaks of the mountains on the day that Grateful Peace escorted Lady Melina Shield to her first meeting with the Dragon Speaker.

Peace was an educated man—few Illuminators were not, given the range and variety of texts they encountered from their youngest days at the desk. Even so, he felt his bowels chill at the distant rumble. His parents had controlled their large, unruly brood with a variety of threats regarding the wizard-spawned horrors that dwelt in the vast reaches of the Sword of Kelvin Mountains, and whenever he heard winter thunder he was once again a very small child.

Lady Melina did not appear to hear the distant rumbles. Bright, alert, and, as far as the thaumaturge could tell, not a bit nervous, she walked with quick and eager steps toward the Speaker's Tower.

She looked quite nice in a gown of autumn gold velvet trimmed in black. That she chose to wear the colors of House Gyrfalcon said something, Grateful Peace knew. He wondered what. Was she reminding them of her noble birth and status? Was she asserting her continued alliance to her homeland? Or was the choice simply habit, what she was accustomed to wearing for matters of state?

Even after they had climbed the long spiral stair—Apheros had ruled against revealing to her the secret of the lift—Lady Melina had lost little of her energy. Grateful Peace found himself admiring her despite himself. The New Kelvinese capital city was set high in the Sword of Kelvin Mountains and strong men had found themselves reduced to short, panting breaths until their hearts and lungs adjusted to the altitude.

When the herald announced them, the Dragon Speaker rose

with stately majesty to greet them. In his robes of office, Apheros was a towering figure, magnificent in scarlet silk trimmed with gold. His long-jawed face was painted black but for a hint of crimson rimming each eye and silver, bat-winged dragons sparkling on each cheek.

A gold dragon clung to the top of his head, claws digging into the Dragon Speaker's scalp so that a thin trickle of blood oozed from beneath them. The dragon's eyes glittered so realistically that the reptile seemed alive and watchful. Any moment, it seemed, the dragon might bend its sinuous neck and whisper secrets into the Speaker's ear.

Grateful Peace knew something of the artistry that went into creating this effect. Apheros *was* a tall man, but the shoes he wore hidden beneath the hem of his robe were what gave him that unreal height. His face paint was not purely black, but included a subtle shading of greens and browns that sharply defined his features despite the apparent monotone.

The gold dragon was, of course, not alive. It was an heirloom of the Founders' days, set onto a skullcap shaped anew with each Speaker to precisely fit that Speaker's head.

Peace wished he could have known the face artist who had thought to add the blood coming from beneath the dragon's claws. It added a certain horrid realism. Indeed, he knew otherwise quite sturdy thaumaturges who admitted not liking to look directly at the Dragon Speaker when he was in full formal garb because of this single touch. They claimed the damp-seeming trails of blood made them queasy.

Lady Melina, however, was not showing any such weakness. Upon entering the audience chamber she had sunk into a deep curtsy such as was used to honor monarchs in Hawk Haven. She did not move until Apheros spoke.

"Rise, visitor."

The language he used was New Kelvinese. He might have spoken Pellish, but that would have been a concession to a foreigner. In any case, Apheros's command of languages was nowhere near as good as Peace's. It would break the carefully constructed illusion of power if the Dragon Speaker trotted out his halting command of the other language.

Lady Melina rose and stood with her head thrown slightly back, studying the Dragon Speaker's face. Perhaps Apheros was somewhat put out by this inspection, for he moved to the business at hand more rapidly than Peace had anticipated.

"The time has come," Apheros began in deep, resonant tones more thrilling than any commanding bellow could be, "to unseal that which you have carried so faithfully to this land. As reward for your determined efforts, it has been decided to grant you, Lady Melina Shield, the great honor of opening each box and revealing what has been hidden within."

Peace concealed a smile. Actually, Apheros and his intimate counselors had been concerned by the fact that—as far as any of their artisans could tell—the boxes were in no way trapped, were each closed with a fairly simple mechanical lock, and were sealed only with a wax impression of Queen Valora's coat of arms.

Fear that there was some more subtle protection upon the boxes rather than a desire to honor Lady Melina was what prompted this generous gesture. Otherwise, the boxes would have already been opened and their contents studied. After all, why let the foreign woman have a chance at them if her knowledge would prove unnecessary?

If Lady Melina was aware of what a dubious honor she had been granted, she gave no sign. Dipping another curtsy, she murmured in New Kelvinese:

"Thank you, Honored Apheros."

Her accent only made her humility the more charming. Apheros gave a haughty nod.

"Herald, summon the Primes."

The Primes were the thaumaturges representing each of the sodalities. Added to their number were the Dragon's Three, the Speaker's own chosen counselors. Apheros would have preferred to limit the witnessing to this latter group, but his precarious hold on the office made it unwise for him to risk alienating his allies.

The Primes wore full face paints, designed not only to display the patterns of their sodalities, but meant to minimize any personal tattooing. In this gathering, they were not themselves, but their sodalities.

Lady Melina watched with interest as the thaumaturges processed in, her brow furrowing with concentration as she sought to identify each pattern. As this was all the introduction she was to get to this august body, Peace thought she was wise.

He himself would not have kept her so uncertain of her own status, but Apheros had been firm. No honors or privileges would be granted to the foreigner until she had proven herself necessary. Otherwise, should the need arise to dispose of her, awkward questions might be asked by the members of the conclave who, rightly, might fear that their own privileges would no longer protect them.

After the procession had ended and the Primes had seated themselves on the high-backed, gilded chairs set along the curved walls of the tower room, Peace drew back to his own seat. This was to one side toward the back, at an angle from which he could study the gathering without being obvious himself.

He knew that by Hawk Haven's standards his place was a low one and saw one of Lady Melina's slender brows arch in momentary surprise. Doubtless she was reassessing his importance in view of this information.

Angered, Peace contemplated enlightening her as soon as they were alone together—finding some subtle and cutting way of explaining that being the Dragon's Eye was among the highest honors. Then he decided not. Let her learn the truth and grovel when she realized how she had slighted one of the powerful.

After the thaumaturges had settled into the statue-still poses etiquette demanded when display rather than debate was the order of the day, a pair of the Dragon Speaker's staff clerks—one of them Kistlio—carried out a low table and set it in front of Lady Melina. A chair was brought next.

Apheros had not wanted to give Lady Melina even this, but Peace had argued otherwise, saying that if she was not to suspect the ambivalence of her position she must be granted at least some courtesies. Lady Melina, however, ignored the seat. She remained standing, taut as a drawn bow, awaiting the first box.

Kistlio brought forth the largest of the three, a long, broad rectangular box that, despite its relative breadth, was so lacking in depth as to seem nearly flat. He also carried the ring of keys the New Kelvinese smiths had made to replace those the vanished Baron Endbrook had carried away.

A flicker of anxiety touched Grateful Peace as he thought of the absent baron. None of the search parties had located Endbrook, nor had the New Kelvinese spies heard anything about him. Doubtless, as the guard insisted, Baron Waln Endbrook was buried in some snowdrift or had drowned trying to cross the White Water River.

Dismissing thoughts of the baron, Peace returned his attention to the center of the room.

Lady Melina was fitting the first key into the lock. She had to struggle to turn the lock—not surprisingly, given the weather through which the boxes had been carried. Still, Peace found he was holding his breath.

All around the chamber not a person moved. A Songweaver shut her eyes as if in anticipation of an explosion. Then, with a solid metallic click, the lock snapped open.

"I think it was a bit rusted," Lady Melina said apologetically.

At her words, Grateful Peace noted a general release of tension among the brightly garbed ranks, but his gaze was drawn inexorably to where Lady Melina was now raising the lid of the box. Whatever lay within was swaddled in fabric, so she lifted out the entire bundle and slowly unwrapped the contents.

Like used bandages, the cloth coiled in a heap at her feet. At last there was a glint of silver, a hint of color. When the last piece of cloth slid to the floor, Lady Melina held her discovery out so that all gathered could see it clearly.

It was a silver mirror, set into a long-handled ivory frame. The ivory was intricately worked with patterns of twining vines, open blossoms, and impish faces. In places the surface had been stained with pigment and set with tiny gemstones, the color just enough to bring out the details without obscuring the perfection of the carving itself.

In his deepest heart, Peace knew this mirror to be a fit vessel for sorcery.

The next box brought before Lady Melina was also fairly flat, but much smaller, hardly long enough to span her hand from the heel of the palm to the tips of her fingers. The lock worked after a slight struggle and this time several of the thaumaturges forgot dignity—and prudent fear—enough to lean forward to watch as it was opened.

There was not so much padding in this box, just a layer on the top that Lady Melina lifted out and set to one side. For a long moment she stared in puzzlement at what was revealed. Then she remembered her manners and lifted the artifact out, holding it up for general examination.

It was a comb—not an ornamental comb used to adorn an elaborate coiffure, but a simple comb such as anyone might use to tidy up. It was crafted from a smooth, highly polished wood in rich shades of reddish brown. The comb was quite attractive in its simple way, but no one could deny its essentially utilitarian nature.

Had Lady Melina herself not been so evidently puzzled—and equally evidently trying to conceal that puzzlement—Grateful Peace might have wondered if she had made a substitution at some point during her journey. However, had she done such a thing, surely she would have picked something else with which to fool them—a slim wand or an elegant dagger—certainly not a comb.

The final box was square, and about the size of Lady Melina's palm. This time the lock clicked open smoothly. Peace wondered in passing if the practical Kistlio had dabbed in a bit of oil after seeing the struggles with the previous two locks.

From the moment Lady Melina opened the lid, those directly alongside her could glimpse a gleam from the contents, for what the box held had not been swathed or padded. There was no need; the interior of the box had been shaped to hold, the lid's interior quilted with satin.

Still, the artifact within was so small that it was not until Lady Melina took it upon herself to parade around the room, holding up the box so that each Prime might see the contents, that Peace got a clear look.

A ring rested within, a ring cast from pure gold and set with a bluish white moonstone that seemed to glow with a pale light of its own. The curved surface of the moonstone had been carved in the likeness of an enigmatically smiling face, its eyes half-hooded, though whether in laughter or in mockery Grateful Peace could not feel certain.

Upon closer inspection, Peace realized that the setting that held this unsettling gem was no simple band. The prongs that clasped the moonstone in place were the fangs of a snarling beast that held the moonstone in its jaws.

The creature so represented might have been a bear or perhaps a wolf, though its mouth was stretched so wide that any likeness to an actual animal was more fancy than otherwise. The beast's eyes were represented by perfect rubies, so tiny that it seemed beyond possibility that any human hand might have faceted them, but faceted they were so that they caught the light and gave it back sparkling as with rabid fury.

Unlike the comb, the ring seemed—as with the silver mirror—a worthy vessel for enchantment. The enigmatic expression of the moonstone countenance remained with Peace even after Lady Melina had passed on around the room. He contrasted it with the snarling beast that held it.

What power was concealed behind that smile? Might it glow with light? Might the stone hold the secret of slowing the moon in her nightly voyage? Might the carved face speak in riddles that held enchantments within their convoluted prose?

Grateful Peace saw a trace of his own wonder and excitement on the face of Kalvinia, representative for the Sericulturalists, and schooled himself to impassivity. Lady Melina already knew more than enough about his own hopes. No need to add to her store of knowledge. He still wondered that he had spoken so freely to her.

The Dragon Speaker stared longest and hardest at the ring, then he gestured Lady Melina back to her place. Obediently, she returned, this time taking her seat. She did not lay as much as a single finger on the three artifacts, but arrayed them in their boxes on the table in front of her so that all might glimpse them. Then she spoke unbidden for the first time:

"Now we see what we have, honored thaumaturges. Where do we go from here?"

The foreign woman's expression as she looked around the room was as enigmatic as that of the moonstone ring—except in her case there was no doubt that her smile held just the slightest trace of mockery.

IMMEDIATELY AFTER Firekeeper had related Elation's report regarding Lady Melina's movements, the company had left Gateway, riding along the northeast road toward Dragon's Breath until nightfall and resuming the journey again almost before dawn had lit the sky.

It was on that second day that Elise realized with pleasure that her body had hardened to the long days in the saddle, that the journeys between Silver Whale Cove and Eagle's Nest, between Eagle's Nest and the North Woods, had been nothing but training for this moment.

With that knowledge came a certain odd freedom. Until it wasn't needed, Elise hadn't realized how much of her attention was centered on guiding Cream Delight—though most of the time the mare was content to follow the other horses' lead—on shifting to avoid aching muscles or to avoid other little discomforts.

Now that her mind was released from these distractions Elise began to work through just what they must do when they arrived in Dragon's Breath.

"When we get there," she said, her words breaking a lazy silence, "what are we going to do? I've been told that Dragon's Breath is a big city. We can't go door to door asking after Lady Melina. For that matter, her presence there may be a secret."

"Should it be?" Derian asked. "After all, Hawk Haven and New Kelvin are allied—even the events that led up to King Allister's War didn't break that alliance."

"Strained it," Elise agreed, "but didn't break it. Unhappily, given the secrecy of Lady Melina's departure, I don't imagine that she'll be making her presence widely known."

"I agree with Lady Elise," Sir Jared said. "Lady Melina could have traveled as a tourist, perhaps seeking distraction from her grief over the deaths of husband and brother. Instead she traveled in secret. We have our suspicions why, of course."

"We *know*," Firekeeper growled.

Unlike the rest of them, the wolf-woman traveled mostly on foot, saying that jolting about on horseback was more wearying than running. When she did need a rest, she clambered up on top of one of the mules and perched on its back, a cloak about her shoulders, looking rather like a gargoyle on a castle wall. She had trotted up near Elise when that young lady had begun speaking, so now Elise grinned down at her.

"*We* know," Elise agreed, "and Lady Melina is going to want no one else to have a chance to guess. Meddling with magic is still frowned upon in Hawk Haven and Bright Bay. Her brother the duke, if no one else, might get very stern with her if she did further damage to House Gyrfalcon's reputation."

Derian was currently riding point, Roanne prancing as if she fancied she was leading a parade. He craned around in his saddle, his lean body flowing with the horse's gait and reminding Elise how much more she had to learn about riding.

"We've been over this before," Derian said. "Elise's original question has been troubling me for a while—ever since I saw Gateway and realized how very different the New Kelvinese are from us. How are we going to find Lady Melina without her knowing we're looking for her?"

"I have a thought . . ." Wendee Jay said softly. Then she paused.

There was a hesitancy to Wendee's manner that surprised

Elise a bit. The other woman had proven herself chatty, quite a comfortable person to be around and, if not a substitute for Ninette, an adept replacement. Then Elise realized that Wendee wasn't sure just where they—Sir Jared and herself in particular, she suspected—drew the line at servants putting themselves forth.

Firekeeper might have a title, but she dismissed it except as another name to which she would reluctantly answer from time to time. Derian might be a king's counselor, but he was a carter's son without title and his noble connections were patronage, not family.

This matter, however, had been raised by Elise—the future Baroness Archer—and clearly Wendee was uncertain if her advice would be welcome.

"What is it, Wendee?" Elise asked, trying to project warmth and reassurance into her tone. "Don't hold back. I may have studied New Kelvin, but my knowledge is limited. You are the only one of us who has done more than cross to a border town."

Wendee seemed even more uncomfortable.

"Actually," she said, "what I had to say wasn't about New Kelvin, not really. It relates, but it's something else."

"Go on," Elise prompted, wishing Ninette were along. Ninette could have privately assured Wendee that Elise wasn't a snob, but for Elise to do it herself would sound like just the thing a perfect snob *would* say.

I'll just have to prove to Wendee by my actions that I don't think less of her because she doesn't hold a title.

"Well," Wendee said, "is it important that Lady Melina not know we're looking for her? I mean, I understand why you didn't want her to know at first—when you weren't certain your suspicions were justified—but now . . . It's like Lady Firekeeper says, you *know*."

Elise mulled over this, nodding her head so that Wendee would not take her silence as rejection.

"That's a very interesting thought," she said. "I hadn't seen things that way."

Derian frowned. "But what do we do if Lady Melina gets the wind up and runs?"

"We chase!" Firekeeper said fiercely, jumping lightly as if she might bolt across the fallow fields that very moment, like a dog after a hare. "Wingéd folk should be watching Lady Melina and the treasures. They see, we run, we catch her!"

Derian grinned. "I bet you would and then the New Kelvinese would chop you into little, tiny pieces. Still, I like what Wendee's saying. It should make Lady Melina easier to find if we're not hiding ourselves, and if she does bolt . . ."

He shrugged.

"We chase," Firekeeper repeated firmly.

"So how are we going to find Lady Melina?" Elise asked again. "Even if we don't need to hide, it's not going to be easy. I suppose we could set up a residence and start entertaining on a lavish scale, but I don't have the resources for that. My father, you may recall, doesn't even know I'm here."

Instantly, Elise wished she hadn't reminded them, but no one commented. Derian did nod a bit resignedly, but even he didn't protest. Maybe since Elise had acted as a translator the night before, his reluctance to have her along had begun to ease.

True, Wendee possessed a fair command of New Kelvinese, enough to get by, but her vocabulary was frequently archaic and often she lacked the words for common terms like "chamber pot" or "spoon." Elise supposed these didn't come into use very often in high drama.

"There's a way we could sort of entertain," Wendee offered, "without needing more funds than we've brought with us."

Elise grinned. "Good! I was dreading writing my father."

Wendee relaxed. "We make ourselves a part of local society—a fairly visible part. People should come to us, then."

"Getting to be part of the local culture won't be easy," Derian commented dubiously. "As we've seen, the New Kelvinese don't exactly embrace foreigners."

"Actually . . ." Wendee paused thoughtfully. "I thought that Doc might hold the solution to all our problems."

"Me?" Doc started. Elise noticed that he managed to look

astonished, pleased, and worried all at once. "How could I?"

"Go into practice," Wendee said, "as a healer."

"But New Kelvinese herb lore is respected in every land!" Doc protested. "Some of my best drugs come from here. How could I compete?"

"You have the healing talent," Wendee replied, "and that would make you special in any land."

"They must have their own doctors with the talent," Doc said, not protesting, just stating a point.

"They may or may not," Wendee said with a shrug. "The point is, the talent makes you useful beyond the average apothecary. In any case, I'm not so certain that the talents are common in New Kelvin. Did you ever see *The Tragic Romance of Tiliata and Mermetio*?"

"I'm afraid I missed that one," Doc admitted. Elise liked how the faint trace of a grin visible beneath his beard made his face light up. "It sounds like quite a show."

"Oh, it is," Wendee enthused. "I played Tiliata in a production some years ago. The play deals with a romance between two lovers . . ."

"It would," Doc teased, "by definition."

Elise felt a flash of envy. Doc never teased her—but then he might have known Wendee for years.

Wendee frowned at the knight. "This is serious."

"Sorry."

"Tiliata is a maiden, a member of the Sodality of Herbalists. Mermetio—the youth she loves—is a rising member of the Choir of Songweavers. They fall in love—an innocent enough passion—but soon after his voice begins to change."

Doc and Derian exchanged sidelong glances, which Wendee valiantly ignored. Her voice took on a certain melodramatic tone as she related the story.

"Desperate to help Mermetio maintain his place—for if his voice broke dangerously he would be forced to find a new sodality, and the pair's hoped-for marriage would be long delayed—Tiliata makes Mermetio a potion. Unfortunately, she is a mere apprentice and doesn't realize that the same concoction that will stabilize his voice will also geld him. Mermetio loses interest in her and she—facing not only her lover's abandonment but the wrath of her superiors—poisons herself."

"And your point?" Doc prompted.

Wendee glared at him.

"My point is that if they had doctors with the healing talent Tiliata could have paid one to cure him. That isn't even mentioned as an option. There are dozens of incidents like that in modern New Kelvinese drama—people maimed or mortally wounded—and never once is a person with the healing talent summoned. That only happens in traditional drama—stories set in the days before the Burning Death—what they call the plague."

Doc nodded, sketching a gracious bow in the air above his saddle's pommel.

"You have a point, Goody Wendee. I apologize for my doubts. Very well. Let's seek out the local equivalent of the Street of Apothecaries and Healers."

He frowned then. "I wonder if I need a guild membership to practice?"

"I don't know," Wendee admitted. "We can look into that when we get there. I guess if you can't be licensed, we'll just have to do without."

Doc didn't look happy about this aspect of the plan, but Elise didn't let such a minor wrinkle keep her from being charmed.

"We'll rent a few rooms," she said confidently, "ground-floor ones if we can find them. I'm certain that if Lady Melina is in town someone will tell us—people always tell foreigners about other foreigners."

She spoke with assurance, having witnessed similar exchanges in Bright Bay and even at home in Hawk Haven. People were always asking where you were from and then asking if you knew someone else from the same place.

Suddenly, the days that must pass before they reached Dragon's Breath seemed an eternity. She longed to thump Cream Delight with her heels and go racing along the roads until they reached the city of sorcery.

Firekeeper seemed to sense her burst of enthusiasm.

"I wish we could fly," she said wistfully, "like Elation."

The wolf-woman pointed above to where the golden-eyed peregrine shifted lazily on the air.

"So do I," Elise said softly, as if they were sharing a great secret. "So do I!"

XXIV

THE MAN WHO HAD greeted Baron Endbrook outside Smuggler's Light proved to be Longsight Scrounger, one of the leading figures in the pirate organization. Nor had it been complete chance that he had been waiting to meet the baron. Lookouts had spotted Waln almost as soon as he entered the swamp; reports of his progress had been passed along to the lighthouse.

"We might even have pulled you out if you'd blundered into a boghole," Longsight said. "Then again we might not have."

He grinned at his own joke, showing a jagged front tooth, broken some said when he bit another pirate's arm to the bone during a brawl.

Longsight had taken Waln into the lighthouse and encouraged him to bathe and dine. It was only after Waln had suddenly nodded up from a guilty drowse following an excellent meal of fish poached in white wine that he thought to wonder whether the door to his room was locked.

The baron decided not to bother checking. He'd walked into the pirates' lair freely. It was up to them to decide whether he was their guest or their prisoner. For now he needed rest more than freedom, and sleep was not denied him.

Waln's dreams were full of storm-tossed seas through which he piloted a ship crewed by skeletons. Eventually the ship was wrecked against rocks the crystal blue of Lady Melina's eyes.

He swam to shore, where he spent an eternity slogging through swamps in a thick fug of summer heat. He struggled on endlessly, pushing through vines that wrapped around his limbs, twisted around his throat.

Several times he nearly strangled, but always the pressure relented just before his heart burst from lack of air.

When Waln awoke, clear light was shining in through the narrow window in his room. A girl with hair the color of fire or fine brandy was seated at his bedside reading a book. Seeing he was awake, she put down the book and dashed away—presumably to fetch some adult. Only when she was gone did Waln realize that the girl had been Citrine Shield.

He slept again before anyone returned to speak with him. When he awoke, the light had dimmed and a man waited nearby. Waln could not recall seeing him before, but judging from how the man reached over and took his wrist to test his pulse Waln thought he must be some sort of healer.

"Fess Bones," the other said by way of introduction. "Here, drink some of this—it's just water."

Waln did as he was told, realizing he felt wrung-out, so weak that he could hardly get his fingers to close around the handle of the heavy pottery mug. Fess Bones helped him, wiping the water that dribbled down Waln's chin as neatly as a mother might.

"You've been sick these past two days," Fess reported. "Fever rose the very night you arrived. You slept the night through and all the day following. Woke once this morning—we thought you were with us—but the fever dragged you down again. It's evening now. How do you feel?"

"Thirsty," Waln croaked. "Weak."

"You can have more water in bit. Let your stomach learn to swallow what you just drank. I'll see if the kitchen has any broth and tell Longsight you're awake and likely to live."

Fess was back some indeterminate time later with a container of warm fish stock.

"Longsight says you're to rest. He'll talk with you come morning."

Waln wanted to disagree. His task was too important. He

needed to get news to Queen Valora, but when he tried to speak his throat would not obey him. He let Fess Bones spoon fish stock into him, drank more water, drifted back to sleep.

When Waln awoke once again, darkness had fallen. Someone else sat vigil with him, just visible in the flickering candlelight—a weathered old crone with a scar through her right eyebrow and the top of her left ear missing. She gave him water and broth, helped him use the pot, then settled back in her chair to nap.

Waln himself was at last wide awake. In some ways he felt more alert than he had since meeting with Lady Melina at the post-house, his mind clear, his thoughts cogent. He wondered if his family had missed his letters or had simply believed that some vagary of winter shipping had delayed them, wondered how he could get a message to Queen Valora, wondered how she would take the news of Lady Melina's betrayal.

The queen was certain to be angry—furious. A sudden realization chilled Waln as if the fever was returning. What if Queen Valora took her anger out on him?

Somehow the thought had never occurred to him. He'd fled toward her, trusting the queen to avenge the wrongs done to him and, through him, to her. Why had he never seen that Queen Valora would most likely strike out at the nearest person holding part of the blame?

Lying on his back in the dark room, listening to the rasping snores of the old pirate woman in the chair beside his bed, Baron Endbrook frantically reworked his plans.

Before, in some vague fashion he had thought to take ship for the Isles, to let Queen Valora assume responsibility for the entire mess. Now Waln realized that if he hoped to return home with some shreds of his reputation intact, he must act at once. Fortunately, the very secret nature of his embassy for her made it unlikely that Queen Valora would inquire after him too publicly lest embarrassing information come to light.

He had time. The thought comforted him. He had time, time to put pressure on Lady Melina, to regain the artifacts, to make his own deal with the New Kelvinese to activate the artifacts or—better—to simply get off this cursed mainland. Queen Valora could find another ambassador.

After he had the artifacts back, then Waln could tell Queen Valora the truth. If nothing had been lost but a little time, surely she would be willing to accept that the heirlooms' secrets had not been unlocked—especially when she realized how close she had come to losing them entirely.

All through the long hours of darkness Baron Endbrook lay awake. When dawn filtered pale and chill through the narrow window the crone ceased her snoring. She moved flaccid lips over bare gums and smiled pinkly at him.

"Sleep well, ducks?"

"Well enough, mother," Waln replied politely. "Do you think Longsight will see me today?"

The crone cackled mirthlessly.

"Oh, yes, he'll see you. The question is will you be wanting to see *him* again once he's done with you."

DERIAN WAS AMAZED how the deeper they traveled into New Kelvin the less he felt he understood the country. It was as though this strange and uninviting land had receded farther away now that they rode their horses across it.

In an effort to fight this sensation of alienation, Derian paid close attention to the terrain. He forced himself to notice how the land began to rise as they turned north toward Dragon's Breath, how the towns became more infrequent as the land became rockier.

Their first day or two out of Gateway, the little group had ridden through farmland or through forest. The style of the houses and barns had been odd—functional, but built with a different sense of beauty. The colorful facial decorations worn even by field laborers out mending fences or attending to some other routine task had made the New Kelvinese seem like drawings brought to life rather than living, breathing people he might understand.

Their group seemed to be the only ones on this stretch of the road who weren't purely local travelers going from one town to the next. Moreover, the New Kelvinese didn't seem to like strangers, ignoring Derian's pleasant greetings or at most responding with a grunt.

Even the innkeepers, who might have been expected to be more friendly, even if only for reasons of business, were taciturn and curt. Privately, Derian was glad that Elise wanted to practice her New Kelvinese. He could stand back a few steps and let her bear the brunt of the foreigners' rudeness.

Certainly, their situation didn't seem to trouble Elise nearly as much as it did him. Derian wondered if that was because everything about this journey—from spending the day mostly in the saddle to doing without a personal maid—was weird and different.

After the first two days of travel, the farms had been markedly smaller, devoted to kitchen gardens, poultry, and flocks of sheep or, later, goats. Terraced fields challenged the mountain slopes, revealing the extent of the labor needed to grow anything at all in this inhospitable land. Had it not been for Firekeeper and Blind Seer, their band would have been reduced to eating goat cheese and turnips—that being all the inns had to offer, or at least all they were willing to sell to foreign travelers.

Rooms seemed to be in short supply as well, but Derian had made certain they would be prepared for camping. Usually Elise could find out which landowner wouldn't be offended by their pitching tents. Yet, although food and shelter could be dealt with, Derian was almost overwhelmed by the burden of being quartermaster, guide, and, by default, leader of their expedition.

Doc might have had seniority, but except in medical matters he was not inclined to take charge. Elise possessed noble rank, but was completely inexperienced. Firekeeper was Firekeeper—impossible and unpredictable—one moment as tractable as a lamb, the next vanishing for hours.

As the road to Dragon's Breath became lonelier and the winter skies more overcast and bleak, Derian realized he was beginning to rely on Wendee Jay as something like a second-in-command. Wendee, at least, had lived on the road without servants—she was, in fact, like him, more a servant than a master. Without a second thought she would comb and braid Elise's long hair, chivy Firekeeper into line, stir a supper pot, and handle a hundred other small tasks that weren't evident until they went undone.

She was also far better than Derian at delegating responsibility—ordering Doc and Elise to attend to jobs Derian would have taken on himself. Somewhere deep inside, Derian was still in awe of those two, not so much for themselves as for their titles and noble connections. Wendee seemed to feel no such awe, telling Elise to mind the fire or sending Doc to fetch water from a stream.

Moreover, Wendee was an accomplished entertainer. When the monotony of travel grew too great, Wendee would recite from plays or poems, tell them anecdotes—some rather risqué—from her days in the theater, or, often in response to Firekeeper's pleading, relate what she knew about New Kelvin.

She was doing just that one afternoon as the horses and mules toiled their way up a particularly steep stretch of road that would eventually lead through a tight pass that Derian privately worried would already be snow-blocked. A trader back in Gateway had told him that this was often the case, but Firekeeper had been impatient to arrive in Dragon's Breath, not wanting to take the longer route that would avoid this particular pass.

Derian considered sending someone ahead to scout. Blind Seer would have been his first choice, but the wolf had vanished, as he often did near midday. Elation was drowsing atop one of the packs. He could ask Firekeeper to send the peregrine ahead to report, but the bird saw things differently than the humans did and had proven a poor judge of the needs of the ground-bound.

He weighed his options. If he asked Firekeeper to send Elation, the wolf-woman might decide to go off on her own initiative. Derian decided that he didn't want Firekeeper straying too far off in this unfamiliar land. In fact, if Wendee's stories could keep the wolf-woman close rather than wandering off to find Blind Seer, all the better.

"They paint their faces," Wendee was saying when Derian stopped worrying and paid attention again, "in many patterns, most of which have deep meanings, though I think some are simply for decoration. The tattoos are different—at least if I've understood the plays rightly. Tattoos mark some big decision, an unchangeable course of action."

"Like a marriage?" Elise asked.

Derian noted that though she didn't color, she also made a point of not looking ahead to where Doc was riding point.

Wendee laughed lightly. "Oh, far more permanent than that, Lady Elise. Marriages end—mine did."

"Did your husband die?" Elise asked. Derian could see she was already feeling sorry for the other woman.

"No," Wendee replied, "we divorced. Turned out we didn't suit."

Elise looked rather shocked. Derian grinned. For all her worldliness in some things, the heir to the Archer Barony could be rather naive. Divorce was not unheard of, even in the upper classes, but he supposed it was more easily arrived at by those who were not merging large amounts of property and great names in addition to the lives of the people involved.

"Then you're raising your children alone?" Elise prompted tentatively, as if she were prying into a great secret.

"That's about the measure of it," Wendee agreed, apparently feeling no discomfort at discussing the topic. "The girls live with me and when I must be away, I make arrangements for their care."

Firekeeper tugged at the cuff of Wendee's trousers.

"You were telling about tattoos," she reminded.

Wendee gave the wolf-woman a tap on the head.

"And you shouldn't interrupt."

Firekeeper looked offended.

"Elise did first! You were talking about tattoos."

Derian intervened, swallowing his own laughter.

"Firekeeper *does* have a point, Wendee, and minimal tolerance for small talk."

He was surprised at the chiding look Wendee Jay turned toward him.

"Well, she'd better acquire some then, shouldn't she?" she asked tartly. "If Lady Firekeeper's going to accept the advantages of being an earl's daughter, then she'd better learn more about social graces than that it's not polite to snatch the meat off someone else's plate."

Derian was angry—all the more so because of the trust and reliance he'd vested in the relative newcomer. He'd worked hard to get Firekeeper to even that point! He'd like to know if Wendee could have done as much with the snarling, inarticulate, nearly naked wolfling masquerading as a fifteen-year-old girl that the earl had thrust on *him*!

"You think you know . . ." he was beginning when Doc interrupted.

"Heads up, folks," he said in the strong, level voice he normally reserved for critical medical emergencies. "I saw something—maybe human—moving in the rocks ahead of us."

Firekeeper bounded from where she had been trotting at Wendee's stirrup to Doc's side.

"Where?" she snapped.

"Left," he said. "Near the rock shaped like a bear."

The wolf-woman darted off the road and vanished into the rocks. Elation shrieked once and sprang into the air after her.

An arrow struck the road in front of them almost before the two were gone. It quivered there, impaled in the dirt, the danger it implied seeming an impassible barrier.

"Grab the mules," Derian ordered, shouldering Roanne up alongside Doc's horse. He didn't pause to see if anyone obeyed.

"Warning shot," Doc said tersely. "Bandits will want our horses and mules. The rest of us aren't so safe."

Derian nodded and swung out of his saddle. None of the others had waited for orders to do the same.

"Keep a horse between you and them," he said rather unnecessarily. "We'll have to trust Firekeeper."

"Should we back up?" Elise asked. She was very pale, but her voice didn't tremble.

Derian started to nod; then he saw the two bandits who stepped out into the road to block their retreat.

They were as ugly as ogres from a tale meant to scare a child into good behavior. Their faces were painted the sickly greenish-yellow of an overcooked egg yolk; their eyes were rimmed in hangover red. Black lines gave one curling cat whiskers, the other bat wings that "masked" the upper half of his face.

The whiskered one said something in rhythmic New Kelvinese. Derian didn't need a translation to tell him that the bandit was ordering them not to move; the gesture he made was universal. What hurt was that he was laughing at them.

More bandits were coming out from hiding now. At least six were visible, each with features painted in some horrid pattern of red, green, and black.

Bat Mask jerked a mule's lead rope from Wendee's hand and shouted something to someone out of sight. Then he turned to them and spoke sharply in New Kelvinese. At the conclusion, he cupped his hand alongside his mouth and made a beckoning gesture with his free hand.

Elise translated in a low, flat voice.

"He says to call back the boy—I think he means Firekeeper—call her back or he'll, he'll . . ."

Her voice quavered. Wendee finished.

"He'll gut the carrot-head boy."

Derian swallowed hard. He wished Elise and Wendee hadn't translated anything. They might have played dumb. On the other hand, the long knife in Bat Mask's hand looked very sharp and he might have decided to demonstrate just who his threat was directed against. Derian was acutely aware that only he could be called "carrot-head."

The bandit made a jerking motion with the blade and said something else.

"He says call her now," Wendee reported. "He'd rather not

kill anyone. We're young and ... something about Waterland."

"Slaves," Doc guessed tersely. "He'll sell us as slaves."

Without a pause Sir Jared then shouted:

"Firekeeper, they want you to come back. They'll kill Derian if you don't! Be careful."

A high, mournful wolf's howl came in reply. Then a human voice called:

"Tell them I come."

Derian's heart sank. If Firekeeper returned, hope was dead. If she didn't *he* was dead. Either way, the situation was grim.

Their one remaining chance rested with the Royal animals— Elation and Blind Seer. The bandits might not have noticed the hawk; they didn't know about Blind Seer. Unfortunately, the giant wolf wouldn't act if doing so would endanger his pack mate. Only if Firekeeper was dead would the wolf attack, and then his vengeance would be terrible.

Firekeeper emerged from a cluster of rocks just as Bat Mask was raising his knife to Derian's throat.

"Stop!" she shouted. "I am here."

Such was the force of the wolf-woman's personality that the knife did drop. Whiskers strode out to drag her over to the rest. She walked more quickly then, defying his right to touch her.

Whiskers pointed to the sky, made a swooping gesture with one hand. Firekeeper tilted her head at him, truly puzzled.

"Elation," Derian said quickly. "He wants you to call Elation."

As if resenting Derian's initiative, Whiskers dropped a rough hand onto Firekeeper's forearm where a hawk would perch. She jerked away and he grabbed for her shoulder. The feral woman was faster than he expected, so all he did was bump against her chest.

This was enough. Confusion then enlightenment were visible, even through the paint.

He guffawed, said something to his companions, grabbed Firekeeper and poked again. She bit him on the hand. When he jerked it back, howling at the pain, Firekeeper walked with dignity to stand between Derian and the bandits.

The other bandits were ridiculing their bitten comrade. Whiskers snarled something at them, then gave a short, angry laugh and grabbed at his crotch. Neither Wendee nor Elise translated the speech he gave then. It wasn't necessary.

Of them all only Doc spoke and he only to curse. Slapping the healer across the mouth, Bat Mask ordered them all to silence. As the bandits herded them along the road, Derian's thoughts swirled in frantic panic.

They know our "boy" is a girl. They're going to rape the women—Elise, Wendee, Firekeeper. They might have anyway, but they'll do so now for sure. The one Firekeeper bit has to prove he has balls.

Wendee and Elise were so pale that their own faces might have been painted pure white. Wendee looked strained, torn between anger and fear. Elise was simply terrified. Too brave to sob aloud, still she couldn't keep silent tears from rolling down her cheeks.

She's a virgin. Derian thought. *I bet she is. I don't think Jet got very far with her—that's why he was visiting the camp followers. She's a virgin. I guess Firekeeper is, too, but she doesn't know what they have in mind, won't guess until they start. Will she even understand then?*

His mind flickered to another track.

Should we tell them? Doc said they were going to sell us to Waterland as slaves. Do virgins sell for more? Would it matter to them at this point? Judging from the way they're acting, they're horny as stallions in springtime. Wonder if they've any women in their band. Didn't see any, but who can tell through winter clothes and painted faces?

The bandits were leading them up a track so steep the horses stumbled. Derian saw Roanne slip to one knee; he turned to help the mare, and one of their captors hit him across the face. Derian reeled back, cursing, tasting blood on his lip.

Damn them. They'll ruin the horses. Ruin the women. Wonder what they'll do to me and Doc? Don't like how that one guy was looking at me. I thought dying was the worst thing.

Maybe we should tell them about virgins. Might save a couple of them. Then poor Wendee . . .

His thoughts shied away from the image.

The bandit camp was in a hollow against a rock face, an open area sheltered from the weather on all sides and nearly undetectable until you were right upon it. The rock face itself sank back so deeply that it might conceal a cave. Certainly it was as good a shelter as some houses Derian had seen.

They were herded off to one side of the open area into a pen clearly meant for holding human prisoners. The sides were made of wooden poles set far enough apart that the captives would always be visible, but set far too close for anyone to squeeze out. The door was made along the same lines and locked with a sliding bolt.

Nothing more sophisticated was needed, for guards took position on raised platforms set against the rock face. From these they could raise an alarm or put an arrow through any who tried to escape.

Moving in the easy routine of laborers returning from a job well done, the bandits settled their loot. The horses were penned on the other side of the open area. A fire was built up in the center. No one came to meet the returning party, so apparently the entire band had gone along on the raid.

Holding one of the wooden bars in each fist, Derian counted.

Eleven. Two stripping the gear off the horses. One building the fire. One getting water—High-stepping Stallion. I'm thirsty—three guarding us. Guess I should be complimented. That's almost one for one. Of course, they have bows and short swords, and we have nothing. Bet Firekeeper's steamed about them taking her Fang. One's wrapping the bitten fellow's hand. That's nine. Where are the other two?

His question was answered almost as soon as he framed it into thought. The two remaining bandits emerged from the sheltering rock face carrying furs and blankets. They'd heaped these on the ground near the fire before Derian realized what this meant.

They're going to do it in public. The girls won't even have the dignity of privacy. I've got to do something!

Try as he might, he couldn't think of anything. Neither, apparently, could Doc. The knight stood at the edge of their prison staring out, his expression wooden. His eyes reflected the burning fire, fueling it with hate.

He'll go mad, do something to get himself killed if they touch Elise. It's bad for me; they're my friends. Terrible for him—he's loved her practically since he met her and now he's got to watch her be . . . I've got to do something!

Wendee stepped forward from where she'd been crouching next to Elise, subduing her own fear by comforting the younger woman. Her remedy seemed to have been effective. Elise's sobs had quieted. She sat crumpled on the ground, holding a confused and frustrated Firekeeper by one hand.

"Maybe they'll want one at a time," Wendee whispered. "Give the child some hope."

She went and leaned sideways against the fence. Despite the chill, she'd pulled back her winter coat and was showing off—as if by accident—the voluptuous curves of her figure. In the midday sun, her hair loosed from its traveling knot shone golden.

Not long after, Whiskers crossed to their prison. All the others, excepting their guards, had gathered in a semicircle around the heaped blankets. A few began a rhythmic clapping, slower than the beating of Derian's racing heart. The rest joined in, standing in attentive silence that was more horrid than any rude comments could have been.

Wendee forced her lips into a stiff parody of a welcoming smile. Knowing the door would be opened at least for a moment, Derian gathered himself to spring, saw Doc doing the same, knowing all the time that it was hopeless.

Better than being alive to watch it happen, Derian thought, and hated himself for being a coward.

As the bolt was shot back, Derian's blood hummed so loudly in his ears that he didn't even hear the clapping. Then, as if it had grown there, the butt of an arrow blossomed in Whiskers's throat.

A shrill shriek at the same moment announced Elation's

arrival. One of their guards tumbled from his perch above their pen, the peregrine still attached to his face, her talons raking to the beating of her wings.

Blind Seer attacked without a sound. Turning on his heel, Derian saw the massive grey blur that impacted the second guard, knocking him off the ledge. The wolf didn't pause, but continued his spring toward the third guard.

Doc fumbled the gate open and seized Whiskers's knife. He ran toward where the guard Blind Seer had knocked from the ledge was struggling to rise.

"Get the bows!" he blurted back at Derian.

Firekeeper was gone. No longer needing to worry about the guard's punishing arrows, she had swarmed up one side of their prison and dropped down on the other side.

Derian saw her stringing the dead man's weapon and fitting an arrow to the string, her expression calm, even thoughtful.

Derian turned to gather up Elise. The bandits were temporarily confused, but that confusion was already moderating into fear and fear into anger. Their rescuers had accounted for three guards and Whiskers. Firekeeper would doubtless kill or disable another few. Even so, that left too many, especially as they were armed and the prisoners were not.

Elise was already on her feet, her tear-streaked face curiously serene, as if shock after shock had left her with nothing but the moment. Derian dragged her out to the comparative shelter of some rocks behind where Firekeeper stood.

Blind Seer, his muzzle and chest red with blood, leapt down beside Firekeeper and crouched by her feet for just an instant. Then he sprang away and was gone.

Derian recalled watching the wolf train with Firekeeper as she had learned to handle sword and shield, knew that Blind Seer understood all too well the danger of arrows. He hoped the wolf was circling to attack from some safer angle.

More arrows than Firekeeper could have shot had found their mark. Derian looked through their former prison to where Doc had gone. The guard lay still. Wendee held the man's sword with an ease that suggested some experience with the weapon. Doc was fumbling with the man's bow.

Cursing the cage that separated them, Derian darted from cover and over to Doc. An arrow slicing just behind him announced that at least one of the bandits had regained his bow. A shrill cry from Elation suggested that he wouldn't be in a condition to fire it much longer.

By the time Derian had taken the bow from Doc and nocked an arrow, the remaining bandits had taken shelter behind some rocks on the other side of the open area. None had apparently reached the cave—a good thing, since if they got into there it might be impossible to get them out.

And like any vermin, Derian thought angrily, *they've probably dug an escape tunnel.*

He sent an arrow across the open space, saw it shatter itself against the rock, and held his fire. The guard's quiver had been full, but there was still nothing to waste.

Again Derian counted and was amazed by the carnage a few minutes had presented. Four had died with the first attack—if you counted the one Blind Seer had knocked from the ledge and Doc and Wendee had finished. Arrows had claimed four more out in the open.

Judging from the blood trail leading from a dropped bow to the rocks, Elation had hit another, so of the three that were unaccounted for, at least one was severely wounded.

Firekeeper must have been making a similar assessment, for now she called across to him.

"Few left. They come out soon."

Derian had no opportunity to ask what she meant. A howl, loud and full, such as a wolf uses to drive the prey, sounded from behind the rocks where the bandits had taken shelter. In their corral, the horses and mules tried to run, pressing against the rails with such frantic terror that Derian feared they would harm themselves.

The bandits were no more immune to such terror. Though their own dead lay sprawled on the ground in front of them, the bandits fled from that terrible howl. Perhaps, to give them some credit, they had glimpsed the grey form that had ripped an armed man open with a single, slashing bite. Perhaps they preferred the clean death given by arrow or sword to that end.

Even knowing as he did that the howl came from a friend, Derian felt himself shudder. Pity slowed his attack, but Fire-keeper felt no pity. Two arrows found their mark. Two bandits fell. The third, dragging himself blindly behind a ruined face, became the prey of the wolf.

Derian turned away, retching at the carnage, yet washed through with joyful relief. They'd survived. He hadn't had to find a solution, but somehow they'd survived.

He started, remembering that first arrow, the one that had taken Whiskers as he opened their prison door.

"Who . . ." he started to ask.

A cloaked and hooded figure came climbing down from the rocks behind their prison.

"Hi!" the stranger said cheerfully, pushing back his hood. "I say! That was rather close, what?"

Derian gaped. The stranger was Edlin Norwood.

❀

ELISE SAW THE EXPRESSION on Derian's face. Something in the redhead's astonishment cut through the numbness that had seized hold of her soul when she realized what the bandits intended for her and made her able to speak again.

She smiled. "Edlin!"

Sir Jared echoed her. "Edlin! Cousin, what are you doing here?"

"Glad to see me?" the bright-eyed young man said with a broad grin. He might have been meeting them on a dance floor rather than a battlefield.

"Definitely," Jared replied. "But how did you come to be here?"

Edlin scuffed the dirt with the toe of his boot, suddenly a boy expecting to be reprimanded.

"I heard you talking to my father," he said defiantly, "about Lady Melina and what Firekeeper was going to do. I wanted to help but I knew you wouldn't have me, so I followed along, what?"

"Did your father know what you were going to do?" Sir Jared asked incredulously.

"Not really," Edlin said. "I told him I was going out to train some of the dogs for tracking in the snow, that I'd be out a couple days. I think he was peeved because I was supposed to help with the house party, but he doesn't really want me marrying any of those girls so he let me go.

"I went," Edlin continued, taking a deep breath, then speaking all in a rush on the exhalation, "and then I left the dogs with Race Forester. He wanted to come with me, but I wouldn't let him. He says 'Hi' though. Anyhow, I left a note for my father and told Race not to deliver it until I'd been gone three days. Then I hied after. Tracked you, you know, but didn't let you know I was there."

"I'll say we didn't!" the knight replied.

Elise noted that Jared now looked torn between amusement and anger. There was something else there as well—envy? Elise wondered if she'd read him right.

"I knew," Firekeeper said a trace smugly.

She had been pawing through the bandit corpses to find her Fang and was now strapping the knife back into place.

"I knew," she repeated, "but I no say. I think it funny."

The wolf-woman looked suddenly uncomfortable.

"Now I don't." She gave a stiff bow. "Thank you, Brother Edlin."

Edlin bowed to her in return, a gallant, sweeping gesture that couldn't quite hide the foolishly adoring expression on his face.

Elise, who had been dreading another suitor—Sir Jared, undeclared as he was, was almost too much, especially given how she was feeling right now—swallowed a guilty giggle.

She hadn't realized that Edlin was besotted with Firekeeper. No wonder he'd known his father wouldn't let him join their company. Given Edlin's impulsive streak, he'd doubtless already asked his father for permission to wed his adopted sister—and been soundly refused.

A warm affection for this romantic spirit—an affection she most certainly would *not* have felt if he were pursuing her—came into her heart. Elise welcomed it all the more as it did something to press back the numb terror that flooded back into her when she recalled how close . . .

She shivered, hiding it in a brief bow—an odd feeling, but her riding breeches made a curtsy seem ridiculous—to Edlin.

"Thank you for saving us," she said softly. "I don't know if we could have escaped without your help."

"Oh, I don't know, what?" the young man said, but it was clear from the color that rose to his cheeks that he was pleased. "Firekeeper's friends weren't sitting on their haunches waiting for me to save the day. You might say we had the same idea."

"How did you plan?" Derian asked. "Did you talk to them?"

Edlin shook his head, removed his bow from where it had been slung over his shoulder, efficiently unstrung it.

"Nope. I just followed their lead. I figured they could get the closer ones, but not the guy coming at that cage, so I went for him. You know the rest."

"I guess we do," Derian said, looking around at the corpse strewn area. "And thank you. I was wishing I could do something—I don't know what I would have done . . ."

Elise saw a memory of desolation in Derian's eyes and realized for the first time that she and Wendee had not been the only ones to suffer.

Surprisingly, Edlin looked ashamed.

"I should have found some way to stop them before they caught you," he muttered. "I'm really sorry you had to go through all of that."

Sir Jared, on whose face Elise now recognized a trace of the same shame and desperation, clapped him on the shoulder.

"You did what you could and it's all right in the end."

He, too, scanned the open area.

"The question is what do we do now? Move on or take shelter here for the night?"

Wendee Jay, who had been staring at the bloody field as if at a revelation of truth, spoke one word.

"Go."

Derian—more practical or perhaps more schooled in the realities of war—glanced up at the angle of the sun.

"There's nowhere to camp between here and well on the other side of the pass. I was counting on having time to inspect that pass and then make plans. We won't have that option. I'm afraid our best choice is to stay here."

"With all these bodies?" Wendee asked tremulously.

"We move them," Firekeeper said with the assurance of one to whom all dead bodies are nothing more than meat. "No bodies. Elation see a rock hole to drop into."

Sir Jared gave an ironic smile. "Doubtless that 'rock hole' is where many of the bandits' own victims were buried. I think that's an appropriate grave."

Derian nodded. "I'll join the burial detail as soon as I check the horses and mules. The bandits were rough on them and Blind Seer's howl didn't help."

"It did!" Firekeeper exclaimed indignantly.

"It didn't help the horses," Derian clarified with the seemingly infinite patience he kept for the wolf-woman. "It certainly helped us. Doc, Lord Edlin—could you help Firekeeper? Wendee and Elise can see what shape our supplies are in and maybe see if we can eke out our own supplies with the bandits.' "

Elise was glad to have a task to do, anything to keep the memory of her own fear away. That fear bothered her almost as much as the possibility of rape had done. She had always imagined she would do better in a time of crisis—in the war she had even managed to do the ugly work of a surgical assistant though she had thought she hated the sight of blood.

To have become a huddled, sobbing chit ashamed her, and as she flushed at the memory, she remembered something else.

"Wendee," she said softly as they hurried to where the bandits had dropped the goods stripped from their animals near the fire—doubtless for inspection after . . .

Elise hurried her thoughts away from that.

"Wendee," she repeated, "I didn't thank you, I want to thank you . . ."

"Think nothing more of it," the older woman said almost

curtly. "I'm glad I didn't need to go through with it."

"But, what you did was so brave," Elise persisted.

"Was it?" Wendee asked. "Or was I just more afraid of the waiting?"

"I heard what you said to Derian," Elise said firmly. "You were brave. I'm going to tell Duchess Kestrel when we get back to the North Woods—and I'll reward you myself. I have . . ."

"Don't," Wendee said.

She knelt down next to one of the mule packs, fumbled to open the straps with hands that trembled despite the heat of the bonfire.

"I don't want to remember," Wendee continued, "and a fuss would make me remember. All those plays, all those poems, all those grand stories of heroism. I never realized that no matter what they did—all those people I admired so and tried to be—I never realized that inside they were likely near puking their guts out from fear."

Elise wrapped an arm around Wendee's shoulders. She felt the other relax slightly and only then realized how tense she herself had been.

"At least you stood on your feet," Elise said, not letting a trace of bitterness or self-pity touch her voice, "like one of those heroes. Not like me. I think you can still face them with pride."

Wendee stared blankly at her, then began laughing shakily.

"Well, if I ever go back to the theater," she said, unbuckling the strap, "I'll play those parts differently. Or maybe I'll stick to comedy."

"Oh, I don't know," Elise said, working on another pack, "I sometimes think that what happens in those stories is only funny to those of us watching from the outside. I'm not sure how funny it would be to live."

"True," Wendee agreed. She took a deep breath, then surged on, deliberately practical. "This pack looks in pretty good shape. I think we can trust that the bandits were being careful until they saw what goodies we had."

Elise nodded. "Let's take a look in their shelter. It's going to be a bit gruesome going through their things, but . . ."

"We won," Wendee asserted firmly. "Any law of the land would say that it's our right."

"I wonder if the law's the same in New Kelvin?" Elise said thoughtfully.

"Who cares?" Wendee replied with a shrug. "No one's around to ask. We'd better get going. Cleanup is moving along pretty fast."

Elise caught a glimpse of Firekeeper and Blind Seer dragging a rather large body across the rocky ground. Firekeeper had hold of the man's shirt; the wolf had his jaws clamped through a shoulder. They moved like a team in harness, the wolf trusting the woman to see behind him.

"I wonder if she knew," Elise whispered. "What they were going . . ."

She couldn't make herself finish the phrase, didn't need to. Wendee shook her head.

"I hope not. There's an innocence to her—bloody hands and all—an innocence worth preserving. Let's not explain."

Quickly, as if she needed a change of subject, Wendee said:

"I've been thinking over what you were saying about how a comedy would feel to those in it, living the events. It reminded me of something my first teacher told me, something from Lazzaralo Denisci's writings . . ."

When the burial detail returned, the goods scavenged from the bodies wrapped in an old cloak, they found the two women seated by the fire. They were heating up bread and beans from the bandits' store and discussing drama theory with a concentrated intensity that defied interruption for any other matter.

Only Firekeeper was puzzled, but she was so often puzzled by human ways that she dismissed this last as just one more mystery.

XXV

THEIRS WAS A MEETING of bullies—of strong men who used that strength unmercifully to control those weaker, but who also were willing, almost eager, to surrender to the control of one stronger than themselves. Such a desire to surrender is at the secret heart of most bullies—but does little to comfort those they pound to submission.

Longsight Scrounger was not the lord of the pirates. Indeed, it was a matter of debate whether that legendary personage existed. What Longsight was was a good sailor, a better pilot, a mean hand with a sword or club, and, finally, a man possessed of a talent—a singular skill for finding things. Longsight could find fresh water, a lost piece of jewelry, sometimes even something as vague as the best path or a safe cove.

Had Longsight not been a bully, he might have become a dowser, a wealthy man honored throughout the Isles and perhaps beyond, but Longsight craved power more than he did respectability. Among the pirates, his gift gave him a slight edge. Those stronger than him valued his talent as an intangible asset, worth cultivating even if they despised the man. Those weaker than him feared Longsight not only because of his own not inconsiderable strength, but because the looming shadow of those others who considered him a tool difficult to replace.

The arrangement was one that satisfied Longsight perfectly and he came to the room where Waln sat up in bed to meet him with the equanimity of one who knows he has the upper hand and will enjoy using it to deliver a beating.

Waln Endbrook had learned to hide the bully beneath a veneer of fine clothing, beneath his ownership of a merchant fleet, beneath the influence money can buy, but he had never ceased to be a bully at heart. His wife, Oralia, knew that— fearing and loving him as only a willful woman broken can love. His servants knew that and worked harder to avoid his wrath.

His children had yet to make the discovery, for Waln doted on them and punished his servants rather than his darlings. Someday they would learn, however, and a new battle would be joined. Waln might even end up the loser, but that day was long in the future.

For now, Waln hardly thought of his children, his wife, his money and influence. When he did he thought of them as things at his disposal, extra fists with which to batter his opponent. Although he knew enough of Longsight Scrounger to respect him, he also trusted in his own strength.

Longsight might have sensed this as he strolled into the sickroom, for the cocky greeting he'd intended—a clever bit about Waln having survived the fever maybe just to give their hangman a bit of practice—melted on his lips.

Instead he hitched up the chair, spun it around, and sat backward, with its ladder back between him and Waln. He asked much more neutrally:

"So, how are you feeling?"

"Weak as a kitten and sour as vinegar," Waln replied, which was neither completely true nor completely false.

Certainly he wasn't himself—no man could be who'd traveled the distance he had half-fed and poorly clad with winter freezing his bones by day and by night. Still, he'd lived hard enough as a youth to know that a couple of days' good feeding and rest and he'd be himself again.

There was no advantage to telling Longsight that, so Waln contented himself with a faint, self-deprecating smile.

Longsight, feeling more confident, grinned at him.

"So, how'd you end up like that? Last time I saw you, you were riding high and mighty with a noble lady at your side."

Lady Melina's name, unspoken, rested like a threat between them. There had been no way to keep her identity from the pirates, not with her daughter kept among them and her with that damned gemstone on her forehead.

Waln hadn't worried. There would have been no advantage to the pirates in spreading the information, not while Waln held the upper hand. Now, however, the knowledge was transforming into a threat.

Concisely, as he had rehearsed through the dark hours of the night with only the snoring crone for audience, Waln recited an edited version of events. He had to stay close enough to the truth for Longsight to know what he must to help him, but he didn't need to tell all.

For one, Waln didn't need to tell how he'd been panting after the woman like a dog after a bitch in heat. Instead, the way Waln told the story, Lady Melina had ensorcelled him and made him her slave. Only the threat to his own life had broken the spell, necessitating his mad dash, leaving some—unnamed—valuables in the evil woman's possession.

The odd thing was, this version of events made more sense to the baron than the reality he knew. Lady Melina *was* a nice-looking piece, but he'd seen better, had better—much better. His own wife was more attractive if it came down to that.

There was Lady Melina's high birth and the lure of that conquest, but would that have been enough to make him act like an idiot? Intellectually, Waln knew that had been the case. On some deeper level, he could almost feel the tendrils of enchantment that had wrapped around his soul and made him act as he otherwise would not have.

For a fleeting moment, Waln wondered if perhaps he should take his account—this version of it—before Queen Valora. However, now that his head was clear, prudence won out—that and the discovery that he had acquired an aversion to powerful women.

Waln had expected Longsight to sneer at him, to ridicule and mock him for his weakness. What he hadn't entertained was the possibility of being believed. Longsight, however, was nodding slowly, as solemn as judgment.

"We've seen something of her mother's power these long days since you left the girl, Citrine, with us."

The baron noted that Longsight's knuckles, where he grasped the back of the chair, grew white as he told the tale.

"One of my young bucks—looking, he says, to please me, but I think he meant to steal it for himself—backed the girl into a corner and was setting about cutting that jeweled diadem from her head.

"The girl set up such a screaming that we heard it from the light to the cellar. Even when my buck—Red Stripe, they're calling him now—put his hand over her mouth and near suffocated her the girl just kept screaming. Shrill as a seagull she was, but not near as melodious. Even after she shouldn't have had air to yell, she kept hollering and wailing.

"I came thumping up the stair in time to whack Cime—him that's Red Stripe now—on the head before he killed the girl out of fear. As soon as she calmed down, the girl herself told us what happened—and later I checked the story with Cime before sending him for a lashing, so I know it's true."

Longsight's voice dropped low and fearful.

"The girl ended with saying—prissy as a schoolmarm I had back when I was a lad, she was—'My mother bound that stone to me when I was just a baby. I've worn it since, though at times I've hated the thing. I'd give it to you if I could, but take it from me and I'll die.'

"I tell you, Waln, my blood ran cold to hear a child talk that way. There was truth in it. That's why I have no problem believing that the Lady Melina trapped you by sorcery. If she'd do such to her own child, she'd do it to a stranger."

Amazed by this bit of good luck, Waln considered that perhaps he *should* have expected this reaction. No profession he knew—except possibly the legendary market gamblers of Waterland—created such faith in superstitions as that of the sailor. It grew out of challenging wind and water, from all the little rituals one fell into almost unconsciously when trying to propitiate that which could drown you without thought or malice.

Waln adapted his tactics swiftly, unwilling to risk Longsight's awed terror transforming into angry resentment at his own fear.

"I'm going to get my own back from Lady Melina," Waln

announced sternly, "whether she is a sorceress or not, but it's a foolish man who sticks his hand in a fire knowing he'll be burnt. Not until I've got her softened up will I go after her."

Longsight's eyes narrowed and he looked stern, but Waln noted the nervous way his tongue traveled around his teeth, pausing at the broken one, as if testing all were there.

"I can't send any men with you," Longsight said. "Winter is when the Light is most defenseless—the swamp firms some with the cold and the waters near the shore are yet navigable. My trust is holding this place and I will not weaken it for you—even if you go after that sorceress."

Or, thought Waln with irony, aware of his own growing confidence, *perhaps especially if I do.*

"I wouldn't expect *that* of you," he said aloud, trusting to his own strength that Longsight would let the hint of mockery pass. "I want to use your network, not your men. Lady Melina needs to be softened, as I said. All I want, for now, is someone to deliver a message."

"A message?" Longsight looked interested.

"That's right." Waln's smile became cruel. "Before I agreed to escort her to New Kelvin, I extracted safeguards from Lady Melina, meant to assure her good behavior. One of them you hold here—the girl, Citrine."

Longsight nodded, but again his tongue flickered round his lips.

"Now the lady trusted to have me murdered as she had my man Driver murdered. Then she would have ransomed back her daughter from your keeping."

At least I believe she would, thought Waln with a trace of uneasiness, for on this belief lay the foundation of his new plan.

"I want to send Lady Melina a reminder that her daughter is in my keeping—and an assurance that though she must believe me dead, that I am very much alive and ready to oppose her."

Longsight grinned. "You believe she is in Dragon's Breath?"

"I do," Waln said, "or if she is not, that there will be those in the Dragon Speaker's service who will know where she is. Can you get a message there—a message and a small package?"

"I can," Longsight replied. "I'll even wait to charge you postage till the spring."

"No need," Waln said airily. "When I am stronger, I can draw funds from a contact in Port Haven."

Longsight looked pleased.

"We'll keep the girl on trust till we're paid," he said with a sudden return to toughness.

Waln knew he had won for now, but he didn't dare alienate Longsight—not just yet. He made a show of lowering his gaze as if the concession had been forced from him. In reality, he had never intended to take Citrine away from the lighthouse. She was much more secure there than any place he could hide her.

"Of course, Longsight. However you wish."

Longsight was pleased. Without fully standing, he managed to twirl the chair under him so that he could lean against the back.

"Tell me now, Baron Endbrook, what size package do you need to send?"

"Nothing very large," Waln assured him, "just a lock of hair—and a finger or two."

FIVE DAYS HAD PASSED since the comb, ring, and mirror had been taken from their boxes before the witnessing Primes. In that time, initial optimism that the wisdom of New Kelvin would force the three artifacts to quickly reveal their secrets had vanished.

Five days had passed if you counted the actual day of the unboxing—as those who opposed Lady Melina's involvement did, four days if one only counted the subsequent days.

Grateful Peace was among those inclined to reckon that four

days had passed. Certainly nothing productive had been done that first day. Oh, the artifacts had been weighed and measured, the materials of their construction subjected to minute, if cautious, examination, but no real, practical work had begun until the next day.

Testing had begun with the ring, for there wasn't a single New Kelvinese who had grown to adulthood without hearing wonderful tales of enchanted rings that held within their compact shapes magics beyond imagining.

The gold from which the ring was crafted was not the purest—a piece of information that, while it had disappointed the poets among them, had given Peace reason for hope. As he saw things, who would want a ring made of pure gold? Pure gold was soft, so malleable that it could be bent beneath the slightest finger pressure. A ring made of pure gold would never hold an inscription; settings would fall from the prongs bent to hold them. The metal itself would become easily scratched or scuffed, thus diminishing the very beauty for which the metal was valued.

Tollius, of the Sodality of Smiths, argued that the Founders could have enchanted pure gold to unusual hardness, but Peace was not convinced. Why waste enchantment if a less pure alloy would do? Many of the writings implied that a single artifact could contain only so much magical force. If this was the case, then an enchantment to harden pure gold would take up space that could have been used for something much more interesting.

No, never mind the arguments raised by his associates, Peace found the quality of gold used for the ring a reason for great optimism.

The carved stone in the ring's setting proved to be—as it had seemed under casual observation—a moonstone. This stone lived up to the expectations of those who believed that only the best and purest would be used in an enchanted artifact.

Pearly white touched with mysterious hues of blue and pink, the gem's color shifted with the light. The moonstone gave the impression of shining from within, as if it soaked up light and gave it back from within its secret heart.

Unhappily, this was just an illusion. Carried within a darkened room the gem failed to shine at all, but this did not make anyone lose hope. The ring remained a promising artifact. Already factions were quietly politicking to forbid Lady Melina to take the ring as her promised reward.

The mirror was nearly as satisfactory as the ring—indeed there were those who found it more so. They recited tales of mirrors used for scrying, for communication with distant places, for magnifying the heat and light of the sun (as in the tale of the Star Wizard's battle against the Dragon of Despair—the very dragon who was said to be bound beneath the city of Dragon's Breath and to heat with its fiery breath the waters that steamed from beneath the earth).

The reflective surface of the mirror proved to be polished silver, not glass. The frame had been fitted together from intricately interlocking pieces of ivory. There was some debate as to the source of the ivory, for it seemed to hold a more delicate color than the whale's teeth that were the usual source, but no one questioned that it *was* ivory.

Posa, the thaumaturge who represented the Illuminators and was one of Peace's oldest friends, created a small stir when she declared that there were minute particles of ground gemstones in the pigments that had been used to tint the ivory. Some declared that these were necessary elements of the sorcerous formulation and so a clue to how the Founders bound magic into an artifact. Others, like Peace himself, wondered if they might not have been included simply because they were pretty.

Even the comb, upon more detailed inspection, showed more promise than it had initially. After scrupulous inspection and much arguing and calling for yet one more specialist, no one, not the wood carvers, the botanists, nor the antiquarians, could identify the wood from which it had been made.

Moreover, this wood proved to be surpassingly hard and amazingly heavy. Yet there was no doubt that the material *was* wood, for it possessed a definite grain never found in any other material. Traces of bark were evident along the edge opposite the tines.

Unhappily, these initial discoveries were not followed by some quick revelation of how to activate the magic the artifacts must hold within them.

To facilitate investigation, Apheros appointed a conclave of sorcerers from those sodalities that seemed to have the most to contribute to the investigation. The conclave members were given assistants who could do the more menial tasks, such as making simple drawings or hunting out references from the huge library that had been carefully preserved since the days of the first Healed One.

Although the conclave initially concentrated their efforts on the ring, within a few days they split into three teams. Still, though they discovered more details about each artifact's construction, they failed to unleash the forces bound within.

Grateful Peace, in his joint capacities of a senior Illuminator and the Dragon's Eye, was appointed a member of the initial conclave. When the teams were created, he politely refused a place on any single team. His excuse was that as an Illuminator, what he could contribute best were the odd scraps of knowledge he had accumulated during his years as a copyist.

This was completely true. Posa was already working with the team assigned to the mirror; as her expertise in the matter of inks and pigments was legendary, Peace could add nothing more.

Needless to say, Peace had ulterior motives behind his refusal. Drifting from group to group, listening to their discussions, observing their interplay, he was in a position to coordinate the information. Doubtless some—including Lady Melina—thought him nothing but a toady and spy for the Dragon Speaker. Peace didn't mind. He had long delighted in being undervalued.

As the days passed, Peace detected a current that tugged at the fringes of his attention, a subtle shifting of the internal dynamics of the various groups. A force was influencing the activities of the conclave, directing the course of the various investigations with a word, a hint, a smile.

This subtle manipulator was, unsurprisingly, Lady Melina Shield.

Her influence evolved gradually so that at first Peace did not trust his own impressions, but once he was aware of them, her actions were unmistakable. Lady Melina was making allies of some of the most important thaumaturges in New Kelvin. Perhaps she merely sought to preserve her life, for she must have suspected that her usefulness to Apheros would vanish as soon as the magic within the artifacts was unlocked. That made perfect sense. Peace even respected the lady for her foresight.

Grateful Peace wondered if he should draw the Dragon Speaker's attention to this development. He hesitated. Lady Melina was doing nothing wrong. Indeed her suggestions were facilitating the investigation. She had a gift for the flattering word that made a criticism acceptable, for the suggestion that interrupted a pointless debate, the encouragement that drew out the thoughts of a shy theorist.

If he did report her, Peace thought, might not his words seem nothing more than petty jealousy that she was wielding the influence that should be his as a member of the Speaker's inner circle?

Moreover, despite Apheros's initial aloofness toward her, the Dragon Speaker was now obviously quite pleased with Lady Melina. Her arrival and the unveiling of the three artifacts had distracted the thaumaturges from the issue of whether to continue pursuing the old ways or to move into new. His office was more secure than it had been for some time.

The signs of Apheros's favor were obvious even to those who did not have Peace's discerning and suspicious eye. No longer did Lady Melina dine from a tray in the isolation of her chamber. No longer did she make do without servants. If she was not dining at the Dragon Speaker's table, she was the guest of some other important thaumaturge, sometimes even of the Healed One himself. Her servants were drawn from the ranks of the well-trained and polished. Kistlio was appointed her secretary.

Grateful Peace had come in for little of the lady's attention since the day she—quite wrongly—assessed him as unimportant. Now, watching the changing dynamics within the court, he did nothing to alter her feelings. He knew it was unlikely that any of his peers would advise her of the truth about him. Lady Melina would not be so crass as to state her opinion of Peace aloud, for he did hold title and rank.

When they met—which was frequently—she was polite and solicitous. However, Grateful Peace no longer came under the intense focus of her crystal blue eyes; he was no longer the one she barraged with questions.

Unwilling to admit he was jealous, Grateful Peace told himself he was relieved. As the five days became six and the six seven, he realized that he *was* relieved. He also began to suspect that Lady Melina was involved in some project far more interesting to her than unraveling the secrets held by the three artifacts.

If he hadn't had those first days alone with her, he might have suspected she was a spy for her king or his heir, her daughter. Her fierce, quickly dampened anger when Sapphire had been mentioned convinced Peace that there was no love lost between mother and daughter—that there had not been since the daughter had rebelled against her mother a few moonspans before.

No, Lady Melina was not working for Hawk Haven. Clearly, given her willingness to conspire in the murder of Baron Endbrook, she was not working for Queen Valora. Bright Bay, its king completely and willingly under the influence of Hawk Haven, was not a separate player in this game.

Perhaps she played for the influence of House Gyrfalcon. Perhaps, as Peace had thought initially, she meant to preserve herself against assassination. However, as he considered Lady Melina and what he was learning of her devious inclinations, more possibilities occurred to him.

Perhaps Lady Melina meant to unlock the secrets held in the three artifacts and then, with the aid of some willing lackey, steal them away. Perhaps she meant to secure the best single artifact for herself and was making allies against the day she would need to argue her case before the gathered Primes.

Perhaps she hoped to remain in New Kelvin even after the three artifacts were activated and her immediate purpose fulfilled. That would be safer than returning to Hawk Haven, where she was already quite unpopular. Lady Melina was not the type to accept the lower social role to which foreign residents of New Kelvin were relegated. Perhaps she merely meant to make enough highly ranking contacts to assure that she would continue to move in the best circles.

As the days passed, Grateful Peace considered these things even as he moved about the Granite Tower, where the experiments on the artifacts were being conducted.

He thought about his suspicions when he paused to puzzle over an inscription found concealed in the leaves of the mirror's carving. Considered more as he marveled over the revelation that the "wood" of which the comb was made also partook of the qualities of stone. Worried even as he discussed the possible implications of the little compartment discovered behind the moonstone face of the ring.

The more he studied her, the more alien Lady Melina seemed, her very body language a mask behind which her true intentions were hidden. As her tongue became more facile in New Kelvinese, she used her native language less. She had her lady's maid decorate her face with touches of color, especially about her eyes, which daily became more and more the focus of her face.

Most of the thaumaturges were delighted, seeing this as her submission to the greatness of New Kelvinese culture. Peace was not so certain.

The more acceptable Lady Melina became by local standards, the more Grateful Peace sensed that she wore a mask— a mask he could not even guess how to lift so that he could see the true face she concealed behind its elaborate, empty form.

THERE HAD BEEN other bodies down in the bottom of the cleft in the rock where they had thrown the bandits: old bodies whose bones had snapped and cracked under the burden tossed down onto them, bodies not so old whose rotting the cold might have slowed but had not stopped.

If, as Firekeeper had been taught, it was wrong to kill humans unless in self-defense—or defense of the homeland, which was like defense of the self, at least as Derian confusingly explained it—then the killing of the eleven bandits had been not only necessary but good.

Prepared to rejoice as after a successful hunt, Firekeeper had been unsettled by the predominantly somber mood of her companions. There was relief, but no joy. Only Edlin Norwood seemed to feel any satisfaction at all, but before they had finished the meal Elise and Wendee had prepared for them, he, too, had gotten caught up in the pervading mood of gloom.

Firekeeper, not liking this at all, had slipped from the fireside to run with Blind Seer. The Royal Wolf was feeling quite pleased with himself—his mood was at least more what she had expected.

Over and over again Blind Seer bragged about his prowess, relating how he had run across the rocks, never once slipping though pockets of snow and ice made the surface treacherous.

"And then I leapt," he howled, a baying bark in the notes, "I leapt, limbs stretching so that I could feel the strength and power in my mighty muscles. With a mere toss of my head, I sent one man—armed, mind you, armed with a bow whose deadly hail of arrows might have torn through my fur to paint the stone with the scarlet of my blood—I sent that man crashing to the hard rocks below.

"Then I leapt again and this time my fangs ripped into the bandit's flesh. I ripped, I tore, but my great might was not needed. The fragile human ripped in two, streaking my fur with the tribute of his lifeblood . . ."

Really, Firekeeper enjoyed the boastful recital, but after she'd heard it—or variations on it—three or four times, she made a leap of her own. She caught the blue-eyed wolf off guard and together they rolled about on the cold, hard ground. The violent exercise washed from her the last of the impotent fury she had felt when the bandits had forced her to return lest she be the cause of Derian's death.

"Even more than war," she said to Blind Seer as they were catching their breath after their romp, "I have decided that I don't like bandits. I don't like this taking of a person so another person cannot act freely. War is ugly, wasteful, and foolish, but banditry is hateful. I am glad the bandits are dead and I cannot understand why the others are not singing their triumph around the fire."

"Humans!" Blind Seer snorted.

"They were brave!" Firekeeper persisted. "Edlin gliding over the stone to deliver death with his arrows. Doc, Wendee, Derian, even unblooded Elise, they were all brave. Why do they sit hanging their heads and acting like yearlings who have tried an elk and been kicked in the head for their presumption?"

Blind Seer shook his great shaggy head, a gesture he was attempting to learn so he could communicate at least a little with the humans in whose company he so frequently found himself.

"Humans," he said, "are incomprehensible—all but you, dearest . . . and you," he added quickly when he saw Firekeeper raise her fist to thump him, "you are a wolf in all but form."

DISHEVELED AND TIRED but inwardly happy, Firekeeper returned to the others. It was nice to come to a fire you didn't need to kindle yourself, nice to have a bit of warm food set aside for you. Being with humans wasn't all bad.

Derian broke what was evidently, judging from how the others started at the sound of his voice, a long silence.

"I am wondering," he said, his voice low and rough, "if I am responsible for what happened to us today."

Doc asked, his voice shaped by puzzlement, "What do you mean, Derian?"

"I mean, I'm wondering if by asking around Gateway about best routes and all the rest I tipped off someone who contacted the bandits. A fast rider could have beaten us here—especially one who knows local shortcuts—or a carrier pigeon could have carried word ahead."

"Don't," Elise said in clipped tones that, despite their lighter note, held something of her father in them, "take onto yourself more than your due. Winter trade is common—though more comes through Plum Orchard than through Stilled. These bandits may regularly raid this pass—a strike or two that takes in goods, livestock, and resalable persons would set them up for quite a while."

Derian smiled what Firekeeper thought was a rather stiff and unnatural smile.

"Maybe that is so," he admitted, "but I've been worrying. They were so well prepared, took us so easily . . ."

"Don't," Elise repeated. "They might have had a spy at the last inn or along the road. Try not to beat up on yourself for something that you weren't to blame for, and that came out all right in the end."

Listening as she licked the bean gravy from her fingers, Firekeeper thought that the last sentence sounded as if it were addressed to someone else, but though she looked at every face, she couldn't figure out for whom the words were meant.

When they left the next morning, the mules were somewhat more heavily burdened than they had been on arrival, their panniers stretched out with fresh booty.

Wendee Jay had insisted that they must reward themselves for their victory. Though the trade goods and dry foods were a poor substitute for the liver-stealing, belly-swelling gorge and romp that usually followed a good hunt, Firekeeper had seconded her with enthusiasm. Surely there should be some celebration!

The bandits had not been wealthy, but the best from their hoard was worth carrying away. Firekeeper carried soft fox pelts and folded squares of silk over to where Derian packed them away. There had been jingling sacks with small bits of jewelry and coins, too. She'd tried a bangle on herself, liking how the metal flashed in the clear winter light, but it slowed her hand, so she put the trinket by until a special occasion arose.

They found the pass clear—suspiciously clear, as if the bandits might have shoveled and packed in anticipation of making a fast escape with their new possessions. Even so, they traveled for the best part of the day before reaching the place where this road intersected the north/south trade road that would take them into Dragon's Breath.

A town had grown up where the two roads met and Firekeeper was impressed and—though she would have died rather than show it—intimidated by the three-and four-story stone buildings.

Firekeeper remembered her first view of West Keep, where Derian had begun her education in human ways, how the towering stone building had seemed like a living creature made all of stone. She remembered how terrified she had been when she had first visited Eagle's Nest, the single event that had most solidly driven home to her how very many humans there were and how insignificant she was among them.

But now she considered herself sophisticated in such matters. She had seen three cities—if you included the twin towns of Hope and Good Crossing—and had dwelt in two different castles. She didn't want to be impressed any longer with the massive structures humans could make out of stone and wood.

She didn't want to, but she was.

It helped that Elise was open in expressing her own awe and wonder, that Wendee pointed to the sculptures with unfeigned glee, recognizing in their shapes familiar figures from the plays she had acted in years before.

The men affected to be less impressed—at least at first. The encounter with the bandits had made them grim, as if determined that no threat would escape their vigilance. Edlin was the first to break, forgetting to rein in his mount in his astonishment at seeing set into the side of some public building a cut-glass window so elaborate that it made the ones in his father's study seem prentice work by a very uncertain hand.

The vendor whose cart Edlin narrowly missed shook a fist

at him, showering the young man with invective that turned into smiles of pride when Edlin grimaced apologetically and pointed to the window by way of explanation.

And this was just in a town a day's ride from the capital!

The next day they reached the vicinity of Dragon's Breath too late to go inside the walls, but, as with Eagle's Nest, a city had grown up outside the official wall. They found rooms in a—for New Kelvin—friendly inn. The owner condescended to tell them that their first duty in the morning was to register with the city guard.

"It is to your own protection," he explained laboriously in Pellish. "Foreigners not have manners and do stupid thing. You register as foreigner, guard tell you how not to break law and custom. If you do then, they be more forgiving because you have try to be civilized."

"Well!" Wendee said, drawing in her breath with an indignant snort. "Really!"

Elise nodded. "It's as if they expect us to spit on the carpets."

"And let the dogs piss in the hallways," Edlin agreed. "If I'd brought any of the hounds with me, by the buzzing-winged Hummer, I'd be tempted to do just that. Imagine!"

Firekeeper frowned.

"I think is good," she said. "They tell us how to be."

Five sets of eyes turned to stare at her quizzically—six, when Elation, who had gone to sleep on the back of Derian's chair, opened her own golden-rimmed eyes to study the wolf-woman.

Firekeeper struggled to explain.

"Is this," she said. "When I do as wolf do, Derian tell me is bad manners. So though I think wearing shirt in hot and sticky summer is as stupid as a late-summer-born pup in winter, I do to be polite."

She looked sternly at them, asking them to accept the magnitude of her sacrifices in the cause of good taste.

Derian grinned at her.

"And these days," he said, "you even let someone else finish their meat before stealing the bone—what amazing tact!"

Firekeeper grinned back at him.

"Who know what thing is to New Kelvinese people what is shirt to wolf? You not know either."

Edlin blinked. Despite his evident admiration of the wolf-woman, he was the one who still had the most trouble understanding her manner of speech. Wendee, perhaps owing to her practice in making sense of the chattering of small children, had far less trouble.

"You do have a point," she admitted. "And the law is the law."

"I wonder," Elise mused in the tone she reserved for purely philosophical points, "what they would do if we didn't report and then later broke some local ordinance. Could we plead ignorance and thus avoid punishment?"

"Let's" said Doc dryly, "not try that."

He looked away quickly then. Firekeeper was getting tired of the prolonged mating dance between him and Elise. She'd be glad when spring arrived and they got down to business.

She wondered if there would be anyone for Doc to fight. Elise's father, maybe? He seemed to take the place of the One Male in her pack. Did humans even do such things? Hadn't Sapphire and Shad mated out of season?

Firekeeper frowned and bit her lower lip. Impulsively, she started to ask, then remembered how carefully everyone was avoiding discussing an attraction that was obvious—at least where either Doc or Elise might overhear. She resolved to wait and ask Wendee or Derian when the others weren't near.

The next morning as the sun was rising the wolf-woman strolled out of the small stable in which she and Blind Seer had been sleeping. As their own horses and mules were the only animals present, this had been reasonable—even wise, for no one would trouble their gear when the big "dog" was known to be on guard.

She bent over, tousling the bits of straw and hay from her hair, wondering if she could possibly get Derian or Wendee to draw her a hot bath. The idea was attractive, so she straightened up, eager to make her request before Wendee had a chance to get involved with something else.

Her movement was interrupted in midstretch as she saw the skyline ahead of her. Dragon's Breath rose two or three times larger than Eagle's Nest, a multilevel sprawl that ascended up the mountain slopes. Glass caught the light from the rising sun as it slid through gaps in the Sword of Kelvin Mountains.

The awe Firekeeper had felt the day before when they had arrived in the outlying town was nothing to the wondering fear that filled her as she looked at this city that was her destination.

Colors the rainbow never dreamed of adorned walls and doorways. Domes of beaten copper or faceted glass caught the sun's light, granting it polish and refinement. Brick and stonework shaped intricate patterns that teased the eye as if leading it through a maze.

For a moment, Firekeeper had a hint of what the world must have been like in the days before the Old Country rulers vanished back into their own lands. She understood the terrible power the Royal Beasts had combated—and had retreated before. Then that revelation mercifully retreated, and she was left instead with a sense of vastness and desolation.

So many buildings! So many people! How in all of this was she to find Lady Melina Shield?

And how—even if she found her—was she to steal anything at all from out of this massive human stronghold?

XXVI

As EAGER AS FIREKEEPER WAS TO FIND LADY MELINA, steal the three items, and hurry back west, her first glimpse of Dragon's Breath transformed her impatience into care—rather as a wolf who has scented what she thought was a solitary deer might pause to reconsider her tactics when she realizes that what she has surprised is a rutting buck with a twelve-point rack.

While Derian, with Elise as translator, undertook the tedious and confusing task of registering their party as foreign traders, Wendee and Doc were put in charge of finding them a place to stay.

Edlin was assigned to grooming their assorted beasts, a job he did with something like good grace. His role in saving them from the bandits had helped make him one of their number, but he was aware that he was an interloper and was eager to prove his continued worth.

Edlin hinted to Firekeeper that he'd enjoy "Little Sister's" company down in the stable, but Firekeeper wasn't about to encourage his puppyish affection. With Blind Seer ghosting behind her, she joined Doc and Wendee.

The innkeeper had loaned them one of his sons, a youth with enough of both languages to act as a translator in case Wendee's New Kelvinese wasn't sufficient. In turn, Wendee's New Kelvinese was sufficient to assure that the boy didn't distort their needs for his own gain.

The innkeeper's boy led them immediately from the quieter fringes of town to a secondary market area outside the ancient walls. Inside the main walls—as in Eagle's Nest—stabling for the horses and mules would be prohibitively expensive. Moreover, the boy explained, that part of the city had become the purview of the sodalities. Very rarely did any building come up for rent, and the market there welcomed only the products of the sodalities themselves.

Firekeeper followed a few steps behind the rest, trying not to show her terror at being surrounded by this sprawling city. She took some comfort from knowing that Blind Seer was trailing them, seeing how well he could conceal his presence from the daylight world.

"Given the pong of trash and night soil," the wolf said, "even though cold has deadened some of the reek, I should not alert the duller noses. We will be helped in that the New Kelvinese limit the numbers of herbivores on the streets during the day—fewer to catch my scent and be properly terrified."

"And the dogs?" Firekeeper had asked. "These people do keep dogs."

"I'll growl 'em to silence," the wolf replied confidently.

Firekeeper knew that in reality Blind Seer was no happier than she about their surroundings, but like her he had changed since their first venture into what humans persisted in calling "civilization." Moreover, he had promised to help her in the undertaking the Royal Beasts had laid upon her, and he could not do that from outside Dragon's Breath.

Elation, as usual, was gone on some business of her own. She might be following Derian; then again, she might be hunting out some of the wingéd folk—perhaps the very crow who had followed Lady Melina north.

Actually, as they twisted through the streets, Firekeeper began to have a sneaking suspicion that Blind Seer could have walked openly at her side with Elation perched on his back and no one would have noticed. Even to her, limited as her exposure to human customs had been, the people of Dragon's Breath seemed *weird*.

The stories Wendee had told along the road had prepared her somewhat for the wide use of face paint, but she decided that no mere tales could have prepared her for the reality of the wildly colored faces—or for the smell of the preparations used to achieve the effect.

There didn't seem to be one single preparation in use, but many involved oils and dyes that had quite strong odors. Spices, nutmeats, flower petals, pulverized minerals all mixed together into an olfactory storm that made Firekeeper struggle not to pinch her nostrils shut.

And then there was the clothing. Much of it resembled the long straight robes Wendee had purchased in Gateway—although more brightly colored. Sometimes two or three such robes had been layered over each other to provide protection from the cold. Other passersby wore long coats trimmed in fur or brilliant tapestry brocades.

These, however, were the comparatively normal New Kelvinese.

Firekeeper nearly lost sight of her companions the first time a truly exotic figure paraded past. It was a man—at least it seemed to be male—clad all in bronze-colored tights. These tights were not merely formfitting. They were padded so that the man's limbs had *more* form, so they were exaggeratedly defined. Stylized muscle groups along the man's arms, legs, and chest had been worked out with careful anatomical detail; his penis protruded before him like a spear, balls swaying below with every stride.

The man's face had been stained reddish-bronze, his eyes rimmed in black, his nose tip painted so that it appeared to spread across his face in an oddly bovine fashion. The enormous headgear he wore continued the illusion. Flaring ears and long bronze horns created the impression—even for Firekeeper, who usually saw reality and had difficulty seeing mere art—of a bipedal bull.

She swiveled around as the man went by and saw that his outfit included a tail that, rather than dragging limply on the ground behind him as she might have expected, bounced and waved like a natural tail of flesh and bone.

What astonished her almost as much as the bull-man was that no one else seemed to notice him, no one but herself, Wendee, and Doc. Even the innkeeper's son, who was young enough that he should have been delighted by such a colorful figure, passed the bull-man without slowing, pausing only when he realized that he had nearly lost those he was intended to guide.

After they had threaded through the streets for a bit longer, Firekeeper realized why these exotic figures raised no comment. Many they passed on the crowded streets in this part of town could have rivaled the bull-man in complexity of costume and pure gaudiness of finery.

Within the next hour Firekeeper saw so many wildly attired figures that she finally didn't bother to turn and stare after each one. There were people dressed as birds or beasts, people dressed as the night sky in robes set with mirrors, people parading beneath amazing hats—some so large that they required support yokes resting on the wearer's shoulders.

Nor were the domestic animals immune to the general passion for costuming things as what they were not. The horses wore—at the very least—horns jutting from their foreheads or antlers on their headstalls. Their coats had often been colored some unusual shade. Firekeeper had a sudden insight to where the dyes once used to color Princess Sapphire's Blue must have been bought. She wondered if Lady Melina had been inspired by her youthful visit to New Kelvin.

Oxen with intricately curling horn sheaths hauled carts covered in bells and streamers. Even the dogs—though they encountered few of these—were adorned with things that glittered and flashed. Only the birds were, by and large, untouched by the human passion for decoration and seemed drab and plain by contrast.

Within a few hours after noon, Derian and Wendee had located a landholder who seemed interested in renting a portion of her premises to them.

She was a fat woman with rolling chins that effectively disguised the location of her neck. Because of the New Kelvinese custom—fairly universally observed as far as Firekeeper could tell—of shaving the front of her head to a point just above the tips of her ears, the woman appeared to have an extremely large head—or at least a vast expanse of face.

This face was stained bright pink, the color of certain late flowers—the flowers that must compete for the attention of bees who have been jaded by the entire spectrum of spring and early summer. Her eyebrows were stained a darker pink, as were her lips. The blue eyes that confronted the world from this wash of rose were startling in contrast.

Somehow, Firekeeper whispered to Blind Seer, *I expected them to be red, like those of a rat seen at night.*

The wolf snuffled his agreement. *"At least her gown is green. More pink and I would think we had opened a door into the sunrise."*

"I am," the pink-faced woman announced haughtily, "Hasamemorri."

She spoke Pellish with a formality that suggested that she had learned it much as Elise had learned New Kelvinese, from books and tutors rather than from daily use.

Wendee said something in New Kelvinese, doubtless a request about the property they had been told Hasamemorri had to rent.

Hasamemorri raised a carnation-pink eyebrow, possibly, Firekeeper thought, considering their previous encounters, at Wendee's archaic phrasing. Wendee, however, had learned it was better to show at least some knowledge of the local language. The locals were either amused or flattered. They took not being told that one among them spoke New Kelvinese—as the trio had learned at their first stop—as an insult.

Hasamemorri said something else. Though she didn't invite them inside, Firekeeper saw her relax slightly.

"Curious about us," Blind Speaker commented. "And she has stabling for the horses. This time I checked."

Firekeeper nodded thanks. They'd wasted a long hour negotiating with a promising landholder only to learn too late that although he owned stable space it was currently leased out. She didn't pass the news on to Wendee. Wendee had learned enough to ask early on.

Wendee continued to speak in New Kelvinese for another phrase or so; then she switched to Pellish.

"I'm sorry, ma'am," she said. "I can't say what I need to in your fine language."

"I doubt," Hasamemorri replied fairly amiably, "that the texts of the great playwrights contained the words you need for discussing a rental. Would you and your companions come within?"

Doc nodded acceptance. Firekeeper spoke quickly before anyone could accept for her.

"Please, Wendee, Doc—I want to stay out here and watch the people."

Wendee gave a quick glance toward Hasamemorri, but the pink lady seemed pleased rather than offended.

"Let the child remain without," she said grandly. "Come into my parlor."

A cup of something hot and smelling lightly of mint was sent out to her. It wasn't tea, quite, but it wasn't alcoholic, so

Firekeeper sipped it as she watched the New Kelvinese go by. She tried to think how she would paint herself if she were to pass as a New Kelvinese. None of the designs she saw appealed to her, but the imagining amply amused her.

Doc and Wendee emerged in good humor.

"We have a place and at a decent rent, too," Wendee said as they walked briskly back to the inn. "It turns out that Hasamemorri has trouble with arthritis or something in her knees."

"Nothing that losing a few hundred pounds wouldn't help," Doc muttered.

"And Doc made much of the pain recede," Wendee continued blandly. "In return for his continued services, we're to have the entire ground floor—Hasamemorri prefers the upper apartments. There's a kitchen we can share and she'll even loan us a maid once a week and allow us to combine our laundry with hers for a small additional charge."

Much of this information rushed through Firekeeper's mind as water would over a rock. Still she grasped the essentials.

"And the horses and mules?" she asked, just to be safe.

"There's a good stable out back," Wendee assured her. "We have to supply our own feed and labor, but that's no trouble."

"Good," Firekeeper said. "Now we can find Lady Melina. People will hear of Doc and come to us with stories."

"I doubt it will take long for us to get a line on her," Wendee agreed optimistically. "Right, Doc?"

Doc, perhaps contemplating an undefined period of time during which he must daily contemplate Hasamemorri and her abused knees, replied with unaccustomed fervor:

"I sincerely hope so!"

ARRIVAL IN DRAGONS BREATH dispelled the last of the cloud that had clung to Elise since the bandit attack.

They moved from the inn to Hasamemorri's house the very

afternoon that Wendee and Derian rented the space. The land-lady descended like a pink cloud to supervise their arrival, although she seemed disappointed that they didn't have more baggage.

"Perhaps," Wendee said with a soft giggle as she hurried past Elise with a double armful of groceries, "she thought we would be burdened down with exotic foreign trade goods—salted fish, maybe."

Elise grinned, her happiness continuing unabated when the next day dawned and the work of settling in began in earnest. Hasamemorri might be disappointed, but Elise was not.

Everything about the house—including their pink-painted landlady—filled her with delight. Elise had always enjoyed reading about foreign lands. Bright Bay, cousin as it was to Hawk Haven, had proved to be something of a disappointment. New Kelvin most definitely was not, and now she had escaped the shelter of the inn and was actually living among the native people. It was all she could do to keep from hugging herself with excitement.

The large central hallway that split the ground floor of the house into two parts was transformed into their waiting area. The room to the left of the front door was to be Doc's consulting room. The chamber to the right would double as a short-term infirmary and dispensing area.

At night Edlin would sleep in the consulting room; Derian and Doc would share a chamber that backed onto the infirmary. Elise and Wendee would share the nice, well-lit side room that, owing to its glass skylight, would become a surgery when one was needed.

Firekeeper had made clear that she didn't want any special space in the house reserved for her. If the night grew cold, she would sleep in the kitchen. Otherwise, she preferred the stables. As this provided protection for their horses and mules, no one—not even Edlin—protested that these were quarters far beneath the rank of a lady.

Edlin, Elise thought with a wry smile, was learning some-thing about the reality of the girl he thought he adored—learning that she was often taciturn, that when she did speak she was often disturbingly literal, and that she was as loyal as the sun was bright—most especially to Blind Seer, but also to those humans for whom she felt responsible.

At this very moment, Edlin, however, was presumably too busy to moon over his wolfy lady. Wendee had somehow tricked her young master into supervising the maids Hasamemorri had graciously loaned them. As this meant assisting with the lifting and water carrying—Doc was being a stickler for cleanliness, especially in the surgery and consulting rooms—Edlin was kept quite busy.

Firekeeper and Derian had been excused from anything to do with setting up the household and medical practice. Their job was to learn everything they could about Dragon's Breath. Since the innkeeper's boy had been quite happy to continue as guide and translator, Elise was free to translate for Doc—a necessary task, since without assistance he could not understand anything his patients said to him.

Even before they hung the Healer's Guild emblem out over the door, Sir Jared set very strict limits as to whom he would see. As her very first task, he asked Elise to letter a sign in New Kelvinese stating his limits.

"I am not a miracle worker," he explained, steadily sorting the supplies Wendee had bought for him in the market earlier that morning. "I cannot cure any illness. I cannot make tumors melt away. My gift is for strengthening. I can help a broken bone to mend more quickly; I can convince the blood to replenish itself at a greater rate. I can give the body's own soldiers courage to carry on their fight against an invader but I cannot, *cannot* . . ."

He almost shouted the word.

"I *cannot* do miracles. Moreover, I will not try. Even the little things I can do drain me so that I sleep at night as one dead. I will not waste the capacity I do have to help fussing over those who are beyond my powers."

Elise reached out an impulsive hand to hold one of Doc's. She felt his long, dexterous fingers wrap around hers, grateful for the human contact, forgetting for a moment anything but that they were two people.

This was the man she knew and liked, the man who had taught her how to bind wounds and to mix healing ointments. On the eve of the early battles of King Allister's War, he had also taught her how to recognize a person capable of being treated from one who could not be. That had been a terrible lesson, one that had been given its first test when her own dear cousin Purcel had been brought in from the field.

"I understand, Doc," Elise said softly, "and I'll make certain the patients understand, too."

Sir Jared nodded and when he pulled his hand out of hers it was not with that sudden, embarrassed jerk that she had come to dread but simply because he needed it to unpack a box of cloth bandaging strips.

"Derian did take care of our paperwork with the local guilds?" he asked.

Elise nodded, busying herself with sketching out Doc's manifest on a sheet of wood with a stick of charcoal. One good thing about New Kelvin—there was never a shortage of writing materials. Anticipating their need, Hasamemorri had loaned her tenants some interesting color sticks in which the pigments were suspended in wax. They weren't as versatile as paint and had a tendency to smear, but they also didn't need long to dry.

Elise paused to squint critically at her draft, rubbing out the end of a line where the letters had started to slope.

"Yes, he and Wendee went out this morning. They registered us with the local—I guess you'd call it mayor's office— and picked up a list of the regulations we'll be expected to abide by. Then they went over to the Healer's Guild and paid for your license."

"Any problems?"

Elise heard Doc pause in his unpacking as if anticipating trouble.

"Not really," she assured him. "They were happy to take our money. Derian and Wendee were very careful to explain that you would be doing more than simply binding wounds and dispensing potions. Derian said that the Healer's Guild officer seemed intrigued rather than challenged."

"That reaction's interesting in itself," Doc said thoughtfully. "I wonder if Wendee's conjecture that the talents don't flourish here is indeed true."

Elise finished the rough lettering for her sign. In the interests of speeding the opening of their business, she'd kept the legend brief and to the point.

> SIR JARED SURCLIFFE, HEALER.
> SPECIALIST IN BROKEN BONES, WOUNDS,
> AND COMMON AILMENTS.
> NO MIRACLES!

"What do you think?" she asked, holding it up for Doc's inspection.

"Neat and concise," he said approvingly. "Since you'll be continuing to assist me, my lady, I'll give to you the task of separating the patients into those we can treat and those we cannot."

Elise—threatened at first by the seeming formality implied in "my lady"—warmed to the inclusive "we."

"I can try," she said.

"Good." Sir Jared rubbed his hands briskly. "Now, my hope is to reserve my talent for where it is truly needed. The rest of our patients we will treat by more usual methods."

"Right," Elise said. "Shall I send in your first patient? There's a friend of Hasamemorri waiting upstairs in her parlor."

Doc looked about his makeshift consulting room.

"I suppose you may as well get her. You can color in the sign later."

That first day—their first full day of residence in Hasamemorri's house—they saw three people. First came the friend of Hasamemorri's—an elderly woman with very bad swelling of the joints. Doc gave her a powder for the pain and an ointment for her joints.

Their second patient was the result of a chance accident a street away. A young man had been caught between a cart and a wall when the donkey pulling the cart was frightened by a sudden noise. Someone had noticed Edlin hanging out the emblem required by the Healer's Guild and brought the injured man there, not caring about credentials as much as proximity.

Elise's battlefield experience kept her from blanching when the pale, blood-smeared youth was hauled in on a makeshift stretcher constructed from someone's winter cloak. She knelt by him out in the street, checked for blood on his lips, the odor of bowel on his breath.

The brownish red stain the young man had used to pattern his face was distracting, but a gentle inspection with her fingertip was enough to show her what was dye and what was blood.

Doc heard the commotion and came to the door, but he didn't rush to take her place.

"Do we have a chance?" he asked, almost conversationally.

"I think so," she replied.

"Have his friends bring him into the consulting room. The surgery isn't ready yet."

With that, Doc retreated. In the background, Elise could hear him bellowing to Wendee for hot water. With the part of her mind that wasn't completely absorbed in directing the bearers, she made a note to make certain that water was always kept warm on the hob for just such emergencies.

The youth looked more badly injured than he really was. Most of the blood proved to be from abrasions. His worst injuries were cracked and broken ribs, but those that were broken had missed the lungs. There was no bowel perforation.

An hour after he had been carried in he was set in the infirmary, sound asleep from one of Doc's potions.

Their third visitor arrived a few hours after the young man had been brought in, when Doc was sitting in his consulting room drinking very strong tea and recovering from the ordeal.

Knowing how exhausted Doc was, Elise nearly sent this patient away. Superficially, he looked quite healthy. Then he held up one of his hands. It was withered, the muscles gone, the fingers collapsed loosely onto themselves.

"I'm sorry," Elise said to him, wishing her New Kelvinese weren't so formal. She thought it made her sound more severe than she wished. "Sir Jared cannot heal old injuries. His ability is limited to strengthening the body when it must battle new wounds."

The man—she had trouble judging his age because of the concentric lines of yellow and orange he had drawn about his eyes and mouth—frowned. His dull blond hair was drawn back into a tight braid and his loose robe hid the shape of his body.

"I saw that on the sign," he said. "Still, I would speak with Sir Jared. I will pay for a consultation."

Something in the patient's gaze—his eyes were a weird, pale shade without tint of their own—made Elise feel that she could not send him away. There was an aura of command about him that made her suspect he was not accustomed to being denied.

She longed to pass the decision onto Doc, but that wouldn't be right.

"Very well," she said. "Sir Jared is recovering from a surgery and must look in on his patient in a bit, but he is available now."

The man glided past her into the consultation room without further comment, without even bothering to knock. Elise followed him in, signing her apology for the interruption to Doc over the visitor's shoulder.

"Sir Jared doesn't yet speak New Kelvinese," she explained when their visitor looked back at her quizzically, as if wondering why she was still there. "I will translate if you wish."

"I do," he said, "for I lack your tongue. I am Oculios." He continued bowing to Doc and then, a bit uncertainly, to Elise herself.

Elise translated. "He says his name is Oculios."

Doc nodded, said, "Oculios," with a slight smile.

He did pretty well. There was something wrong about how he shaped the vowels. He made the "o" sound too flat—a touch more "ah" than "o"—but it was recognizable.

Elise settled herself into being nothing but a mouth as Oculios continued speaking:

"I used my deformity to win the sympathy of your pretty assistant. Although," he said, casting a quizzical glance at her from those beringed eyes, "I don't think it worked. However, I have not come to consult you about that old wound."

"Good," Doc replied after Elise had finished, "because I can't do anything about that. Out of curiosity, what happened to the hand?"

"An accident with some heated chemical," Oculios answered after Elise had repeated Doc's question, "when I was younger. I am a member of the Sodality of Alchemists, though I myself am an apothecary by trade."

"Ah, the competition has arrived," Doc murmured.

Elise expected Sir Jared to tell her not to translate that last statement—it sounded a bit obnoxious—but when he didn't, she did her job, not even softening the phrasing as she might have. The addition of a word like "honored" or "respected" or "long admired" would go a long way—and wouldn't be a lie, either, for she knew that Doc did admire New Kelvinese medicines.

Still, Doc wasn't stupid. If he had reasons for being blunt, even a bit rude, she wasn't going to mess up his gambit.

Oculios smiled faintly. "Actually, I am not. Not really. I prefer not to set bones and deal with raw wounds. I lack the training—even if my infirmity didn't make such work practically impossible. In fact, I refer such patients to others. Actually, I am here for two reasons."

He began to tick them off by raising a finger on his strong hand.

"One, I am here as a representative of my sodality. That's an organization quite different from a guild."

Elise frowned slightly, then spoke in her own right.

"Could you explain that, sir? I've never managed to understand that point and my books and tutors—they all seemed to assume that I did." She grinned. "Actually, I'm not certain that my tutor really understood either."

Oculios gave her a sudden smile—the first such that didn't seem like a bit of studied politeness. It turned the lines around his mouth into rippled crescents.

"I can do so," he said. "First, may I have your name? I am aware that I dismissed you unfairly as a mere apprentice to the healer, Sir Jared. You are clearly his partner."

Elise blushed. To herself she furiously tried to excuse the reaction as mere embarrassment at not having made proper introductions. Deep inside, she knew she had colored at hearing herself named so innocently in such an intimate relationship to Sir Jared.

"One moment, Oculios. I must tell Sir Jared what we have been saying."

She provided a quick summary.

Doc nodded. "Good. These sodalities sound important. Learn what you can about them and don't mind pausing every line or so to translate for me. I'll take a summary when you're done."

Elise decided that since this meeting was going to take a while, she may as well be seated. She made a neat curtsy to their visitor as she did so.

"I am Lady Elise Archer," she said.

"Lady Archer," Oculios said, not rising, but dipping his head in the seated equivalent of a bow. "Now, to explain. The guilds here are much like they are in your land—as I understand them, that is—organizations for regulation of business, setting reasonable prices for services and standards of quality for whatever is being sold."

"That seems a fair definition," she agreed.

"Here," Oculios continued, "the guilds are informally associated with various sodalities. The sodalities specialize in related skills, but specialize in the magical elements of those skills."

Elise shivered at this open mention of the forbidden art of magic. If Oculios noticed her reaction, he chose not to comment.

"Most of my art," he said, "consists of tasks a healer or herbalist in your own land would recognize. However, I also am devoted to endeavoring to perpetuate knowledge left to us at the departure of the Founders. In the case of my sodality, we attempt to combine elements into potions and preparations that our records tell us the Founders once used."

"Attempt?"

Elise felt the word slip out before she could school it back.

Oculios went stiff and formal. The lines around his eyes and mouth became rounded, like ripples spreading from a pebble dropped into a still pool.

"In our land, as in yours, much information was lost and damaged during the Burning Death. Where New Kelvin differs from Hawk Haven is that we have regathered much of that knowledge and have it available for our use."

Elise schooled her expression into something wide-eyed, awed, and maybe just a bit scared. Oculios relaxed slightly, apparently pleased by her respect.

"Additionally, it is from the sodalities that the Primes are elected—and from the Primes that the Dragon Speaker is elected."

Elise nodded, on firm ground again. She had studied this peculiar system of government with interest. The Dragon Speaker seemed to be the *real* king of New Kelvin, but the Speaker ruled at the whim of these Primes. She had thought that the Primes were nobles, but apparently they were more like master crafters who might or might not also dabble in magic.

"One moment," she said, wanting time to adapt her own mental map. "Let me translate."

"So," Sir Jared commented when she had finished. "Oculios is not here as a competing healer, but as a representative of their ruling class."

"Do you want me to translate that?"

"Might as well."

She did. Oculios stretched his lips into one of his formal smiles.

"That is true to a point. My sodality is greatly interested in your use of magic to assist in healing. The form is different than our own, but still it falls in our purview. We would like to study Sir Jared at work."

"That's fine," Doc said, "as long as it doesn't get in the way of my treatments."

"Such," Oculios replied earnestly, "would be counterproductive. My second reason for coming here is purely personal. I am interested in knowing whether Sir Jared would care to purchase preparations from my pharmacy."

Elise translated, and Doc thought for a moment.

"You know," he said finally, "that would be useful. I can only spend so much time grinding powders and combining ointments. Wendee certainly doesn't have the knowledge to buy all the raw materials I need, as she bought bandages and the like this morning. I would have had to buy medicines eventually—if we get business, that is."

Oculios laughed when Elise translated this last.

"Never doubt that you will," he said. "Already the news of the foreigner with the interesting powers is spreading. The work you did today on the young man will help—if he recovers with unusual speed that is."

Sir Jared's professional pride was pricked.

"Would you like to join me?" he asked, rising. Something in his bearing reminded Elise of Earl Kestrel. "I need to check on my patient about now."

"Gladly."

The young man was resting nicely, well enough that Sir Jared asked that word be sent to his parents that he could be taken home that very day.

Although Oculios tried to hide his reaction, he was obviously deeply impressed. After they returned to the consulting room, he spent the next hour negotiating with Sir Jared, working out a trade that involved his goods for the opportunity for himself and selected members of his sodality to observe Sir Jared at work.

The end result was highly satisfactory to them all; indeed, Elise felt as if they might have taken advantage of the man. She said as much to Sir Jared after Oculios had departed.

"Don't worry about him," Jared said with a hearty laugh.

"He'll doubtless be reimbursed for his materials from his sodality treasury and gain in importance for having secured exclusive rights to my time. Did you notice how careful he was to contract for that?"

Elise was relieved. Oculios wasn't the most comfortable person she had ever met. Indeed, his open claims to doing magic made her skin crawl. Still, he had been impressed with Doc and quite ready to pay honestly for Doc's time.

Shortly before the dinner hour, their accident victim's parents came to take him home. There was no negotiating over pay. They simply left a small canvas bag containing the accepted guild rate for such work on the bedside.

They also left a small silk purse containing what Hasamemorri told them was a good-luck token. It was shaped like a man's torso cast in porcelain and glazed a pretty, shimmering blue. Since the token had a hole drilled through it like a bead, Elise strung it on some silk cord and hung it in the window alongside the door, where it was visible from without through the lightly frosted glass side panel.

Hasamemorri, when she descended from above, was temporarily startled at the sight. She studied the swinging token for a moment, then nodded in satisfaction, her fat chins rippling like the congealed gelatin from around a roast.

"Quite nicely done—a foreign touch. It should be good for business."

"Why?" Elise asked. "I thought foreigners weren't liked in New Kelvin."

Teeth were barred in a smile that seemed very white against the pink flesh.

"They are not," Hasamemorri admitted, "but still you are interesting just the same. You are so provocative with your bare faces and odd clothing, but you do magic as well, so you are not as hostile as most foreigners are. You are more like us."

Elise thought she understood, and understanding made her uncomfortable. Doing magic was frowned upon in Hawk Haven. It was not just more unzoranic, like fancy titles. It was *wrong*.

The talents were different—they weren't magic—they were just like having another sense, like having good hearing or perfect pitch or something. They weren't really magic.

Were they?

IT WAS ONLY when the package arrived for Lady Melina that Grateful Peace realized how serious things were becoming.

The package arrived in midafternoon eleven days after the unveiling of the comb, mirror, and ring. Luncheon was over—Lady Melina had dined in small company with the Dragon Speaker and several of his associates. Although she was still learning the various titles belonging to the members of the Primes—a task complicated by the fact that many of them had more than one title—she still treated Peace more dismissively than any wise person would a member of the Dragon's Three.

This dismissal continued to suit Peace, for it freed him to watch her. This was precisely what he was doing on the day the package arrived.

He was pacing the secret gallery behind Lady Melina's suite, making liberal use of the peepholes. His desire, formed quite cynically and rationally, was to catch her involved in some act she would not wish known—he wasn't sure quite what that would be, but he was certain he would recognize it if he saw it.

A liaison, perhaps, or a treasonous conversation of some sort, maybe against the current Dragon Speaker, maybe a plot to steal the ring or comb or mirror—or all three. The problem Peace faced was that, realistically seen, all of these would be more damaging to the New Kelvinese participants than to Lady Melina.

Liaisons were not illegal in New Kelvin—not unless they violated someone's contractual rights and the damaged party wished to press complaint. Could a foreigner be treasonous?

Only, Peace supposed, against their own nation. Anything else was simply political maneuvering.

Still, Peace did not give up hope that he might catch Lady Melina at a disadvantage. If he succeeded, then he would have something with which to blackmail her, with which to make certain that when she went home the items would remain here.

And also a way to make certain that she would go home.

This was how Grateful Peace was thinking on the day that the package arrived for Lady Melina. It came by special messenger. She never received anything by regular mail, although she had commented that if the process of unlocking the magic in the three items took much longer she would need to make arrangements to get in touch with her family.

The messenger was not a man Peace recognized, anonymous in his striped robe and rather generic face paint. He gave the package to Lady Melina and departed quickly.

After the door closed, Lady Melina returned to her favorite seat upon the sofa. She hefted the package on the palm of her open hand, as if trying to judge the contents by the weight. A slight, mysterious smile just touched her lips.

Peace lifted the spyglass he had ready with him for just such an instance. He shifted to a peephole from which he knew he could get a view of the contents.

Lady Melina cut the heavy twine that tied the parcel shut, undid the waxed wrapping cloth on the outside, then undid the lighter cloth wrapping on the inside. The box itself was crafted from a dark polished wood, the latch sealed with wax. The wax bore an impression, as from a ring.

Grateful Peace focused his spyglass more tightly and got a clear look at the seal: a wavy line with seemingly random bumps in it, a line that curved around to meet itself at its beginning. He felt a slight chill of recognition: Endbrook— the emblem of Lord Waln, whom all had given up for dead.

Moving more quickly now, Lady Melina inspected the latch. It opened with a snap that Peace heard quite clearly even from his hiding place.

Lady Melina raised the lid and stared down at the contents. Two slim peach-colored things rested in the box, nestled in a bed of some rough crystal. Each was vaguely crescent-shaped and tipped at the wider end with reddish brown. After a moment, Peace realized that they were human fingers—small ones, as from a child's hand.

Next to them rested a small gemstone, multifaceted and possessed of a deep reddish gold hue. A citrine, Peace thought, or a topaz. He knew gems well, having often portrayed them in his days as an active illuminator. Pinned beside the gem, so that it encircled it, was a curl of hair the precise color of the jewel.

Only when the box was jerked suddenly from out of his line of sight did Peace lower his telescope and look at Lady Melina's face. Beneath the paint she was beginning to affect even when she was alone he could see that her expression was serious, even mildly affronted.

Lady Melina sat very still for about a quarter of an hour, the box open in her lap, its grisly trophies visible for so long that Peace had ample opportunity to inspect them. A child's fingers, fairly recently cut, preserved, doubtless, by the cold weather and by the salt crystals in which they had been packed. Fingers from a left hand, he thought, but he couldn't be certain.

Eventually, Lady Melina rose and carried the box to the fireplace. She laid the fingers among the coals and stood watching as they blackened and charred. Peace caught a faint whiff of burning flesh, and wrinkled his nose in distaste. Lady Melina only blinked slightly as if the smoke had stung her eyes. When the fingers were nothing but two black curves, she broke up the remains with a poker and stirred them into ash.

Tossing the salt onto the flames, which it turned temporarily blue, Lady Melina put the box with her belongings, the gem in her jewel case. Then she rang for a servant and returned to her seat on the sofa. When a young woman appeared, Lady Melina looked up from the book she had reopened across her lap and said:

"There's a bad odor in the room, Tipi. Could you bring some rose petals to strew on the fire?"

The maid bowed and vanished.

Peace continued to watch, paralyzed with disbelief. Lady Melina had a daughter named Sapphire—the Crown Princess of Hawk Haven. He knew that her son and heir apparent was named Jet. Was it impossible that she also had a child named Topaz—or maybe Citrine?

He thought she might. That seemed to fit with his recollections.

Two fingers from a child, a lock of hair, a stone that gave a name, the seal of Baron Endbrook—a threat, a warning, a promise of future harm . . . or a notification of harm done.

Whatever had been in that box, surely Lady Melina had read the signs as easily as Peace himself had done.

"Give back what you have stolen or the child will suffer."

And she had calmly burnt the fingers and returned to her research.

Not even the scent of rose petals could make the air seem sweet after that.

XXVII

FIREKEEPER WAS LEARNING the exhilaration of a new kind of chase. Assisted by Elation, by Bold—the crow who had so patiently tracked Lady Melina to Dragon's Breath—and by Derian, the wolf-woman exalted that she was drawing closer to her goal.

Dragon's Breath was no longer merely an intimidating cluster of stone walls, stinking alleyways, and twisting streets. Under the enthusiastic tutelage of the innkeeper's boy, it had resolved into landmarks, even into districts. Oddly, by the time seven days had passed, Firekeeper knew this city far better than she had ever known Eagle's Nest.

Driven by a need to know this new territory in which she was forced to hunt, Firekeeper made herself go out every day, made herself listen as the innkeeper's boy recited the names of buildings, of streets, even of important people. Her dreams swirled with peculiar-sounding place names, twisted them around their Pellish meanings.

Aswatano, the Fountain Court. Gyria Aitulla, the Wizard's Tower. Urnacia, the Sand Melter.

Nor did the feral human confine her prowling to daytime. Each night when her comrades believed her sound asleep in the stable, Firekeeper slipped out into the darkness. Blind Seer pacing beside her was enough to dissuade any of the curs who scavenged through the icy streets.

Something inhuman in her own body language kept two-legged predators at bay. Indeed, they may have disbelieved what their own eyes glimpsed in the glow of moon or starlight. In a concession to the winter cold, Firekeeper now wore her trousers long enough to be tucked into the tops of her boots. Her vest was now lined with fur, but she disdained sleeves lest they drag against her arms. A brown wool cap trimmed with fur was suffered to cover her head—a concession not to cold but to the tendency of the trailing ends of her roughly cut hair to get in her eyes.

So lightly clad, so silent in her movement was she that any human prowlers might have believed they glimpsed some wizard's summoning roaming the streets by night on its master's business, and even the worst elements of Dragon's Breath's nightside knew better than to tangle with wizard's work.

By daylight, Firekeeper and Blind Seer did not dare go too close to the palaces in which the most highly ranked members of the various sodalities worked their art. These were beyond the purview of any foreigner except by specific invitation. By night Firekeeper was under no such constraint. She melted into the shadows and vaulted over polished walls, prowling through the winter gardens and leaving behind only the occasional mark of a slim booted foot—and even these only rarely, for Race Forester had taught her how to eliminate the gross marks of her passage.

One night in the garden of the Beast Lorists she was confronted by a brace of tame snow leopards. These massive cats were more naturally gifted in weaponry, but there was a difference between them—they were tame, but Firekeeper was not.

The wolf-woman knew, too, the difference between courage and foolhardiness. She found no dishonor in fleeing a more powerful opponent. After confusing the snow leopards and luring them into a tangle of shrubbery, Firekeeper climbed up and over the wall. Come morning, the leopards' keepers found their charges angry and frustrated, but could offer no better explanation than that some fisher or weasel had come to taunt them in the night.

But even before she knew its true nature, one cluster of buildings teased at Firekeeper, tempting and promising wondrous things. These were Thendulla Lypella, the Earth Spires, the place where the Healed One, king of New Kelvin, lived, the center from which the Dragon Speaker ruled.

Thendulla Lypella stood at a high point at the city's northernmost edge, a cluster of tall, slim towers that reduced to seeming insignificance the complex of interconnected buildings at their base. The towers were crafted of smoothly polished stone and glowed pure white in some lights, pale silver in others, twilight-blue when the sun was at its palest. Some were topped with cone-shaped roofs, shingled in intricately patterned slate. Others were flat-topped, ringed with crenellated battlements that reminded Firekeeper of broken teeth.

No more than a half-dozen people, their young guide told Derian and Firekeeper with peculiar pride, knew their way through the entire complex.

Derian had commented that this seemed a highly inconvenient way to run a center of government, to which the innkeeper's son had replied with that peculiarly New Kelvinese air of superiority that not everyone could learn the mazes that connected the Earth Spires, for they were deliberately kept confusing through the use of magic.

Firekeeper wondered whether this was true. By means of magic—or sometimes by means of *ancient* magic—seemed to be the boy's most common explanation for anything complicated or confusing. One rather messy night, she'd learned herself about the existence of underground sewers of which the boy was apparently ignorant. *He'd* bragged that the city's waste was carried away by magic.

Magic or not, the area surrounding Thendulla Lypella did seem the best guarded of any point in the city. As of yet, the wolf-woman hadn't found a way inside. The walls were inconveniently high for climbing. Even if she had managed to find foot- and toeholds on their smoothly finished sides, their tops sloped to a gradual peak that discouraged gripping fingers.

Each of the five gates was constantly guarded, even the broad one nearest to the kitchens where boring things like food supplies and clean laundry were delivered. Firekeeper supposed she could hide herself in one of the supply carts if necessary, but that would mean leaving Blind Seer behind. A slim young woman might hide amid bags of clean sheets; a huge wolf could not.

Firekeeper was beginning to hope that she would not need to penetrate Thendulla Lypella at all when Bold located the artifacts.

The crow had spent much of each day patiently soaring around each of Thendulla Lypella's polished stone spires, inspecting each of the buildings below, which—though small in comparison with the spires themselves—sometimes rose to as many as five stories. With a patience and determination for which his kind was not widely celebrated, Bold landed on windowsills or perched on the edges of parapets—anything to get a glimpse inside.

The peregrine Elation acted as the crow's guardian, and kept him on course when the maze of walls confused him and threatened to send him back over terrain already covered. Elation longed to join the search herself, but knew that she was a showy bird of a type coveted by humans. Moreover, she did not understand the language of New Kelvin and lacked the crow's facility for learning.

In the end, that knowledge of language proved to be the key, though as Derian later commented, no one without wings could have hoped to overhear the conversation that had cinched the crow's suspicions.

Bold had perched on one of the crenellated battlements of a certain tower that for some days had attracted his attention. What had first drawn his attention had been the interesting smells eddying from its vicinity.

First, there was burning, as of many braziers and warming pans. Nearly to a one—Firekeeper did not feel herself a fit judge—the humans felt that even New Kelvinese, mad as they were about tradition, would not choose to winter in tower rooms when, as observation showed, there were plenty of empty rooms equipped with chimneys and other such modern conveniences. So Bold had begun to center his search around this tower.

What was being burned was even more interesting. Bold and Elation scented not just wood and charcoal, as one might expect if a sudden influx of visitors had necessitated these towers being turned into living quarters. They smelled herbs and spices, bone and blood, even melted metals. Had the reek been in the vicinity of the Alchemists' Hall—they were too wise to the dangers of their craft to maintain anything as lofty as a palace—the birds might not have questioned it, but here among the Earth Spires it was an unusual combination.

The spire's windows were opened from time to time, as if a cross draft was welcome despite the chill it brought. Unfortunately, the smooth façade of the structure as a whole had not included jutting exterior windowsills in its design. When the winds whipped about the structures, Bold was often beaten away from his precarious perch and had to make his laborious return on wings that ached increasingly with the passage of days.

He took to perching on the parapets to rest, protecting himself from the winds by huddling between the crenellated battlements. Taking pity on him, Elation dropped the crow things to eat, including things a falcon found rather nasty, like bread soaked in bacon fat. She knew, however, what such flying took out of even her and admired the smaller bird's persistence.

Had it not been for his jealous refusal to abandon one such

morsel, Bold would probably have flown away when the two humans emerged onto the parapets. This would not have been cowardice, but reflex. A wild bird, even a Royal Crow, did not linger near humans willingly.

The two humans were apparently seeking a breath of air untainted by smoke and other foul odors, for they reeked of burnt bone and hot metal. They were clad alike in serviceable robes of pale grey, their sleeves tied back from their hands. Their faces were uniformly scarlet, though tattooing showed through the paint. The whites of their eyes were nearly as red as the smeared paints on their faces. Yet for all this, they were cheerful.

"That last may have done it," said one. "I swear I saw an image move within the glass."

"As did I," his companion agreed. "A faint figure but sure. It was deep blue, like a midsummer sky at evening. There was nothing of that color in the room for the mirror to reflect back to us."

"I concur," the first said. "All of us wear working paint and robes: red and dirty white. The walls are grey stone, the carpets old and their colors muddy. Nothing could have given back that hue."

The two men went on in this fashion for some time, repeating as excited people will the details of their victory, embellishing with some small anecdote or flourish until Bold felt as if he had been within the room.

Piece of bread now swallowed, the crow hopped from foot to foot, wondering if he should fly away to spread the news he had or wait to hear more.

"That makes one of the three," the first continued, stilling the crow in his impatience. "The ring and the comb have yet to yield their secrets."

"And even the mirror only begins," blinking his bloodshot eyes. "We are at the beginning of a long road."

"But now," the first encouraged him, "we know this is a road worth traveling. We know for certain that the foreign woman has not led us astray for some odd purpose of her own."

"True," the second replied, then added with some haste, "but then I never doubted her veracity and trustworthiness."

"Never!" the first agreed.

It seemed to Bold that they glanced around uncomfortably, especially at the door they had left blocked open behind them.

"We should be going in now," the first continued. "The thaumaturges will be eager to make another attempt."

"Indeed."

"Leave the door open or closed?"

"Close it for now. We could use the ventilation, but I'm not taking initiative. Tempers are too short."

The sealing of the heavy door closed off any further sound, but Bold had already leapt into the air. A black arrow with glinting eyes, he swept from the heights, plummeting down with all possible speed.

Elation's dive was swifter still, and the peregrine banked at the crow's side.

"News?" she shrieked.

"Find the wolf-child!" Bold replied. "I'll be at the stables. How my wings hurt!"

But the falcon was already gone, and so the crow preserved his pride.

When Firekeeper heard Bold's report she didn't know whether to be elated or dismayed. True, the artifacts were found, but how was she to get to them? The spire in which the New Kelvinese were working was at the heart of the cluster.

Praising Bold, she went to find her comrades. Maybe they would have some solution to what seemed to her an insoluble puzzle.

When Firekeeper came panting up to him with her news, Derian arranged a meeting in Doc's consulting room. Hasamemorri had already shown herself vastly curious about the peculiar activities of her foreign tenants, hauling her tremendous bulk down the stairs on any excuse.

Usually Hasamemorri restricted her visits to the shared kitchen or to offering comfort to the patients in the infirmary. She was far too much in awe of Sir Jared to invade his consulting room without invitation or appointment.

Business was over for the day—barring an accident like the one that had done so much to spread the word of Doc's talent. The evening meal had also been finished—Wendee's preparations being of the sort that could not wait without being ruined.

Happily, Derian thought, *Firekeeper still has that wolfish reverence for food. Even though she's nearly out of her skin with worry, she won't let food go to waste. I don't think she thought much of the mushroom omelet, though.*

Now, however, both meal and washing up completed, the household gathered in the consulting room. Wendee handed around mugs of tea—some exotic blend that Oculios the alchemist had given to Doc. It smelled like the spices Derian's mother hoarded for special baking projects, carrying within the warm scent an unexpected surge of longing for home.

Stirring a dripping spoonful of honey into his cup, Derian looked over to where Firekeeper sat on the floor, her hand resting on Blind Seer's head. The wolf was apparently asleep. Bold and Elation sat rather more alertly on the perches that Lord Edlin had made for them, Bold turning a piece of bread over and over in his claw as if looking for the best place to begin eating it.

Both Elise and Doc looked as if they would welcome a good night's sleep rather than a tactical counsel. Although their medical practice didn't quite have customers lining along the street, they had attracted an unprecedented amount of business in a mere handful of days.

Last night, both had been up late helping deliver a baby. Mother and child had survived, much to the astonishment of the midwife, who had loudly protested against the father's bringing in not only a foreigner but a *male*. Elise's fluency and tact had both been tested on that call.

Turning to Firekeeper, Derian asked, "Do you want me to summarize what you told me earlier?"

The wolf-woman nodded gratefully. As was often the case when she was excited, she had lost a good deal of her command of the language.

Derian noted Wendee's slightly disapproving frown. She felt that Firekeeper needed to overcome her tendency to depend on others to smooth the way through awkward human interactions. This time, Derian chose to ignore Wendee's advice—though largely he agreed.

"The big news first," he said. "Firekeeper has located the missing artifacts."

An indignant caw that needed no translation interrupted him before he could go further.

"Excuse me," Derian corrected himself. "Bold located the missing artifacts—or thinks he has. Elation, however, is inclined to agree. She went back for a second look after she found Firekeeper and told her to wait for Bold at the stables."

No one interrupted as Derian summarized the account Firekeeper had given him earlier, not even Lord Edlin, who had shown a disconcerting tendency to verbal ejaculations along the lines of "What?" and "Astonishing!" This time the young heir apparent to the Kestrel Duchy simply sat grinning foolishly, as if he was listening to some bardic lay rather than being intimate to an unfolding crisis.

I suppose we're all somewhat to blame for that, Derian thought. *We've kept Lord Edlin in the background ever since he joined us, even though the very manner of his joining us should have made us see his value. I suppose it's that grin of his and the way he makes calf-eyes at Firekeeper. He seems like such a boy.*

When Derian finished, however, it was Edlin who spoke first.

"Well, that's really wonderful," he said, grinning from ear to ear. "Wonderful! Wonderful! But, I say, what are we going to do next? I don't imagine that Elation and Bold can just nip in there and fetch out these artifacts? They don't sound too big, not if what Bold heard is right—a ring, a comb, and a mirror, what?"

Derian found himself turning to the birds, as if they could speak, but of course it was Firekeeper who replied. Her expression said quite clearly that though she hadn't understood half of Edlin's babbling, she had caught the gist.

"Bold no think they can," she said seriously, something in her manner making clear that the matter had been discussed at length. "He say the door to the top close from down."

"Do you mean the door from the roof closes from below?" Wendee asked.

"That right," Firekeeper said impatiently. "So I say."

Wendee didn't say anything further, but her expression commented eloquently, *"Not quite, Lady Firekeeper."*

Edlin went on cheerfully. "Well, if it closes from below, I guess it opens from there too, what?"

Firekeeper blinked at him, then nodded.

"Windows," she continued, "there are, on each—" She frowned, hunting for a word. "—level of tower. Windows are closed most of time and when open windows have—" She waved her hand in the air, miming some obstruction.

"Bars?" Edlin guessed brightly, as if this was some party game.

Firekeeper frowned at him.

"Not just bars, I think." She glanced around the room, her gaze coming to rest on the patterned wooden screen that Doc used to grant privacy when a patient was too shy to undress before him.

"More like that, I think," she said.

Elation made a staccato cacking sound. Firekeeper nodded and corrected herself.

"Like that but with bigger holes," she said. "Still, holes too small for even Royal Crow."

Now it was Bold's turn to interrupt. His caw was accompanied by a rippling of his feathers that Derian felt certain carried as much meaning as the sounds he made.

"Bold say," Firekeeper translated patiently, "that he could get through and maybe out with something small—like a ring is small—but not with mirror or comb if they any size. Crows," she added, "are great thieves."

Elise, leaning back in her chair with her eyes half-closed, asked drowsily:

"Have either Bold or Elation actually seen the artifacts? Maybe they are all small enough to be squeezed out through the screen."

"Not have see," Firekeeper replied. "Will try later. Seems that work goes on in tower even after dark has come."

"Good," Elise said. "The birds can see in the dark then?"

Firekeeper paused, then said:

"No more than me, but they not need much light to fly to tower and tower have light inside."

Derian refrained from commenting that Firekeeper saw far better in the night than he himself did.

"I say," Edlin said. "Won't they be taking a risk, though? What about owls?"

Elation screeched in obvious indignation, but something about Bold's shrinking posture seemed to say that the Royal Crow had indeed considered the possibility.

"They go," Firekeeper said, her stern brown gaze firmly on the two birds. "Elation protect Bold."

"From what I gathered back at Revelation Point Castle," said Doc, rather unexpectedly, "I don't think we're going to find that all of these artifacts can be squeezed through the window lattice even by a very clever crow. How do we get to them? From what Bold reported, it sounds as if the New Kelvinese have learned how at least one of the artifacts works. I don't like the idea of giving them time to figure out the others."

That brought even Elise out of her doze.

"How long do you think we have?" she asked anxiously.

"I don't know," Doc said, "but I can't help but wonder if in magic, as in medicine, finding the right course of treatment is more than half the cure."

Firekeeper looked confused.

"You mean if they make mirror do magic, soon they make ring and comb and mirror all do magic?"

"That's what I'm afraid of," Doc admitted.

In a single supple movement, Firekeeper rose and crossed to the window. She unlatched it and flung it open. In response to some command unheard by the humans, crow and falcon swept out the window into the night. Blind Seer was a bound behind them.

"I say!" said Edlin admiringly.

"They go," Firekeeper explained as she closed and latched the window, "and start more scout. Blind Seer go and listen in case they have trouble."

"What can he do?" Derian asked. "Aren't the walls too high for him to get inside?"

"He can do nothing," Firekeeper admitted, a trace of her own frustration showing, "but at least we will know."

She settled herself onto the hearth rug again.

"Now, how we get inside?"

Various plans were suggested but all came up against the same problem—even if one or more of their company did get inside, no one knew how to find their way about. The inn-keeper's boy's statement that the interior of Thendulla Lypella was a maze kept coming back to trouble them.

"And even," Elise said, rubbing her eyes as she repeated a point raised earlier, "if we do get someone inside, only two of us speak the language with some facility—and neither Wen-dee nor myself are the people I would pick for a dangerous raid."

"Not plan to talk," Firekeeper growled. "Plan to take."

"Nice in theory," Wendee said dryly, "but it may not be so easy."

"I say," Edlin said, somewhat diffidently. "It seems to me that our problems fall into two categories, what?"

They all turned to look at him.

"Well, there's how to get inside—we've worked out several possibilities for that: the laundry or grocery way, checking out the sewers, finding a way over the walls, hunting for secret passages . . ."

He grinned. This last had been his own suggestion.

"We've figured we can do disguises, too. So that's one category. The other problem is how to find our way around when we're inside."

"That's right, my lord," Derian said politely.

"Well, I say," Edlin said. "Is there any reason we can't make a map? I mean, the birds—when they come back—they've been up over the place. They can tell Firekeeper what they've seen and she can write it down for us."

Firekeeper looked at Edlin with the same sort of astonishment most people would show if a dog started talking sense. Then she frowned.

"I no can write," she admitted a bit shamefacedly.

Her failure to learn to read and write was a matter of ongoing contention between her and her various advisors. Only recently had she admitted that there might be a use for the skill, and then only privately to Derian.

Derian hastened to intercede before what seemed like quite a good idea could be ruined by a technical detail.

"We can work something out," he said. "You could translate for the birds and I could do the writing. Actually, we may want to draw a map. I'm not much good at that but . . ."

"I am," Edlin interrupted, blushing slightly. "I mean, I've had some training. Part of the education to be a war leader someday, you know."

"Then," Firekeeper said with some reluctance, studying her adopted brother through narrowed eyes, "we work together like a pack."

Edlin beamed.

Even through his relief that at least an intermediate solution had been found, Derian resolved to stay in the vicinity while the map was being worked on, just in case. Firekeeper might be needed to translate for the birds, but he suspected that *he* might be needed to translate for Lord Edlin.

GRATEFUL PEACE would have brought his concerns about Lady Melina before Apheros immediately, but the Dragon Speaker was in conferences and could not be interrupted—at least for anything short of a declaration of war or some other major disaster.

Suspicions about the moral character of an ally, especially one whom Apheros was coming to increasingly favor, did not fall into that category.

Before Grateful Peace could obtain the private audience he required, news came from the Granite Tower that the mirror had been forced to yield up at least some of its secrets.

Peace hastened to witness the report of the research group before the Healed One and Dragon Speaker. The meeting was scheduled to permit the researchers time to change from their drab working robes and scarlet face paint to something more suitable for such an important audience.

Peace, however, could not get Apheros alone even for a moment. He was too busy preparing himself for the audience. Finally, Peace resigned himself to waiting until later.

Lady Melina, her eyes now glittering crystalline ornaments around which a serpentine pattern made its painted course over the upper portion of her face, was the modest and self-effacing heart of the trio who reported their success to Apheros. Yet for all that either of her companions—Posa the Illuminator and Zahlia the Smith—spoke three sentences to any one from her, Peace had the eerie sensation that Lady Melina was the one who commanded.

"After several days spent attempting promising rituals and incantations left to us in the writings of the first Healed One," said Zahlia in impressive rolling cadences far richer than the shouts she used when working over her forges, "we accepted the suggestion of our esteemed foreign advisor, Lady Melina Shield, and attempted to combine our incantations with manipulation of various carved portions on the frame of the mirror itself."

Posa took up the report, offering first a slight bow to Lady Melina, as if acknowledging that she only sang her praises.

"Early investigation had revealed that several portions of

the mirror's frame concealed small compartments. Analysis of these compartments showed that despite the passage of time and many years in clumsy barbarian hands, traces of powder remained.

"We analyzed the powder and, when merely manipulating the mirror did not prove sufficient—even when combined with the wondrous incantations of the first Healed One—we tried refilling the compartments with appropriate powders."

Lady Melina smiled upon king and minister both.

"To our joy and wonder," she said, her voice filling the chamber despite the superficial softness of its tone, "the experiment worked. A shadowy figure clad in a blue robe of a hue that all confirmed was not present in the tower room at that time appeared in the face of the mirror."

Zahlia took up the tale again, seemingly unaware that she had been upstaged for the most important single part. As she droned on about the duration that the apparition had appeared, about plans to renew the attempt and confirm what was essential, and similar details, Peace scanned the room as was his custom and duty.

On the faces of those privileged to witness this audience he saw a variety of responses—astonishment, pleasure, awe, joy, even a trace of jealousy from those members of the Defeatists who had been loudly proclaiming that magic was not the means to power and prosperity.

His training alerted him to something peculiar about the dynamics of the gathering, even before his conscious mind could isolate what it was. As Zahlia and Posa droned on, embellishing on their plans and all but openly bragging about their success, Peace isolated the wrongness.

All about the room, the little person-to-person interactions that would be usual at such an audience—even one where the Healed One was present—were reduced. They still went on where those of comparatively lesser importance were grouped—a nudge, a wink, a quick whisper or scribbling of a note. Among those of highest rank—even those members of the Defeatists who should be thinking of how to shift this development to their own advantage—there was nothing.

They listened to the speakers with rapt attention, nodding or frowning when appropriate, even laughing at an inadvertent pun on Posa's part, but still there was a singular lack of spontaneity among them. Peace noticed how their gazes continually drifted to the trio of speakers—even when it might have been more appropriate for one or more to be glancing at the Healed One or Apheros—to judge their reactions.

After a time, Grateful Peace became certain that it was not the entire trio they were looking toward, but rather to Lady Melina alone.

Once he became aware of the wordless pull the foreign woman was exerting, Peace himself realized that he had to struggle not to look into her eyes whenever she glanced in his direction.

Each time her gaze drifted through the quarter of the room where he was seated, Peace found himself fighting a luxurious lassitude similar to the sensation of drifting off into sleep. He succeeded mostly because of the nature of his location in the room—as usual he was set off to one side where he could watch and report rather than in the front—and because Lady Melina continued to dismiss him as less than important.

Or maybe, Grateful Peace thought, a cold chill penetrating to the very center of his heart, *she believes me already lulled and thinks that she need not renew her hold on me. What sorcery might she have worked during our long talks in the sleigh on the way to Dragon's Breath? Certainly, I talked more freely to her then than I usually would to some dubious foreigner.*

The idea was so startling and so terrifying that Peace nearly lost track of what was being said. Long practice made it possible for him to scan the room without seeming to move even his eyes. What he saw frightened him to the core.

Apheros, the Dragon Speaker, listened to the report with solemn dignity, gravely shifting his attention from one speaker to the next. Yet to Peace, who had known him for years— who had long ago been chosen as a member of this Dragon's Three—there was a diminution of the animating spark.

This was the Apheros the outer world regularly saw—the

act he put on his constituents. What was missing was the true Apheros, the signs of which Peace had long ago learned to watch for. Anger and arrogance were as natural to Apheros as were gravity and dignity—and more normal. They were the fires from which his ambition to power had been lit: anger when things were not done as he thought they should be, arrogance that his way was best.

And his gaze never drifts to me as it usually would, Peace thought. *That's what I've been missing! That casual looking that is not looking, the checking to learn what I have seen so that he may anticipate trouble or encourage a supporter. Apheros is like an actor expertly playing the part of a politician, but the politician is not there.*

The thaumaturge had no doubt who was writing Apheros's script. His only question was how she had managed it. Surely it had something to do with how her gaze restlessly played over the room. Under the guise of awed foreign visitor inspecting the gathering of the Primes, she was keeping her hand tight on invisible reins.

With a sudden chill Grateful Peace realized that here in this very chamber sorcery was being performed, sorcery so subtle that perhaps only a victim on the edge of the spell's power could have detected its workings.

This realization was followed by one even more terrible. After a lifetime devoted to the reawakening of the power of magic within his land, Grateful Peace looked upon the invisible force of sorcery and realized that if this was magic he wanted nothing to do with it.

Treasonous as the thought might be, Peace recognized that what he felt as he looked upon true magic was not desire, but fear.

XXVIII

MAKING A MAP OF THENDULLA LYPELLA proved
to be a laborious process. First of all, it could not be
escaped that the birds saw differently not only from humans, but from each other. The falcon's eye was keener,
meant to distinguish the movements of field mice and
rabbits among often self-colored surroundings.

The eye of the crow was more oriented toward the general,
more, Derian thought, like that of a human. Where Elation
saw movement, Bold saw *difference*—that which had not been
present at an earlier time. This was necessary, of course, for
a creature who made many of its meals from carrion.

Moreover, neither crow nor falcon tended to distinguish
man-made landscape features from natural features. That these
two were Royal Beasts, sophisticated beyond their lesser cousins and educated by experience, made the task simpler. After
a few requests, they learned to state whether the feature they
were describing was natural or created—or at least if they
were uncertain.

Had Derian not been responsible for Firekeeper's earliest
education in human society—a time when she, too, had struggled to grasp that oddly shaped hillsides might be made by
humans and called houses or castles—he might have given up
in frustration.

Then there was the problem of Firekeeper herself. Although
she was learning to use maps, even beginning to accept that
flat two-dimensional sketches might represent a much more
complex reality, it was another matter to have her to look upon
the work in process and tell whether or not art represented
reality.

Oddly enough, the birds themselves intervened before the

situation could become a deadlock. They were accustomed to seeing the landscape from above and thus had less trouble accepting the "bird's-eye view" that cartographers had adopted as a convention.

Once they understood how a circle might represent an entire tower, how a pair of lines might represent a road, how a thicker line might represent a wall, they were quite willing to critique Edlin's efforts. Bold, with his sharper eye for detail, was the harder to satisfy, but in the end even the crow was satisfied.

The spire in which Bold had pinpointed the New Kelvinese at work was situated among many surrounding buildings. Distances would have been difficult to estimate, for the wingéd folk rarely worried about any distance that could be traversed in a short flight, but here the towering height of the spires themselves assisted.

Lord Edlin had little trouble estimating the spires' relative heights and distances from each other, a thing Firekeeper found untellingly annoying.

"If he do that," she complained to Derian after they had finished and the birds had been sent off to continue gathering information, "why we do all this with the wingéd folk? He just draw from his own eyes then. Surely even he see that towers must rest on earth even if we cannot see that."

Derian shook his head. They had stepped outside for a breath of fresh air. The air was crisp, the light almost impossibly clear and bright. He had seated himself on a bench backing the stone wall of the house. Cold seeped up through his coat and trousers.

"Don't be a pig, Firekeeper," he replied wearily—the mapping had been hard on him, even if he hadn't had to draw a line. To him had fallen the job of translating for Firekeeper as she translated for the birds.

"We needed to know what lies *between* the spires," Derian went on. "Many of them—as you well know—are mounted on the tops of other buildings. Since we can't fly, we're going to need to go in from the bottom up. That means knowing what's at the bottom—where the paths are, where the guards are, where the cover is, even where we might create the best distraction from outside."

Firekeeper grimaced, but accepted Derian's reprimand without protest. It was, Derian thought, one of the advantages to her wolf mentality. She accepted criticism and correction—when merited—far more easily than most humans her age did.

Fleetingly, Derian thought of his sister, Damita, and her increasingly frequent arguments with their mother. Dami was a few years younger than Firekeeper, but as she grew into her woman's body she was less willing to accept her mother's guidance, was more and more eager to prove herself an adult.

But Firekeeper, Derian thought with a sudden flash of understanding, *doesn't need to prove that to anyone. She's proven herself to wolves and humans alike—and now apparently to the Royal Beasts as well or they wouldn't have given her this task.*

Thinking of Damita made Derian fleetingly homesick. He knew that Elise had begun writing home now that it would be impossible for Baron Archer to force her to return. Derian thought he should start doing so himself.

If I can find the energy, he thought, heaving himself to his feet. Firekeeper—and the ever-present Blind Seer—had vanished while he was lost in thought and when he opened the kitchen door he could hear her inside chivying Edlin.

"But what is that?"

"A map of the exterior of the spire we need to get inside," Edlin replied.

Derian waited for him to add "What?" or "I say!" or another of his numerous verbal ticks, but none followed.

Firekeeper said slowly, "But the tower—tower is spire, yes?"

"Pretty much," Edlin said, "though usually spires are thinner, pointed on top. Towers can be any tall building, either part of a building or standing on their own. Spires are usually on the tops of towers, right?"

Derian hurried back inside. It sounded like trouble was brewing. When he entered the surgery, which, because of its superior lighting, had been turned into a drafting room, he found that Firekeeper had crossed to a window and was look-ing out across the skyline toward the complex in question.

"Why," she continued, ignoring Derian's entry, "do we then call Thendulla Lypella the Earth Spires? Some have points, but some do not."

"I say," Edlin said, moving to stand next to her, "you're right, you know. There are as many towers as spires. I really don't know why they call it that."

Derian interrupted.

"You'd need to ask Elise about that," he said, "or Wendee. They're our translators."

"Oh."

Firekeeper gave one more hard stare out the window, then drifted back to inspect Edlin's latest sketch.

"This is the tower-spire?" she asked. "The one we need to get into?"

"That's right," Edlin replied. "From what you told me ear-lier—from what Bold and Elation told you, what?—I knew how many levels there were. I can even see some of the win-dows from here. I thought we might like a sketch onto which we can add our notes—you know—this window looks in on a small room, this onto a big one, what?"

"I say!" Derian said. "That's a great idea."

Only after the words had escaped him did he realize he'd fallen into unconscious mimicry. Edlin's pattern of speech was contagious. He bit his lip, terrified that the young lord would take offense, but Edlin had only heard the praise.

"Pretty good, eh?" he said complacently. "It should help save time. No need to go charging in through a door if we know it leads to a closet or something."

Relieved that he hadn't given offense, Derian forbore from commenting that a window wasn't likely to be wasted on a closet. Edlin's logic was good, even if he wasn't the best at expressing what he meant.

Firekeeper, however, stood scowling at the drawing.

"But it is," she waved her hands in the air, miming straight lines, "like this—a box. The tower-spire is a round."

"Cylinder," Derian said automatically.

Edlin shook his head at her.

"Never happy, what?"

He picked up the stick of charcoal he'd been using to rough out his drawing and sketched in a few more lines. Derian wasn't sure how he managed, but suddenly the elongated rectangle possessed a visible quality of roundness.

Firekeeper blinked at the drawing, tilting her head slightly as if willing her mind to accept the representation. Then she smiled.

"Yes! That is more like, but this is—what?—maybe one half?"

"About a half," Edlin agreed. "I can't draw the entire spire in one drawing. It doesn't really have sides—not like a house does—but there's more to it than I can show. I could make a model . . ."

He selected a piece of paper and drew what to Derian's eyes seemed like a few random lines; then he rolled it into a cylinder and set it on one end. The lines marked where the windows were on the tower.

Firekeeper hit her thigh in a sharp clap of applause.

"I see!" she crowed.

"That's right," Edlin said approvingly, letting the cylinder fall flat again. "But for what we need, it's better to be less literal. It's hard to make notes on something standing up and harder still to read them, right?"

"Right," Firekeeper agreed firmly.

It was apparent to Derian that Edlin had just leapt again in her estimation—perhaps even higher than he had done after their skirmish with the bandits. After all, Edlin had been helpful, but she and Blind Seer were proven the more effective fighters. Human arts, especially when they were useful ones, impressed the wolf-woman more.

Feeling slightly unsettled, Derian wondered if Edlin might actually succeed in his irregular courtship of his peculiar adopted sister. Certainly, for all his foolish mannerisms, Edlin had noticed what Firekeeper liked and was playing to those likings.

Unbidden, Derian remembered how the wolf-woman's lips

had brushed his cheek when she had departed for the western wilds. Derian fought down the memory, forcing himself to consider what Earl Kestrel would think if Edlin actually won Firekeeper's hand—for surely that reaction mattered more than what Derian himself might think or feel.

Seeking distraction from these uncomfortable thoughts, Derian glanced to where Blind Seer rested on the hearth rug, head on paws, blue eyes fixed unwinkingly on the young lord. Derian felt an uneasy surge of fear as he tried to decide what *Blind Seer* might feel about the idea of his pack mate joining with a human.

The giant wolf had become such a usual part of Derian's day that the young man no longer really saw him. He forced himself to do so now and felt his blood chill. Weeks of travel had honed away the fat the wolf had accumulated through easy living in the cities. Even through a thick winter coat, muscle was evident. As if sensing Derian's inspection, the wolf yawned in lazy arrogance, showing gleaming fangs set in jaws that could break a man's arm as a afterthought.

Derian felt visceral, atavistic fear flow through him. Looking upon Blind Seer, even though the wolf was at rest, he knew who was the hunter, who was the prey.

It seemed to Derian, as he watched Blind Seer's gaze, never wavering from Edlin Norwood, that Blind Seer knew so, too.

THE POSSIBLE SECRETS OF THE COMB were the matter under discussion that day, two days after Lady Melina and her associates had reported their success with the mirror.

On the day that had followed the initial report, the mirror, yielding to a complex series of rituals, had revealed itself as a device for scrying. Its range, however, appeared to be limited both by distance and by the scryer's own knowledge of the area being scried.

Despite this evident limitation, success—as heady as any

drink distilled or brewed—kept the researchers working night and day. Some felt that the right combination of powders would increase the mirror's range, others felt certain that the mirror possessed other powers whose secrets they would learn in time.

Following the lead of those who had been working with the mirror, the team dedicated to the ring had begun mixing various powders and secreting them in a minute compartment that had been discovered when the moonstone was slid free from its setting in the beast's jaws.

Once or twice, the stone had glowed with a pale, eldritch light, thus encouraging the researchers in their belief that—as with the mirror—the proper powders combined with the right words or the correct manipulation of the ring itself would grant them success.

The comb, however, had stubbornly refused to yield anything to those who had set themselves to discover the manner of its workings. Pry as they might, they could find no compartment into which an energizing powder might be placed.

Stoneworkers from among the most skilled members of the Sodality of Lapidaries had been called in to offer their opinions as to what material the comb might have been crafted from.

After some study, these had insisted that the material was both stone and plant—simply put, a plant that had been transformed into stone. They even claimed that originally the wood had been some form of oak, thus gaining the ire of the botanically minded among the researchers, who resented their arrogant certainty.

Moreover, there were those who insisted that this muddled the entire question of which type of spells were applicable. The first Healed One had dictated great volumes on the ways and traditions of magic. He had even broken with the long-established traditions of the Founders and set down some spells in writing.

Usually, as was the nearly universal custom of the colonial powers, those colonists who had shown promise in the magical arts had been sent back to the Old Country to be taught. They were only permitted to return home once they were initiated and their tongues sealed so that they might not unwittingly reveal that which would be dangerous to the untutored.

However, all of the material set down by the Healed One was firmly based on a single foundation—that magical power was best understood when studied in discrete units. These units had become the basis for the thirteen sodalities. Unhappily for those who must work with the comb, the fact that it was made of both stone and yet somehow of wood meant that it crossed the boundaries of two sodalities—the Lapidaries and the Herbalists—and these were jealous of their secrets.

Had it been the Lapidaries and the Smiths who had been so challenged there probably would not have been as many difficulties. These sodalities considered themselves closely allied. Among those who worked with the earth and those who worked with that which grew from it, however, there was a long rivalry, its origins lost in the days of reestablishment following the Burning Death.

Impatient with delays, the Dragon Speaker had commanded that these differences be set aside. Acidly, Apheros had reminded them that the teams working on the mirror and ring had progress to show whereas those who had devoted themselves to the comb had nothing.

Lady Melina had insinuated herself into this meeting by offering her services as a mediator between factions. Even had she not ensorcelled many of those involved, Peace thought sourly, her offer would have been accepted. The truth was, it was a good offer—a wise offer—for she alone stood outside of these rivalries and could not be said to entertain favoritism even by extension or alliance.

Peace himself was present in his role as a member of the Dragon's Three. He noted with a certain degree of ironic detachment that Lady Melina had begun to treat him with a touch more interest and deference. One of her tools, he supposed, must have told her precisely who the Dragon's Three were and how influential they could be.

Grateful Peace forced himself to be courteous to Lady Melina even though in reality her very proximity made his blood crawl. Claiming a touch of snow-blindness, he had taken to wearing tinted glasses even when indoors. The sensation of dwelling in ever-present twilight was a fair price to pay for the assurance that Lady Melina would experience some difficulty if she tried locking her gaze with his.

Moreover, the glasses made it easier for Peace to do the watching which was his primary role in Apheros's power system. Behind the tinted glass, his gaze might be resting anywhere, creating the impression that he was always watching. Honestly, he was a bit sorry that he hadn't thought of the idea before.

"I recall a tale," said old Columi, the round-bodied, round-headed emeritus of the Sodality of Lapidaries, " 'twas but a child's tale, but it 'twas about a comb and may have some bearing on this matter."

Urged on by the other members of the team, Columi went on:

"It was about a princess," he said, "or some such royal lady. She was in flight from enemies. I don't recall quite how it came about, but she had been forced to flee with little but what she had on her person. One of these things was a comb."

"A magical comb?" asked one of the listeners eagerly.

"The story doesn't precisely say," Columi admitted, "but it must have been one, for when the princess's pursuers—I'm fairly sure it was a princess, but it might have been a queen—drew close, she took the comb from her pocket and flung it down behind her steed. From where the comb fell, a mighty forest all of oaks, each growing as close to the other as the teeth had been on the comb, sprang into existence."

Peace watched with a trace of amusement as a half-dozen sets of eyes—Lady Melina's included—looked with a certain degree of respect upon the comb that rested on the center of the council table.

"And?" prompted Nelm of the Herbalists. "And what happened next?"

Columi looked at him in astonishment.

"Why the queen—or princess—escaped, at least for a time.

She had to work other tricks before she got completely clear of the bad lot who were after her."

"And the forest—the oak forest out of the comb," asked sweet-faced Kalvinia of the Sericulturalists, "did the forest remain thereafter?"

Columi frowned. "Don't recall. Don't think the tale says. Do you think it matters?"

"It might," Kalvinia replied, twirling around her fingers a braid of hair as light and as delicate as her own silk, "if the comb's powers can only work once. It would prove difficult if we suddenly had a forest burst into being in the middle of this tower room."

"Now, I don't precisely see . . ." Nelm was beginning, when there came a knock on the door.

They were holding their conference in a room on the second level of the Granite Tower. It was a large room, roughly half the breadth of the tower itself. Naturally it was rounded except for a single long, straight wall. The door to the central corridor was in this wall, and even as Nelm rose to answer the knock, the door was opened from without.

Young Kistlio, the former Illuminator and Peace's own sometime assistant, stood without. In the days that had passed since his own awareness of Lady Melina's powers had solidified, Peace had singled out Kistlio as one of those most completely under the foreign woman's power.

Where once he had been cool and aloof to her as was proper and correct, Kistlio now fawned. Peace did not know whether this meant that his nephew's mind or will or whatever it was that Lady Melina affected with her spells was weaker than the norm, or whether the woman had employed greater force in his enchantment.

A few others had commented on Kistlio's evident devotion to his new mistress. Many thought that this was precisely because she *was* the youth's mistress—in a far more carnal sense than was formally meant by the term.

Peace, however, had spent enough time spying on Lady Melina to feel fairly certain that whatever she did to assure Kistlio's excellent service, sexual favors were not included.

Indeed, she seemed as chaste as a winter snowbank—a thing that had disappointed the thaumaturge, for he had hoped to use her sexual activities to create resentment and anger between those she favored, and even between those she did not.

Kistlio burst into the room with a physical energy that reminded Grateful Peace just how young he was. The sleeves of his blue-black robe fluttered with the wind of his passage. His face, painted in a routine white on black geometric pattern assumed when on errands and the like, showed a slight smudging along one cheek, as if Kistlio had forgotten to school his hands.

This shocked Peace. Learning to never touch one's face in a fashion that might damage the paint was one of the earliest lessons any civilized person was taught. Even in rural areas where semipermanent stains were more common than the elaborate paints used by those who followed more intellectual pursuits, the mannerisms persisted and, indeed, were considered the first mark of good breeding.

Of course, he could have been jostled in a crowd, Peace thought, trying to comfort himself. He was fond of Kistlio. The boy had potential. That Lady Melina might ruin him . . .

Unbidden the image rose to mind of two small severed fingers, peach-colored crescents reduced to stinking ash.

"Lady Melina," cried Kistlio, all but flinging himself at her feet, "I bring you great news!"

Lady Melina, who had not spoken through all the long discussion except when a word was needed to turn away some bit of bickering, now turned to the boy.

"Stand straight," she said a trace severely, then softening added, "Now, what news is it you have for me?"

"Some of your countrymen have come to Dragon's Breath," Kistlio said proudly. "One at least is a sorcerer—though I am sure not of as great power as yourself. This one is a healer and all the city is singing his praises, for at a touch bones knit of themselves and wounds cease to bleed."

Lady Melina looked less than delighted at this news, but Kistlio did not seem to notice. Indeed, Peace noted that although there were several people of rank and merit in the chamber—himself included—Kistlio spoke as if no one were present except for Lady Melina.

"I heard of these strangers in the marketplace," the boy continued, "and went to look upon them. Other than the healer, there seems to be one other with power. She is a young woman, hardly more than a girl, and from what those living nearby told me she commands fearsome beasts—even as legend says those with the power of beast lore once did."

Although Peace kept his head angled as if watching only the boy, his gaze was on Lady Melina's face. The red stain she wore after the custom of New Kelvin kept him from reading her complexion, but he could have sworn that she shook—though whether in fury or in fear he could not be sure.

"And why do you tell me this?" Lady Melina asked, her voice unnaturally calm. "Surely there have been those from my country come here before."

Kistlio faltered, as if for the first time realizing that his news might be less than welcome.

And so he might have had the sense to consider, Peace thought bitterly, *had you not taken his will, Lady Melina. But when you steal will and mind, you steal sense as well.*

"I thought," the boy floundered, then continued more steadily, "I thought that the great lady might have use for those who, like her, practice the ways of foreign magic. I thought she might harness their powers to hers and make them serve her for her greater glory and for the glory of our land."

Lady Melina regained her composure during this brave little speech. Reaching out, she patted Kistlio on one shoulder.

"You have confused mere talent with art," she said gently. "These who you have seen possess something that is not common in my land but is not unheard of either. These talents are born into a person as might be eye color or perfect pitch or some other natural thing. Although talents have the semblance of sorcery, they are no more sorcerous than is the perfectly repeated song of a nightingale.

"Have you forgotten," Lady Melina asked, her tone taking on just a hint of reprimand, "that the study of sorcery is forbidden in Hawk Haven? I myself have been the solitary scholar of what is seen there as a horrid and dreadful art. So, my boy, I thank you for these tidings, but I do not believe I can turn these visitors to our use."

Kistlio gave Lady Melina a deep bow, one that signified not only acknowledgment of her words but his heartfelt relief at being forgiven.

He began to back away, anticipating dismissal. Lady Melina signified that she would have him wait.

"Tell me," she said, her tones as soft yet as binding as a silken cord, "tell me, did you learn the names of these strangers? Since they are from Hawk Haven, they may be known to me."

"Sir Jared Surcliffe is the healer," Kistlio replied, a trace of his earlier pleasure in bearing her news making his lips stumble over the unfamiliar syllables. "The one with the gift for beast lore . . ."

"No lore," corrected Lady Melina gently, "merely an affinity. Indeed, if I know the one of whom you speak, she is nearly a beast herself, poor, mad child."

"This mad woman," Kistlio continued obediently, "is called the Firekeeper."

"So I guessed," Lady Melina hissed. "I have met her before. Do these two have comrades?"

"Several," Kistlio confirmed. He looked a trace unhappy. "Though I did not get their names, gracious lady."

"I may be able to guess," Lady Melina said, "but I would be pleased if you learn them for me. Do not say for whom you ask—simply ask."

"That should be easy, Lady Melina," the boy said. "All their neighbors delight in speaking of them. They say having foreigners on their street is the best amusement winter can offer. One never knows what strange thing they will do next."

Lady Melina frowned at this. Doubtless she could not forget that she, too, was a foreigner, for all her mimicking of civilized ways. Perhaps she wondered what entertainment she might provide for an idle moment's gossip.

"Learn the foreigners' names," she commanded. "Now

leave us. Our small business has interrupted my distinguished hosts and colleagues long enough."

For the first time, Kistlio seemed to see those assembled— all of them of sufficient importance to merit his deepest respect at other times. He swept them collectively a deep bow, granted Lady Melina yet another obeisance, and left.

Although the door into the corridor was thick, Peace imagined he could hear the boy's booted feet running down the corridor. Doubtless he was heading outside once more, never mind the cold and the gathering dusk.

"I humbly apologize," Lady Melina said, displaying a convincing facsimile of just those emotions. "Shall we continue?"

As if they were puppets on a stage set, the team members picked up their discussion nearly where it had left off.

"As I was saying," Nelm said, "I don't precisely see how this tale Columi just told us relates to our specific problem. Does he wish us to throw down the comb? What words should we say? Must we be pursued by enemies to make the magic work? Would it only work for a woman?"

Kalvinia immediately began to reply but Peace did not bother to listen. He could not escape the feeling that something important had just passed.

You knew who those people were, Lady Melina, he thought. *But whether what you felt at hearing of their coming was fear or anger, I cannot be sure. Still, I am certain of one thing: either you fear them or you hate them—maybe both. Either way, that makes them people I need to know.*

He considered. His fellow in the Dragon's Three—one Xarxius, formerly of the Stargazers—had been head of the expedition sent as observers to the war to the south that Hawk Haven and Bright Bay now called King Allister's War—as if one man deserved either the credit or the blame! Stonehold more reasonably refused to even name it a war, calling it simply the Battle of the Barren River.

Now that Peace thought on the matter, Xarxius had made himself very scarce of Lady Melina's company. Peace had hardly considered that this might be deliberate. Winter was a busy time for trade in heavy items like glass, which could be moved more easily over snow-packed roads. As a specialist in foreigners, Xarxius was always very busy in winter.

Maybe Xarxius had *meant* to avoid Lady Melina. Peace would seek him out as soon as this meeting was over.

For now, he settled back in his chair and with patience born of long practice turned his full attention to the raging debate on the magical merits of a comb.

GRATEFUL PEACE INVITED XARXIUS to dine with him that same evening. Surprisingly, Xarxius was not already committed, and he agreed to come by Peace's chambers when his business was completed.

Each of the Dragon's Three had been given one of the spire-topped towers within Thendulla Lypella for his own use. As he had come into Apheros's service many years before, when Apheros had been elected the Dragon Speaker, Peace had ample opportunity to discover any secret places or spy galleries.

He had found some, but there were none in the rounded tower room to which he took Xarxius. It was a room that in the winter he used most commonly by day, for its great beauty was in the floor-to-ceiling windows—each a full nine feet in height—that graced the circular room at regular intervals.

After dark the windows—even when heavily curtained—made the room rather chilly. However, Peace ordered his servants to stoke up the stove that squatted in the center of room. The stove, unlike the windows, was of modern manufacture. Either the Founders had not used this room after dark in the cold seasons or they had possessed some magical means for heating.

The smiths, however, had melded function and artistry, casting the stove in the shape of some amphibious beast from legend and enameling the metal in shining white and green. The fire was fed through the creature's wide, frog-like mouth, and glass spheres set in its bulging eye sockets shone with internal light.

Although Peace was fond of the stove—it had been among the first things he had commissioned for his own use—this was not why he chose to meet Xarxius here. The existence of the windows made it obvious that the walls contained no spy holes. The heavy curtains that were usually drawn across the windows were open now, making quite plain that no one hid behind them. In all ways, the room proclaimed itself secure.

When a servant announced Xarxius's arrival, Peace saw his guest grasp the significance of Peace's preparations.

"Draw the curtains," Peace ordered the servant, "then leave us. We have everything we need. See that we are not interrupted except on direct command of the Dragon Speaker himself."

He glanced at Xarxius as he gave this last command, but Xarxius nodded his agreement. The two men spoke of little as the servant went about his labors, chatting idly of the meeting Xarxius had just attended with some financiers from Waterland, eager to secure a trade concession for the coming spring.

Xarxius was some ten or twelve years older than Grateful Peace, but his features fell into lines and wrinkles beyond even those years. Many had unkindly compared him to a hound dog, for with his long broad nose, soulful brown eyes, and, most of all, the bags beneath those eyes, he did rather resemble one of those phlegmatic beasts.

That appearance was deceptive. The only character trait Xarxius shared with a hound dog was persistence when on the trail. He was clever and witty, yet wise enough to conceal this from those who could be fooled. He was also brutal enough to take advantage of such misjudgments.

It was largely owing to Xarxius and those on his immediate staff that New Kelvin still wielded economic independence. Without great care, the smaller mountain kingdom would doubtless have been swallowed up by the ruthless plutocracy of Waterland, their neighbor to the east.

Since tonight Xarxius had come to Grateful Peace directly after his meeting with some Waterland financiers, as would be expected, his face paint was an exemplar of misdirection. Subtle shading gave the impression of a constant smile, shadowing about his eyes made his expression difficult to read. Wild curls of color placed at random distracted from the more subtle art in such a disturbing fashion that the viewer's eyes unconsciously returned to that comforting—if illusory—smile.

As one who had begun his own career doing facial decoration, Peace revered the artistry of Xarxius's adornment. At another time, he might have asked who had originated the design, but tonight he had something more immediate to discuss.

When the last curtain was drawn and the servant dismissed, Peace locked the door behind him. Xarxius barred his teeth at him in a broad, doggy grin.

"Somehow I don't think you've asked me here so I can tell you about the excellent prices I obtained on a contract to make the window glass for the new palace of the Supreme Affluent."

"I fear not," Peace replied, gesturing toward one of the broad-armed chairs set near a small oval table a comfortable distance from the stove, "although I am certain that you worked wonders. There is nothing the plutocrats of Waterland like less than actually spending their money."

Xarxius laughed in agreement and accepted the goblet of white wine Peace poured for him. Tempting scents rose from the covered dishes as Peace carried them over to the table and began to serve the meal.

"I have asked you here," Peace continued, ladling beef simmered with mushrooms and cream, "because I fear a threat to the Dragon Speaker's rule."

"Do the Defeatists still challenge him?" Xarxius asked, helping himself to fresh bread. "I am astonished. I had thought that the arrival of the three artifacts and the actual awakening of power in the mirror would have stilled their voices—at least for now."

"Their voices are stilled," Peace agreed. He put the serving dishes to one side of the table and took his seat. "The threat comes from another source."

Xarxius cocked an eyebrow at him.

"Oh? What source?"

As was his wont, Peace answered indirectly.

"What do you know of Lady Melina Shield?"

"Ah, our honored visitor." Xarxius sampled a mushroom,

nodded his approval of the flavor. "She is the youngest daughter of a Great House of Hawk Haven. Her brother is the reigning Duke Gyrfalcon. She is recently widowed, but has several children left to comfort her—five according to some counts, four according to others."

Thinking of the severed fingers, Peace said, "I don't understand."

"Lady Melina," Xarxius continued, his voice gruff and hearty, rather like a friendly barroom gossip, not a specialist in foreign policy, "bore five living children, four girls and a boy. The eldest girl, however, was the victor in the recent competition to be adopted as heir to the throne of Hawk Haven—old King Tedric being without living issue.

"By custom, King Tedric has adopted this young woman—the Crown Princess Sapphire—so according to some counts, that leaves Lady Melina shy one child."

"And those who remain are?"

Xarxius looked quite curious about this interest in a foreigner's family, but supplied the information without pause.

"Jet—the heir to the family's small fortune—Ruby, Opal, and Citrine."

"Ah."

Peace sighed deeply. He held up a hand when Xarxius appeared ready to ask some questions of his own.

"Bear with me, old friend. I fear before we part this evening I will have answered all your questions and more. Tell me, have you heard of a Sir Jared Surcliffe and some woman called the Firekeeper? Who are they and what is their relation to Lady Melina?"

Grateful Peace fancied he saw a glimmer of understanding in Xarxius's deep-shadowed eyes as the other sipped his wine, pausing, perhaps, to frame his answer in light of some private knowledge of his own.

"Sir Jared Surcliffe," Xarxius said, as if reciting from some dossier visible only to himself, "is a cousin of House Kestrel, the land that lies across the White Water River on our southwestern boundary. Although without fortune himself, he has the patronage of Earl Kestrel. He is gaining renown as a healer in his own right and is said to have been favored by Crown Princess Sapphire and her newlywed husband after they were injured in the recent assassination attempt—this despite some unhappiness on the part of the established healers of Bright Bay.

"Firekeeper—there is no 'the' preceding the name as far as I have heard—is also connected to House Kestrel. She is the adopted daughter of Earl Kestrel—in this capacity she is known as Lady Blysse. However, I have been told she prefers the other name.

"Lady Blysse's preadoption lineage is somewhat more in doubt. Many believe her to be the daughter of King Tedric's youngest son, Prince Barden, who was disowned by his father after he disobeyed his father's wishes and attempted to establish a colony west of the Death Touch Mountains. Others doubt this, stating she could be one of any number of children taken along on the expedition.

"Whatever the case, like Princess Sapphire, Firekeeper was considered a possible candidate as King Tedric's heir. Although he did not choose her, rumor says that she remains a favorite of his."

Xarxius ate a few bites of his meal, then ran his tongue lightly around his lips before continuing.

"It is also said that Firekeeper is in some way magically gifted—though fearing sorcery as they do, those of Hawk Haven do not state it precisely that way. What is not in doubt is that she commands two beasts—a peregrine falcon and a timber wolf—who obey her slightest whim. I saw the girl myself when I was an observer at the recent war, and while I was in no position to judge whether she is magically gifted or not, I will say without question that she is very odd."

Grateful Peace nodded. Xarxius's account was filling in gaps in what he recalled.

"One more question," Peace said. "Then I promise to tell let you dine while I tell you all I know. I also promise to answer any questions you may present."

"Fair," Xarxius agreed. "Ask."

"What—if any—relationship do these two have with Lady

Melina Shield? I don't just mean kinship—though I know the Hawk Havenese count this as important. I am also interested in matters of personal history."

"Well," Xarxius drawled, and Peace could see the true smile within the paint, "Lady Blysse—this Firekeeper—did slay Lady Melina's brother."

Peace blinked and Xarxius, with a chuckle, continued:

"Lady Melina's brother was Prince Newell, the widower of Tedric's second child, his daughter Lovella. Although it has been kept somewhat quiet—probably in the interests of sparing House Gyrfalcon embarrassment—Prince Newell attempted to murder King Tedric during the final battles of King Allister's War."

Peace nodded. He remembered reading a report of this, though he didn't think the report had emphasized that Prince Newell was a Shield. He thought he might have assumed that Newell was of Tedric's own house. It was so difficult to keep these foreign relationships straight! Moreover, Peace's own duties involved internal politics, not external.

"Prince Newell would probably have succeeded," Xarxius said around a mouthful of bread, "but this Firekeeper somehow got wind of what he was doing and interrupted him. I understand that she herself was nearly slain in the process."

Smiling ironically, Peace nodded again.

"So Lady Melina has reason to hate this Lady Blysse."

"Reason enough," Xarxius agreed. "Now, tell me, is it coincidence that you ask me these questions just a few days after my own informants reported to me that this very Lady Blysse and Sir Jared—along with several companions—have come to Dragon's Breath and are dwelling here? Their apparent purpose is to pursue the practice of medicine, but my informants tell me that Lady Blysse and an intimate companion—one Derian Carter, who incidently is an advisor to King Tedric—have been prowling the city as if seeking something."

"It is no coincidence," Grateful Peace replied. Concisely, but omitting not one essential detail, he told Xarxius about the news Kistlio had brought that afternoon and how Lady Melina had reacted.

"And you feared for the safety of our honored guest," Xarxius said when he finished. "How admirable!"

Peace did not have to have known his fellow Three for these past fifteen years to hear the hint of sarcasm in his voice.

"I think not," he said. "I have reason not to fear *for* Lady Melina, but to fear *her.*"

Xarxius stared at him for a long moment. Then slowly, portentously, he nodded assent.

"I, too, fear her. I know, I know," he added hastily, "I was among those who agreed that her interesting proposal was worth pursuing—although I noted to Apheros that a mind which could come up with such an intricate plan involving so many levels of betrayal bore careful watching."

Xarxius's voice dropped to a hound-dog bay. "But I never believed that she possessed such power as she has shown here."

"You've seen it, too, then!" Peace's voice nearly broke with relief. He had expected to spend long hours convincing Xarxius of the reality of what he had observed.

"I have." Xarxius frowned. "I thought that I had even seen her mark on you, old friend, but I must have been mistaken."

Peace shook his head.

"You were not. She set that mark upon me—possibly as we traveled from the Stone Giant Inn to Dragon's Breath—but whatever her power is it must need some maintenance. With bigger fish to catch, she let me idle in her nets. I slipped through the meshes."

Xarxius sighed deeply. "Lady Melina may have overextended herself, too. Both Apheros and the Healed One are definitely under her influence. Many of the Primes are at least open to her suggestion—open enough to eliminate their normal dislike of a foreigner."

"And some are more receptive than that," Grateful Peace added. "There are those who look to Lady Melina for guidance and reassurance. Yet even as they do so, they seem unaware."

Xarxius nodded. "I saw what was happening, but I didn't know what I could do—one man, alone. Finally, I decided that the wisest course for me was to avoid her as much as possible and to do everything I could to hasten the awakening of the artifacts. Then she would take her share, go home, and we could return to our usual lives."

Grateful Peace took a deep breath.

"Xarxius," he said seriously, "I'm not sure that Lady Melina intends to go home . . ."

The hound-dog face stared at him in disbelief. With immense care, Peace told him what he had seen, ending with those two severed fingers and the news that Baron Waln Endbrook was almost certainly alive.

XXIX

"SO WE HAVE A MAP," Elise said, inspecting Edlin's completed work that evening after dinner, "and it seems to be a fine one. Now what do we do with it?"

Their makeshift household was gathered in Doc's consulting room. The kitchen—filled with the warmth of both ovens and hearth, scented with the spices Wendee had used in preparing that night's dinner—would have been more comfortable, but Hasamemorri or one of her maids was always trotting in or out.

Tonight, when they needed to plan the next stage in their campaign, they required privacy. Chairs had been carried in for all but Firekeeper. The polished maple table on which Doc's instruments were usually spread had been pulled away from the wall and the chairs set about it. Edlin's map had been tacked to the wall in sight of all.

"What do we do with this map now that we have it?" Elise repeated.

She knew she sounded cross, but somehow she couldn't help herself. The first patients had arrived at dawn. Although the usual round of winter complaints—coughs and wheezes and stuffy heads—could have been treated with powders and poultices purchased from any reliable alchemist, Doc's reputation as a miracle worker was such that any with money to spare arrived at their door.

Since Elise had agreed to sort the patients into categories—leaving Sir Jared free to treat those who truly needed him—it fell to her to tell over half of those who lined their hallway that the doctor would not see them, that he recommended that they go to the nearest alchemist (Oculios in this case) and purchase the appropriate preparations.

Most departed meekly, as if knowing that what had prompted them to come here in the first place had been curiosity more than anything else. Some, however, grew obstreperous. More than once Lord Edlin had been called away from his cartography and forced to bodily oust some complaining wretch.

Fortunately, Edlin seemed amused at being asked to act as a house guard. They had yet to meet anyone who could both wrestle with a strapping young nobleman and convincingly maintain their complaint that they were so infirm that they *must* see the doctor.

"Well, it's a map," Edlin said, looking at her with concern. "We use it to plan our campaign, what?"

He beamed at her. He had every right to be pleased with his handiwork. The reports of crow and falcon had been transformed into straight walls and curving towers. Colored pencils had been used to tint different structures so they could be referred to at a glance. Guards were indicated in red; areas where people—servants and such—tended to cluster had been shown by green dots.

Somehow what Lord Edlin had created was more than a static map—it was a drawing representing a living community, a reminder that the place they must seek to infiltrate was filled with people going about their daily business.

Elise despaired of their ever being able to get more than ten feet inside the gates without being detected. From those patients she did not send away, she had gathered that even to most residents of the city Thendulla Lypella was a mystery, a fine, secret place where the primes met in conclave, the Healed One resided, and from which the Dragon Speaker coordinated the complex resources of the kingdom.

Even the few who had worked inside or knew someone who had worked in the citadel could tell little. Servants were not encouraged to wander outside of where they performed their responsibilities. Those who waited upon those personages privileged to be given residence within the walls were usually housed within. It was said that the most private areas were tended by slaves purchased from Waterland. These unfortunates never left Thendulla Lypella.

"So we can make plans," Elise said. "Well, very good, let's do just that. Well?"

She realized that everyone was staring at her and had the grace to color. Finally, Derian, braver than the rest or perhaps merely more accustomed to the whims of females spoke:

"We all agree that our target is the tower Lord Edlin has shaded in blue, right?"

There were nods all around.

"Unhappily for us, it is not freestanding. Rather it tops a large, rectangular structure—a structure that may or may not be connected to those closest to it."

Derian rose from his chair, pointing with a slim stick swiped from the kindling basket to the light lines Edlin had shaded to indicate places where the information their avian spies had given them was less than perfect.

Elation, perched on the back of his chair, squawked some comment or protest. Firekeeper shushed her. No one else seemed to notice.

My first council of war, Elise thought. *How odd. I just realized that this is my first council of war. When I am the Baroness Archer I will be expected to attend many of these— unless I want to be dismissed to the ranks of the noncombatants as my mother and Uncle Aksel Trueheart always are. When Sapphire is queen will she respect those who love conflict less than she? King Tedric does, but Sapphire . . .*

Elise straightened in her seat, recognizing the second component contributing to her crossness. It wasn't just that she was tired. That was part of it, but the truth was, she was afraid, afraid deep down inside, because she knew that whoever was chosen to go inside those walls she must accompany them— she, because she alone spoke the language well enough to pass for a native.

And I want to sit back with the ladies, sit back as I did whenever we went hawking. Ever and always I have left the real risks to others. My grandfather was raised to the ranks of the nobles because of his courage—I pray to the green-eyed Lynx that some of his blood still runs in my veins.

Sir Jared, braced from the several cups of strong tea he had drunk with his dinner, leaned closer to get a better look at the map.

"It seems to me," he said, "and I'll be the first to admit that I am no tactician, that the gate there—south of the big orange building—is the most promising. It has only two guards on it and seems fairly close to our goal."

Firekeeper laughed softly.

"So think I, Doc," she said, "until I go look at it with my eyes. That gate need only two guards because all building near have many windows looking out at it. Also, gate faces on a busy street. It is for . . ."

The wolf-woman looked at Derian, seeking a word she lacked.

"Processions," Derian supplied, "parades and the like. It seems to be largely ceremonial in function. I can't recall having seen it opened, and a few cautious questions to our young guide seem to confirm that it is used infrequently."

"Just goes to show," Doc said, not at all nonplussed at having his suggestion so thoroughly shot down, "how a map is one thing, but knowledge is another."

Wendee seemed about to offer a suggestion of her own, when there came a knock on the front door. She saw Elise automatically start to rise and pressed her down with a friendly hand.

"Stay put, Lady Elise. You've been answering that all day while I drank tea in the kitchen."

Elise smiled at her gratefully.

"Sure, Wendee. When you're not running off to the market, cooking for a winter-lean household, and taking care of the mending, cleaning, and all else. Then you might have a cup of tea."

Wendee chuckled as she left, saying, "I'll tell them you're not home, Doc."

When she returned a few moments later, her face was oddly pale and all traces of laughter were gone. She closed the door deliberately, but even when the heavy oak was between her and the hallway, she spoke in hushed tones.

"There's a man out there—a rich one I'd say from his clothes. I couldn't see his face—he kept his hood up even when he stepped inside—but there's something about him that says he's used to being obeyed. He wants to see all of us. He knows our names and everything."

"Not a patient then?" Doc queried.

"I don't think so."

Derian quickly pulled loose the pins that tacked the map to the wall and hid it away.

"Do we see him?" he asked.

Firekeeper nodded. "He knows our names, better we know his—and his odor, too—than to go jumping from shadows."

Elise felt herself agreeing and heard Wendee depart. She reentered a moment later escorting the stranger. The cloak he wore was thick black wool, its hood pulled to shadow his features. In the flickering lamplight, it was easy to fancy that he had no face at all.

Derian glanced at Doc and Elise as if expecting one of them to take charge. When neither did so—Elise, still recovering from her momentary fancy, seemed to lack the will—he spoke:

"Greetings. Who are you and what brings you to us?"

The cloaked figure shifted slightly as if studying them all.

"Bold words, blunt and direct, such I would expect from a mere youth who counsels kings."

They waited for the stranger to say more. When he did not, Derian prompted.

"You seem to know us, sir. Who are you?"

Almost reluctantly, the man let his hood drop back. His face had been shaded in degrees of grey and black through which could be seen several tattoos. Like all the upper-class New Kelvinese, his hair was shaved to a point roughly above his ears. The hair remaining was as white as sun-bleached bone. His eyes were impossible to see behind tinted glasses.

Elise judged their visitor to be somewhere past fifty, healthy, but not given overmuch to exercise. She realized that these last assessments were the result of her recent work. Before she would have said that he was too ordinary-looking—if one left out the facial decorations and peculiar hairstyle—to be handsome, but too distinguished to be plain.

"My name," their visitor said, "is Grateful Peace and I come to you in what I hope is shared cause, for I am the enemy of one of your countrywomen—of Lady Melina Shield."

Grateful Peace looked at the gathered foreigners before him with a consternation he felt certain that he had managed to hide before they detected it.

There were six in all in the group: three women and three men. Additionally, there were three animals in the room. Two were birds—one surely the peregrine falcon of which Grateful Peace had already heard, the other a large, black bird, either a raven or crow. He thought raven from its size, though it seemed to lack the heavier beak of the raven, possessing instead the slimmer lines of the crow. Maybe it was some southern variety he had not encountered.

Peace had little attention to spare for the birds, however remarkable they might be. Xarxius had told him that Lady Blysse, the Firekeeper, was accompanied by a wolf, but no words could have prepared Peace for the reality of the animal who—at his entrance—had risen to its feet and now stood glowering at him with uncannily blue eyes. It was a timber wolf, most surely, its thick coat in hues of grey, touched with brown and bits of white, but a timber wolf the size of a pony.

The wolf filled the room with its presence, yet none of the humans seemed to notice it, none but the dark-haired young woman who sat on the floor beside it, one hand resting lightly on the wolf's flank, the other hovering in the vicinity of a large knife belted at her waist.

Peace was curious about her, but some sixth sense he had gained as the Dragon's Eye told him that she was not the one to address first. Instead he directed his attention to the others.

The two remaining women were fair. The elder of the fair women was the one who had opened the door to him and spoken with him in New Kelvinese that seemed to mix archaic phrases with the more modern argot of the marketplace. She was quite attractive, possessed of a full, womanly figure and bright eyes that he fancied could show laughter easily.

There was no laughter in her now, however. She stood by the door through which she had admitted him to this inner chamber, having shut it as soon as he had crossed the threshold. She made no move to act further, but looked to her companions for guidance.

This came not from the redhead who had spoken to him on his arrival, but from the second of the fair-haired women—a young woman, barely out of girlhood and showing the potential for great beauty.

It was this woman who, despite her youth, recovered first from the evident shock of the announcement with which he had greeted them. Rising from her seat, she addressed him in his own language.

"I am Lady Elise Archer," she said, "as you already seem to know."

"I know the names, certainly," Peace replied, "but am grateful to have your aid at attaching them to their correct owners."

Actually, Xarxius's briefing, augmented by a report he had fetched from his own chambers, had given Peace a fair idea of who must be who. The formality of introductions, however, should give everyone a moment to adjust to the implications of this sudden meeting.

"And, please," Peace added, "while I deeply appreciate the

courtesy you do me in addressing me in the language of the land, I am fairly fluent in your language and am willing to continue our conversation in it—more than willing. I would prefer it. I have no idea what spies may watch your house, but I feel assured that few will speak your language well. My people are . . . reluctant to learn other languages."

Lady Elise shifted tongues easily.

"Very well," she said. "Let me continue introductions. This—the lady who met you at the door—is Wendee Jay, a retainer of Duchess Kestrel and our trusted advisor."

Peace offered a bow after the fashion of Hawk Haven, and Wendee Jay responded with a graceful curtsy.

"Pray, Goody Wendee," Peace said, hoping he was selecting the correct title, "be seated."

Wendee did so, perching at the edge of her chair, as if she expected to leap to her feet any moment.

"This," Elise continued, gesturing to the third woman, "is Lady Blysse Norwood, granddaughter of the duchess, daughter of her heir, Norvin Norwood."

The third woman rose from the floor with a lithe grace that spoke of strength in its easy motion. One hand remained on the wolf, the other near her knife. She was dressed after the fashion of neither Hawk Haven nor New Kelvin, but in some style all her own. Her feet were bare, as were her arms where they extended from a fine leather vest. She wore trousers rather than a skirt, and these too were leather and showed evidence of hard use.

Yet it was not her strange manner of dress, nor even her self-contained watchfulness, that made Grateful Peace study her in slightly horrified fascination. There was a manner about this woman—Lady Blysse, as she had been introduced—that did not seem human. In some ways her body language was as contained as that of an Illuminator before a desk covered with priceless paints and liquid leaf, yet when she did move, as when she rose to greet him, it seemed as if her muscles had been trained in another school and only reluctantly yielded to human constraints.

Lady Blysse nodded at him, acknowledging the introduction, but not bothering to reply. Yet even as Lady Elise moved to her next introduction, Grateful Peace was aware that the dark gaze of Lady Blysse did not leave him—nor did the blue-eyed gaze of her wolf.

Next to be introduced—in strict order of precedence some small part of his mind noted—was Edlin Norwood, Lord Kestrel. This young man ruined the favorable impression granted by his rather handsome angular features by observing events with a slightly open mouth and an expression of mild, foolish astonishment. He, it transpired, was the heir to Earl Kestrel, elder brother to Lady Blysse.

Sir Jared Surcliffe, the healer, came next. He showed some family likeness to Lord Kestrel, though only when one looked for it. There was an air of competence about him that Peace—who had not expected either such a small or such a relatively youthful group—took comfort in.

Mentally, Grateful Peace made note of the investment House Kestrel had put into this expedition. Two children of the house, one near relation, one servant. Clearly, New Kelvin's neighbor across the White Water had some interest in the matter at hand. It meant that Peace would need to take great care, for he had no desire to spark a retaliatory strike from over the border. The Gateway to Enchantment, though a small town, was a vital economic center.

Last, Lady Elise came to the tall red-haired youth who Peace had already deduced must be Derian Carter, the advisor to King Tedric. Like Lady Blysse, Derian had risen when Grateful Peace entered, but this was not a nervous gesture. He retained a poise that Peace quite admired in one of his years. Although Derian was clearly interested in their guest, he showed neither the awe of Lord Edlin nor the nervousness of Wendee Jay nor even the guarded watchfulness of Lady Blysse.

Like a good counselor, Derian Carter was waiting to hear what would be said. Only then would he judge. Peace felt certain that despite young Carter's tradesman's name and lack of title, whatever he said would weigh heavily with his comrades. He resolved then and there to sway young Carter at any cost.

Peace nodded to the six—*or perhaps*, he thought, *I should think nine, for the animals are watching me with as much attention as the humans.*

"May we be seated?" he asked. "What I have to say cannot be said quickly and there is no need for formality, I hope."

Lady Blysse moved and seated herself on the edge of the table that dominated one side of the room.

"You say," she said, cutting through whatever gentle diplomacies the others might have offered, "you are Lady Melina's enemy. Why? She come here at your inviting."

Peace nodded.

"At the invitation of my government," he said, "an invitation which I initially favored. Now that I have had over half a moonspan to get to know Lady Melina—half a moonspan that has been quite filled with events through which I can judge her true character—I am no longer so certain I want her to remain. Unhappily, I am nearly alone in my feelings. Lady Melina herself has made certain that those who would be most likely to request her departure are most firmly in her camp."

He did not miss the significant glances that passed between some of the company—nor that both Lord Kestrel and Wendee Jay seemed confused and afraid rather than enlightened.

"Why," Derian suggested, "don't you start at the beginning, sir? Are we to understand that Lady Melina is in New Kelvin at your suggestion?"

"Rather," Peace said, "at her own. It happened like this. When King Allister of the Pledge took possession of Revelation Point Castle certain heirlooms belonging to the family of Gustin the First were no longer in the Royal Treasury."

"I guess that's fairly common knowledge in this group, sir," Derian agreed.

"Well, that theft would have occurred somewhere around the end of Falling Leaf Moon—what is that in your calendar?"

Lady Elise replied promptly, "Deer Moon. The next is Lynx Moon."

"Very well," Peace said, giving her a nod of thanks. "Early

in Lynx Moon we—that is the Dragon Speaker, to be precise—received an anonymous letter suggesting that if Queen Valora approached our country asking for help awakening the power in the items that we refuse and insist that in order to do so the items be accompanied by someone who could assist with awakening them."

There were a few murmurs at this, but no one interrupted. Peace continued:

"As you may imagine, there was much debate over this letter, much conjecture as to its source. However, we were intrigued. Rumor of King Allister's loss had hardly reached us before this missive. We resolved to bide.

"In time an ambassador from Queen Valora did come to us. He hinted at the possession of magics, but it rapidly became clear—we searched his baggage most thoroughly—that he did not have the artifacts with him. We told him to depart and not to return without both the items and one who was conversant in magical lore. At that time, none of us had the faintest idea who our correspondent might have been, but we had no doubt that whoever it was would not have sent us that message without also playing the other end of the field."

Sir Jared spoke, "And what would you have done if the ambassador had returned without this expert? Sorcery is a condemned art among all the colonies founded by Gildcrest—and the Isles may be counted among these."

"If the ambassador bore with him the artifacts," Peace said, "we would have negotiated. However, that did not prove to be a difficulty. When next we heard from Baron Waln Endbrook—that was the name of the ambassador . . ."

Peace saw from the expressions around him that this information came as no surprise.

"When next we heard from Baron Endbrook, it was notification that he would be with us again at the end of Dead Leaf Moon or near the beginning of New Snow Moon."

"Boar Moon and Owl Moon," murmured Lady Elise.

"He would be bringing with him both the artifacts and the promised expert. In nearly the same post came a letter from our mysterious correspondent. This time she identified herself as one Lady Melina Shield. She did not offer her credentials to us, instead she acted as if her notoriety was already known to us . . . as indeed it was.

"At that time, one of the most commonly told tales out of Hawk Haven—though it had many variations—was how the Princess Sapphire had broken the sorcerous bindings laid upon her by her mother. Our own ambassadors could testify to the pale oval on the princess's brow, to the common belief by all and sundry that this was the scar marking where Lady Melina's talisman had been ripped away.

"Our interest, then, in Lady Melina had already been aroused. Many a convivial dinner had degenerated into argument over the question of whether this was evidence of active sorcery or merely a tale believed by credulous barbarians."

Peace paused. "Forgive my seeming rudeness. I merely try to show you how it was with us. Let me simply state that there were those among us who were quite eager—above and beyond the fact that Lady Melina herself had contacted us—to meet the lady and to question her."

"I say!" exclaimed Lord Kestrel. "I can see that. My father had left me back to manage the old estates while he went off to war, but let me tell you that when I heard the gossip, I was pretty eager to get a squint at the witch myself. I mean, I'd known her since I was a kid, and we'd scared ourselves silly with stories about the things she probably did, but now we knew."

He glanced around, noticed the barely concealed impatience on the faces around him, and stopped.

"Sorry 'bout that, just wanted you to know I understood."

Peace gave the young lord his most gracious smile.

"Yes, that was kind of you, Lord Kestrel. You must understand that to us there is no stigma attached to practicing magic. We admire it. You may have been frightened by those stories. We were fascinated—a fascination that may have led us to behave unwisely."

He coughed slightly. At this, Wendee Jay leapt to her feet.

"We've forgotten to offer you anything to drink. Go on with your story. I've the kettle on the hob and can put some tea together in no time. Don't worry about me. I'll catch on pretty quick."

She darted from the room so rapidly that Peace was surprised. Then he realized that Goody Wendee was probably fleeing him—his avowed interest in magic must make him seem as repulsive to these people as would an interest in torture. The other five held their ground, however, nor did they seek to stop him from speaking, so Peace went on.

"We felt fairly certain that Lady Melina had arranged for Queen Valora to think of her when a sorceress was needed. Most likely, she simply sent another of those anonymous letters. However, she might have simply trusted to her reputation. I understand that upon her return from the war people hissed at her in the streets, that she was so shunned in some quarters that she finally retired to her family holdings."

Lord Kestrel nodded. "I say, that's true of the city folk in Eagle's Nest, at least. My mother told me something about that, you know. *Mother* thought how the lady was treated a disgrace, herself, and went out of her way to make Lady Melina feel welcome."

"In any case," Peace said when the others had glowered Lord Kestrel into silence, "we were inclined to welcome Lady Melina. She, however, had more than simple welcome in mind. Out of what she presented as simple national loyalty to Hawk Haven, she expressed a reluctance to have any of those artifacts returned to Queen Valora, for Queen Valora would certainly turn them against both Hawk Haven and Bright Bay.

"Lady Melina continued beyond this mere statement of patriotism, stating that she would help us eliminate Ambassador Endbrook and obtain the artifacts. Although she was willing to help with this, she did request that we give to her what had already been promised by Queen Valora: that is, one of the three artifacts for her own.

"Lady Melina's plan was neatly arranged: simple and direct. I must admit that we might even have worked some similar ruse ourselves. Queen Valora, you see, overestimated the esteem in which New Kelvin holds her. She seems rather blinded by her own passions—her rage at those who had exiled her,

her need to have more power at her control. We are not. More-over, Queen Valora had taken measures to secure Lady Melina as her faithful ally, so she had even less reason to fear treachery."

Peace noted that Derian Carter looked quite worried at these words.

"You have a question, young sir?"

"No. Don't let me interrupt."

Peace raised an eyebrow, but continued.

"I myself was sent to bring Lady Melina to Dragon's Breath. I speak your language well and could be more easily spared than my diplomatic colleague, whose talents were needed elsewhere. We made our move against Baron Endbrook. He was swifter to sense danger than we had believed he would be. He managed to flee, but in his bid to save his life he was forced to abandon the artifacts. The night into which he fled was winter-cold and snowy. Although several days' searching did not turn up his body, at the time we believed him dead."

Lady Elise repeated softly, "At the time . . . I must say, Duke Peace, your story gets more interesting all the time."

Grateful Peace actually had to suppress a grin. He was beginning to like these young people. They possessed such an interesting mixture of wisdom—or at least the diplomatic equivalent of street smarts—and innocence.

He transformed his grin into a kindly smile.

"I am pleased that you find it so, Your Ladyship, and, please, there is no need to title me 'duke.' "

Elise frowned slightly. "I apologize if I demoted you, sir. My language teacher told me that 'duke' was the equivalent of your title."

"In some ways," Peace agreed, "it might be so, but unlike a duke I do not hold my position for life, only at the pleasure of the Dragon Speaker, and even the Dragon Speaker holds his title only at the pleasure of the Primes."

"Confusing," Lady Elise said, "but clearly this is not the time to discuss fine points of linguistics."

"No," Peace said, permitting a touch of sorrow to shade his

tone. "I fear not. As I was saying, we thought Baron Endbrook dead. Indeed the majority of my colleagues have not been enlightened as to my belief that he yet lives. You see, the manner of my learning was such that I do not care to have the information spread about where the wrong ears might hear it."

Wendee Jay returned with a pot of tea and tray of cups. While she poured, Peace resumed his tale—for it was a tale, rather than a report. In a good report a watcher did not slant the facts. Here, however, Peace was not functioning as a watcher, and he felt it his right to slant the facts for their best effect.

He'd been careful not to make his own people seem too noble, too generous of spirit. Lord Kestrel might have been fooled by such high-flown rhetoric, but from the start Peace had doubted that either Derian Carter or Sir Jared would be. Now he added Lady Elise to his list of those who understood rather more than one would expect.

"I escorted Lady Melina and the three artifacts to Dragon's Breath. Initially, Apheros—that is the current Dragon Speaker—was inclined to treat Lady Melina with some disdain. However, somehow—and I firmly believe sorcery was at work—she insinuated herself into his inner circle with amazing ease. She also won the trust and favor of the Healed One—our hereditary monarch—apparently in the course of one evening. I cannot say how she did this, for the visit was relatively private and I was not among the guests.

"Since then," Grateful Peace continued, "Lady Melina has moved from barely tolerated foreign guest to a leader among those who are working to unlock the secrets of the artifacts. Her influence is subtle rather than direct, but I am a watcher of long standing and I see the pattern which is developing. My fear is if she can achieve so much in a period of time hardly greater than half a moonspan, what will she have managed in a full moon or in two or three? As events stand now, Lady Melina is not likely to be asked to leave until all three of the artifacts have been awakened. Only one has begun to reveal its secrets. Much time may pass before the others do the same."

Grateful Peace pressed his palms together and bent his head, staring at his own dark-painted reflection in the polished tabletop. With all his might, he sought to create the impression of a man so far gone in fear that he would attempt anything.

It wasn't hard. After his conversation with Xarxius, he *was* afraid.

A rough, slightly husky voice broke his act.

"What are the things?" it said. "These three artifacts. What are they? How big are they? Can they be carried away?"

Grateful Peace raised his head and found that the speaker was Lady Blysse. She still perched on the edge of the table, but there was a tightness about her—a tightness akin to a drawn bowstring or a coiled snake.

Peace answered carefully. "They are fairly small: a ring, a comb, and a mirror—a hand mirror with a carved ivory frame and a face of polished silver, such as a fine lady might keep on her dressing table."

"I want them," Lady Blysse said, her dark eyes meeting his and holding them.

Peace felt the challenge in that gaze and met it with his own. He held her eyes with his own as he spoke, but the young woman—hardly more than a girl, he realized—never wavered.

"You can have them," he agreed evenly. "I, personally, no longer want them. Others among my people may disagree."

"What you want, then, if not artifacts?" Lady Blysse asked.

Peace let his gaze drop, trying to make it seem as if he was just searching for his teacup, but he had a feeling that Lady Blysse was not fooled in the least.

"I want Lady Melina gone from New Kelvin," he declared, raising the cup. "Take her from my country, alive or dead. I don't care which, but take her away. I believe she has ambitions here—perhaps even extending to rulership. I believe she has ensorcelled my leader and my king. Once I thought sorcery was the answer to all problems. Now I see differently. In Lady Melina's hands, magical power may bring destruction to all I hold dear. Take her away!"

He let his voice drop.

"Or kill her."

The reply that came seemed unaffected by his declaration.
It was simply two pragmatic words from Lady Blysse.

"You help?"

This was not quite what he had hoped for, but it was sufficient. Grateful Peace nodded and sipped his tea. It was quite
good, a local blend with a faint taste of new-mown hay and
the sweetness of wildflowers.

"I will," he said, "but I do not want my role to be known.
Depending on the nature of her control, even when Lady Melina is gone there may be some who will resent those who
ousted her. That is why I would prefer foreign agents—agents
who can be believed to have acted for their own motives. If
you remove her, in turn, I will help you acquire the artifacts.
I am no longer so certain I want foreign magic active within
New Kelvin."

Derian Carter, who had risen to get his own tea, now spoke.

"Wait a bit," the redhead said, still standing, one callused
hand holding the cup, the other tracing the pattern of the wood
grain in the tabletop. "Firekeeper, we've gotten ahead of ourselves again."

Lady Blysse growled ever so softly.

"Not for me," she said. "This is what I want."

Derian held his ground. Grateful Peace was impressed, but
then maybe the young man was used to growling from this
strange feral creature.

Derian wagged a finger at her.

"Mice want the cheese," he said softly. "Think about that."

Lady Blysse scowled, but said nothing more.

Derian Carter turned to Peace.

"This is fascinating," he said bluntly. "You come offering
to help us steal what—frankly—your people were prepared to
do murder and even risk war to steal in the first place. All you
want is the removal of one woman who, it seems to me, you
could dispose of yourself. There's more here than meets the
eye. I want to see the rest before we commit ourselves."

Peace nodded. "That is only reasonable. I am willing to talk further, to answer any question you ask."

"Any of you have questions?" Derian asked.

"One in particular," Sir Jared replied. "What makes our honored guest think Lady Melina won't return home of her own accord when the work on these artifacts is complete? Even if you decide to break your agreement with her and keep all three artifacts for yourself, she cannot complain without ruining her reputation beyond repair. Even her brother the duke is likely to publicly disown her if she makes it known she has been practicing magic. Queen Valora would probably spend half her treasury to avenge the betrayal."

"Are those alone not reason enough for her to not wish to return to Hawk Haven?" Peace asked.

"Maybe," Sir Jared agreed. "But Lady Melina need not say where she has been. Even if someone ratted on her, she could simply look pathetic and claim that someone seeks to harm the Princess Sapphire by slandering her mother."

"Are not the princess and her mother estranged?"

"They are, but that doesn't mean that anyone's forgotten the relationship. Sapphire doesn't wish to disown her sisters and brother . . ."

Peace caught a flicker of distaste pass over Lady Elise's features at Sir Jared's mention of this brother and made a note to ask Xarxius what history might lie between them.

". . . And so she must remain in contact with Lady Melina, for Lady Melina is head of that household and will continue so until her death."

"And Queen Valora's vengeance?"

Sir Jared shrugged. "Queen Valora may be pretty peeved, there's no question of that, but is she willing to risk her very shaky truce with Hawk Haven and Bright Bay over it? Would her people even support her? Most of them share our heritage and with it our distaste for those who would practice magic. If Queen Valora makes a public issue of why she hates Lady Melina, then her own desire to use sorcery will probably become public. I'd guess Lady Melina would make certain that it did. With that excuse, Stonehold would probably support an effort to retake the Isles. Waterland, too."

From the mildly surprised expressions on one or two of the faces around the table, Peace deduced that the healer was not usually given to such long speeches. He factored that—and the passion it implied—into how he framed his own reply.

"So you think that, even with the enemies she has made, Lady Melina could return to Hawk Haven?"

"I do. The question is, what is it you know that makes you so certain she isn't planning to do so?"

With a show of reluctance, Grateful Peace cleared his throat.

"There was something I saw. I alone was witness, but I swear to you by the bones of the first Healed One that I am telling the truth."

Even Lady Blysse was listening now, her pique put aside for the moment.

"I have mentioned to you that when Lady Melina first arrived in Dragon's Breath, Apheros wanted no special honors shown to her?"

"You said something of that," Derian Carter agreed.

"He was actually rather rude," Peace went on almost apologetically. "Lady Melina was refused personal servants and was quartered in rooms we keep for guests. These rooms . . ."

He paused, as if he was about to give away a great secret. Actually, he was fairly certain that most of those "guests" who were invited to stay within the Earth Spires probably suspected that they were spied upon. Uneasily, he wondered if Lady Melina had as well. If she did, that made her action not merely a private declaration of intent but a challenge.

All this flashed through his mind even as his lips continued to move.

"These rooms," Peace repeated, "have been specially prepared so that little that goes on within them cannot be seen or, at the very least, heard. Lady Melina was given one of the best—one that offers no privacy at all to the dweller.

"I went frequently to watch her. Watching, you see, is my . . . There is no precise word for it in your language—'job' or 'profession' comes close, but so does 'vocation' and so, in a little sense, does 'honor' or 'rank.' "

He shrugged. "I am the watcher for the Dragon Speaker—

the Dragon's Eye. It is an old and honored position, one that predates the current kingdom and goes back to the Founders' time. It is my job to see what the Speaker cannot see, to sit where he cannot sit, to note what he cannot note, to draw conclusions that he is in no position to make. As watcher, I know all the hidden ways through the Earth Spires—if anyone does, that is, but their builders.

"I was fascinated with our foreign guest—all the more so in that she seemed to lose interest in me soon after her arrival. I think it was my good fortune to have her underestimate the importance of a watcher. Like Lady Elise, she may have made a study of our land, but such a post does not get put into history books."

Elise nodded agreement. "It's the first I've ever heard of it. I don't think we even have an equivalent unless you count scouts in time of war."

Peace noted Lady Blysse's expression of impatience and returned to the matter at hand. In any case, he had no wish to diminish the mood he had been so carefully building.

"Four days past, as I was watching, a messenger came to Lady Melina bearing a package. The package contained a box—a box sealed with the seal of Waln Endbrook, the baron of the Isles whom I had believed dead. The box contained four things: a gemstone, a lock of hair, and what I later realized were two freshly cut fingers from the hand of a child."

He paused, listening for expressions of horror. The perfect silence that greeted him was even better.

"The gemstone was the color of a fine brandy, reddish gold in hue. Lady Melina inspected it and the lock of hair—which was nearly the same color—then turned her attention to the fingers. She looked at these for a long moment, then consigned them and the lock of hair to the fire. When these were ash, she returned to her book. The gemstone was put in her jewel box. Later, I arranged to have it checked by a lapidary. It was a citrine."

"Citrine!" Lord Kestrel was the only one to find his voice. "I say, doesn't Lady Melina have a daughter named Citrine?"

"She does," Derian said, and his voice trembled with either

grief or rage. "A daughter she took away when she left Eagle's Nest with Baron Endbrook, a daughter whose location we do not know."

Lady Blysse cried out as if in physical pain and sprang to her feet.

"You said, Derian, you said you thought Lady Melina might have given Citrine as . . ." She lost the word and stammered in frustration, "As Blind Seer is to me. Did she give her for nothing?"

Derian nodded. "That's what the man is telling us, Fire-keeper. That Baron Endbrook thought he could trust Lady Melina to play fair with him because he had her daughter. When he got away, he sent a message reminding her. My guess is he expected her to send some word that she was willing to work with him again."

The redhead had been speaking in carefully measured phrases, as if he did not trust himself to think too closely about what he was saying.

"And," Derian continued, turning to Peace, "you're telling us that she did nothing but burn the fingers?"

Peace nodded solemnly, though inwardly he was rejoicing. He had hoped the news would have some effect, but he had hardly hoped for this level of fury. Indeed, he'd need to take care that the fury did not boil over or that in their anger they did not leave Dragon's Breath with the task for which he needed them undone.

"Nothing," he admitted, "of which I know. Of late, however, I have come to distrust the reliability of my network of informers. Many that I trust seem to be under the lady's spell.

"In any case," Peace added, as if seeking to comfort them, "only four days have passed since she received the message. Baron Endbrook would not yet expect her reply."

"Do you know where he is?" Lady Elise asked sharply.

"I do not," Peace said, "but I am assuming that he is outside of New Kelvin. Soldiers under my orders have searched closely within."

"Then Citrine may still be alive," Lady Elise said. Her eyes were bright with unshed tears, but her voice was steady. "We have time."

"Time only," Peace put in, "if you go to her swiftly. I fear that only one person in New Kelvin may know where the child is hidden."

"Lady Melina," Lord Kestrel breathed. "Of course! We must go to her and get the truth—by force if necessary."

The young lord sprang to his feet.

"There is not a moment to lose!"

Derian Carter pushed Lord Kestrel back into his chair with a firm, though not unkind, hand.

"We'll lose more than time, my lord, if we don't lay our plans carefully."

He glanced at his companions.

"Do we work with this man?"

Peace noted that he did not say "trust."

One by one, six heads nodded agreement. There was no argument, no debate. The only sound was a squawk from the crow, which had been drowsing on its perch.

"Very well," Derian said, turning to Peace. "Let's get on with it. What's your plan?"

Yes, Peace thought as he began to outline what he intended. *I am indeed beginning to like these young people. What a pity that if they choose to do as I suggest most of them will probably end up dead.*

XXX

FIREKEEPER FELT A CERTAIN THRILL when she realized that the hunt would take place that very night.

At first there had been some talk of delaying, of making further plans. The great log in the hearth had split in two and begun to crumble to ruddy cinders as the humans discussed possible ways to achieve their goal.

There were difficulties. Grateful Peace could not say for

certain just when—if ever—the research teams left off their work on the three artifacts. Some experiments required hours of observation. These were usually scheduled to run through the night, and one or two researchers remained to tend them.

Grateful Peace wanted them to go after Lady Melina and to trust him to retrieve the artifacts. No one—Firekeeper least of all—liked this idea, so Peace was forced to abandon it. Reluctantly, the thaumaturge was forced to agree that whatever plan they settled on must include means to achieve both goals.

That simple decision, apparently, made things more difficult rather than—as Firekeeper had thought it would—easier.

One difficulty that the white-haired man with his smell of grease and old silk *had* solved for them was how to get inside Thendulla Lypella. Grateful Peace knew of a tunnel—a tunnel branching from one of the sewers Firekeeper had already discovered—that would take them beneath the walls and under the complex. From this tunnel they could emerge into one of several cellars.

However, even this didn't solve all their problems.

Using the map Edlin had drawn, Grateful Peace showed them that the building in which Lady Melina was living and the building holding the artifacts were not the same.

Following this revelation, there was much argument over which goal should have priority—for their group was too few in number to make splitting up a realistic option.

Needless to say, Grateful Peace felt that kidnapping Lady Melina should come first. Firekeeper, however, knew her duty—retrieving the artifacts must come first. The others varied in opinion, but gradually one and all were convinced that perhaps kidnapping Lady Melina should come first. After all, she was the only one who knew where Citrine was, and if she escaped . . .

This last argument won Firekeeper—albeit reluctantly—over. The wolf-woman was fond of the round-faced little girl, remembered their long conversations in the springtime meadows above Eagle's Nest Castle, remembered, too, that Citrine and her cousin Kenre Trueheart had been the first friends she had made on her own. She thought that gave the girl some claim to her energies, a claim that competed fairly with the one held by the Royal Beasts.

After all, Firekeeper told herself when she thought uncomfortably of how the Beasts would react if she failed, it wasn't as if she was choosing to rescue the girl *rather* than steal the artifacts. She intended to do both.

Her own decision made, Firekeeper grew restless when the planning continued. To her indignant surprise, Blind Seer chided her for her impatience.

"Don't be such a pup," the great wolf growled. *"When you lived in the wilds did you dig after a rabbit without first blocking the exits from its hole?"*

"No," Firekeeper replied a trace sullenly.

"Here we are hunting not a rabbit but a den of weasels—weasels we must stalk without waking them, weasels we must catch without hurting. Surely that merits a little thought in advance."

"They are thinking more than a little!" she protested.

Blind Seer huffed at her. *"You are still such a pup! I tell you, this is more dangerous than any hunt we have ever attempted. My fur stands on end just thinking of it. Rather would I go into a she-bear's den in spring and attempt to eat her cubs than do what we must do here."*

"But you are with me?" Firekeeper asked anxiously.

"I have sworn before our people to be with you," the wolf assured her. *"But I do not think they knew what they were asking when they sent you out."*

To Firekeeper's surprise, Edlin Norwood was the one who halted the seemingly endless cycle of plan, counterplan, and refinement.

"I say," the young lord said, "but isn't it getting rather late? I mean," he went on diffidently, "shouldn't we get a move on?"

"Are you saying, Lord Kestrel," asked Grateful Peace, a touch of astonishment in his voice, "that we should essay this challenge tonight?"

"Well, I do think so, rather," Edlin replied boldly. "I mean, tonight you got out of there, no one the wiser. Will you be so free another night? What I'm trying to say is that you're at the beck and call of this Ass-fellow . . ."

"Apheros, the Dragon Speaker," Elise corrected quickly, clearly horrified at this lapse in diplomacy.

Edlin didn't seem to notice her dismay. He simply grinned his thanks for the correction and continued speaking.

"Right, Apheros, well, what if he needs you, Grateful Peace, tomorrow night? What if he wants you to do some watching or whatever it is you do? What if there's some big experiment in the laboratories you need to supervise? What if—and don't get me wrong, old chap, but these things do happen—what if Lady Melina gets her hooks into you again? I mean, we know about the way in through the sewers and all, thanks to you, but we don't really know how to get through them right and how to come out right and a dozen other things. I say we go for it tonight—right now. We have hours and hours of darkness left and folks there in the tower will be getting tired and well . . ."

Edlin trailed off, a bit confused by the flood of his own eloquence.

"Lord Kestrel," Grateful Peace replied slowly, "does have a point. As I told you earlier, I took my fellow Three, Xarxius, into my confidence this evening as the fastest means of learning about you. I trust Xarxius as much as I do any man . . ."

"And that," Blind Seer muttered, *"is not very much at all."*

". . . But a servant could have passed on word of our meeting and conclusions might be drawn. However, I will say that I think it unlikely we were betrayed—my servants, after all, are loyal to me. A much more real threat to our success may occur if Lady Melina chooses to act against you."

"Against us?" asked Edlin, surprise making the words sound rather like a gulp.

"You," Peace agreed. "I recognized her anger when she learned that you were residing in the city. It is not impossible that she might choose to have action taken against you. Something as simple as voiding your residence permit—a voiding based on some minor technicality, nothing that could be traced to her—could force you to leave Dragon's Breath. Even if you were able to hide nearby in the mountains—an onerous task this time of year—our chances for a successful raid would be reduced. If she insisted that you be escorted to the border . . ."

"She could do this?" Derian asked.

Firekeeper noted with some satisfaction that her red-haired friend was clearly worried. If Derian was worried, then it was likely they would move tonight.

"Apheros could, or the Healed One." Peace shrugged. "I can think of a dozen ways that such an escort could be arranged without giving reason for you—or your government— to take offense. Since I believe neither Apheros nor the Healed One are able to refuse Lady Melina anything, it is much the same."

"Then tonight," Elise said, wonder and no little fear in her voice. "Tonight we must be ready."

"Within the hour I should say," Grateful Peace replied. "I came to you straight from my meeting with Xarxius. We have talked for some hours. Most of the residents of the Earth Spires will have retired. I wish we could know how many are at work in the Granite Tower."

Firekeeper grinned.

"I can have that learned," she said, leaping to her feet. "Elation will fly at night, as will Bold. They can report to us here. I will tell them to look especially for Lady Melina. No need for us to go to her place—her room—if she is with the artifacts."

The wolf-woman felt some satisfaction at Grateful Peace's evident surprise. He hid his reaction well, but there was a momentary widening of his eyes that told her much. The thaumaturge's scent—now that she had learned to separate it from that of his cosmetics—altered, too. She did not need to hear Blind Seer's tail thumping muted applause on the boards behind her to know that she had pulled off a coup.

Still swelled with wolfish pride, Firekeeper woke the birds, explained their task, and promised rewards for swift return and detailed reports.

Cold wind swirled in through the window when she opened it to set the birds free. Above the sky was dark, the stars undimmed, for the majority of the city lights had long since been extinguished.

Once, Derian had told her that the Waterlanders believed that the stars held the undying spirits of all who had walked on the earth. These spirits were thought to look down on the living with interest. Sometimes they even granted wishes.

Firekeeper turned her face to the stars and wished with all her heart that tonight's venture would be successful.

ELISE SAW GRATEFUL PEACE'S SURPRISE when Firekeeper suggested sending the birds out to scout, but she doubted that anyone else—except possibly the wolf-woman herself—had noticed. She decided that explaining that Firekeeper was really able to talk to animals—and probably being disbelieved for her pains—would waste valuable time.

The thaumaturge also apparently thought that the time for questions was past, for though his lips parted momentarily, they closed again without a word being spoken.

"Let us be at it then, friends," Grateful Peace said, the last word softening what had been a distinctly autocratic tone of voice. "I have shown you the buildings that hold our targets. I have also done my best to tell what you should do when you get inside. Let me emphasize once more that I would prefer that my involvement be minimal."

"Fine," Firekeeper growled to Elise's dismay. "Be this minimal. Let us get on with the hunt. The birds can find us in streets. I have told them to be looking."

"Well and good," Grateful Peace replied without any of the pique Elise had feared he would feel. "However, there is one thing that must be done before you can get on with your hunt. Without a disguise of some sort, you would not go ten feet without being stopped."

"Disguise?" Firekeeper tilted her head to one side in inquiry. "That word . . . I forget."

Wendee Jay rose as Derian began to explain. Elise turned to the thaumaturge with a question of her own.

"Do we really need disguises, sir?" she asked. "It's not as if we're trying to infiltrate the Granite Tower. We're simply going in as raiders."

"Night raiders smear blackening on their faces lest the reflection be seen," replied Peace, indicating his own features with a graceful flourish of his long fingers. "In the same fashion, the longer you can pass for people who belong in Thendulla Lypella, the more time you will have to obtain your objectives.

"Remember," he added seriously, "not only must you get in, you must also get out."

Elise bit her lip. Wendee's return saved her from needing to reply.

"We bought most of these in Gateway, Lord Peace," Wendee said, displaying the bundled robes and the boxed cosmetics, "though I've added some since."

Perhaps in response to Elise's surprised expression, Wendee added:

"They're lovely things, Lady Elise, and I thought if we didn't need them here, we'd take them home with us."

Elise patted her hand. "You've done well, Wendee."

Peace was less pleased, but his displeasure was less at Wendee than at the mixed nature of their purchases.

"These," he explained, indicating their Gateway purchases, "are flimsy things—woven expressly for sale to foreigners. You'd never see such in the Earth Spires. These, however," he tapped a few robes, "are of fine quality. Goody Wendee definitely has judgment.

"Together," he concluded, "they are as mismatched as yellow stripes on a stallion."

"We hardly need to make a fashion statement, what?" said Lord Edlin. "Just to get in and out again."

Grateful Peace nodded. "But the mixture will make the getting in, much less the getting out, harder to do. Still, we shall manage. Happily, Goody Wendee has laid in a large supply of red tones."

Wendee blushed. "I thought they would do for cosmetics when we got home. Much less outlandish than the blues and purples, lovely as those are."

"Whatever your reason," Peace said, "they will serve well. The working costume in the research tower is a red-painted face and grey robe—not a deep grey, a pale shade close to that of undyed material."

"Why?" asked Derian, looking as if he was slightly surprised to hear himself asking.

"Because, young counselor," Peace replied, "the red is striking—a visual warning even to peripheral vision that someone else is near. The paint or stain is laid on thinly enough that facial expressions can be easily read through the color to help eliminate misunderstanding."

I wonder, Elise thought, *if that means the rest of the time they actively court misunderstanding?*

"Grey robes," Peace continued, "are easily cleaned or at least easily re-dyed. Now, my thought is to disguise those of you who are going in as researchers. Although the teams contain many important people, each sodality has sent over lesser members to do the scut work—sweeping up, grinding components, and the like. No one can be said to know everyone, so you should pass—at least for a time."

"Two questions," Derian said, raising his fingers. "One, you say 'those of you who are going in.' Are you suggesting we leave someone behind?"

Peace shook his head.

"Not precisely behind," he said. "Rather, I suggest that one or two of your number be delegated to pack your belongings and clear out of this house. Doctor?"

"Yes?"

"Have you the means to drug your landlady and her servants?"

Elise, knowing Doc's strict medical ethics, pivoted to look at him, ready to step in before he could say something too damaging to their cause.

The indignation she expected to find on his hawk-nosed features was not there. Instead, Sir Jared was nodding agreement and understanding. Something about his expression reminded her that he was a cousin to Earl Kestrel—a man whose devotion to scheming was as sincere as it was efficient.

Jared said, "I can do it more easily if they'll drink what I have. Wendee, did you notice if Hasamemorri was awake when you went to get the costuming supplies?"

"She was," Wendee said, looking up from where she had been sorting the reds from the other colors. "I heard her speaking to her maid about fetching a bit more firewood."

Wendee's blue eyes twinkled with wicked glee.

"I wouldn't be surprised if she heard our late caller arrive and is staying awake deliberately in hopes of learning what emergency has brought him."

"Very good," Doc said. "When you can tear yourself from your labors, come with me. I think we'll be sending them up some refreshments along with our apologies for the disturbance."

"Wait," Derian said. "I mean, do you think we should leave Dragon's Breath tonight?"

"That's right," Peace replied a touch acidly. "Surely you don't think that if you are successful Apheros will wait until morning to call and ask what you have been about?"

Derian sighed. "No, I suppose not. Who should stay to clear us out of here?"

"Pause and think on that," Peace advised. "What was your other question?"

To Elise's astonishment, Derian looked positively uncomfortable.

"The disguises," he muttered.

"Yes?"

"About them," Derian said. "Do they include shaving our heads?"

Even before the thaumaturge replied, Elise knew what the answer would be.

What will my mother think?

"Of course," Grateful Peace replied. "Only peasants wear all their hair—and usually only those who must labor out-of-doors. It is quite out of fashion among the sodalities to wear front hair."

There was a startled silence. Somehow, even when everyone had been considering disguises earlier on, no one had anticipated this contingency.

Wendee said slowly. "In the theater, we wore false head-fronts made from waxed cloth, but they had to be custom-fitted and even so they looked right fake up close."

Running her hand over her already ragged haircut, Fire-keeper gave a hoarse chuckle.

"Never will I have a good coat," she said with a rueful smile. "That I were a wolf!"

Wanting a moment to adjust to this new inevitability, Elise returned to the matter raised by Derian's first question.

"Who of us shall stay and who shall go?" she asked.

"I go," Firekeeper said firmly. "And Blind Seer with me. From what this Grateful Peace say, Blind Seer will have some places to hide and if he do not . . ."

She shrugged.

"The power of the wolf," Grateful Peace replied, "is certainly worth some risk. How many among you speak our language?"

"I do," Elise said, her hand moving involuntarily to touch her hair. "And Wendee does as well."

"I've picked up a little over the last few days," Derian said, "but it's spotty."

Grateful Peace tugged at the snowy length of his white braid.

"I suggest that both of the ladies go, then," he said. "Being able to understand what you hear may be more valuable than any skill with weapons."

"All ladies," Firekeeper said, indicating herself.

"That," the thaumaturge said with a trace of a sigh, "has already been settled."

"I say!" protested Edlin. "We can't send in three ladies without a man to protect them. It just isn't done!"

Elise was suddenly furious—or maybe she was just scared, but it certainly felt like fury.

"Would you say the same to Princess Sapphire?" she asked. "Duchess Merlin commanded troops during the final battle of King Allister's War. Where were you?"

She felt some satisfaction when Edlin gaped at her, but unhappily the young lord recovered quickly.

"*They* are trained in the arts of war," Edlin retorted, "but I recall that you won't even hawk!"

"Hopefully," Doc cut in, "this will remain a raid and never need the arts of war. Firekeeper, however, will not have trouble if fighting is needed. What is your training in that area, Wendee?"

Wendee brushed her hands across her skirts, the very picture of efficiency.

"I've had some training with both knife and sword," she replied coolly. Then her expression grew worried, "Though I must admit that I am rusty, and I've never really been in battle."

Doc nodded and turned to Edlin.

"So you see, cousin," he said. "These ladies are not the frail flowers you had thought. Lady Elise may not have a warrior's training, but I know from experience that she will not faint at the sight of blood."

Elise had her indignation under control now, so when she spoke to Edlin it was in a much gentler tone.

"You're right, Edlin, I don't care for blood sport, but I can use a bow. What descendant of Purcel Archer could escape learning that? I doubt that skill will be needed, but I promise to try to stay with what I do best."

Edlin looked unhappier still when Doc took up the thread again.

"In any case," he said, "we will not be sending in the three female members of our party alone but for the wolf. I will be going with them. Not only have I seen my share of combat, but a healer should be where harm may happen. That leaves you and Derian to get our gear together and outside city limits."

"Both of us!" Edlin protested. "I say!"

Elise noted that Derian was fingering his forehead, an expression equal parts embarrassment and relief on his features.

"Doc's right, Lord Edlin," he said. "We need to move out all those horses and mules—not to mention having to pack and load our gear. That almost exceeds what I would expect of two men. It would be impossible for one—especially since we will probably have only a few hours. Isn't that right, Lord Peace?"

Grateful Peace nodded solemnly.

"I fear so. You may begin while we start costuming—but hold. Are either of you young men skilled with a razor?"

Derian shrugged. "Enough to scrape my chin."

Edlin nodded. "About the same, I'm afraid."

Laughing, Elise cut in.

"No need to keep these men from their tasks, sir. I've learned to shave well in preparing patients for Sir Jared."

"Very good."

They split then into three groups: Doc and Wendee to prepare the drugged tea so that Hasamemorri and her maids could not comment on their leaving and possibly delay them; Derian and Edlin (still grumbling) to begin packing; the remainder to begin transforming themselves into some believable facsimile of New Kelvinese.

THE BIRDS RETURNED just as Grateful Peace was about to shave Elise's head. He had shaved Sir Jared's head first, all the while verbally supervising Wendee's makeup. Now Wendee, her cosmetics in place but for the final coat over her yet unshaved head, was applying Firekeeper's paint.

Elise had taken on shaving Firekeeper, for the wolf-woman had refused to let a stranger holding something as sharp as a razor come close to her. The shaving had been followed by a general trim, for Firekeeper had insisted on her back hair being trimmed as well—a thing that Grateful Peace had thought wise, noting politely that no one would voluntarily wear such a ragged coiffure.

Her face partially painted, clad still in her vest and trousers, when a rap came on the glass Firekeeper rose from where Wendee was applying the red paint to her face and opened the window. Falcon followed by crow fluttered in and took their respective perches.

Elation faced the wolf-woman full on with one gold-rimmed eye and squawked something suspiciously like laughter. In reply, Firekeeper spat into the fire.

"She really does understand them, doesn't she?" Grateful Peace commented as he lifted the razor.

Trying to ignore the gentle tug of the razor against her hair—the blade was so sharp that what she felt was more a vibration than an actual cutting—Elise held her head very still as she answered:

"She does, and they do her. I think they understand all of us somewhat, but that is because they have learned our language while Firekeeper speaks theirs."

"Do you understand them?"

Elise remembered not to shake her head.

"No, not any more than people usually understand animals. Blind Seer and Elation seem to be trying to learn to communicate directly with us through gesture—nodding or shaking their heads—though with the falcon the motion involves the entire body."

"Interesting."

The New Kelvinese fell silent then, concentrating on his delicate task. Elise sat frozen, dreading the seemingly inevitable nick of razor against her scalp. It never came.

Eventually, Grateful Peace dusted the top of her head with the palm of his hand and said:

"Would you like to see how you look?"

"I think not," Elise replied honestly. "Not quite yet. Can you do my makeup?"

Peace nodded.

"I can begin, but I will need to attend to Goody Wendee's hair unless you intend to do so."

"You're much faster than I am," Elise laughed, aware that the sound held a nervous lilt.

She felt acutely aware of the passage of time, knowing that every moment brought her closer to a challenge she was uncertain she was really prepared for. With a hot flush of shame, she recalled how she had collapsed when they had been taken prisoner by the bandits. Would she fall apart now?

Doc didn't think so. Firekeeper hadn't questioned her participation. Even so, Elise found herself sneaking glances at the wolf-woman, looking for some sign that the other shared her doubt.

Firekeeper looked distinctly odd with her new haircut and partially painted face. The absence of front hair made her head look somehow longer. It also robbed her of much of her femininity.

Is that because only men go bald and now we look like balding men? Elise thought a trace hysterically.

Firekeeper turned back to Wendee, indicating with a gesture that the older woman could return to applying the makeup. As Wendee stroked the red paint onto Firekeeper's shaven head with fingers that had lost none of their expertise, the wolf-woman spoke:

"What the wingéd folk tell is good and not good. Good is that there are few people in the upper portions of the tower. Not so good is that in lower part," she gestured toward Edlin's map, "is a room with many people in it."

Elise felt Grateful Peace's fingers stop their work for a moment as he turned to glance at the map. They picked up the tempo again almost immediately.

"That is a conference room. It takes up about half of that level of the tower. The rest is given over to a corridor and two smaller rooms which I believe are being used for little more than storage."

Firekeeper grunted acknowledgment.

"Think you that we can go past without those inside knowing?"

"Quite possibly," Peace agreed. "I could even go inside the room and pretend to be interested in the course of their debate."

Elise heard a ring of pride in his voice.

"I go everywhere and no one dares question. While I am in the conference room I can check whether they have one of the artifacts with them."

"Good," Firekeeper replied. "How much longer till we go?"

Grateful Peace paused again in his work.

"If Goody Wendee is nearly finished with your makeup and Lady Elise can complete my work here, we should not be long."

"Please, take care of Wendee's hair," Elise said. "I'll finish my own makeup and check Firekeeper's."

"Here, then," said Peace, "is a mirror. I believe Sir Jared is done with it."

Jared replied, "That's right. I'm going to get my kit together. I want to carry at least a few bandages and such."

As she accepted the mirror, Elise realized that she was avoiding turning in Sir Jared's direction. At Peace's suggestion, he had removed his beard and mustache. The one glimpse of him she had caught had made him seem quite the stranger. She didn't know what he'd think of her.

One thing seemed certain—if he'd fallen in love with her for her beauty, this shearing was certain to kill that love.

Elise managed to keep from gasping with horror when she saw her own reflection. Grateful Peace had pulled her hair back into a queue before beginning his shaving. Therefore it was a nearly hairless, scarlet-faced demon who blinked out at her from the mirror. If Elise hadn't grown somewhat accustomed to finding the features beneath the omnipresent New Kelvinese ornamentation she would not have known herself.

"Take the red stick," Peace said to her, his hands never pausing in their rhythm, "and darken the line of your brows. Give your features some definition by filling in the creases alongside your mouth. Paint in your lips as well, but do so lightly. If you apply too much, you'll end up with paint on your teeth."

Having a specific task steadied Elise. As she complied with the thaumaturge's orders, he continued:

"The most important thing all of you must remember if you are to pass for one of us is that you *must* keep your hands away from your face. We learn this from our earliest childhood so that it is automatic. The constant rubbing of lip or eyelid or bridge of nose that you people do sets you apart."

Wendee agreed. "That's just what my director told us. When we did *Parted by the White Water* he said that the best way to show that Guyus was New Kelvinese even when he wasn't wearing any paint was to make certain he never raised his hands above neck level. It was amazing how effective it was."

Before long, they were ready. Peace had selected the most appropriate robes from Wendee's collection and supervised their donning so that the fabric remained untouched by the paint. Because of the cold and because of the possible need for a fast escape, the robes were donned over trousers and shirts. It transformed them all—even curvaceous Wendee Jay—into bulky androgynous figures.

Weapons were concealed beneath the robes. These were few enough, mostly knives. Bows would be useless indoors and, in any case, the researchers would not be armed. Lady Melina was another matter.

The women were more or less accustomed to long skirts, but Doc clearly felt encumbered. Hearing him curse as he stumbled, Elise turned to him.

She saw his eyes widen as he took in her new appearance and fancied that his expression mirrored her own. However, as he said nothing, neither did she.

"Take smaller steps," she counseled. "You are striding as if in breeches or trousers. That's why you keep treading on your hem."

Doc tried to do as she had advised, achieving a mincing gait that sent Firekeeper into peals of laughter.

"No, Doc, smaller steps, not tiny—you look as if your boots are too tight!"

Sir Jared grumbled, "I'll never manage this!"

Grateful Peace turned a serious face toward him.

"If you think not, Sir Jared, then you must remain."

Relief flooded Elise as Sir Jared straightened and glowered at the New Kelvinese.

"I am going," he said. "I just hope I don't end up on my backside in the snow."

"We won't be out in the snow for long," Peace assured him. "As we have prepared, I have considered possible routes. Initially, I thought to take us above ground until we were fairly near the Earth Spires. However, this would create more opportunities for you to be seen. Your disguises are adequate, but not perfect. Therefore, we will descend at a point closer to this neighborhood. Once below ground, I want you to tuck up your robes."

"So we don't walk on them?" Doc asked wryly.

"Not only that," Peace said. "I will be doing the same. It would not do for any of us to track in sewer dirt. Footwear can be scraped or, at worst, discarded, but robes cannot be."

They said their farewells to Derian and Jared. Both young men wore matching expressions, mixing apprehension with guilt.

"I say," Edlin said, pumping Elise's hand—she'd had to forestall him from an embrace lest he smear her paint—"I feel a complete cad letting you go without me."

"You'll have trouble enough," she reminded him, "getting everything out in time. Are Hasamemorri and her maids asleep?"

"Like babes," he assured her. "I prowled up there a moment ago."

Edlin glanced over to where Firekeeper stood by the door, her hand resting lightly on Blind Seer's head.

"Take care of Little Sister," he said with affected lightness.

"No need," Firekeeper replied, though Elise could have sworn she wasn't near enough to hear. "We take care of ourselves. You and Derian take care and we see you when we come."

As they took their leave, Elise noted that Derian bore on

his cheek the faintest mark of two red lips. Firekeeper, then, *had* said her good-byes.

Despite their cloaks, which they wore with the hoods pulled up around their heads, the night air was so cold that the moisture from their breath froze in tiny crystals on the wool.

"It is colder than usual for this time of year," Grateful Peace commented conversationally. "Good. All but those with important business will be indoors."

He led the way to a side street at the end of which a trapdoor interrupted the orderly cobbles.

"Service entrance," he explained, raising the ring. "The traps are a bit heavy."

Elise was surprised that Firekeeper, who normally enjoyed showing off her considerable strength, let Sir Jared be the one who came forward to help raise the stone. Then she saw that the wolf-woman was in conference with Elation.

The falcon departed in an explosion of wings and Firekeeper padded over to join them.

"Elation say," she informed them, "that Lady Melina is there—not in her room—she is in tower."

As Elise descended the ladder into the depths, she glanced up and glimpsed Firekeeper's expression in the moonlight. The wolf-woman's eyes were shining and her teeth were bared, deadly white against her reddened face.

XXXI

 SUBCONSCIOUSLY, GRATEFUL PEACE HAD EX-pected the sewer to be cold and dank. In reality, it was actually somewhat warmer than the area above, insulated as it was by the living rock upon which the city was built.

Nor was the subterranean tunnel terribly clammy. Even

though the temperature here was somewhat warmer than Peace had expected, it was cold enough to draw most of the moisture from the air. It had even frozen the stench—somewhat.

He began to lead the way down the rounded length of the tunnel, guiding his small band along the narrow but perfectly serviceable walkway that ran along both sides. Each of them carried a torch from the ample supply stocked by the city's sewer workers.

Peace began to lead, but he had hardly taken two steps when the girl, Firekeeper, pushed him gently to one side. She and the wolf glided to the front.

"I can see in this light," she explained in the soft voice people always seem to use when in darkness, the type of voice that acknowledges that darkness carries with it the purest element of the unknown, "if I not look into the torch fire."

Grateful Peace let her pass.

He had wondered how the wolf was going to get down into the tunnel. The ladder was very steep—hardly more than a series of metal rungs beaten into the wall. The platform below was slightly wider than the walkway they now traversed, but hardly wide enough to allow a leaping wolf a margin for error.

He had thought of several alternatives. Somehow he had never considered that Lady Blysse would *carry* the wolf, supporting it with one arm, guiding herself down the rungs with the other.

That would take superhuman strength, amazing confidence, and trust, so he had never considered it as an option. But she *had* done it, and if he had not watched the operation with his own eyes he still wouldn't believe it.

True, at the end Firekeeper had been panting hard and the front of her print robe was covered with grey wolf hair, but she had done it. She hadn't even messed her face paint too badly, though there were small patches of red on the wolf's flank where his fur had pressed against her face.

Grateful Peace followed the wolf-woman along the tunnel. It was rounded, a great pipe that in an emergency could carry far more water than it usually bore. It had been designed with snowmelt floods in mind, perhaps, or perhaps in anticipation that someday Dragon's Breath would become a far larger city than it had ever been or ever would be.

Peace didn't really know which was the answer.

We humans are such odd creatures, he thought. *Consider the energy we spend speculating on things that are not, that may never happen, that cannot be. Is that what sets this young woman apart from us? She seems to live precisely in the moment, on the cusp of each breath.*

"Which way?" came the husky voice from out of the near darkness in front of him.

They had come to a crossing of the tunnels. A new one entered from the east. A bridge had been built here for the convenience of those who must sometimes descend to carry away what blocked the easy flow of this subterranean river.

"Go straight," Peace replied. "We continue north almost all the way."

A grunt was his only reply; then there was the faint sound of soft-soled boots on stone and the occasional click that he imagined might be the tapping of the wolf's toenail against the floor.

In reality, he might be imagining it or transferring sounds from behind to in front. The acoustics here were tricky. He'd heard that the Sodality of Songweavers sent their apprentices into the tunnels alone and after dark as part of their test to be accepted as thaumaturges. If they could navigate by sound alone, they were promoted. If not, they could remain in the choir, but were never promoted.

It might be true. Some of the finest musicians in the choir never wore the thaumaturge's mark. On the other hand, it might just be one of those stories that all the sodalities spread around lest their associates think them too soft, too undemanding.

Occasionally, their party passed under another trapdoor. Each time, Firekeeper would pause beneath it, unspeaking, waiting to be told if this was the one. She did the same at each crossroad. Eventually, her silence got on Peace's nerves.

She's watching me, he thought. *I'd forgotten what it is like to be watched. I wonder if she is doing it deliberately.*

Something of her grin, just glimpsed in the torchlight as she once again turned away and began padding down the tunnel, made him think this was so.

Eventually, they came to a cluster of tunnels radiating from a central point. In the flickering light of their gathered torches, several trapdoors could just be glimpsed.

"We're under the Earth Spires now," Peace said. "Although I do not expect to meet with anyone, progress now in complete silence. I am not the only one who uses these ways."

The air stunk now with a greater concentration of fecal matter. It bore a hint of another scent, too, sulphur blended with a hint of molten copper and a dry musk unlike anything else known.

The sewer workers called it the breath of the dragon. The Sodality of Lapidaries said it was simply a concentration of the same gases that warmed the hot springs and caused mud to boil in certain pools. Certainly, the area surrounding the Earth Spires was rather more active than the rest of the city. This was either because the Star Wizard really imprisoned a dragon here or because the Founders had liked hot water nearby for their baths and experiments.

Either way, Peace was accustomed to the smell. His companions were not. He had to hush them again when they made disparaging comments about the rotten-egg reek. Whispers sometimes carried farther in these tunnels than did louder sounds. Why they did so was a mystery, but mystery or not, it was still truth.

Firekeeper was now staying closer to him. At first Peace thought she was afraid; then he realized that she was simply closing on the circle of light, getting her eyes accustomed to it so that if they emerged into a lit place she would not be disadvantaged.

She must sense—He stopped himself in midthought. *Sense! By the skull of the first Healed One—realize, not sense. I am falling under some superstitious reverence for the creature. True, she speaks to animals. True, she is more like something from one of the tales of the Founders' time than I had ever seen before, but there is no magic to her. She is simply strange. She is intelligent enough to realize that we must reach our way up fairly soon, that's all.*

Even so, Peace realized he was unnerved. Firekeeper alone would not have done it, but Firekeeper's powers combined with what he had seen Lady Melina do, with what he had heard that Sir Jared could do. . . . It rocked the foundations of his reality.

All my life I have believed myself part of the sorcerers' empire. Now I must face the truth that sorcery is not in us—not at least that I have seen. The kingdom of sorcery lies just across the White Water River and the great irony is they pretend to hate magic!

Firekeeper was waiting under another trapdoor. Peace checked the signs carved into the stone beside it. He nodded and unfastened his cloak.

"This is the door I want," he said softly. "Let me go first. I'll see if anyone is there. Leave your cloaks behind when you come up. They wouldn't be worn in the building."

He didn't say more, hoping they understood that even if someone was in the cellar they would not find it odd if the Dragon's Eye rose from the depths—or if they found it odd, they would not comment.

Reaching up, Grateful Peace set his torch in the sconce prepared for precisely this purpose. Little bits of burning ash fell on his sleeve and died in the cold of the fabric. Finding the first rungs of the ladder took him a moment, but after that he could have climbed from memory.

He mounted silently, pushed back the trapdoor, caught the scent of a cellar room that was almost never opened.

The key word here, of course, was "almost."

BLIND SEER INSISTED on being the one to follow the thaumaturge up the ladder.

"If there is trouble," the wolf said, *"I will end it in two*

snaps. In any case," he added practically, *"who but you would be strong enough to catch me if I fell?"*

Firekeeper gave in without protest. The straight ladder had been useless for getting the wolf down, but going up the toe-holds proved to be just sufficient. Of course, it didn't hurt that they had essayed similar ladders during their nightly prowls.

She followed the wolf without a backward glance. Of course the other three would follow. What else could they do?

Emerging into the dimly lit cellar, Firekeeper threw her head back both to sniff—though catching any scent in this odor-filled place was a challenge—and to better feel the movement of the air. Along the sides of her face and against the skin of her shorn head, she could feel a current. It was too slight to be a breeze, but enough to indicate that somewhere an aperture stood open.

Grateful Peace had carried his torch—its flame dancing slightly in that same air current—to where a door was outlined against the darker stone.

Blind Seer stood hardly more than a pace behind the thau-maturge, ready to attack should the man prove treacherous. Firekeeper doubted Peace knew the wolf was so close; otherwise it was unlikely that he would calmly stand there, his ear pressed to where he had opened the door just the barest slit.

Grinning slightly, she moved to join them.

"Anything?" she asked in a soft voice.

To his credit, Grateful Peace did not start, nor did he show surprise when he found the great wolf right behind him. The acrid scent of suddenly released perspiration gave him away, but Firekeeper didn't blame him. As she saw it, he would be mad *not* to fear the wolf.

Peace shook his head.

By this time the other three had climbed up the ladder and closed the trapdoor behind them. By torchlight, Peace gave them all a quick inspection, straightening the fall of a robe, touching up the red on their faces. Firekeeper suffered him near, knowing that her exertions had marred her paint. She longed for the moment when she could scrub her skin clean, eliminate the greasy scent of the stuff, and return to normal.

Not trusting that the custodial staff would have oiled the door hinges, Peace did so, using an ointment he had carried along from Wendee's supply. Then he looked sternly at Fire-keeper.

"This time," he said, "*I* lead the way."

Firekeeper blinked at him, but did not argue. She hadn't planned on leading here in any case. She felt much safer knowing that Grateful Peace was aware of her Fang at his back.

All but one torch—the one Doc carried at the very rear—was extinguished. Then, with Peace leading, they ascended the stone stairs. Blind Seer fell back to melt into the shadows behind Doc. Firekeeper missed his warmth at her side, but knew that he was safer there—and that if there was trouble nothing would keep the wolf from her.

Although the building above rose around the base of the tower, here the stairs coiled round the outer rim of the tower's foundation. The stone treads were worn, showing a slight dip toward the center, chipping and scoring along the edges where heavy things had been dragged. They were neither steep nor shallow, holding in them the measure of lost people.

As she ascended, Firekeeper concentrated on not stepping on the hem of her robe while remaining alert for any danger. Her mouth was dry as it never had been when she hunted in the wilds and she recognized the dryness as the taste of fear.

Although the wolf-woman strained every nerve, she heard nothing, sensed nothing as they mounted. At last they reached a solid door, its planks bound with iron. A whiff of colder air coming from beneath the door told her that they had reached a level above ground.

Peace paused and looked back.

"Ground floor," he said softly. "The conference room is one above."

No one asked any questions. He was merely reminding them of what they had reviewed before departing Hasamemorri's house. Once again, Peace oiled the hinges, eased open the door. It swung into the stairwell, forcing Firekeeper to drop back a step or two to give it clearance.

Almost without thinking, she switched her Fang into a throwing grip. The knife was not very accurate when thrown—the cabochon-cut garnet at the base of the pommel threw off the balance—but it would do.

Again, there was nothing ahead of them but emptiness. Firekeeper's nerves were screaming, begging for something to attack, something to do.

Puppy! she scolded herself scornfully. *Are you truly nothing but a puppy?*

She lapsed into watchfulness as she followed Peace into the corridor. From Edlin's maps she knew that this must be part of the larger building that extended around the base of the tower. She raised her head to listen, but heard no movement from the corridors that crossed out from this one.

At the far end of one corridor there was a glow of pale light and snatches of lazy conversation in New Kelvinese. She couldn't understand a word, but it did not seem to bode harm for them.

Peace had told them that this ground floor was being used as sleeping space for the researchers. If so, no doubt most were resting, dreaming of future success. A few, night owls by preference or perhaps winding down after some exertions, must be chatting in a common area.

They will never know we were here, Firekeeper thought.

Grateful Peace led them down a corridor to the left—to the north, Firekeeper thought, remembering the map. He paused before a door, larger and heavier than the cellar doors.

"Outside," he whispered.

Firekeeper nodded, showing she remembered. This was the door they would have gone through had Elation not reported that Lady Melina was in the tower. It was the door they would still go through if the situation Elation had reported had changed.

They had settled this matter while traveling through the sewers, and now she slipped outside to meet the falcon.

As they had planned, Elation was waiting, sitting hunched

on the branch of a twisted tree bare of all but a few tattered leaves clinging to its upper reaches.

"*Lady Melina?*" Firekeeper asked.

Elation fluttered her wings.

"*Still in there. She is three levels above this one. There are six with her working over something small. Bold watches and would call if she had left.*"

"*My thanks.*" Firekeeper slipped back inside, nodded once, pointed upward, and held up three fingers.

Peace nodded, smiled a smile that was more a baring of teeth against the blackening of his face, and motioned them on. The stairwell to the upper levels curved against the outer walls of the tower. At the top was a stout door, but its locks were not meant to keep Peace out.

As they moved into the corridor, Firekeeper could immediately tell the difference from the lower floor. Fat candles with several wicks burned in wall sconces shaped after the fashion of grasping hands. The corridor smelled of musty wool from the rug. The scent of strong tea and sweets eddied from beneath a large double door on one side of the corridor.

"Conference room," Peace mouthed.

As planned, he went to the door, unlocking it when he found it locked.

That is a form of power, Firekeeper thought. *Not only being able to unlock doors, but having no one question your right to do so.*

She glanced at her companions. Elise had followed her up the stair and so now stood closest. Her lips were slightly apart as if she had been panting, but that was the only sign of fear she showed.

Wendee was more obviously afraid, her gaze darting back and forth as if she expected one of the doors to fly open and their enemies to set upon them. Still, she held her ground, her attitude not of panic, but of readiness.

Doc had extinguished his torch before leaving the stairwell, but his right hand remained curved as if still holding its weight. He had remained near the stairwell door, holding it just the slightest bit ajar so as to hear if anything came from below.

Blind Seer crouched near Doc's feet. His jaws were parted in a wolfish grin, his tongue lolling slightly. Any who came through that door would find a welcoming committee so terrifying that he might not even find breath to scream.

Glancing at Elise, Firekeeper touched the lobe of her ear and pointed toward the door. Elise looked worried for a moment, then nodded. She pressed her ear to the keyhole, her furrowed brow looking very odd with the bare skin above it.

After listening for a moment, Elise raised one hand, making a mouth of the fingers and moving them so that they suggested steady conversation under way inside. Suddenly, she stiffened and pulled back, indicating to the others that they should hang back as well.

The door opened and Peace said something to those inside as he stepped through. His tone was relaxed and easy, but Firekeeper did not let down her guard until he had come through—alone.

He gestured for them to enter the stairwell, paused long enough to lock the door behind him. As he did so, he said:

"They are making plans, nothing more. The artifacts are above. Lady Melina works with the ring. The comb and mirror are locked in a safe on the floor one above her."

Firekeeper wished that Elation had volunteered whether any stayed above to guard the safe, but then neither of the wingéd folk could have known where the items were stored.

As the next floor was not in use—as least as far as Peace had been able to discern—they passed by that door. The stair spiraled around until they had mounted to the level where, according to both Elation and Peace's informants, Lady Melina labored to awaken the secrets of the ring.

Here Firekeeper became aware of a conflict of loyalties. Yes, Lady Melina was within—and with her one of those things the wolf-woman had come to retrieve. Above, however, quite possibly unguarded, were the two remaining artifacts.

Should she pass by an easy chance to obtain them just to go after Lady Melina? Wouldn't going in where her team was awake and alert be certain to cause a commotion—a commotion that might bring help from below or from alert guards posted outside?

The more the wolf-woman considered, the less wise going through that door seemed, yet even now Peace was preparing to unlock it. She laid a hand on the man's black-robed arm, drew her Fang from the Mouth that held it.

She pressed her lips close to his ear.

"Wait!" she ordered.

STANDING A FEW PACES BEHIND FIREKEEPER, Elise heard the wolf-woman order Grateful Peace to stop at the very instant he would have unlocked the door. A sparkling reflection, ruddy in the candlelight, told her that the wolf-woman had not trusted her voice alone to be enough to assure obedience.

The tip of Firekeeper's knife rested against Grateful Peace's throat and no one who had seen her at work that night would have doubted she had the strength to slice not only through skin but through spine as well.

Peace had frozen in place, but now he dared shape a single word.

"Why?"

Firekeeper's brows knotted. As was often the case when she was pressured, speech—at least human speech—did not come easily to her.

"If we do," she managed, "noise will come. So will others. Before we have the things . . ."

She jerked her head to indicate above.

Elise understood and was impressed by Firekeeper's forethought.

"She means," she whispered hurriedly, "that if we go in where there are six or seven people, there will be an alarm. She wants to get the items from above first."

Grateful Peace licked his lips, a sure sign—given what he had told them of New Kelvinese mannerisms—that he was tense. Elise feared that he would do something unwise. After all, he was a man accustomed to being obeyed, one of the most important men in his kingdom.

Would he realize the risk he would be running if he challenged Firekeeper? At times like this she was more wolf than human and from what Elise had grasped of wolf ways, there was only one way to deal with a challenger.

Elise held her breath for what seemed like an eternity.

"I believe," Grateful Peace managed, "that a change in plans is in order."

"What," Wendee asked—rather bravely, Elise thought, given the wild look in Firekeeper's eyes—"will we do if they decide to leave while we are upstairs?"

Elise watched carefully while Firekeeper, who had removed her knife from Grateful Peace's throat and motioned them away from the door, considered.

"Blind Seer," the wolf-woman replied, "will wait here to guard. No one will leave."

As the doors to these upper tower rooms opened almost directly into the stairwell, the wolf took up his station on one of the broad treads.

If someone comes up the stair ... Elise thought, then shrugged. Anyone coming up those stairs tonight was in for a nasty surprise, wolf or no wolf.

Leaving Blind Seer, the five humans mounted up and around the curve to the next door. Peace took out his keys and looked to Firekeeper for permission.

The wolf-woman nodded tersely and drew her knife, poised to spring should the room be occupied.

It was.

Two young people, a man and woman, both tattooed across their faces, though the patterns of those tattoos were blurred from where scarlet paint had been inadequately removed, had started up from the floor, apparently when the key turned in the lock.

What they had been doing was quite obvious. Both were

completely nude; the youth still knelt between his partner's thighs. When they saw the dark-painted features of the Dragon's Eye, their initial embarrassed flush faded into something pale and sickly.

Grateful Peace strode into the tower room, his voice resonating through the almost empty chamber and filled with righteous anger. Firekeeper padded after him, staying where his bulk would conceal much of her advance.

Embarrassed, Elise hung back, taking as her excuse the need to make certain that the door into the stairwell was securely closed behind them so the sound of Peace's voice would not carry below.

For the first time, she was glad that her face was painted red. This way Doc could not see her blush.

"So which of you is on watch tonight?"

The youth, scrabbling for his discarded robe, said weakly: "I am, sir."

"And your partner?"

"She's not my partner. I mean she is . . . I mean, sir, that she isn't assigned to this watch. I asked her to keep me company."

"But wasn't someone assigned to that task?"

Elise had the feeling that Grateful Peace was guessing, basing his queries on previous experience.

"Yes, sir, but I . . . I . . . It isn't his fault, sir. I told him I'd be all right alone. He very much wanted to get some sleep, sir. Prime Tallus has had him working double time . . ."

The youth trailed off. Elise found herself admiring him for managing to say so much while standing buck naked in front of one of his superiors.

Peace appeared to consider.

The girl had grabbed one of the blankets that had been heaped on the floor and wrapped it around herself, but physical cover had not granted her courage. The boy—for Elise was willing to guess he was not much more than seventeen—took advantage of Peace's silence to slip on his own robe and fasten the carved wooden toggles up the front.

"I have come to take the two artifacts in the safe to the

Dragon Speaker," Peace said at last. "I will permit you to open the safe."

The boy hesitated, but Peace did not look as if he would brook any argument. In any case, whatever bit of procedure was being violated in this request—and Elise sensed that *something* Peace had just said wasn't quite right—the young man wasn't in a very good moral position to ask questions.

Head bowed as if seeking to avoid looking more than he must into the thaumaturge's pale, angry gaze, the youth crossed to where a large, ornate metal box rested on a stand in one corner of the room.

The case had been embellished with teeth and claws so that it resembled some very compact monster. Brightly polished copper claws gripped the edges of the door.

Trying not to watch too closely—after all, she didn't know whether this was supposed to be a routine with which she was familiar—Elise missed exactly what the young man did that caused the claws to snap away from the door.

Peripherally, she was aware that the young woman had retreated several steps and now was trying to put on her gown without relinquishing the cover of the blanket.

Elise wondered if she should offer to help but decided not to draw any more attention than necessary to herself.

Now the young man was doing something with the metal monster's teeth. The door to the box sagged slightly within the brackets that held it. He slid it to one side and retrieved two wooden boxes from within.

We're going to do it! Elise thought excitedly.

Then everything went wrong.

PEACE SAW THE VERY INSTANT THAT sudden revelation touched the young man's eyes. He had just handed over the two boxes and was moving to close the safe. Whether that was the moment he got his first clear look at Peace's unorthodox escort or simply the moment that he regained some of the confidence that had vanished when Peace's entry interrupted his tryst, Peace might never know.

"Wait a moment, sir," the young man said just a trace awkwardly. "I really should notify the team downstairs that you are removing the artifacts."

"That isn't necessary . . ." Peace rapidly rummaged through his memory, found the youth's name—Indatius of the Artificers. ". . . Indatius. I need no clearance."

"But *I* do, sir," Indatius said with impressive determination. Perhaps he had decided that there was no way his indiscretion could be overlooked so at least he wasn't going to be caught violating another procedure.

Peace had not been a watcher these many years without knowing implacable stubbornness. He nodded.

"I see," he said, hoping to stall.

Indatius, however, was ahead of him. He grabbed the heavy door of the safe and wrenched it from its tracks. It hit the wooden floor with a resounding, reverberating clatter that would without question bring someone from the room below to investigate—or at least to complain.

Indatius backed away from Peace—without, however, attempting to take the boxes from him.

"I'm sorry, sir," he began, "but this is all wrong. I don't recognize your assistants and . . ."

A low, ominous howl from below interrupted whatever Indatius might have been about to say. Sir Jared wrenched open the door to the stairwell.

Firekeeper, almost visibly balanced between staying near the artifacts and answering that call, teetered for only a moment. Then, moving with more speed than Peace would have credited even her, she snatched the boxes containing the mirror and the comb from his hands.

Backing away as smoothly as if she could see behind her, Firekeeper thrust one box into Elise's hand, the other into Wendee's. Then, without word or pause, she was running down the stairs, her own, shriller howl echoing back through the stone corridor.

Peace realized that the behavior of this strange, feral woman had provided him with an excuse for his own actions. He could always claim to have been forced to guide the Hawk Havenese into the tower. It wasn't the best of explanations, but it would do for now.

Spinning on his heel, he pointed toward where Elise and Wendee stood, too surprised for this brief moment to flee.

"After them!" he shouted.

As Indatius bolted past him, eager to redeem himself, Peace caught the young man a solid thump behind his ear. Indatius reeled. Peace sent him down. Only then did he recall Indatius's lover.

Wendee Jay, however, had not forgotten her.

After stuffing the slim box that held the comb into the waist of her robe, Wendee had scooped up some of the piled blankets from the floor. In one smooth move, she tossed them over the girl's head. In fact, Wendee might have acted even before Peace had succeeded in bringing down Indatius.

If so, Peace thought with that cruel detachment that came to him in a crisis, *Goody Wendee, too, may have done her part to save my reputation.*

"Bind her and the boy," he heard Elise order with a coolness that astonished him. "I'm going down to see what made Firekeeper howl like that. Doc may need my help."

Peace ran after Lady Elise, so close upon her heels that the trailing golden braid that was all that remained of her once magnificent hair almost touched him as it flew out behind her.

They reached the landing below only moments after Firekeeper's howl had sounded. Immediately, the reason for that anguished cry became evident.

Blind Seer lay on his side in the open doorway, his silvery grey fur awash with blood. The blood flowed from both head and throat, hiding the actual wounds beneath the gory flood.

Sir Jared knelt beside the wolf, laboring with such focused intensity that the beast must not yet be dead. As Lady Elise paused beside the healer, her knuckles rose to her mouth to stifle a scream.

Firekeeper was nowhere to be seen. Assuming that she had

gone ahead into the room, Grateful Peace sidled past the bleeding hulk on the doorsill and stepped into the room. Long training in noticing everything around him collected the details before he had time to register what they meant.

Superficially, the large, round chamber was arrayed much as he would have expected it to be. Tables littered with various items of alchemical gear stood untouched. The retorts bubbled calmly over their braziers. Thin glass tubes carrying distilled liquids through some prearranged sequence remained unbroken.

That was where normalcy ended.

Four grey-robed figures huddled against the wall farthest from the doorway, the whites of their eyes wide with terror and grotesquely accented by scarlet paint. A body sprawled in a pool of blood just a few steps from the doorway showed why they feared to draw closer.

Peace opened his mouth to summon the doctor from his lupine patient, but a second glance told him this one was beyond help. That same glance brought home to him who it was who lay there dead.

It was Kistlio, his sister's son, the eager young clerk who had been seduced into Lady Melina's service. Voice trembling slightly with sudden grief, Peace demanded:

"What happened here?"

Rafalias of the Lapidaries replied, her voice still shrill with panic.

"We were working, in here, on the ring . . ."

"Yes," Peace prompted.

"There was a sound from above, a dreadful thumping. Lady Melina . . ."

For the first time, Peace registered that Lady Melina was not among those huddled figures. Nor was Firekeeper. Now he knew what had been important enough to draw the young woman from her wounded pet's side.

". . . wasn't very happy. We'd been hearing thumping up there all evening—softer, but that last had been enough to make the glassware rattle. Evaglayn was so startled she dropped a retort."

Rafalias pointed to where the broken glassware had been swept against the wall.

"Yes?" Peace prompted.

He forced himself to listen closely. If he didn't, he was going to start thinking about a bright-eyed young man who was now dead because his uncle had not seen the truth in time. Dead because his uncle had treated with foreign killers rather than deal with the problem through more usual channels.

"Lady Melina wasn't very happy," Rafalias faltered, repeating herself before she found the thread of her tale. "She told Kistlio to go see what was wrong and to get the names of those who were creating such a commotion. She was swearing that she herself would report the disturbance to the Dragon Speaker at the very moment Kistlio opened the door."

Rafalias couldn't seem to find the voice to continue but Evaglayn, a pretty, if grave, young woman who was a senior apprentice from the Beast Lorists, took up the tale.

"A wolf stood without, a wolf as large as . . ." Evaglayn pointed with trembling hand. "You can see it yourself."

Peace nodded, impatient now. He was bursting with a desire to do something, but to act without knowing what had gone before would be idiocy.

"It growled," Evaglayn said, "and anyone with any sense would have frozen where he stood, but Kistlio could never be slowed nor stopped when Lady Melina needed service. He drew his knife and slashed down at the beast, slicing it across the head near one eye. The wolf howled in pain and anger and lunged forward."

Evaglayn may have remembered then that Kistlio was Grateful Peace's nephew, for now she spoke more gently of him.

"Kistlio was very brave, though. He kept slashing at the wolf, forcing it back a few steps. Yet there was no hope that a single man armed only with a knife could defeat such a creature. Kistlio lies where the wolf left him."

Rafalias, perhaps sensitive to the lack of dignity she showed in letting an apprentice—no matter how senior—speak in her place, took up the tale.

"As Kistlio fell, Lady Melina grabbed the ring from where it rested on the table and thrust it into her robes. From the table she seized a hand axe Nelm had been using earlier to chop scented woods for the braziers. Running forward, she intercepted the wolf and swung at him, catching him hard in the flank.

"The wolf snapped at her, but Lady Melina gave the oddest laugh—high and nasal like the whinny of a frightened horse. She seemed to address the beast in her own language. He paused and when he did so, Lady Melina skipped past him and through the door. The wolf made as if to follow, staggered a few steps, and collapsed where even now he lies."

"We could see," Rafalias went on a trace apologetically, "that there was life in the monster yet, so we kept our distance."

"Wise," Grateful Peace said dryly. "Very wise. So none of you went after Lady Melina—even though she appears to have departed with a priceless artifact."

They gaped at him then, all four, and in their slowness to recognize Lady Melina's possible culpability, Peace saw again the effectiveness of the foreign woman's magic.

"Someone did go after her," replied Evaglayn slowly, "moments after the wolf had fallen. I caught a glimpse of scarlet paint and very short hair—oh, and a robe in some print, not a proper researcher's grey as we wear here."

"Quite a lot to notice as someone hurries past the door," Peace said. He felt curiously distant from all this, yet vaguely judicial—though for the moment he had no idea who was on trial.

"The person I saw paused by the wolf for a moment," Evaglayn replied defensively. "Paused and laid a hand in its blood, but whoever it was stayed no longer than that."

Grateful Peace turned away from them, no longer interested. Kneeling, he turned over Kistlio's body. The boy had died from a single clean swipe at his throat. He must have bled out almost before he hit the floor.

Had Kistlio known he had failed the woman he so unnaturally adored?

Something in the expression on the young man's face told Peace that he had.

XXXII

WHEN SHE HEARD BLIND SER'S CRY OF PAIN, Firekeeper froze in place. Hooks of obligation tore cruelly into her heart. One bound her to the artifacts; the other, stronger and deeper, pulled her almost physically toward wherever Blind Seer was.

Thought, as most would understand it, did not play a part in her subsequent actions. All the wolf-woman desired was to loosen the hook that held her to this place.

Her hands darted forth and seized the boxes from the hands that held them. She wheeled to run, found she could not bare her Fang with her hands full, and thrust the boxes into the keeping of those who—even through the fog of impulses filling her mind—she knew could be trusted.

That action loosened the hook sufficiently that she was free to run to Blind Seer, but—swift as she had been—she saw as soon as she rounded the curve of the stair that she was too late.

The Royal Wolf lay on the floor, his fur soaked with the blood that still flowed from countless wounds. Firekeeper's nose could not be fooled into hoping that the blood was not the wolf's, for though she smelled human blood, most of what clung to the wolf was his own.

As she crouched beside Blind Seer, one blue eye flickered open.

"Lady Melina," he panted. "The ring."

"Did she do this?"

With a weak thump of his tail, Blind Seer answered, "Yes." Firekeeper glanced into the round tower room, confirming what she had already guessed—perhaps a chance trace of perfume in the air had told her before she thought to ask. Lady Melina was not among those who huddled within, nor was hers the corpse that lay facedown on the floor.

Behind her, she could hear Doc running down the stairs. Knowing well that he could do more for Blind Seer than she could, Firekeeper felt the hook of obligation anchor itself into her heart once more.

"I'll get her," she promised, "and the ring."

Blind Seer said only, "Remember, she is not a wolf."

Her hand still wet with the wolf's warm blood, Firekeeper leapt over him and down the curve of the stair.

As she passed the door on the conference-room level, she heard curses and exclamations. They didn't interest her, except in some small corner of her mind that noted there could be unfriendly pursuit. What had seized her attention was a draft of fresh cold air from below.

Someone had opened the outer door. Did Lady Melina race for aid or merely to her den?

The wolf-woman slowed as she emerged into the cold night and a bit of black detached itself from the surrounding blackness.

Bold the crow cawed, "We saw. Elation follows Lady Melina. I will lead you."

Firekeeper managed a nod of thanks, but held up her hand for a moment's respite. She pushed the door to the Granite Tower closed behind her and shoved a boulder from those collected at the base of the tree against it.

There must be other exits from the tower—even if only the one in the cellar—but this might slow pursuit.

Squawking his approval, Bold took wing. As she followed, seeing the crow as motion against the air rather than as shape or form, Firekeeper thought she knew where they were going.

Grateful Peace's descriptions returned to her, confirming that Lady Melina had fled to her den, rather than seeking help.

The stillness of the complex confirmed the wolf-woman's guess. In the near distance, Firekeeper could hear the guards posted at the ornate front gate talking with casual boredom among themselves. Had Lady Melina wanted aid, she could have found it there. So she wanted something else more.

The ring.

Firekeeper's early life had not shaped her mind to think in twists, but recently she had been given ample lessons in such thought. Even as the need to preserve the ring gave Lady Melina excuse for flight, the desire to steal it—to preserve it for her sole use—would be ample reason to turn away from easy assistance.

Bold banked to a halt before a door that even now stood ajar. Elation perched on the door's upper edge.

"I stopped her," the peregrine said with pardonable pride, *"from closing this and locking it behind her—she had a key— but the corridors within are too narrow for my wings."*

"Go." Firekeeper commanded even as she stepped inside. *"Help the others to safety. They have two of the artifacts. I will get the third and follow."*

She didn't wait for a reply, but darted instead up the stairs. Lady Melina's scent was hot, but the wolf-woman didn't need that as a guide; her memory held Grateful Peace's directions.

Peace had told them that the building stood nearly empty. It was reserved exclusively for foreign guests. After one visit, not many such guests chose to stay within Thendulla Lypella, if they were given a choice, for their freedom was so restricted that it was as if they dwelt within a luxurious prison.

Some, Peace had said ironically, might even suspect that arrangements had been made to watch them.

All but the most essential staff slept elsewhere and even those should be asleep. Since Lady Melina had not alerted the gate guards, Firekeeper doubted she would awaken someone as useless as a maid.

The wolf-woman pelted up the stairs after her prey, her booted feet making soft scuffing noises against the stone, her trailing, bloodstained robe torn away in front—for she had ripped it as she ran to keep it from tangling her feet.

She could feel the short hairs on her neck stand up when she turned down a corridor and saw a partially open door at one end. Noise came through that opening: frantic whimpers and gasping breaths. With shining eyes, Firekeeper ran toward her prey.

Bursting through the open door with such speed that even had anyone crouched behind or beside the portal she would have passed them before they could strike, Firekeeper spun to a halt on a patch of thick carpet before a low sofa.

Lady Melina knelt by a fireplace, her hands pressed against the stones. On her right hand, Firekeeper saw a large ring that didn't quite fit and guessed that this was the third artifact. On the stone bench that flanked the fireplace rested a small hatchet, its blade stained with Blind Seer's blood.

Firekeeper paced forward and Lady Melina stood to meet her, turning rather too quickly, as if she sought to hide something behind her.

Her face had been painted as garishly as that of a New Kelvinese. Not for Lady Melina the simple scarlet worn for work; this color wove a serpent's path emphasizing the upper portion of her face.

Searching for the face beneath the paint, Firekeeper sought Lady Melina's eyes. She found them, cool and pale, glittering from the depths of two sinuous coils.

The wolf-woman felt an odd desire to shout aloud in triumph, but the sight of the bloody hatchet on the hearthstone chilled her spirit. Lips peeling back from her teeth in a snarl, Firekeeper growled:

"That—" She pointed to the ring. "Give!"

"Why?" Lady Melina replied almost casually. Then her voice rose sightly, excitement coursing through its controlled notes.

"Can it be that you know its secret?"

Firekeeper only stared at her, confused.

"No, I see that you do not," Lady Melina laughed. "I see that you are merely a dog fetching for her master."

Firekeeper bristled, but Lady Melina continued on, even pausing long enough to take a seat on the raised hearth.

"I wonder who sent you, pup? Uncle Tedric? Allister Seagleam? Probably. They seem to command you and yet . . ." Her voice fell into a silky, insinuating softness. "And yet you do not know that what you seek at others' command holds in it the power to grant your heart's desire."

Despite her fury, Firekeeper discovered that she could no more keep from listening than she could will the sun to rise.

"See this?" Lady Melina held out her hand so that Firekeeper could see the ring clearly. "A moonstone held in the jaws of a beast. The New Kelvinese were not slow to pick up on the symbolism, but I think they feared the power we would unleash . . ."

She chuckled. "No pun intended."

Firekeeper growled, but though some part of her clamored that she should seize the ring and be gone—leaving Lady Melina's head on the floor in token of her coming—she could not seem to stir.

"The moon is an almost universal emblem for change," Lady Melina went on. "Here it is held in the mouth of a beast. Moon/change/beast. It is a simple enough sequence, don't you think?"

Shaking her head was the hardest thing Firekeeper had ever done.

"We haven't yet found the trigger," Lady Melina admitted. "I've suggested mingled blood . . ."

Blood!

The word burned through Firekeeper's mind, the thunder of her own blood in her ears was like a storm beating against the shore. Amid the noise, she didn't hear what Lady Melina said next, only knew that the ring was being extended toward her, glowing in the firelight as Lady Melina moved it slowly back and forth, back and forth.

"Come, Firekeeper, take the ring," Lady Melina urged softly. "You've always wanted to be a wolf, haven't you? This holds the means. Of course, if you return the ring to King Allister, you'll never have that power, will you?"

The thunder of the waves was ebbing now, being replaced with a gentler susurrus, a sleepy rhythm that held the rocking of a cradle, the swaying of the bough, the caress of waves against a beach.

Firekeeper half raised her hand toward the ring and wondered at the heaviness in her limbs.

"Stay with me, Firekeeper," Lady Melina said gently, "stay with me and I will help you find your dreams. We will discover how to awaken the ring. Then you can have all you desire."

Firekeeper's foot slid forward as if of its own accord. Behind her, a rattling blended into the soft rhythm in her head; even the metallic clink as Lady Melina's left hand slid the hatchet into her grip couldn't break her sense of sleepy peace.

She would be a wolf, a wolf at last. She and Blind Seer would run through the woods, laughing as they plowed chest-deep through the snowdrifts.

Something worried at the edge of her tranquility when she thought of the blue-eyed wolf. She saw him haloed in red, but then the red transformed into the glow of the setting sun behind him. Then they stood shoulder to shoulder, singing the moon as she rose.

Smiling, Firekeeper was stepping forward when the crash of glass against wood and stone ripped through the sound of Lady Melina's voice. A shriek sliced the air.

"Firekeeper!"

An intense shock of pain in the vicinity of her right hip, coming almost as one with the shrill cry, jolted Firekeeper from her dream.

She stood within arm's reach of Lady Melina, but this Lady Melina was anything but tranquil.

The sorceress still wore the ring upon her right hand, but the blue-white stone was covered by Bold. The crow had perched upon Lady Melina's upper arm and now sought to drag the ring from the woman's hand.

Lady Melina might have shoved the bird away, but for the fact that she needed her remaining hand to ward Elation from her face. She had dropped the hatchet in her panic and instantly Firekeeper realized what had caused the pain in her hip.

Neither was Lady Melina a trained fighter, nor had she expected the dual thickness of leather where vest met trousers beneath Firekeeper's tattered robe. Doubtless she had been aiming higher—for the soft abdomen or the vulnerable throat—but Elation's attack had thrown her aim off just enough.

Firekeeper dove into the fray.

The peregrine couldn't achieve the height she needed for one of her stooping dives, but she had sufficient room to batter at Lady Melina with her wings. Already, Elation's claws had drawn blood, blood that beaded against the paint on Lady Melina's face, creating the eerie impression that the sorceress's own blood had rejected her.

Firekeeper staggered slightly as she registered the deep bruise that would be forming where the hatchet had impacted against the bone, but an almost insane fury was replacing the artificial tranquility Lady Melina had created.

The wolf-woman never doubted that she—like so many others—had fallen prey to Lady Melina's particular sorcery. She recalled her own triumph as she had sought, wolf-like, to intimidate her opponent with her stare and knew that in doing so she had opened herself to her enemy's attack.

Remember, she is not a wolf.

Burning with shame, she heard Blind Seer's warning—a warning she had discarded. Had it not been for the intervention of the wingéd folk she would be bleeding out her life at Lady Melina's feet.

Fang in hand, Firekeeper pushed the peregrine aside. Ignoring the new trickle of blood from where a talon had scored her forearm, she pressed the knife blade against Lady Melina's throat.

As from a great distance, she heard Bold's hoarse chuckle of triumph as he tugged the ring free. Heard the flap of his wings as he bore away his prize—never knowing how much temptation he was taking out of reach.

But Firekeeper had eyes only for Lady Melina. Keeping her own gaze away from the fatal crystalline paleness of the sorceress's gaze, she was ready to push the blade home when she heard Elation—who was perched somewhere behind her—say:

"Citrine."

Firekeeper stayed the thrust.

"Where is Citrine?" she asked hoarsely.

Lady Melina did not feign ignorance.

"Will the information win me my life?"

"No, but it may win Citrine's own."

Lady Melina paused; then, to Firekeeper's astonishment, she began to shake—a deep trembling accompanied by the tang of fresh sweat and the faint odor of urine.

"I don't want to die!" the woman wailed.

Firekeeper growled, "Tell me!"

Lady Melina could not crumple—not without driving the knife into her own throat—but her muscles seemed to lose all strength. Close to Lady Melina as she was, Firekeeper could feel the muscles slacken, driven beyond the rictus of terror into the limpness of despair.

"I'll show you where Citrine is!"

"No."

"She's . . . Please, you can't want to rob a little girl of her mama!"

"You stall. Tell!"

"A house," Lady Melina gasped.

Tears now coursed down her cheeks, splashing hot against Firekeeper's hand. Inadvertently, she drew her hand back slightly, but the Fang still remained within easy reach of that vulnerable throat.

Perhaps mistaking distaste for mercy, Lady Melina gulped out a few words.

"To the east of Hawk Haven, near the swamps. That's where we left her. I don't know . . ."

Her voice trailed off into racking, panicked sobs. Then, as if her bones had melted, she slid from the hearthside bench onto which she had been pressed.

Lady Melina raised her face to Firekeeper, but she did not try to meet the wolf-woman's eyes, keeping her own downcast in fear. Her posture eloquently spoke of her vulnerability— exposing her throat to the killing blow.

"Please," the sorceress whimpered. "Spare me! Spare me . . ."

The last was barely audible.

Firekeeper tried to raise her Fang to drive it into that soft, white throat, but she could not make her hand move.

This time, however, there was no external control at work. In her deepest heart, Firekeeper *was* a wolf, and no sane wolf ever killed an opponent who had surrendered.

"*I can't . . .*" she said to Elation.

"*You can't let her live. This one is mad. She left her daughter to die. She tried to kill Blind Seer—he is sorely wounded.*"

"*I can't . . .*" Firekeeper moaned.

Lady Melina, eyes still downcast, arms outstretched, rose on trembling legs. She backed until she stood pressed against the stone, her fingers scrabbling as if she would dig herself a burrow there.

"*If you can't then,*" Elation shrieked, beating her wings and rising into the air, "*I can!*"

But there was not space, even in this large chamber, for the peregrine to stoop and dive as she would have outside. As she floundered, seeking to adapt her strike, there was a loud click.

Lady Melina cried out, this time not in fear but in triumph. A portion of the stone slid from behind her and she backed into a tunnel—doubtless one of those very tunnels of which Grateful Peace had bragged.

Firekeeper recovered swiftly from her shock at seeing surrender transform into flight. Lady Melina darted into the darkness on the other side of the wall.

When Firekeeper would have dashed after her, Elation landed so heavily on her shoulder that the wolf-woman was thrown off balance.

"*No!*" Elation shrieked. "*We have the ring. We know where the child is. Don't throw your life away.*"

Firekeeper staggered under the weight of the bird. Her hip shouted its own argument against an extended chase through unknown territory.

"*The others,*" she asked. "*I told you to get the others away.*"

"They are away, but needed no help from me to see the wisdom of retreat. Bold saw them beginning their descent from the tower. Blind Seer," the peregrine added in response to an unasked question, *"was with them. By now—unless Grateful Peace has betrayed them—they should be clear of this place and on their way outside the walls."*

Firekeeper nodded. *"Then we, too, must be away."*

They eschewed attempting to return to the tunnels, even though the Granite Tower was unbelievably quiet. Elation flew around it and reported that the top floor held two people quite definitely bound, while the next held four sitting down who might well be bound. The next lower floor remained dark—and so presumably empty—while the bottom floor of the tower proper was empty on one side. The other held a room full of people who seemed to be splitting their energies between arguing and trying to pry open a window that might not have been opened for centuries.

Firekeeper thought about finding another cellar and seeing if there was another trapdoor, but in her heart of hearts she was soundly tired of stone buildings, sewer tunnels, and all the rest. Instead, Elation bore the rags of Firekeeper's robe to the top of a shadowed portion of wall, far from where the commotion was centered.

With the cloth to pad the top where someone had strewn glass and other unpleasant things, Firekeeper struggled over the wall. Alternately staggering and limping, with the birds flying ahead to warn her of strangers, the wolf-woman made her weary way to where she could only hope her friends would be waiting.

THEY HAD APPOINTED an old sheepfold well outside the farthest outskirts of Dragon's Breath as their meeting place. It was a good choice, far enough that they should not be noticed, not too far to be reached by people on foot.

The only problem, Derian thought, *with meeting places is that first everyone has to get there.*

Initially, frantic preparation had kept his mind too full even for worry. Not only did he and Edlin need to pack every item belonging to their household, but there were supplies to lay by and—because Derian was an honest man—payment to leave for Hasamemorri as an apology for raiding her larder.

The horses—and more especially the mules—had resisted being packed and loaded at such a peculiar hour. Sleepy, stable-warm, well fed, the last thing any of them wanted was to be dragged out into the crisp, chill night.

Roanne had nipped Derian on the sleeve, snaking her ears back against her skull to express her disapproval.

Skilled as he was at dealing with both horses and mules, Derian found himself missing Firekeeper. A few words from her—or a growl from Blind Seer—would have reminded the hoofed stock who was in charge.

Firekeeper, Derian thought wryly, *but I wouldn't be arguing.*

One pleasant surprise, however, had been Lord Edlin's competence. Derian had expected to need to chivy him along at every stage, but, although Edlin could act like the greatest idiot ever to walk the earth, he proved remarkably steady once a crisis was at hand.

I should have expected that, Derian thought, chiding himself. *Edlin came through when the bandits captured us. It's just so easy to forget he has any skills at all when he spends so much of the time walking around with his mouth half open.*

Moreover, the hunting expeditions that were Lord Edlin's passion had honed his skills with both riding horses and pack mules. He might never be Derian's equal—Derian, after all, had been working in the trade since he could toddle at Colby Carter's heels—but he was an apt partner.

"If you ever get tired of lording," Derian said to Edlin when between them they had convinced one particularly obstinant mule to accept its load, "I'll speak to my father about giving you a job."

Edlin, grinning foolishly, actually looked pleased.

I wonder why Earl Kestrel didn't take Edlin west, Derian thought. *Maybe he wanted him to learn how to run the estate without Daddy near, but maybe Earl Kestrel hasn't had the chance to see what Edlin can do.*

Getting past the city guard had been its own form of torture. Derian had rehearsed his spiel over and over as they led their pack train through the nearly deserted streets. He felt that he had to say just enough to sound casual, but not so much that later he would be singled out for his panicked babbling.

It was something of a pity that neither Elise nor Wendee could be spared to go with them, but Derian firmly agreed that those who could understand what was being said around them needed to go into Thendulla Lypella. After all, it wouldn't do to have someone ask a question or snap a command, then for no one but Peace and one other to understand what had been said.

Still, it meant that he and Edlin would be remembered as foreigners when alarm was raised. That would set pursuit all the more swiftly on their heels.

As much as Derian had dreaded it, their encounter with the guards proved to be anticlimatic. Drowsy and cold, the three guards didn't much want to leave their warm gatehouse or the game they were playing.

Derian caught a glimpse of an elaborately painted board covered with polished stones in various colors when he went to the gatehouse to turn in his paperwork. The guard—having no orders to keep anyone from leaving Dragon's Breath—barely glanced at the documents before thrusting them into a wooden tray by the door.

He did, however, give Derian's naked face a second glance, his own white-and-light-blue-patterned features awakening momentarily with an expression of mild distaste.

Heart still pounding and head light with relief, Derian swung back into Roanne's saddle and urged the lead mule into a fast walk, certain that any moment he would hear a voice calling out for them to halt.

Then had come the long, tense ride to the sheepfold. He and Lord Edlin hadn't dared press the animals too rapidly.

Frozen ground invited all manner of catastrophes—strains, sprains, and even broken legs. To insure against disaster, they kept to the margin of the road where packed snow offered better footing than did the carefully tended sleigh course down the center.

Three or four sleighs passed them within the city limits, but once they passed beyond the outskirts, not even the road custodians seemed to be up and about.

The worst part of that part of the journey was neither the cold nor the sleepiness that threatened to steal over Derian now that the demands on his attention had eased. It was worrying that he and Edlin would arrive too late—that they would arrive and find the others waiting impatiently or, even worse, that they would arrive and find representatives of New Kelvin's weird government waiting for them.

Derian fretted over such contingencies, his thoughts beating out this rhythm of fear with some of the same steadiness that the horses and mules tramped over the snow.

It might have helped if he could have talked to Edlin, but the lord rode at the tail end of the train, urging on the stragglers and keeping a rear watch.

Finding the sheepfold empty seemed so impossible that Derian had just sat for a long moment and stared. Afterward, he guessed that his expression must have been every bit as foolish as any Lord Edlin had ever managed, but Edlin, trotting his mount to the front, didn't even grin.

"We're here, what?" he said cheerily. "Well that's fine, just fine. I thought we might get here and find the others come and gone with nothing but a note to tell us where to meet them."

Derian, suddenly panicked by a possibility he hadn't considered, glanced frantically around. Edlin leaned from his saddle to slap him on the shoulder.

"Don't worry, old boy. No tracks. We're first. Let's get the beasts inside the fold, what?"

Doubtless the sheepfold had been built here precisely because the location was far enough outside the city limits that none of the city regulations applied, yet close enough that herders starting out early could have their flocks to market in a timely fashion. There was even a spring of fresh water and a rough shelter.

Horses and mules accepted the snowy sheepfold with little grace, despite the fact that New Kelvin's attentive road custodians had cleared it since the last major snowfall.

"I say," Edlin said, returning from the spring, over which he had needed to break the ice before drawing water, "it's a good thing we're not like Firekeeper—able to understand beast talk and all, what? The critters are probably cursing like soldiers. After all, we drag them out of a warm stable and send them off through the snow in the dead of night. Shame we can't heat them some mash or something."

Derian shook his head. "Don't dare risk it, they might end up with colic if we fed them, then took them out on the road again too soon."

He stomped his feet and looked back along the dark, silent road.

"I wonder where the others are," he said.

"Me, too," Edlin replied. "Wish we were with them, what? Much better than this freezing wait."

Derian nodded somberly.

Edlin brightened. "No reason why you and I shouldn't have something hot to drink, though, while we wait, I mean. There's dry wood in that shelter—I saw it when I went to the spring. I'll put on kettle—there's one there—and we'll have something to take the chill off *our* bones and put the rest to the side for when the others get here."

If they get here, Derian thought uneasily as he moved to water the animals. *If they get here.*

WHEN BLIND SEER TOTTERED TO HIS FEET and, growling, made clear that he would prefer to move under his own power, Elise thought she'd start crying with guilty relief— relief because this was the first clear sign they'd had that the wolf would live, guilt because she had been wondering how they would ever manage to carry him when they began their retreat.

Indeed, if they could carry him.

Thinking of how Firekeeper would react if she learned that Blind Seer had been abandoned was enough to make Elise wonder rather nervously if she could manage to carry the wolf at least a short distance.

Doc certainly couldn't do so. He had lavishly used his talent to set Blind Seer's wounds on the way to healing—maybe too lavishly. Elise didn't want to think what they would do if someone else was hurt.

But at least Blind Seer was on his feet. The wolf's quickly shaved flank bore so many stitches that he resembled a skin toy rather than a living creature—or would have had there not been so much blood clinging to his remaining fur.

Worse still was the area around his left eye. Kistlio's knife had cut the lid and damaged the orb. Doc had done his best—dabbing the region with alcohol before loosely bandaging that side of the wolf's head—but it was too soon to know whether the livid, swollen area would succumb to infection.

After binding the couple upstairs, Wendee Jay had sneaked down the stairs to scout, going far enough that she could hear what might lie ahead while remaining unseen behind the curve.

When Wendee came back up, her tired eyes were worried.

"I heard pounding on the door below," she reported. "From what I could gather—and the words weren't clear—the folks down there know they are locked in and are not at all pleased about it."

Grateful Peace, turning from where he was locking the door to the third-floor room behind him, turned up his lips in a wry expression that was not so much a smile as an admission that events had gotten beyond him.

"I used a key," he said, "that locks a lock most do not know is there. Had we not made so much noise, they probably would have continued their debate unknowing. Now, however . . .

He shrugged. "They will eventually force the lock. We must leave as soon as possible."

"Ready here," Doc said, rising and shouldering his repacked kit.

"As is your patient," Grateful Peace said, leading the way down the stair. "You are indeed a miracle worker."

"Hardly," Doc replied dryly.

Grateful Peace chose not to argue.

"Goody Wendee," he said, "was there any noise from the ground floor?"

Wendee nodded.

"I think so."

"Then let me go first," Peace said. "My reputation is ruined with those above—or will be when they have time to think—but most of those who are rooming on the ground floor are so junior to me that they will not dare give challenge."

Elise, marveling at his confidence, wondered, too, how much was bluff.

One thing was certain. Any hope Grateful Peace had for salvaging his place here rested on proving Lady Melina's treachery. From the moment he had locked the four remaining researchers into the tower, he had relinquished any hope of pretending to have been coerced into working with the foreigners.

Clutching the box holding the mirror—it was too big to thrust into a pocket as Wendee had the comb—Elise followed Grateful Peace down the curving stair.

Her ears strained, not only to hear what Grateful Peace was about, but for the sound of Firekeeper's return.

"What are we going to do," said Wendee, who must have been thinking along similar lines, "if Lady Blysse doesn't return?"

Elise shook her head uneasily, but Sir Jared had an answer.

"We go on," he said. "Of all our company, Firekeeper is the best able to escape on her own. With two of the artifacts in our possession, we would be betraying her trust if we didn't try to get away with them."

Wendee looked so shocked that Elise nearly strangled on a shrill, hysterical laugh.

"Remember how Firekeeper took on the bandits?" Elise said when she had her voice under control again. "She'll be all right."

Wendee nodded, somewhat reassured. Elise wished she believed her own words. Firekeeper was tough, but she was hardly invulnerable. Moons had waxed and waned before she had fully healed from the injuries she had taken fighting Prince Newell.

This time, Doc wouldn't be there to treat the wolf-woman if she did get hurt, and Blind Seer wouldn't be there to bring help.

And then there was Lady Melina . . .

Elise found herself shivering and, to distract herself, focused exclusively on the moment.

Ahead she could hear Grateful Peace speaking in New Kelvinese, his accents far more pretentious than any he had ever used when speaking to her.

"I commend you," said he, "for your alertness. Yes, there has been a difficulty. For that reason, I have locked the upper levels. They are to *remain* locked until I return. Do not pay any mind to whatever anyone on the other side of those doors will say to you. They are not in control of themselves."

Elise felt herself grinning.

"Does what happened have anything to do," asked a voice that sounded like a young voice trying very hard not to sound young, "with the artifacts?"

Elise could almost hear Grateful Peace's meaningful nod. Its shape was reflected in the awed and slightly terrified intake of breath that came in response.

"However," Peace went on, "I trust that by the time the sun is nooning all will be well. I suggest . . ."

The word could have been "command."

"I suggest that you return to your sleeping quarters and get what rest you can. Tomorrow promises to be a very busy day."

There was a chorus of "Yes, sirs" and other polite noises, then a pattering of feet as at least a dozen people did their very best not to be the last one before the gaze of the Dragon's Eye.

"Come," Peace said more softly in Pellish. He poked his head around the corner of the stair and motioned for them to hurry. "We dare not delay."

"Lady Firekeeper . . ." Wendee began, but Peace shook his head decisively. "No. She must find her own way."

With Peace in the lead, they descended again into the cellars. Wendee went down next, assisting Blind Seer. Elise followed and helped Doc manage the ladder.

At the bottom, as they were all reclaiming the cloaks they had stowed in a dark corner and Peace was lighting a torch, Elise turned to Sir Jared.

"Doc," she asked, keeping her voice soft, "do you have room in your pack for this?"

She held up the box containing the mirror.

He nodded wearily.

"Put it in for me, will you, Elise? I don't think I could get the pack off just now."

Elise felt terrible about burdening him further, but the box didn't weigh too much and she needed to have her hands free . . . just in case.

They trooped through the icy darkness in silence, lit only by the one torch they had taken time to light. Peace said nothing until they had left the spiderweb of tunnels beneath Thendulla Lypella for the greater sewer network.

"Much," he said, motioning them to a halt, "depends on what has happened with Lady Melina, if Lady Blysse has . . . neutralized her, then we may have hours before anyone comes for us. If she has not, pursuit could come quite soon.

"Ultimately, this sewer empties outside the city. That is how I suggest we go. However, our exit will be neither easy nor pleasant."

"Oh?" Elise asked, distrust flooding her.

After all, Peace had betrayed his own people. Why shouldn't he betray them? She thought of the mirror and the comb. Peace could redeem himself quite nicely if he returned them, couldn't he?

"Lady Elise, my fellows would be fools to leave a potential roadway such as this unguarded. However, on a cold night like tonight, the guards may be less than attentive. Unfortunately, the exit from the tunnel is covered with a heavy grille work gate. My keys will open it, but I do not think we can open it without attracting attention to ourselves."

Wendee said leadenly, "Then we're doomed."

"Not quite," Peace replied. "There is a smaller exit hatch, similar to the one through which we entered the tunnels. My keys will also open that door, but one problem remains."

"What?" Elise asked.

"The hatchway enters directly into the guardhouse."

"Oh."

Doc asked, "Do we have any choice?"

"We could exit within the city," Peace said, "but I do not fancy our chances of traversing the city without causing comment. Even if no one has heard about the thefts we are a rather disreputable-looking lot."

"We're doomed," Wendee repeated. Then, with visible effort, she put on a brave manner. "So we might as well follow the course that dooms us less quickly. I'm for the tunnel into the guardhouse."

Everyone else nodded—even Blind Seer.

They went on without speaking for some time. As she trudged along in the back, Elise found the night's exertions catching up to her. Who would have known when they'd settled down that evening to discuss how best to retrieve the artifacts that some hours later they would have two of them?

Two and hopefully three.

Elise could feel exhaustion threatening her. It had been a long day and promised to be a longer night. She was cold, and her feet—which she had been on much of the day—ached abysmally.

Her head ached, she wanted to weep, to whine like a child, anything but tramp through this cold tunnel with its reek of sewage.

It seemed too much, unfair, that the only reward she could anticipate at the end of the journey was a possible fight followed by further flight, this time through the snow and wind. Presumably they'd ride until hiding became necessary, and then where would they go? Where would they hide?

Ahead, the light of the single torch Grateful Peace carried burned steadily. At least here there was no wind. At least here no one was chasing them. At least here . . .

Elise straightened and forced a grin. If this was as good as it was going to get, well, then, she'd better appreciate it.

What had she been telling herself—that it was unfair that she had to put up with these conditions?

Well, who insisted you come along, Lady Elise Archer? she asked herself.

No one but me was her silent reply.

And in any case, what's fair? Was it fair that Sapphire and Shad were nearly murdered on their wedding day? Was it fair that King Allister had to deal with treachery along with his coronation? What is fair?

"Life isn't fair," she muttered to herself.

Doc, hearing the sound but certainly not the words, paused and looked back at her in concern.

"Are you all right, Elise?" he asked.

"I'm fine," she said, giving him a determined smile. "After all, it's pretty pleasant here, out of the wind."

IT WASN'T REALLY NIGHT ANYMORE when they arrived outside the city; it was predawn. At this time of year when winter had set her seal on the world, that meant it was still very dark, and very cold.

It was predawn inside the tunnels, too, Elise thought, but the thing was, time didn't seem real there, underground. It was just dark and vaguely smelly and the only light in the world came from the flickering torch that Peace had several times renewed from custodial caches along the way.

Elise blew on her fingers and wished for a hot cup of tea.

"Is it true that people sleep most heavily just before dawn?" she asked. "My father told me that once."

"I've heard that, too," Wendee replied. "But I don't know how true it is."

They could talk in a normal tone of voice here—they had to, if they wanted to be heard. As they had trudged along underground, their route had brought them into broader and broader tunnels.

Now they walked alongside what Peace told them had once been a river—a small river, but a very real one. The river had run from the mountains through Dragon's Breath. Some time during the rule of the Founders, it had been sent underground. Tunnels had been built over it.

Where it once carried snowmelt, now it mostly carried sewage. The snowmelt was diverted into reservoirs, though enough was let through to rinse the sewage on its way. The system was more complicated than that, but that was the basic idea.

The liquid in little tunnels had been frozen on top and maybe all the way under, too. Here there was a skin of ice on top. Underneath, the tainted water ran. When it reached the grille work gate, it splashed out into a big river, which carried the waste away. The noise was steady and, best of all, covered the sound of talk.

Elise made a face as the wind brought the sewer smell their way. She didn't know if she'd ever drink from a New Kelvinese river again—not unless the water was boiled and distilled.

How she'd like a cup of tea!

Peace had actually done pretty well by them. There had been food—mostly bars of dried fruit mixed with grains or nuts—in some of the custodial stores. The thaumaturge hadn't known if these were official supplies or some worker's way of making his labor more pleasant.

Either way, having something to eat went a long way toward making them all feel more confident. Peace had found fresh water, too.

Peace had also insisted on rest stops. During these, he'd had them clean off the scarlet paint. Descriptions of the fugitives might well mention that stain.

Hearing how much they disliked the feel of the paint, Grateful Peace didn't insist that they replace it in full. Instead, with a greenish color stick he gave them each a couple of "tattoos." He explained that the average New Kelvinese read tattoos automatically, and would remember what these had said far more readily than details like height or hair color.

Elise's face now said that she was dedicated to a minor cult she'd never heard of before this night. Wendee's said she was a member of some historical society.

But now they'd come to the end of the sewers. Doc—looking much stronger now—was holding the torch so that Grateful Peace could oil the trapdoor. It was supposed to be kept oiled—this being a fairly important part of the sewer system—but Peace wasn't taking any chances on people doing what they were supposed to do.

As she watched the thin man with the bone-white braid trailing down his back, Elise had the feeling that beneath his calm he was even more unsettled by recent events than she was. Like her, he had chosen to be here, but unlike her, she didn't think that he'd planned for the night's venture ending with him exiled from the kingdom he'd served for most of his life.

Elise felt oddly sorry for Grateful Peace. Then the time to feel sorry was over. It was time to head up and out into whatever awaited them.

XXXIII

 RUSTY IRON RUBBED ROUGH GRANULES into Elise's fingers as she hung from the ladder with one hand and pushed up the trapdoor with the other.

The thaumaturge was above already, prowling somewhere in the semidarkness, searching out the residents, checking if any stood watch. He had explained that no one would question his presence, for the Dragon's Eye went every-where. However, he preferred that their group's presence not be known if at all possible, for he felt there was still a slight chance that he would be able to redeem himself before his people—a chance that grew more tenuous each time his role in helping the outlanders was confirmed.

Their plan had been that if there was no indication that Grateful Peace had been discovered, the rest were to begin their ascent. They had to do without more complex signals, for any sound Peace might make would awaken the sleepers, and Peace had been forced to close the trapdoor behind him because of the noise from the falls.

Inside the stone guardhouse the noise from the sewage falls was muted. Even so, the solid little building wasn't silent. Silence would have been preferable, for the same dull rumble that covered the sound of their own cautious movements made Elise uneasily aware how easy it would be for someone to sneak up behind her.

Quickly she turned her head, right, then left. Nothing but vague, unmoving shadow shapes were revealed. Not precisely comforted, but certain that at this moment no one was near, Elise bent over the trapdoor and motioned for the others to climb up after her.

She heard a rasping scrape, followed by a pained whine as Blind Seer hauled himself through the trapdoor. The wolf's stiff straining movements were so unlike the lithe grace with which he had mounted a similar ladder only a few hours before that Elise felt her heart catch in sympathetic pain.

In quick succession, Wendee, then Doc—both of whom had waited below to assist the wolf with his ascent—emerged from the trapdoor. When Doc was through, Elise closed the door.

Her abortive sigh of relief nearly choked her when a high-pitched but strong voice spoke from the center of a dark rec-tangle Elise had taken for a closed door:

"Don't move nor even breath or I'll land a crossbow quarrel soundly in your liver."

Blind Seer, who had been scenting the air, growled—a low

sound, full of anger and frustration. None of the others commented even to that extent.

"Now we," the voice continued, "have our sympathies with escaping slaves, even those who don't come announced, but there is a price for sympathy. Do you have it with you?"

With some surprise, Elise heard her own voice answering: "We do, but it's under our wraps."

What's going on here? she thought frantically. *Where is Peace? Escaped slaves? I think I understand, but what are they going to do to us when they find we don't have their price?*

She didn't waste energy wondering how they had been detected. The guards must be so accustomed to the noise from the falls that they didn't even hear it anymore. Some sound out of the ordinary must have alerted this woman.

From elsewhere, she heard the slap of shod feet coming down stone stairs. A man's voice called, "Tymia? What's going on?"

"Alarm," Tymia, as their captor turned out to be named, replied economically. "I've three here and a big dog. Bring a lamp, will you?"

"Right."

Where is Peace? Has he left us here?

Elise tried to frame a bluff, but she knew she was floundering—it was hard to bluff when you knew so little. Their time of residence in Dragon's Breath hadn't been long enough to learn the fine details of slavery in New Kelvin. She hadn't even seen a slave, though she did know that most were owned not by individuals but by organizations.

The price this Tymia had mentioned was doubtless paid in currency, but what would be considered a fair amount? Would she be expected to bring out a coin or a purse?

And where was Peace?

Not one but three new figures were revealed in the glow of the lamplight, a woman and two men. All were young, all wore sleepwear—soft trousers and shirt—augmented by boots and weaponry. One man carried a crossbow. The man with the lamp had a sword belt sloppily girded around him. The woman bore both sword and crossbow, though neither was carried in a ready position. Rather it looked as if she had snatched up her weapons from habit rather than volition.

All four—including Tymia, who was revealed for the first time as other than a shadow—were older than Elise, but still hardly beyond their mid-twenties.

Tymia, who wore a uniform, though one loose around the collar and a bit rumpled, stepped forward, studying them with an intent interest that became concern as she got a better look at her captives. Elise remembered seeing a similar expression on the face of young Indatius in the Granite Tower, and dreaded what was coming.

Whatever slaves typically looked like, it was quite clear that she, Wendee, and Doc did not fit the profile. It said something about how odd they must look that Tymia didn't spare a glance for Blind Seer—and that was her mistake.

The great grey wolf didn't leap—his injuries were too great for that—but in the enclosed room he hardly needed to do more than rush forward. His intelligence was evident in that he did not go for Tymia herself but for her crossbow.

A sharp cracking snap proved that wherever else he was wounded, his jaws were just fine.

Elise didn't wait for a second opportunity to act. Bending her head slightly, she rushed at the man who bore both lamp and sword. He brought up his sword in a halfhearted block, but Elise took her tactics from Blind Seer's book.

Wheeling widely away from the sword, she dove for the lamp and knocked it from his hand. It hit the floor solidly. The newly lit wick snuffed out, sending the room back into darkness.

Here Elise and her companions, who had spent so many of the recent hours in semidarkness, were less inconvenienced than the four guards. However, the guards had the advantage of knowing the layout of the room—and of being armed. Moreover, they were skilled fighters—a distinction none in Elise's company, except possibly Doc, could claim.

The former lamp-holder wheeled after Elise, seeming to follow her by the very movement of the air. As he grabbed at her, she felt the flat of his sword blade slide over her arm as he grappled for position.

She kicked out, by luck catching him in the kneecap. He yelled, but the sound was more angered than pained. It blended with Tymia's shrieks as she backed away from Blind Seer, who, having disarmed her, was apparently pressing her in the dark.

There were other yells as well. Wendee and Doc had not left Elise to attack alone, but they had been several steps behind her, even as the remaining two guards had been behind the one Elise had attacked.

Much confused fumbling followed. A thud announced that someone had slipped in the lamp oil and fallen to the floor.

Elise, however, had little attention to spare for this. Her opponent had grabbed her trailing braid and was using it to reel her head in close to his hand.

Ignoring the sharp pain, she tried to pull away, but he had wrapped a length or so of hair around his hand. Again she tried to kick out, but was jerked up short.

"None of that," he warned. "Or I won't bother with keeping you alive."

Moving without conscious thought, Elise sagged.

Her captor leaned to catch her—discommoded by the fact that he'd imprisoned one hand in her hair, while his sword occupied the other. Elise ignored the pull against her braid, though the pain brought tears to her eyes—and fell further forward.

Instinctively trying to keep his balance, the guard shifted to put his sword arm around her waist. At the moment she felt his hold, but before he could straighten, Elise lifted her feet from the floor. She might not weigh over much, but to her already unbalanced captor, it was enough.

He toppled, falling partly on top of her, flailing to keep from cutting himself on his own sword. He let go of her hair, though his fingers remained painfully tangled.

Knowing too well where he was by the heat of his breath, Elise brought up her elbow. Groaning, he jerked back and she was free.

Firekeeper or Sapphire would probably have knocked him cold, but Elise knew her limits. Skipping back, she assessed the situation.

Tymia's shrieks had turned into moans of fear, but from the sound of them Blind Seer had not killed her. Scuffling in one corner told that either Doc or Wendee or both still occupied the other guards.

Light, Elise thought. *We need light.*

She fumbled her way toward the trapdoor, hoping to find Doc's kit there. He kept candles for emergencies, along with flint and steel. Elise was no great hand with a tinderbox, but she had learned to manage on campaign.

Then, as if in direct answer to her unspoken wish, there was light. Grateful Peace stood in a doorway, a three-pronged candelabrum in one hand.

By the triple candlelight, Elise saw that Blind Seer crouched over Tymia. The guard was nearly mad with fear, but offered no immediate threat.

The remaining female guard was out cold. Wendee and Doc stood equidistant from the crossbowman, apparently unsure in the darkness how best to close.

When the candlelight flooded the dark room, the man turned to face this new threat. His cocked bow followed his motion as might a pointing finger. When the guard saw a stranger, he pulled the trigger.

Peace screamed and staggered. Once again, there was darkness.

THE WOLF-WOMAN LIMPED into the sheepfold sometime before dawn. Elation and Bold had stayed with her much of the way. They said they didn't trust her sense of direction, but Firekeeper knew that what they didn't trust was her temper should she encounter anyone. Ever since Lady Melina had tricked her, the wolf-woman's self-loathing had grown so that anyone who crossed her path might well be hurt.

And Bold had made things no easier for her by insisting that Firekeeper carry the ring. The crow's reasons were completely practical. Small as it was, the ring was still an encumbrance the bird did better without. Firekeeper could hardly refuse such a simple request, but she couldn't help but feel that *she* would be better off without it as well.

Or was it that she still couldn't escape the dream that she would be better *with* it?

The moonstone grasped in the beast's jaws had seemed to shine with promise, speaking to the wolf-woman in Lady Melina's voice, reciting the wonders that could be Firekeeper's for the taking. Firekeeper had stuffed the ring deep into a trouser pocket, but if she didn't guard against it, she could hear the voice: wheedling, promising, tempting her to betrayal and theft.

To distract herself, she concentrated on the pain in her hip, on the cold leaking through her boots, on the image of Blind Seer lying bloodied over the doorsill into the tower room. These things silenced the voice—at least a bit—but did nothing to sweeten her temper.

The peregrine and the crow had traded off keeping an eye on their human, each taking some time to hunt. The crow, scavenger and carrion eater that he was, had fared far better than the falcon. However, though lacking the excellence of an owl's night vision, the peregrine had managed to startle a rabbit.

Firekeeper had no stomach for the fare when Elation brought her a portion, nor did she accept the hot honeyed tea that Edlin held out to her almost as she arrived. Instead, she looked around, noted that her pack was shy several members, and growled:

"Where are they?"

"I don't know," Derian replied. Unlike Edlin, he seemed to sense her anger. "I wish I did."

"Bold say," she indicated the crow with a toss of her head, "they go into tunnels again. They should be here."

"Don't blame me!" Derian snapped.

Firekeeper felt her lips curling in a snarl, then looked more closely at the redhead. Derian's fair skin was almost translucent despite its weathering. Grey circles beneath his eyes spoke of a wakeful night—and of worry.

She bit her lip.

"Blame me. Lady Melina get away. Bold get ring, but I let her go."

She dragged her cold fingers across her face, feeling the red weals she left behind them though her nails never touched the skin. It reminded her of the paint she'd scoured away with sand and ice water hours before. She could still feel the traces clotting near her hairline like old blood.

"I must find them," she said, "before Lady Melina do."

Edlin rose, setting his mug by the fire.

"Let me come with you," he said eagerly.

"No."

She was gone before even his ready lips could shape another phrase. Only when she was out in the snow once more did she realize that she had no idea where to look.

Bold dropped from the sky.

"Let me scout," he said. *"I'll head back toward the city. Why not call for the wolf?"*

The crow's suggestion was a good one, but when Firekeeper howled, there was no reply—none but Edlin's faint shout from behind her. Determinedly, Firekeeper began to trudge back toward the city. She did not take precisely the route she had before—that one had begun on the east side of the city before tracing its way south.

Now she angled her way somewhat to the west. She knew that Elation and Bold had both made periodic checks along the road as they hunted. They would have seen the others if they were along it. Bold would check again now.

The sky gained not so much color as the underglow of approaching light as Firekeeper slogged on. Long ago, she'd learned how to ignore pain, but she was all too aware of the inconvenience offered by her shortened step, her many bruises. She began to regret refusing the hot sweet tea.

That was a human act, not a wolf one, she sneered at herself. *Since when has a wolf refused to eat? What are you becoming, Little Two-legs, neither human nor wolf but the worst of both worlds?*

The lightening sky took on the pale hue of the moonstone, taunting her with the possibilities she had refused. She raised her head once again to howl her desperate cry.

At first, when the answer came, she could hardly believe it. Then, forgetting the pain in her hip, Firekeeper began to run, howling again and again as if somehow Blind Seer might lose her.

GRATEFUL PEACE DID NOT so much come conscious as come aware, and even that awareness was marred by a certain sense of unreality. He was upright and moving—apparently without his own volition, and with a strange jolting motion.

His legs were splayed and warmer than most of him, which was very cold. His back was less cold than his front and leaned against something that vibrated at a different tempo than the jolting motion of his forward progress.

Almost as soon as he was aware of these things, he was aware of considerable pain in his upper body in the vicinity of his right collarbone. His right arm hung very limp, so very limp that he found himself wondering if it had been immobilized. Trying to move it, though, set his head to racing and his heart to pounding with such ferocity that he nearly blacked out.

When the red and purple pounding in his head relented, Peace decided—a deliberate decision of which he felt rather proud—to open his eyes. He was met with a wash of pale colors: white, grey, a touch of blue.

Early-morning light, he thought. *I am out-of-doors. Some-one has taken my glasses.*

A moment later, he registered a bit more.

I am on a horse.

He realized then that two rode the horse: himself and someone he was leaning against. That other one balanced Peace
against himself, a thing that seemed to take all his energy. The
shaking Peace had felt was nothing so simple as the other's
breathing. It was the bone-deep trembling of pure exhaustion,
exhaustion so deep that it demands sleep and keeps it at bay
only by absolute will.

Sir Jared, Peace thought, *holds me on this horse though he
himself is almost too tired to sit straight.*

He listened. The motion of the horse was accompanied by
a rhythmic crunching, not perfectly matched, however. Years
of building from sound the pictures his eyes could not see
offered him a tentative explanation.

*The women walk at the horse's head, breaking the snow
and guiding it. The wolf may be with them, but if it is, I wonder
that the horse is not more restive.*

"Where . . ." he croaked, and discovered then that his mouth
was so dry that he could hardly shape a sound.

From behind him, he heard Sir Jared's voice, flat with exhaustion, call:

"He's coming around."

The horse was permitted to stop then. It didn't seem much
to mind. A brisk crunching in the snow, and Lady Elise's
bright young voice asked:

"How are you?"

Peace moved his mouth but no sound came.

"Wait." Then, "Open up."

Snow was put gently into his open mouth. It melted so
rapidly, Peace suspected he was feverish. Like a baby bird, he
opened his mouth in mute entreaty.

More snow came until his mouth was no longer dry.

"Thank you," Peace croaked. "What happened?"

"We're out of the guardhouse," Elise replied in a brisk tone
that told him she was not saying everything. "Don't worry,
we didn't kill them, though that Tymia's going to hate wolves
forever. We locked them in their own cells. Someone should
come along and let them out eventually, I guess."

She was speaking too fast, too brightly, leaving something

out. Peace hadn't been a watcher for this long without learning to hear the unspoken behind the words. He didn't press.

"We stole a horse—they only had one, probably for delivering messages—put you two aboard. We're staying off the road, but I'd guess we're almost to the sheepfold."

Her tone said quite clearly that Lady Elise didn't have any idea where they were or how far they had come.

"Blind Seer," Wendee Jay added, her voice coming from somewhere near the horse's head, "went to find the others so they won't worry."

Remembering the stitched-together hulk of half-blind wolf, Grateful Peace didn't think that the hope in Wendee's voice was merited in the least. Probably the brute would go find a cave or fluffy snowbank and sleep off his injuries. Still, dogs were known to be very loyal. Maybe wolves were, too.

"My glasses?" he asked.

"Broken," Lady Elise replied apologetically, "when you fell. We kept the pieces, but there hasn't been time to try to mend them."

"Of course," Peace murmured. He was drifting off again. Fighting sleep didn't seem worth the effort. When the horse started moving again, he struggled with an idea, but all he could manage was a vague notion that fear held the shape of pigeon wings.

THE WOLF PROVED HIMSELF WORTHY of the others' belief in him. Sometime later—Peace wasn't sure how long—Peace became aware of Lady Blysse's husky voice.

". . . to him?"

There was horror and pity in her tones. Then he learned of whom and of what she spoke, and the horror and pity became his own.

"We were ambushed in the guardhouse at the end of the sewer," Lady Elise said. The horse had not stopped its forward motion. "Or something like that. We tried to sneak in and found they had an alarm rigged up. We fought them."

Peace could hear the pride in her voice.

"We wouldn't have done too well if three of them hadn't been half-dressed and fresh from bed and the fourth hadn't been dozing. It was dark and just when we needed light the most, Peace came up with a candelabrum."

Wendee took up the tale.

"Doc and I had been trying to get near this one fellow, but, well, Doc was pretty beat and I was . . . well, scared because I knew the man had a crossbow."

"Good to be scared, then," Firekeeper said seriously, and Peace had the eerie feeling that she was looking at him.

"The bowman," Wendee continued, "turned when he saw the light. I don't know if he fired on purpose or whether his bow just went off."

"On purpose," Elise said definitely. "Doc said so."

"But he fired. His aim wasn't great, but . . ."

Her voice trailed off.

"I see," came Firekeeper's voice.

"Grateful Peace dropped the candles then," Wendee went on, adding with a true sense of drama, "and only pure luck kept them from dropping in the lantern oil."

"That was across the room," Elise corrected.

"Anyhow," Wendee said with a faint note of reproof in her voice, "Doc and I jumped the last guard. I grabbed him and Doc kicked his feet out from under him. The guard went down hard . . ."

There was a nervous giggle.

"With me still on top of him. That knocked him out cold."

"I'd gone over to Peace," Elise said, taking up the thread, "and I saw right away that things were both better and worse than we'd thought. He was out cold, not dead as we'd thought, but the reason he was out was that the arrow had caught him right where it opened up the artery into his arm. When he'd fallen, he'd shattered so many bones . . ."

Peace listened horrified, heard her swallow, and add almost apologetically.

"He really isn't very young. Bones break more easily when you're older. Doc felt if we tried to save the arm, we'd lose the man for sure. As it was, Doc nearly killed himself saving Grateful Peace. He was already so weak."

Peripherally, Peace heard the narrative continue, describing how Wendee—with Blind Seer as enforcer—had imprisoned the guards and found a horse, but he couldn't keep his attention on what was being said.

His arm? But he could feel it! It was a little stiff, it ached, but they couldn't have taken it off! He could feel it!

Even as he tried to convince himself otherwise, Grateful Peace knew the truth. His right arm—his drawing arm—the arm that had been his way to prosperity and prominence . . .

His arm was gone.

And then, as if things could not be worse, Peace remembered why fear had the shape of pigeon wings.

WARNED BY BOLD.—or at least by Bold's reappearance, and Derian was becoming very good at guessing what frantic hopping up and down combined with hoarse cawing might mean—Derian and Edlin had the mules reloaded and the horses tacked up by the time Firekeeper returned with the remainder of their company.

Pale morning light showed them for what they were—injured, exhausted, and completely unsuited for a further press, but press they must. Even had any been inclined to stop, the words Grateful Peace forced out between fever-swollen lips would have enlivened the most exhausted blood.

"Pigeons," he murmured. "In a few hours at most."

Derian frowned, but Edlin caught on at once.

"Carrier birds, I say! He's right, you know. As soon as they figure out that we're not anywhere in the city, they'll send out messenger pigeons to all the guard posts."

Firekeeper smiled cruelly from where she had perched on a laden mule.

"I send Elation," she said, "for pigeons."

"Not a bad idea," Derian agreed, swinging into Roanne's saddle, "but Elation can't hope to catch every pigeon."

"It's a shame," Elise said, her tartness excusable given how Doc looked, "that your Royal Beasts didn't send you out with a bit more support."

Firekeeper looked as if she agreed.

If the Beasts hadn't sent out much help, nature conspired to offer some unlooked-for—and almost unappreciated—aid in form of ugly weather that swirled down from the mountains later that morning. Light flurries turned into a steady fall of big white flakes. These, as the day warmed, became sleet and freezing rain.

Footing for the horses and mules was—especially on the steeper parts of the road—uncertain enough that Derian frequently called out for the healthy to dismount and lead their animals.

At these times, Derian tossed Roanne's reins to Elise, who rode either beside or behind him, depending on the going, and slogged back to take control of the mules. Firekeeper aided him at these times. Her particular form of encouragement— apparently threats that any mule that so much as thought of acting up would find itself dinner for herself and Blind Seer— might not have been kind, but it was effective.

When she was not harassing the mules, Firekeeper would trot ahead, finding some sheltered point where she could kindle a fire. She had the gift for encouraging a blaze, even in the damp—no doubt why the wolves had called her Firekeeper.

The promise of hot, sweet tea was almost as much of a stimulant as the tea itself, and permitted the group to push on despite lack of sleep. These rest stops, welcome as they were, seriously depleted the supplies Derian had laid in, but he refused to worry. One day—today—was all he needed to worry about. Quite likely the New Kelvinese would make certain he didn't have many more days to worry about if he worried so much about tomorrow that he neglected today.

During that day's long haul Lord Edlin, trained in the harsher weather of the North Woods, earned Derian's undying gratitude. On his own volition, Edlin positioned himself close to Doc—who, though somewhat recovered from his expenditure of talent, was still weak—and to Grateful Peace. When either man showed signs of fading, there was Edlin taking control.

Derian began to wonder if the young lord had some talent of his own, but during a break for a sticky mouthful of honey and nuts, chased by a mug of hot tea, Edlin refused any such honor.

"Too stupid to stay in out of the snow," he said cheerfully. "That's me, what? Good thing, this time, though that I've the experience. Helps, what?"

The same weather that froze their faces inside their hooded cloaks, that sapped their strength along with their heat, also helped preserve them from discovery.

The few travelers they passed were interested only in getting to their own destinations. Whereas in fairer weather they might have paused to pass the time of day and thus noted the foreign character of their fellow travelers, now they only slogged past, encased in their own private misery and layers of ice.

Pigeons, too, would not fly in this weather. Even the homing imperative was nothing against the instinct to survive. Derian suspected that Elation, who had circled back to Dragon's Breath, and the Beast Lore cotes from which a feverish Peace had told them any message was sure to be sent, was likely to be having a thin time of it.

Although in no great shape himself, Blind Seer forged ahead. His eerie howls—transmitting information to his pack mate—became such a familiar sound that even high-strung Roanne ceased to start. For himself, Derian found them a comfort.

When nightfall drew near, Firekeeper asked Blind Seer to find somewhere they might pass the night. As much as they needed to put distance between themselves and Dragon's Breath, they needed even more to eat and sleep, and to give the animals a chance to recover.

The wolf-woman came to Derian as dusk was thickening, making their nightmare progress almost impossible.

"Ahead is a barn, empty. There is hay there and wood."

"How far?" Derian asked.

"Not too," she reassured him.

Despite this reassurance, it was almost too far, especially for those among them who did not, like Firekeeper and Edlin, prefer the out-of-doors. Over and over again, Derian found himself oddly grateful for the very real threat to their lives and freedom. Without this, he suspected that one or more would simply have given up.

The barn was drafty. The roof was missing several boards on the south side, but there was ample room for everyone on the dry northern side. They set up tents in the open areas, providing not only privacy, but something to hold personal warmth.

The horses and mules provided additional heat as they crowded round, munching on slightly musty hay. Derian made certain that the horses got the better feed. The last thing they needed was a case of colic.

Perhaps the greatest indication of the universal relief at being in out of the weather was that not one of the equines so much as flattened an ear when Blind Seer padded by and took a place alongside one of the two fires Firekeeper had kindled.

Bad weather should have driven the game into cover, so Derian decided not to question just where Firekeeper had found the brace of fat ducks and three plump rabbits she supplied for their dinner.

The wolf-woman was still limping, but she refused to be pampered. Indeed, Derian noticed that she seemed more than a bit unhappy with herself, eager to make amends for sins that no one else had even charged her with.

Doc insisted that everyone eat something before being permitted to sleep. After that, there was a general crawling toward tents, and soon exhausted snoring joined the sounds of the livestock.

Derian was as tired as the rest, but as often happened when he had overexerted himself he could not get his mind to relax. He settled for placing himself on watch.

Doc was also wakeful. Grateful Peace was coming to some

sort of crisis, and with a physician's patient watchfulness, Doc had set himself to see the other man through. They were joined by Firekeeper.

"Blind Seer," she said to Doc, glancing with open affection at the sleeping wolf, "say you nearly kill yourself to save him. Thank you."

Doc nodded. "He nearly was killed protecting us and trying to stop Lady Melina. It's all one and the same."

"His eye?" Firekeeper asked, tilting her head to one side inquisitively.

"I don't know," Doc replied. "The swelling could be a good thing, protecting the eye while it heals. There's no great amount of pus, no bleeding, but I can't make promises."

Firekeeper nodded glumly.

"He told me to remember that Lady Melina wasn't a wolf," she said. "And I forgot—twice. Twice she used that to defeat me."

They'd already heard her account of how she had pursued Lady Melina, how Bold and Elation had saved her and regained the ring, how she had let Lady Melina escape.

"Don't blame yourself," Derian said gently.

"Who else can I blame?" she asked bitterly. "Not Bold, not Elation—without them I would be dead. Not Blind Seer—he warned me."

Doc leaned over and touched Grateful Peace's forehead.

"Fever's breaking. Riding in the cold today may have kept him from burning alive, but it will take its toll. How's the soup coming?"

Derian checked the small kettle where the livers and hearts from their evening meal simmered in snowmelt.

"It's taking on color," he said.

"Good. Ladle some into that mug. I want it to cool a bit before I spoon it into him."

As Derian complied, Doc went on:

"Firekeeper, I've been thinking about what Lady Melina told you—about where Citrine might be. She's almost certainly in the eastern part of Hawk Haven, probably down by the shore."

"You think so?" Firekeeper asked.

Derian relaxed from a tension he hadn't even been aware was holding him stiff, for the self-loathing had left the wolf-woman's tone, replaced by the eagerness she always demonstrated when action was contemplated.

"You know that Princess Lovella died going after enemies of Hawk Haven, right?"

"Yes," Firekeeper nodded eagerly, "and you were with her and were made knight for bravery."

"Well, those enemies were pirates and smugglers, allies of Bright Bay at that time, which is why we were so eager to be at them."

"Yes?"

"They had a stronghold, an old lighthouse in the swamps that spread north of Port Haven, near where the White Water meets the ocean. I've been thinking, like I said, and the more I think, the more likely it seems to me that Baron Endbrook may have stored his hostage there."

"Why?"

There was no challenge in Firekeeper's tone, only a desire for information.

"The Islanders have long been allies of the pirates, that's one reason. Secondly, the weather is bad for deep-water sailing, bad enough that I don't think he would have risked her on a voyage to the Isles. I want your help checking this."

"How?"

"Elise gave me the idea."

Derian grinned slightly as Doc's tone warmed slightly, the way it always did when he spoke of Elise. Apparently, seeing her unwashed, half-shaved, and cranky had done nothing to diminish his admiration.

"Earlier, she mentioned that the Beasts should have given you more help. Well, I found myself musing over what we could do if we had a few more of your wingéd folk. Then I thought, well, we still have Bold with us and I've gathered that there are others who keep an eye on things."

Firekeeper nodded.

"If Bold would go ahead of us, down to the swamps, maybe talk to some of the seagulls or something . . ."

From Doc's tone, Derian could tell that despite the fact that he'd nearly killed himself to save Blind Seer, he felt ridiculous suggesting asking animals to do a job that would take conscious thought and planning.

"They could check if Citrine is at the lighthouse," Doc concluded. "That would save us a considerable amount of effort and then, if she is there, if a bird or two would carry messages to both King Tedric and King Allister . . ."

Doc swallowed hard.

"Well, not only could we rescue Citrine, maybe we could finish what Princess Lovella started, maybe we could put out Smuggler's Light."

BOOK

THREE

XXXIV

OWL MOON HAD BEEN SHOWING her first quarter when Baron Endbrook had sent a messenger to Dragon's Breath with a box for Lady Melina Shield. When Owl Moon had shone fat and round, he had imagined the lady receiving the box and its grisly contents. By the time Owl Moon had waned to a quarter once more, Waln was eagerly awaiting her reply.

Yet he had not been idle as those days passed.

Though pirates and smugglers by profession, scofflaws by choice, killers when needed, there were few among those hardened men and women who dwelled in the Smuggler's Light who had not been shocked by Waln's cool mutilation of young Citrine Shield's hand.

That he had done the deed himself, rather than ordering some lackey to do it for him, had only raised him in their estimation. Given the lives they led, the pirates often mistook the sensation of fear for that of respect.

Since his days as a gutter bully, Waln had learned how to capitalize on others' fears. He would not let the opportunity escape him now.

Even as Fess Bones was binding up the weeping girl's hand, Waln had swaggered down into the common area that occupied the second story of the lighthouse.

Longsight Scrounger, who to this moment had reigned supreme over those gathered in this illicit stronghold, didn't like seeing his vassals shrink from another. Had he been a dog, his hackles would have risen and his lips curled back from his teeth.

Longsight and Waln had been fencing with each other from the moment Waln had arisen from his sickbed, but to this moment neither had struck decisively. They had growled and snarled, snapped and sniffed about for weaknesses, but neither had attacked.

Had Longsight been a different kind of man, Waln might not have even challenged him—he had no desire to be a pirate king. Longsight, however, could not work with anyone else. Either he worked *for* others or, preferably, they worked for him.

Perhaps the shadow of Queen Valora's influence as much as anything about Waln himself had cautioned Longsight to hold back any attempt to openly dominate Waln, but now faced with what he perceived a challenge to his authority Longsight forgot queen, wealth, and title.

Without their ennobling aura, he saw only a large man, somewhat pale from illness, a man who dared strut into Longsight's hall as if he owned it.

"I must admire you, Waln," Longsight Scrounger sneered, his voice silky as a whiplash drawn lazily over the skin it anticipates cutting, "for how you discipline little girls. So firm! So direct! No wonder Queen Valora uses you for her errand boy. She must recognize a well-trained nursery hand."

Waln didn't speak a single word in response to this taunt.

Never pausing in the lazy stride with which he'd entered the common room, Waln strolled over to where Longsight sat in a high-backed cushioned chair at the best table among those arrayed about the hall.

Right until Waln raised his hand, Longsight might have thought the other man too flustered to fight back. Then lightning strike of Waln's hand as he brutally backhanded Longsight across one side of his face gave answer.

Longsight's head snapped back and impacted with the hard wooden back of his chair. For a bare breath it seemed that he might have been stunned; then Longsight rose to his feet, pushing the chair behind him so that it toppled over and crashed to the floor.

The common room of Smuggler's Light was decorated rather after the fashion of a large tavern. Now it resembled one more than ever as tables were dragged back and chairs scooted aside to open a makeshift arena for the combatants in the center of the floor.

Not one of those men and women who in other circumstances would have followed Longsight Scrounger to the death rose to offer him aid. Not one protested Waln's attack upon their leader. Only the old crone who had been by Waln's bed when he had awakened cried out—and that shrill sound might well have been fierce excitement rather than protest.

Bets were laid on—though few bet in favor of Waln. Rather the pirates bet on how long it would take Longsight to knock the challenger down, how many blows Longsight might need, whether a dirty trick or two might come into play.

To one side of the room, Lucky Shortleg could be heard loudly bemoaning that he had not time to set proper odds.

Yes, the bets were on Longsight. The pirates knew him, knew his ferocity, his tenacity, his skill in a dirty brawl. Those who knew Waln at all knew him as a shipping magnate, a man who possessed wealth and title. They had no idea how he had won those prizes.

Fess Bones—coming down into the commotion after wrapping Citrine's hand in layers of gauze and dosing the girl with a powerful sleeping draught—Fess Bones found many who were willing to take his bet that Baron Endbrook would be the one to stagger from the makeshift arena.

Fess Bones set himself up for life with his winnings from that betting. It was Longsight Scrounger who, when all was ended, spat teeth onto the floor and then collapsed onto the scarred wood, sliding into a puddle of his own blood and spit.

Some sixteen days later, when Fleet Herald, the messenger Waln had sent to Lady Melina, returned to Smuggler's Light, it was Baron Endbrook who stood at the top of the lighthouse overlooking the swamp, and Longsight—recovered from the worst of his beating, though inclined to whistle between broken teeth—who answered the door and then scurried away.

A more loyal lieutenant than Longsight Scrounger Waln could not have asked for, not if he ordered himself one out of his own warehouses. Like Waln himself—who served Queen Valora out of self-interest, tinged with fear—Longsight respected those more powerful than himself. When he had thought Waln physically vulnerable, he had been willing to dismiss title and wealth. Now these became two more chains that bound Longsight like a whining cur at his master's heel.

If Fleet Herald was surprised at this change to the order of things, he said not a word. He merely dipped his bow deeper than he might have and licked his lips nervously.

Looking down at the cringing messenger, Waln felt deep foreboding replace the comfortable self-satisfaction that had been his daily diet since he had defeated Longsight and stomped a few opportunistic types who had thought to take him on when he was—presumably—weakened.

"I expected you days ago," Waln growled at Fleet. "What is your report?"

Fleet made no excuses nor apologies. He knew—as Waln himself did—that he had made excellent time, especially given the winter weather and the nature of his mission.

"The lady sent no reply to your message, sir," he said in as soft a voice as he dared.

"None!" Waln bellowed.

This had been a possibility he had contemplated only in his gloomiest moments. A doting father himself, he had thought the threat to Lady Melina's daughter would bring him some message from the lady. In his brighter moments, Waln had even contemplated a future where the messenger returned with the three artifacts.

Waln considered the possibility that Fleet had stolen the artifacts, but dismissed it at once. Longsight had recommended Fleet precisely because the man was utterly trustworthy in this type of job and had made himself valuable by being so. Fleet would not risk his reputation for cursed artifacts that he—like any sane man—doubtless feared.

Nor did Fleet Herald have a kingdom to support him—as did Queen Valora or Lady Melina—if he turned thief.

"Are you certain there was no message?" Waln asked, giving Fleet every opportunity to say something that would mitigate the circumstances.

"None, Baron." Fleet straightened and met Waln's eyes. "I

waited a full day lest she change her mind, but she sent no word to me, nor did she send out any other messenger. From what I gathered, she must have put what you told her from her mind, for she simply went about her duties."

Waln swallowed a groan of despair. He'd been playing at pirate. Now, it seemed, he might need to turn pirate. Certainly, there would be no returning to the Isles—to his family and fortune—without those artifacts . . .

Not unless he made every effort to regain them. Queen Valora might forgive him then.

Waln had received Fleet in his private chambers, a decadently overfurnished room that took over the entire space once devoted to housing the light. He'd wanted to be alone to savor his triumph and to contemplate his next move.

How could he counter when the Lady Melina refused to play?

Or what if she didn't intend to play his game, but to write the rules for one of her own?

"Go," Waln said to Fleet. "Get some hot food, a good night's sleep. Tomorrow I'm going to want to know everything—no matter how minor—you learned about Lady Melina and her position in New Kelvin."

Fleet gulped nervously as he made yet another slovenly bow and retreated. Waln, turning to watch him go, saw someone on the landing without—someone who had been bold enough to sneak upstairs and listen.

Sunlight caught fire from the gemstone on her brow as Lady Melina's youngest daughter looked in at him. Citrine's big blue eyes were wide and slightly crazed. She waved her maimed hand at him in a parody of greeting.

She was laughing.

IF I LIVE TO BE AS OLD AS KING TEDRIC, Elise thought, *I will never forget that journey.*

A glimmer of wry humor colored her next thought, *Though I might wish to do so.*

For three days they had pushed hard, taking side roads whenever possible, riding during the hours they were least likely to meet anyone. As they had descended along the edge of the Sword of Kelvin Mountains, heading not only south but to lower altitudes, the weather had warmed—not enough to offer comfort, but enough that they were forced to contend with mud and slush in the daylight hours.

Sleigh travel was heavier on the roads at night, so night was when they took cover. Always the sense that they were just one step ahead of the alert preyed on them. More than once, Elise had awakened from nightmares where the New Kelvinese guards were at the door to whatever barn or shack they had sheltered in.

Indeed there had been times when, bent over Cream Delight's neck so that she could gather what heat she could from the mare, Elise had felt certain that the alarm must have gotten ahead of them. Every time Firekeeper or Blind Seer brought word of a cluster of houses, an inn, or a larger than usual traveling party, Elise had been certain that their desperate bid for freedom had ended.

Even Elation's return to them two days into their journey had given Elise only a little reassurance. The Royal Peregrine had reported that the New Kelvinese had searched the vicinity around Dragon's Breath for a half-day before finding the imprisoned guards at the end of the sewer tunnel and thus confirming the means of escape from the city.

The heavy snowfall had made it impossible for the New Kelvinese to send out pigeons or to confirm the direction in which the fugitives had gone. When the snow let up, only a few of the reluctant birds could be convinced to fly. Those that had taken off had met with a quick end.

Elation couldn't be certain she had gotten all the pigeons, for she had wisely waited to stoop upon them when they were out of sight of the Beast Lore covey. Riders had been sent out with orders to leave word of the fugitives along the road. The same weather that had made their own journey a misery had slowed these riders as well.

Elise was not comforted by Derian's conjecture that the riders would not be as desperate as the fugitives. He reassured his companions that the messengers would be inclined to take advantage of a gossip-hungry innkeeper's offer of a glass of something hot or comfortable shelter when night drew on.

Derian spoke reassuringly enough, telling anecdotes from his own experience, but Elise noted that the redhead often glanced back along their trail and that more than once Bold was sent to see if any pursued.

Bold had to serve as their aerial spy. As soon as Elation had rested—and Firekeeper had little patience with the peregrine, saying that she was already fat on rich pigeon flesh—the falcon was sent east to the swamps in hope that she would learn something of Citrine Shield's precise whereabouts.

When today had dawned, clear and bright, the falcon had not returned, but Firekeeper was unworried. The bird could go much faster and more directly than any of them, but she still needed to rest and hunt.

Derian had reminded them when they set out that they were only a half-day's journey from Zodara. Despite the exotic sound, Zodara meant something like "Trader Town," and was the easternmost crossing between Hawk Haven and New Kelvin. They had chosen to come here, rather than returning to Gateway, because from Plum Orchard they were days closer to the area where Citrine had last been seen.

Unhappily, coming into Zodara meant that they could not hope to sneak across unnoticed. They had come into the town quite openly—the New Kelvinese put their guards at the riverside, not their own interior.

Zodara was a much larger trade crossing than the Gateway to Enchantment and at this time of year became quite busy. The White Water slowed—as much as that angry body of water ever slowed—when portions upstream froze. Moreover, heavy cargoes, like the glass for which New Kelvin was renowned, were more likely to reach their destinations if slid over snow rather than jolted over stony roads.

This meant that Zodara was quite busy. With Derian's coaching, Elise secured them stabling near the southeast edge of town. The man who owned the warehouse looked at them without curiosity, dismissing them with the typical New Kelvinese disdain for foreigners. However, Elise doubted that he was so dismissive that if an alarm was raised he wouldn't remember them.

The winter weather meant that no one thought it peculiar that they kept their heads covered, so Elise's New Kelvinese haircut went unremarked when she and Derian ventured out into the town to check out their options for getting across.

Elise wasn't terribly hopeful that they could find someone who would carry them to Plum Orchard—she figured they would need to take their risks on the public ferry—but trade goes two ways.

Within a few hours, Derian had recognized a trader with whom his father did some business. Promises of payment and hints of intrigue had fired both this woman's greed and her sense of adventure. By late that afternoon they were all loaded aboard a series of flat-bottomed boats—even Blind Seer, though the wolf had to submit to being caged.

Evening saw them unloaded on the friendly shores of Hawk Haven.

Plum Orchard was a simple town—though at this time of year, swollen as the population was with merchants and their goods, it really qualified as a city. The cobblestone houses and shops looked so reassuringly normal after nearly a moonspan of New Kelvinese architecture that Elise nearly burst into tears.

They took rooms at a coaching house owned by cousins of Derian's mother. In light of the family connection, the owners found room for the rather large group and their animals despite the influx of merchants in Plum Orchard.

A large payment taken out of the New Kelvinese coin earned by Doc's efforts in Dragon's Breath—and easily exchanged here so close to the border—rewarded Derian's relatives for making the travelers welcome and encouraged them to keep from gossiping about their rather remarkable guests.

Elise was fascinated when she realized that to their hosts the most remarkable of these guests was not Derian, though they honored (and slightly envied) him for his counselor's ring, nor was it either herself or Edlin, though they both claimed titles and the promise of sizable inheritance, nor—and this was remarkable in itself—was it Firekeeper and her wolf.

The one whose presence awakened wonder and awe in these sophisticated innkeepers was Grateful Peace. They knew far more of New Kelvinese custom than was usual in Hawk Haven and recognized him for a man of quality and education—a man who, after the custom of New Kelvin, had risen to power more on his own merits than on his ancestry.

But Derian's cousins had been paid for silence and Elise felt sure that they would keep that silence.

For the first time since leaving Hasamemorri's house five days before, Elise had a really hot bath. She scrubbed the last traces of scarlet paint from her skin before tumbling between clean linen sheets. Her last thought before falling asleep was that she would have felt perfectly normal once more had it not been for her hair—or rather her lack of hair.

Early the next morning, Wendee Jay, frowning at her own reflection in the mirror, raised the same subject.

"I don't think I can go home until this has grown out. My little Merri will scream."

Had it not been for a certain defiant humor in the other woman's tone, Elise would have thought her completely serious.

"My parents," Elise replied, "are going to have quite a bit to say about my new style, too. I wonder if bonnets might come back into style?"

They laughed unsteadily. Small hats were definitely "in," but these were mostly ornaments, meant to draw attention to the head. The heavy, all-concealing bonnet belonged to the realm of marketwomen and older ladies, though it was considered permissible for travel.

Firekeeper thumped a couple of times on the door panel and came in. She, too, was scrubbed clean and freshly clothed. Her face, however, seemed to glow with something more than just scrubbing.

"Doc say," she announced, actually pirouetting in place, "that Blind Seer's eye will live!"

Elise felt an answering glow light her own face and Wendee clapped her hands together. Despite his injuries, the great grey wolf had insisted on acting as forward watch for their group. Whereas on the journey out Elise suspected he had often slept for several hours a day, trusting his greater speed to permit him to catch up, this time Blind Seer had been nearby every hour they were on the move.

Only the heaviness of his sleep each night and the quantities of food he required gave hint to the tremendous toll his exertions took on him.

"He will have scar through lid and around eye," Firekeeper continued, "that will always show, but both will work."

The wolf-woman looked truly happy for the first time since she had failed to catch Lady Melina. Elise hoped that Firekeeper was on the way to forgiving herself.

"Blind Seer laugh at me," the wolf-woman continued, her tone sour but her eyes still dancing, "and say, why I keep this silly hair. He say cut it off and have done. Hair will grow back."

She held out a razor. "Would one of you cut it off?"

As Elise accepted the razor, it occurred to her for the first time that Firekeeper was as vain as any woman. Her disinterest in fashion, her open disdain for what she considered the more ridiculous aspects of clothing, her own idiosyncratic manner of dress, all these had blinded Elise to the truth.

Now, as she set about shaving the rest of Firekeeper's tatty hair to an even length, leaving just the bare fuzz of five days' growth against her scalp, Elise realized that Firekeeper would like nothing more than a thick mane of hair.

"How about you?" Firekeeper asked as she viewed the end result of Elise's barbering in the mirror. "Will you go short in front, long in back?"

Elise considered.

"I think so, Firekeeper. I don't have your courage. A tight

braid wrapped close and the contrast won't be so obvious. Wendee?"

"I'll follow your lead, my lady." Wendee laughed a trace nervously. " 'Tis bad enough being bald in front without being bald all over."

Firekeeper ran her fingers over the stubble on her scalp, then shrugged.

"I not even had enough to make braid. Maybe someday."

She sounded distinctly wistful.

That trace of femininity vanished, however, when a shrill scream sounded from outside the window.

"Elation!" Firekeeper shouted and ran down the stairs.

They could hear her thudding over two at a time in her haste to get the peregrine's report.

Wendee sighed. "Don't think me coldhearted, Lady Elise, but I was so hoping for a day to let my behind rest from the saddle."

Elise nodded. "You're a kind woman to say so. Citrine is my own cousin and I'd been hating myself for wanting nothing more than to rest. Still, it seems that Elation is going to keep us honest to our better selves."

As she slipped on her outer clothes and hurried outside to hear what the falcon had to report, Elise felt a thin finger of worry touch her heart. They'd been counting on Elation to find Citrine.

What if the falcon had failed?

❀

FIREKEEPER'S BARE FEET SLAPPED on the wooden treads of the staircase as she raced to meet Elation. Outside, the ground was cold and hard, but she was too excited to miss her boots.

Elation was perched on a narrow fence rail, busily shredding a plump rat that had abandoned its comfortable housing under the floor of one of the hay barns upon finding that barn un-accountably inhabited by a wolf.

Raising her head from her still warm repast, Elation fixed Firekeeper with one of her gold-rimmed eyes.

"I have found Citrine," she cried triumphantly. "As Doc guessed, she is to be found in a stone tower in the swamps to the east. She is pale and fragile, but still lives. I saw another thing there as well."

"I am certain you saw many things, mighty conqueror of the clouds," Firekeeper said, lavish with her praise.

Not only did the falcon deserve it, but flattery eased her along like oil on a hinge.

Elation, finished now with the rat, preened, wiping away the worst of the gore.

"I saw a man arriving," Elation said, "a man I had seen in Dragon's Breath some days after our own arrival. He had made himself noticeable to me then, for my eyes are sharp and I miss nothing. I had seen that he had hair beneath the knit cap—hair where a New Kelvinese permitted access into Thendulla Lypella would have had none."

Firekeeper gasped her admiration aloud, encouraging the peregrine to continue.

"He also did not walk like a New Kelvinese. They all mince because of those robes and tight shoes they wear," the falcon continued, exaggerating somewhat. "He walked like a man of Hawk Haven . . . or perhaps from Bright Bay. In any case, like a man from a place where trousers and boots are worn, not robes and curly-toed slippers."

"Peace doesn't wear curly-toed slippers," Firekeeper protested, temporarily distracted.

"He does in court and among his fellows," Elation retorted placidly. "I saw him."

Firekeeper shook the distraction away.

"So there is contact between New Kelvin and Baron End-brook," she mused aloud.

"Rather between Endbrook and New Kelvin," Elation corrected, "for I saw that this man was treated as one of the flock at the lighthouse. Nor is Baron Endbrook happy at the news the man carried to him."

"When did you see this?" Firekeeper asked.

"The sun was high then," Elation replied. "When I had seen all I could see, I flew here directly. I rested some when darkness came, then flew much of the next day. Last night, I rested again. When I arrived, I located your lodgings by the mules in the pasture."

"Less than two full days," Firekeeper said. "I am impressed. Even for a falcon of your power and tenacity, that was a flight of which to sing."

Elation preened, though her feathers were clean by now.

Blind Seer, pretending to doze in the thin winter sunshine, sniggered.

"I *am* impressed," Firekeeper repeated. "From what Derian and his maps tell me, we afoot will need four or five full days to cover the same distance."

ELATION'S ARRIVAL had found their company somewhat scattered. Doc had been tending to Grateful Peace and making arrangements for the crippled thaumaturge to be moved to Doc's family holdings in the Norwood Grant.

Peace had survived the journey, but that was the best that could be said for his condition. Ideally, he should have been allowed to stay in one place and heal, but the danger to his life should he remain so close to the border was very real.

As Firekeeper understood it, the New Kelvinese One—Apheros the Dragon Speaker, a ruler who was not a king, who served a king but was more powerful than that king . . . this Apheros would not simply let Grateful Peace disperse from the New Kelvinese pack.

Peace's actions would be seen as more heinous than stealing meat from a weaning pup and for them the penalty would be death. Whether or not assassins, such as those who had come to Sapphire and Shad's wedding, would be sent could not be ascertained, but in any case, Peace would be safer away from the border.

Derian, for his part, was replenishing their sadly depleted supplies. Edlin was assisting him—at Derian's invitation.

However, with Bold's help, Firekeeper collected her stragglers before the morning was much older. In a private room with a thick door and Bold outside the windows to make certain none snooped on their conference, she informed them of what the peregrine had discovered.

"So," the wolf-woman concluded, "how soon can we leave?"

Derian frowned thoughtfully.

"I'm nearly finished with my purchases. There are farms along the way, even a tavern or two with rooms to let. We don't need to carry as much."

Edlin nodded agreement and seemed to be about to launch into one of his incomprehensible speeches when Doc spoke up.

"Have we thought this through?" he asked. "So we go. What are we going to do when we get there?"

Firekeeper honored Doc for his healing talent—a talent he had insisted on using to her benefit as soon as he had recovered some, so that her hip no longer ached and the bruises were fading to a nasty purplish green. Because of how she honored him, she held back her exasperation.

"We must ride for days and days," she reminded him gently. "Maybe we can plan on the road?"

Doc nodded a trace impatiently.

"We can and shall," he said. "However, do you really think that the few of us can take Smuggler's Light?"

Firekeeper was sincerely puzzled.

"We not take this light. We take Citrine. She is very small."

"Firekeeper," Doc persisted, "they won't give her to us, not just for asking, nor do I suspect that she's going to be particularly easy to steal away. This matter has advanced beyond our ability to handle it alone."

"I say! I'd wondered about that," Edlin said diffidently. "I mean, this Endbrook is an ambassador, what? Wouldn't our going after him—and I know you, Sister, you're not going to let him hurt Citrine and then go free as air—I don't particularly want to let him go myself . . . But what I was saying is, wouldn't our going after him create a diplomatic incident?"

Firekeeper felt her patience melting.

"Not again!" she wailed. "Isn't anything simple?"

"Maybe among the wolves," Edlin said kindly, "but not among humans, what?"

"And not among wolves either," Blind Seer added from where he lay beside her on the floor. *"If it was, you wouldn't be here. By the way, have you considered how you're going to get the artifacts you gave to Elise and Wendee away from them? They sleep with them at night and wear them under their clothing by day."*

"Shut up!" Firekeeper growled at him.

The humans blinked at her and she slouched down.

"Not for you, Edlin," she apologized, for it was clear that everyone thought she'd been snarling at Edlin.

"That's all right," he beamed.

Firekeeper sighed.

"This diplomatic incident," she said, sounding out the words carefully, "how do we prevent it and rescue Citrine still?"

She had expected this simple question to start another long wrangle, but Doc surprised her by saying:

"I have an idea. It will take some cooperation from your wingéd-folk allies, Firekeeper, but I think it's time we brought in Princess Sapphire. Citrine is, after all, her little sister. Sapphire's not likely to refuse a call to come to her aid. If the crown princess decides an ambassador is out of line, she can act against him . . ."

"Boot him out, you mean," Edlin translated happily.

"That's right," Doc concurred. "She can also bring in some of the Royal Guard to enforce her wishes."

Elise asked a trace hesitantly, "But didn't Princess Lovella fail to take Smuggler's Light with an army?"

"True," Doc replied, "but Sapphire isn't Lovella—and she'll have Lovella's failure to learn from. Sapphire won't be looking to take the tower, just to remove two of its residents. I think the pirates may see reason and surrender Baron Endbrook and Citrine if their choice is that or losing the light house."

"I could ask Elation to carry words," Firekeeper said, glancing over at the peregrine, "but she is one. Do you need more that you speak of allies?"

Doc nodded. "I also suggest that a message be sent to King Allister. From court gossip following the wedding, I know that he was planning to have ships patrol the coast lest Queen Valora get ambitious. He may be able to divert a ship or two to cover the coastal side of the swamp—just close enough in so that we can inform Baron Endbrook that there's no escape that way."

Elation moved uneasily on her perch, lifting first one foot, than the other.

"I cannot be everywhere." she said. *"Nor do I care for the idea of flying over the sea searching for ships. I begin to understand why Doc speaks of 'allies.' "*

"So do I," Firekeeper replied, impressed and unsettled at the scope of Doc's vision. *"You will someday be among the Mothers of your people,"* she continued. *"If you went with Doc's message to King Allister, could you convince some of the Royal Gulls to seek out the ships?"*

"I could try," Elation said, *"but I can no more promise for a seagull who isn't here than I can promise for the wind."*

"Elation will try," Firekeeper said aloud, "but she cannot promise. Bold could carry the message to Eagle's Nest. He is not a falcon nor yet is he known to Princess Sapphire, but you can make the writings talk for him. Consider what you will write and write it small. I go and speak with Bold."

She leapt to her feet and hurried outside, not wanting the others to see how Doc's idea had troubled her world. A few moons ago, Doc had not known of the Royal Beasts. Now he had swallowed the idea that there were beasts intelligent enough to serve his needs and was turning them to his use.

Somehow she felt that Grateful Peace was not the only traitor to come back out of New Kelvin.

XXXV

KING ALLISTER OF THE PLEDGE had escaped to the castle roof. Somehow, he had never imagined that the greatest irritant of his new kingship would be a houseful of adolescent women.

Royal politics he understood—he'd lived them all his life. Great-Aunt Seastar with her continual angling for position was a problem. So was his perennially offended royal physician. Lord Rory had never forgiven Allister for permitting Sir Jared to treat the newlyweds. So were a multitude of lords and ladies of various stripes of nobility, all determined either not to lose privileges that had been their family's since the days of Gustin I, or to gain new privileges under the new—and presumably manipulable—monarch.

But these things Allister understood. These things he'd been prepared for in some shape or form since Queen Valora first set him to try for the throne of Hawk Haven—never dreaming, of course, that he would end up instead with her throne.

What he didn't understand were young females. He'd brought back four with him from Hawk Haven, and they seemed to have unfolded like the petals of an exotic flower ruffling into multiples of itself. The proliferation had started with a tea party or so, become circles dedicated to embroidery or dancing or some other delicate pursuit.

Pearl had told him that many of the local nobles were offended because *their* daughters had not been invited to stay at the castle. Gossip said that King Allister expected *both* of his sons to marry foreign women, and this had encouraged every mother in the kingdom with a remotely eligible daughter to find some excuse to bring her by the court.

Tavis was besieged by every type of woman imaginable. Blushing maidens so shy they could hardly speak above a whisper were at least not offensive, but watching coquettes play their flirtatious games with a youth hardly into his sixteenth year was enough to make Allister's blood boil.

Minnow and Anemone were no better than the rest—though, of course, they were not interested in their brother. However, the hunt for his favor had made them prematurely aware of their own importance in the marriage races. A few moonspans ago at the wedding they had hardly known how to move in a formal gown. Today Allister had seen Anemone modeling a dress—a gift to her from some well-wisher—that made her look far too sophisticated for his tastes.

Until, that is, he had protested too bluntly and she had dissolved into tears, racing for her room trailing brocaded silk and lace after her.

Pearl had given him a look that held a mixture of exasperation and understanding before hurrying after the girl.

And Allister had headed for the roof.

There was a spot on one of the crenellated battlements that he particularly liked when he needed to think. Higher than much of the surrounding castle, it provided a good view of both the bay and the town. Whyte Steel approved of it for security reasons—a single guard could hold the base of the tower, though two were usually posted there. Allister couldn't complain. He hadn't forgotten the assassins.

Hood pulled up around his ears, Allister was leaning back against one side of the battlements, looking out over the ocean, when a peregrine falcon plummeted out of the sky behind him and perched on the stone.

Allister's first thought was *Here's a danger Whyte didn't anticipate, or he wouldn't have let me up here either!*

The falcon, however, broke from its stoop short of the king and perched on the edge of the battlement.

Allister thought that the bird looked vaguely familiar. As it cocked his head to look at him, he felt certain. He'd never seen a peregrine as large, but for one. It studied him with a certain regal arrogance and then emitted a chuffing, churling noise that so seemed a greeting that he responded.

"Elation, isn't it? Lady Blysse's bird?"

It hunched its shoulders and shrieked softly. Then it lifted one taloned foot. For a moment, Allister thought it was going to preen. Then he saw the lead capsule tied to the leg.

The bird lowered its head and rubbed against the capsule, churring encouragingly—or at least Allister hoped the noise was meant as encouragement. He felt rather nervous for his fingers as he brought them within reach of that cruelly curved beak and those deadly sharp talons, but the bird held its ground and suffered him to remove the capsule—indeed, it seemed grateful to have it gone.

With a preliminary stretching of its wings, it dove off of the tower. King Allister watched it plummet downward, then level off and soar gracefully as if glad to be free of its burden.

Curious and unwilling to face the probable distractions that would meet him if he descended, Allister hunkered down so that the wind might not blow the contents of the capsule from his hands and used his belt knife to cut open the lead.

As he had expected, there was a small curl of parchment within. On it was written in painfully tiny print:

King Allister—

If the Ancestors still smile on us, Elation will get this to your hands. Citrine Shield has been taken hostage by those who hold Smuggler's Light. To save her we need their ships prevented from departing into the ocean.

We understand that you have ships patrolling the coast north to the Waterland border, lest certain parties get ideas. Pray divert one or more of these ships to the area near the lighthouse. Keep any ship from leaving.

Explanations can be given to any emissary you would send, but we must beg you act without more than this. Our role is not official, but we will also be begging aid from King Tedric. We do not expect to be refused as Citrine is his heir's sister.

Elation can bear news to us. She will find you a carrier if you wish messages borne to your ship captains. Pray, do not delay. The life of a little girl—at the very least—rests on prompt action.

This peculiar note was signed "Jared Surcliffe, Knight of the White Eagle."

Allister was reading the note over for the second time when Elation landed again on the battlement. He noticed a pair of gulls riding the wind slightly above his tower. They were not calling or complaining as would be usual when confronted with a bird of prey in their territory. The king did not think this was coincidence.

"Come," he said to Elation. "I have a reply for you to carry."

He started to hold out his cloaked arm, remembered how cruelly talons could pierce even leather, and added:

"Do you by chance know where my private library window is? There is a balcony outside."

The hawk shrieked, but whether this was "yes" or "no" he couldn't be certain.

He compromised by saying: "I will have a red scarf hung out when I am ready. Please, take your leisure and hunt your fill in the meantime."

The peregrine leapt in the air with such promptness Allister had to believe he had been understood. The gulls followed one at a time, peeling off like soldiers in formation.

Shaking his head in wonder, Allister headed down the stairs, his footsteps becoming more and more rapid as he approached the bottom. He shook off several attempts to claim his time, stopping only to speak with Calico, his court clerk.

"Two tasks for you," the king said. "First, find out how quickly *Waveslicer* can be made ready for departure. Second, find Queen Pearl. Tell her I would speak with her—not immediately, for I must write several letters first, but at her earliest convenience."

Calico bowed. Curiosity was writ large on his patched face, but he valued the king's trust too much to pry.

King Allister had just finished drafting a reply to Sir Jared and three missives to the captains of those ships that should be in closest proximity to the Smuggler's light, when a knock came on his door. Pearl entered on the heels of her knock.

"Read this, my dear," Allister said, pushing across to her the missive Elation had brought, "but hold your questions while I check these letters."

Queen Pearl did so, her round face becoming quite grave before she finished. When Allister looked up from his own correspondence, he saw that her eyes were bright with unshed tears.

"What madness is this?" she asked, her voice calm and steady. "Who has laid hands on this child?"

"I don't know," Allister admitted. "I know no more than do you. My guess is Queen Valora is somehow at the bottom of this. Her assassins failed to kill Sapphire and Shad, and for some reason she has settled on working her revenge on Citrine. That, however, is just a guess."

"And you will send the ships as Sir Jared requests?"

Allister tapped the instructions he had just written and began to roll them into thin spills that could be inserted within carrying tubes.

"They are here along with a reply for Sir Jared. He doesn't mention timing, but my hope is that any assault from the land will be held until my vessels are present to close off escape by water."

Pearl laid a finger to one side of her face and nodded.

"Surely," she said comfortingly, "that is not an unreasonable hope. Why request support and then not wait for it to arrive?"

"My thoughts exactly."

"But why would anyone go after Citrine without waiting?"

Allister rose and opened the doors onto his balcony, answering Pearl as he secured a red kerchief onto a bit of ornamental carving. Outside, the wind had risen and he was glad to close the door behind him and return to his desk by the fire.

"Because, I fear, Sapphire is hotheaded and impulsive. I don't know what fondness she feels for this youngest sister, but even if she cares little for her . . ."

"I think she rather likes her," Queen Pearl interrupted.

". . . she is quite likely to go to her rescue, even if only to revenge the insult paid to herself."

"Would Sapphire be so impulsive?" Pearl asked, then answered herself. "Of course she would be."

"But that is just a guess," Allister continued. "I desire more information. To get that, I must go to where the conflict is. You will reign in my absence."

"You can't go!"

"Yes," he replied firmly. "Tavis is too young to act as my emissary. Shad is in Hawk Haven. I hate to admit this, but as of yet there is no one immediately available in Bright Bay— other than your father, who is too old for such a voyage— who shares both prominence of rank and my trust. We have been in power too briefly. Therefore, I must go myself. Sapphire and Shad are my heirs as well as Tedric's. Their actions reflect on me—more so if I am not present to deny my sanction to any wilder course they may contemplate."

"I understand," Pearl said. "You will take *Waveslicer*?"

"Precisely. The shoals that flank Hawk Haven's bit of coastline would force a larger vessel to divert further out to seas. I am sending messages to the captains of the *Boisterous*, *Damselfly*, and *Sea Stallion*. *Boisterous* is to patrol the ocean side of the shoals to prevent a ship from escaping through there to the Isles. The other two are to come in closer to shore."

"Hawk Haven," Allister continued a trace smugly, "has a navy, but their people are not sailors like ours. Most of their vessels will be in dry dock for the winter. I suspect that is one reason Sir Jared appealed to me."

"One reason?" Pearl prompted gently.

"The other may be something to do with Sapphire or with Valora or some other mystery I don't yet know enough about to understand."

Pearl sighed and pushed her hands through her hair.

"Since there may be danger to Sapphire's other sisters," she said, her tone that of one who plans aloud, "I must restrain Ruby and Opal from going too far afield, and place strong guard on them when they do. That should prove interesting."

Allister looked up from sealing the message capsules. "Interesting?"

"I believe Opal is forming an attachment. She will not like being so heavily chaperoned. No matter. I was intending to have her freedom curtailed in any case. She cannot be permitted to form any alliances without her mother's permission. It is time she learned the drawbacks of her increased prominence."

Allister rose. "It is difficult to imagine any one of Lady Melina's daughters doing anything without their mother's permission."

"Yes," Pearl agreed slowly, "and that rather makes little Citrine's case all the more interesting. Where is her mother in all of this?"

"I expect to hear momentarily from Hawk Haven," Allister admitted. "Surely Lady Melina will have already appealed to Sapphire. She would not wait for Sir Jared to do so."

"True."

Feeling as if he might be about to make a fool of himself, Allister went and opened the door onto the balcony again. He had dreaded finding nothing there, but Elation was waiting. As he came out, bracing himself against the cold, she gave a shrill cry and two gulls dropped from the skies and landed near.

As if demonstrating what was expected, the peregrine stretched up her body so that the king could easily secure the message capsule. He held his palm flat so that Elation could see the three that remained.

"I'd hoped to send messages to three of my ships," he said. "Could you find another messenger?"

Elation stiffly shook her head—the motion was more a leaning of her entire body from side to side, but the meaning was unmistakable.

"Ah." Allister frowned thoughtfully. "That was probably too much to ask. Could one of the gulls carry two capsules?"

Again the falcon indicated "no."

"Wait then," he said. "I need to make a change."

He hurried back inside and adapted the message he had

written for the *Sea Stallion*'s captain, indicating that he should pass on her orders to the *Damselfly*'s captain at the first opportunity.

"That should work," he explained to Pearl. "They're sailing in company."

He went outside again, Pearl accompanying him this time despite his protests that she'd take a chill.

"I don't want to miss this" was all she would say.

Allister turned again to Elation:

"Your message is for Sir Jared. Do your companions here know how to recognize the ships *Boisterous* and *Sea Stallion*?"

Elation nodded, a gesture that involved squatting low as if to cover her feet with her feathers then raising her torso as high as possible, and repeating the motion a few times. From slightly behind and beside him, Allister heard Pearl gasp in amazement. He fancied the peregrine was pleased.

"This capsule," he continued, "is for the *Sea Stallion*. She should be sailing closer to the coast."

One of the gulls edged closer. It was markedly more apprehensive than the falcon and Allister guessed that while Elation was accustomed to at least some human handling, the gulls were truly wild.

Thinking of this and recalling how he had seen gulls use their beaks to neatly flense flesh from the carcasses of whales and sharks, he had to fight to keep his hands steady as he fastened the capsule to the gull's leg.

"This capsule," he said, turning to the other gull, "is for the *Boisterous*. Weather permitting, she's out in deeper water, closer to the Isles."

Neither gull offered any indication that they had understood him.

"I guess," he said, stepping back to Pearl's side and sliding his arm around her shoulders, "we'll need to trust Elation to translate if needed."

The peregrine shrieked something unintelligible, and without further ceremony the three birds took flight. Elation caught a wind and moved north. The gulls soared higher and headed out to sea.

Clad only in an indoor gown, Pearl was trembling from the chill air, but she insisted on watching until the birds were out of sight.

"That may be," she said, "the most amazing thing I can ever hope to see."

"More amazing," Allister said, drawing her back inside and to the fire, "than Lady Blysse and her wolf?"

"More," Pearl said, "for these came of their own will with no human guidance. Their behavior makes me wonder how much we have been overlooking. Have they been here all along?"

Allister found that the idea made him uneasy, but as there was nothing he could do about it—short of trying to drive every bird from the castle, and that was manifestly insane—he put both idea and discomfort from him.

He and Pearl spent several minutes discussing matters she might need to deal with in his absence; then Calico knocked at the library door.

"The *Waveslicer* can sail at dawn," he said, "winds permitting."

"We always sail 'winds permitting,'" Allister said with a smile. "Very good. Tell the captain I will be with her an hour before we sail. I will bring two guards with me, but otherwise trust her vessel to supply my other needs."

"Very good, Sire."

Calico paused and, when nothing further was forthcoming, asked diffidently:

"May I know the reason for your departure, Sire? I wish to be of aid and already rumors are spreading."

"Already?" Allister was astonished.

"Your private craft readied at such short notice, Sire," Calico replied. "It could not go without comment."

"I suppose not."

Allister gave Calico an edited version of the truth that included pirate action with possible political overtones but left out Citrine's situation—he and Pearl had decided that Ruby and Opal would be better off not knowing. That he had received his news from an apparently intelligent hawk he also left out. Let Calico assume he had a skilled spy network that even the clerk didn't know about. Such would only add to most of his subjects' respect for him.

"Queen Pearl will take over matters of business in my absence," the king concluded. "With your support, I trust there will be no difficulties that cannot be met."

Calico straightened with pride.

"I will give the queen every assistance."

"I never doubted that for a moment."

KING ALLISTER WAS PREPARING to depart before first light the next morning when a rap came upon his dressing-room door.

"The king," his valet called out sharply, "is not receiving. He must catch the tide."

"I bear an urgent message for His Majesty," came the reply, its tone as uncompromising as the valet's, "from the crown prince."

King Allister waved a hand and the valet reluctantly opened the door. One of the guards stood without.

"Delivered just this moment," he said, passing the king a packet wrapped in oiled cloth. "The messenger had spent himself and nearly broke his horse's wind getting it here, so I took it upon myself to spare him the stairs."

"Good thinking. Thank you and give him my thanks. If I'm to catch my ship, I may not have time to speak with him myself, but Queen Pearl will give him audience if needed."

"Yes, Your Majesty."

Allister didn't need to instruct that the messenger be given food and a bed. He could trust his servants to do that as a matter of course. The guard withdrew and Allister opened the packet. Within were several sheets of paper, closely written in what Allister recognized as his son Shad's neat, angular hand.

Knowing the tide would not wait upon his leisurely perusal of the contents, Allister permitted the valet to continue dressing him—a thing he normally deplored as the ultimate expression of laziness.

Dear Father,

By now you may have received a note from Sir Jared Surcliffe. If you were in doubt as to whether or not to do as he requests therein, I herein request you to do so at the request of your fellow monarch, King Tedric of Hawk Haven.

That being said, I should say that I have no doubt that you will have done so without prompting.

There was a blot here, as if the writer had been interrupted.

Sapphire, reading this over my shoulder, tells me that I am being unnecessarily cryptic, that I must tell you what you are to do in case Sir Jared's letter did not reach you. Very well. We request that you direct any vessels you have operating in the vicinity of Hawk Haven—as you requested permission to do this autumn in light of then just completed events—to proceed to the vicinity of the former lighthouse known as Smuggler's Light.

Once there, your captains should be instructed to keep any and all vessels, no matter the registry, from departing without being searched. The cargo they are searching for is a girl of some eight years, one Citrine Shield. They should be informed that she may be disguised, drugged, or otherwise unable or unwilling to identify herself.

Allister lifted his foot so that his valet might slide his boot onto it. A small smile twisted the corner of his lips. He could imagine Sapphire dictating those orders to Shad. They certainly didn't sound like his son.

The king feared Sapphire would be disappointed in her father-in-law. He had given no such detailed orders—only that ships were to be held against departing. To say more would be to stir up rumors with which he did not care to deal, especially if the matter could be resolved more quietly.

He continued reading:

Although we ourselves were only informed of matters this morning, we are departing within an hour or so, riding with all haste to the swamps north of Port Haven. If you wonder at our decisiveness, know this.

For some time now, Sapphire has been worried about her sister Citrine. More lonesome for her sisters than she would have believed possible, she had inquired after the possibility of Citrine paying a winter's visit. At first her brother, Jet, put her off with vague excuses. This did not do for long.

Not long ago, Jet was forced to admit that not only did he not know where Citrine was—except that she was in Lady Melina's keeping—he did not know where Lady Melina was either. She has apparently been out of touch with her son and heir since mid-Boar Moon. With any other person, this might be excusable. With Lady Melina, who has delighted in dominating her family . . .

There was a thick crossing out several words in length, then the text continued.

. . . this is a matter for speculation if not outright concern. Therefore, Sapphire was already worried when Sir Jared's news arrived.

This missive will be sent to you by a series of fast riders, these riders directed to press night and day so that you might hear of our actions and be encouraged to have your fleet join us in resolving this matter.

I must go. My horse is ready, my wife champing at the bit.

Allister smiled at this last despite the serious nature of the correspondence. Folding the letter and returning it to its sleeve, he found himself dressed.

"Thank you," he said to the valet. "Take a few days' leave in my absence. You deserve it."

"My thanks, Your Majesty."

Pearl was waiting for him without. Allister embraced her and slid the letter into her hand.

"Read at your leisure, my dear. It is mostly Shad's personal views on the matter that sends me to sea. I don't think they need be shared with the court."

Pearl gave him a wan smile and tucked her fingers into the crook of his arm.

"Tavis and the twins are up and ready to see you off," she said.

The next several minutes were occupied with purely domestic matters—indeed, with some of the most intimate moments the family had shared since the coronation.

Then King Allister departed through the sea gate and from there directly on board the *Waveslicer*. One of the virtues of Revelation Point Castle was that it possessed a deep enough harbor that all but the largest ships could come directly to the dock.

He stood on deck waving for a moment; then, at the urging of Perce Potterford, the guard Whyte had placed in command of the pair who were to accompany the king, Allister went into his cabin. He heard the creak of the lines and the slap of the canvas as the sails caught the wind.

An urgency that hadn't been with Allister while he still had tasks to perform seized him now. Had he thought it would have helped matters, King Allister of the Pledge would have pulled a line or helped haul up the anchor himself.

He knew, however, that his appearance would only make the crew nervous. Sighing, he pulled out a stack of documents that Calico had thrust upon him, and composed himself to wait.

WINTER SUNLIGHT, bright and clear but without much heat, peered through the foliage as if seeking to spy upon Firekeeper and Blind Seer. For the last several days, woman and wolf had been acquainting themselves with the unfamiliar terrain surrounding Smuggler's Light.

Until she had seen Smuggler's Light for herself, Firekeeper had not wanted to wait to rescue Citrine—diplomatic considerations or not. Her first sight of the structure, some two days before her companions arrived, had quite quelled her enthusiasm for taking on the pirates alone.

The uncertain footing and sinkholes that made the swamp a death trap for those humans who dared venture beyond the damp meadows into the swamp proper provided minimal risk to the wolf-woman. She had the good sense to trust Blind Seer to pick out a path for her. He did this with greater ease than even he might have anticipated, because—although they did everything possible to eliminate their trail—humans *did* use the swamp.

In summer, the general wetness might have eliminated even a scent trail. In winter, with much of the surface water frostbound, those who used the trails were more easily followed. In summer, the fecund greenery would have provided further barriers, masking trails with vines and opportunistic grasses. In winter, though the evergreens kept their needles, the bayberry, ash, and oak that had adapted to thrive in the brackish conditions had shed their leaves. The grasses had died back or had been devoured by foraging deer and rabbits.

Canebrakes still blocked lines of sight, however, as did tall stands of cattails. These slim reeds with their heavy tails on top swayed in the wind, fascinating Firekeeper, who had never seen them in such quantity, nor of such size.

But though she delighted in the swamp much as she had the marsh near Revelation Point Castle, the wolf-woman's main purpose for investigating the terrain so carefully was so that she might rescue Citrine. She treasured a private vision of herself going to meet Derian and the rest upon their arrival, holding Citrine by one hand.

Wolf-like, she thrived on the praise of her pack mates; human-like, she imagined that praise before it was earned, carefully building images until the event seemed merely a formality. Her first sight of Smuggler's Light shocked those imaginings from her forever.

Smuggler's Light so dominated the surrounding area that Firekeeper had trouble believing that many of the people in the area had forgotten it had ever been built. As tall as many of the tallest structures she had seen in Dragon's Breath, the lighthouse was a deceptively slender cylinder of smoothly dressed stone capped with a windowed room at the very top. Vines dense enough to cover the stone, but not thick enough to bear weight, gave the stone a diaphanous cloak.

As had Thendulla Lypella in New Kelvin, Smuggler's Light also had structures around its base. These were also made of smoothly dressed stone and were connected to the lighthouse like spokes onto the hub of a wheel. In the spaces between these spokes were fenced yards. From some of these Firekeeper could smell chickens, ducks, goats, pigs, and rabbits. Others showed some evidence of having been gardens—fallow now but for cabbages, kale, and, probably, root vegetables.

There was no scent of either horses or cows. Doubtless the occupants trusted their comings and goings either to boats or to any one of the numerous foot trails Blind Seer had found threaded through the swamp.

Firekeeper—more sophisticated now in fashions of human building—doubted that the original lighthouse outbuildings had possessed such solid iron-sheathed doors, nor that the windows had been made with shutters that—once drawn closed— defied any to open them while at the same time providing those within with ample slits from which to fire arrows.

She wondered some at finding these shutters drawn, but decided that those within could be seeking any possible insulation from the winter cold. Smuggler's Light—whatever its merits—was not overly generously supplied with chimneys. Doubtless it was rather chilly within.

The entire complex was built upon an island of solid, rocky ground that emerged from the surrounding swamp into a perceptible hill. The channel surrounding the hill had been dug out, providing the lighthouse with a moat wider than Derian was tall. A deep channel to the east assured both that water from the ocean would keep that moat filled even during a severe drought and that boats could get directly to the lighthouse.

When Firekeeper first saw this moat, she found no bridges across it. A later, more careful, inspection revealed the makings for bridges concealed on the island near where each of the trails through the swamp ended. These bridge makings, however, were not only concealed—they were stored far enough from the moat's edge that they could not be "borrowed" from the wrong side.

A cleared zone on either side of the bank meant that no one could sneak up unobserved—at least no normal person could. Firekeeper and Blind Seer came that first time by night and if any watcher had glimpsed them, he would have thought them merely two of the wild creatures that the swamp drew into itself each winter when foraging without became sparse.

Seeing the place, Firekeeper gave up any hope of stealing Citrine away without help. Indeed, she wondered if anyone, even Sapphire with an army to aid her, could breach these defenses. She no longer questioned that Princess Lovella had died trying to take the place. Indeed, she felt considerable respect that the princess had even dared try.

The rest of Firekeeper's companions, traveling at a more leisurely pace and by daylight rather than night, arrived in the vicinity of the swamp two days after Firekeeper and Blind Seer.

In anticipation of their arrival, Firekeeper had found them a sheltered copse, mostly of second-growth evergreens, in which to pitch their camp. The copse provided shelter from both easy observation and the winds. These, while less fierce than they had been in the Sword of Kelvin Mountains, were still a matter to be reckoned with where comfort was concerned.

There was fresh water near the copse, courtesy of an old well. Most of the well's stone lining had fallen in, but the water remained pure, without the slightest taint of salt.

Upon their arrival, Derian and Edlin both found ample evidence that years before there had been a farmstead here: the foundation of a house, a section of vine-covered wall, partially burnt timbers overgrown with weeds where they were not given to rot, a dented tin mug. No one, however, had lived here for a long time—probably the ruins dated to before the smugglers had set up housekeeping in the swamp.

During the journey east, Derian had purchased fodder for both horses and mules. With this stored in what might well have once been a root cellar, there was no need to let the beasts out to graze. Firekeeper and Blind Seer supplied the humans with venison; Edlin snared rabbits in the fields.

All in all, especially after the terrible journey along the Sword of Kelvin Mountains, they were quite comfortable. Here they would wait, doing their best to keep out of sight until Princess Sapphire arrived. Bold had brought the news that Sapphire was indeed coming and on his own initiative had gone to watch the post-road for signs.

Elation arrived a day after the others, bearing the news that she had delivered her message to King Allister and that he had been receptive. Messages had gone out to three ships, and, Elation believed, the king himself meant to follow.

"But how," Firekeeper asked, "will this place be broken? It is a fortress that makes Thendulla Lypella in New Kelvin seem as open as a meadow after the deer have cropped it short. Those within have food. They must have good water, and here there is no tunnel to let us inside."

She reported this last rather glumly, for much of her energy for the last few days had been spent searching for just such a tunnel. However, though foxes, mice, and rabbits all dug escape holes from their burrows, the smugglers were like turtles or porcupines, trusting instead to their armor.

At least Edlin, busy again with his drawing materials and

paper, was kept busy mapping the results of her explorations.

"How we get in," Derian replied, "is not for us to decide. Sapphire and Shad will act—and King Tedric probably told them what to do."

He tried to sound confident, but Firekeeper could see that he was quite worried. It showed in the manner in which he moved: quick and agitated. She knew why Derian felt as he did. Sapphire really was brave, but she could be impulsive, too.

What if her impulsiveness led to Citrine's death?

That night Firekeeper prowled the swamp again. Despite the cold, she stripped to her skin and swam the moat. On the other side, the edgy sensation of fear kept her warm.

She wished Blind Seer were with her so that she might steal some of his heat, but the wolf had remained on the other side lest his closeness panic the domestic animals into raising an alarm.

Restlessly, the wolf-woman paced close to the stone walls. Even if someone watched from the glass-walled room at the top, this close to the walls she was invisible. She walked around the circle, checking for any door or window that might admit her.

She slipped into the chicken coop, but the door that permitted the humans to come and tend the birds was locked and barred.

In the goat pens she took a blanket and wrapped it around her. At least her shaved head meant that her hair was not dripping down her back. Here, too, the door to the interior was locked—and this despite a fence built to keep predators away from the goats. A fence like that would keep most humans out as well.

Firekeeper wondered at a level of caution that combined locked doors and tight fences. Humans, to her knowledge, were not usually so careful of routine security. They made doors and did not shut them, installed locks and did not turn the keys—not unless they were afraid of something.

Pressed against the stone of Smuggler's Light, Firekeeper wondered.

Were the pirates afraid?

If so, what had made them so? Had something or someone given them warning?

Frowning, she left the blanket to the goats, slipped back through darkness, and swam the moat again, leaving no more of a ripple than might an otter.

Blind Seer had stood guard over her clothing and whimpered his concern until she donned them once more.

"Stupid, pup," he said. "What good will you do Citrine if you die of cold?"

"I won't," she replied.

The wolf ignored her.

"And have you forgotten the promise you made the Royal Beasts? When will you reclaim the other treasures?"

Fleetingly, Firekeeper thought of the ring. If she could awaken its powers she wouldn't be fighting cold now. Even if she had swum the moat, as a wolf she would have shaken herself dry, then run a little to warm her blood. Her underfur would have protected her even while the outer dried.

She had no underfur and her underclothing had only taken the damp into themselves and now lay soggy against her skin.

Ah, well, at least she could run. There was a fire back at the camp. Food, too. She wouldn't die of cold.

Blind Seer loped easily beside her, alert lest she miss the trail, but even in his alertness he kept after her about the artifacts.

"What will you do when Sapphire and Shad arrive, and one of them claims the artifacts for King Allister? What will you do when King Allister himself arrives?"

"How will they know we have them?"

"Elise will tell them. She smells of fear if she so much as looks toward the bundle in which she keeps the mirror. You are fortunate that she took it from Doc's pack. If he had it, you might never get it back."

"Even if Sapphire and Shad learn that we have the artifacts, they won't dare claim them," Firekeeper replied with more confidence than she felt. "Their people fear magical things. They daren't make a public fuss."

The wolf persisted, "You must take them from Wendee and Elise. Then you can claim to have lost them or hidden them or thrown them in the swamp. Otherwise, the only one you can give to the Beasts is the ring—and they will not be pleased."

Firekeeper felt herself warming, though some of the heat was temper.

"In good time!"

"Before Sapphire arrives," the wolf insisted. "Or I will know what I have begun to believe—you fear those things of metal and gems."

Firekeeper did not reply. She knew he was at least partially right—she did fear them, but not as Elise and Wendee did. They feared them for their potential; she feared them for their promise.

She was able to put Blind Seer's words from her for a bit, for when they returned to the camp, Bold was waiting.

"He's been back an hour or so," said Edlin, who had drawn the late watch. "I say! This *is* our crow? Bold, I mean."

"It is Bold," Firekeeper agreed, hanging over the glowing coals of the fire as if she could transfer the heat directly into her veins.

Bold squawked at her, a trace indignant that she had gone to the fire before speaking to him.

Firekeeper apologized and then listened. She turned to Edlin, who had been watching, curiosity animating his every feature.

"Princess Sapphire and her troops are coming," she said. "They should arrive some hours after the sun."

Edlin rubbed his hands together briskly.

"I say! Now we'll see some action, what?"

Firekeeper nodded.

"You must rest," she said, "if you wish to be strong for action. I'll watch now."

Edlin shook his head.

"This is my watch. You get some rest. You look like a drowned kitten."

Indignant, Firekeeper crawled into her pup tent and stripped. Blind Seer wriggled in beside her.

She slept restlessly. When she did slip into dreams, they were peopled with the Royal Beasts.

At first the Beasts said nothing, only stared. Eyes that should have been green or gold or deep brown were all as blue as Blind Seer's, the left split in two by the red line of a healing scar. Then an angry whisper arose:

"We have done so much for you and now you betray us!" accused a rippling chorus of voices. *"Wolf-child. Hah! We see. Human blood rises in the end."*

The dream went on and on, reclaiming Firekeeper with uncontestable strength each time she struggled toward waking.

The camp stirring shortly before dawn brought her to full wakefulness at last. Feigning sleep, she heard Edlin sharing Bold's news with each as he or she awoke.

Through the door slit, she watched, biding her time. At last it came. The camp was mostly empty. Derian was tending the horses and mules. Wendee and Elise were fetching water. Edlin was checking his snares.

Doc was in the camp, but in his tent, dressing. She would need to risk him seeing her, but if he did he should think nothing of it. She was often in and out of the tent the other two women shared, for Wendee kept her clothes—Firekeeper could not be bothered with such trifles.

Glancing around, she padded across to the other tent. Once inside, she found the mirror easily enough, wrapped in a bundle of Elise's clothing. The comb was harder to find.

Indeed, Firekeeper was about to give up, thinking that Wendee had kept the comb with her to assure its safety. However, the Hawk Haven aversion to things magical proved the wolfwoman's ally. Wendee had not wanted to carry the comb with her—far from it, she had wanted to insulate herself from whatever baleful influences it might contain.

Firekeeper found the comb wrapped in silk, held between two small flat pieces of wood, as if it might somehow cut its way free if not restrained. Grabbing the comb, wrappings and all, Firekeeper stuffed it into the back of her trousers. The mirror was tucked into her vest.

She was out of the tent before Blind Seer's low howl told her that the women were returning, nor did she pause. Not pausing to answer cheerful cries of good morning, she waved and loped in the direction of the swamp.

Once there, she and Blind Seer didn't need to go far to find a tangled place where the humans would never go. She cached the three artifacts in the crotch of a vine-shrouded tree. Somehow, leaving the ring was hardest. She wanted more time to study it, hoping that it would answer her need as it had not answered the mere curiosity of the New Kelvinese. Nonetheless, she left it.

When Firekeeper returned to camp, Elise and Wendee intercepted her before she had reached the fire.

"Firekeeper," Elise said, her tone mingling accusation and fear, "the mirror and the comb . . . did you take them?"

Firekeeper nodded. She'd already decided that the best way to handle this was to brazen it out.

"Yes." She smiled warmly. "Thank you for holding them for me. I mean to take them sooner from your care, but I have been so worried about Citrine."

Elise didn't look happy.

"Firekeeper, those things belong to King Allister. You do realize that?" she said.

Wendee spoke at the same moment, so that her words overran Elise's like water over rocks.

"What are you going to do with them?" she asked. "Do you have any idea?"

Firekeeper chose to answer Wendee rather than Elise. Even then, the wolf-woman wasn't completely honest, for her mind was filled with the soft blue glow of the moonstone ring.

"I don't know," she answered.

Bitterness lay on her tongue as she spoke. For some reason she was reminded of the Story of the Songbirds.

XXXVI

ALTHOUGH THE PRISM AND MIRRORS that had once caused firelight to gleam with the intensity of a captured sun were long gone, still the glass-windowed room at the top of Smuggler's Light remained a spectacular place from which to view the sunrise.

It began with a wash of pinks and pale yellows against the grey of the predawn sky. As the sun itself was invisible—hidden behind the curtaining wall of trees that grew between the lighthouse and the ocean—one might imagine the transformation was taking place without any physical agent.

By the time the sun's orb had topped the tree line, the aura of mystery had vanished, replaced by light in a thousand shades of gold.

Today was cloudless, the light as clear and bright as a newly minted coin, but this brilliance did nothing to cut through the darkness crowding Waln Endbrook's soul. He would have preferred rain or sleet or even hail—though this last would have necessitated drawing shutters over the glass. Instead, he was given a shining light without warmth, clarity without promise.

Pacing, he scowled, and his chance-met reflection in a windowpane scowled back at him. A sense of approaching doom gnawed at him, unalleviated by his awareness that he might have brought that doom onto himself.

Some days past, alarmed by his sudden insight that the reason Lady Melina had not replied to his threat was that she intended to offer threat of her own, Waln had ordered that every door into Smuggler's Light be kept locked, that every window within reach of the ground be shuttered.

The pirates were still permitted to come and go as they wished, but few had business to take them out-of-doors in this winter weather. They remained inside, crowding into the darkened rooms on the lower floors, going about their tasks and muttering as the dimness and the chill entered their hearts.

Those who did go out were not permitted to carry keys with them and were ordered to have the moat bridges drawn up behind them if they did depart. That this was—as Waln knew from the cringing Longsight—a standard precaution didn't seem to matter. The pirates sensed that what had been a routine measure had become an active defense.

Waln had ordered watch to be kept all around the tower, night and day. Again this was a standard procedure; again the pirates sensed that his reiteration of the need indicated that he suspected some specific threat. They grumbled as they watched, seeing things that were not there—especially those who must watch by night. Their tales fed rumors, and rumors fed the general uneasiness.

But the pirates feared Baron Endbrook, and so they obeyed. Their code was such that a single man or woman might have challenged him, but a mutiny was not likely—at least not on such slim provocation. They were moderately comfortable, well fed, and rested. Sailors one and all, they were accustomed to a captain's autocratic reign.

The seeds for a mutiny were there, however, and Waln saw them watered by the half-mad grin of little Citrine. What he had done to her was the club that had beaten them; somehow she might yet be a weapon turned against him.

RESTLESS, IMPATIENT FOR HE KNEW NOT WHAT, Derian curried Roanne's coat until the chestnut gleamed like polished copper. He was taking out a dandy brush for some fine work when Elation's shriek alerted him to the falcon's arrival.

The peregrine glided down to rest on one of the rails of the makeshift corral Derian and Edlin had constructed. The young lord had proved apt with an axe, less so with knots, but grinningly eager to learn. The end result was a lashed rectangle that used trees as posts, secure enough to hold the horses and mules from wandering, though not strong enough to resist if they made a concerted effort to get free.

Having heard from Firekeeper that the swamps contained their share of pumas, Derian thought it best not to so secure the herbivores so that they would become a tavern for the satisfaction of wandering wildcats.

Elation squawked when he came over and sleeked her feathers with one hand. He still felt a glow of joy—tinged with pride—that the peregrine permitted him the privilege. She could have as easily taken off one of his fingers.

A distant rumble of horse hooves told Derian that Elation had not joined him only for company.

"Thanks," he said. "I'll go tell the others."

He found all but Edlin in camp. Wendee, Elise, and Firekeeper were in a tight knot off to one side, apparently in the midst of some heated discussion. He wondered if Firekeeper was resisting changing her clothes again.

Doc stood by the fireside, pouring himself tea.

"Heads up," Derian called. "Company—probably the princess or some of her people."

That broke up the colloquy at the camp's edge. The three women returned in step. Elise looked worried, Wendee apprehensive, and Firekeeper as impassive as a stone—only the way she tangled her fingers in Blind Seer's ruff gave indication that she was less than tranquil.

About a dozen riders swept to the edge of their camp. Sapphire and Shad rode at the core.

With his horseman's eye, Derian noted that their mounts all showed signs of strain, but that none had been pressed beyond endurance.

Sapphire rode the Blue—an indication that she, at least, had kept the same mount since Eagle's Nest. The warhorse snapped square yellow teeth when one of the other horses accidently ventured too close, then stamped with uneasy malice when it caught sight of Blind Seer. Sapphire calmed her steed easily, almost idly, but then she had always been a fine horsewoman.

The crown princess glanced around their little camp and a smile touched one corner of her mouth. Only after she had surveyed it and approved its neatness did she look at the group gathered to welcome her. Elise and Wendee wore kerchiefs that concealed the worst of the mutilation to their hair, but, despite the cold, Firekeeper went bareheaded, her shaven head visible for all to see.

Derian saw the crown princess's eyes narrow, but when she spoke her words were routinely conversational.

"Nice place here," she said. "I thought to have my troops set up camp in the field beyond."

She gestured west and slightly south.

"Good choice," Derian replied. "There's fresh water in the area. I don't know where there might be more."

"Captain," Sapphire said, nodding to one of her riders, "bring on the rest of the troop. Tell them to set up an orderly camp. No one—and I mean no one—is to venture into the swamp without our direct orders."

Derian bit back a smile as Sapphire included Prince Shad in her last comment. The Bright Bay sailor sat his horse well, but his training had been to command at sea. Clearly he was content to let his wife handle matters on land. Derian admired Shad's composure. Most young men—and Shad was only slightly older than Derian himself—would have needed to prove themselves, if to no one other than themselves.

"You've kept well out of sight," Sapphire commented, swinging down out of the saddle and tossing the Blue's reins to the nearest rider. "My advance scout—" she nodded toward one of the riders, "—had some trouble finding you."

"We thought it wisest," Derian said, bowing respectfully as he spoke. "Firekeeper's been in the swamp, but no one other than Lord Edlin has ventured beyond the edges."

"Edlin?" Sapphire's brow furrowed. "That idiot's here?"

Defense for the young lord came from an unexpected quarter.

"My brother," Firekeeper said calmly—and she offered no bow, "is no idiot."

Sapphire's blue eyes flashed, but she caught herself before she descended into an unfitting wrangle. Seeing that his wife was temporarily out of words, Prince Shad intervened smoothly.

"Fitting that you defend your brother," he said, dismounting and offering Firekeeper a warm smile, "since we are here to rescue our sister. Tell us all that has happened. How did you come here? How did you learn of this situation? The note Sir Jared sent was understandably short on particulars."

Sapphire recovered herself enough to nod.

"Glynn," she said to the rider who held the Blue's reins, "why don't the rest of you join the others in setting up camp? Unless there's real need, don't trouble us."

Glynn, a handsome woman with thick dark hair drawn up into a knot at the back of her head, nodded and turned her gaze—reluctantly, Derian thought—from her inspection of the little camp and its inhabitants.

As all but the prince and princess took their leave, general greetings were exchanged. Wendee Jay was introduced, and her connection to both Duchess Kestrel and Firekeeper explained.

Once, Derian thought, his mood balanced between relief that Sapphire had checked her temper, and amusement, *Sapphire would have thought a servant beneath her knowledge.*

He felt a twinge of satisfaction that he had been one of those who had forced the proud woman to alter her view.

Lord Edlin sauntered in, three rabbits dangling from his hand, as they were settling themselves about the fire.

"I say!" he said. "I thought it might be royalty come to call when Bold came squawking after me. Hello, cousins!"

His bow was more a waist-level bounce than a courtly obeisance. From her expression, Firekeeper was forgiving Sapphire for thinking her adopted brother an idiot.

"Don't mind me," Edlin said, sitting himself on the fringes of their circle. "I'll just sit here and clean my catch."

He began to do so immediately, tossing the offal to the crow and wolf—Elation was too proud to descend to such—as relaxed as if this were some hunting trip and not the advent of a desperate venture whose ending no one could even guess.

"Tell us everything," Prince Shad repeated. "How did you come on Lady Melina?"

They told their tale much as it had happened, for it became clear that skipping any detail would lead to questions. Only Firekeeper edited her part, playing down her trip west until it sounded as if she had merely decided to go after the artifacts as something of a lark.

Derian caught a glimpse of Elise's expression—a glower moderated by evident worry—before the young woman smoothed it from her face.

Something has happened between them, he thought. *Something to do with the artifacts.*

Telling took hours, for they could not explain how they got into Thendulla Lypella without explaining about Grateful Peace and they could not explain about Grateful Peace without explaining something about the governmental structure of New Kelvin. Unlike Elise, neither Sapphire or Shad had ever been very interested in foreign countries—though Shad, as a sailor, knew something of Waterland and other seafaring nations.

Had Derian not known Firekeeper well, he might have thought she slept there on the ground, her head pillowed on Blind Seer's flank, but he did know her and the tension he had sensed in her earlier had not left, it had merely been subdued.

When, at last, they ended their tale with an account of how they had decided to come east after Citrine, Sapphire sighed and spoke.

"Well, Mother certainly has taken a great deal upon herself," she said, "and so I certainly can't blame you for doing the same. Why didn't you come to us sooner?"

From where she lay, her eyes still closed, Firekeeper said: "Diplomacy. Too slow."

Shad, perhaps fearing that this time Sapphire would not keep her temper, cut in quickly.

"Inelegantly put, my dear, but Firekeeper does have a point.

If the matter had been resolved through diplomatic channels we'd still be trying to confirm that Lady Melina was in Dragon's Breath, and that the New Kelvinese had been in possession of the artifacts. By the way, who has them now?"

"I do," Firekeeper said, this time opening her eyes and sitting up. "They are safe. Safer than Citrine now that pirates must notice horses and camps and troops all over here."

She waved to indicate the military camp that had taken shape very efficiently despite the semifrozen ground.

"How long do we wait to go for her?"

Sir Jared, who had been mostly content to let others do the narrating, now intervened.

"Firekeeper is again inelegant," he said quickly, "but she does have a point. She's been scouting the area around Smuggler's Light and from her reports Edlin has been roughing out a map. Defenses are even better than they were two years ago when I was here with Princess Lovella."

This firm but gentle reminder that he was the only veteran present of that ill-fated campaign gave Doc's words unwonted authority. The question of the artifacts was put aside—though Derian did not doubt it would be raised again—and the matter of rescuing Citrine approached with new urgency.

"Lord Edlin," Prince Shad said, "you're a cartographer?"

His skill in this area had been mentioned during the earlier report and now Edlin beamed.

"I do fairly well, what?" said the young lord with a grin.

"You'd be honored in Bright Bay," the crown prince continued. "Sailors love maps almost as much as they love ships. Let us see your latest effort."

This, when produced, was less colorful than the Dragon's Breath map, but, since Edlin had packed along his drawing supplies, it was still a work of art. Even Sapphire looked impressed as the map was unrolled and the corners weighted down with rocks so that all could see it.

"The birds do help with getting the overview," Edlin explained happily, "and Firekeeper is a joy for noting varied terrain and rises and such. I've done my best to shadow in the high ground and the worst of the bogholes and such. I've even had her tell me some of the major landmarks."

Shad traced some of the darker green lines.

"There seem to be several quite clear routes to Smuggler's Light."

"Not so clear," Firekeeper said, sounding disgruntled, "but there, yes."

Derian sensed that it was his turn to cut in.

"Firekeeper sees things no average scout would," he explained. "Even Race Forester was astonished by her wood's lore. I suggest that rather than depending on the map, you have her first take your scouts along any route you want to use—get them used to it."

To his relief, Shad was nodding.

"Like harbor pilots," he said. "Good idea. Now that we've finished discussing the more—uh—delicate matters . . ."

Like cursed artifacts, you mean? Derian thought sarcastically. *And unauthorized espionage within the borders of technically friendly nations—stuff like that?*

"Now that we've finished with those matters," Shad continued, "and don't really need to discuss them again for now, I think it would be a good idea to invite some of our troop commanders to join us. From what I gathered during the war, land commanders expect to confer and such, not like at sea."

Of course at sea, Derian continued his silent commentary, *it's rather harder to get everyone together, isn't it? Every man isn't an island, but every ship does a pretty fine imitation.*

What he said aloud was:

"Would Your Majesties prefer us to adjourn to your camp? I see that the royal pavilion has been raised."

Sapphire shook her head.

"Better not to encourage eavesdropping. In any case, if the pirates haven't noticed us yet, Firekeeper's right, they will. A spy would find sneaking up on this camp, especially with Blind Seer and Firekeeper here, pretty impossible."

She's buttering up Firekeeper, Derian thought, amazed. *When she arrived, the two of them were like alley cats spitting at each other. Now it's praise and flattery. I wonder what she wants?*

Over a meal delivered by the royal couple's camp stewards, their augmented group discussed the various approaches to Smuggler's Light—their advantages and disadvantages, the need for building portable bridges, the question of how to get troops across the killing ground fairly intact.

The longer they talked, the further they defined the situation; the further they defined the situation, the less certain Derian felt that they would find any way inside. Smuggler's Light seemed an impenetrable fortress. The pirates held not only the high ground, but the most valuable playing piece on the board, and, to make matters worse, if Firekeeper was right, they were prepared for trouble.

Shad and Sapphire had arrived in midmorning. The sky was dusking into evening when Princess Sapphire pushed a hand through her thick blue-black hair and said:

"The situation looks pretty desperate, doesn't it?"

One of her squad commanders, a veteran of Princess Lovella's failed attack, spoke for them all.

"It does, Your Majesty. The place is better protected than before. We don't know how many people are in there, but they don't need many to hold it."

Sapphire nodded agreement, shared a glance with Shad that—to Derian's eyes—looked positively conspiratorial.

"My little sister is in there," she said. "Citrine is only eight. I'd like her to see nine, but I don't want to waste the lives of good, brave people just for that."

Everyone was staring at Sapphire now. Firekeeper, Derian thought uneasily, looked positively angry. Probably only Sapphire's fulsome praise a bit earlier was making her listen.

"So we have a plan," Sapphire continued, "a plan for softening them up. We didn't go into it before for two reasons. First of all, it was important that we learn what we're up against. Even if this plan works, we're going to need to make a show of arms at some point. Secondly, we couldn't instigate this plan until after dark, so we had time."

She paused to swallow some hot mulled wine, and Shad picked up right where she had left off.

"The pirates have every advantage," he said. "Good walls,

supplies, all the rest. Taking that place means a siege—possibly a long one."

Derian saw the squad commanders exchange glances. Obviously none of them fancied spending the winter parked on the edge of—or directly in—a swamp. On the other hand, it beat getting riddled by arrows from smuggler's light. They straightened and paid closer attention.

"However, we can shorten the time needed for that siege," Shad continued. "As Lady Blysse has learned from her scouting, they are still storing the majority of their livestock in pens between the buildings at the lighthouse's base. If some or all of these were slain or set free, they would lose their fresh food.

"True, they would not need to feed the livestock then, but take note of what they have there: goats and pigs will eat almost anything—in fact, I wouldn't be surprised if they're using them to clean up their scraps. Chicken feed—well, that's proverbial. Rabbits might be more of a problem, but they could slaughter them early and not be too put out. I wouldn't be surprised if they augment the duck food with material from the swamps.

"Therefore, if we get rid of their livestock, we cut deeply into their supplies far more rapidly than we would if we simply waited."

The scout commander nodded. "I could send in my people, but even so there would probably be casualties."

Firekeeper laughed huskily.

"Let me go," she suggested, "me and Blind Seer and I don't think there be casualties—unless you mean ducks and pigs."

Princess Sapphire nodded.

"We'll take you up on that offer," she said. "It's precisely what we were hoping for."

Counting on, Derian thought. *No wonder you started flattering her!*

The commander of the scouts looked disgruntled and Sapphire was quick to soothe him.

"This is meant as no insult to your scouts, Wheeler," she said. "Lady Blysse is—simply put—unique. She has already been across the moat. Blind Seer can either watch her back or join her."

The enormous wolf's jaws gaped in what Derian would swear was laughter. Clearly he thought the entire thing was a tremendous joke.

"Blind Seer come with," Firekeeper said. "Bold can watch."

Sapphire went on as if there had been no interruption.

"They can go by night, Wheeler. Moreover, if anyone sees Blind Seer's footprints . . . Well, that moves us into our next tactical element."

Wheeler stroked the bridge of his nose thoughtfully, his face lighting up and his expression becoming almost merry as he considered what his princess was saying.

"I offer no further objections, Princess Sapphire."

"Well, does anyone else wish to offer any objections to that stage of the plan?" Shad asked. "If not we'll move onto our next element."

A female voice, trembling slightly as at its own temerity, took advantage of the prince's purely formal pause.

"I do," it said.

Wendee Jay, who had been in and out of the council circle occupying herself with some of her more routine tasks, now stepped boldly into the light. She curtsied deeply and then spoke her protest in a breathless rush.

"Last time Lady Firekeeper swam the moat, Your Majesty, she thought no one noticed, but I did and she was chilled to the bone. I'm not saying that she can't do what you ask, but some provisions should be made for preserving her health—otherwise you'll have her coughing out her lungs."

Derian quietly applauded Wendee. It was *hard* to speak up front of people you'd been taught since childhood were your betters.

Firekeeper looked over at Wendee.

"You noticed?"

"I was awake in my tent and heard you come back and speak with Lord Edlin. *He* may not have noticed, but I saw you were shaking. I was about to come out and insist that you get into something warm when you decided of your own accord to go to bed. The next day, you told us where you'd been and I put the facts together."

Edlin looked abashed at the look Wendee gave him.

"Sorry," he said. "I was excited about the crow being back, what?"

"Any thoughts on how we could deal with this?" Shad asked. "I think Goody Wendee raises a valid point."

"Lady Blysse could carry dry clothing in an oiled bag," one of the commanders suggested.

"Better she use some sort of bridge," another protested. "Keep her out of the water at all costs. It is Wolf Moon, after all, no time to be swimming in ocean water."

"Firekeeper?" Shad looked at the wolf-woman, soliciting for her opinion.

"A bridge is big," she said, her hand gesture showing that what she meant by "big" was closer to "awkward," "but the water is cold. If I take time now, I could make something to carry and lay across moat."

Wheeler, the scout officer, rubbed his hands together in approval.

"Let me put some of my people on it, my lady. They've skill in this. No need for you to reinvent the wheel and those I have in mind can be trusted not to breathe a word that they're building more than a prototype for future action."

Firekeeper caught the gist of his offer and graciously nodded her acceptance. Wheeler excused himself to give the necessary orders.

"Good," Sapphire said. "Now, as some of you have doubtless guessed, the second major element in our siege tactic is the need to break down the smugglers' will—their morale. As I see it, by whatever right Baron Endbrook has claimed a place there, he is a relative newcomer. Initially, the smugglers will view us as their enemies, but after Firekeeper has rid them of their foodstuffs and proven that they are not so impervious to attack as they think, then Prince Shad and I will send a message to them."

Shad continued, "We want Citrine Shield alive and safe. That's what started us down here. When we consulted with

King Tedric and Queen Elexa, though, they rapidly showed us that there is a bigger picture here—a more complicated question. In short, Baron Endbrook cannot be permitted to operate on Hawk Haven land without penalty. If we let him do so, we send a message to Queen Valora—a message that she will interpret not as caution but as weakness."

"Moreover," Sapphire said, picking up on Shad's point so smoothly that Derian couldn't help but imagine prince and princess rehearsing exactly what they would say, who would make which points, "it would be to our advantage to break the pirates' hold on Smuggler's Light. As long as rule of the sea was split between Bright Bay and Waterland, the pirates were a nuisance, but one we could deal with in our own time.

"Baron Endbrook has shown us that the pirates are willing to operate as the Isles' ally. We must show this cannot be. Therefore, if at all possible, we must take Smuggler's Light. If we cannot—and I am willing to admit we may not be able to—then we should at least leave them a clear message that the days of tolerance are over!"

She brought her hand down on her thigh as she concluded, a dramatic gesture that was not all affected. It was perfectly in keeping with her persona as the warrior princess, the heroine of ballad and song.

There was no applause, but the respectful silence that greeted her proclamation—outrageous as it was in view of what they had learned about the smugglers' defenses, in view of past defeats—was more acclamation than any cheering could be.

The meeting broke up soon after that. The commanders went to tell their squads an abbreviated version of plans. It had been decided that it would only help matters if a pirate spy learned of the plans to break Smuggler's Light. For that reason anyone seen leaving the swamp—except for Baron Endbrook and Citrine Shield, of course—was to be permitted to go.

In winter's hold, the pirates would find summoning reinforcements difficult. In any case, they were unlikely to wish to declare open war on Hawk Haven. Smuggler's Light was a good base, but it was not the pirates' only base—and now they might well feel they had a claim on Queen Valora.

Before departing for their own pavilion, Shad and Sapphire paused to say good night.

"That was a good plan, cousins," Elise said, rising onto her toes to kiss Sapphire's cheek.

Sapphire glanced from side to side, but there was none but their own small company to overhear her.

"To tell the truth," she said, "wiser heads than ours concocted it. King Tedric was the one who suggested much of it. Your father, Elise, helped us refine it along the road."

"Father is here?"

Elise looked not so much pleased as terrified.

"He is. By his own choice, Baron Archer stayed from council. He said it was essential that our commanders think Shad and I are completely in charge."

"You are," Doc said softly. "You are."

Shad nodded. "I've commanded a vessel—a small one—but the responsibility is nothing to this."

"And I," Sapphire said, her voice hushed, "thought I would be delighted, but I find myself continually thinking what Uncle Tedric said before he let me go."

"What?" Elise asked.

"He told me to be careful, that he didn't want to lose another daughter to that blasted lighthouse."

Sapphire's voice broke on the words. Then she straightened and shook back her hair.

"And if we do things right, he won't. Where is Firekeeper?"

Derian spoke up, "Building bridges or, rather, watching them be built."

"I won't meddle further," Sapphire said. "Firekeeper will know best how much time she needs and when she's ready to leave."

"And we," Shad said, "need to go 'round the campfires and speak to our troops. Rumor moves fast and dangerously at times like this."

They strolled away, hand in hand, for a brief moment just two people who had been married for only a few moonspans and who, in that time, had repeatedly faced death and hardship. Then they reached the light of their own, larger, camp and almost visibly became crown prince and crown princess again.

"I'm so glad I'm not them," Elise said.

Derian thought he heard Doc murmur, "So am I."

He might have been mistaken, though, because when he looked over at the healer, Sir Jared's features were as expressionless as those of a graven image.

❧

OCCASIONAL CLOUDS SLID OVER THE SKY. There was little moonlight, so little that Firekeeper didn't need to consider it before setting her bridge in place, arranging the elements just as the scouts had taught her.

Going barefoot for better balance, she crossed. Blind Seer followed. The temporary cloud cover was breaking as she hid the bridge near where the smugglers kept their own bridging materials. Anyone looking out from within should see—even in daylight—nothing unusual. Of course, if plans went correctly, by daylight both the wolf-woman and her bridge would be long gone.

Needing no bridge, Elation and Bold had gone ahead. Bold swooped in front of various windows, reporting that he thought there could be watchers behind some of the shutters. The very shutters that protected those within from attack, however, would limit their line of sight.

Two of the lighthouse's residents did keep watch in the glass-walled room at the very top, but Bold reported them less than perfectly attentive. In any case, though they could see for a distance around them, what lay at the lighthouse's feet would be more difficult to see.

Elation disdained keeping watch. The peregrine wanted to be in on the hunt.

"Where do we begin, muddy-feet?" the falcon asked.

Firekeeper paced so that she was within the lighthouse's

shadow, moving low to the ground so that if by any chance she was glimpsed she would be mistaken for an animal. She recalled the layout of the pens from her earlier visit.

Six rectangular buildings, spaced evenly apart from each other, radiated out from the round base of the lighthouse, creating six fan-shaped yards between them. Three of these were devoted to gardens. The remaining three, set with a garden between them, held livestock.

Poultry was stupid. Pigs were slow—through fearsome when roused. The rabbits were in hutches, but the goats ranged with more freedom.

"Goats, I think," she said. "And I will release the rabbits for your hunting, Elation. Remember to still your cries!"

The falcon made a short, indignant squawk.

Blind Seer hung back while Firekeeper, using those clever fingers which the Royal Beasts had praised, opened the gate into the area that held the goats and rabbits.

She paused to listen, but no alarm was raised. That was good. Although neither she nor Blind Seer had scented dogs, they had not been able to eliminate the possibility that they were present. Perhaps the pirates had not wished to have their location given away by barking.

The slaughter that followed was quick and efficient, so much so that Elation protested that the wolves had kept all the fun for themselves.

Firekeeper did not reply. While Blind Seer scraped manure over the carcasses to ruin the meat for delicate human palates, she moved onto the pigs. The huge, fat creatures were sluggish with sleep and her Fang opened several throats before they even knew she was among them.

Blind Seer took care of the rest.

She had left the poultry for last. Foxes would have been kept out of the carefully built coops, but not the wolf-woman.

Ignoring Elation's indignation—for the peregrine considered birds her rightful prey—Firekeeper slipped inside, her fingers twisting necks with ruthless efficiency. It seemed a pity to waste so much good food when the camp held so many to feed, so she filled an empty grain sack with the fattest of the bodies.

So far, no alarm had been raised. Indeed, the only guardian they had met was a slim tabby cat who had doubtless been hunting for pickings of his own. Hissing warning and defiance, he had slipped away and Firekeeper had been happy to let him go. If the humans grew hungry, let them eat cat.

Grinning fiendishly, Firekeeper risked opening the garden fences. These—meant to keep out rabbits and deer—again offered no challenge to her.

Wolves are great diggers and Blind Seer plowed the loose soil around cabbages and root vegetables with enthusiasm. Some food might be scavenged after his work, but it would be filthy and scarred.

They took their time, trusting Bold to warn them, choosing stealth over speed, for even if an alarm was raised, they felt certain they could escape.

When the work was done, Firekeeper waited for another cloud, then replaced the bridge. Tossing the bag containing the chickens to the other side of the moat, she paused. Blind Seer seemed to read her thoughts.

"I didn't spoil all the meat," he replied slyly. "I had some hopes of dinner."

She grinned. Another sack was quickly filled with dead rabbits. A young goat was easily slung across her shoulders. Blind Seer hoisted another in his jaws, trotting as lightly as if unburdened.

It was a pity they had to leave so much, but there was no helping it. Firekeeper took some comfort in the thought that the moat—though an effective barrier for humans—would not keep out all the scavengers. Unless the smugglers worked quickly, Bold's relations would claim the rest. A winter-hungry puma would find the moat easy to leap.

After first hiding the bridge, Firekeeper hauled their booty away from Smuggler's Light. Once they were in the depths of the swamp, Firekeeper cached the sacks of poultry and rabbits in a tree. Cold would keep them for a while. Then she gutted the goats, giving the innards to Blind Seer, who accepted them as delicacies.

She didn't forget to give the wingéd folk their share, but try as they might, neither bird could match the wolf's voracious appetite. Firekeeper's own belly growled at the hot, bloody scent, and she satisfied it with a few strips of still warm liver. Proper eating could wait.

At last, liberally gore-splattered from her shaven head to her bare feet, Firekeeper hoisted the goats across her shoulders and let Blind Seer lead the way back to camp.

Doubtless Wendee would scold her for the mess she had made of her clothing, but even with that looming on the horizon, Firekeeper was completely happy.

XXXVII

CACKLING FROM THE OLD CRONE roused Waln from an uneasy sleep.

"Why are you laughing, old woman?" he snarled.

He had stopped using the courteous address "mother" after learning that the old woman actually was Longsight Scrounger's own mother, but had yet to learn her real name.

Grinning so broadly that her pink gums with their occasional tooth showed plainly, the old woman laughed.

"Can't you hear the ravens? Can't you hear the crows? 'Tis an omen—everyone's saying it, all but the cooks. They're weeping and wailing."

She scuttled out before Waln could ask more, leaving behind her a pot of hot water. He'd decided to forgo his morning tea unless he could brew it himself, lest some rival poison him. Shaking a few leaves of mint into the water, Waln walked to the closed and shuttered window. Without, he could hear the hoarse squabbling of ravens and as he peered out a dark-winged shape passed his line of sight.

Hastening into his clothing and gulping the tea so fast that he tasted it as nothing but heat in his throat, Waln headed downstairs, schooling his feet so that he would not be seen to hurry. That simple act took nearly all his self-discipline, for the closer he came to the lower levels the louder came the sounds of argument and debate.

When Waln emerged into the large, round base of the light-house which served as the common room, he found himself the immediate focus of a swarm of unhappy and frightened people who crowded up to him before he could step off the landing at the base of the stairs.

Fragments containing snippets of information shattered against his ears like hail stones.

". . . all dead!"

"Blood over everything . . ."

". . . spoiled. Unfit for a dog . . ."

"Prints the size of a horse's hoof . . ."

"A host of moles couldn't . . ."

"Starve . . ."

Raising one arm into the air, Waln drew in a deep breath and bellowed for silence. Then he cast about until he spotted Longsight Scrounger. The lean man smiled ingratiatingly, ducking his head like a dog expecting to be kicked.

"Longsight, you speak first," Waln ordered, still shouting though the silence was absolute. "The rest of you hold your tongues till I ask to hear."

Straightening now that he had his master's attention, Longsight looked confident, almost as arrogant as he had when he had ruled the Light.

"It's like this, Baron," Longsight said, "to make it short. Something got into the pens in the night. There's not as much as a chicken left alive nor a cabbage that hasn't been uprooted. Cook says that she can make something from the vegetables, but most all of the meat has been spoiled. What the ravens and crows didn't get at has been filled with muck and manure."

Waln didn't want to give credence to this report. It was too incredible for belief, but the nodding heads in the crowd gathered around him confirmed that Longsight was—at least in general—correct.

Some mouths were working in a fashion that made Waln think that there were details yet to be revealed. He ignored these gossips and cast around for someone to blame.

"And who was on watch last night?" he growled, his voice rumbling low in his throat.

Five of the pirates stumbled forward with a jerky motion that made Waln suspect they had been shoved.

All five showed signs of exhaustion brought to wakefulness by a sudden shock. He'd seen the like shipboard when a storm or attack had roused all hands on deck to deal with the crisis. Doubtless the watchmen hadn't been in bed long—if at all—before someone had raised the alarm.

One was pushed forward to act as spokesman for the group.

"We were, Your Baron, sir," he said. He was called Red Stripe or, sometimes, Cime, and stood low in the hierarchy, doubtless why he had been forced under Waln's gaze.

"And this slaughter happened without any of you hearing or seeing a thing?" Waln said with brutal contempt.

"Yes, sir."

Red Stripe stared at his feet.

"Where were you?"

"I had a drifting watch, sir, going from window to window just as you ordered, sir. I didn't see a thing, sir, didn't hear a peep."

When Waln only glowered at him, Red Stripe offered an excuse.

"The walls are thick, Baron, and at your orders all the windows were locked and shuttered. Not much sound gets through that, Baron, sir, by your leave. It was dark, too, the moon ain't giving much light, and there were clouds."

Waln could see traces of sympathy on a few faces in the crowd. Lest sympathy give rise to rebellion, he strode off the landing and walloped Red Stripe across one side of his face.

The man reeled back. Now Waln saw no sympathy on any face—only fear.

He stepped back up onto the landing and scanned the company.

"So," he said, making his voice singsong, like a child's making an excuse, "it was dark and it was cold and you couldn't hear a thing ..."

The few sycophantic titters were silenced when Waln shifted to his on-deck bellow.

"So something comes and does havoc in the night, and that's the piss-poor excuse you offer. Would I have set a watch if I didn't think there was a reason to do so?"

There was no reply. He repeated his question, even louder.

"No, Baron," the luckless Red Stripe muttered.

"That's better."

Waln scanned the room. Most of the smugglers were united with him, ready to blame those who had failed the watch. A few, however, were still itching to tell him something. He'd listen, but first ...

He wheeled on the cook, a greasy woman with a cook's traditional rolls of fat. She was a Waterland native who—rumor said—had turned cannibal when stranded in a lifeboat some years before. It had been unclear whether her victims had been living or dead when she chose to dine on them, so she had been exiled for her transgression rather than executed for murder.

"Cook, you say the meat has been ruined?"

"Buried in shit, Baron," came the blunt reply, "where it isn't torn to shreds."

"Very well. Have someone cut you some nice fresh ham. Our faithful watchers deserve a fit breakfast for their night's work. Season it appropriately. Are there any eggs?"

Cook grinned, appreciating the humor.

"All broken and mixed with straw, Baron."

"What a fine omelet that should make!" Waln said with false heartiness. "Let our watchers have omelet with their ham. Make certain they eat every bite."

Cook chuckled. As she was turning to obey, Waln asked casually:

"The contents of the larders are fine, I suppose?"

"Dry stuff," Cook said, "and salted. Nothing touched, though, if that's what you're asking."

Waln nodded.

"Very good. Arrange for the rest of the meals after our faithful five have had their breakfast."

"Yes, Baron."

Having finished with the watchers, Baron Endbrook turned to the gossips. They'd be careful how they told what they had to say lest they, too, end up eating shit and straw rather than wholesome food.

"You!" he said, pointing to a big-boned, fair-haired woman. "You've been waiting to get a word in. Go ahead."

The woman sauntered forward, enjoying her moment on center stage and clearly unafraid that he would find fault with her report.

"Baron Endbrook," she began with polite deference, "I was one of the first awake this morning, one of the first outside. Everything is just how Longsight tells you, but there's more he didn't tell."

She paused and Waln nodded for her to go on. Judging from the expressions about the room, about half had heard this tidbit and the other half were eager to learn.

"I'm Stonehold-born," the woman said, explaining in those words both her build and pale blonde hair, "and farmed a bit before turning to the sea. My first thought after I saw what had happened was to see what had done the damage."

She paused dramatically, stretching her interlaced fingers, and popping her knuckles into the expectant quiet. Waln let her have her moment. It did him no harm.

"I was taken with the smoothness of the meadow round from the start," she said, "for given the destruction you would have thought an army had been through. There were traces here and there, but to a casual glance there was nothing to show what had passed. Not so in the pens, not so at all. There the dirt was churned and trampled, dug and soft, welcoming prints. I found them, too."

She raised two fingers.

"Two sets only, Baron, at least that I could tell. One was of a set of small bare feet, the other from a wolf so large I'd never even imagined the like—not even in my nightmares. These two alone seem to have done the hunting, these two alone all the killing."

Loud, panicked murmuring arose as the Stoneholder stepped back, satisfied to give up the stage now that her report was complete. Her smug smile showed that the effect of her words was all she had hoped.

Waln had felt the color drain from his face, but he steadied himself. There was only one pair who could have left those marks. Best he admit it and minimize the impact of the news.

He was opening his mouth to speak when a high, shrill giggle cut through the noise.

"I know! I know! I know who it is!"

She'd been in the back of the room, so he hadn't seen her before this moment. Now Citrine Shield clambered onto one of the tables and stood dancing from foot to foot, waving her maimed hand in front of her so none could miss it.

"So do I!" Waln bellowed, but he might have held his tongue. No one was listening.

"It's Firekeeper! Firekeeper! And Blind Seer with her! They're my friends!" The little girl laughed hysterically. "They've come to get me."

She waggled the index finger of her maimed hand at Waln.

"You don't want to see Firekeeper when she's angry! Ask Prince Newell! Ask his ghost, rather!"

Longsight Scrounger had pushed his way through the gathered pirates and now he hauled the girl off the table. The thump he gave one round cheek silenced Citrine, but from across the room Longsight's own mother cackled.

"Look sharp now, my boy," the crone said, her cracked voice full of concern. "Don't break the little lass. Her friends are coming for her and they'll not be kind to those who hurt the little dear. I've always been her friend so I'm not afraid but those who've hurt her . . ."

The implied threat melted into broken, vindictive laughter. Longsight let Citrine slide from his arms and onto the floor. The girl struggled to her feet and ran—weaving a bit—to the shelter of the old woman's arms.

The eyes that turned on Waln now were fearful indeed, but less so at him than at what he had brought upon them. Anger glinted here and there. More than one hand drifted near a sheathed dagger.

Waln sensed he was losing control of the situation. At that very moment he was saved by a thunderous pounding on the lighthouse door.

SINCE SHE COULDN'T AVOID meeting Baron Archer, not without stirring up rumors that they were at odds, Elise decided that her first duty on the day following that upon which Sapphire had arrived with her troops was to hunt out her father. To be completely honest, she wasn't certain that they *weren't* at odds.

Elise had written to say that she was safe and to tell her parents not to be angry with Earl Kestrel for letting her go, emphasizing that she'd given her host little choice. However, the peculiar combination of circumstances that had led up to her departure from the Norwood Grant for New Kelvin didn't permit detailed explanations. Even a sealed letter could be read and too much was at stake for her to risk a diplomatic incident.

Before departing the camp, Sapphire had suggested that Elise wait until the next morning to seek out Baron Archer as, at Sapphire and Shad's request, he was in charge of posting sentries around the fringes of the swamp. After all, the current policy of letting the pirates leave the area did not include not keeping track of the situation, and those disaffected enough to steal away might be willing to sell information.

Elise had slept restlessly the night before, unable to relax when images of Firekeeper prowling through the dark right up to the pirates' doorsill kept intruding. An hour or so after Firekeeper had departed, she had given up the pretense and joined the others around the campfire.

Firekeeper had arrived some interminable time later, absolutely covered in blood and with two gutted goat carcasses slung over her shoulders the way a more ordinary maiden would wear a garland of flowers. She had seemed honestly astonished that they had been worried, had even insisted on going back into the swamp to fetch out two large bags—one filled with dead poultry, the other with equally dead rabbits.

Only after Edlin had agreed to take on the grisly task of gutting and skinning the lot had Firekeeper permitted Wendee to haul her off so that the lady's maid could reassure herself that all the blood was indeed—as Firekeeper swore—someone else's.

A small smile quirked Elise's mouth as she recalled Firekeeper's protests, but she thought that the wolf-woman didn't particularly enjoy being blood-covered and filthy—she just wasn't repulsed by it as Elise herself would be.

Indeed, Elise had noticed that Blind Seer—contrary to the popular image of the savage wolf—was quite fastidious. Immediately after hunting he would be completely begored—as if he had waded chest-deep into his kill. Soon after he fed, however, the wolf would seek out the closest running water and wade in as deeply as possible so that the current might scrub him clean.

Such thoughts distracted Elise as she went about her morning grooming. She wondered what Ninette would think when she saw how independent her mistress had become, and smiled.

Finding Baron Archer was amazingly simple. The Archer coat of arms, a gold field emblazoned with a man shooting scarlet arrows from his bow, fluttered on a pennant over her father's field pavilion. What she had not counted on was finding Jet Shield first.

Afterward, Elise would chide herself for being so foolish as not to realize that Sapphire—and Citrine's—ambitious and glory-hungry brother would have insisted on being part of the rescue mission. His disgrace during King Allister's War would only make Jet more determined to enhance his damaged character.

However, Elise had so effectively dismissed her onetime true love from her thoughts and memories that his voice speaking her name was her first reminder of his existence.

"Elise," Jet said in his deep, sensual voice—a voice that could, if he wished, make every word seem as intimate as a caress. "Or should I say, Lady Archer? No, let it be Elise."

As she had been avoiding use of the formal title that she must assume on her coming birthday, Elise could hardly protest. Turning so quickly that her skirt and cloak swirled about her, she found Jet emerging from what must be his own tent.

He wore black, as always, a dull black in this case, befitting a man whose sister was endangered. Even in this, he looked strikingly handsome. His thick dark hair resisted being pulled back into a queue. His dark eyes hinted at suppressed passion.

Not so long ago, Elise would have nearly swooned at the smile that curved his lips, a smile that hinted of past intimacies while promising eternal discretion. Now she was simply annoyed to find Jet slowing her progress.

With a smoothness that amazed her—for she had thought her hands tucked securely in her muff—Jet took her hand and lightly kissed the fingers.

"I am so pleased to see you again, cousin."

He paused slightly before using the familial address, as if hinting that he might have said "darling" or "love" but for the possibility of listening ears.

Elise drew her hand back and tucked it securely into her muff, intertwining the fingers lest he draw it forth again. She was so astonished by Jet's behavior—he acted as if they were still courting!—that she said what she was thinking.

"What are you doing here? Sapphire didn't mention you were among her troops."

Momentarily, Jet's dark eyes flashed at what Elise realized with guilty hindsight he must take as an insult. Jet could hardly have expected Elise to know he was among the company, but he had certainly expected Sapphire to mention his presence—and his rivalry with his sister was so long-standing that he would balk automatically at being named one of "her" troops.

"If Hawk Haven is to go to the rescue of my littlest sister," he said, recovering after the briefest of pauses, "then certainly I must be among her soldiers."

"Of course," Elise said. "Duty to our families is of paramount importance. In fact, I was about to call on my father. If you will excuse me . . ."

After his own melodramatic speech, Jet could hardly delay her. With a flourishing bow and elegantly voiced hopes that he would have the privilege of her company sometime soon, he let her pass.

Elise arrived at her father's pavilion without further interruptions. She found Perr, her father's body servant, without, packing away the pans in which he had doubtless cooked the baron's morning meal.

"Good morning, Lady Elise," he said, giving her his usual bow.

She tried to read her father's mood from his servant's greeting, but Perr had never been a great intimate of hers and his manner was, as always, correct and without undue familiarity.

"Good morning, Perr," she replied. "Is my father in?"

"The baron is, my lady. One moment while I see if he is receiving."

As Ivon Archer might have been dressing or otherwise indisposed, Elise tried not to read too much into the delay. Perr emerged quickly enough.

"The baron says he will be happy to see you, Lady Elise. Please go inside. I will follow with tea. Have you breakfasted?"

"I have Perr," Elise said, feeling a touch more hopeful. "Thank you."

Ducking under the cloth door panel, Elise found herself in the very pavilion in which she had lived during King Allister's War. Perr occupied the side chamber that she had shared with Ninette, but otherwise it was much as it had been.

Baron Archer had apparently been dressing, for he was ty-ing his neck cloth as he came from his bedchamber.

"Elise," he said, holding out his hands to her.

She put her own in his, while shaking down the hood of her outdoor cloak. Baron Archer paused in the process of giving her a parental embrace and gaped at her.

"What have you done to your hair?" he asked, the question more exclamation than mere inquiry.

"I cut it, Father," Elise replied meekly. "In New Kelvin. It was necessary if we were to get into Thendulla Lypella without raising undue suspicion."

"You cut it," he repeated, something odd in his tone. "To get into Thendulla Lypella."

"Yes, sir."

Belatedly, Elise realized what the new note in her father's voice was. It was pride. Ivon Archer was fairly bursting with pride in his daughter!

Perr entered the pavilion at that moment, bearing a tea tray. The baron dismissed him, asking him to make certain no one drew close enough to overhear their discussion. This done, Baron Archer set Elise on a camp chair and poured her tea with his own hands.

"I know something of the situation," he said. "Princess Sapphire has been good enough to take me into her confidence. Now I wish to hear everything from you."

Floating on the unexpected euphoria of her father's approval, Elise recounted everything that had happened since her departure from the Norwood Grant. She glossed over her early discomfort, and tried to make light of the encounter with the bandits. Something of her terror during the last must have crept into her voice despite her efforts, however, for she saw Baron Archer's eyes narrow and saw his fists clench in unvoiced anger.

Elise didn't forget—she couldn't have even if she wanted to do so—to highlight the other's roles: Firekeeper's courage and reluctant patience, Derian's steady competence, Wendee's wonderful combination of practical management and artistic flourish, Edlin's unexpected depths. She tried not to praise Doc above the others, but here as elsewhere she knew that her voice betrayed her. Her admiration for the man was so complete—he was strong yet giving, brave without being brash—that she knew it flowed into her voice.

Baron Archer neither chided nor questioned her about her feelings. He respected her heart's privacy and reserved his questions—and he had many—for the tactical matters. He was also very curious about Grateful Peace.

Elise was telling him about how Peace had been taken to Sir Jared's relatives when Perr called from without:

"Baron Archer, there is a messenger here. The crown prince and princess request your attendance at the command tent. They also wish to know if you know where Lady Archer might be found."

Baron Archer rose, saying, "Tell the messenger that I will attend upon Their Majesties immediately and that Lady Elise is with me."

"In that case," the messenger replied, turning to them as the baron held the tent flap for Elise. "The prince and princess request your attendance as well, Lady Archer."

They went, walking side by side. Elise gloried in her father's approval. She wasn't naive enough to believe that it would be unfaltering, but it felt good to know she had earned it. Maybe she did have what it would take to be a Baroness Archer who wouldn't shame her ancestors' spirits.

For just a moment Elise felt she had the answer to her dilemma regarding Sir Jared. Then the guard outside Sapphire and Shad's pavilion hailed them and her momentary insight slipped elusively away.

The crown prince and princess were waiting inside along with a small group that included most of those who had been involved in yesterday's tactical meeting but did not include—Elise noted with a certain amount of glee—Jet. She nodded to her camp mates, but no one violated the formality of the royal presence with small talk.

After a few other latecomers had arrived and all had been welcomed, Sapphire turned to business.

"I am pleased to inform you that the first stage of our plan to dishearten the smugglers seems to have gone without a hitch."

Elise glanced at Firekeeper, who looked rather smug. Sapphire continued:

"Knowing that they would likely notice the disruption as soon as dawn broke, we sent a messenger bearing a letter containing our terms for surrender soon after first light."

Shad lifted a document from the table.

"In the absence of secretaries and all the rest," he said with a disarming smile, "let me read you the text."

"Greetings—

"We of Hawk Haven have decided to tolerate no longer your illegal residence upon our lands and within a structure built at the desire of the Crown, said structure being the lighthouse popularly known as Smuggler's Light.

"You are hereby notified that you must vacate said property and its environs by next sunrise. If you do not do so, we will take forcible measures to make certain that you vacate the lighthouse—up to and including making certain that you vacate your lives.

"Although your behavior has incurred our displeasure, we are willing to permit you to depart with your personal property and without fear that you will be detained for the crimes you have committed against this kingdom if you surrender alive to us the following two persons: Baron Endbrook of the Isles and Citrine Shield of Hawk Haven.

"If said persons are not surrendered to us promptly and alive, then the residents of the lighthouse may expect that all efforts will be made to detain them and to incarcerate them for their crimes. If said persons are surrendered, all residents of the lighthouse may have their freedom as long as they depart our borders and those of Bright Bay within a reasonable period of time.

"Note that we are aware that said Baron Endbrook and Citrine Shield were alive and residing within said lighthouse

as of the writing of this letter. Do not attempt to convince us otherwise. Equally, murder of said persons as an expedient manner of delivering them into our custody will be most brutally punished.

"By this time you will have noticed the damage worked upon your gardens and livestock. Consider this a token of our seriousness.

"A messenger bearing a white flag of truce may safely enter our camp west of the swamp at any time before next dawn and expect to be treated fairly. After that time, we will recognize neither flag nor messenger but treat with you as the criminals that you are."

Shad looked up from his reading.

"We've signed it," he said with a slight grin, "with every flourish and title we could come up with between us, including such that indicate that we are acting under King Tedric's aegis."

Wheeler, commander of the scouts, was the first to speak.

"It's firm," he said, his tone adding, "Perhaps a bit *too* firm," though Wheeler was either too polite, or too politic, to say so.

"It is firm," Shad agreed. "We felt that it must be. From what I know of pirates, these people are likely to break into factions under stress. If we permit them overmuch time to decide and too many loopholes, we are creating reasons for factions to form."

Wheeler nodded, but Elise could tell he would have preferred a more subtle approach. Fleetingly, she recalled Sapphire and Shad playing that strategy game—navy and pirates?—while they convalesced. She hoped they had not mistaken reality for a game.

A few more questions were raised, mostly having to do with what precautions had been taken to keep the lighthouse under observation, what should be done about those seen sneaking away now that an ultimatum had been issued, and the like. However, as the letter had already been sent, there was not much that could be debated.

Elise glanced at her father, but Baron Archer looked quite satisfied. She wondered if he had known of the contents of the letter in advance, and, considering what Sapphire had said earlier about how he had conferred with them on the ride from Eagle's Nest, thought he might have known at least the gist, if not the precise contents.

After the meeting was dismissed, Baron Archer excused himself from his daughter.

"I am going to ride the rounds of those archers I have posted around the swamp's western and southern perimeters," he explained. "They'll be getting restless by now and needing to be rotated."

He bowed over her hand and departed. Elise fancied that she heard him whistling as he walked away, though the sound was cut short, as if Baron Archer realized that such action was beneath his dignity.

She turned toward her own camp. If there was to be fighting, she would not be in the thick of it, but she and Doc would be needed to assist the field-hospital staff. In that case, she must be as rested and clearheaded as any of those who would fight.

Briskly, Elise stepped up her pace, hoping that Sapphire and Shad's bold feint would work and that no more blood would be shed.

XXXVIII

 THE NEXT DAWN CAME—the deadline for surrender—but no one emerged from the lighthouse.

No one at all, and that was odd. Smuggler's Light had several doors. One at the side of each of the buildings around the base led out into the gardens or livestock pens; there was also the lighthouse's original door, a broad, weathered panel now reinforced with iron.

Early the morning before, soon after Firekeeper's sabotage had been discovered by the inhabitants, there had been much activity outside the lighthouse. It seemed that pretty much everyone who lived in the lighthouse had wanted to see the destruction for themselves.

Later, under the direction of a rangy, knobby-jointed fellow, work crews had emerged, some to scavenge edible food, some to dig pits to bury that which was ruined beyond use.

Based on these comings and goings, Captain Wheeler's scouts had been able to make a fair assessment of how many resided within Smuggler's Light. The number of inhabitants had been higher than any had imagined—a fact that no one greeted with particular delight.

Now, however the doors remained closed; the shutters stayed folded over the windows. Deserters had been expected—even prepared for—but not one person had left.

From Firekeeper, who had the news from her wingéd friends, Derian Carter knew that at least some of the smugglers remained inside. The wolf-woman also assured him that no one had escaped via some other route—a tunnel under the moat, for example. All night, she and Blind Seer had restlessly patrolled the swamp, augmenting the watch kept by the more usual scouts. Like them, she had seen no one depart.

Dawn turned into a clear, bright winter morning. When not one shred of pink remained in the skies and the sun had finished mounting from the east, the crown prince and princess called a tactical meeting in their pavilion.

Derian, perhaps in deference to his place as one of King Tedric's counselors, was included. So was Firekeeper.

The wolf-woman whined some, saying she was tired from her long night's vigil, that she would never keep awake through all the human talking. After Blind Seer nipped at her heel, however, she brightened and trotted after Derian.

"Maybe," she said with a grin, "I sleep better because of all the talking. Otherwise, I worry too much."

"Just don't snore," Derian retorted. "Otherwise I'll have to kick you."

The pavilion was crowded enough to be comfortably warm, but the emotional temperature was less pleasant. Those summoned to the meeting milled about, talking in low voices to each other and avoiding the royal couple. Derian could understand why.

Sapphire was clearly not in one of her sweeter moods. Derian would have been willing to bet that she blamed herself for things not going according to plan. She stood off to one side, deep in a heated conversation with the more senior commanders—Baron Archer among them. Only their low voices kept Derian from classifying the discussion as an outright argument.

Standing by himself a few paces away, Prince Shad looked both worried and distinctly worn. Derian felt an outrush of sympathy for the prince. Not only did Shad bear his own concerns, but Sapphire's more personal ones as well. Moreover, Shad bore the additional onus of being from Bright Bay.

Early that morning, as Derian had tried to overcome his private disappointment that the ploy hadn't worked as planned, he had wandered restlessly through the military camp. More than once he overheard fragments of nearly treasonous conversation among the soldiers, the gist of which was that the pirates hadn't surrendered because they had somehow learned that their ocean escape route was guarded by ships from Bright Bay.

Bright Bay, at least as the gossip went, had been—as everyone knew or claimed to know—allied with the pirates before King Allister's War. Now the pirates trusted their former allies to let them slip through the barricade. Why, then, should they surrender? They were just waiting for the right moment and would escape to sea.

Such rumors shouldn't have had the strength of spit and spider silk, but the truth was that many of those who fought for Hawk Haven were uncomfortable with the alliance with Bright Bay. Bright Bay had been the enemy in their parents' day and in their grandparents' day. It was too soon to trust.

Moreover, most of the soldiers had never served on a ship or even been to sea. To them the ocean was an alien element. By association, those who were at home upon the waves were as dangerous and unreliable as the waters themselves.

Something in Shad's posture, a certain level of unspoken defiance, led Derian to believe that Shad had heard these rumors.

The crown prince must feel very alone, Derian realized. His wife—really his only close friend in Hawk Haven—was isolated from him by her own concerns, leaving him to face by himself the growing hostility of those who claimed to be his subjects.

Thoughts such as these made Derian put himself forward more than he might have in another situation. Normally, he dreaded more than anything being thought a social-climbing commoner, an ass-kissing sycophant. Putting those fears aside, Derian crossed to where Prince Shad stood, ostensibly reviewing a map, but really providing an excuse for those who were avoiding him to do so.

"Your Highness," Derian said, offering a deep bow.

Shad laughed a touch stiffly, but he lowered his map.

Derian noted it was Edlin's original of the swamp and the area around the lighthouse. Last night, Edlin had been making rough copies by lanternlight, all the while chatting away about how he hoped that their only purpose would be to provide him with a chance to practice drafting.

"No court manners here, Counselor," the crown prince said.

Derian winked at him.

"I'm just trying to teach Firekeeper her manners, Prince Shad."

As Firekeeper had simply collapsed along one side of the tent, her head pillowed on Blind Seer's flank, Derian had excuse enough for the jest.

One corner of Shad's mouth quirked in an almost unwilling grin.

"She looks beat," he said.

"She is," Derian admitted. "No one is harder on Firekeeper than she is herself. She also cares more deeply for Citrine than most people realize."

Shad nodded a bit absently.

"We won't leave Citrine there," he said, his tone so low as to be almost inaudible. "No matter what people say, we won't leave her in there!"

Derian hazarded laying a hand on the prince's arm.

"I never thought you would," he said. "Neither did Firekeeper. If she did, she wouldn't be asleep now. She'd be awake and trying to find a way to handle this all by herself."

For a moment the grim lines around Shad's eyes softened. He looked Derian directly in the eyes.

"Thank you," he said softly. Then, more loudly, turning to the company at large, "It looks as if everyone is present. Shall we come to order?"

As the mob was resolving itself into a tidy arc facing the royal couple, the prince tapped Derian lightly on one arm.

"If I could impose on you, Counselor, as you are not with the military portion of this operation, I would like you to stay here and hold the map for all to see when needed."

Derian nodded and stepped back a few steps. He remained near to hand, but effaced himself as he had learned to do when serving Earl Kestrel. Grateful Peace's description of his role in the Dragon Speaker's court came to mind.

Very well, Derian thought, a trifle amused. *Now I am a watcher, too.*

The meeting began with the briefest summary of events that everyone present knew all too well.

But now we all know them in the same words, Derian thought, wondering if he could explain this to Firekeeper. *Probably not. She thinks too much in emotion and impulse to understand the value we put on words.*

Then he remembered the terrible pain in Firekeeper's eyes when she had admitted to him her discovery that Royal wolves could lie, and he wasn't so certain.

When the meeting shifted from what had been done to what should be done, the tone became acrimonious. In his self-appointed role as watcher, Derian saw things that he might not otherwise. How many of those other meetings had been shaped by his fear that he might not have anything to say if called upon, or worse yet, by his desire to think of something worth saying?

He banished even those self-recriminations and set himself to watching—and listening. Almost mystically he became aware of the patterns of interaction between those gathered: glances exchanged, a nudge with an elbow, a warning kick— gentle as the brushing of an eyelash but as potent as a shout.

These little signs and a dozen more he saw, though he did not comprehend all the subtleties of their patterns any more than a dragonfly lightly touching on the surface of a pond sees the larger pattern caused when ripples interact.

But he saw and was captivated by the heady power of watching.

There were those here who thought mostly of what this meeting, this campaign meant to them. There were those who considered further—of what it might mean to the kingdom or even to the region. There were those who could not get beyond their immediate frustration at being ruled over by those they thought of as children.

Nor were these ripples all discrete. Sometimes more than one pattern rippled from a single person.

Derian made himself concentrate on the immediate issue rather than on the subtle patterns of power. Basically it resolved itself into a simple question: What was the best way to respond to the pirates' defiance of the terms set forth in the letter?

Despite variations as to what strategy should be employed, opinions fell into two general camps—either lay a siege or attack.

The greatest argument against a siege was that no one knew how long the smugglers could hold out or, as Sapphire somewhat acidly added, what might happen to Citrine over the course of a long siege.

The greatest argument against an attack was that the smugglers would have the advantage, at least for the first several forays. They held the fortification. Moreover, the dense growth and soft earth of the surrounding swamp meant that siege weapons could only be brought in with great difficulty.

And again there was the question of what they would do to their hostage once battle was joined. Citrine might well be the first casualty.

Derian had a fleeting image of the lighthouse, ringed by its moat, the moat itself ringed by troops in Hawk Haven's scarlet and silver. Over it all, like a grisly banner, hung the crow-picked corpse of a little girl, only recognizable by the gem-stone that still glimmered from beneath the rags of her hair.

He shuddered and hoped that if anyone saw they would think he was taking cold. At least no one had suggested that they give the whole thing up as a bad job and head home.

At least two hours passed in debate as points were repeated and refined. Then Firekeeper woke from her nap. She propped herself up next to Blind Seer. Still seated on the floor, she yawned, ran her hands across the fuzz that was beginning to cover her scalp, and stretched.

Only those few closest to her noticed, and these looked down at her with ill-disguised expressions of disgust, which did not lighten when Firekeeper took advantage of a break in the debate to comment:

"I say we go in. We must for Citrine, but why must we batter at their doors?"

Sapphire looked down at the wolf-woman, her bad temper not in the least mollified by two hours of fruitless discussion.

"What do you mean, Lady Blysse?"

Derian winced internally, though he kept the expression from his face. It was always a bad sign when Sapphire reverted to calling Firekeeper by her more formal name.

Firekeeper leapt lightly to her feet, not in the least put out. She even bobbed something like a bow in Sapphire's direction.

"I mean," she said lightly, "why should be batter at their feet when these are made of stone but their head is made of glass?"

Sapphire frowned; then her expression brightened.

"The lighthouse, you mean. It has a stone footing, but the

top floor where the light was is walled in glass."

Firekeeper nodded, remembering enough of her manners not to say something like "What else could I mean?"

Sapphire's momentary cheerfulness vanished.

"But we cannot reach those windows. We don't have wings like Elation does."

Firekeeper nodded. "I am thinking on that. Still, when I went and hunted the place, I stayed near the walls because even if they had seen me . . ."

Unspoken as the words were, her posture proclaimed a bragging "Not that they would have."

". . . they could have done little to hurt me without coming out to me."

Firekeeper's bared teeth—nothing like a smile—and the way she touched her belted Fang made clear what would have happened to any who dared come out after her.

"To go up to the windows," Firekeeper continued, flagging slightly in her unusual burst of eloquence, "we must be close to the rock."

Firekeeper's proposal, inelegantly phrased as it had been, stirred up a brief flurry of debate, most of it—Derian was unhappy to see—centered on debunking it.

Prince Shad, however, was not so easily dissuaded.

"Climbing ropes or rope ladders would get us to the top," he said into the polite silence that fell whenever either he or Sapphire spoke. "The biggest problem would be anchoring them."

"And getting those who would climb them across to the lighthouse unscathed," said one of the siege's most vocal proponents.

Firekeeper, ever thoughtless of those who had not earned her respect, waved a dismissive hand.

"No problem," she said. "We go by night."

The man gaped at her and a new flurry of protest would have begun then and there had Princess Sapphire not turned a very cool blue gaze on those who would protest.

"Any thoughts on how we might get those ropes anchored?"

Her tone made clear that any thoughts on any other topic were not welcome.

Baron Archer said, "We might work something with arrows, Princess, but I'm not certain any of our bows have the range and the power. Another problem would be securing the ladders, even if we broke through the window glass."

Looking exquisitely unhappy, Firekeeper said:

"Plan as if those ladders or ropes—no more than two or three to start—were hanging down."

She turned to leave. Princess Sapphire called after her:

"Where are you going, Firekeeper? This is your plan."

"I go," Firekeeper said, her expression no less unhappy, "to work how those ropes will fly."

She forestalled further questions by moving toward the door. When Blind Seer rose to follow her, not even the most sycophantic member of the gathering tried to stop her.

There certainly something to be said for having a wolf on your side, Derian thought, and hoped that Firekeeper was indeed the wolf on Hawk Haven's side, as devoted to that kingdom's efforts as Blind Seer was to the wolf-woman's own safety.

Eventually, Sapphire and Shad decided to trust that Firekeeper would deliver what she promised. A night attack did have its advantages—among them the unspoken one of giving the smugglers more time to sweat and maybe even to surrender.

They ordered their commanders to plan for both a more usual ground assault and for one that would include sending a team in through the glass windows at the top. Some debate was raised as to the possibility that these, too, might be shuttered, but everyone seemed to think that this could be worked around.

Prince Shad, as comfortable as a squirrel in the treetops when confronting riggings, set up a testing ground for those who wanted to volunteer for the topside assault. It consisted of a rope ladder attached not all that firmly to the one remaining wall of the former farmhouse. Alongside it hung a rope with knots interspersed down its length.

Derian wandered over to watch, arriving in time to see one candidate succeed, and another brilliantly and memorably fail.

Doc and Elise had volunteered to be on hand to treat those who might injure themselves during the trials. Derian gave them a nod and a grin as they hurried off to check the man sprawled on the ground, then strolled over—with a confidence he didn't precisely feel—to stand near the prince.

Shad nodded to Derian, motioning him over.

"Come to watch?"

"Come to audition," Derian said, "if that's permitted for someone not enrolled in a militia unit."

Shad hid his surprise quite well.

"It's permitted," he said, "since I permit it. Can you really manage it, or are you being supportive of Firekeeper?"

In answer, Derian walked over to where the ropes were slung. He'd put on soft boots so he'd be able to feel with his feet and light doeskin gloves that kept his hands warm without crippling his sense of touch.

The rope ladder—like so many rope ladders he'd climbed into haylofts and silos—proved no real challenge. Indeed, it bounced less than many of those he'd climbed, since he could always brace himself against the wall.

It took him a moment to remember how to get the right start on a rope, but once he was up he swarmed to the top nearly as nimbly as a sailor.

"Sign him up!" Shad called to the sergeant who was assisting him. Then to Derian, "Have you been to sea?"

"Never," Derian said, pleased that his muscles hadn't forgotten their training, "but my dad had a thing about rope ladders to the haylofts—said it kept down the traffic when the girls had to manage their skirts."

He winked and the prince gave a knowing chuckle.

"And when I was a boy," Derian said, "one of our favorite games was to climb a rope up over the haycart and swing out for a soft landing. We did something similar at the swimming hole in the summer. I must admit, I never thought those games would come in so handy."

Shad nodded, his attention on the next candidates.

"Handy, yes," he said, "though I wonder if your father would think so if he knew that those games would put you in the front of a battle."

Derian, thinking of how Colby Carter still mourned the siblings he had lost in earlier battles, really couldn't answer.

Prince Shad waved to the sergeant.

"Take that one and we'll have enough. Tell those I've chosen that they're to beg or borrow strong, soft gloves and boots—if they don't have them already. We meet in one hour to discuss tactics."

When Derian started to withdraw, Shad put a hand out to stop him.

"Hold a moment, Counselor," he said. "I have to ask you—here where no one can overhear us—what do you think Firekeeper is up to? Do you think she can indeed get us in?"

Derian frowned.

"Two questions, Prince, and two questions for which I have no definite answers. If you would accept guesses instead . . ."

Shad nodded.

"Then my guess is that Firekeeper is trying to convince some of what she'd call the wingéd folk—birds who are to other birds what Blind Seer is to the wolves we know—to carry ropes up for us. I saw her talking with Baron Archer a while ago and my guess is that she was learning if his archers could make the hole. Then the wingéd folk could carry the ropes up and maybe anchor them somehow. They could also guard from above while we climbed."

Shad's eyes shone.

"That's wonderful! I remember the crow who brought Sapphire her letter. It was a marvelously intelligent bird. Do you think Firekeeper can make them?"

"It's closer to 'convince' than 'make,' " Derian replied carefully. "Firekeeper is always saying how they are not hers."

Sometimes, he thought, leaving that dangerous idea unspoken, *what is more accurate is that she is theirs.*

Shad was so delighted that Derian couldn't keep from saying a bit more.

"Take care how you voice your pleasure, Prince," Derian

said. "I sense that Firekeeper is not completely happy about making public how intelligent the Royal Beasts can be. Even if she pulls this off, it might not be a bad idea to spread a rumor that the animals are her trained pets or something."

"I thought," Shad said slowly, "that she was offended if you referred to Blind Seer or Elation as her pets."

"True," Derian assured him. "Absolutely the correct etiquette—to her face. However, well . . . When I first met Firekeeper, less than a year ago, her relationships with animals fell into pretty much two categories: those you ate and those you befriended. I remember that she thought we were pretty clever for bringing horses along so we wouldn't need to hunt our meat. It took me a while to show her they had other uses."

"And," Shad said with a laugh that was a touch too hearty, "she clearly still prefers not to ride."

"I suspect that when she finds the right horse," Derian said, "her opinion will change. For now, though, most horses shy when they see Blind Seer and prove more a problem than otherwise.

"The point I'm trying to make, Prince," Derian continued, returning to his original subject, "is that Firekeeper never thought of using animals to do tasks for her—the way we use horses, oxen, hunting birds, dogs . . ."

"And," Shad said, understanding more quickly than Derian had thought he would, "she is unhappy with the idea that we might transform her wingéd folk into mewed hawks, her wolf companion into a war dog."

"Precisely," Derian agreed. "It might be possible, too, but to do so we would need either to befriend them . . ."

Images of Elation drowsing on a chair-back in his room flitted through his mind.

". . . Or enslave them. If we did the latter, we would make Firekeeper our enemy. She is my friend, but I can say without hesitation that she would make such a vicious enemy that we would welcome Lady Melina back into our homes."

Shad opened his mouth as if to protest, then snapped it shut.

"You may be right. I just remembered how she single-handedly slew all the livestock at Smuggler's Light."

"And came home laughing and thinking it all a great game," Derian reminded him steadily, "except that so much meat had to be wasted."

LATER THAT DAY, Firekeeper came to Prince Shad just as he was dismissing his squad of climbers. Derian had been about to leave with the rest—in addition to the prince and himself there were eight others—when he saw the wolf-woman making her way to the across the meadow. He hesitated, touching Shad lightly on one arm.

"Prince," he said, "I think you may wish to wait a moment. Firekeeper . . ."

He pointed.

"Red Fox!" Shad exclaimed in soft-voiced surprise. "I never saw her coming and it's broad daylight yet. How did you?"

"I happened to be looking the right way," Derian said dismissively, "and I've learned to keep an eye open for her. Wolves have a sense of humor, you know."

"I didn't know," Shad said curiously.

"They do," Derian grinned. "Mind, it's not very subtle. It falls more into the 'hide behind a tree and jump out at you' category than anything else . . . so you can understand why I've learned to look for her."

Firekeeper was close enough that she must have overheard the last, but she didn't choose to comment. Her expression remained serious, holding a trace of the unhappiness Derian had seen earlier. For a moment, he thought she was going to admit defeat, but her first words dispelled that notion.

"I see your climbing," she said, offering the prince an abbreviated bow. "Good. There will be ropes."

She outlined her plan then and there. In substance, it was much like what Derian had envisioned. Baron Archer had agreed to delegate archers to break the windows. Bold and Elation would drop the ropes into place, then fly a high guard.

"Am sorry," she said, "I not get more help, but gulls refused and is no time to find others."

Shad smiled reassuringly.

"You've done brilliantly," he said, "and this is best. I'll let the word go out that you're having two of your trained beasts help us."

A flash of anger lit Firekeeper's eyes. Then she seemed to understand. A small smile chased the misery from her features.

"That is good," she replied. Then she returned to the more immediate problem. "Still one thing. How to make the ropes hold. Someone in meeting mention something but I not know the word."

"Grapples," Shad said. He made a series of hooks with his fingers. "Rather like this but made of metal. The rope is fastened to the base. I must see if we have any with us that will be of a weight the birds can lift. If not, the farrier will have to manage something."

He offered them a weary smile.

"I had better go. First I need to tell Sapphire and our commanders that I will be taking in a group through the top. Then I need to speak with the quartermaster and the farrier."

"I'll do that," Derian offered. "You concentrate on the people. I can handle gear."

Shad accepted with a nod and began to walk toward the encampment. Derian's route was slightly different. He glanced at the wolf-woman.

"And where are you off to, Firekeeper?"

"Am going to see Captain Wheeler," she said. "And tell him that I will run front guide through swamp if he wishes."

"Think he'll accept?"

She nodded confidently.

"He rather have me and Blind Seer in front," she said with a wicked grin, "than know that there are wolves in the darkness where he not see them."

❧

THE LETTER HAD PROVIDED Waln with a way out—though certainly not the way those who had written it must have assumed he would take. It had been delivered into his hands, its passage through the common room shifting attention from Citrine back to Waln himself.

Breaking the seal, Waln read the long text. Initially, the contents panicked him. He couldn't see a way around the trap that had been laid for him. A strong impulse to fold the letter away took command of him. He was in the very course of doing so when he felt an inkling of the way out.

He laughed, a deep belly laugh that invited everyone present to join in the joke. A few did, though the laughter tapered off uncertainly as they realized that they had no idea what the joke was.

Masking his face with a broad smile, Waln shook out the letter. He almost wished he wore spectacles so he could make a production of putting them on. Omitting that, he angled himself so that the best light was on the page.

"We've received a letter," he said. "I've heard of good gimmicks in my time, but this one about beats them all for brass. Let me read it to you."

Without further hesitation, he read the letter aloud. Normally, Waln didn't consider himself terribly good at such things, but the same manic impulse that had prompted him to bull this through gave him style.

He read, not overdoing it, but shifting his tone slightly to make certain phrases such as "no longer to tolerate your illegal residence upon our lands" and "forcible measures" sound vaguely ridiculous.

When he came to the passages demanding the surrender of himself and Citrine Shield as a guarantor of safety for those who wished to depart, he laughed so hard that he wiped tears from his eyes.

"As if they'd keep *that* promise!" he said, before returning to the text.

He concluded with a rolling recitation of the honors and titles attached to the signatures. Since many of the pirates viewed such nobles' flourishes as unzoranic, these did not intimidate as was apparently intended. Rather they seemed empty braggadocio, like the strutting of a rooster.

"Pretty good rack for a couple of fawns," Waln commented.

A brief, heated discussion of the letter's contents followed. By its end, Waln felt that he could sort the company of smugglers into three parties.

One consisted of those who—although they had heard the letter—did not believe for a moment the likelihood that the terms within would be kept. Many of these had committed crimes in their native lands and had turned to piracy after fleeing. Although a few, like the cannibal cook, might have done nothing illegal in Hawk Haven—other than smuggling, that is—they still did not expect a warm welcome from the local authorities.

A second group simply didn't like being ordered from what they, with some justice, regarded as their property. These were firm believers in the unchallengeable strength of Smuggler's Light. A few were veterans of the battle during which Princess Lovella had been killed. While the members of the first group viewed the letter with distrust, this group grew angrier the further Waln read. They were insulted that anyone thought they could just be ordered away.

The third group—and quite possibly the largest—were not greatly swayed by Waln's eloquent reading. They still viewed him as an intruder—the source and the focus of all their immediate woes. They would quite happily have turned him over to Princess Sapphire and Prince Shad.

What stopped them was that Waln's surrender had not been all the letter demanded. They would have handed over Waln and Citrine, too. They might even have surrendered themselves and trusted the offer of escape. However, what they could *not* do was surrender those from the first two groups—those who were not inclined to surrender themselves.

As many of these were among the largest, meanest, and strongest of the lot, and as the two groups who did not wish to heed the terms set out in the letter equaled or outnumbered those who might have given in, the point was moot.

It did not take much arguing for those who might have given in to realize that their lives weren't worth the air in their lungs if the others thought they might turn traitor. The more vocal ceased to argue. The less vocal never spoke up.

Waln noted them, though, noted them carefully. Although he did not single them out, he did make certain that none of them were given guard duty on the ground floor, that none of them were given the best of the weapons from the armory, and, most importantly, that none of them got within arm's reach of *him*.

Citrine, however, he kept close within reach. He didn't trust someone—not even among those whose interests were at least technically allied with his own—not to steal her away in order to work some sort of trade.

Many, he knew, thought that Princess Sapphire would lose her fire for battle when her little sister was returned to him. All Waln needed to do was look at the girl's maimed hand to realize that in his estimation Princess Sapphire was likely to become more eager for his head rather than less.

If Sapphire offered to leave Smuggler's Light alone in exchange for Waln, Waln knew that his days of leadership would be over. Even he could not expect to bully into submission the assembled might of the pirates.

Gone were the days that Waln Endbrook had hoped to regain the artifacts or repair his standing with Queen Valora. Right now all he wanted was to keep alive.

If he could retain the respect of the pirates, he might manage to escape when the sailing weather improved, and to then set up a new life for himself somewhere—maybe to the south, past Stonehold's brutal coast. Waln had heard rumors that there was rich land there, and Lady Melina's necklace would provide him with starting capital. Eventually, he could pay someone to bring Oralia and his children to him.

But first he needed to survive, and in order to survive, he needed to remain in control.

Waln was grateful that the letter gave them so much time in which to reply. He spent the first part of the day setting up defenses, working in consultation with the most skillful of the pirates and taking the advice of those who knew the place best.

There had been some thought of requesting help from those

pirates who were wintering in other strongholds. The easternmost edge of the swamp along where it met the ocean concealed several boathouses in which vessels were dry-docked. Getting one of these ready would be a chore, but it could be undertaken. However, an inspection of the seas from the heights of the lighthouse soon caused this plan to be discarded.

The long-glass showed several ships flying Bright Bay's green and gold flag patrolling the area where the channel from the lighthouse emptied into the ocean. Although a small vessel might have a chance of getting away, one of the size needed to brave the winter swells would almost certainly be spotted, if not by night, then certainly by day.

With both escape and reinforcements ruled out, Waln found himself well supported as he readied the lighthouse for a defensive battle. He had never really been a fighter, but he had captained ships and managed a large shipping concern. Both took the ability to coordinate others. It helped that Waln also had the talent for making others do much of the work and planning, all the while leaving the impression in their minds that he was the font of great ideas.

By nightfall Smuggler's light was secure, the residents divided into shifts, what supplies that could be salvaged prepared and stocked away. Drinking water would not be an issue, for a well stood at the heart of the common room, tapping into the same source of fresh water that kept the swamp moist and brackish at all times of year.

As a means of displaying his confidence, Waln retired to sleep come nightfall. Yet even here he was not taking the great gamble it might seem. One of his tactical suggestions had been that a couple of large rooms on the second floor be turned into dormitories—so that those of unshakable loyalty could keep an eye on those less trustworthy.

No names had been named, but he managed to word things so that the mere suggestion that one wanted to sleep in privacy suggested less than sterling loyalties. This done, Waln took a cot by the door. Citrine was given a pallet right next to him. To assure her not going anywhere, Waln put her in a harness, like one might use to restrain a big dog.

He fell asleep that night to the ugly music of men snoring undercut by Citrine's muffled sobs.

XXXIX

THE NEXT MORNING PASSED SLOWLY, each moment resonating with a tension so prevalent that it was almost palpable. When noon had come and gone with no further message from the enemy and no action glimpsed on their borders, the pirates grew relieved, then cocky.

Waln fed this cockiness, preferring it to the tension. As he paced his rounds of the lighthouse—praising some, chiding others into greater vigilance—more than one confidant was privileged to share his "private" image of the young prince and princess wringing their hands and mewling over what should be done.

Although the lack of immediate counterattack quelled the fears of those who would have surrendered at the letter's behest—and subjected them to a good deal of teasing from their "braver" fellows—Waln was careful not to let vigilance slip. He took advantage of the noonday meal to address those who were not on watch about the need for continued watchfulness.

"They must do something," he said, "make some little feint in order to save face. How else will they avoid the shame of being called Princess Pig-butcher and Prince Cattle-killer?"

Waln made his tone fatherly and surveyed the assembled crew—whom privately he viewed as an ill-assorted and untrustworthy bunch—with apparent pride.

"You are the lords and ladies of the seas, the masters and mistresses of the trade lanes. I would not have one of you shed a drop of blood because we let our guard down. Let them shed the blood! Let them do the dying!"

A raucous cheer answered him and vigilance through the afternoon was redoubled. Bets were passed as to when the attack would occur, and the coming of the enemy troops as eagerly anticipated as the final lap of a horse race.

By the second nightfall, some of the headiness had ebbed, replaced by a stoic watchfulness that Waln found more reassuring.

If this went on much longer, he would send out a raiding party with some of the hottest heads and the most unreliable elements. Trudging through the swamps would cool the hotheads, and if a few of the unreliable escaped they were hardly much of a loss.

He went to his cot in the dormitory that night quite ready for sleep. No one would attack by night. It simply wasn't done. Even if they did, their torches and lanterns would give them away long before they reached the lighthouse.

"Sweet dreams," he murmured to Citrine as the girl laid herself on her pallet.

He even meant it.

WALN WAS AWAKENED by a chorus of shouts from both above and below. As he rolled over and shoved his feet into his boots, he realized that the shouting had been preceded by a crashing noise as of broken glass—the sound that had actually pressed him to wakefulness, though the shouting had come close upon it, like thunder after lightning.

Dragging Citrine along by her harness, Waln rushed out into the corridor, long dagger in hand.

Behind him other sleepers were reaching for boots and shirts, comparing notes on what they had heard. A few were close behind him.

The sleeping room was near the staircase—the door of which had been spiked open as a precaution against anyone getting imprisoned on a specific floor, From above, Waln could hear metal clashing on metal, the sound of glass breaking, screams like the shrieks of a hawk. Judging from the muted quality of the sound, it was coming from the top floor, where the light had once stood.

From the common room below, the sound was more chaotic, as if rather than confronting a specific enemy, the watchers on that level were trying to prevent something. A smutty smell of burning came faintly to his nostrils. A dull, rhythmic booming announced that a ram had been brought into play.

At the landings of the third and fourth floors above Waln, two of those assigned to watch bolted forth so unconsciously in sync with each other that they looked like pull toys on a single string.

"What in the deep blue is going on!" Waln bellowed.

Tris Stone, a woman who it was said had murdered her unfaithful husband in a particularly gruesome fashion, looked at him wild-eyed.

"An attack! They've bridged the moat on all sides!"

Waln didn't bother to ask why no one had seen the enemy's approach. There'd be enough time for recriminations and punishment when this battle had been won.

He didn't allow himself to think that they might not win.

WITHOUT ASKING, Firekeeper had assigned herself to Prince Shad's wall-climbing team. She felt certain of her welcome. After all, without her help there would *be* no entry through the upper level. It was her plan and it seemed to her that she should be present to see it through.

Blind Seer was less than happy about her intentions. He would have preferred her to stay on the ground and fight by his side. However, when Firekeeper explained her reasons he relented.

"There must be one of us," she said, sitting beside him on the ground some distance from the camp, "who is prepared to do nothing but find Citrine. Prince Shad and his climbers—if I know anything of humans—will be distracted. I will not.

When we encounter enemies, I will brush past them and find Citrine. They, worried about questions of courage and 'clear lines of retreat' and other such things, will be delayed."

Blind Seer rolled onto his back so that she could scratch his belly. After a thoughtful sigh, he conceded.

"And what shall I do, then?"

"Watch from the ground," Firekeeper said promptly. "That lighthouse has more doors than a hive has bees. Baron Endbrook strikes me as the type of coward who may try to run while others fight his battles. He might manage this if mere humans opposed him, but not against you."

Blind Seer rumbled his pleasure.

"I cannot watch everywhere," he cautioned.

"I know that, sweet hunter, but those blue eyes of yours see far better than anything humans have—especially by night. I plan to ask Bold to scout for you. He will not be needed above once we are inside."

"Bold only? What of Elation? That bird has rested from her journeys hither and yon. I weary of her bragging."

This last was said affectionately. In truth, Blind Seer felt nearly as much pride in the falcon's doings as she did herself. Nor had he forgotten his gratitude to both Elation and Bold for protecting Firekeeper during her escape from Thendulla Lypella.

Firekeeper hesitated, her fingers pausing in their scratching.

"If she would be of use to you," she said at last, "I would ask her to scout. However, if you can manage with only the crow . . ."

"If!" the wolf said indignantly.

"If you can," Firekeeper said, resuming her rhythmic scratching of the wolf's chest, "then I thought to ask Elation to defend Derian as best she can. I would not rob Fox Hair of this chance to prove himself before a One of his pack, but for all his courage during the past war Derian is not yet a blooded warrior. I fear that when the time comes to trade blows with sword or knife, he will falter and be killed."

"Wise," Blind Seer said. "There is some thought behind those doe eyes of yours."

He rolled when she would have punched him, coming up lightly and wagging his tail.

"Come and run with me," he said, bouncing a bit. "You have been serious too long."

Firekeeper shook her head, resisting, though Blind Seer darted away and back again, wagging his tail as if inviting her to grab hold.

"Later," she said, "when all this is over. I have too much to worry me."

Blind Seer relented, but she could see he was disappointed.

"You are becoming as grim as a she-bear with two cubs," he grumbled. "Remember your promise."

"I will," she said.

Fleetingly, she remembered the moonstone ring.

Perhaps, sweet hunter, I will truly run with you and not trail along behind.

THE ATTACK WAS SET to begin well after nightfall. In order to minimize the need to show lights, the troops advanced into the swamp at twilight, stopping a fair distance from their destination, beneath where the canopy—from Elation's perspective—protected them from being seen, even from above.

Dark lanterns were permitted, as were hot drinks. Elation and Bold periodically checked, making certain that no one showed a light that could give them away.

At the prearranged hour, Firekeeper and the scouts—Edlin the newest and proudest recruit among their number—led the way deeper into the swamp. Despite paths marked out with guidelines and infinite care, one or two soldiers stumbled into the morass and had to be dragged free and dried.

The cold weather, however, protected them from the worst of the swamp's hazards. The poisonous snakes and insects were dormant for the winter. The stinging nettles and rash-inducing plants had lost their leaves.

The attackers approached from four different points. Three groups were to advance and, using thin blades and rods, break the ground-floor windows. Then they were to set torches—

now smoldering in carefully covered buckets and pots—to the shutters and drop coals inside.

There was no real hope that a fire would catch within; rather, the hope was that a panic might arise that would lead to a door being opened. At the very least, this would prove a distraction from the attackers' other activities.

A fourth group—under the command of Princess Sapphire, who had reluctantly admitted she couldn't climb a rope on a dare—was to assault the original lighthouse door with a makeshift ram cut from a massive poplar that might have once sheltered the farmyard.

Again, they did not hope to burst in the door, but with this as the apparent focus of their attack, attention and fighters should be diverted from the fifth group.

This, of course, was the one led by Prince Shad, the band of climbers, including Firekeeper, who would go in through the top. Baron Archer and the best of his band would break the windows with specially prepared blunted arrows. Then they were to drop back and provide cover for the squad on the ram, for these would be unable to protect themselves.

Of Firekeeper's former companions, Derian was with Shad. Edlin was with the scouts and, later, would join the archers. Doc and Elise, of course, were with the hospital crew. Wendee Jay had elected to stay with them. Firekeeper did not doubt that the latter's steadiness would be greatly valued if injuries mounted.

She was parting from the scouts, her hand buried in Blind Seer's fur in silent farewell, when a familiar voice said rather diffidently:

"I say, won't you give your brother a kiss for luck, what?"

Firekeeper knew well that what Edlin felt toward her was more than brotherly affection. For a moment she considered turning away without a word. Then she recalled that, like Derian, this was Edlin's first taste of battle.

She lifted herself on her toes and kissed Edlin lightly on one cheek.

"Good luck, Brother."

She melted into the darkness before he could say more. As

he trailed her, Blind Seer seemed less than pleased.

"You didn't kiss me!" he sniffed.

She knelt and wrapped her arms around him.

"You I expect to see again, fool! Him I am not so sure."

Blind Seer gave her a sloppy lick on one cheek and then went to begin his patrol.

The ascent of the lighthouse went more smoothly than Firekeeper had dared hope. In her mind she renamed Shad "Spider" for the incredible dexterity with which he climbed the knotted rope. Derian, going up third on one line, made the climb easily as well.

Although—remembering her avowed purpose for making the ascent—Firekeeper had agreed to let those better armed and trained climb before her, she itched for her chance. She had practiced some on the farmhouse wall, and although different types of climbing were second nature to her, she did wonder how well she would manage when the time came.

She got to the top—though no one would dub her spider for her grace, and her leather trousers saved her from a nasty scraped knee. As she mounted, Elation's shrieks and Bold's rough caws warned her that she was ascending into a battle.

Coming to the top, Firekeeper poised on the broad window ledge, waiting for a clear spot of floor to jump down. Chance let her make it for herself when one of the defenders, stumbling back from an attacker's blade, came within range.

With a sharp thrust of her Fang's pommel, she knocked the man cold, leapt down and over him, and charged into the shadowed stairwell.

Another might have been blinded here, but Firekeeper had learned to see in the dark. She saw the darker darkness that was the ascending man and kicked out. Her foot was bare—she had forsaken boots for comfort when climbing—but her heel was hard and made contact directly with his forehead. He fell back, landing against another and causing him to stumble in turn.

Firekeeper was tempted to take time to finish them, but nei-

ther man had Citrine. Below, the thudding of the ram against
the door seemed like the beating of the lighthouse's own gigantic heart, as if the stone walls had come to life and were
siding with the attackers.

The odor of smoke would have kept even Blind Seer
from tracking Citrine by scent, but the traces eddying in
were not enough to do more than make Firekeeper's eyes
water slightly.

She dashed past the fourth-floor landing, past the third, certain from the minimal noise that no one of importance was
here, and that those who remained here were occupied in trying to attack those on the ground below.

Reaching the second floor, the wolf-woman paused for a
moment at the dormitories. They reeked of unwashed bed lin-
ens, but their only occupants proved to be a handful of panicked pirates.

One of these darted forth to offer their group surrender,
but Firekeeper cared only that Citrine was not among them.
Ignoring the man's pleas, she rushed down, feet slapping on
the smooth polished stone, her ears alert for the little girl's
voice.

At last she heard it as she burst into the open on the
ground-floor landing. Most of the pirates were scattered
about the room. Some stood by the door, watching in horror
as the metal bound wood splintered beneath the repeated
blows. More were gathered in front of the windows, damp-
ing coals, trying to get an angle from which they might stab
or shoot those without.

In passing, Firekeeper hoped that the troops remembered
what they had been told about keeping close to the walls. Then
her attention centered on where a big man stood near the center of the room, Citrine crumpled in a weeping heap at his
side.

Firekeeper howled as the wolf howls to intimidate the prey
and rushed across the room. Her advent was too sudden and
too startling for any of the pirates to react swiftly. Moreover,
at that moment, a panel in the door buckled and snapped beneath the force of the ram.

The general rush in her direction was redirected toward the door. Firekeeper reached the man—he could only be Baron Endbrook, though she had never seen him—and pressed her Fang against his throat. She would have pushed it home that instant, never mind the shower of blood, but he wheezed out a single word.

"Wait!"

She froze, pressing hard enough that blood oozed around the blade.

Baron Endbrook took this as a prompt.

"I have to trade," he hissed, "for my life."

Firekeeper barred her teeth.

"Nothing," she snarled. "No diplomacy!"

"Lady Melina's necklace!" he screamed.

Firekeeper froze. The desperation in his eyes told her that if this was a feint, it was one he thought he could somehow make good. That alone was enough to make her spare him—for the moment. She had been among those who had assisted Sapphire in freeing herself from Lady Melina's enchantment and she knew that without proof Melina no longer had the necklace, similar freedom for Citrine and her siblings might well be impossible.

Howling her frustration, Firekeeper turned the blade in her hand, bringing her balled fist down to punch into the hollow between his upper ribs. Baron Endbrook gasped and sunk to his heels, surrendering.

Firekeeper slashed the rope that bound Citrine to him. She could hear the clumping of booted feet on the stairs and knew that Prince Shad and his men were behind her. The door was cracking underneath the ram.

Bending, she gathered Citrine into her arms and held her close, sheltering the child's weeping form as the battle was joined, raged, and ended almost in a heartbeat.

THUMPING DOWN THE STAIRS a few paces behind the bulk of Prince Shad's more seasoned fighters, Derian could hardly comprehend what he was seeing.

At one end of the huge, round room an iron-bound door was splintering under the blows of the ram. From two side rooms soldiers wearing Hawk Haven's scarlet and silver were rushing into this central chamber. In the center of this chaos stood Firekeeper, Citrine clasped in her arms, Baron Endbrook collapsed at her feet.

Later, Derian would learn that some of the pirates, hoping for amnesty and seeing Baron Endbrook attacked, had flung open the outer doors to admit the enemy. What it seemed at the time was that somehow Firekeeper's solitary presence had been enough to end the battle. This impression was not reduced when Blind Seer, Bold soaring over him, had leapt into the room and come to stand at her side.

Firekeeper, however, kept everything in perspective. She waited for the worst of the chaos to end, for the remaining defenders to be disarmed and herded into a corner under guard, and for Sapphire to turn her way. Then she smiled and held out Citrine.

"Your sister needs you," she had said, her voice ringing out so that all fell silent to listen.

Sapphire, bloodied yet wearing that battle aura that was already making her a legend, crossed and took the girl into her arms. Someone started a spontaneous cheer into which Firekeeper raised her own voice.

It's as if she realizes that Sapphire needs to be flattered else she'll become an enemy. If she does realize this my wolf-woman has learned a great deal.

When that ruckus died down, Firekeeper gestured derisively toward where Baron Endbrook sat on the floor, Blind Seer keeping watch over him with the air of a wolf who very much wants to bite the sheep.

"This one say," Firekeeper continued, "he have something to offer for his life. You is princess. You is decide."

Derian winced, wondering if Firekeeper deliberately lost her grammar under such circumstances.

Sapphire handed Citrine to Shad, who had come to stand beside her, his expression as grim as the wolf's. She glared down at Baron Endbrook and said:

"What is it you have to offer us?"

"Your mother's necklace," Waln gasped. "I have it hidden away. I demanded it and your sister as hostages against Lady Melina's good behavior. She gave them—and seems to have renounced them."

Even with everyone in the room—pirate and soldier alike—straining to catch what was being said there was a murmuring. Most had not realized to what extent Lady Melina was involved in Citrine's misfortune.

There goes keeping that quiet, Derian thought, *but then silence is probably not the best course in this matter. I suspect news of where Lady Melina is will get across the border. She isn't exactly hiding herself away.*

Sapphire blanched at the mention of the necklace. She might have renounced her mother's hold, but that necklace was a powerful talisman nonetheless—and it held the Citrine's eventual freedom in its glittering arc.

"And what do you want for it?" she asked. "Your life?"

"My life," Waln Endbrook said, a trace of his former dignity returning, "and my freedom."

"I cannot offer you a pardon for what you have done here," Sapphire said, "and would not if I could. That is King Tedric's to give, for in allying yourself against our enemies you have forsaken any diplomatic privileges you had been given."

"Enemy?" Waln said haughtily. "Are you saying the Isles are your enemy? Or New Kelvin?"

"No." Sapphire's smile was both polite and cruel. "These smugglers and pirates. These are our enemies."

Waln hung his head, knowing himself beaten. Had Citrine not lived, had the pirates not been present in such numbers to tell of his actual doings, he might have tried to bluster. Derian could see it in his face.

Watching, again, he laughed to himself.

He felt a heaviness on his shoulder as Elation glided in for a landing.

"It's almost over, girl," he said softly. "I can see it."

She nipped the finger he raised to stroke her feathers, but so gently that it felt like the needle bite of a kitten's milk teeth.

Sapphire had been conferring with Shad, Baron Archer, and several other ranking nobles. Citrine had been turned over to Jet, who was trying hard to look both compassionate and heroic. Neither expression was natural to him, so all Jet ended up looking was foolish.

"Baron Endbrook," Sapphire said at last, "as much as I would like to deal with you on my own, the decision is not mine to make. However, come with us to Eagle's Nest and we will put your case before King Tedric. I, certainly, will offer my hope that he accept your trade—I have reasons for wanting that necklace, but I am not the monarch."

Not yet, her stormy blue gaze said, reminding Waln that here was yet another formidable woman with whom he must deal.

Baron Endbrook nodded. "I give my word to go with you, and I promise to keep it," he added bitterly, "better than your mother did hers."

"One thing more," Sapphire said, and something in her bearing made the captive baron wilt where his sense of his own wrongs had been enough to make him at least a shadow of his former self.

"Yes, Princess," Baron Endbrook said meekly.

"Jet Shield, who is Citrine's guardian since Lady Melina is not here, has made a demand of me. It is a demand I feel I cannot refuse even though since my adoption by King Tedric I am technically not of his family. Even so, in a matter of family justice, I feel competent to make a ruling."

Derian thought that Jet looked more confused than anyone else present, but in this circumstance, at least, his habitual posing stood him in good stead. Realizing that Sapphire was using him for some end of her own—and doubtless thinking he could expect favors in return—Jet straightened and tightened his hold on Citrine.

"Speak for me, Princess," Jet said in the vibrant tones that had thrilled many a lady's heart. "I am overcome with emotion."

If Sapphire felt any gratitude for this accomplished acting, she gave no sign of it. Her attention was solely for the now trembling baron.

"I have said I could not rule as to whether you could buy your life . . ." she said, drawing out the moment. "However, you have taken something from Citrine and it is only fair that we take the same from you in return."

A murmur, half-approval, half-shock rippled through the gathered soldiers. Baron Waln gave a low moan, but that was all. He neither begged nor pleaded nor threatened, only turned his head away when Sapphire stretched his hand on a makeshift block.

Nearly as neat as a surgeon, she cut free the two smallest fingers on the baron's left hand.

Absolute silence fell as she completed the mutilation, silence broken by a shrill cry from Citrine.

"He cut off a lock of my hair, too!" the little girl called out with all the anger and frustration she had kept buttoned inside. Then she burst into tears and buried her face in Jet's collar.

Jet looks, Derian thought unhappily, *as helpless as I feel.*

THE GENERAL CELEBRATION that spread as the troops prepared to spend the rest of the night at Smuggler's Light took longer to reach the hospital. The victory had not been without cost—though given what could have happened, the bill was light indeed.

Elise, kneeling beside the last of the wounded to come out of surgery, making him comfortable until he could be moved into the lighthouse, looked up at Doc. He was very worn, his face pale even in the lamplight.

"He'll make it," she told him.

"I know," came the reply, "though I wasn't sure for a while and we'll need to mind infection."

The man—one of Elise's father's archers who had been hit by some of the return fire from the third floor of the lighthouse—grinned weakly and held out a hand.

"Thanks, Doc."

Sir Jared took the offered hand and pressed it.

"My pleasure, I assure you."

A deep voice spoke from the shadows.

"I'll take over now," Baron Archer said. "Prince Shad sent me over with a team to shift the patients into the lighthouse. You two need to get some rest. I understand that neither of you have been assigned a watch tonight."

The baron grinned, his expression only faintly visible in the poor light.

"The senior medical officer seemed to think you have both done enough—especially for volunteers."

Doc and Elise accepted their dismissal and began to walk toward the lighthouse. Now that the fighting had ended, spare lanterns had been set to light the path. It made for an odd effect, Elise thought idly. Feet were lit nearly as brightly as daylight, but anything above waist level was cast into comparative shadow.

Ahead, Smuggler's Light was a swarm of activity. Still charged with the excitement of the night battle, many of the troops were celebrating with some of the ale that had been found in the storeroom.

"I can't handle that noise yet," Doc said with a weary sigh. "Go on ahead, Elise. I'll find myself a rock somewhere and sit until I can bear it."

Elise took his arm, tingling at her own boldness. Earlier that evening, as they had worked side by side preparing for the coming assault, she had finally caught hold of the thought that had teased her earlier.

"Let me walk with you," she said, and he didn't refuse.

Now, Elise realized, might be the only time she had to speak with Doc privately. Come morning, they would move back into the larger camp. Their own private mission completed—though she realized that the matter of the artifacts had yet to be completely settled—Elise suspected that her father would insist on her coming with him first to Eagle's Nest, then home to the family estates.

That his desire would be based in a wish to brag about her and her exploits to Lady Aurella—and to anyone else who came within hearing—might make Baron Archer's insistence tolerable, but it did mean that Elise's brief freedom was ended.

Protected by the darkness, she allowed herself something of a wry smile. Freedom. In some ways she was as trapped as those pirates who were now being held in one of the rooms of their own former fortress, and like them, the walls that held her in were those of her own home.

She could feel Doc's exhaustion in the bone-deep trembling that gently shook the arm she held. He was so tired. Perhaps it was unfair to speak with him now, but it might be more unfair not to do so while they had the chance.

By stumbling against it, they found a rock large enough to hold them both, too large, in fact, for the smugglers to have hauled it away when they were clearing the ground around the lighthouse. It was low to the ground, however, barely higher than a footstool. Given Smuggler's Light's elevation, it would have offered little cover, if any.

"I think," Doc said after a time, "that I remember this rock. It was near where Princess Lovella fell. It must be the same. There weren't many upon the island."

After a long pause he said:

"It is much more pleasant being here with you than it was with the princess."

He couldn't even muster the energy to laugh at his own feeble wit. The effort came out like a dry cough.

Belatedly, Elise remembered the brandy flask stuffed into one of the pockets of the apron she wore over her dress.

"Brandy?" she asked, drawing it out. "I also have cold

tea. It is heavily dosed with honey and in my opinion tastes foul."

"Brandy," Doc replied, accepting the flask and knocking back a fair swallow. "I'd rather sleep tonight."

The night air was crisp, the skies clear and bright.

A few weeks ago, Elise thought, *I would have found this cold. Now, after the Sword of Kelvin Mountains, it seems comfortable.*

Doc seemed to divine the course of her thoughts, for he asked:

"Are you cold?"

"No," she laughed. "I was just thinking how pleasant this is after our trip through the mountains. There's no wind, no sleet, no ice, and no one chasing us. I think I've learned something about comfort."

Doc chuckled. "I suspect it's a lesson like that more than anything else that makes Firekeeper so tolerant of bad weather. She's had to put up with worse conditions and has learned from them."

"I've learned another lesson, too," Elise said, sensing that this was the opening she must take if she was not to lose her courage.

"Oh?"

"I've realized that someday I'll be Baroness Archer," she said. "I knew in my mind all along that was what I was to be, but I don't think I ever knew what it meant. I learned this trip that it's not just a title—it's a responsibility. My father has been trying to show me that for years, but it never sunk in before."

"What changed you?"

"No one thing," Elise said. "Part was watching other people be responsible. Without Derian taking responsibility for all the small details together we would have failed. There were other things: watching you with your patients, Firekeeper with her single-minded sense of purpose. I couldn't help but contrast that to Edlin, who was along for a lark—for an adventure. I realized that for all my words, I was more like him than I wanted to admit."

She sighed and forged on.

"I saw Grateful Peace give up his place in the Dragon Speaker's court for what he thought was right. That made a tremendous impression. So did realizing that Lady Melina had abandoned her responsibilities—as a mother, as a head of house—for her own desires."

She sighed and toyed with the hem of her apron. Beside her, Doc sat listening, so carefully attentive that she could hear his measured breathing. After a moment she went on:

"My father has been trying to show me how much depends on me being a responsible baroness. Until this trip, I never realized what that would mean. There are people out there whose future and whose family's futures will be affected by what I do, by the choices I make. That's terrifying. The only thing that must be more terrifying is being one of those people and wondering if some silly chit of a girl is going to grow up or if she's going to ruin your lives out of nothing more malicious than thoughtlessness."

Jared laughed softly.

"You're awfully hard on yourself, Elise."

She shook her head, though he couldn't see the motion.

"Not at all, Jared. I might have ruined them. Think what would have happened to them if I'd married Jet! Do you think he'll be a good caretaker?"

She answered herself.

"Not unless he learns to think for himself and about what his actions mean for others. Maybe he will now that Lady Melina's gone, but when I was swooning after him I wasn't seeing a person, I was seeing an image with a handsome face—a conquest—the young man all the other girls wanted.

"I," she ended with heat, "was an idiot."

"You," Jared retorted, "were a girl not yet to her majority, under considerable pressure to think herself grown, and . . . well, maybe a bit of an idiot."

They both laughed, then Elise drew in a deep breath.

"I may be out of line, Doc, but I've been under the impression that you're . . . fond of me."

"More than fond," he said, perhaps too drained to maintain polite deception. "I love you."

"I appreciate the compliment," she said, "I really do, more than I can say. I like you. I respect you. I might even love you. That's Elise speaking. The future Baroness Archer—she's someone I hardly know yet. I need to know her better before I let myself make any commitments for the future."

Elise realized that tears were running down her cheeks and sniffed them back, angry with herself.

"I'm not doing this very well," she said. "I . . . What I'm saying is that I can't make any choices, any decisions, not for a long time. Eventually, I need to marry, to marry while I'm young enough to produce healthy children. Given that my mother seems to have the Wellward weakness in that area, I probably should marry before I'm twenty-five, just in case I'm infertile, too."

Sir Jared patted her hand.

"Easy, now. I'm not asking you anything. I never would."

Elise sniffed, then laughed, the tendency to tears backing away.

"That's what Mother said. She said if any asking was done I'd need to do it because you were too much the gentleman."

Jared chuckled. "Wise woman. I appreciate the compliment, though I might have called myself an insecure coward, not a gentleman."

"You're a gentleman," Elise said. "And what I'm trying to say is that if I was just Elise, I'd probably do something impulsive and romantic and propose to you right now and argue out the consequences with my parents later. Since I'm finally facing up to who and what I really am—though I hope the ancestors let me keep my father for a long time yet—I'm not going to do any such thing. I'm not even going to promise. I might marry Edlin. I might marry some fat merchant thirty years older than me with no social connections but lots of money."

"Not that!" her listener said in mock horror.

"All right, not that, but you understand what I mean."

"Yes. You're telling me that I may smile to know that I have my dearest one's affection, and may hope for no more."

He squeezed her hand, then let go.

"That's quite a lot, actually."

Putting a hand on the rock, he pushed himself to his feet.

"Come along, Lady Archer, before the gossips think I have indeed had more."

Elise rose.

"You *are* a gentleman."

"Not at all. I suspect your reputation will be protected in any case by my pallor. I could barely raise myself to my feet, much less . . ."

He trailed off. Elise could almost see his blush.

As it turned out, their reputation was protected by more than Jared's exhaustion. When they were nearing the tower, Wendee Jay stepped to intercept them.

"Baron Archer," she said, "suggested that I have been with you all the time."

"Kind of him," Sir Jared said gravely. "And of you. My thanks."

Elise shook her head in amazement.

"Yes. Thank you."

As a trio, then, they entered the lighthouse and into the glow of the general celebration.

XL

ABOARD *WAVESLICER* THE NEXT MORNING, King Allister of the Pledge learned of the victory at Smuggler's Light. The news was flashed out at dawn by heliograph from the top of the lighthouse. In addition to announcing the victory, it thanked his vessels most warmly for their part in holding the coast secure.

Although the message seemed perfectly in order, the pirates were more than clever enough to try such a feint, so King Allister ordered his ships to hold their stations. He himself insisted on leading a shore party. His guard protested, but Allister waved the protests away.

"No, Perce. I'm going and not by a later boat. We have their message, and from everything we can see by long-glass, the lighthouse is the smugglers' no longer."

Besides, he thought, *this is Shad's first major victory and I'll throw this damn crown in the bay if being king means that I must stop being a proud father.*

As the landing craft was rowed up the smugglers' sea channel, Allister had ample opportunity to study its design. He thought he detected several concealed boathouses along its length and made note to pass this information on to Shad and Sapphire.

Despite his bodyguard's evident apprehensions, they made the lighthouse without being attacked—though Allister thought that their approach was noticed. This was confirmed when, on arriving at the island that held the lighthouse, they were met by a delegation that contained both crown prince and crown princess.

Shad and Sapphire embraced him warmly.

"I'm pleased to see you both looking so well," Allister said as they walked up the slope toward the lighthouse. "Last time I saw you, you both still looked a bit peaked. Obviously marriage agrees with you."

"Or winter campaigning," Sapphire said, but her bluff words didn't quite cover her blush or the smile she gave Shad, "and what a campaign it has been!"

"How is your sister?"

Sapphire looked less happy.

"Alive, but whole neither in mind nor body. The bastard . . ."

She bit back the words with visible effort.

"It's a long tale and not all my own. We're moving our wounded and our prisoners out of the lighthouse and to drier land. We plan to move to less open quarters in Port Haven today. Our first task this morning was to signal your vessels and send a rider to King Tedric. He'll need to know of our success and we want his advice as to what to do with the prisoners."

"Sapphire," Shad said, "has no stomach for executions—nor, I must admit, do I."

"Good," Allister replied. "Anyone who does would make a poor ruler. Unhappily, sometimes a ruler must make that decision."

They discussed the situation of the pirates and smugglers as they crossed to the Smuggler's Light. Some were truly hard cases, others were simply sailors gone bad. A few were slaves escaped from Waterland who had bought their freedom from being resold by the pirates by joining in their ventures.

Only when they had reached one of the long, rectangular rooms that radiated off the base of the tower did Sapphire and Shad begin the long history that had led them to this point. The room had been chosen for its relative warmth—it backed onto the kitchens, which had been turned into infirmaries—and for its promise of privacy. For that reason, Shad and Sapphire held nothing back.

Queen Valora's treachery was reported, and the truth of that report confirmed by a broken man with a bandaged hand who Sapphire introduced with spitting scorn as Baron Waln Endbrook, ambassador from the Isles to the courts of New Kelvin. Allister could hardly believe that this was the same man he vaguely recalled being introduced to at the Hawk Haven wedding.

"I hate him," Sapphire said as he was led away. "He mutilated Citrine's hand—cut off two fingers. He left her here in the keeping of smugglers and pirates, knowing she would be sold into slavery if he didn't return."

"That's one execution," Shad added, "neither of us would have trouble ordering. Unfortunately, he has the means to buy his life."

They told him then of Lady Melina's part in the plot, of the securities she had given so that Baron Endbrook—on behalf of Queen Valora—had been willing to trust her. They brought in Derian Carter to tell the part he and his companions had played, and though the young man was a long time over the telling, King Allister had a feeling that something was being left out.

He didn't interrupt, however, for Shad and Sapphire had shifted to the part of the story that involved them most closely. They told how Sir Jared's message had confirmed their own worries, how they had charged forth to the rescue, how the rescue had been effected.

During this part of the tale, they ceased being self-conscious and became what they were—two young people, barely into their third decade, who had risked much and succeeded where all others had failed. Allister liked them for their enthusiasm and even for their bragging. They hadn't held themselves in the reserve, nor taken undue risks, but had chosen parts where they were needed.

I think, despite all the ways we could have gone wrong, he thought, *that Uncle Tedric and I may have chosen wisely. Ancestors guide them when we are no longer here to do so!*

By the time the long telling had ended, all but the soldiers being left to hold the lighthouse against the pirates' possible return had departed the swamp. Word was sent that the slower contingent carrying the wounded was already under way to Port Haven.

"We can follow more swiftly," Shad said. "Anything more you want to know, Father?"

"One thing," King Allister replied. "Where are those damned artifacts?"

There was an uncomfortable pause; then Derian Carter spoke up.

"Firekeeper asked me to tell you—all three of you," he fumbled as if uncertain of what titles to use.

"Go on, son," Allister said, "no need to stand on formality here in private."

"She said to tell you that she'd like an audience with you,

not here, out in a bit of swamp. It's about the artifacts. She has them, you see."

DERIAN KNEW HE WAS FLUSHING as he delivered his peculiar message, but he couldn't help it. Maybe Firekeeper thought nothing of ordering kings and royal heirs apparent hither and yon—especially out into swamps at the dead of winter—but *he* did!

He could tell that King Allister's bodyguard, standing to that point impassive against the wall near the door, thought something of it too, and it wasn't a kind thought. Visions of recent assassination attempts danced in his eyes and he frowned.

"Really, King Allister," the guard said, stepping forward, "I must protest. Sir Whyte Steel would never permit such a thing and I cannot either."

"Enough, Perce!" King Allister snapped with what Derian thought was truly the royal note to his voice. "I register your protest. However, the lady in question is very odd and very honest. If she wants us in the swamp for whatever reason, I, for one, am going."

Derian was relieved to see that Shad and Sapphire were of one mind with King Allister.

"Firekeeper is odd," Sapphire said to the guard, "but as you may recall from our wedding, she is also firmly on the side of our safety."

Perce had to be content with this, but Derian could see that he felt the responsibility strongly.

"I'm coming with you," he said in a tone that brooked no disagreement.

Derian shrugged. "I don't see how Firekeeper could mind one more. We're quite the little party."

In addition to the three rulers, Firekeeper had requested that all the members of the group that had gone into New Kelvin come as well. This had caused some argument, for Elise and Doc felt that their place was with the wounded. The military surgeons, however, gave them leave.

"We'd been prepared to handle this without your assistance," one reminded Doc. "And if we have a few more casualties because your talent let live some who otherwise would have died, we shoulder that burden gladly enough."

So Firekeeper got her way. She usually did, Derian thought rather sourly.

Blind Seer rather than Firekeeper was waiting to guide them—a thing King Allister's bodyguard viewed with increased distrust and dismay.

Edlin saw Perce's expression and said cheerfully:

"Takes a bit of getting used to, what? Still, he's as trustworthy as I am, just not as sunny to look at."

Shad was quick to introduce Edlin, the only member of the party King Allister had not met before.

"Edlin Norwood, Lord Kestrel, Father."

"Norvin Norwood's son?" King Allister said. "I am pleased to meet you. Your father directed a cavalry troop for me in the past war."

"And left me at home to manage the harvest, what?" Edlin said. "Still, I've bloodied my sword in this little fracas, you know. Not too bad. Grandmother's still holding the reins at home; Father's managing well enough. Maybe I'll do a turn as a scout or a sailor, what?"

Derian saw King Allister blink as Edlin babbled—doubtless thinking, as everyone did, how unlike were father and son. The king's response, however, was the soul of courtesy.

"If you wish to go to sea and your father can spare you, I'll speak with one of my captains."

"I say, that's wonderful!" Edlin beamed. "I think we'll need more Hawk Haven sailors as time goes on, can't keep relying on your good navy, you know."

Derian heard King Allister say softly to his son, "He speaks like a complete idiot, but there's sense in his head."

"He's a first-rate cartographer, too," Shad responded in the tones of one who offered a great compliment.

Firekeeper awaited them on a little island—hardly more than a few stable hummocks gathered around a cluster of rocks. A channel of mud and slimy water separated her from them, and Blind Seer's posture made quite clear that both woman and wolf intended for them to remain apart.

Without preamble, Firekeeper began.

"I have the artifacts," she said, taking the three precious items from a feed sack and spreading them on the largest of the rocks.

Reactions varied. Derian's companions looked at them with distaste mingled with familiar fear. King Allister's bodyguard actually took a step toward his monarch, as if expecting a comb, a ring, and a mirror to suddenly transform into ravening beasts and rip out the man's throat.

Derian admired Perce for his bravery. Clearly, his first impulse had been to shrink back.

Sapphire studied the artifacts as if wondering what there was to them that would make a mother abandon her children, a noblewoman choose exile from her birth land.

King Allister and Shad, however, viewed them with curiosity colored with distaste.

"A ring," Shad said. "We were right on one."

Allister nodded. "And the long one was a mirror, not a mask or fan. I never would have guessed, not in a million years or with all the wisdom of the Silver Whale, that the last was a comb."

"What do they do?" Sapphire asked.

Derian waited for Firekeeper to speak, and when she didn't—when indeed a thinning of her lips made clear that she did not plan to speak—he spoke for her.

"Grateful Peace, the New Kelvinese thaumaturge I told you about, said that the mirror was the only one which had begun to relinquish its secrets. They believed it was a scrying device of some sort. The impressions they were getting were weak and blurred, so I don't know how useful it would be."

Sapphire frowned slightly. "And they had figured out nothing about the others—not even with all their magic?"

"The magic of New Kelvin," Derian said carefully, "may be more in their hopes than in reality. Certainly, we saw little enough evidence of it."

"That is neither here nor there at this point," Sapphire said. Then she sighed. "Though I suspect it will be of great importance in the future. Why have you brought us here, Lady Firekeeper?"

Firekeeper nodded, appreciating the bluntness and apparently not hearing the irritation in the princess's tone.

"These," she said, gesturing to her companions, "are here to tell you that these are indeed the things we took from New Kelvin. I ask Baron Endbrook if ever he see them, but he say he only see boxes so he cannot say for sure if these are what he brought in from his queen. Grateful Peace say, though, that these are the things he see opened and these are the things he see worked on. I have no reason to think he lie."

King Allister said, "Very well, we have confirmed that these are—to the best of anyone's knowledge—the very items that Queen Valora removed from my treasury, that were taken into New Kelvin, and were retrieved from there by you and your companions. What next?"

In answer, Firekeeper removed a steel-headed hammer from where she had hidden it behind a stone. Without comment, she brought it down, this time with all her considerable strength onto the face of the mirror. The polished silver bent and buckled, the ivory frame popped from the edge and lay in pieces.

Next she smashed down on the comb. It might have indeed been carved from stone rather than wood, but its delicacy could not resist the violent force turned against it. Where the hammer hit, the polished stone turned to powder. The remaining pieces scattered across the rock, one flying so far that it dropped into the mud.

"What," Sapphire screamed, "are you doing!"

"Am killing these," Firekeeper said, and her hand, holding the hammer poised above the ring where it rested in a hollow on the rock, trembled. "My people fear them. Your people fear them. I think such should die no matter what wonders . . ."

And to Derian's amazement the wolf-woman's voice broke as from a great unspoken grief.

"No matter what wonders," she repeated, faltering, "they can work."

Elation shrieked once, loudly, as she might before stooping upon her prey. Firekeeper stared at the bird, wild-eyed, then nodded.

Again, the wolf-woman brought the hammer down, this time with such force that the moonstone vanished in a puff of blue-white dust and the gold that held it was flattened, becoming almost flush with the stone she used for her anvil.

The stone itself cracked beneath the force of that final, angry blow, and Firekeeper leapt to her feet. Her trousers were muddy from where she had knelt, but she found purchase enough on the soft dirt to shove the rock so that it slid beneath the water and began to sink into the muddy bottom. Then she flung the remnants of the mirror and comb out into the swamp, where they plopped and sank beneath the ooze.

Firekeeper stared at them.

"That is all," she said. "Go."

Edlin opened his mouth.

"Go!" she repeated with a growl that Blind Seer echoed.

Derian spoke, feeling his words were incomplete for the occasion.

"I think Firekeeper needs to be alone. She'll join us when she's ready, either here or in the North Woods."

He saw the wolf-woman nod her shaven head, a gesture so full of grief and exhaustion that he longed to comfort her. Blind Seer wuffed softly and wagged his great bush of a tail once.

"You watch her, fellow," Derian said, brushing his hand along the wolf's spine.

None of the others uttered so much as a word of farewell, but turned and filed back toward solid ground. As Derian followed, he felt obscurely comforted. Blind Seer would watch over Firekeeper—that he could trust when there was nothing else in all the world to be trusted.

❧

WITH DULL EYES Firekeeper watched her friends depart. She knew their plans, had heard them discussed earlier that day. Elise was going back with her father; the rest would take a few days to see Port Haven, then ride back to the North Woods. There had been much enthusiastic chatter regarding staying in proper inns and waiting out snowstorms where there would be hot cider and music.

She had no heart for such things—indeed, inns with their crowds and smoke and noise held little enchantment for her at the best of times. These were not the best of times. Her dreams had vanished beneath the hammer's head, vanished when Elation had shrieked:

"The woman lies!"

The peregrine's cry had reminded Firekeeper in whose words she was placing such hope.

The mirror and comb had been destroyed by muscle strength alone—much as Princess Sapphire had destroyed the gem through which her mother had controlled her. The ring, however, had been broken by the sheer force of the wolf-woman's anger—not at Lady Melina, but at herself for being so nearly seduced by the woman's lying words.

Yet had they been a lie? Now she would never know.

Elation squawked at her.

"Do you truly go to the North Woods or do you go west to tell the Royal Beasts what you have done?"

"I won't go west," Firekeeper said. "I think I will go to the North Woods, though not at once."

"Why won't you go west?" Bold asked. "The Beasts will honor you for your courage and tenacity. I myself will sing your praises."

Firekeeper felt a smile trying to surface at the thought of a singing crow, but the smile died without reaching her lips.

"I have done what they asked," she said in explanation, "but maybe not in the manner of their asking. They said that I was to bring the artifacts to them and they would secure them against misuse. Instead I myself have secured them against misuse by destroying them. Right now I don't have the patience to debate such fine points with those who still see me as an odd pup with fingers."

Elation laughed. "Then I will carry the news to them. Bold and I will spread your news to the ears that wish to hear it. Then I will join you in the North Woods. There is good hunting there and I wish to see what Derian does to improve Earl Kestrel's stables."

"Tell us your message," Bold agreed. "I will sing to all, not just to the Mothers of my kind."

"Tell them," Firekeeper said slowly. "Tell them that I have kept my promise. The things are found and though I will not bring them back, they are broken beyond use—they will hurt no one."

To her eye, the shattered ruins of the moonstone ring were still visible, though the rock that held them was being swallowed by the swamp. The beast's features were battered and dented, but she could see them, remember how she had hoped to make them her own.

Looking at the ruined ring, Firekeeper was not so certain that no one had been hurt. Certainly, her own heart was breaking.

Blind Seer came up to her as she finished speaking, nudging her with his head, forcing her to look him in those unwolfish eyes, blue as a mountain pool but holding sight.

Seeing the still livid scar that bisected the wolf's eyelid, Firekeeper was forced to admit that she was not the only one who had accepted loss to fulfill this promise. Blind Seer could have been truly blinded—or killed.

The great grey wolf nudged her again.

"Catch me," he suggested, beginning to run, leaping from hummock to hummock.

Firekeeper reached for his tail as it trailed behind him. It slipped through her fingers, but in the reaching she did indeed begin to run.

Blood flowed through her veins, tracing the crack in her broken heart, making it whole, though leaving behind a scar.

GLOSSARY OF CHARACTERS[1]

Agneta Norwood: (H.H.) daughter of Norvin Norwood and Luella Stanbrook; sister of Edlin, Tait, and Lillis Norwood; adopted sister of Blysse Norwood (Firekeeper).

Aksel Trueheart: (Lord, H.H.) scholar of Hawk Haven; spouse of Zorana Archer; father of Purcel, Nydia, Deste, and Kenre Trueheart[2]

Alben Eagle: (H.H.) son of Princess Marras and Lorimer Stanbrook. In keeping with principles of Zorana I, he was given no title, as he died in infancy.

Alin Brave: (H.H.) husband of Grace Trueheart; father of Baxter Trueheart.

Allister I: (King, H.H.), called King Allister of the Pledge, sometimes the Pledge Child; formerly Allister Seagleam. Son of Tavis Seagleam (B.B.) and Caryl Eagle (H.H.); spouse of Pearl Oyster; father of Shad, Tavis, Anemone, and Minnow.

Alt Rosen: (Opulence, Waterland): ambassador to Bright Bay.

Amery Pelican: (King, B.B.) Spouse of Gustin II; father of Basil, Seastar, and Tavis Seagleam. Deceased.

Anemone: (Princess, B.B.) formerly Anemone Oyster. Daughter of Allister I and Pearl Oyster; sister of Shad and Tavis; twin of Minnow.

Apheros: (Dragon Speaker, N.K.) long-time elected official of New Kelvin.

Aurella Wellward: (Lady, H.H.) confidant of Queen Elexa; spouse of Ivon Archer; mother of Elise Archer.

---

[1]Characters are detailed under first name or best-known name. The initials B.B. (Bright Bay), H.H. (Hawk Haven), or N.K. (New Kelvin) in parentheses following a character's name indicate nationality. Titles are indicated in parentheses.

[2]Hawk Haven and Bright Bay noble houses both follow a naming system where the children take the surname of the higher ranking parent, with the exception that only the immediate royal family bear the name of that house. If the parents are of the same rank, then rank is designated from the birth house, greater over lesser, lesser by seniority. The Great Houses are ranked in the following order: Eagle, Shield, Wellward, Trueheart, Redbriar, Stanbrook, Norwood.

Barden Eagle: (Prince, H.H.) third son of Tedric I and Elexa Wellward. Disowned. Spouse of Eirene Norwood; father of Blysse Eagle. Presumed deceased.

Basil Seagleam: see Gustin III.

Baxter Trueheart: (Earl, H.H.) infant son of Grace Trueheart and Alin Brave. Technically not a title holder until he has survived his first two years.

Bee Biter: Royal Kestrel; guide and messenger.

Bevan Seal: see Calico.

Blind Seer: Royal Wolf; companion to Firekeeper.

Blysse Eagle: (Lady, H.H.) daughter of Prince Barden and Eirene Norwood.

Blysse Kestrel: see Firekeeper.

Bold: Royal Crow; eastern agent; sometime companion to Firekeeper.

Brina Dolphin: (Lady or Queen, B.B.) first spouse of Gustin III, divorced as barren.

Brock Carter: (H.H.) son of Colby and Vernita Carter; brother of Derian and Damita Carter.

Calico: (B.B.) proper name, Bevan Seal. Confidential secretary to Allister I. Member of a cadet branch of House Seal.

Caryl Eagle: (Princess, H.H.) daughter of King Chalmer I; married to Prince Tavis Seagleam; mother of Allister Seagleam. Deceased.

Ceece Dolphin: (Lady, B.B.) sister to current Duke Dolphin.

Chalmer I: (King, H.H.) born Chalmer Elkwood; son of Queen Zorana the Great; spouse of Rose Rosewood; father of Marras; Tedric, Gadman, and Rosene Eagle. Deceased.

Chalmer Eagle: (Crown Prince, H.H.) son of Tedric Eagle and Elexa Wellward. Deceased.

Chutia: (N.K.) Illuminator. Wife of Grateful Peace. Deceased.

Citrine Shield: (H.H.) daughter of Melina Shield and Rolfston Redrbriar; sister of Sapphire, Jet, Opal, and Ruby Shield.

Colby Carter: (H.H.) livery stable owner and carter; spouse of Vernita Carter; father of Derian, Damita, and Brock Carter.

Columi: (N.K.) retired Prime of the Sodality of Lapidaries.

Culver Pelican: (Lord, H.H.): son of Seastar Seagleam; brother of Dillon Pelican. Merchant ship captain.

Damita Carter: (H.H.) daughter of Colby and Vernita Carter; sister of Derian and Brock Carter.

Derian Carter: (H.H.) also called Derian Counselor; assistant to Norvin Norwood; son of Colby and Vernita Carter; brother of Damita and Brock Carter.

Deste Trueheart: (H.H.) daughter of Aksel Trueheart and Zorana Archer; sister of Purcel, Nydia, and Kenre Trueheart.

Dia Trueheart: see Nydia Trueheart.

Dillon Pelican: (Lord, B.B.) son of Seastar Seagleam; brother of Culver Pelican.

Dirkin Eastbranch: (knight, H.H.) King Tedric's personal bodyguard.

Donal Hunter: (H.H.) member of Barden Eagle's expedition; spouse of Sarena; father of Tamara. Deceased.

Edlin Norwood: (Lord, H.H.) son of Norvin Norwood and Luella Kite; brother of Tait, Lillis, Agneta and Blysse Norwood.

Eirene Norwood: (Lady, H.H.) spouse of Barden Eagle; mother of Blysse Eagle; sister of Norvin Norwood. Presumed deceased.

Elation: Royal Falcon, companion to Firekeeper.

Elexa Wellward: (Queen, H.H.) spouse of Tedric I; mother of Chalmer, Lovella, and Barden.

Elise Archer: (Lady, H.H.) daughter of Ivon Archer and Aurella Wellward; heir to Archer Grant.

Evaglayn: (N.K.) senior apprentice in the Beast Lore sodality.

Evie Cook: (H.H.) servant in the Carter household.

Faelene Lobster: (Duchess, B.B.) new head of House Lobster; sister of Marek, Duke of Half-Moon Island; aunt of King Harwill.

Farand Briarcott: (Lady, H.H.) assistant to Tedric I, former military commander.

Fess Bones: a pirate with some medical skills.

Firekeeper: (Lady, H.H.) feral child raised by wolves, adopted by Norvin Norwood and given the name Blysse Norwood.

Fleet Herald: a pirate messenger.

Fox Driver: (H.H.) given name, Orin. Skilled driver in the employ of Waln Endbrook.

Gadman Eagle: (Grand Duke, H.H.) fourth child of King Chalmer and Queen Rose; brother to Marras, Tedric, Rosene; spouse of Riki Redbriar; father of Rolfston and Nydia Redbriar.

Gayl Minter: see Gayl Seagleam.

Gayl Seagleam: (Queen, B.B.) spouse of Gustin I; first queen of Bright Bay; mother of Gustin, Merry (later Gustin II), and Lyra. Note: Gayl was the only queen to assume the name "Seagleam." Later tradition paralleled that of Hawk Haven, where the name of the birth house was retained even after marriage to the monarch. Deceased.

Glynn: (H.H.) a soldier.

Grace Trueheart: (Duchess Merlin, H.H.) military commander; spouse of Alin Brave; mother of Baxter Trueheart.

Grateful Peace: (Dragon's Eye, N.K.) also, Trausholo. Illuminator; Prime of New Kelvin; member of the Dragon's Three. A very influential person. Husband to Chutia.

Gustin I: (King, B.B.) born Gustin Sailor, assumed the name Seagleam upon his coronation; first monarch of Bright Bay; spouse of Gayl Minter, later Gayl Seagleam; father of Gustin, Merry, and Lyra Seagleam. Deceased.

Gustin II: (Queen, B.B.) born Merry Seagleam, assumed the name Gustin upon her coronation; second monarch of Bright Bay; spouse of Amery Pelican; mother of Basil, Seastar, and Tavis Seagleam. Deceased.

Gustin III: (King, B.B.) born Basil Seagleam, assumed the name Gustin upon his coronation; third monarch

of Bright Bay; spouse of Brina Dolphin, later of Viona Seal; father of Valora Seagleam. Deceased.

Gustin IV: (Queen, B.B.) see Valora I.

Gustin Sailor: see Gustin I.

Harwill Lobster: (King, the Isles) spouse of Valora I; during her reign as Gustin IV, also king of Bright Bay. Son of Marek.

Hasamemorri: (N.K.) a landlady.

Hazel Healer: (H.H.) apothecary, herbalist, perfumer resident in the town of Hope.

Heather Baker: (H.H.) baker in Eagle's Nest; former sweetheart of Derian Carter.

Holly Gardener: (H.H.) former Head Gardener for Eagle's Nest Castle, possessor of the Green Thumb, a talent for horticulture. Mother of Timin and Sarena Gardener.

Honey Endbrook: (Isles) mother of Waln Endbrook.

Hya Grimsel: (General, Stonehold) commander of Stonehold troops.

Indatius: (N.K.) young member of the Sodality of Artificers.

Ivon Archer: (Baron, H.H.) master of the Archer Grant; son of Purcel Ar-

cher and Rosene Eagle; brother of
Zorana Archer; spouse of Aurella
Wellward; father of Elise Archer.

Ivory Pelican: (Lord, B.B.) Keeper
of the Keys, an honored post in
Bright Bay.

Jared Surcliffe: (knight, H.H.) knight
of the Order of the White Eagle; possessor of the healing talent; distant
cousin of Norvin Norwood who
serves as his patron. Widower, no
children.

Jem: (B.B.) deserter from Bright
Bay's army.

Jet Shield: (H.H.) son of Melina
Shield and Rolfston Redbriar;
brother of Sapphire, Opal, Ruby, and
Citrine shield. Heir apparent to his
parents' properties upon the adoption
of his sister Sapphire by Tedric I.

Joy Spinner: (H.H.) scout in the service of Earle Kite. Deceased.

Kalvinia: (Prime, N.K.) thaumaturge,
Sodality of Sericulturists.

Keen: (H.H.) servant to Newell
Shield.

Kenre Trueheart: (H.H.) son of Zorana Archer and Aksel Trueheart;
brother of Purcel, Nydia, and Deste
Trueheart.

Kistlio: (N.K.) clerk in Thendulla
Lypella. Nephew of Grateful Peace.

Lillis Norwood: (H.H.) daughter of
Norvin Norwood and Luella Stanbrook; sister of Edlin, Tait, Agneta
and Blysse Norwood.

Longsight Scrounger: pirate, leader
of those at Smuggler's Light.

Lorimer Stanbrook: (Lord, H.H.)
spouse of Marras Eagle; father of
Marigolde and Alben Eagle. Deceased.

Lovella Eagle: (Crown Princess,
H.H.) military commander; daughter
of Tedric Eagle and Elexa Wellward;
spouse of Newell Shield. Deceased.

Lucky Shortleg: a pirate.

Luella Stanbrook: (Lady, H.H.)
spouse of Norvin Norwood; mother
of Edlin, Tait, Lillis, and Agneta
Norwood.

Marek: (Duke, Half-Moon Island)
formerly Duke Lobster of Bright Bay
but chose to follow the fate of his
son, Harwill. Brother of Faelene, the
current Duchess Lobster.

Marigolde Eagle: (H.H.) daughter of
Marras Eagle and Lorimer Stanbrook. In keeping with principles of
Zorana I, given no title as died in infancy.

Marras Eagle: (Crown Princess,
H.H.) daughter of King Chalmer and
Queen Rose; spouse of Lorimer

Stanbrook; mother of Marigolde and Alben Eagle. Deceased.

Melina Shield: (Lady, H.H.) reputed sorceress; spouse of Rolfston Redbriar; mother of Sapphire, Jet, Opal, Ruby, and Citrine Shield.

Merri Jay: (H.H.) daughter of Wendee Jay.

Merry Seagleam: see Gustin II.

Minnow: (Princess, B.B.) formerly Minnow Oyster. Daughter of Allister I and Pearl Oyster; sister of Shad and Tavis; twin of Anemone.

Nanny: (H.H.) attendant to Melina Shield.

Nelm: (N.K.) member of the Sodality of Herbalists.

Newell Shield: (Prince, H.H.) commander of marines; spouse of Lovella Eagle; brother of Melina Shield. Deceased.

Ninette Farmer: (H.H.) relative of Ivon Archer; attendant of Elise Archer.

Norvin Norwood: (Earl Kestrel, H.H.) heir to Kestrel Grant; brother of Eirene Norwood; spouse of Luella Stanbrook; father of Edlin, Tait, Lillis, Agneta, and Blysse (adopted).

Nydia Trueheart: (H.H.) often called Dia; daughter of Aksel Trueheart and Zorana Archer; sister of Purcel, Deste, and Kenre Trueheart.

Oculios: (N.K.) apothecary; member of the Sodality of Alchemists.

One Male: formerly Rip; ruling male wolf of Firekeeper and Blind Seer's pack.

One Female: formerly Shining Coat; ruling female wolf of Firekeeper and Blind Seer's pack.

Opal Shield: (H.H.) daughter of Melina Shield and Rolfston Redbriar; sister of Sapphire, Jet, Ruby, and Citrine shield.

Oralia: (Isles) wife of Waln Endbrook.

Ox: (H.H.) born Malvin Hogge; bodyguard to Norvin Norwood; renowned for his strength and good temper.

Pearl Oyster: (Queen, B.B.) spouse of Allister I; mother of Shad, Tavis, Anemone, and Minnow.

Perce Potterford: (B.B.) guard to Allister I.

Perr: (H.H.) body servant to Ivon Archer.

Posa: (Prime, N.K.) member of the Sodality of Illuminators.

Purcel Trueheart: (H.H.) lieutenant Hawk Haven army; son of Aksel

Trueheart and Zorana Archer; brother of Nydia, Deste, and Kenre Trueheart. Deceased.

Purcel Archer: (Baron Archer, H.H.) first Baron Archer, born Purcel Farmer, elevated to the title for his prowess in battle; spouse of Rosene Eagle; father of Ivon and Zorana Archer. Deceased.

Race Forester: (H.H.) scout under the patronage of Norvin Norwood; regarded by many as one of the best in his calling.

Rafalias: (N.K.) member of the Sodality of Lapidaries.

Red Stripe: also called Cime; a pirate.

Reed Oyster: (Duke, B.B.) father of Queen Pearl. Among the strongest supporters of Allister I.

Riki Redbriar: (Lady, H.H.) spouse of Gadman Eagle; mother of Rolfston and Nydia Redbriar. Deceased.

Rolfston Redbriar: (Lord, H.H.) son of Gadman Eagle and Riki Redbriar; spouse of Melina Shield; father of Sapphire, Jet, Opal, Ruby, and Citrine Shield. Deceased.

Rook: (H.H.) servant to Newell Shield.

Rory Seal: (Lord, B.B.) holds the title Royal Physician.

Rose Rosewood: (Queen, H.H.) common-born wife of Chalmer I; his marriage to her was the reason Hawk Haven Great Houses received what Queen Zorana the Great would doubtless have seen as unnecessary and frivolous titles. Deceased.

Rosene: (Grand Duchess, H.H.) fifth child of King Chalmer and Queen Rose; spouse of Purcel Archer; mother of Ivon and Zorana Archer.

Ruby Shield: (H.H.) daughter of Melina Shield and Rolfston Redbriar; sister of Sapphire, Jet, Opal, and Citrine Shield.

Saedee Norwood: (Duchess Kestrel, H.H.) mother of Norvin and Eirene Norwood.

Sapphire: (Crown Princess, H.H.) adopted daughter of Tedric I; birth daughter of Melina Shield and Rolfston Redbriar; sister of Jet, Opal, Ruby, and Citrine Shield; spouse of Shad.

Sarena Gardener: (H.H.) member of Prince Barden's expedition; spouse of Donal Hunter; mother of Tamara. Deceased.

Seastar Seagleam: (Grand Duchess, B.B.) sister of Gustin III; mother of Culver and Dillon Pelican.

Shad: (Crown Prince, B.B.) son of Allister I and Pearl Oyster; brother of

Tavis, Anemone, and Minnow spouse of Sapphire.

Steady Runner: a Royal Elk.

Steward Silver: (H.H.) long-time steward of Eagle's Nest Castle. Her birth-name and origin have been forgotten as no-one, not even Silver herself, thinks of herself as anything but the steward.

Tait Norwood: (H.H.) son of Norvin Norwood and Luella Stanbrook; brother of Edlin, Lillis, Agneta and Blysse Norwood.

Tallus: (Prime, N.K.) member of the Sodality of Alchemists.

Tavis Oyster: (Prince, B.B.) son of Allister I and Pearl Oyster; brother of Shad, Anemone, and Minnow.

Tavis Seagleam: (Prince, B.B.) third child of Gustin II and Amery Pelican; spouse of Caryl Eagle; father of Allister Seagleam.

Tedric I: (King, H.H.) third king of Hawk Haven; son of King Chalmer and Queen Rose; spouse of Elexa Wellward; father of Chalmer, Lovella, and Barden; adopted father of Sapphire.

Tench: (Lord, B.B.) born Tench Clark; right-hand to Queen Gustin IV; knighted for his services; later made Lord of the Pen. Deceased.

Thyme: (H.H.) a scout in the service of Hawk Haven.

Timin Gardener: (H.H.) Head Gardener for Eagle's Nest Castle, possessor of the Green Thumb, a talent for horticulture; son of Holly Gardener; brother of Sarena; father of Dan and Robyn.

Tipi: (N.K.) slave, born in Stonehold.

Toad: (H.H.) pensioner of the Carter family.

Tris Stone: a pirate.

Tymia: (N.K.) a guard.

Valet: (H.H.) eponymous servant of Norvin Norwood; known for his fidelity and surprising wealth of useful skills.

Valora I: (Queen, the Isles) born Valora Seagleam, assumed the name Gustin upon her coronation as fourth monarch of Bright Bay. Resigned her position to Allister I and became queen of the Isles. Spouse of Harwill Lobster.

Valora Seagleam: see Valora I.

Vernita Carter: (H.H.) born Vernita Painter. An acknowledged beauty of her day, Vernita became associated with the business she and her husband, Colby, transformed from a simple carting business to a group of associated livery stables and carting services; spouse of Colby Carter; mother of Derian, Damita, and Brock Carter.

Viona Seal: (Queen, B.B.) second wife of King Gustin III; mother of Valora, later Gustin IV.

Wain Cutter: (H.H.) skilled lapidary and gem cutter working out of the town of Hope.

Waln Endbrook: (Baron, the Isles) also, Walnut Endbrook. A prosperous merchant, Waln found rapid promotion in the service of Valora I. Spouse of Oralia; with her, father of two daughters and a son.

Wendee Jay: (H.H.) retainer in service of Duchess Kestrel. Lady's maid to Firekeeper. Divorced. Mother of two daughters.

Wheeler: (H.H.) scout captain.

Whiner: a wolf of Blind Seer and Firekeeper's pack.

Whyte Steel: (knight, B.B.) captain of the guard for Allister I.

Yaree Yuci: (General, Stonehold) commander of Stonehold troops.

Zahlia: (N.K.) member of the Sodality of Smiths. Specialist in silver.

Zorana I: (Queen, H.H.) also called Zorana the Great, born Zorana Shield. First monarch of Hawk Haven; responsible for a reduction of titles—so associated with this program that over emphasis of titles is considered "unzoranic." Spouse of Clive Elkwood; mother of Chalmer I.

Zorana Archer: (Lady, H.H.) daughter of Rosene Eagle and Purcel Archer; sister of Ivon Archer; spouse of Aksel Trueheart; mother of Purcel, Nydia, Deste, and Kenre Trueheart.

Look for

THE

DRAGON

OF

DESPAIR

by Jane Lindskold

available in hardcover August 2003
from Tor Books

BURNING A TRAIL through the sky, the comet was brighter than any single star, almost brighter than the moon. Certainly, it appeared more purposeful.

There was no doubt about the purposefulness of the young woman who sat watching the comet from atop one of the smooth stone outcroppings that erupted here and there through the forest floor like whales frozen in the act of breaching. Her arms were wrapped around her bent knees so that she made a single form, almost like a rock herself, but unlike the rocks her gaze was fixed on the light in the sky.

To Firekeeper, who knew the stars through all their shifting annual panorama as a city-born woman would know the streets around her own house, the comet was a source of unending fascination and not a little uneasiness. She didn't like either feeling one bit.

Night after night, she found herself drawn to some dark, quiet place where she could watch the comet, as if by watching it she could keep the heavens from doing something else unpredictable. Although the spring nights were yet chilly and damp here in the Norwood Grant at the northwestern edge of the Kingdom of Hawk Haven, Firekeeper didn't find them uncomfortable. She'd lived unprotected through much harsher weather.

Blind Seer, her closest friend, often sat with Firekeeper on these vigils, though the wolf didn't really understand the woman's fascination.

"A light in the sky," Blind Seer grumbled on this night as on so many others. *"That's all it is. Come and run with me. We could terrify the deer."*

Firekeeper uncoiled herself sufficiently to swat the wolf lightly across the bridge of his long nose.

"*Let them raise their fawns in peace*," she said, "*so there will be food for the year to come. Surely you haven't fallen so low that you must hunt sucklings and their mothers.*"

"*I was more thinking of the young bucks, spring mad in the pride of their new antlers. They need humbling.*"

Her eyes never leaving the fat white comet with its glowing tail, Firekeeper answered. "*And you a Royal Wolf, greatest of the great, are setting yourself the task of improving Cousin-kind? Our parents would be ashamed.*"

Their argument was interrupted by the sound of feet steadily advancing along the forest trail. Neither wolf nor woman moved, for the tread was as familiar to them as the tall red-haired youth who appeared around a bend in the trail a moment later.

"I thought I'd find you out here," Derian Carter said, greeting them with a casual wave of the hand that was not occupied balancing a tin-screened candle lantern. "Watching the comet again? I promise you, it won't go anywhere."

"Elation tell you where I am," Firekeeper replied, knowing this must be so. She had many places from which she watched the comet. Animal wariness kept her from frequenting any one place too often. Elation, however, could have easily found her.

The peregrine falcon had taken a liking to Derian. Although Elation could not talk to Derian as she could to Firekeeper, she had found ways of making him understand simple things. Derian, in turn, simplified matters greatly by accepting, as most of Firekeeper's human acquaintances still did not, that the bird was as intelligent as most humans.

"Elation might have," Derian admitted before changing the subject. "There's news from across the White Water River. A single courier made the crossing late this afternoon. He came to Duchess Kestrel, figuring she'd pay well to know the last several months' gossip from New Kelvin."

Firekeeper was interested in spite of her initial pique at having her vigil interrupted.

"From New Kelvin?"

The neighboring country was separated from Hawk Haven by a river broad and rocky enough to be difficult to cross even in the best weather. Once snowmelt had swelled the river, the two nations had been effectively cut off for better than a moonspan. Only lately had the river begun to ebb, though weeks would pass before normal commerce resumed.

Derian nodded.

"And from how both the duchess and the earl remained closeted with the courier through dinner, the courier had news worth the tokens the duchess has ordered drawn from the Norwood Grant treasury."

"And what did the courier say?" Firekeeper prompted, almost, but not quite, forgetting the comet.

"I don't know," Derian replied, "but we have been requested to meet with Duchess Kestrel and her son as soon as possible. Can you leave your comet unwatched?"

Firekeeper gave him a slight smile, though she knew Derian could not see it in the darkness.

"I can."

A GROUP OF SEVEN were to meet in Duchess Kestrel's study—eight, if you counted Blind Seer, which Firekeeper most certainly did. As she waited for the rest to assemble and stop their idle chatter, the wolf-woman studied her surroundings, automatically noting exits and defensible corners.

This was a room Firekeeper had visited only once before. Unlike the nearby chamber claimed by her son for a similar purpose, the duchess's study was light and uncluttered, its furniture crafted from pale woods rubbed to a high polish and scented with beeswax. The stone-flagged floors were covered in jewel-toned New Kelvinese carpets that seemed to glow in the lamplight. The broad, south-facing windows were curtained in heavy brocade woven in shades of soft golden brown and beige.

In her younger days, Saedee Norwood, Duchess Kestrel, had been a warrior who had won her spurs in a particularly nasty border skirmish with Bright Bay. There was a statue in the garden commemorating those deeds. It depicted a slim-hipped young woman brandishing a sword, an arrogant tilt tó her proud head.

But those battles had been long ago. The only trace remaining of that woman was the selfsame sword hanging on the wall behind the desk where the duchess daily dealt with the business of running the large land grant that she had inherited from her father. Bearing children—two of whom had survived to adulthood—had spread Saedee Norwood's once slim form. Bearing the responsibilities of her position had graven lines in her face.

Yet, Firekeeper thought as she watched the duchess greet those she had summoned, perhaps not all traces of that young warrior had vanished. The arrogant lift of the duchess's head was much the same, though tempered with a restraint that might have been alien to her younger self.

There was a similar arrogance in the bearing of the duchess's son and heir, Norvin. Earl Kestrel was a small man—indeed, his mother was taller—and maybe some of his apparent arrogance came from refusing to be seen as weak in a world where strength and size were usually equated.

Firekeeper knew the earl fairly well. It had been he who had led the expedition she had accompanied out of the western wilderness. Initially, she had thought Norvin Norwood taken up with nothing but his own advancement. Later, she had come to realize that—interested as Norvin was in promoting his own good and that of his family—he was also a commander whose troops respected him, a master whose vassals found him fair, and a parent who, though dictatorial at times, strove not to smother his children.

In the eyes of the human world, Firekeeper was one of those children—adopted by the earl soon after his return from the west. Firekeeper did not think of the earl as her father—that place in her heart belonged to the wolves who had raised her—nor did she particularly think of the earl's four children as her siblings. One of these, however, Norvin Norwood's eldest son and heir, had earned the wolf-woman's mingled affection and exasperation.

Edlin Norwood entered the room even as Firekeeper thought of him, his breezy friendliness a decided contrast to his father's and grandmother's studied restraint. Nor did he particularly resemble them, lacking their prominent hawk-like nose. Edlin did share his father's dark hair—though the earl's mixed silver with the jetty black—and the earl's pale grey eyes. Still, no one watching Edlin as he bobbed a quick bow to his grandmother and then collapsed bonelessly into a comfortable chair would have taken him for his father's son.

But Firekeeper respected Edlin. He had been with her and Derian in New Kelvin early in the winter just past and had proven that there was more to him than met casual inspection. However, if Edlin's deeds in New Kelvin had earned Firekeeper's respect, they did nothing to reduce her frustration with him. Soon after Firekeeper had arrived at the Norwood Grant the previous autumn, Edlin had taken a very unbrotherly fancy to her. He'd even—so Firekeeper had heard rumored—told his father he wished to marry her.

The earl had refused without even consulting Firekeeper—though his decision proved much to Firekeeper's relief—but his father's refusal hadn't ended the matter for Edlin. Often he would watch Firekeeper, sometimes covertly, more often forgetting himself and gaping with slightly open mouthed admiration.

Why Edlin fancied her Firekeeper hadn't the least idea. In a society where women were admired for social grace and elegance—even those who, like Saedee Norwood or Crown Princess Sapphire, had won honor on the battlefield—Firekeeper possessed neither. She donned long gowns, jewels, and other such finery only under duress. Rather than displaying herself to her best advantage on some couch or embroidered chair, she preferred sitting as she was now, on the floor, her arm flung around Blind Seer, her short hair tousled from wind and weather.

Fortunately for Firekeeper, Saedee Norwood had forbidden anyone—even her son—to force Firekeeper to change her ways too drastically. As long as Firekeeper would gown when necessary, used proper utensils when dining at table, and remembered not to bolt her food, the duchess claimed herself content. Firekeeper, in turn, sought to please the duchess, preferring to offer evidence of her willingness to learn human ways on her own, rather than having them forced upon her.

Such attempts to please were not alien to Firekeeper's nature. Wolves always submit before those who have power over them. To them this is an expression of respect, not a humiliation. Saedee Norwood did not ask for belly-pissing cringing, only the human equivalent of a jaw-licking tail wag.

Moreover, like her son, Saedee Norwood had proven herself worthy of Firekeeper's respect. The wolf-woman had observed how the duchess enforced the right of individual decision not only for Firekeeper, but for other members of her household as well. At a time when a hundred years of fairly stable government was bequeathing social ritual and restraint as its gift to the younger generation, Saedee was old enough to remember when this had not been so—and wise enough to sacrifice the benefits she could have garnered from a calcifying social order for the greater benefits gained from a vital and active family.

Thus Saedee had made her son, Norvin, her partner in running the Norwood Grant at a time when several of her contemporaries were struggling to maintain a firm hold over their growing households. Equally, she used her authority over her son to keep him from rebuking Edlin too severely for his own idiosyncratic style.

But then, as Firekeeper had learned from Wendee Jay, the Kestrel retainer who served as the wolf-woman's personal attendant, Saedee Norwood herself was an unconventional woman. No one knew who had been the father of her children—Norvin, Eirene, and several others who had not survived beyond infancy. Saedee had not only kept this information to herself—she had also refused to marry, even when offered advantageous alliances for her house.

Firekeeper stretched, wondering just a little about the pedigree of this human family with whom she found herself allied.

Edlin's arrival brought the gathering's number to six. Derian had arrived with Firekeeper and Blind Seer, and both duchess and earl had already been present. Now a slight rap on the door announced the last arrival.

Grateful Peace was a slender and elegant man, almost effete to Firekeeper's way of seeing things. His hairline had receded so far back that he was nearly bald. What hair he retained was bone white. His facial features were startling—adorned as they were with the bluish green lines of several tattoos. Spectacles perched on the bridge of his thin nose and gave him a round-eyed appearance at odds with his air of quiet watchfulness.

He had come from New Kelvin the previous year, self-exiled for choosing to act against the policies of the government he had served for the previous decade and a half.

A solid hit from a crossbow bolt had forced the amputation of Grateful Peace's right arm. While he recuperated, he had wintered at the Surcliffe family vineyards east of Duchess Kestrel's holding. However, when the snowmelt had begun, Duchess Kestrel had invited Peace to join herself and her family at their residence—deliberately waiting to offer her invitation until the White Water River was so swollen that there would be no easy commerce between the Norwood Grant and New Kelvin for at least a moonspan. Grateful Peace was an outcast from his homeland, and no one doubted that there was a price on his life.

Nor, Firekeeper thought, *would Peace be easy to hide. Even though he has stopped painting his face, nothing can hide the tattoos. Though he styles his hair more as men wear it here, still his very bearing and manner of standing is different. He walks awkwardly in trousers, as if his legs still need to feel the touch of robes to know when to break his stride.*

Duchess Kestrel did not keep them waiting long after Grateful Peace had arrived.

"I assume that all of you have already heard about the courier who arrived today. 'Courier' may be too polite a term," she added with wry smile. "However, it will do.

"One item of his news was rather shocking," the duchess continued. "Before I reveal it, I must ask that you not speak of it to anyone other than those gathered here. I have chosen to reveal it to you because I would like your advice regarding what course of action I should take."

Nods around the semicircle facing the duchess's desk confirmed the willingness of the gathered to keep her confidence. When Firekeeper realized that this was no general gossip session—as she had first imagined when Derian had spoken to her out on the grounds—she wondered why Duchess Kestrel had wanted her here.

Duchess Kestrel did not offer to answer this unspoken question, only accepted their unspoken promises of silence with a nod of her own.

"Very well," she said with a slight, involuntary sigh. "Melina, once of House Gyrfalcon, has married. Her new spouse is the Healed One, the hereditary monarch of New Kelvin."

Saedee Norwood declaimed these words as if she expected them to cause a sensation, nor was she disappointed. After a moment of shocked silence, there was a tumult of questions and expressions of dismay. Firekeeper believed that she herself had kept silent, but after a moment she realized that the rumbling growl she heard was coming from her own throat.

No wonder. If there was a human Firekeeper hated and despised, it was Lady Melina Shield. She had trouble thinking of the woman by another name, although Lady Melina had been disowned and exiled and so lost both title and right to her House name. Melina had tricked and used Firekeeper—a thing for which the wolf-woman blamed herself as much as she blamed Melina, though this realization made her feel no less bitter.

Earl Kestrel had raised a hand to still the babble and, with a glance at his mother, took it upon himself to answer some of the questions.

"First," he said, his tones clipped, "we are certain that this information is correct. The courier came originally from Dragon's Breath, the capital city of New Kelvin, where the information is, apparently, not common knowledge. However, he has a sister working within one of the Earth Spires and she gave him the news."

Grateful Peace interjected a comment of his own before the earl could continue.

"Keeping such a marriage secret would be less difficult than you of Hawk Haven might imagine," he said, his Pellish excellent but flavored with a melodious accent, rather as if he expected the words to have more syllables than they did. "The Healed One is a semi-sacred person. He appears in public rarely and his affairs are not for common gossip."

"Thank you," Duchess Kestrel said. "You have anticipated one of my own questions. I had wondered how such information could be kept from the people. Certainly servants, at least, would gossip."

"The secret could not be kept perpetually," Peace replied, "but for a few months, perhaps while the Healed One assured himself of support from the Dragon Speaker and some key thaumaturges, for that time it could be kept quiet—a thing rumored, but not confirmed. Many of the servants in Thendulla Lypella"—he used the New Kelvinese name for the Earth Spires, the towering buildings that held the New Kelvinese government—"are slaves and never leave the property. However, as this courier of yours has shown, even slaves have contacts outside of the walls."

After making certain that Grateful Peace had finished, Earl Kestrel continued his discourse.

"Not only are we certain that the news is genuine," he said, "we are fairly certain that we are the first Great House to receive the information. The White Water River remains quite swollen. The courier who came to us risked his life in his hope of reward for being the first."

"As you all must realize," the duchess added, smoothly taking up her son's account, "this information could have serious ramifications for our government."

"Our government?" asked Derian. "You mean for the king?"

Duchess Kestrel nodded. "A woman born of Hawk Haven's nobility has married a foreign monarch. Moreover, Melina is from House Gyrfalcon, first among the Great Houses. Even more significantly, Melina is the mother of one of King Tedric's heirs."

Firekeeper felt herself growling again. Crown Princess Sapphire was indeed Lady Melina's birth daughter, though she had been cruelly used by her mother. Now it seemed that, despite the adoption that should have taken Sapphire far out of her mother's reach, Melina was exercising power over her once more.

Derian frowned, but Firekeeper thought that his concern was less for Sapphire than for King Tedric. Since the autumn before, when King Tedric had honored him by making him one of his counselors, Derian had developed a deep personal loyalty to the monarch of Hawk Haven.

"We will tell the king this news, won't we?" Derian asked.

"Certainly," Duchess Kestrel answered. "Only yesterday I had a packet of letters from Eagle's Nest. Not one mentioned Melina's marriage, nor have the post-riders brought in any news. Therefore, we must act on the assumption that the news has not yet reached the king."

"I say," Edlin said, straightening slightly. "Why would a king need to keep a wedding secret?"

All eyes turned to Grateful Peace.

"A wedding to a foreigner," the former thaumaturge replied, "would most certainly need to be kept secret, at least until the government decided how to present the matter to the public. As you may recall from your visit to our land, we of New Kelvin entertain a somewhat inflated view of our worth in comparison to that of other people."

"Right-o!" Edlin said, grinning. "Sorry. Overlooked that, don't you know."

Earl Kestrel shook his head, disapproving as always of his son's casual attitude. He himself, as Firekeeper knew, would never admit forgetting something—at least as long as he could pretend otherwise.

"May I continue with the business at hand, Edlin?"

"I say!" Edlin said. "Of course you can, Father! I'd be the last to stop you."

Blind Seer was the only one to snigger aloud and only Firekeeper knew the wolf was laughing.

"This news has the potential," Norvin Norwood continued,

"to have severe ramifications for our entire kingdom. Princess Sapphire is new to her position. Her mother is feared. This strengthening of Melina's position could greatly weaken the crown princess's support. Therefore, it is important that the news reach the king and his heirs as quickly as possible. The more time they have to prepare, the more wisely will they react."

His pale grey gaze came to rest on Firekeeper and for the first time she understood why she had been included in this gathering.

"Firekeeper," the earl said, "do you think you could get Elation—that peregrine of yours—to carry a packet to the king?"

Firekeeper stiffened. She had dreaded a request like this since the year before when Elation had deigned to carry a report to King Allister of Bright Bay. For hundreds of years, since before the Plague that had sent the Old World rulers back across the sea and left their colonists to fend for themselves, the Royal Beasts had sought to hide themselves from a humanity that had initially treated with them as friends only to later attack them as enemies.

Her own emerging from across the Iron Mountains with Blind Seer and Elation had been the beginning of the end to that secrecy. True, few knew that the tales that were now widely told were true, not merely a minstrel's fancy, but among those who suspected the truth were some of the most powerful men and women in Hawk Haven. They would not hesitate to use whatever tools they might if those tools would stay a crisis.

"No," the wolf-woman replied bluntly. "I will not. Elation will not. The Royal Beasts are not your servants, any more than King Tedric is their servant. Why not send a pigeon?"

Duchess Kestrel answered for Earl Kestrel, who was frozen with displeasure.

"There are three reasons that sending a pigeon would not be wise. First, it's a bad season for the birds as the weather is very changeable. Second, we have only one bird left who will return to Eagle's Nest and, by our contract with the king, we must keep one in case we need give warning of invasion. Third, this information is too serious to trust to a potentially insecure courier."

Saedee Norwood smiled in a fashion that Firekeeper thought was more akin to a baring of teeth.

"Indeed, the courier who brought this information to us is being detained for a few days. We have him quite comfortable, but have taken care that those who wait on him are the least likely to share gossip."

The duchess turned a kinder smile upon the wolf-woman.

"But Firekeeper, I don't understand your reluctance. Princess Sapphire is your friend. You stood for her at her wedding. Surely you should help her now."

Firekeeper growled, but an idea was taking shape in the back of her mind. She let it grow and answered the first point.

"Sapphire is her own friend first, then Shad's, and the king's, then her family's. Maybe then she remember a few others. No matter, that." Firekeeper bit her lip, for making speeches in human talk was still hard for her. "Everyone know Sapphire's mother—even King Tedric—when she is made crown princess. Why L . . . Melina matter now that Sapphire belongs to king?"

What followed was a long discourse on politics, alliances, and the rest, begun by the duchess and her son, but with Grateful Peace adding a few words here and there before it was ended.

Most of what they said went over Firekeeper's head, but she gathered that what Lady Melina had done was so terrible because she had placed herself at the head of another government. At least this would be how many in Hawk Haven and Bright Bay would interpret Melina's actions, though Grateful Peace was quick to say that Melina would not be nearly as powerful in New Kelvin as a monarch's spouse would be in Hawk Haven.

"If she was any but Lady Melina," Firekeeper said to Blind Seer, *"I would be comforted by what Peace says, but Lady Melina will rule where others think themselves the One."*

"So you will have Elation carry their message?" The tilt of the wolf's ears expressed wariness, as if he had scented a puma lurking in the trees.

"Not quite," Firekeeper replied.

She waited until the humans had finished their lecture, then offered the compromise she had come up with a few minutes before.

"Elation not carry message," she said, "nor will I ask her, but I will carry."

She held up a hand to forestall the protests that began almost before she finished speaking.

"I am fast as usual post-horse," she said, "not the gallop relays, no, but as horse jogging on roads, and I not need stay on roads. No great rivers is between here and Eagle's Nest. I can go if not as fast as peregrine flies, as straight."

She stopped, pleased with the image.

Earl Kestrel frowned.

"Blysse, it is time you realized the less than suitable impression such behavior makes. My suggestion keeps your dignity and position in mind—as your own does not."

Firekeeper smiled at him, knowing well that it was his own dignity, as her adopted father, that Norvin Norwood was worried about. What parent doesn't wish to control his children?

"Either I go," she said with polite firmness, "or message no go fast."

Earl Kestrel didn't immediately cease trying to convince Firekeeper to do things his way, but eventually the duchess put a hand on his shoulder.

"Norvin, as easily make water run up hill as try to change her mind. You can't do it. Let us accept this compromise. Firekeeper, when will you go?"

Firekeeper shrugged. "This now, if you wish."

The duchess gave a gracious nod. "Within an hour or two will do. I wish to write out a report and to request that Grateful Peace dictate one regarding his perception of the New Kelvinese reaction when this news becomes widely known."

Derian Carter, who had listened attentively, clarifying terms for Firekeeper during the more theoretical political discussions, now cleared his throat.

"I can't travel as quickly as Firekeeper," he said, "but I could follow on horseback. I'd been intending to go south soon anyhow, to place an order with my father for mounts for the Norwood stables before he heads to the spring market in Good Crossing. I could carry another copy of the message and speak for you, clarifying points as Firekeeper might not be able."

Earl Kestrel nodded, some of his sourness vanishing.

"We had intended to ask you to do much the same," he said approvingly. "As a ring-wearing counselor to the king, you will be able to gain a private audience."

Derian inclined his head in a bow of respectful acknowledgment.

"He's not as intimidated by our Norvin as once he was," Blind Seer chuckled. Like Firekeeper he was fond of Derian, and like any wolf he enjoyed seeing a cub grow into his fur and tail.

Blind Seer's comment made Firekeeper think of something new. Although it didn't pertain precisely to the matter at hand, it was related and she thought she might as well raise it now.

"Blind Seer and I go to Eagle's Nest, then," she said aloud, "and from there when telling king is done and questions answered, then Blind Seer and I, and maybe Fox Hair if he wish, we go west across the mountains and see my pack."

She didn't phrase this as request, but Earl Kestrel chose to reply as if she had.

"That would be fine," he said. Clearly, if the wolf-woman wouldn't serve him, she might as well be out of sight. His annoyance at her was apparent in how he quickly changed the subject. "Mother, I was thinking, Derian could carry with him a coop of our carrier pigeons. Therefore, if the king needs to reply he can do so that way as well as by courier."

"I say," Edlin interjected, speaking in Firekeeper's ear so as not to interrupt the duchess's reply to the earl. "I say, Firekeeper, can I go with you to see the wolves?"

He looked so eager Firekeeper almost hated refusing him.

"No," she said. "Even Fox Hair will be a problem, but I know he has oath to fill and I would guide his steps. Two humans may be too much."

She stopped then, realizing she had almost said more than she had intended. Edlin, happily, had fixed on the first part of her statement.

"Oath to fill? What?"

Derian nodded. "I vowed at the end of King Allister's War to return to the place where Prince Barden's expedition died and set up a marker for all the dead. Lord Aksel Trueheart has agreed to research the names for me and even to help with preparation of gravestones."

Earl Kestrel, finished with his private discussion with the duchess, had heard Derian's explanation.

"You never mentioned this to me," he said sternly.

"It was a private vow," Derian replied almost apologetically. "When I lettered temporary markers for the battlefield I kept thinking of those graves we left. As you know, we listed the names of those we knew among the dead—Prince Barden and his wife, a few others—but we didn't have a full list of the expedition with us."

Norvin Norwood nodded. Although he had led the expedition to find a prince, he had not been concerned enough about the commoners in the group to carry along their names.

"My sister, Eirene," the earl said, his voice breaking slightly, "was Barden's wife. I would like to send some small trinkets for her grave."

"I would also," the duchess said so quickly that Firekeeper was certain she was swallowing tears. "Sweet Eirene . . ."

Firekeeper sensed the duchess's gaze resting on her and shifted uncomfortably, knowing what the old woman was wondering. Part of the reason Earl Kestrel had convinced his mother to adopt the wolf-woman into the Kestrel line was that there was a good chance that Firekeeper was Barden and Eirene's daughter, Blysse.

The wolf-woman had no idea whether this was true or not

but the idea, as always, made her vaguely uncomfortable. She leapt to her feet, suddenly eager to be away.

"I get some small things," she said, "and come back for these letters."

No one stopped her as she darted out the door.